PENGUIN CLASSICS

THE PORTABLE EDGAR ALLAN POE

EDGAR ALLAN POE was born in Boston on January 19, 1809, the son of itinerant actors. Orphaned in 1811, he became the ward of John and Frances Allan of Richmond, accompanying them to England in 1815 and then returning in 1820 to Richmond, where he completed his early schooling. In 1826 he attended the University of Virginia, but gambling debts forced his withdrawal, and after a clash with his foster father, Poe left Richmond for Boston. There in 1827 he published his first book of poetry, *Tamerlane and Other Poems,* and enlisted in the U.S. Army as "Edgar A. Perry." After tours of duty in South Carolina and Virginia, he resigned as sergeant-major, and between two later books of poetry—*Al Aaraaf, Tamerlane, and Minor Poems* (1829) and *Poems* (1831)—he briefly attended the U.S. Military Academy. Court-martialed and expelled, he took refuge in Baltimore with his aunt, Maria Clemm, and there began to compose fantastic tales for newspapers and magazines; in 1835 he obtained a position in Richmond at the *Southern Literary Messenger.* Perhaps already secretly wedded to his thirteen-year-old cousin, Virginia Clemm, he married her publicly in 1836. At the *Messenger* Poe gained notoriety by writing savage reviews, but he also raised the journal's literary quality and enhanced both its circulation and reputation. In 1837, however, economic hard times and alcoholic lapses cost Poe his job; he moved to New York, where he completed a novel, *The Narrative of Arthur Gordon Pym,* published in 1838. By then, Poe had relocated to Philadelphia, where he wrote "Ligeia" as well as "The Fall of the House of Usher" and "William Wilson." During successive editorial stints at *Burton's Gentleman's Magazine* and *Graham's Magazine,* Poe developed plans to establish a high-quality monthly periodical. He also published his first book, a volume titled *Tales of the Grotesque and Arabesque* (1840), and later produced the first modern detective story, "The Murders in the Rue Morgue," as well as the prize-winning cryptographic tale, "The Gold-Bug." In 1842 his wife suffered a hemorrhage that marked the onset of tuberculosis. Poe returned to New York in 1844 and reached the peak of his productivity, publishing such tales as "The Premature Burial" and "The Purloined Letter." He gained fame in 1845 with his poem "The Raven," and that year also saw the publication of two books: *Tales* and *The Raven and Other Poems.* But the weekly literary newspaper he had managed to acquire, *The Broadway Review,* collapsed at the beginning of 1846. Moving to nearby Fordham, Poe continued to write and to care for Virginia until her untimely death in 1847. In his final years, he composed the sweeping, cosmological prose-poem, *Eureka* (1848), as well as some of his most renowned poetry, including "The Bells," "Eldorado," and "Annabel Lee." After a ruinous bout of election-day drinking, Edgar Allan Poe died in Baltimore on October 7, 1849.

J. GERALD KENNEDY is William A. Read Professor of English at Louisiana State University and a past president of the Poe Studies Association. He earned his doctoral degree at Duke University, where he was elected to Phi Beta Kappa. His books on Poe include *Poe, Death, and the Life of Writing* (1987) and *"The Narrative of Arthur Gordon Pym" and the Abyss of Interpretation* (1995), as well as two edited collections of essays, *A Historical Guide to Edgar Allan Poe* (2001) and (with Liliane Weissberg) *Romancing the Shadow: Poe and Race* (2001). In an early book titled *The Astonished Traveler: William Darby, Frontier Traveler and Man of Letters* (1981), he reconstructed the career of a prolific antebellum geographer and magazinist. Kennedy's work on literary modernism includes *Imagining Paris: Exile, Writing, and American Identity* (1993) and two edited collections, *Modern American Short Story Sequences* (1995) and (with Jackson R. Bryer) *French Connections: Hemingway and Fitzgerald Abroad* (1998). He has served many years on the board of the Ernest Hemingway Foundation. Fellowships from the John Simon Guggenheim Foundation, the National Endowment for the Humanities, and the Louisiana Board of Regents have supported work on an expansive study of national destiny and the cultural conflicts that vitiated American literary nation-building, 1820–1850.

The Portable Edgar Allan Poe

Edited with an Introduction by
J. GERALD KENNEDY

PENGUIN BOOKS

PENGUIN BOOKS
Published by the Penguin Group
Penguin Group (USA) Inc., 375 Hudson Street, New York, New York 10014, U.S.A.
Penguin Group (Canada), 90 Eglinton Avenue East, Suite 700, Toronto,
Ontario, Canada M4P 2Y3 (a division of Pearson Penguin Canada Inc.)
Penguin Books Ltd, 80 Strand, London WC2R 0RL, England
Penguin Ireland, 25 St Stephen's Green, Dublin 2, Ireland (a division of Penguin Books Ltd)
Penguin Group (Australia), 250 Camberwell Road, Camberwell,
Victoria 3124, Australia (a division of Pearson Australia Group Pty Ltd)
Penguin Books India Pvt Ltd, 11 Community Centre,
Panchsheel Park, New Delhi – 110 017, India
Penguin Group (NZ), 67 Apollo Drive, Rosedale, Auckland 0632,
New Zealand (a division of Pearson New Zealand Ltd)
Penguin Books (South Africa) (Pty) Ltd, 24 Sturdee Avenue,
Rosebank, Johannesburg 2196, South Africa

Penguin Books Ltd, Registered Offices: 80 Strand, London WC2R 0RL, England

This edition first published in Penguin Books 2006

22 24 26 28 30 29 27 25 23 21

ISBN 978-0-14-303991-4
CIP data available

Printed in the United States of America
Set in Sabon

Contents

POEMS   393

LETTERS   443

CRITICAL PRINCIPLES   523

OBSERVATIONS   571

As a writer enamored of "the foreign subject" Poe must have resented Burton's announcement of a $1000 literary contest that included $250 for five tales illustrating different eras in American history or portraying U.S. regional differences. His contempt for Burton prompted him to tell a friend: "As soon as Fate allows I will have a magazine of my own—and will endeavor to kick up a dust."

That idea became increasingly irresistible. In 1840, as Rodman's apocryphal journal was unfolding in monthly installments and as Poe unscrambled cryptograms for *Alexander's,* he also devised a plan to start his own periodical. In *Burton's* he decided to play the literary sleuth by accusing Harvard professor Henry Wadsworth Longfellow of plagiarizing from Tennyson. Poe also published a fine new poem of his own, "Sonnet—To Silence," as well as "Peter Pendulum, the Business Man," a biting satire perhaps aimed obliquely at Burton but more obviously targeting American commercial greed. In March, Burton lamely reneged on the announced premiums for original works, and two months later, intent on building a new theater, he prepared to sell his journal. Poe seized the moment to print a prospectus for his own periodical, to be called the *Penn Magazine,* but when Burton saw the circular, he accused Poe of disloyalty, fired him, and demanded repayment of money already advanced. The dismissal provoked a blazing reply in which Poe warned Burton, "If by accident you have taken it into your head that I am to be insulted with impunity I can only assume that you are an ass."

Out of work, Poe enlisted contributors and subscribers for his proposed journal, which he envisioned as having a "lasting effect upon the growing literature of the country." He found a new ally in Frederick W. Thomas, a Cincinnati novelist and Whig partisan who campaigned in Philadelphia for presidential candidate William Henry Harrison. Another sympathetic figure was George Graham, who edited the *Saturday Evening Post,* owned *The Casket,* and in October acquired *Burton's.* Graham generously lauded Poe's plans for the *Penn,* and when illness forced Poe to postpone the project, Graham solicited his work for his amalgamated monthly, *Graham's Magazine.* In the first issue, Poe's "The Man of the Crowd" signaled the beginning of an important connection with Graham, for when a bank crisis in early 1841 forced another delay in the

Penn, Poe gratefully assumed responsibility for book reviews in *Graham's* at an annual salary of eight hundred dollars. But the monthly also provided a venue for new tales: developing the city mysteries premise of "The Man of the Crowd," he invented the modern detective story in "The Murders in the Rue Morgue" in April, and the following month published "A Descent into the Maelström." Poe also contributed a series on cryptography, "A Few Words on Secret Writing," that grew from his writing for *Alexander's.*

Convincing Graham that they could together create a prestigious, high-quality monthly featuring American writers exclusively, Poe began in June 1841 to solicit contributions from notable authors—Irving, Kennedy, the poet Fitz-Greene Halleck, and even the much abused Longfellow. But privately he admitted to Thomas his growing irritation with Graham, and for the next two years pursued a clerkship in the administration of President John Tyler, successor to Harrison (who died soon after his inauguration). Poe was disillusioned by the absence of an international copyright law to protect the work of American authors and to prevent U.S. publishers from selling "pirated" English works. He was also appalled by the "namby-pamby" character of *Graham's,* which added fashion plates and—at the end of 1841—two female editors to a staff that already included Charles Peterson. Poe nevertheless claimed responsibility for the journal's commercial success and continued to write reviews, read proofs, and contribute tales (such as "Never Bet the Devil Your Head") as well as a new series on handwriting called "Autography." He also wrote an "Exordium to Critical Notices" questioning the campaign for "national literature" while warning of America's "degrading imitation" of British culture. But in January 1842, a devastating event destroyed Poe's tranquil home life: His young wife (then only nineteen) suffered a massive pulmonary hemorrhage while singing at the piano. "Dangerously ill" for weeks, she seemed to recover, yet relapses confirmed that Virginia, like Poe's mother, had been stricken with consumption.

Vacillating between denial and anger, Poe sought forgetfulness in drink; sometimes absent from work, he quarreled with Graham about money. He still pursued the dream of a magazine of his own, urging Thomas to propose to President Tyler a journal edited by Poe that might "play an important part in the politics of the day." When not overwrought, he carried out assignments for *Graham's*, interviewing Charles Dickens in Philadelphia in March and producing for the May issue the famous review of Hawthorne that enunciated Poe's theory of the tale based on unity of effect. He also published two stories betraying domestic anxieties: "The Oval Portrait," which depicts an artist too busy to notice that his wife is dying, and "The Masque of the Red Death," which represents fatal contagion as an unexpected intruder.

But another interloper, a fifth editorial associate added by Graham—Reverend Rufus W. Griswold—apparently precipitated Poe's departure from the magazine staff. Griswold had included Poe's work in his *Poets and Poetry of America*, the first comprehensive anthology of its kind, and Poe and Griswold expressed mutual cordiality but privately despised each other. At Griswold's hiring, Poe abruptly resigned, claiming that the magazine's feminized content—"the contemptible pictures, fashion-plates, music and love tales"—had motivated his departure, but he plainly refused to work with Griswold and saw his arrival as a threat to his own editorial influence.

Without steady income, Poe resumed old quests and cultivated new connections. Thomas spoke of an impending appointment at the Philadelphia Custom House, but Poe nevertheless visited New York seeking an editorial position—though inebriation undermined his efforts there. To Georgia planter and poet Thomas Holley Chivers, he proposed a lucrative partnership, still hoping to launch the *Penn Magazine*. Poe's focus on the journal intensified in November, when hopes for a government position faded. Hearing that James Russell Lowell was founding a Boston magazine, Poe offered to become a contributor, forwarding a new poem, "Lenore," and an essay, "Notes Upon English Verse." Lowell also published "The Tell-Tale Heart" in his short-lived *Pioneer,* and upon its demise Poe announced to Lowell his own plan to create "the best journal in America." He was soon contracting with a Philadelphia publisher of "ample capital" named Thomas Clarke to produce a high-quality magazine now titled *The Stylus*. In response to the "great question of International Copy-Right," it would feature American writers exclusively, resisting "the dictation of Foreign Reviews." Poe seemed once more on the verge of realizing his great dream, but again he destroyed his prospects for success.

An administrative change at the Custom House persuaded Poe that he could secure a government job by appealing directly to the president in Washington. He had expected Thomas to arrange the necessary interview with Tyler, but Thomas was ill, and upon reaching Washington, Poe began drinking heavily. His boorish behavior offended his friends, the president's son, and a visiting Philadelphia writer named Thomas Dunn English. In desperation, Poe's ally Jesse Dow implored Clarke, a temperance man, to rescue Poe from humiliation. Poe returned to Philadelphia on his own steam, however, making an immediate, conciliatory visit to the publisher. But Clarke had seen enough and soon retracted his offer to publish *The Stylus*. In the wake of this misadventure, English included a derisive portrait of Poe in his temperance novel, *The Doom of the Drinker,* a work commissioned by Clarke.

But Poe's situation was not altogether hopeless. His tale "The Gold-Bug" won a hundred-dollar prize offered by the *Dollar Newspaper*. Reprinted in many papers, the story garnered more recognition for Poe than any previous publication; one Philadelphia theater immediately staged a dramatic adaptation. In August the author resumed a loose affiliation with *Graham's,* his sporadic reviews serving to repay loans from the publisher. That same month the *Saturday Evening Post* published "The Black Cat," Poe's own temperance tale about the perverse compulsions incited by drink. As *The Doom of the Drinker* appeared in serial form, Poe found a new source of income: He became a public lecturer, speaking on American poetry to large crowds in Philadelphia, Wilmington, Newark (Delaware), Baltimore, and Reading. In early 1844 his staunch support of the copyright issue drew a letter from Cornelius Mathews of New York, who sent his pamphlet on that subject and perhaps an invitation to join the American Copyright Club. Having imposed too often on too many people in Philadelphia, Poe moved in April to New York.

The author created an instant sensation in Manhattan when his "Balloon Hoax" appeared as a dispatch in an extra edition of the *Sun*. The public clamored for news about the transatlantic flight, but James Gordon Bennett of the rival *Herald* detected a ruse and forced a retraction. The uproar, however, only confirmed Poe's talent for what he called "mystification" and excited his creativity. That summer he told Lowell of the "mania for composition" that sometimes seized him; since December 1843 he had composed "A Tale of the Ragged Mountains," "The Spectacles," "Mesmeric Revelation," "The Premature Burial," "The Oblong Box," "The Purloined Letter," " 'Thou Art the Man,' " and "The System of Doctor Tarr and Professor Fether," as well as "The Balloon Hoax" and several shorter pieces. Like "The Gold-Bug," most of the new tales portrayed American scenes, and Poe declared that he was writing a "Critical History of Am. Literature." For a small Pennsylvania newspaper he was also writing a chatty column called "Doings of Gotham." Once indifferent to American subjects, he manifested a pragmatic shift in focus. That spring Poe again proposed to Lowell coeditorship of a "well-founded Monthly journal" featuring American authors; he reminded Chivers of a similar offer, and in late October he cajoled Lowell a third time while sending proposals for both the magazine and a new, multivolume collection of tales to Charles Anthon, an influential New York professor.

Disillusioned by Whig partisanship and cheered by the copyright campaign of Young America, a group of rabid Democrats, Poe lent token support to the Democratic Party in 1844, befriending the head of a political club and writing the lyrics to a campaign song. He commented wryly on the contest between Whig Henry Clay and Democrat James K. Polk in his metropolitan gossip column, and in November began contributing "Marginalia" to the partisan *Democratic Review*. But he privately mistrusted the expansionist agenda of Polk, and in a tale partly inspired by the election of 1844 satirized the chief rationale for U.S. imperialism—belief in Anglo-Saxon cultural superiority—in "Some Words With a Mummy."

Even as he was caricaturing the predicament of the American magazinist in "The Literary Life of Thingum Bob," Poe accepted a position in October with N. P. Willis's *Evening Journal*, where his celebrated poem "The Raven" first appeared in January 1845. Widely discussed, reprinted, and parodied, the poem made Poe a celebrity, yet its evocation of unending melancholy also marked a rehearsal of his impending bereavement. He distracted himself from constant worry about Virginia by playing the literary lion in

New York salons and by plunging into daily journalism. But his squibs for the *Mirror* and subsequent contributions to a new newspaper, the *Broadway Journal,* curbed his productivity in fiction, which in 1845 amounted to only four new tales, including "The Imp of the Perverse" and "The Facts in the Case of M. Valdemar." But his newfound fame, partly excited by Lowell's biographical sketch of Poe in *Graham's,* gave him greater editorial freedom, which he used to renew his attacks on Longfellow. He extended his assault on the professor poet in a well-attended February lecture on American poetry, but he also remained adamant about copyright, and that month published "Some Secrets of the Magazine Prison-House," his most searing analysis of literary property and the economic thralldom of American authors. Evert Duyckinck, leader of Young America, rewarded Poe's advocacy of copyright by publishing first *Tales* and then *The Raven and Other Poems* in his Library of American Books.

Soon after his "Prison-House" manifesto, Poe joined the staff of the *Broadway Journal,* which was owned by John Bisco and Charles F. Briggs. There he accelerated the Longfellow war by adopting a pseudonym (or so it appears) to stage a notorious debate with himself about the revered poet. Briggs initially countenanced Poe's monomania on plagiarism, but by May became alarmed by his renewed drinking after a long abstinence. Lowell and Chivers, who both visited New York that spring, testified to his reckless dissipation. But Poe managed somehow to revise many of his tales and poems for reprinting in the weekly, and among his numerous reviews he celebrated the poet Mrs. Francis Sargent Osgood, with whom he was carrying on an ostensibly platonic, semipublic "amour" sanctioned by his ailing wife. Wishing to give the journal a "fresh start," Briggs planned to relieve Poe of his editorial role and find a new publisher, but when his partner disagreed, Briggs withdrew, and Bisco named Poe editor, offering him half of the meager profits. The crisis came in October: that month Poe made his infamous appearance at the Boston Lyceum, reading not a promised new poem but rather the early, esoteric "Al Aaraaf." The outcry from that fiasco had not subsided when Bisco capitulated and sold out to Poe, who through loans from friends became sole proprietor of a failing literary journal. Despite the attraction of his revised, reprinted works and his biting editorial commentaries—

in which for weeks he taunted his Boston critics—the *Broadway Journal* was in a death spiral. Beset by debts, Poe ceased publication on January 3, 1846, the final issue ironically reprinting his early tale "Loss of Breath."

Illness, poverty, and scandal dogged Poe throu... 1846. For *Graham's* he composed "The Philosophy of Comp..." an exaggerated account of how he wrote "The Rave... ... Elizabeth F. Ellet stirred a controversy involving ... ...ood's love letters to Poe that ostracized him from the ... ...n of Anne C. Lynch. The episode also provoked a bi... ... with Thomas Dunn English, who had moved to Ne... ...d become an unlikely ally in the Longfellow wars b... ...oe at a volatile moment. Rumors of Poe's insanity a... ...s worsening condition prompted their move to healthi... ...ings in Fordham, where they rented a country cott... ...well, Poe prepared for *Godey's* a series on the "N... ...rati," flattering friends and abusing enemies in pith... also continued his "Marginalia" series but comp... ...notable new tale—perhaps inspired by his feud w... ...ed "The Cask of Amontillado." The "Literati" sk... ...ing English as an ignorant charlatan elicited a sland... ...for which Poe eventually received a legal settlement. ... ...46 he increasingly became an object of private gossi... ...ublic derision by "little birds of prey"; alluding to his ... ...nunciation of drink, he called Virginia his "*only* ...w to battle with this uncongenial, unsatisfactory, and ...ul life." In letters to Philip Pendleton Cooke and George W. Evelith, he nevertheless revealed his determination to publish *The Stylus*, the "one great purpose" of his literary life. But at year's end that goal seemed remote; both Poe and Virginia were bedridden in Fordham, attended by Mrs. Clemm and Marie Louise Shew, a friend with nursing experience.

For Virginia, the end came on January 30, 1847. On her deathbed she asked her husband to read Mrs. Shew a poignant letter from the second Mrs. John Allan, confessing that she had turned Poe's foster father against him. Virginia's death and burial prostrated Poe, and although he composed a poem ("The Beloved Physician") for Mrs. Shew when she nursed him back to health, he wrote little else in 1847. His lawsuit against English briefly provided distraction from grief and, after a favorable ruling, relief from penury. That summer Poe visited Thomas in Washington and called at the office of *Graham's* in Philadelphia, perhaps to deliver a new review of Hawthorne that appeared in the November issue. His only significant literary composition since Virginia's death, however, was "Ulalume," a mystical poem transparently inspired by her loss. He received attentions from several literary women and composed for Sarah Anna Lewis the anagrammatic poem, "An Enigma." Across the Atlantic his work had attracted the attention of Charles Baudelaire, the poet whose translations would enshrine Poe as a literary deity in France.

Recovering his vigor, Poe turned again in 1848 to the grand, unfinished project of launching a monthly magazine; he printed a prospectus and planned a tour to attract subscribers. He intended to feature his long-deferred study of "Literary America," providing a "faithful account" of the nation's "literary productions, literary people, and literary affairs." Simultaneously he was penning *Eureka,* a cosmological prose poem, to elaborate his insights into life and death, matter and spirit, God and humankind. To finance his tour he gave a lecture called "The Universe" in February, but according to Evert Duyckinck, his "ludicrous dryness" actually "drove people from the room." Hoping to extract a salable tale from his magnum opus Poe sent the futuristic satire "Mellonta Tauta" to *Godey's,* which published it thirteen months later. He also contributed more "Marginalia" to *Graham's* and tried to ignore journalistic taunting by English. Having completed a year of mourning, Poe found himself increasingly pursued by literary women, and he contemplated remarriage. The kindnesses of Mrs. Shew (a married woman) inspired a valentine poem, and Poe drafted a version of "The Bells" at her home, but his pantheism so troubled her that she broke off the friendship. A widow, Sarah Helen Whitman, published a valentine poem to Poe in the *Home Journal,* and he reciprocated by sending her a poem recalling a glimpse of her in 1845. Another married poet, Jane Ermina Locke, came to Fordham to meet Poe and invite him to lecture in Lowell, Massachusetts. During a July visit there he lectured on American poetry and met Annie Richmond, a young married woman who quickly became his muse and confidante. The encounter inspired part of "Landor's Cottage," a landscape sketch composed later that year. Upon his return to New York, Poe found bound copies of *Eureka* awaiting him.

taken a sobriety pledge did she agree to marry him. Poe's joining the Sons of Temperance marked a desperate bid to change his ways and repair his reputation. In poor health, yet sustained by Mrs. Shelton's acceptance, he departed for New York, presumably to accompany Mrs. Clemm to Richmond for the wedding. But in Baltimore, his first stop en route, Poe imbibed excessively, and on October 3, an election day, he was discovered at a polling place "rather the worse for wear." Transported to Washington College Hospital, he remained intermittently delirious for four days and died on October 7, 1849.

❖

In a checkered career of barely two decades Poe produced more than sixty poems, some seventy-odd tales, one completed novel, a long prose poem of cosmological theory, and scores of essays and reviews. He introduced into poetry, criticism, and prose fiction many innovations that altered literary culture. Poe's greatest achievement as a writer, however, transcends his technical or formal innovations. Working in the context of U.S. nation building and territorial expansion, the rise of a capitalist market economy, the decline of religious authority, the development and secularization of mass culture, and the advent of modern scientific skepticism, Poe (in the words of Sarah Helen Whitman) "came to sound the very depths of the abyss," articulating in his tales and poems "the unrest and faithlessness of the age." As compellingly as any writer of his time, Poe intuited the spiritual void opening in an era dominated by a secular, scientific understanding of life and death. If Kierkegaard analyzed philosophically the condition of dread that accompanied the "sickness unto ' literary expression to modern doubt reka may be seen as a late, desperate   ....ut from the laws of physics—from the implacable materiality of science itself—a theory of spiritual survival. In his most stunning poetry and fiction he staged the dilemma of the desolate self, confronting its own mortality and beset by uncertainties about a spiritual afterlife.

Thanks in part to Reverend Rufus Griswold, the nemesis whom the author perversely designated as his literary executor, Poe's posthumous reputation was originally clouded by moral condemnation. Griswold's notorious obituary, recast as a preface to the otherwise reliable edition of Poe's works he supervised in the 1850s, acknowledged his contemporary's genius but also portrayed him as a morbid loner, a drunken lunatic wandering the streets muttering "curses and imprecations." Poe's early defenders included George Graham and N. P. Willis as well as Mrs. Whitman, who in 1860 issued *Edgar Poe and His Critics,* an acute estimate of his lasting significance. The publication of a multivolume edition of his works in French by Baudelaire established his fame abroad and made Poe the patron saint of the symbolist movement. Later in the nineteenth century John H. Ingram and George Woodberry wrote pioneering biographies, and as the twentieth century began, James A. Harrison produced the first scholarly edition of Poe's collected writings. During the twentieth century, new biographies by Arthur Hobson Quinn and more recently by Kenneth Silverman have incorporated fresh information and critical perspectives. John Ward Ostrom's edition of Poe's letters, and the compilation of the *Poe Log* by David K. Jackson and Dwight Thomas, as well as the definitive edition of Poe's collected writings by T. O. Mabbott and Burton R. Pollin, have marked important milestones in scholarship, while critical studies of the past seventy-five years have enriched and complicated the appraisal of Poe's work. Derogation of Poe's achievements by such luminaries as Henry James, T. S. Eliot, and Aldous Huxley as well as Poe's exclusion from several studies of the so-called American renaissance have underscored his problematic status. Yet he remains irresistibly compelling, the undying appeal of his strange tales and poems testifying to his enduring international significance.

Chronology

CHRONOLOGY

1809 Born in Boston to actors David Poe and Elizabeth Arnold Poe. Father born in Baltimore, son of Irish-born emigrant David Poe, Sr., American quartermaster during the Revolutionary War. English-born mother came to United States in 1796; wedded David Poe in 1805. Older brother William Henry Leonard Poe born in 1807.

1811 Mother dies of tuberculosis in Richmond, one year after birth of daughter, Rosalie. Father had abandoned family; likely died of tuberculosis in 1811. Richmond merchant John Allan and wife Frances become foster parents of Edgar; grandparents in Baltimore care for brother Henry, while Mackenzie family of Richmond welcomes Rosalie.

1815 Accompanies John and Frances Allan to England, where Allan opens a branch of his mercantile firm, Ellis and Allan, in London. Edgar visits Allan family relatives in Scotland and the following year enters boarding school in London as "Edgar Allan."

1816 Paternal grandfather David Poe, Sr., dies in Baltimore.

1818 Enters Reverend Bransby's Manor House School in Stoke Newington.

1820 Economic reverses compel Allan to close his London branch and return with family to Richmond, where Poe enrolls in Richmond Academy using his family name.

1822 Composes an ode for departing teacher, Joseph H. Clarke; cousin Virginia Clemm born in Baltimore.

1823 Enters William Burke's school; meets Jane Stith Stanard, mother of a friend.

1824 Mourns death of Mrs. Stanard; makes six-mile swim in James River.

1825 Allan inherits a fortune, purchases a Richmond mansion; Poe becomes engaged to Sarah Elmira Royster.

1826 Enters University of Virginia; excels academically but incurs gambling debts; returns to Richmond, where Mr. Royster forbids daughter's marriage to Poe.

1827 Quarrels with Allan and leaves home; sails to Boston under an alias; enlists in U.S. Army as Edgar A. Perry. Calvin F. S. Thomas publishes *Tamerlane and Other Poems;* Poe sails to South Carolina for duty at Fort Moultrie.

1828 Seeks release from army commitment; Elmira Royster marries Alexander Shelton; Poe and his unit relocate to Fortress Monroe, Virginia.

1829 Receives promotion to sergeant major and plans to seek appointment to West Point. Foster mother, Frances Allan, dies in Richmond. Poe hires military replacement and receives honorable discharge; moves to Baltimore, lodges at hotels and with relatives, seeks publisher for new poetry volume. Hatch and Dunning publish Poe's *Al Aaraaf, Tamerlane and Minor Poems.*

1830 Receives appointment to U.S. Military Academy; excels in French and mathematics. John Allan remarries, leaves New York without contacting Poe, forbids further communication.

1831 Devastated by Allan's rejection, Poe neglects military duties, faces court-martial, receives dismissal. Finds New York publisher for third volume of verse; Elam Bliss issues *Poems,* purchased by 131 cadets. Poe moves to Baltimore, takes up residence with grandmother and aunt, writes tales in response to newspaper contest. Brother William Henry Leonard Poe dies of consumption. John Allan, Jr., born in Richmond. Baltimore beset by cholera epidemic; Poe experiences long illness. Delia S. Bacon wins *Saturday Courier* contest.

1832 Philadelphia *Saturday Courier* publishes "Metzengerstein" and four more tales by Poe. John Allan, in failing health, revises his will. Second Allan son born. Poe tutors cousin Virginia, seeks employment.

1833 Baltimore *Saturday Visiter* announces literary contest; Poe submits several new tales and poems. "MS. Found in a Bottle" wins fifty-dollar prize for fiction. John Pendleton Kennedy offers Poe's "Tales of the Folio Club" to a Philadelphia publisher. Poe does odd jobs for Kennedy and the *Visiter.*

1834 *Godey's Lady's Book* publishes "The Visionary" (later called "The Assignation"). Poe rebuffed by Allan in last meeting in Richmond; Allan dies six weeks later, leaving Poe without an inheritance. Thomas W. White launches *Southern Literary Messenger*. Henry C. Carey declines to publish Poe's tales.

1835 Kennedy aids destitute Poe; recommends him to White as prospective employee. Poe contributes "Berenice" and other tales to *Messenger*, writes reviews, offers advice to White. Grandmother Elizabeth Poe dies in Baltimore. Poe travels to Richmond to apply for teaching position; assists White; suffers suicidal crisis; returns to Baltimore, perhaps to marry Virginia secretly. Returns to Richmond with Virginia and Mrs. Clemm as housemates; resumes work at *Messenger*, publishes many reviews, reprints his tales and poems, and expands journal's national reputation.

1836 Marries Virginia in public ceremony; enjoys acclaim as editor, despite White's refusal to confer title; publishes many reviews, notes, and essays. Harper & Brothers decline to publish "Folio Club" tales; advise Poe to write novel. White threatens to fire Poe for drinking.

1837 White dismisses Poe. *Messenger* publishes two installments of Poe's novel, *The Narrative of Arthur Gordon Pym*. With wife and mother-in-law, Poe moves to New York, completes novel, and secures contract with Harper & Brothers. Panic of 1837 postpones publication of *Pym*; Poe remains unemployed and impoverished.

1838 Relocates to Philadelphia; unsuccessfully seeks employment. Harper & Brothers publish *Pym*; novel receives mixed reviews. Poe publishes "Ligeia" in Baltimore *American Museum*. Allows Thomas Wyatt to use his name as author of textbook on seashells.

1839 Obtains position at *Burton's Gentleman's Magazine*; meets Philadelphia literati; publishes "William Wilson" in *The Gift* and "The Fall of the House of Usher" in *Burton's*. Lea & Blanchard publish Poe's *Tales of the Grotesque and Arabesque* in December. Poe issues challenge in *Alexander's Weekly Messenger* to solve any cryptogram submitted by readers.

1840 Begins serialization of "The Journal of Julius Rodman" in *Burton's;* solves cryptograms in *Alexander's;* accuses Longfellow of plagiarism. Burton dismisses Poe for issuing *Penn Magazine* prospectus; project elicits encouragement from many quarters. Poe meets Frederick W. Thomas; contributes "The Man of the Crowd" to newly created *Graham's Magazine;* suffers prolonged illness that delays *Penn.*

1841 Financial crisis further postpones *Penn.* Poe takes job on *Graham's* staff; publishes "The Murders in the Rue Morgue" and "A Descent into the Maelström." Meets Rufus Griswold; plans to edit new monthly magazine in collaboration with George Graham and solicits work from noted American authors, but privately seeks government appointment through Thomas. *Graham's* publishes Poe's features on "Secret Writing" and "Autography."

1842 Virginia Poe suffers pulmonary hemorrhage that signals consumption; Poe drinks to relieve sorrow. Interviews Charles Dickens; resigns position at *Graham's.* Renews efforts to obtain patronage job through Tyler administration; makes abortive visit to New York seeking editorial work. Fails to receive government appointment; publishes "The Mystery of Marie Rogêt," based on death of Mary Rogers in New York.

1843 James Russell Lowell's *Pioneer* publishes "The Tell-Tale Heart." Poe enlists publisher Thomas C. Clarke as partner in projected magazine now called *The Stylus.* Drinks heavily during disastrous visit to Washington in quest of patronage appointment; offends Thomas Dunn English there; loses support of Clarke, who commissions English to write temperance novel. Wins one hundred dollars in *Dollar Newspaper* contest with "The Gold-Bug"; fails to obtain government position; delivers lecture, "American Poetry," in several cities. English's serialized novel, *The Doom of the Drinker,* caricatures Poe.

1844 Enters most productive year as writer; moves to New York; creates sensation with New York *Sun* hoax on transatlantic balloon flight. Explores new strategies to launch *Stylus;* writes "Doings of Gotham" dispatches for Columbia (Pennsylvania) *Spy;* publishes "The Purloined Letter" and joins editorial staff of *Evening Mirror.*

1845 Develops connections with Young America group and Evert Duyckinck; publishes "The Raven" and becomes literary celebrity; joins staff of *Broadway Journal,* acquiring part ownership, and

A Note on Texts

The texts of Poe's published works are in the public domain. In this edition, taking advantage of recent textual scholarship and generally following the principles of modern bibliography in establishing the texts to be published, I have endeavored to present the most readable and reliable versions of Poe's works. That is, I have attempted to reproduce the last published version over which the author had editorial control. For the fiction and poetry, I have mostly relied on the Redfield edition of *The Works of the Late Edgar Allan Poe,* edited by Rufus W. Griswold. Whatever animus Griswold bore for Poe (and betrayed in his introductory memoir), he took the trouble to reproduce, in most cases, the latest versions of each work, sometimes inserting subsequent authorial revisions that Poe had inscribed marginally in late publications of his work. Yet the Redfield edition did not incorporate all of those revisions, and in several tales and poems I have included further emendations thanks to electronic texts provided by the Edgar Allan Poe Society of Baltimore. I thank Jeffrey A. Savoye for his kind cooperation.

Griswold's edition of 1850–56 also included a number of misprints and typographical errors, which I have silently corrected. For the sake of readability, I have also added accents omitted from foreign words and (in a very few cases) corrected spelling errors. I have also compared my versions of the poetry and tales with those established by Thomas O. Mabbott, sometimes adopting editorial revisions made by Mabbott and in a few cases correcting his texts. (Parenthetical dates in the table of contents denote first publication.)

My texts for the critical essays and opinions—some of which

appeared in Griswold's edition—ultimately derive from the original
periodical sources. These writings were not revised by Poe and so
present few editorial problems. For the letters, I have relied on the
texts established by John Ward Ostrom in the two-volume 1948
Harvard edition, used with permission of the Gordian Press,
which now holds the copyright.

The Portable Edgar
Allan Poe

TALES

TALES

Poe considered the domain of the short prose tale less "elevated" than that of the poem but more extensive and thus more conducive to innovation. He noted that the author of a tale "may bring to his theme a vast variety of modes or inflections of thought." The seventy-odd narratives that he published between 1832 and 1849 represent a surprisingly diverse body of fiction marked by ongoing experimentation and compulsive revision. Throughout his career Poe continued to rewrite even his greatest stories; as late as 1848, for example, he was still recasting "Ligeia." For the title of his first volume of stories, he used the terms "grotesque" and "arabesque" to characterize their "prevalent tenor," the former connoting deformity or ugliness and the latter fantastic intricacy. He regarded his arabesque tales as more serious productions, "phantasy-pieces" associated unfairly by critics with " 'Germanism' and gloom." Elsewhere he identified "tales of ratiocination" (detection) and "tales of effect" (sensation) as notable varieties of prose fiction, having already produced key examples of both. Although he critically disparaged allegory, he ventured into that mode in such works as "William Wilson" and "The Masque of the Red Death." Poe's experiments in short narrative also included prose poems, spiritualized dialogues, and landscape sketches. He purposely blurred the line between the expository essay and the tale, between fact and fiction, in both "The Premature Burial" and "The Imp of the Perverse." Essays such as "The Philosophy of Furniture" have sometimes been included among his tales, as have certain anecdotal reviews. Some of the articles that he composed to accompany magazine illustrations can likewise stand as independent tales.

Poe's contributions to the tale as a literary genre include what is often regarded as the earliest theory of the short story form, four paragraphs (see pp. 534–36) tucked in a review of Hawthorne's *Twice-Told Tales*. His emphasis on "single effect" to intensify Gothic sensation led him to compose unified narratives in which orchestrated actions, images, and impressions culminate in a striking conclusion. In such tales as "Ligeia," "The Fall of the House of Usher," or "The Facts in the Case of M. Valdemar," the ending produces horror through shock: a sudden, final transformation exceeds expectation. If Poe did not originate surprise endings in the tale, he popularized and perfected them. More significantly, perhaps, he experimented with first-person narration and demonstrated the unsettling effect of an irrational, unreliable narrator, whose gradual, seemingly inadvertent betrayal of derangement undermines his own version of events while implying another. From "Berenice" to "The Cask of Amontillado," Poe created I-narrators who calmly and methodically disclose their mad compulsions, producing in "The Tell-Tale Heart" and "The Black Cat" his most penetrating analyses of psychopathic violence.

Poe also developed narrative prototypes for science fiction and the modern detective story. In an early work ("The Unparalleled Adventure of One Hans Pfaall"), he mixed science and satire to describe a balloon flight to the moon, but in a later, more plausible narrative ("The Balloon Hoax"), he embraced strict verisimilitude, extrapolating from scientific data to chronicle an imagined flight across the Atlantic. In "MS. Found in a Bottle" he traced an incredible voyage toward an immense vortex at the South Pole, and in his only full-length novel, *The Narrative of Arthur Gordon Pym*, he incorporated (and plagiarized) scientific observations by actual South Sea explorers to "authenticate" a fantastic account of the polar region. Such scientific hoaxes as "The Facts in the Case of M. Valdemar" illustrate his credo that "the most vitally important point in fiction" is that of "earnestness or verisimilitude." Poe used the semblance of reality to mystify his reader, serving up palpable fiction as positive fact. His fascination with criminology and investigative ratiocination, already apparent in "The Man of the Crowd," yielded a trio of Parisian crime tales featuring C. August Dupin. Exercises in rational analysis also figure in "A Descent into the Maelström," "The Gold-Bug," and "The Oblong Box."

Although often associated with Gothic tales of terror, Poe devoted roughly half of his fiction to humor, producing satires, burlesques, parodies, and spoofs. Several of these pieces now seem too silly, affected, or topical to engage modern readers, and a handful appear to be dashed off for the sake of money alone. But certain comic narratives cleverly lampoon the sensational tale as popularized in *Blackwood's Magazine,* and other farces mock national myths and illusions. Even supposedly serious tales include grimly comic touches: Poe's love of jokes and puns gives manic hilarity to "The Cask of Amontillado," and a similar sardonic humor animates "Hop-Frog," while "The Premature Burial" ends with an unexpected joke on the reader.

During the first decade of his magazine career, Poe devoted himself almost exclusively to foreign subjects: predicaments or conflicts grounded in Old World places—Venice, London, Paris, and other locales vaguely European. Nearly all of his greatest tales—such as "Ligeia," "The Fall of the House of Usher," or "William Wilson"—impute to foreign settings a strangeness that supplements the uncanny effect of narrative events. From "Metzengerstein" through "The Masque of the Red Death" and "The Pit and the Pendulum," Poe portrayed a distinctly imaginary Europe marked by decadence, rivalry, tyranny, and corruption—by the very evils from which the young republic naively supposed itself liberated. But by the early 1840s, literary nationalism had made American subjects and materials nearly obligatory, and beginning with "The Gold-Bug," set in South Carolina, Poe pragmatically shifted his fiction toward domestic scenes and situations. Yet he refused to rewrite history for the sake of American mythmaking and argued defiantly that national literature was a contradiction in terms. Convinced that "the world at large [is] the true audience of the author," Poe continued to prefer foreign themes and crafted several late European tales—such as "The Cask of Amontillado"— dramatizing universal human passions.

Predicaments

Predicament

MS. FOUND IN A BOTTLE

*Qui n'a plus qu'un moment à vivre
N'a plus rien à dissimuler.*

— QUINAULT — ATYS.[1]

Of my country and of my family I have little to say. Ill usage and length of years have driven me from the one, and estranged me from the other. Hereditary wealth afforded me an education of no common order, and a contemplative turn of mind enabled me to methodise the stores which early study diligently garnered up. Beyond all things, the works of the German moralists gave me great delight; not from any ill-advised admiration of their eloquent madness, but from the ease with which my habits of rigid thought enabled me to detect their falsities. I have often been reproached with the aridity of my genius; a deficiency of imagination has been imputed to me as a crime; and the Pyrrhonism of my opinions has at all times rendered me notorious. Indeed, a strong relish for physical philosophy has, I fear, tinctured my mind with a very common error of this age—I mean the habit of referring occurrences, even the least susceptible of such reference, to the principles of that science. Upon the whole, no person could be less liable than myself to be led away from the severe precincts of truth by the *ignes fatui* of superstition. I have thought proper to premise thus much, lest the incredible tale I have to tell should be considered rather the raving of a crude imagination, than the positive experience of a mind to which the reveries of fancy have been a dead letter and a nullity.

After many years spent in foreign travel, I sailed in the year 18—, from the port of Batavia, in the rich and populous island of Java, on a voyage to the Archipelago of the Sunda islands. I went as passenger—having no other inducement than a kind of nervous restlessness which haunted me as a fiend.

Our vessel was a beautiful ship of about four hundred tons, copper-fastened, and built at Bombay of Malabar teak. She was freighted with cotton-wool and oil, from the Lachadive islands. We had also on board coir, jaggeree, ghee, cocoa-nuts, and a few cases of opium. The stowage was clumsily done, and the vessel consequently crank.

We got under way with a mere breath of wind, and for many days stood along the eastern coast of Java, without any other incident to beguile the monotony of our course than the occasional meeting with some of the small grabs of the Archipelago to which we were bound.

One evening, leaning over the taffrail, I observed a very singular, isolated cloud, to the N.W. It was remarkable, as well for its color, as from its being the first we had seen since our departure from Batavia. I watched it attentively until sunset, when it spread all at once to the eastward and westward, girting in the horizon with a narrow strip of vapor, and looking like a long line of low beach. My notice was soon afterwards attracted by the dusky-red appearance of the moon, and the peculiar character of the sea. The latter was undergoing a rapid change, and the water seemed more than usually transparent. Although I could distinctly see the bottom, yet, heaving the lead, I found the ship in fifteen fathoms. The air now became intolerably hot, and was loaded with spiral exhalations similar to those arising from heated iron. As night came on, every breath of wind died away, and a more entire calm it is impossible to conceive. The flame of a candle burned upon the poop without the least perceptible motion, and a long hair, held between the finger and thumb, hung without the possibility of detecting a vibration. However, as the captain said he could perceive no indication of danger, and as we were drifting in bodily to shore, he ordered the sails to be furled, and the anchor let go. No watch was set, and the crew, consisting principally of Malays, stretched themselves deliberately upon deck. I went below—not without a full presentiment of evil. Indeed, every appearance warranted me in apprehending a Simoon. I told the captain my fears; but he paid no attention to what I said, and left me without deigning to give a reply. My uneasiness, however, prevented me from sleeping, and about midnight I went upon deck. As I placed my foot upon the upper step of the companion-ladder, I was startled by a loud, humming noise, like that occasioned by the rapid revolution of a mill-wheel, and before I could ascertain its meaning,

I found the ship quivering to its centre. In the next instant, a wilderness of foam hurled us upon our beam-ends, and, rushing over us fore and aft, swept the entire decks from stem to stern.

The extreme fury of the blast proved, in a great measure, the salvation of the ship. Although completely water-logged, yet, as her masts had gone by the board, she rose, after a minute, heavily from the sea, and, staggering awhile beneath the immense pressure of the tempest, finally righted.

By what miracle I escaped destruction, it is impossible to say. Stunned by the shock of the water, I found myself, upon recovery, jammed in between the stern-post and rudder. With great difficulty I gained my feet, and looking dizzily around, was at first struck with the idea of our being among breakers; so terrific, beyond the wildest imagination, was the whirlpool of mountainous and foaming ocean within which we were engulfed. After a while, I heard the voice of an old Swede, who had shipped with us at the moment of our leaving port. I hallooed to him with all my strength, and presently he came reeling aft. We soon discovered that we were the sole survivors of the accident. All on deck, with the exception of ourselves, had been swept overboard; the captain and mates must have perished as they slept, for the cabins were deluged with water. Without assistance, we could expect to do little for the security of the ship, and our exertions were at first paralyzed by the momentary expectation of going down. Our cable had, of course, parted like pack-thread, at the first breath of the hurricane, or we should have been instantaneously overwhelmed. We scudded with frightful velocity before the sea, and the water made clear breaches over us. The frame-work of our stern was shattered excessively, and, in almost every respect, we had received considerable injury; but to our extreme joy we found the pumps unchoked, and that we had made no great shifting of our ballast. The main fury of the blast had already blown over, and we apprehended little danger from the violence of the wind; but we looked forward to its total cessation with dismay; well believing, that, in our shattered condition, we should inevitably perish in the tremendous swell which would ensue. But this very just apprehension seemed by no means likely to be soon verified. For five entire days and nights—during which our only subsistence was a small quantity of jaggeree, procured with great difficulty from the forecastle—the hulk flew at a rate defying computation, before rapidly succeeding flaws of wind, which, without equalling the first violence of the Simoon, were still more terrific than any tempest I had before encountered. Our course for the first four days was, with trifling variations, S.E. and by S.; and we must have run down the coast of New Holland. On the fifth day the cold became extreme, although the wind had hauled round a point more to the northward. The sun arose with a sickly yellow lustre, and clambered a very few degrees above the horizon—emitting no decisive light. There were no clouds apparent, yet the wind was upon the increase, and blew with a fitful and unsteady fury. About noon, as nearly as we could guess, our attention was again arrested by the appearance of the sun. It gave out no light, properly so called, but a dull and sullen glow without reflection, as if all its rays were polarized. Just before sinking within the turgid sea, its central fires suddenly went out, as if hurriedly extinguished by some unaccountable power. It was a dim, sliver-like rim, alone, as it rushed down the unfathomable ocean.

We waited in vain for the arrival of the sixth day—that day to me has not arrived—to the Swede, never did arrive. Thenceforward we were enshrouded in patchy darkness, so that we could not have seen an object at twenty paces from the ship. Eternal night continued to envelop us, all unrelieved by the phosphoric sea-brilliancy to which we had been accustomed in the tropics. We observed too, that, although the tempest continued to rage with unabated violence, there was no longer to be discovered the usual appearance of surf, or foam, which had hitherto attended us. All around were horror, and thick gloom, and a black sweltering desert of ebony. Superstitious terror crept by degrees into the spirit of the old Swede, and my own soul was wrapped up in silent wonder. We neglected all care of the ship, as worse than useless, and securing ourselves, as well as possible, to the stump of the mizen-mast, looked out bitterly into the world of ocean. We had no means of calculating time, nor could we form any guess of our situation. We were, however, well aware of having made farther to the southward than any previous navigators, and felt great amazement at not meeting with the usual impediments of ice. In the meantime every moment threatened to be our last— every mountainous billow hurried to overwhelm us. The swell surpassed anything I had imagined possible, and that we were not instantly buried is a miracle. My companion spoke of the lightness of our cargo, and reminded me of the excellent qualities of our ship; but I could not help feeling the utter hopelessness of hope itself, and prepared myself gloomily for that death which I thought nothing could defer beyond an hour, as, with every knot of way the ship made, the swelling of the black stupendous seas became more dismally appalling. At times we gasped for breath at an elevation beyond the albatross—at times became dizzy with the velocity of our descent into some watery hell, where the air grew stagnant, and no sound disturbed the slumbers of the kraken.

We were at the bottom of one of these abysses, when a quick scream from my companion broke fearfully upon the night. "See! see!" cried he, shrieking in my ears, "Almighty God! see! see!" As he spoke, I became aware of a dull, sullen glare of red light which streamed down the sides of the vast chasm where we lay, and threw a fitful brilliancy upon our deck. Casting my eyes upwards, I beheld a spectacle which froze the current of my blood. At a terrific height directly above us, and upon the very verge of the precipitous descent, hovered a gigantic ship, of perhaps, four thousand tons. Although upreared upon the summit of a wave more than a hundred times her own altitude, her apparent size still exceeded that of any ship of the line or East Indiaman in existence. Her huge hull was of a deep dingy black, unrelieved by any of the customary carvings of a ship. A single row of brass cannon protruded from her open ports, and dashed from their polished surfaces the fires of innumerable battle-lanterns, which swung to and fro about her rigging. But what mainly inspired us with horror and astonishment, was that she bore up under a press of sail in the very teeth of that supernatural sea, and of that ungovernable hurricane. When we first discovered her, her bows were alone to be seen, as she rose slowly from the dim and horrible gulf beyond her. For a moment of intense terror she paused upon the giddy pinnacle, as if in contemplation of her own sublimity, then trembled and tottered, and—came down.

At this instant, I know not what sudden self-possession came over my spirit. Staggering as far aft as I could, I awaited fearlessly the ruin that was to overwhelm. Our own vessel was at length ceasing from her struggles, and sinking with her head to the sea. The shock of the descending mass struck her, consequently, in that portion of her frame which was already under water, and the inevitable result was to hurl me, with irresistible violence, upon the rigging of the stranger.

As I fell, the ship hove in stays, and went about; and to the confusion ensuing I attributed my escape from the notice of the crew. With little difficulty I made my way unperceived to the main hatchway, which was partially open, and soon found an opportunity of secreting myself in the hold. Why I did so I can hardly tell. An indefinite sense of awe, which at first sight of the navigators of the ship had taken hold of my mind, was perhaps the principle of my concealment. I was unwilling to trust myself with a race of people who had offered, to the cursory glance I had taken, so many points of vague novelty, doubt, and apprehension. I therefore thought proper to contrive a hiding-place in the hold. This I did by removing a small portion of the shifting-boards, in such a manner as to afford me a convenient retreat between the huge timbers of the ship.

I had scarcely completed my work, when a footstep in the hold forced me to make use of it. A man passed by my place of concealment with a feeble and unsteady gait. I could not see his face, but had an opportunity of observing his general appearance. There was about it an evidence of great age and infirmity. His knees tottered beneath a load of years, and his entire frame quivered under the burthen. He muttered to himself, in a low broken tone, some words of a language which I could not understand, and groped in a corner among a pile of singular-looking instruments, and decayed charts of navigation. His manner was a wild mixture of the peevishness of second childhood, and the solemn dignity of a God. He at length went on deck, and I saw him no more.

A feeling, for which I have no name, has taken possession of my soul—a sensation which will admit of no analysis, to which the lessons of bygone times are inadequate, and for which I fear futurity itself will offer me no key. To a mind constituted like my own, the latter consideration is an evil. I shall never—I know that I shall never—be satisfied with regard to the nature of my conceptions.

Yet it is not wonderful that these conceptions are indefinite, since they have their origin in sources so utterly novel. A new sense—a new entity is added to my soul.

It is long since I first trod the deck of this terrible ship, and the rays of my destiny are, I think, gathering to a focus. Incomprehensible men! Wrapped up in meditations of a kind which I cannot divine, they pass me by unnoticed. Concealment is utter folly on my part, for the people *will not see*. It was but just now that I passed directly before the eyes of the mate; it was no long while ago that I ventured into the captain's own private cabin, and took thence the materials with which I write, and have written. I shall from time to time continue this journal. It is true that I may not find an opportunity of transmitting it to the world, but I will not fail to make the endeavor. At the last moment I will enclose the MS. in a bottle, and cast it within the sea.

An incident has occurred which has given me new room for meditation. Are such things the operation of ungoverned chance? I had ventured upon deck and thrown myself down, without attracting any notice, among a pile of ratlin-stuff and old sails in the bottom of the yawl. While musing upon the singularity of my fate, I unwittingly daubed with a tar-brush the edges of a neatly-folded studding-sail which lay near me on a barrel. The studding-sail is now bent upon the ship, and the thoughtless touches of the brush are spread out into the word DISCOVERY.

I have made many observations lately upon the structure of the vessel. Although well armed, she is not, I think, a ship of war. Her rigging, build, and general equipment, all negative a supposition of this kind. What she *is not*, I can easily perceive; what she *is* I fear it is impossible to say. I know not how it is, but in scrutinizing her strange model and singular cast of spars, her huge size and overgrown suits of canvas, her severely simple bow and antiquated stern, there will occasionally flash across my mind a sensation of familiar things, and there is always mixed up with such indistinct shadows of recollection, an unaccountable memory of old foreign chronicles and ages long ago. * * * * * * * * * *

I have been looking at the timbers of the ship. She is built of a material to which I am a stranger. There is a peculiar character about the wood which strikes me as rendering it unfit for the purpose to which it has been applied. I mean its extreme *porousness,* considered independently of the worm-eaten condition which is a consequence of navigation in these seas, and apart from the rottenness attendant upon age. It will appear perhaps an observation somewhat over-curious, but this wood would have every characteristic of Spanish oak, if Spanish oak were distended by any unnatural means.

In reading the above sentence a curious apothegm of an old weather-beaten Dutch navigator comes full upon my recollection. "It is as sure," he was wont to say, when any doubt was entertained of his veracity, "as sure as there is a sea where the ship itself will grow in bulk like the living body of the seaman." * * * * * *

About an hour ago, I made bold to thrust myself among a group of the crew. They paid me no manner of attention, and, although I stood in the very midst of them all, seemed utterly unconscious of my presence. Like the one I had at first seen in the hold, they all bore about them the marks of a hoary old age. Their knees trembled with infirmity; their shoulders were bent double with decrepitude; their shrivelled skins rattled in the wind; their voices were low, tremulous, and broken; their eyes glistened with the rheum of years; and their gray hairs streamed terribly in the tempest. Around them, on every part of the deck, lay scattered mathematical instruments of the most quaint and obsolete construction.

I mentioned, some time ago, the bending of a studding-sail. From that period, the ship, being thrown dead off the wind, has continued her terrific course due south, with every rag of canvas packed upon her, from her trucks to her lower studding-sail booms, and rolling every moment her top-gallant yard-arms into the most appalling hell of water which it can enter into the mind of a man to imagine. I have just left the deck, where I find it impossible to maintain a footing, although the crew seem to experience little inconvenience. It appears to me a miracle of miracles that our enormous bulk is not swallowed up at once and forever. We are surely doomed to hover continually upon the brink of eternity, without taking a final plunge into the abyss. From billows a thousand times more stupendous than any I have ever seen, we glide away with the facility of the arrowy sea-gull; and the colossal waters rear their heads above us like demons of the deep, but like demons confined to simple threats

and forbidden to destroy. I am led to attribute these frequent es-
capes to the only natural cause which can account for such effect. I
must suppose the ship to be within the influence of some strong cur-
rent, or impetuous under-tow. * * * * * * * * * * *

I have seen the captain face to face, and in his own cabin—but,
as I expected, he paid me no attention. Although in his appearance
there is, to a casual observer, nothing which might bespeak him
more or less than man, still, a feeling of irrepressible reverence and
awe mingled with the sensation of wonder with which I regarded
him. In stature, he is nearly my own height; that is, about five feet
eight inches. He is of a well-knit and compact frame of body, nei-
ther robust nor remarkable otherwise. But it is the singularity of
the expression which reigns upon the face—it is the intense, the
wonderful, the thrilling evidence of old age, so utter, so extreme,
which excites within my spirit a sense—a sentiment ineffable. His
forehead, although little wrinkled, seems to bear upon it the
stamp of a myriad of years. His gray hairs are records of the past,
and his grayer eyes are sybils of the future. The cabin floor was
thickly strewn with strange, iron-clasped folios, and mouldering
instruments of science, and obsolete long-forgotten charts. His
head was bowed down upon his hands, and he pored, with a fiery
unquiet eye, over a paper which I took to be a commission, and
which, at all events, bore the signature of a monarch. He muttered
to himself—as did the first seaman whom I saw in the hold—some
low peevish syllables of a foreign tongue; and although the
speaker was close at my elbow, his voice seemed to reach my ears
from the distance of a mile. * * * * * * * * * * *

The ship and all in it are imbued with the spirit of Eld. The
crew glide to and fro like the ghosts of buried centuries; their eyes
have an eager and uneasy meaning; and when their figures fall
athwart my path in the wild glare of the battle-lanterns, I feel as I
have never felt before, although I have been all my life a dealer in
antiquities, and have imbibed the shadows of fallen columns at
Balbec, and Tadmor, and Persepolis, until my very soul has be-
come a ruin. * * * * * * * * * * * * * *

When I look around me, I feel ashamed of my former apprehen-
sions. If I trembled at the blast which has hitherto attended us,
shall I not stand aghast at a warring of wind and ocean, to convey
any idea of which, the words tornado and simoon are trivial and

ineffective? All in the immediate vicinity of the ship is the black-
ness of eternal night, and a chaos of foamless water; but, about a
league on either side of us, may be seen, indistinctly and at inter-
vals, stupendous ramparts of ice, towering away into the desolate
sky, and looking like the walls of the universe.   *   *   *   *   *

As I imagined, the ship proves to be in a current—if that appel-
lation can properly be given to a tide which, howling and shriek-
ing by the white ice, thunders on to the southward with a velocity
like the headlong dashing of a cataract.

To conceive the horror of my sensations is, I presume, utterly im-
possible; yet a curiosity to penetrate the mysteries of these awful re-
gions, predominates even over my despair, and will reconcile me to
the most hideous aspect of death. It is evident that we are hurrying
onwards to some exciting knowledge—some never-to-be-imparted
secret, whose attainment is destruction. Perhaps this current leads
us to the southern pole itself. It must be confessed that a supposi-
tion apparently so wild has every probability in its favor.[3]

The crew pace the deck with unquiet and tremulous step; but there
is upon their countenances an expression more of the eagerness of
hope than of the apathy of despair.

In the meantime the wind is still in our poop, and, as we carry a
crowd of canvas, the ship is at times lifted bodily from out the sea!
Oh, horror upon horror!—the ice opens suddenly to the right, and to
the left, and we are whirling dizzily, in immense concentric circles,
round and round the borders of a gigantic amphitheatre, the summit
of whose walls is lost in the darkness and the distance. But little time
will be left me to ponder upon my destiny! The circles rapidly grow
small—we are plunging madly within the grasp of the whirlpool—
and amid a roaring, and bellowing, and thundering of ocean and of
tempest, the ship is quivering—oh God! and—going down!

Note.—The "MS. Found in a Bottle," was originally published in
1832, and it was not until many years afterwards that I became ac-
quainted with the maps of Mercator, in which the ocean is repre-
sented as rushing, by four mouths, into the (northern) Polar Gulf, to
be absorbed into the bowels of the earth; the Pole itself being repre-
sented by a black rock, towering to a prodigious height.[4]

A DESCENT INTO THE MAELSTRÖM

The ways of God in Nature, as in Providence, are not as *our* ways;
nor are the models that we frame any way commensurate to the
vastness, profundity, and unsearchableness of His works, *which
have a depth in them greater than the well of Democritus.*

JOSEPH GLANVILLE.

We had now reached the summit of the loftiest crag. For some
minutes the old man seemed too much exhausted to speak.

"Not long ago," said he at length, "and I could have guided you
on this route as well as the youngest of my sons; but, about three
years past, there happened to me an event such as never happened
before to mortal man—or at least such as no man ever survived to
tell of—and the six hours of deadly terror which I then endured
have broken me up body and soul. You suppose me a *very* old
man—but I am not. It took less than a single day to change these
hairs from a jetty black to white, to weaken my limbs, and to un-
string my nerves, so that I tremble at the least exertion, and am
frightened at a shadow. Do you know I can scarcely look over this
little cliff without getting giddy?"

The "little cliff," upon whose edge he had so carelessly thrown
himself down to rest that the weightier portion of his body hung
over it, while he was only kept from falling by the tenure of his el-
bow on its extreme and slippery edge—this "little cliff" arose, a
sheer unobstructed precipice of black shining rock, some fifteen or
sixteen hundred feet from the world of crags beneath us. Nothing
would have tempted me to within half a dozen yards of its brink.
In truth so deeply was I excited by the perilous position of my
companion, that I fell at full length upon the ground, clung to the
shrubs around me, and dared not even glance upward at the sky—
while I struggled in vain to divest myself of the idea that the very

foundations of the mountain were in danger from the fury of the winds. It was long before I could reason myself into sufficient courage to sit up and look out into the distance.

"You must get over these fancies," said the guide, "for I have brought you here that you might have the best possible view of the scene of that event I mentioned—and to tell you the whole story with the spot just under your eye."

"We are now," he continued, in that particularizing manner which distinguished him—"we are now close upon the Norwegian coast—in the sixty-eighth degree of latitude—in the great province of Nordland—and in the dreary district of Lofoden. The mountain upon whose top we sit is Helseggen, the Cloudy. Now raise yourself up a little higher—hold on to the grass if you feel giddy—so—and look out, beyond the belt of vapor beneath us, into the sea."

I looked dizzily, and beheld a wide expanse of ocean, whose waters wore so inky a hue as to bring at once to my mind the Nubian geographer's account of the *Mare Tenebrarum*.[1] A panorama more deplorably desolate no human imagination can conceive. To the right and left, as far as the eye could reach, there lay outstretched, like ramparts of the world, lines of horridly black and beetling cliff, whose character of gloom was but the more forcibly illustrated by the surf which reared high up against it its white and ghastly crest, howling and shrieking for ever. Just opposite the promontory upon whose apex we were placed, and at a distance of some five or six miles out at sea, there was visible a small, bleak-looking island; or, more properly, its position was discernible through the wilderness of surge in which it was enveloped. About two miles nearer the land, arose another of smaller size, hideously craggy and barren, and encompassed at various intervals by a cluster of dark rocks.

The appearance of the ocean, in the space between the more distant island and the shore, had something very unusual about it. Although, at the time, so strong a gale was blowing landward that a brig in the remote offing lay to under a double-reefed trysail, and constantly plunged her whole hull out of sight, still there was here nothing like a regular swell, but only a short, quick, angry cross dashing of water in every direction—as well in the teeth of the wind as otherwise. Of foam there was little except in the immediate vicinity of the rocks.

"The island in the distance," resumed the old man, "is called by the Norwegians Vurrgh. The one midway is Moskoe. That a mile to the northward is Ambaaren. Yonder are Iflesen, Hoteyholm, Kieldholm, Suarven, and Buckholm. Farther off—between Moskoe and Vurrgh—are Otterholm, Flimen, Sandflesen, and Skarholm.[2] These are the true names of the places—but why it has been thought necessary to name them at all, is more than either you or I can understand. Do you hear anything? Do you see any change in the water?"

We had now been about ten minutes upon the top of Helseggen, to which we had ascended from the interior of Lofoden, so that we had caught no glimpse of the sea until it had burst upon us from the summit. As the old man spoke, I became aware of a loud and gradually increasing sound, like the moaning of a vast herd of buffaloes upon an American prairie; and at the same moment I perceived that what seamen term the *chopping* character of the ocean beneath us, was rapidly changing into a current which set to the eastward. Even while I gazed, this current acquired a monstrous velocity. Each moment added to its speed—to its headlong impetuosity. In five minutes the whole sea, as far as Vurrgh, was lashed into ungovernable fury; but it was between Moskoe and the coast that the main uproar held its sway. Here the vast bed of the waters, seamed and scarred into a thousand conflicting channels, burst suddenly into phrensied convulsion—heaving, boiling, hissing—gyrating in gigantic and innumerable vortices, and all whirling and plunging on to the eastward with a rapidity which water never elsewhere assumes except in precipitous descents.

In a few minutes more, there came over the scene another radical alteration. The general surface grew somewhat more smooth, and the whirlpools, one by one, disappeared, while prodigious streaks of foam became apparent where none had been seen before. These streaks, at length, spreading out to a great distance, and entering into combination, took unto themselves the gyratory motion of the subsided vortices, and seemed to form the germ of another more vast. Suddenly—very suddenly—this assumed a distinct and definite existence, in a circle of more than a half a mile in diameter. The edge of the whirl was represented by a broad belt of gleaming spray; but no particle of this slipped into the mouth of the terrific funnel, whose interior, as far as the eye could fathom it, was a smooth, shining, and jet-black wall of water, inclined to the horizon at an angle of some forty-five degrees, speeding dizzily round and round with a swaying and sweltering motion, and sending forth to the winds an appalling voice, half shriek, half roar, such as not even the mighty cataract of Niagara ever lifts up in its agony to Heaven.

The mountain trembled to its very base, and the rock rocked. I threw myself upon my face, and clung to the scant herbage in an excess of nervous agitation.

"This," said I at length, to the old man—"this *can* be nothing else than the great whirlpool of the Maelström."

"So it is sometimes termed," said he. "We Norwegians call it the Moskoe-ström, from the island of Moskoe in the midway."

The ordinary accounts of this vortex had by no means prepared me for what I saw. That of Jonas Ramus, which is perhaps the most circumstantial of any, cannot impart the faintest conception either of the magnificence, or of the horror of the scene—or of the wild bewildering sense of *the novel* which confounds the beholder. I am not sure from what point of view the writer in question surveyed it, nor at what time; but it could neither have been from the summit of Helseggen, nor during a storm. There are some passages of his description, nevertheless, which may be quoted for their details, although their effect is exceedingly feeble in conveying an impression of the spectacle.

"Between Lofoden and Moskoe," he says, "the depth of the water is between thirty-six and forty fathoms; but on the other side, toward Ver (Vurrgh) this depth decreases so as not to afford a convenient passage for a vessel, without the risk of splitting on the rocks, which happens even in the calmest weather. When it is flood, the stream runs up the country between Lofoden and Moskoe with a boisterous rapidity; but the roar of its impetuous ebb to the sea is scarce equalled by the loudest and most dreadful cataracts; the noise being heard several leagues off, and the vortices or pits are of such an extent and depth, that if a ship comes within its attraction, it is inevitably absorbed and carried down to the bottom, and there beat to pieces against the rocks; and when the water relaxes, the fragments thereof are thrown up again. But these intervals of tranquility are only at the turn of the ebb and flood, and in calm weather, and last but a quarter of an hour, its

violence gradually returning. When the stream is most boister-
ous, and its fury heightened by a storm, it is dangerous to come
within a Norway mile of it. Boats, yachts, and ships have been
carried away by not guarding against it before they were within its
reach. It likewise happens frequently, that whales come too near
the stream, and are overpowered by its violence; and then it is
impossible to describe their howlings and bellowings in their fruit-
less struggles to disengage themselves. A bear once, attempting to
swim from Lofoden to Moskoe, was caught by the stream and
borne down, while he roared terribly, so as to be heard on shore.
Large stocks of firs and pine trees, after being absorbed by the cur-
rent, rise again broken and torn to such a degree as if bristles grew
upon them. This plainly shows the bottom to consist of craggy
rocks, among which they are whirled to and fro. This stream is
regulated by the flux and reflux of the sea—it being constantly
high and low water every six hours. In the year 1645, early in the
morning of Sexagesima Sunday, it raged with such noise and im-
petuosity that the very stones of the houses on the coast fell to the
ground."

In regard to the depth of the water, I could not see how this
could have been ascertained at all in the immediate vicinity of the
vortex. The "forty fathoms" must have reference only to portions
of the channel close upon the shore either of Moskoe or Lofoden.
The depth in the centre of the Moskoe-ström must be immeasur-
ably greater; and no better proof of this fact is necessary than can
be obtained from even the sidelong glance into the abyss of the
whirl which may be had from the highest crag of Helseggen.
Looking down from this pinnacle upon the howling Phlegethon
below, I could not help smiling at the simplicity with which the
honest Jonas Ramus records, as a matter difficult of belief, the an-
ecdotes of the whales and the bears; for it appeared to me, in fact,
a self-evident thing, that the largest ship of the line in existence,
coming within the influence of that deadly attraction, could resist
it as little as a feather the hurricane, and must disappear bodily
and at once.

The attempts to account for the phenomenon—some of which,
I remember, seemed to me sufficiently plausible in perusal—now
wore a very different and unsatisfactory aspect. The idea generally
received is that this, as well as three smaller vortices among the

Ferroe islands, "have no other cause than the collision of waves rising and falling, at flux and reflux, against a ridge of rocks and shelves, which confines the water so that it precipitates itself like a cataract; and thus the higher the flood rises, the deeper must the fall be, and the natural result of all is a whirlpool or vortex, the prodigious suction of which is sufficiently known by lesser experiments."—These are the words of the Encyclopædia Britannica. Kircher and others imagine that in the centre of the channel of the Maelström is an abyss penetrating the globe, and issuing in some very remote part—the Gulf of Bothnia being somewhat decidedly named in one instance. This opinion, idle in itself, was the one to which, as I gazed, my imagination most readily assented; and, mentioning it to the guide, I was rather surprised to hear him say that, although it was the view almost universally entertained of the subject by the Norwegians, it nevertheless was not his own. As to the former notion he confessed his inability to comprehend it; and here I agreed with him—for, however conclusive on paper, it becomes altogether unintelligible, and even absurd, amid the thunder of the abyss.

"You have had a good look at the whirl now," said the old man, "and if you will creep round this crag, so as to get in its lee, and deaden the roar of the water, I will tell you a story that will convince you I ought to know something of the Moskoe-ström."

I placed myself as desired, and he proceeded.

"Myself and my two brothers once owned a schooner-rigged smack of about seventy tons burthen, with which we were in the habit of fishing among the islands beyond Moskoe, nearly to Vurrgh. In all violent eddies at sea there is good fishing, at proper opportunities, if one has only the courage to attempt it; but among the whole of the Lofoden coastmen, we three were the only ones who made a regular business of going out to the islands, as I tell you. The usual grounds are a great way lower down to the southward. There fish can be got at all hours, without much risk, and therefore these places are preferred. The choice spots over here among the rocks, however, not only yield the finest variety, but in far greater abundance; so that we often got in a single day, what the more timid of the craft could not scrape together in a week. In fact, we made it a matter of desperate speculation—the risk of life standing instead of labor, and courage answering for capital.

"We kept the smack in a cove about five miles higher up the coast than this; and it was our practice, in fine weather, to take advantage of the fifteen minutes' slack to push across the main channel of the Moskoe-ström, far above the pool, and then drop down upon anchorage somewhere near Otterholm, or Sandflesen, where the eddies are not so violent as elsewhere. Here we used to remain until nearly time for slack-water again, when we weighed and made for home. We never set out upon this expedition without a steady side wind for going and coming—one that we felt sure would not fail us before our return—and we seldom made a miscalculation upon this point. Twice, during six years, we were forced to stay all night at anchor on account of a dead calm, which is a rare thing indeed just about here; and once we had to remain on the grounds nearly a week, starving to death, owing to a gale which blew up shortly after our arrival, and made the channel too boisterous to be thought of. Upon this occasion we should have been driven out to sea in spite of everything, (for the whirlpools threw us round and round so violently, that, at length, we fouled our anchor and dragged it) if it had not been that we drifted into one of the innumerable cross currents—here to-day and gone to-morrow—which drove us under the lee of Flimen, where, by good luck, we brought up.

"I could not tell you the twentieth part of the difficulties we encountered 'on the grounds'—it is a bad spot to be in, even in good weather—but we made shift always to run the gauntlet of the Moskoe-ström itself without accident; although at times my heart has been in my mouth when we happened to be a minute or so behind or before the slack. The wind sometimes was not as strong as we thought it at starting, and then we made rather less way than we could wish, while the current rendered the smack unmanageable. My eldest brother had a son eighteen years old, and I had two stout boys of my own. These would have been of great assistance at such times, in using the sweeps, as well as afterward in fishing—but, somehow, although we ran the risk ourselves, we had not the heart to let the young ones get into the danger—for, after all is said and done, it *was* a horrible danger, and that is the truth.

"It is now within a few days of three years since what I am going to tell you occurred. It was on the tenth day of July, 18—, a

day which the people of this part of the world will never forget—
for it was one in which blew the most terrible hurricane that ever
came out of the heavens. And yet all the morning, and indeed un-
til late in the afternoon, there was a gentle and steady breeze from
the south-west, while the sun shone brightly, so that the oldest sea-
man among us could not have foreseen what was to follow.

"The three of us—my two brothers and myself—had crossed
over to the islands about two o'clock P.M., and had soon nearly
loaded the smack with fine fish, which, we all remarked, were
more plenty that day than we had ever known them. It was just
seven, *by my watch,* when we weighed and started for home, so as
to make the worst of the Ström at slack water, which we knew
would be at eight.

"We set out with a fresh wind on our starboard quarter, and for
some time spanked along at a great rate, never dreaming of dan-
ger, for indeed we saw not the slightest reason to apprehend it. All
at once we were taken aback by a breeze from over Helseggen.
This was most unusual—something that had never happened to us
before—and I began to feel a little uneasy, without exactly know-
ing why. We put the boat on the wind, but could make no head-
way at all for the eddies, and I was upon the point of proposing to
return to the anchorage, when, looking astern, we saw the whole
horizon covered with a singular copper-colored cloud that rose
with the most amazing velocity.

"In the meantime the breeze that had headed us off fell away,
and we were dead becalmed, drifting about in every direction.
This state of things, however, did not last long enough to give us
time to think about it. In less than a minute the storm was upon
us—in less than two the sky was entirely overcast—and what with
this and the driving spray, it became suddenly so dark that we
could not see each other in the smack.

"Such a hurricane as then blew it is folly to attempt describing.
The oldest seaman in Norway never experienced any thing like it.
We had let our sails go by the run before it cleverly took us; but, at
the first puff, both our masts went by the board as if they had been
sawed off—the mainmast taking with it my youngest brother, who
had lashed himself to it for safety.

"Our boat was the lightest feather of a thing that ever sat upon
water. It had a complete flush deck, with only a small hatch near

the bow, and this hatch it had always been our custom to batten down when about to cross the Ström, by way of precaution against the chopping seas. But for this circumstance we should have foundered at once—for we lay entirely buried for some moments. How my elder brother escaped destruction I cannot say, for I never had an opportunity of ascertaining. For my part, as soon as I had let the foresail run, I threw myself flat on deck, with my feet against the narrow gunwale of the bow, and with my hands grasping a ring-bolt near the foot of the fore-mast. It was mere instinct that prompted me to do this—which was undoubtedly the very best thing I could have done—for I was too much flurried to think.

"For some moments we were completely deluged, as I say, and all this time I held my breath, and clung to the bolt. When I could stand it no longer I raised myself upon my knees, still keeping hold with my hands, and thus got my head clear. Presently our little boat gave herself a shake, just as a dog does in coming out of the water, and thus rid herself, in some measure, of the seas. I was now trying to get the better of the stupor that had come over me, and to collect my senses so as to see what was to be done, when I felt somebody grasp my arm. It was my elder brother, and my heart leaped for joy, for I had made sure that he was overboard—but the next moment all this joy was turned into horror—for he put his mouth close to my ear, and screamed out the word 'Moskoe-ström!'

"No one ever will know what my feelings were at that moment. I shook from head to foot as if I had had the most violent fit of the ague. I knew what he meant by that one word well enough—I knew what he wished to make me understand. With the wind that now drove us on, we were bound for the whirl of the Ström, and nothing could save us!

"You perceive that in crossing the Ström *channel*, we always went a long way up above the whirl, even in the calmest weather, and then had to wait and watch carefully for the slack—but now we were driving right upon the pool itself, and in such a hurricane as this! 'To be sure,' I thought, 'we shall get there just about the slack—there is some little hope in that'—but in the next moment I cursed myself for being so great a fool as to dream of hope at all. I knew very well that we were doomed, had we been ten times a ninety-gun ship.

"By this time the first fury of the tempest had spent itself, or perhaps we did not feel it so much, as we scudded before it, but at all events the seas, which at first had been kept down by the wind, and lay flat and frothing, now got up into absolute mountains. A singular change, too, had come over the heavens. Around in every direction it was still as black as pitch, but nearly overhead there burst out, all at once, a circular rift of clear sky—as clear as I ever saw— and of a deep bright blue—and through it there blazed forth the full moon with a lustre that I never before knew her to wear. She lit up every thing about us with the greatest distinctness—but, oh God, what a scene it was to light up!

"I now made one or two attempts to speak to my brother—but, in some manner which I could not understand, the din had so increased that I could not make him hear a single word, although I screamed at the top of my voice in his ear. Presently he shook his head, looking as pale as death, and held up one of his fingers, as if to say '*listen!*'

"At first I could not make out what he meant—but soon a hideous thought flashed upon me. I dragged my watch from its fob. It was not going. I glanced at its face by the moonlight, and then burst into tears as I flung it far away into the ocean. *It had run down at seven o'clock! We were behind the time of the slack, and the whirl of the Ström was in full fury!*

"When a boat is well built, properly trimmed, and not deep laden, the waves in a strong gale, when she is going large, seem always to slip from beneath her—which appears very strange to a landsman—and this is what is called *riding,* in sea phrase. Well, so far we had ridden the swells very cleverly; but presently a gigantic sea happened to take us right under the counter, and bore us with it as it rose—up—up—as if into the sky. I would not have believed that any wave could rise so high. And then down we came with a sweep, a slide, and a plunge, that made me feel sick and dizzy, as if I was falling from some lofty mountain-top in a dream. But while we were up I had thrown a quick glance around—and that one glance was all sufficient. I saw our exact position in an instant. The Moskoe-ström whirlpool was about a quarter of a mile dead ahead—but no more like the every-day Moskoe-ström, than the whirl as you now see it is like a mill-race. If I had not known where we were, and what we had to expect, I should not have recognised the place at all. As it was, I involuntarily closed my eyes in horror. The lids clenched themselves together as if in a spasm.

"It could not have been more than two minutes afterward until we suddenly felt the waves subside, and were enveloped in foam. The boat made a sharp half turn to larboard, and then shot off in its new direction like a thunderbolt. At the same moment the roaring noise of the water was completely drowned in a kind of shrill shriek—such a sound as you might imagine given out by the waste-pipes of many thousand steam-vessels, letting off their steam all together. We were now in the belt of surf that always surrounds the whirl; and I thought, of course, that another moment would plunge us into the abyss—down which we could only see indistinctly on account of the amazing velocity with which we were borne along. The boat did not seem to sink into the water at all, but to skim like an air-bubble upon the surface of the surge. Her starboard side was next the whirl, and on the larboard arose the world of ocean we had left. It stood like a huge writhing wall between us and the horizon.

"It may appear strange, but now, when we were in the very jaws of the gulf, I felt more composed than when we were only approaching it. Having made up my mind to hope no more, I got rid of a great deal of that terror which unmanned me at first. I suppose it was despair that strung my nerves.

"It may look like boasting—but what I tell you is truth—I began to reflect how magnificent a thing it was to die in such a manner, and how foolish it was in me to think of so paltry a consideration as my own individual life, in view of so wonderful a manifestation of God's power. I do believe that I blushed with shame when this idea crossed my mind. After a little while I became possessed with the keenest curiosity about the whirl itself. I positively felt a *wish* to explore its depths, even at the sacrifice I was going to make; and my principal grief was that I should never be able to tell my old companions on shore about the mysteries I should see. These, no doubt, were singular fancies to occupy a man's mind in such extremity—and I have often thought since, that the revolutions of the boat around the pool might have rendered me a little light-headed.

"There was another circumstance which tended to restore my self-possession; and this was the cessation of the wind, which could not reach us in our present situation—for, as you saw yourself, the belt of surf is considerably lower than the general bed of the ocean, and this latter now towered above us, a high, black, mountainous ridge. If you have never been at sea in a heavy gale, you can form no idea of the confusion of mind occasioned by the wind and spray together. They blind, deafen, and strangle you, and take away all power of action or reflection. But we were now, in a great measure, rid of these annoyances—just as death-condemned felons in prison are allowed petty indulgences, forbidden them while their doom is yet uncertain.

"How often we made the circuit of the belt it is impossible to say. We careered round and round for perhaps an hour, flying rather than floating, getting gradually more and more into the middle of the surge, and then nearer and nearer to its horrible inner edge. All this time I had never let go of the ring-bolt. My brother was at the stern, holding on to a large empty water-cask which had been securely lashed under the coop of the counter, and was the only thing on deck that had not been swept overboard when the gale first took us. As we approached the brink of the pit he let go his hold upon this, and made for the ring, from which, in the agony of his terror, he endeavored to force my hands, as it was not large enough to afford us both a secure grasp. I never felt deeper grief than when I saw him attempt this act—although I knew he was a madman when he did it—a raving maniac through sheer fright. I did not care, however, to contest the point with him. I thought it could make no difference whether either of us held on at all; so I let him have the bolt, and went astern to the cask. This there was no great difficulty in doing; for the smack flew round steadily enough, and upon an even keel—only swaying to and fro, with the immense sweeps and swelters of the whirl. Scarcely had I secured myself in my new position, when we gave a wild lurch to starboard, and rushed headlong into the abyss. I muttered a hurried prayer to God, and thought all was over.

"As I felt the sickening sweep of the descent, I had instinctively tightened my hold upon the barrel, and closed my eyes. For some seconds I dared not open them—while I expected instant destruction, and wondered that I was not already in my death-struggles with the water. But moment after moment elapsed. I still lived. The sense of falling had ceased; and the motion of the vessel seemed much as it had been before while in the belt of foam, with the exception that she now lay more along. I took courage, and looked once again upon the scene.

"Never shall I forget the sensations of awe, horror, and admiration with which I gazed about me. The boat appeared to be hanging, as if by magic, midway down, upon the interior surface of a funnel vast in circumference, prodigious in depth, and whose perfectly smooth sides might have been mistaken for ebony, but for the bewildering rapidity with which they spun around, and for the gleaming and ghastly radiance they shot forth, as the rays of the full moon, from that circular rift amid the clouds which I have already described, streamed in a flood of golden glory along the black walls, and far away down into the inmost recesses of the abyss.

"At first I was too much confused to observe anything accurately. The general burst of terrific grandeur was all that I beheld. When I recovered myself a little, however, my gaze fell instinctively downward. In this direction I was able to obtain an unobstructed view, from the manner in which the smack hung on the inclined surface of the pool. She was quite upon an even keel—that is to say, her deck lay in a plane parallel with that of the water—but this latter sloped at an angle of more than forty-five degrees, so that we seemed to be lying upon our beam-ends. I could not help observing, nevertheless, that I had scarcely more difficulty in maintaining my hold and footing in this situation, than if we had been upon a dead level; and this, I suppose, was owing to the speed at which we revolved.

"The rays of the moon seemed to search the very bottom of the profound gulf; but still I could make out nothing distinctly, on account of a thick mist in which everything there was enveloped, and over which there hung a magnificent rainbow, like that narrow and tottering bridge which Mussulmen say is the only pathway between Time and Eternity. This mist, or spray, was no doubt occasioned by the clashing of the great walls of the funnel, as they all met together at the bottom—but the yell that went up to the Heavens from out of that mist, I dare not attempt to describe.

"Our first slide into the abyss itself, from the belt of foam above, had carried us a great distance down the slope; but our farther descent was by no means proportionate. Round and round we swept—not with any uniform movement—but in dizzying swings and jerks, that sent us sometimes only a few hundred feet—sometimes nearly the complete circuit of the whirl. Our progress downward, at each revolution, was slow, but very perceptible.

"Looking about me upon the wide waste of liquid ebony on which we were thus borne, I perceived that our boat was not the only object in the embrace of the whirl. Both above and below us were visible fragments of vessels, large masses of building timber and trunks of trees, with many smaller articles, such as pieces of house furniture, broken boxes, barrels and staves. I have already described the unnatural curiosity which had taken the place of my original terrors. It appeared to grow upon me as I drew nearer and nearer to my dreadful doom. I now began to watch, with a strange interest, the numerous things that floated in our company. I *must* have been delirious—for I even sought *amusement* in speculating upon the relative velocities of their several descents toward the foam below. 'This fir tree,' I found myself at one time saying, 'will certainly be the next thing that takes the awful plunge and disappears,'—and then I was disappointed to find that the wreck of a Dutch merchant ship overtook it and went down before. At length, after making several guesses of this nature, and being deceived in all—this fact—the fact of my invariable miscalculation—set me upon a train of reflection that made my limbs again tremble, and my heart beat heavily once more.

"It was not a new terror that thus affected me, but the dawn of a more exciting *hope*. This hope arose partly from memory, and partly from present observation. I called to mind the great variety of buoyant matter that strewed the coast of Lofoden, having been absorbed and then thrown forth by the Moskoe-ström. By far the greater number of the articles were shattered in the most extraordinary way—so chafed and roughened as to have the appearance of being stuck full of splinters—but then I distinctly recollected that there were *some* of them which were not disfigured at all. Now I could not account for this difference except by supposing that the roughened fragments were the only ones which had been *completely absorbed*—that the others had entered the whirl at so late a period of the tide, or, for some reason, had descended so slowly after entering, that they did not reach the bottom before the turn of the flood came, or of the ebb, as the case might be. I conceived it possible, in either instance, that they might thus be whirled up again to the level of the ocean, without undergoing the fate of those which had been drawn in more early, or absorbed more rapidly. I made, also, three important observations. The first was, that, as a general rule, the larger the bodies were, the more rapid their descent;—the second, that, between two masses of equal extent, the one spherical, and the other *of any other shape,* the superiority in speed of descent was with the sphere;—the third, that, between two masses of equal size, the one cylindrical, and the other of any other shape, the cylinder was absorbed the more slowly. Since my escape, I have had several conversations on this subject with an old school-master of the district; and it was from him that I learned the use of the words 'cylinder' and 'sphere.' He explained to me—although I have forgotten the explanation—how what I observed was, in fact, the natural consequence of the forms of the floating fragments—and showed me how it happened that a cylinder, swimming in a vortex, offered more resistance to its suction, and was drawn in with greater difficulty than an equally bulky body, of any form whatever.*

"There was one startling circumstance which went a great way in enforcing these observations, and rendering me anxious to turn them to account, and this was that, at every revolution, we passed something like a barrel, or else the broken yard or the mast of a vessel, while many of these things, which had been on our level when I first opened my eyes upon the wonders of the whirlpool, were now high up above us, and seemed to have moved but little from their original station.

"I no longer hesitated what to do. I resolved to lash myself securely to the water cask upon which I now held, to cut it loose from the counter, and to throw myself with it into the water. I attracted my brother's attention by signs, pointed to the floating barrels that came near us, and did everything in my power to make him understand what I was about to do. I thought at length that he comprehended my design—but, whether this was the case or not, he shook his head despairingly, and refused to move from his station by the ring-bolt. It was impossible to force him; the emergency admitted no delay; and so, with a bitter struggle, I resigned him to his fate, fastened myself to the cask by means of the lashings which secured

*See Archimedes, "*De Incidentibus in Fluido.*"—lib. 2.

it to the counter, and precipitated myself with it into the sea, without another moment's hesitation.

"The result was precisely what I had hoped it might be. As it is myself who now tells you this tale—as you see that I *did* escape—and as you are already in possession of the mode in which this escape was effected, and must therefore anticipate all that I have farther to say—I will bring my story quickly to conclusion. It might have been an hour, or thereabout, after my quitting the smack, when, having descended to a vast distance beneath me, it made three or four wild gyrations in rapid succession, and, bearing my loved brother with it, plunged headlong, at once and forever, into the chaos of foam below. The cask to which I was attached sank very little farther than half the distance between the bottom of the gulf and the spot at which I leaped overboard, before a great change took place in the character of the whirlpool. The slope of the sides of the vast funnel became momently less and less steep. The gyrations of the whirl grew, gradually, less and less violent. By degrees, the froth and the rainbow disappeared, and the bottom of the gulf seemed slowly to uprise. The sky was clear, the winds had gone down, and the full moon was setting radiantly in the west, when I found myself on the surface of the ocean, in full view of the shores of Lofoden, and above the spot where the pool of the Moskoe-ström *had been*. It was the hour of the slack—but the sea still heaved in mountainous waves from the effects of the hurricane. I was borne violently into the channel of the Ström, and in a few minutes was hurried down the coast into the 'grounds' of the fishermen. A boat picked me up—exhausted from fatigue—and (now that the danger was removed) speechless from the memory of its horror. Those who drew me on board were my old mates and daily companions—but they knew me no more than they would have known a traveller from the spirit-land. My hair which had been raven-black the day before, was as white as you see it now. They say too that the whole expression of my countenance had changed. I told them my story. They did not believe it. I now tell it to *you*—and I can scarcely expect you to put more faith in it than did the merry fishermen of Lofoden."

THE MASQUE OF THE RED DEATH

The "Red Death" had long devastated the country. No pestilence had ever been so fatal, or so hideous. Blood was its Avatar and its seal—the redness and the horror of blood. There were sharp pains, and sudden dizziness, and then profuse bleeding at the pores, with dissolution. The scarlet stains upon the body and especially upon the face of the victim, were the pest ban which shut him out from the aid and from the sympathy of his fellow-men. And the whole seizure, progress and termination of the disease, were the incidents of half an hour.

But the Prince Prospero was happy and dauntless and sagacious. When his dominions were half depopulated, he summoned to his presence a thousand hale and light-hearted friends from among the knights and dames of his court, and with these retired to the deep seclusion of one of his castellated abbeys. This was an extensive and magnificent structure, the creation of the prince's own eccentric yet august taste. A strong and lofty wall girdled it in. This wall had gates of iron. The courtiers, having entered, brought furnaces and massy hammers and welded the bolts. They resolved to leave means neither of ingress or egress to the sudden impulses of despair or of frenzy from within. The abbey was amply provisioned. With such precautions the courtiers might bid defiance to contagion. The external world could take care of itself. In the meantime it was folly to grieve, or to think. The prince had provided all the appliances of pleasure. There were buffoons, there were improvisatori, there were ballet-dancers, there were musicians, there was Beauty, there was wine. All these and security were within. Without was the "Red Death."

It was toward the close of the fifth or sixth month of his seclusion, and while the pestilence raged most furiously abroad, that the Prince Prospero entertained his thousand friends at a masked ball of the most unusual magnificence.

It was a voluptuous scene, that masquerade. But first let me tell of the rooms in which it was held. There were seven—an imperial suite. In many palaces, however, such suites form a long and straight vista, while the folding doors slide back nearly to the walls on either hand, so that the view of the whole extent is scarcely impeded. Here the case was very different; as might have been expected from the duke's love of the *bizarre*. The apartments were so irregularly disposed that the vision embraced but little more than one at a time. There was a sharp turn at every twenty or thirty yards, and at each turn a novel effect. To the right and left, in the middle of each wall, a tall and narrow Gothic window looked out upon a closed corridor which pursued the windings of the suite. These windows were of stained glass whose color varied in accordance with the prevailing hue of the decorations of the chamber into which it opened. That at the eastern extremity was hung, for example, in blue—and vividly blue were its windows. The second chamber was purple in its ornaments and tapestries, and here the panes were purple. The third was green throughout, and so were the casements. The fourth was furnished and lighted with orange—the fifth with white—the sixth with violet. The seventh apartment was closely shrouded in black velvet tapestries that hung all over the ceiling and down the walls, falling in heavy folds upon a carpet of the same material and hue. But in this chamber only, the color of the windows failed to correspond with the decorations. The panes here were scarlet—a deep blood color. Now in no one of the seven apartments was there any lamp or candelabrum, amid the profusion of golden ornaments that lay scattered to and fro or depended from the roof. There was no light of any kind emanating from lamp or candle within the suite of chambers. But in the corridors that followed the suite, there stood, opposite to each window, a heavy tripod, bearing a brazier of fire that projected its rays through the tinted glass and so glaringly illumined the room. And thus were produced a multitude of gaudy and fantastic appearances. But in the western or black chamber the effect of the fire-light that streamed upon the dark hangings through the blood-tinted panes, was ghastly in the extreme, and produced so wild a look upon the countenances of those who entered, that there were few of the company bold enough to set foot within its precincts at all.

It was in this apartment, also, that there stood against the western wall, a gigantic clock of ebony. Its pendulum swung to and fro with a dull, heavy, monotonous clang; and when the minute-hand made the circuit of the face, and the hour was to be stricken, there came from the brazen lungs of the clock a sound which was clear and loud and deep and exceedingly musical, but of so peculiar a note and emphasis that, at each lapse of an hour, the musicians of the orchestra were constrained to pause, momentarily, in their performance, to harken to the sound; and thus the waltzers perforce ceased their evolutions; and there was a brief disconcert of the whole gay company; and, while the chimes of the clock yet rang, it was observed that the giddiest grew pale, and the more aged and sedate passed their hands over their brows as if in confused revery or meditation. But when the echoes had fully ceased, a light laughter at once pervaded the assembly; the musicians looked at each other and smiled as if at their own nervousness and folly, and made whispering vows, each to the other, that the next chiming of the clock should produce in them no similar emotion; and then, after the lapse of sixty minutes, (which embrace three thousand and six hundred seconds of the Time that flies,) there came yet another chiming of the clock, and then were the same disconcert and tremulousness and meditation as before.

But, in spite of these things, it was a gay and magnificent revel. The tastes of the duke were peculiar. He had a fine eye for colors and effects. He disregarded the *decora* of mere fashion. His plans were bold and fiery, and his conceptions glowed with barbaric lustre. There are some who would have thought him mad. His followers felt that he was not. It was necessary to hear and see and touch him to be *sure* that he was not.

He had directed, in great part, the moveable embellishments of the seven chambers, upon occasion of this great *fête*; and it was his own guiding taste which had given character to the masqueraders. Be sure they were grotesque. There were much glare and glitter and piquancy and phantasm—much of what has been since seen in "Hernani."[1] There were arabesque figures with unsuited limbs and appointments. There were delirious fancies such as the madman fashions. There were much of the beautiful, much of the wanton, much of the *bizarre*, something of the terrible, and not a little of that which might have excited disgust. To and fro in the seven chambers there stalked, in fact, a multitude of dreams. And these—the dreams—writhed in and about, taking hue from the rooms, and causing the wild music of the orchestra to seem as the echo of their steps. And, anon, there strikes the ebony clock which stands in the hall of the velvet. And then, for a moment, all is still, and all is silent save the voice of the clock. The dreams are stiff-frozen as they stand. But the echoes of the chime die away—they have endured but an instant—and a light, half-subdued laughter floats after them as they depart. And now again the music swells, and the dreams live, and writhe to and fro more merrily than ever, taking hue from the many tinted windows through which stream the rays from the tripods. But to the chamber which lies most westwardly of the seven, there are now none of the maskers who venture; for the night is waning away; and there flows a ruddier light through the blood-colored panes; and the blackness of the sable drapery appals; and to him whose foot falls upon the sable carpet, there comes from the near clock of ebony a muffled peal more solemnly emphatic than any which reaches *their* ears who indulge in the more remote gaieties of the other apartments.

But these other apartments were densely crowded, and in them beat feverishly the heart of life. And the revel went whirlingly on, until at length there commenced the sounding of midnight upon the clock. And then the music ceased, as I have told; and the evolutions of the waltzers were quieted; and there was an uneasy cessation of all things as before. But now there were twelve strokes to be sounded by the bell of the clock; and thus it happened, perhaps, that more of thought crept, with more of time, into the meditations of the thoughtful among those who revelled. And thus too, it happened, perhaps, that before the last echoes of the last chime had utterly sunk into silence, there were many individuals in the crowd who had found leisure to become aware of the presence of a masked figure which had arrested the attention of no single individual before. And the rumor of this new presence having spread itself whisperingly around, there arose at length from the whole company a buzz, or murmur, expressive of disapprobation and surprise—then, finally, of terror, of horror, and of disgust.

In an assembly of phantasms such as I have painted, it may well be supposed that no ordinary appearance could have excited such sensation. In truth the masquerade license of the night was nearly unlimited; but the figure in question had out-Heroded Herod, and gone beyond the bounds of even the prince's indefinite decorum. There are chords in the hearts of the most reckless which cannot be touched without emotion. Even with the utterly lost, to whom life and death are equally jests, there are matters of which no jest can be made. The whole company, indeed, seemed now deeply to feel that in the costume and bearing of the stranger neither wit nor propriety existed. The figure was tall and gaunt, and shrouded from head to foot in the habiliments of the grave. The mask which concealed the visage was made so nearly to resemble the countenance of a stiffened corpse that the closest scrutiny must have had difficulty in detecting the cheat. And yet all this might have been endured, if not approved, by the mad revellers around. But the mummer had gone so far as to assume the type of the Red Death. His vesture was dabbled in *blood*—and his broad brow, with all the features of the face, was besprinkled with the scarlet horror.

When the eyes of Prince Prospero fell upon this spectral image (which with a slow and solemn movement, as if more fully to sustain its *role*, stalked to and fro among the waltzers) he was seen to be convulsed, in the first moment with a strong shudder either of terror or distaste; but, in the next, his brow reddened with rage.

"Who dares?" he demanded hoarsely of the courtiers who stood near him—"who dares insult us with this blasphemous mockery? Seize him and unmask him—that we may know whom we have to hang at sunrise, from the battlements!"

It was in the eastern or blue chamber in which stood the Prince Prospero as he uttered these words. They rang throughout the seven rooms loudly and clearly—for the prince was a bold and robust man, and the music had become hushed at the waving of his hand.

It was in the blue room where stood the prince, with a group of pale courtiers by his side. At first, as he spoke, there was a slight rushing movement of this group in the direction of the intruder, who at the moment was also near at hand, and now, with deliberate and stately step, made closer approach to the speaker. But from a certain nameless awe with which the mad assumptions of the mummer had inspired the whole party, there were found none who put forth hand to seize him; so that, unimpeded, he passed within a yard of the prince's person; and, while the vast assembly, as if with one impulse, shrank from the centres of the rooms to the walls, he made his way uninterruptedly, but with the same solemn and measured step which had distinguished him from the first, through the blue chamber to the purple—through the purple to the green—through the green to the orange—through this again to the white—and even thence to the violet, ere a decided movement had been made to arrest him. It was then, however, that the Prince Prospero, maddening with rage and the shame of his own momentary cowardice, rushed hurriedly through the six chambers, while none followed him on account of a deadly terror that had seized upon all. He bore aloft a drawn dagger, and had approached, in rapid impetuosity, to within three or four feet of the retreating figure, when the latter, having attained the extremity of the velvet apartment, turned suddenly and confronted his pursuer. There was a sharp cry—and the dagger dropped gleaming upon the sable carpet, upon which, instantly afterwards, fell prostrate in death the Prince Prospero. Then, summoning the wild courage of despair, a throng of the revellers at once threw themselves into the black apartment, and, seizing the mummer, whose tall figure stood erect and motionless within the shadow of the ebony clock, gasped in unutterable horror at finding the grave cerements and corpselike mask which they handled with so violent a rudeness, untenanted by any tangible form.

And now was acknowledged the presence of the Red Death. He had come like a thief in the night. And one by one dropped the revellers in the blood-bedewed halls of their revel, and died each in the despairing posture of his fall. And the life of the ebony clock went out with that of the last of the gay. And the flames of the tripods expired. And Darkness and Decay and the Red Death held illimitable dominion over all.

THE PIT AND THE
PENDULUM

Impia tortorum longas hic turba furores
Sanguinis innocui, non satiata, aluit.
Sospite nunc patria, fracto nunc funeris antro,
Mors ubi dira fuit vita salusque patent.[1]
[*Quatrain composed for the gates of a market to be
erected upon the site of the Jacobin Club House at Paris.*]

I was sick—sick unto death with that long agony; and when they
at length unbound me, and I was permitted to sit, I felt that my
senses were leaving me. The sentence—the dread sentence of
death—was the last of distinct accentuation which reached my
ears. After that, the sound of the inquisitorial voices seemed
merged in one dreamy indeterminate hum. It conveyed to my soul
the idea of *revolution*—perhaps from its association in fancy with
the burr of a mill-wheel. This only for a brief period; for presently
I heard no more. Yet, for a while, I saw; but with how terrible an
exaggeration! I saw the lips of the black-robed judges. They ap-
peared to me white—whiter than the sheet upon which I trace
these words—and thin even to grotesqueness; thin with the inten-
sity of their expression of firmness—of immoveable resolution—
of stern contempt of human torture. I saw that the decrees of
what to me was Fate, were still issuing from those lips. I saw them
writhe with a deadly locution. I saw them fashion the syllables of
my name; and I shuddered because no sound succeeded. I saw,
too, for a few moments of delirious horror, the soft and nearly im-
perceptible waving of the sable draperies which enwrapped the
walls of the apartment. And then my vision fell upon the seven
tall candles upon the table. At first they wore the aspect of char-
ity, and seemed white slender angels who would save me; but
then, all at once, there came a most deadly nausea over my spirit,

and I felt every fibre in my frame thrill as if I had touched the wire of a galvanic battery, while the angel forms became meaningless spectres, with heads of flame, and I saw that from them there would be no help. And then there stole into my fancy, like a rich musical note, the thought of what sweet rest there must be in the grave. The thought came gently and stealthily, and it seemed long before it attained full appreciation; but just as my spirit came at length properly to feel and entertain it, the figures of the judges vanished, as if magically, from before me; the tall candles sank into nothingness; their flames went out utterly; the blackness of darkness supervened; all sensations appeared swallowed up in a mad rushing descent as of the soul into Hades. Then silence, and stillness, and night were the universe.

I had swooned; but still will not say that all of consciousness was lost. What of it there remained I will not attempt to define, or even to describe; yet all was not lost. In the deepest slumber—no! In delirium—no! In a swoon—no! In death—no! even in the grave all is *not* lost. Else there is no immortality for man. Arousing from the most profound of slumbers, we break the gossamer web of *some* dream. Yet in a second afterward, (so frail may that web have been) we remember not that we have dreamed. In the return to life from the swoon there are two stages; first, that of the sense of mental or spiritual; secondly, that of the sense of physical, existence. It seems probable that if, upon reaching the second stage, we could recall the impressions of the first, we should find these impressions eloquent in memories of the gulf beyond. And that gulf is—what? How at least shall we distinguish its shadows from those of the tomb? But if the impressions of what I have termed the first stage, are not, at will, recalled, yet, after long interval, do *they* not come unbidden, while we marvel whence they come? He who has never swooned, is not he who finds strange palaces and wildly familiar faces in coals that glow; is not he who beholds floating in mid-air the sad visions that the many may not view; is not he who ponders over the perfume of some novel flower—is not he whose brain grows bewildered with the meaning of some musical cadence which has never before arrested his attention.

Amid frequent and thoughtful endeavors to remember; amid earnest struggles to regather some token of the state of seeming nothingness into which my soul had lapsed, there have been moments when I have dreamed of success; there have been brief, very brief periods when I have conjured up remembrances which the lucid reason of a later epoch assures me could have had reference only to that condition of seeming unconsciousness. These shadows of memory tell, indistinctly, of tall figures that lifted and bore me in silence down—down—still down—till a hideous dizziness oppressed me at the mere idea of the interminableness of the descent. They tell also of a vague horror at my heart, on account of that heart's unnatural stillness. Then comes a sense of sudden motionlessness throughout all things; as if those who bore me (a ghastly train!) had outrun, in their descent, the limits of the limitless, and paused from the wearisomeness of their toil. After this I call to mind flatness and dampness; and then all is *madness*—the madness of a memory which busies itself among forbidden things.

Very suddenly there came back to my soul motion and sound— the tumultuous motion of the heart, and, in my ears, the sound of its beating. Then a pause in which all is blank. Then again sound, and motion, and touch—a tingling sensation pervading my frame. Then the mere consciousness of existence, without thought—a condition which lasted long. Then, very suddenly, *thought*, and shuddering terror, and earnest endeavor to comprehend my true state. Then a strong desire to lapse into insensibility. Then a rushing revival of soul and a successful effort to move. And now a full memory of the trial, of the judges, of the sable draperies, of the sentence, of the sickness, of the swoon. Then entire forgetfulness of all that followed; of all that a later day and much earnestness of endeavor have enabled me vaguely to recall.

So far, I had not opened my eyes. I felt that I lay upon my back, unbound. I reached out my hand, and it fell heavily upon something damp and hard. There I suffered it to remain for many minutes, while I strove to imagine where and *what* I could be. I longed, yet dared not to employ my vision. I dreaded the first glance at objects around me. It was not that I feared to look upon things horrible, but that I grew aghast lest there should be *nothing* to see. At length, with a wild desperation at heart, I quickly unclosed my eyes. My worst thoughts, then, were confirmed. The blackness of eternal night encompassed me. I struggled for breath. The intensity of the darkness seemed to oppress and stifle me. The atmosphere was intolerably close. I still lay quietly, and made effort to exercise my reason. I brought to mind the inquisitorial proceedings, and attempted from that point to deduce my real condition. The sentence had passed; and it appeared to me that a very long interval of time had since elapsed. Yet not for a moment did I suppose myself actually dead. Such a supposition, notwithstanding what we read in fiction, is altogether inconsistent with real existence;—but where and in what state was I? The condemned to death, I knew, perished usually at the *autos-da-fé*,[2] and one of these had been held on the very night of the day of my trial. Had I been remanded to my dungeon, to await the next sacrifice, which would not take place for many months? This I at once saw could not be. Victims had been in immediate demand. Moreover, my dungeon, as well as all the condemned cells at Toledo, had stone floors, and light was not altogether excluded.

A fearful idea now suddenly drove the blood in torrents upon my heart, and for a brief period, I once more relapsed into insensibility. Upon recovering, I at once started to my feet, trembling convulsively in every fibre. I thrust my arms wildly above and around me in all directions. I felt nothing; yet dreaded to move a step, lest I should be impeded by the walls of a *tomb*. Perspiration burst from every pore, and stood in cold big beads upon my forehead. The agony of suspense grew, at length, intolerable, and I cautiously moved forward, with my arms extended, and my eyes straining from their sockets, in the hope of catching some faint ray of light. I proceeded for many paces; but still all was blackness and vacancy. I breathed more freely. It seemed evident that mine was not, at least, the most hideous of fates.

And now, as I still continued to step cautiously onward, there came thronging upon my recollection a thousand vague rumors of the horrors of Toledo. Of the dungeons there had been strange things narrated—fables I had always deemed them—but yet strange, and too ghastly to repeat, save in a whisper. Was I left to perish of starvation in this subterranean world of darkness; or what fate, perhaps even more fearful, awaited me? That the result would be death, and a death of more than customary bitterness, I knew too well the character of my judges to doubt. The mode and the hour were all that occupied or distracted me.

My outstretched hands at length encountered some solid obstruction. It was a wall, seemingly of stone masonry—very smooth, slimy, and cold. I followed it up; stepping with all the careful distrust with which certain antique narratives had inspired me. This process, however, afforded me no means of ascertaining the dimensions of my dungeon; as I might make its circuit, and return to the point whence I set out, without being aware of the fact; so perfectly uniform seemed the wall. I therefore sought the knife which had been in my pocket, when led into the inquisitorial chamber; but it was gone; my clothes had been exchanged for a wrapper of coarse serge. I had thought of forcing the blade in some minute crevice of the masonry, so as to identify my point of departure. The difficulty, nevertheless, was but trivial; although, in the disorder of my fancy, it seemed at first insuperable. I tore a part of the hem from the robe and placed the fragment at full length, and at right angles to the wall. In groping my way around the prison, I could not fail to encounter this rag upon completing the circuit. So, at least I thought: but I had not counted upon the extent of the dungeon, or upon my own weakness. The ground was moist and slippery. I staggered onward for some time, when I stumbled and fell. My excessive fatigue induced me to remain prostrate; and sleep soon overtook me as I lay.

Upon awaking, and stretching forth an arm, I found beside me a loaf and a pitcher with water. I was too much exhausted to reflect upon this circumstance, but ate and drank with avidity. Shortly afterward, I resumed my tour around the prison, and with much toil, came at last upon the fragment of the serge. Up to the period when I fell, I had counted fifty-two paces, and, upon resuming my walk, I had counted forty-eight more—when I arrived at the rag. There were in all, then, a hundred paces; and, admitting two paces to the yard, I presumed the dungeon to be fifty yards in circuit. I had met, however, with many angles in the wall, and thus I could form no guess at the shape of the vault; for vault I could not help supposing it to be.

I had little object—certainly no hope—in these researches; but a vague curiosity prompted me to continue them. Quitting the wall, I resolved to cross the area of the enclosure. At first, I proceeded with extreme caution, for the floor, although seemingly of solid material, was treacherous with slime. At length, however, I took courage, and did not hesitate to step firmly—endeavoring to cross in as direct a line as possible. I had advanced some ten or twelve paces in this manner, when the remnant of the torn hem of my robe became entangled between my legs. I stepped on it, and fell violently on my face.

In the confusion attending my fall, I did not immediately apprehend a somewhat startling circumstance, which yet, in a few seconds afterward, and while I still lay prostrate, arrested my attention. It was this: my chin rested upon the floor of the prison, but my lips, and the upper portion of my head, although seemingly at a less elevation than the chin, touched nothing. At the same time, my forehead seemed bathed in a clammy vapor, and the peculiar smell of decayed fungus arose to my nostrils. I put forward my arm, and shuddered to find that I had fallen at the very brink of a circular pit, whose extent, of course, I had no means of ascertaining at the moment. Groping about the masonry just below the margin, I succeeded in dislodging a small fragment, and let it fall into the abyss. For many seconds I hearkened to its reverberations as it dashed against the sides of the chasm in its descent; at length there was a sullen plunge into water, succeeded by loud echoes. At the same moment, there came a sound resembling the quick opening, and as rapid closing of a door overhead, while a faint gleam of light flashed suddenly through the gloom, and as suddenly faded away.

I saw clearly the doom which had been prepared for me, and congratulated myself upon the timely accident by which I had escaped. Another step before my fall, and the world had seen me no more. And the death just avoided, was of that very character which I had regarded as fabulous and frivolous in the tales respecting the Inquisition. To the victims of its tyranny, there was the choice of death with its direst physical agonies, or death with its most hideous moral horrors. I had been reserved for the latter. By long suffering my nerves had been unstrung, until I trembled at the sound of my own voice, and had become in every respect a fitting subject for the species of torture which awaited me.

Shaking in every limb, I groped my way back to the wall—resolving there to perish rather than risk the terrors of the wells, of which my imagination now pictured many in various positions about the dungeon. In other conditions of mind, I might have had courage to end my misery at once, by a plunge into one of these abysses; but now I was the veriest of cowards. Neither could I forget what I had read of these pits—that the *sudden* extinction of life formed no part of their most horrible plan.

Agitation of spirit kept me awake for many long hours; but at length I again slumbered. Upon arousing, I found by my side, as before, a loaf and a pitcher of water. A burning thirst consumed me, and I emptied the vessel at a draught. It must have been drugged—for scarcely had I drunk, before I became irresistibly drowsy. A deep sleep fell upon me—a sleep like that of death. How long it lasted, of course I know not; but when, once again, I unclosed my eyes, the objects around me were visible. By a wild, sulphurous lustre, the origin of which I could not at first determine, I was enabled to see the extent and aspect of the prison.

In its size I had been greatly mistaken. The whole circuit of its walls did not exceed twenty-five yards. For some minutes this fact occasioned me a world of vain trouble; vain indeed! for what could be of less importance, under the terrible circumstances which environed me, then the mere dimensions of my dungeon? But my soul took a wild interest in trifles, and I busied myself in endeavors to account for the error I had committed in my measurement. The truth at length flashed upon me. In my first attempt at exploration, I had counted fifty-two paces, up to the period when I fell: I must then have been within a pace or two of the fragment of serge; in fact, I had nearly performed the circuit of the vault. I then slept— and, upon awaking, I must have returned upon my steps—thus supposing the circuit nearly double what it actually was. My confusion of mind prevented me from observing that I began my tour with the wall to the left, and ended it with the wall to the right.

I had been deceived, too, in respect to the shape of the enclosure. In feeling my way I had found many angles, and thus deduced an idea of great irregularity; so potent is the effect of total darkness upon one arousing from lethargy or sleep! The angles were simply those of a few slight depressions, or niches, at odd intervals. The general shape of the prison was square. What I had taken for masonry seemed now to be iron, or some other metal, in huge plates, whose sutures or joints occasioned the depressions. The entire surface of this metallic enclosure was rudely daubed in all the hideous and repulsive devices to which the charnel superstition of the monks has given rise. The figures of fiends in aspects of menace, with skeleton forms, and other more really fearful images, overspread and disfigured the walls. I observed that the outlines of these monstrosities were sufficiently distinct, but that the colors seemed faded and blurred, as if from the effects of a damp atmosphere. I now noticed the floor, too, which was of stone. In the centre yawned the circular pit from whose jaws I had escaped; but it was the only one in the dungeon.

All this I saw indistinctly and by much effort: for my personal condition had been greatly changed during slumber. I now lay upon my back, and at full length, on a species of low framework of wood. To this I was securely bound by a long strap resembling a surcingle. It passed in many convolutions about my limbs and body, leaving at liberty only my head, and my left arm to such extent that I could, by dint of much exertion, supply myself with food from an earthen dish which lay by my side on the floor. I saw, to my horror, that the pitcher had been removed. I say, to my horror—for I was consumed with intolerable thirst. This thirst it appeared to be the design of my persecutors to stimulate—for the food in the dish was meat pungently seasoned.

Looking upward, I surveyed the ceiling of my prison. It was some thirty or forty feet overhead, and constructed much as the side walls. In one of its panels a very singular figure riveted my whole attention. It was the painted figure of Time as he is commonly represented, save that, in lieu of a scythe, he held what, at a casual glance, I supposed to be the pictured image of a huge pendulum, such as we see on antique clocks. There was something, however, in the appearance of this machine which caused me to regard it more attentively. While I gazed directly upward at it, (for its position was immediately over my own,) I fancied that I saw it in motion. In an instant afterward the fancy was confirmed. Its sweep was brief, and of course slow. I watched it for some minutes, somewhat in fear, but more in wonder. Wearied at length with observing its dull movement, I turned my eyes upon the other objects in the cell.

A slight noise attracted my notice, and, looking to the floor, I saw several enormous rats traversing it. They had issued from the well, which lay just within view to my right. Even then, while I gazed, they came up in troops, hurriedly, with ravenous eyes, allured by the scent of the meat. From this it required much effort and attention to scare them away.

It might have been half an hour, perhaps even an hour, (for I could take but imperfect note of time,) before I again cast my eyes upward. What I then saw confounded and amazed me. The sweep of the pendulum had increased in extent by nearly a yard. As a natural consequence, its velocity was also much greater. But what mainly disturbed me was the idea that it had perceptibly *descended*. I now observed—with what horror it is needless to say—that its nether extremity was formed of a crescent of glittering steel, about a foot in length from horn to horn; the horns upward, and the under edge evidently as keen as that of a razor. Like a razor also, it seemed massy and heavy, tapering from the edge into a solid and broad structure above. It was appended to a weighty rod of brass, and the whole *hissed* as it swung through the air.

I could no longer doubt the doom prepared for me by monkish ingenuity in torture. My cognizance of the pit had become known to the inquisitorial agents—*the pit*, whose horrors had been destined for so bold a recusant as myself—*the pit*, typical of hell, and regarded by rumor as the Ultima Thule of all their punishments. The plunge into this pit I had avoided by the merest of accidents, and I knew that surprise, or entrapment into torment, formed an important portion of all the grotesquerie of these dungeon deaths. Having failed to fall, it was no part of the demon plan to hurl me into the abyss; and thus (there being no alternative) a different and a milder destruction awaited me. Milder! I half smiled in my agony as I thought of such application of such a term.

What boots it to tell of the long, long hours of horror more than mortal, during which I counted the rushing oscillations of the steel! Inch by inch—line by line—with a descent only appreciable at intervals that seemed ages—down and still down it came! Days passed—it might have been that many days passed—ere it swept so closely over me as to fan me with its acrid breath. The odor of the sharp steel forced itself into my nostrils. I prayed—I wearied heaven with my prayer for its more speedy descent. I grew frantically mad, and struggled to force myself upward against the sweep of the fearful scimitar. And then I fell suddenly calm, and lay smiling at the glittering death, as a child at some rare bauble.

There was another interval of utter insensibility; it was brief; for, upon again lapsing into life, there had been no perceptible descent in the pendulum. But it might have been long—for I knew there were demons who took note of my swoon, and who could have arrested the vibration at pleasure. Upon my recovery, too, I felt very—oh, inexpressibly—sick and weak, as if through long inanition. Even amid the agonies of that period, the human nature craved food. With painful effort I outstretched my left arm as far as my bonds permitted, and took possession of the small remnant which had been spared me by the rats. As I put a portion of it within my lips, there rushed to my mind a half-formed thought of joy—of hope. Yet what business had *I* with hope? It was, as I say, a half-formed thought—man has many such which are never completed. I felt that it was of joy—of hope; but I felt also that it had perished in its formation. In vain I struggled to perfect—to regain it. Long suffering had nearly annihilated all my ordinary powers of mind. I was an imbecile—an idiot.

The vibration of the pendulum was at right angles to my length. I saw that the crescent was designed to cross the region of the heart. It would fray the serge of my robe—it would return and repeat its operations—again—and again. Notwithstanding its terrifically wide sweep, (some thirty feet or more,) and the hissing vigor of its descent, sufficient to sunder these very walls of iron, still the fraying of my robe would be all that, for several minutes, it would accomplish. And at this thought I paused. I dared not go farther than this reflection. I dwelt upon it with a pertinacity of attention—as if, in so dwelling, I could arrest *here* the descent of the steel. I forced myself to ponder upon the sound of the crescent as it should pass across the garment—upon the peculiar thrilling sensation which the friction of cloth produces on the nerves. I pondered upon all this frivolity until my teeth were on edge.

Down—steadily down it crept. I took a frenzied pleasure in contrasting its downward with its lateral velocity. To the right—to the left—far and wide—with the shriek of a damned spirit! to my heart, with the stealthy pace of the tiger! I alternately laughed and howled as the one or the other idea grew predominant.

Down—certainly, relentlessly down! It vibrated within three inches of my bosom! I struggled violently—furiously—to free my left arm. This was free only from the elbow to the hand. I could reach the latter, from the platter beside me, to my mouth, with great effort, but no farther. Could I have broken the fastenings above the elbow, I would have seized and attempted to arrest the pendulum. I might as well have attempted to arrest an avalanche!

Down—still unceasingly—still inevitably down! I gasped and struggled at each vibration. I shrunk convulsively at its every sweep. My eyes followed its outward or upward whirls with the eagerness of the most unmeaning despair; they closed themselves spasmodically at the descent, although death would have been a relief, oh, how unspeakable! Still I quivered in every nerve to think how slight a sinking of the machinery would precipitate that keen, glistening axe upon my bosom. It was *hope* that prompted the nerve to quiver—the frame to shrink. It was *hope*—the hope that triumphs on the rack—that whispers to the death-condemned even in the dungeons of the Inquisition.

I saw that some ten or twelve vibrations would bring the steel in actual contact with my robe—and with this observation there suddenly came over my spirit all the keen, collected calmness of despair. For the first time during many hours—or perhaps days—I *thought*. It now occurred to me that the bandage, or surcingle, which enveloped me, was *unique*. I was tied by no separate cord. The first stroke of the razor-like crescent athwart any portion of the band, would so detach it that it might be unwound from my person by means of my left hand. But how fearful, in that case, the proximity of the steel! The result of the slightest struggle, how deadly! Was it likely, moreover, that the minions of the torturer had not foreseen and provided for this possibility? Was it probable that the bandage crossed my bosom in the track of the pendulum? Dreading to find my faint, and, as it seemed, my last hope frustrated, I so far elevated my head as to obtain a distinct view of my breast. The surcingle enveloped my limbs and body close in all directions—*save in the path of the destroying crescent.*

Scarcely had I dropped my head back into its original position, when there flashed upon my mind what I cannot better describe than as the unformed half of that idea of deliverance to which I have previously alluded, and of which a moiety only floated indeterminately through my brain when I raised food to my burning lips. The whole thought was now present—feeble, scarcely sane, scarcely definite—but still entire. I proceeded at once, with the nervous energy of despair, to attempt its execution.

For many hours the immediate vicinity of the low framework upon which I lay, had been literally swarming with rats. They were wild, bold, ravenous—their red eyes glaring upon me as if they waited but for motionlessness on my part to make me their prey. "To what food," I thought, "have they been accustomed in the well?"

They had devoured, in spite of all my efforts to prevent them, all but a small remnant of the contents of the dish. I had fallen into an habitual see-saw, or wave of the hand about the platter; and, at length, the unconscious uniformity of the movement deprived it of effect. In their voracity, the vermin frequently fastened their sharp fangs in my fingers. With the particles of the oily and spicy viand which now remained, I thoroughly rubbed the bandage wherever I could reach it; then, raising my hand from the floor, I lay breathlessly still.

At first the ravenous animals were startled and terrified at the change—at the cessation of movement. They shrank alarmedly back; many sought the well. But this was only for a moment. I had not counted in vain upon their voracity. Observing that I remained without motion, one or two of the boldest leaped upon the framework, and smelt at the surcingle. This seemed the signal for a general rush. Forth from the well they hurried in fresh troops. They clung to the wood—they overran it, and leaped in hundreds upon my person. The measured movement of the pendulum disturbed them not at all. Avoiding its strokes they busied themselves with the anointed bandage. They pressed—they swarmed upon me in ever accumulating heaps. They writhed upon my throat; their cold lips sought my own; I was half stifled by their thronging pressure; disgust, for which the world has no name, swelled my bosom, and chilled, with a heavy clamminess, my heart. Yet one minute, and I felt that the struggle would be over. Plainly I perceived the loosening of the bandage. I knew that in more than one place it must be already severed. With a more than human resolution I lay *still*.

Nor had I erred in my calculations—nor had I endured in vain. I at length felt that I was *free*. The surcingle hung in ribands from my body. But the stroke of the pendulum already pressed upon my bosom. It had divided the serge of the robe. It had cut through the linen beneath. Twice again it swung, and a sharp sense of pain shot through every nerve. But the moment of escape had arrived. At a wave of my hand my deliverers hurried tumultuously away. With a steady movement—cautious, sidelong, shrinking, and slow—I slid from the embrace of the bandage and beyond the reach of the scimitar. For the moment, at least, *I was free*.

Free!—and in the grasp of the Inquisition! I had scarcely stepped from my wooden bed of horror upon the stone floor of the prison, when the motion of the hellish machine ceased and I beheld it drawn up, by some invisible force, through the ceiling. This was a lesson which I took desperately to heart. My every motion was undoubtedly watched. Free!—I had but escaped death in one form of agony, to be delivered unto worse than death in some other. With that thought I rolled my eyes nervously around on the barriers of iron that hemmed me in. Something unusual—some change which, at first, I could not appreciate distinctly—it was obvious, had taken place in the apartment. For many minutes of a dreamy and trembling abstraction, I busied myself in vain, unconnected conjecture. During this period, I became aware, for the first time, of the origin of the sulphurous light which illumined the cell. It proceeded from a fissure, about half an inch in width, extending entirely around the prison at the base of the walls, which thus appeared, and were completely separated from the floor. I endeavored, but of course in vain, to look through the aperture.

As I arose from the attempt, the mystery of the alteration in the chamber broke at once upon my understanding. I have observed that, although the outlines of the figures upon the walls were sufficiently distinct, yet the colors seemed blurred and indefinite. These colors had now assumed, and were momentarily assuming, a startling and most intense brilliancy, that gave to the spectral and fiendish portraitures an aspect that might have thrilled even firmer nerves than my own. Demon eyes, of a wild and ghastly vivacity, glared upon me in a thousand directions, where none had been visible before, and gleamed with the lurid lustre of a fire that I could not force my imagination to regard as unreal.

Unreal!—Even while I breathed there came to my nostrils the breath of the vapor of heated iron! A suffocating odor pervaded the prison! A deeper glow settled each moment in the eyes that glared at my agonies! A richer tint of crimson diffused itself over the pictured horrors of blood. I panted! I gasped for breath! There could be no doubt of the design of my tormentors—oh! most unrelenting! oh! most demoniac of men! I shrank from the glowing metal to the centre of the cell. Amid the thought of the fiery destruction that impended, the idea of the coolness of the well came over my soul like balm. I rushed to its deadly brink. I threw my straining vision below. The glare from the enkindled roof illumined its inmost recesses. Yet, for a wild moment, did my spirit refuse to comprehend the meaning of what I saw. At length it forced—it wrestled its way into my soul—it burned itself in upon my shuddering reason. Oh! for a voice to speak!—oh! horror!—oh! any horror but this! With a shriek, I rushed from the margin, and buried my face in my hands—weeping bitterly.

The heat rapidly increased, and once again I looked up, shuddering as with a fit of the ague. There had been a second change in the cell—and now the change was obviously in the *form*. As before, it was in vain that I at first endeavored to appreciate or understand what was taking place. But not long was I left in doubt. The Inquisitorial vengeance had been hurried by my twofold escape, and there was to be no more dallying with the King of Terrors. The room had been square. I saw that two of its iron angles were now acute—two, consequently, obtuse. The fearful difference quickly increased with a low rumbling or moaning sound. In an instant the apartment had shifted its form into that of a lozenge. But the alteration stopped not here—I neither hoped nor desired it to stop. I could have clasped the red walls to my bosom as a garment of eternal peace. "Death," I said, "any death but that of the pit!" Fool! might I have not known that *into the pit* it was the object of the burning iron to urge me? Could I resist its glow? or if even that, could I withstand its pressure? And now, flatter and flatter grew the lozenge, with a rapidity that left me no time for contemplation. Its centre, and of course, its greatest width, came just over the yawning gulf. I shrank back—but the closing walls pressed me resistlessly onward. At length for my seared and writhing body there was no longer an inch of foothold on the firm floor of the prison. I struggled no more, but the agony of my soul found vent in one loud, long, and final scream of despair. I felt that I tottered upon the brink—I averted my eyes—

There was a discordant hum of human voices! There was a loud blast as of many trumpets! There was a harsh grating as of a thousand thunders! The fiery walls rushed back! An outstretched arm caught my own as I fell, fainting, into the abyss. It was that of General Lasalle. The French army had entered Toledo.[3] The Inquisition was in the hands of its enemies.

THE PREMATURE BURIAL

There are certain themes of which the interest is all-absorbing, but which are too entirely horrible for the purposes of legitimate fiction. These the mere romanticist must eschew, if he do not wish to offend, or to disgust. They are with propriety handled, only when the severity and majesty of truth sanctify and sustain them. We thrill, for example, with the most intense of "pleasurable pain" over the accounts of the Passage of the Beresina, of the Earthquake at Lisbon, of the Plague at London, of the Massacre of St. Bartholomew, or of the stifling of the hundred and twenty-three prisoners in the Black Hole at Calcutta.[1] But, in these accounts, it is the fact—it is the reality—it is the history which excites. As inventions, we should regard them with simple abhorrence.

I have mentioned some few of the more prominent and august calamities on record; but, in these, it is the extent, not less than the character of the calamity, which so vividly impresses the fancy. I need not remind the reader that, from the long and weird catalogue of human miseries, I might have selected many individual instances more replete with essential suffering than any of these vast generalities of disaster. The true wretchedness, indeed—the ultimate woe—is particular, not diffuse. That the ghastly extremes of agony are endured by man the unit, and never by man the mass—for this let us thank a merciful God!

To be buried while alive, is, beyond question, the most terrific of these extremes which has ever fallen to the lot of mere mortality. That it has frequently, very frequently, so fallen will scarcely be denied by those who think. The boundaries which divide Life from Death are at best shadowy and vague. Who shall say where the one ends, and where the other begins? We know that there are diseases in which occur total cessations of all the apparent functions of vitality, and yet in which these cessations are merely suspensions, properly so called. They are only temporary pauses in the incomprehensible mechanism. A certain period elapses, and some unseen mysterious principle again sets in motion the magic pinions and the wizard wheels. The silver cord was not for ever loosed, nor the golden bowl irreparably broken. But where, meantime, was the soul?

Apart, however, from the inevitable conclusion, *a priori*, that such causes must produce such effects—that the well known occurrence of such cases of suspended animation must naturally give rise, now and then, to premature interments—apart from this consideration, we have the direct testimony of medical and ordinary experience to prove that a vast number of such interments have actually taken place. I might refer at once, if necessary to a hundred well authenticated instances. One of very remarkable character, and of which the circumstances may be fresh in the memory of some of my readers, occurred, not very long ago, in the neighboring city of Baltimore, where it occasioned a painful, intense, and widely-extended excitement. The wife of one of the most respectable citizens—a lawyer of eminence and a member of Congress—was seized with a sudden and unaccountable illness, which completely baffled the skill of her physicians. After much suffering she died, or was supposed to die. No one suspected, indeed, or had reason to suspect, that she was not actually dead. She presented all the ordinary appearances of death. The face assumed the usual pinched and sunken outline. The lips were of the usual marble pallor. The eyes were lustreless. There was no warmth. Pulsation had ceased. For three days the body was preserved unburied, during which it had acquired a stony rigidity. The funeral, in short, was hastened, on account of the rapid advance of what was supposed to be decomposition.

The lady was deposited in her family vault, which, for three subsequent years, was undisturbed. At the expiration of this term, it was opened for the reception of a sarcophagus;—but, alas! how fearful a shock awaited the husband, who, personally, threw open the door. As its portals swung outwardly back, some white-apparelled object fell rattling within his arms. It was the skeleton of his wife in her yet unmouldered shroud.

A careful investigation rendered it evident that she had revived within two days after her entombment—that her struggles within the coffin had caused it to fall from a ledge, or shelf, to the floor, where it was so broken as to permit her escape. A lamp which had been accidentally left, full of oil, within the tomb, was found empty; it might have been exhausted, however, by evaporation. On the uppermost of the steps which led down into the dread chamber, was a large fragment of the coffin, with which it seemed that she had endeavored to arrest attention, by striking the iron door. While thus occupied, she probably swooned, or possibly died, through sheer terror; and, in falling, her shroud became entangled in some iron-work which projected interiorly. Thus she remained, and thus she rotted, erect.

In the year 1810, a case of living inhumation happened in France, attended with circumstances which go far to warrant the assertion that truth is, indeed, stranger than fiction. The heroine of the story was a Mademoiselle Victorine Lafourcade, a young girl of illustrious family, of wealth, and of great personal beauty. Among her numerous suitors was Julien Bossuet, a poor *littérateur*, or journalist of Paris. His talents and general amiability had recommended him to the notice of the heiress, by whom he seems to have been truly beloved; but her pride of birth decided her, finally, to reject him, and to wed a Monsieur Rénelle, a banker, and a diplomatist of some eminence. After marriage, however, this gentleman neglected, and, perhaps, even more positively ill-treated her. Having passed with him some wretched years, she died,—at least her condition so closely resembled death as to deceive every one who saw her. She was buried—not in a vault—but in an ordinary grave in the village of her nativity. Filled with despair, and still inflamed by the memory of a profound attachment, the lover journeys from the capital to the remote province in which the village lies, with the romantic purpose of disinterring the corpse, and possessing himself of its luxuriant tresses. He reaches the grave. At midnight he unearths the coffin, opens it, and is in the act of detaching the hair, when he is arrested by the unclosing of the beloved eyes. In fact, the lady had been buried alive. Vitality had not altogether departed; and she was aroused, by the caresses of her lover, from the lethargy which had been mistaken for death. He bore her frantically to his lodgings in the village. He employed certain powerful restoratives suggested by no little medical learning. In fine, she revived. She recognised her preserver. She remained with him until, by slow degrees, she fully recovered her original health. Her woman's heart was not adamant, and this last lesson of love sufficed to soften it. She bestowed it upon Bossuet. She returned no more to her husband, but, concealing from him her resurrection, fled with her lover to America. Twenty years afterwards, the two returned to France, in the persuasion that time had so greatly altered the lady's appearance, that her friends would be unable to recognise her. They were mistaken, however; for, at the first meeting, Monsieur Rénelle did actually recognise and make claim to his wife. This claim she resisted; and a judicial tribunal sustained her in her resistance; deciding that the peculiar circumstances, with the long lapse of years, had extinguished, not only equitably, but legally, the authority of the husband.

The "Chirurgical Journal," of Leipsic—a periodical, of high authority and merit, which some American bookseller would do well to translate and republish—records, in a late number, a very distressing event of the character in question.

An officer of artillery, a man of gigantic stature and of robust health, being thrown from an unmanageable horse, received a very severe contusion upon the head, which rendered him insensible at once; the skull was slightly fractured; but no immediate danger was apprehended. Trepanning was accomplished successfully. He was bled, and many other of the ordinary means of relief were adopted. Gradually, however, he fell into a more and more hopeless state of stupor, and, finally, it was thought that he died.

The weather was warm; and he was buried, with indecent haste, in one of the public cemeteries. His funeral took place on Thursday. On the Sunday following, the grounds of the cemetery were, as usual, much thronged with visiters; and, about noon, an intense excitement was created by the declaration of a peasant, that, while sitting upon the grave of the officer, he had distinctly felt a commotion of the earth, as if occasioned by some one struggling beneath. At first little attention was paid to the man's asseveration; but his evident terror, and the dogged obstinacy with which he persisted in his story, had at length their natural effect upon the crowd. Spades were hurriedly procured, and the grave, which was shamefully shallow, was, in a few minutes, so far thrown open that the head of its occupant appeared. He was then, seemingly, dead; but he sat nearly erect within his coffin, the lid of which, in his furious struggles, he had partially uplifted.

He was forthwith conveyed to the nearest hospital, and there pronounced to be still living, although in an asphyctic condition. After some hours he revived, recognised individuals of his acquaintance, and, in broken sentences, spoke of his agonies in the grave.

From what he related, it was clear that he must have been conscious of life for more than an hour, while inhumed, before lapsing into insensibility. The grave was carelessly and loosely filled with an exceedingly porous soil; and thus some air was necessarily admitted. He heard the footsteps of the crowd overhead, and endeavored to make himself heard in turn. It was the tumult within the grounds of the cemetery, he said, which appeared to awaken him from a deep sleep—but no sooner was he awake than he became fully aware of the awful horrors of his position.

This patient, it is recorded, was doing well, and seemed to be in a fair way of ultimate recovery, but fell a victim to the quackeries of medical experiment. The galvanic battery was applied; and he suddenly expired in one of those ecstatic paroxysms which, occasionally, it superinduces.

The mention of the galvanic battery, nevertheless, recalls to my memory a well known and very extraordinary case in point, where its action proved the means of restoring to animation a young attorney of London, who had been interred for two days. This occurred in 1831, and created, at the time, a very profound sensation wherever it was made the subject of converse.

The patient, Mr. Edward Stapleton, had died, apparently, of typhus fever, accompanied with some anomalous symptoms which had excited the curiosity of his medical attendants. Upon his seeming decease, his friends were requested to sanction a *post mortem* examination, but declined to permit it. As often happens, when such refusals are made, the practitioners resolved to disinter the body and dissect it at leisure, in private. Arrangements were easily effected with some of the numerous corps of body-snatchers with which London abounds; and, upon the third night after the funeral, the supposed corpse was unearthed from a grave eight feet deep, and deposited in the operating chamber of one of the private hospitals.

An incision of some extent had been actually made in the abdomen, when the fresh and undecayed appearance of the subject suggested an application of the battery. One experiment succeeded another, and the customary effects supervened, with nothing to characterize them in any respect, except, upon one or two occasions, a more than ordinary degree of life-likeness in the convulsive action.

It grew late. The day was about to dawn; and it was thought expedient, at length, to proceed at once to the dissection. A student, however, was especially desirous of testing a theory of his own, and insisted upon applying the battery to one of the pectoral muscles. A rough gash was made, and a wire hastily brought in contact; when the patient, with a hurried, but quite unconvulsive movement, arose from the table, stepped into the middle of the floor, gazed about him uneasily for a few seconds, and then—spoke. What he said was unintelligible; but words were uttered; the syllabification was distinct. Having spoken, he fell heavily to the floor.

For some moments all were paralyzed with awe—but the urgency of the case soon restored them their presence of mind. It was seen that Mr. Stapleton was alive, although in a swoon. Upon exhibition of ether he revived and was rapidly restored to health, and to the society of his friends—from whom, however, all knowledge of his resuscitation was withheld, until a relapse was no longer to be apprehended. Their wonder—their rapturous astonishment—may be conceived.

The most thrilling peculiarity of this incident, nevertheless, is involved in what Mr. S. himself asserts. He declares that at no period was he altogether insensible—that, dully and confusedly he was aware of every thing which happened to him, from the moment in which he was pronounced *dead* by his physicians, to that in which he fell swooning to the floor of the hospital. "I am alive," were the uncomprehended words which, upon recognising the locality of the dissecting-room, he had endeavored, in his extremity, to utter.

It were an easy matter to multiply such histories as these—but I forbear—for, indeed, we have no need of such to establish the fact that premature interments occur. When we reflect how very rarely, from the nature of the case, we have it in our power to detect them, we must admit that they may *frequently* occur without our cognizance. Scarcely, in truth, is a graveyard ever encroached upon, for any purpose, to any great extent, that skeletons are not found in postures which suggest the most fearful of suspicions.

Fearful indeed the suspicion—but more fearful the doom! It may be asserted, without hesitation, that *no* event is so terribly well adapted to inspire the supremeness of bodily and of mental distress, as is burial before death. The unendurable oppression of the lungs—the stifling fumes of the damp earth—the clinging to the death garments—the rigid embrace of the narrow house—the blackness of the absolute Night—the silence like a sea that overwhelms—the unseen but palpable presence of the Conqueror Worm—these things, with thoughts of the air and grass above, with memory of dear friends who would fly to save us if but informed of our fate, and with consciousness that of this fate they can *never* be informed—that our hopeless portion is that of the really dead—these considerations, I say, carry into the heart, which still palpitates, a degree of appalling and intolerable horror from which the most daring imagination must recoil. We know of nothing so agonizing upon Earth—we can dream of nothing half so hideous in the realms of the nethermost Hell. And thus all narratives upon this topic have an interest profound; an interest, nevertheless, which, through the sacred awe of the topic itself, very properly and very peculiarly depends upon our conviction of the *truth* of the matter narrated. What I have now to tell, is of my own actual knowledge—of my own positive and personal experience.

For several years I had been subject to attacks of the singular disorder which physicians have agreed to term catalepsy, in default of a more definitive title. Although both the immediate and the predisposing causes, and even the actual diagnosis of this disease, are still mysterious, its obvious and apparent character is sufficiently well understood. Its variations seem to be chiefly of degree. Sometimes the patient lies, for a day only, or even for a shorter period, in a species of exaggerated lethargy. He is senseless and externally motionless; but the pulsation of the heart is still faintly perceptible; some traces of warmth remain; a slight color lingers within the centre of the cheek; and, upon application of a mirror to the lips, we can detect a torpid, unequal, and vacillating action of the lungs. Then again the duration of the trance is for weeks—even for months; while the closest scrutiny, and the most rigorous medical tests, fail to establish any material distinction between the state of the sufferer and what we conceive of absolute death. Very usually, he is saved from premature interment solely by the knowledge of his friends that he has been previously subject to catalepsy, by the consequent suspicion excited, and, above all, by the non-appearance of decay. The advances of the malady are, luckily, gradual. The first manifestations, although marked, are unequivocal. The fits grow successively more and more distinctive, and endure each for a longer term than the preceding. In this lies the principal security from inhumation. The unfortunate whose *first* attack should be of the extreme character which is occasionally seen, would almost inevitably be consigned alive to the tomb.

My own case differed in no important particular from those mentioned in medical books. Sometimes, without any apparent cause, I sank, little by little, into a condition of semi-syncope, or half swoon; and, in this condition, without pain, without ability to stir, or, strictly speaking, to think, but with a dull lethargic consciousness of life and of the presence of those who surrounded my bed, I remained, until the crisis of the disease restored me, suddenly, to perfect sensation. At other times I was quickly and impetuously smitten. I grew sick, and numb, and chilly, and dizzy, and so fell prostrate at once. Then, for weeks, all was void, and black, and silent, and Nothing became the universe. Total annihilation could be no more. From these latter attacks I awoke, however, with a gradation slow in proportion to the suddenness of the seizure. Just as the day dawns to the friendless and houseless beggar who roams the streets throughout the long desolate winter night—just so tardily—just so wearily—just so cheerily came back the light of the Soul to me.

Apart from the tendency to trance, however, my general health appeared to be good; nor could I perceive that it was at all affected by the one prevalent malady—unless, indeed, an idiosyncrasy in my ordinary *sleep* may be looked upon as superinduced. Upon awaking from slumber, I could never gain, at once, thorough possession of my senses, and always remained, for many minutes, in much bewilderment and perplexity;—the mental faculties in general, but the memory in especial, being in a condition of absolute abeyance.

In all that I endured there was no physical suffering, but of moral distress an infinitude. My fancy grew charnel. I talked "of worms, of tombs and epitaphs." I was lost in reveries of death, and the idea of premature burial held continual possession of my brain. The ghastly Danger to which I was subjected, haunted me day and night. In the former, the torture of meditation was excessive—in the latter, supreme. When the grim Darkness over-spread the Earth, then, with every horror of thought, I shook—shook as the quivering plumes upon the hearse. When Nature could endure wakefulness no longer, it was with a struggle that I consented to sleep—for I shuddered to reflect that, upon awaking, I might find myself the tenant of a grave. And when, finally, I sank into slumber, it was only to rush at once into a world of phantasms, above which, with vast, sable, overshadowing wings, hovered, predominant, the one sepulchral Idea.

From the innumerable images of gloom which thus oppressed me in dreams, I select for record but a solitary vision. Methought I was immersed in a cataleptic trance of more than usual duration and profundity. Suddenly there came an icy hand upon my forehead, and an impatient, gibbering voice whispered the word "Arise!" within my ear.

I sat erect. The darkness was total. I could not see the figure of him who had aroused me. I could call to mind neither the period at which I had fallen into the trance, nor the locality in which I then lay. While I remained motionless, and busied in endeavors to collect my thoughts, the cold hand grasped me fiercely by the wrist, shaking it petulantly, while the gibbering voice said again:

"Arise! did I not bid thee arise?"

"And who," I demanded, "art thou?"

"I have no name in the regions which I inhabit," replied the voice, mournfully; "I was mortal, but am fiend. I was merciless, but am pitiful. Thou dost feel that I shudder. My teeth chatter as I speak, yet it is not with the chilliness of the night—of the night without end. But this hideousness is insufferable. How canst *thou* tranquilly sleep? I cannot rest for the cry of these great agonies. These sights are more than I can bear. Get thee up! Come with me into the outer Night, and let me unfold to thee the graves. Is not this a spectacle of wo?—Behold!"

I looked; and the unseen figure, which still grasped me by the wrist, had caused to be thrown open the graves of all mankind, and from each issued the faint phosphoric radiance of decay, so that I could see into the innermost recesses, and there view the shrouded bodies in their sad and solemn slumbers with the worm. But, alas! the real sleepers were fewer, by many millions, than those who slumbered not at all; and there was a feeble struggling; and there was a general sad unrest; and from out the depths of the countless pits there came a melancholy rustling from the garments of the buried. And, of those who seemed tranquilly to repose, I saw that a vast number had changed, in a greater or less degree, the rigid and uneasy position in which they had originally been entombed. And the voice again said to me, as I gazed:

"Is it not—oh! is it *not* a pitiful sight?" But, before I could find words to reply, the figure had ceased to grasp my wrist, the phosphoric lights expired, and the graves were closed with a sudden violence, while from out them arose a tumult of despairing cries, saying again, "Is it not—oh, God! is it *not* a very pitiful sight?"

Phantasies such as these, presenting themselves at night, extended their terrific influence far into my waking hours. My nerves became thoroughly unstrung, and I fell a prey to perpetual horror. I hesitated to ride, or to walk, or to indulge in any exercise that would carry me from home. In fact, I no longer dared trust myself out of the immediate presence of those who were aware of my proneness to catalepsy, lest, falling into one of my usual fits, I should be buried before my real condition could be ascertained. I doubted the care, the fidelity of my dearest friends. I dreaded that, in some trance of more than customary duration, they might be prevailed upon to regard me as irrecoverable. I even went so far as to fear that, as I occasioned much trouble, they might be glad to consider any very protracted attack as sufficient excuse for getting rid of me altogether. It was in vain they endeavored to reassure me by the most solemn promises. I exacted the most sacred oaths, that under no circumstances they would bury me until decomposition had so materially advanced as to render farther preservation impossible. And, even then, my mortal terrors would listen to no reason—would accept no consolation. I entered into a series of elaborate precautions. Among other things, I had the family vault so remodelled as to admit of being readily opened from within. The slightest pressure upon a long lever that extended far into the tomb would cause the iron portal to fly back. There were arrangements also for the free admission of air and light, and convenient receptacles for food and water, within immediate reach of the coffin intended for my reception. This coffin was warmly and softly padded, and was provided with a lid, fashioned upon the principle of the vault-door, with the addition of springs so contrived that the feeblest movement of the body would be sufficient to set it at liberty. Besides all this, there was suspended from the roof of the tomb, a large bell, the rope of which, it was designed, should extend through a hole in the coffin, and so be fastened to one of the hands of the corpse. But, alas! what avails the vigilance against the Destiny of man? Not even these well contrived securities sufficed to save from the uttermost agonies of living inhumation, a wretch to these agonies foredoomed!

There arrived an epoch—as often before there had arrived—in which I found myself emerging from total unconsciousness into the first feeble and indefinite sense of existence. Slowly—with a tortoise gradation—approached the faint gray dawn of the psychal day. A torpid uneasiness. An apathetic endurance of dull pain. No care—no hope—no effort. Then, after long interval, a ringing in the ears; then, after a lapse still longer, a pricking or tingling sensation in the extremities; then a seemingly eternal period of pleasurable quiescence, during which the awakening feelings are struggling into thought; then a brief re-sinking into nonentity; then a sudden recovery. At length the slight quivering of an eyelid, and immediately thereupon, an electric shock of a terror, deadly and indefinite, which sends the blood in torrents from the temples to the heart. And now the first positive effort to think. And now the first endeavor to remember. And now a partial and evanescent success. And now the memory has so far regained its dominion, that, in some measure, I am cognizant of my state. I feel that I am not awaking from ordinary sleep. I recollect that I have been subject to catalepsy. And now, at last, as if by the rush of an ocean, my shuddering spirit is overwhelmed by the one grim Danger—by the one spectral and ever-prevalent Idea.

For some minutes after this fancy possessed me, I remained without motion. And why? I could not summon courage to move. I dared not make the effort which was to satisfy me of my fate—and yet there was something at my heart which whispered me *it was sure*. Despair—such as no other species of wretchedness ever calls into being—despair alone urged me, after long irresolution, to uplift the heavy lids of my eyes. I uplifted them. It was dark—all dark. I knew that the fit was over. I knew that the crisis of my disorder had long passed. I knew that I had now fully recovered the use of my visual faculties—and yet it was dark—all dark—the intense and utter raylessness of the Night that endureth for evermore.

I endeavored to shriek; and my lips and my parched tongue moved convulsively together in the attempt—but no voice issued from the cavernous lungs, which, oppressed as if by the weight of some incumbent mountain, gasped and palpitated, with the heart, at every elaborate and struggling inspiration.

The movement of the jaws, in this effort to cry aloud, showed me that they were bound up, as is usual with the dead. I felt, too, that I lay upon some hard substance; and by something similar my sides were, also, closely compressed. So far, I had not ventured to stir any of my limbs—but now I violently threw up my arms, which had been lying at length, with the wrists crossed. They struck a solid wooden substance, which extended above my person at an elevation of not more than six inches from my face. I could no longer doubt that I reposed within a coffin at last.

And now, amid all my infinite miseries, came sweetly the cherub Hope—for I thought of my precautions. I writhed, and made spasmodic exertions to force open the lid: it would not move. I felt my wrists for the bell-rope: it was not to be found. And now the Comforter fled for ever, and a still sterner Despair reigned triumphant; for I could not help perceiving the absence of the paddings which I had so carefully prepared—and then, too, there came suddenly to my nostrils the strong peculiar odor of moist earth. The conclusion was irresistible. I was *not* within the vault. I had fallen into a trance while absent from home—while among strangers—when, or how, I could not remember—and it was they who had buried me as a dog—nailed up in some common coffin—and thrust, deep, deep, and for ever, into some ordinary and nameless *grave*.

As this awful conviction forced itself, thus, into the innermost chambers of my soul, I once again struggled to cry aloud. And in this second endeavor I succeeded. A long, wild, and continuous shriek, or yell, of agony, resounded through the realms of the subterranean Night.

"Hillo! hillo, there!" said a gruff voice, in reply.

"What the devil's the matter now?" said a second.

"Get out o' that!" said a third.

"What do you mean by yowling in that ere kind of style, like a cattymount?" said a fourth; and hereupon I was seized and shaken without ceremony, for several minutes, by a junto of very rough-looking individuals. They did not arouse me from my slumber—for I was wide awake when I screamed—but they restored me to the full possession of my memory.

This adventure occurred near Richmond, in Virginia. Accompanied by a friend, I had proceeded, upon a gunning expedition, some miles down the banks of James River. Night approached, and we were overtaken by a storm. The cabin of a small sloop lying at anchor in the stream, and laden with garden mould, afforded us the only available shelter. We made the best of it, and passed the night on board. I slept in one of the only two berths in the vessel—and the berths of a sloop of sixty or seventy tons, need scarcely be described. That which I occupied had no bedding of any kind. Its extreme width was eighteen inches. The distance of its bottom from the deck overhead, was precisely the same. I found it a matter of exceeding difficulty to squeeze myself in. Nevertheless, I slept soundly; and the whole of my vision—for it was no dream, and no nightmare—arose naturally from the circumstances of my position—from my ordinary bias of thought—and from the difficulty, to which I have alluded, of collecting my senses, and especially of regaining my memory, for a long time after awaking from slumber. The men who shook me were the crew of the sloop, and some laborers engaged to unload it. From the load itself came the earthly smell. The bandage about the jaws was a silk handkerchief in which I had bound up my head, in default of my customary nightcap.

The tortures endured, however, were indubitably quite equal for the time, to those of actual sepulture. They were fearfully—they were inconceivably hideous; but out of Evil proceeded Good; for their very excess wrought in my spirit an inevitable revulsion. My soul acquired tone—acquired temper. I went abroad. I took vigorous exercise. I breathed the free air of Heaven. I thought upon other subjects than Death. I discarded my medical books. "Buchan" I burned. I read no "Night Thoughts"[2]—no fustian about church-yards—no bugaboo tales—*such as this*. In short, I became a new

man, and lived a man's life. From that memorable night, I dis-
missed forever my charnel apprehensions, and with them vanished
the cataleptic disorder, of which, perhaps, they had been less the
consequence than the cause.

There are moments when, even to the sober eye of Reason, the
world of our sad Humanity may assume the semblance of a Hell—
but the imagination of man is no Carathis, to explore with im-
punity its every cavern. Alas! the grim legion of sepulchral terrors
cannot be regarded as altogether fanciful—but, like the Demons in
whose company Afrasiab made his voyage down the Oxus, they
must sleep, or they will devour us—they must be suffered to slum-
ber, or we perish.[3]

THE FACTS IN THE CASE
OF M. VALDEMAR

Of course I shall not pretend to consider it any matter for wonder, that the extraordinary case of M. Valdemar has excited discussion. It would have been a miracle had it not—especially under the circumstances. Through the desire of all parties concerned, to keep the affair from the public, at least for the present, or until we had farther opportunities for investigation—through our endeavors to effect this—a garbled or exaggerated account made its way into society, and became the source of many unpleasant misrepresentations, and, very naturally, of a great deal of disbelief.

It is now rendered necessary that I give the *facts*—as far as I comprehend them myself. They are, succinctly, these:

My attention, for the last three years, had been repeatedly drawn to the subject of Mesmerism; and, about nine months ago, it occurred to me, quite suddenly, that in the series of experiments made hitherto, there had been a very remarkable and most unaccountable omission:—no person had as yet been mesmerized *in articulo mortis*.[1] It remained to be seen, first, whether, in such condition, there existed in the patient any susceptibility to the magnetic influence; secondly, whether, if any existed, it was impaired or increased by the condition; thirdly, to what extent, or for how long a period, the encroachments of Death might be arrested by the process. There were other points to be ascertained, but these most excited my curiosity—the last in especial, from the immensely important character of its consequences.

In looking around me for some subject by whose means I might test these particulars, I was brought to think of my friend, M. Ernest Valdemar, the well-known compiler of the "Bibliotheca Forensica," and author (under the *nom de plume* of Issachar Marx) of the Polish versions of "Wallenstein" and "Gargantua."

M. Valdemar, who has resided principally at Harlaem, N.Y., since the year 1839, is (or was) particularly noticeable for the extreme spareness of his person—his lower limbs much resembling those of John Randolph; and, also, for the whiteness of his whiskers, in violent contrast to the blackness of his hair—the latter, in consequence, being very generally mistaken for a wig. His temperament was markedly nervous, and rendered him a good subject for mesmeric experiment. On two or three occasions I had put him to sleep with little difficulty, but was disappointed in other results which his peculiar constitution had naturally led me to anticipate. His will was at no period positively, or thoroughly, under my control, and in regard to *clairvoyance*, I could accomplish with him nothing to be relied upon. I always attributed my failure at these points to the disordered state of his health. For some months previous to my becoming acquainted with him, his physicians had declared him in a confirmed phthisis. It was his custom, indeed, to speak calmly of his approaching dissolution, as of a matter neither to be avoided nor regretted.

When the ideas to which I have alluded first occurred to me, it was of course very natural that I should think of M. Valdemar. I knew the steady philosophy of the man too well to apprehend any scruples from *him*; and he had no relatives in America who would be likely to interfere. I spoke to him frankly upon the subject; and, to my surprise, his interest seemed vividly excited. I say to my surprise; for, although he had always yielded his person freely to my experiments, he had never before given me any tokens of sympathy with what I did. His disease was of that character which would admit of exact calculation in respect to the epoch of its termination in death; and it was finally arranged between us that he would send for me about twenty-four hours before the period announced by his physicians as that of his decease.

It is now rather more than seven months since I received, from M. Valdemar himself, the subjoined note:

MY DEAR P—,

You may as well come *now*. D— and F— are agreed that I cannot hold out beyond to-morrow midnight; and I think they have hit the time very nearly.

VALDEMAR.

I received this note within half an hour after it was written, and in fifteen minutes more I was in the dying man's chamber. I had not seen him for ten days, and was appalled by the fearful alteration which the brief interval had wrought in him. His face wore a leaden hue; the eyes were utterly lustreless; and the emaciation was so extreme that the skin had been broken through by the cheek-bones. His expectoration was excessive. The pulse was barely perceptible. He retained, nevertheless, in a very remarkable manner, both his mental power and a certain degree of physical strength. He spoke with distinctness—took some palliative medicines without aid—and, when I entered the room, was occupied in penciling memoranda in a pocket-book. He was propped up in the bed by pillows. Doctors D— and F— were in attendance.

After pressing Valdemar's hand, I took these gentlemen aside, and obtained from them a minute account of the patient's condition. The left lung had been for eighteen months in a semi-osseous or cartilaginous state, and was, of course, entirely useless for all purposes of vitality. The right, in its upper portion, was also partially, if not thoroughly, ossified, while the lower region was merely a mass of purulent tubercles, running one into another. Several extensive perforations existed; and, at one point, permanent adhesion to the ribs had taken place. These appearances in the right lobe were of comparatively recent date. The ossification had proceeded with very unusual rapidity; no sign of it had been discovered a month before, and the adhesion had only been observed during the three previous days. Independently of the phthisis, the patient was suspected of aneurism of the aorta; but on this point the osseous symptoms rendered an exact diagnosis impossible. It was the opinion of both physicians that M. Valdemar would die about midnight on the morrow (Sunday). It was then seven o'clock on Saturday evening.

On quitting the invalid's bed-side to hold conversation with myself, Doctors D— and F— had bidden him a final farewell. It had not been their intention to return; but, at my request, they agreed to look in upon the patient about ten the next night.

When they had gone, I spoke freely with M. Valdemar on the subject of his approaching dissolution, as well as, more particularly, of the experiment proposed. He still professed himself quite willing and even anxious to have it made, and urged me to commence it at once. A male and a female nurse were in attendance; but I did not feel myself altogether at liberty to engage in a task of this character with no more reliable witnesses than these people, in case of sudden accident, might prove. I therefore postponed operations until about eight the next night, when the arrival of a medical student with whom I had some acquaintance, (Mr. Theodore L——l,) relieved me from farther embarrassment. It had been my design, originally, to wait for the physicians; but I was induced to proceed, first, by the urgent entreaties of M. Valdemar, and secondly, by my conviction that I had not a moment to lose, as he was evidently sinking fast.

Mr. L——l was so kind as to accede to my desire that he would take notes of all that occurred; and it is from his memoranda that what I now have to relate is, for the most part, either condensed or copied *verbatim*.

It wanted about five minutes of eight when, taking the patient's hand, I begged him to state, as distinctly as he could, to Mr. L——l, whether he (M. Valdemar) was entirely willing that I should make the experiment of mesmerizing him in his then condition.

He replied feebly, yet quite audibly, "Yes, I wish to be mesmerized"—adding immediately afterwards, "I fear you have deferred it too long."

While he spoke thus, I commenced the passes which I had already found most effectual in subduing him. He was evidently influenced with the first lateral stroke of my hand across his forehead; but although I exerted all my powers, no farther perceptible effect was induced until some minutes after ten o'clock, when Doctors D—— and F—— called, according to appointment. I explained to them, in a few words, what I designed, and as they opposed no objection, saying that the patient was already in the death agony, I proceeded without hesitation—exchanging, however, the lateral passes for downward ones, and directing my gaze entirely into the right eye of the sufferer.

By this time his pulse was imperceptible and his breathing was stertorous, and at intervals of half a minute.

This condition was nearly unaltered for a quarter an hour. At the expiration of this period, however, a natural although a very deep sigh escaped the bosom of the dying man, and the stertorous breathing ceased—that is to say, its stertorousness was no longer apparent; the intervals were undiminished. The patient's extremities were of an icy coldness.

At five minutes before eleven I perceived unequivocal signs of the mesmeric influence. The glassy roll of the eye was changed for that expression of uneasy *inward* examination which is never seen except in cases of sleep-waking, and which it is quite impossible to mistake. With a few rapid lateral passes I made the lids quiver, as in incipient sleep, and with a few more I closed them altogether. I was not satisfied, however, with this, but continued the manipulations vigorously, and with the fullest exertion of the will, until I had completely stiffened the limbs of the slumberer, after placing them in a seemingly easy position. The legs were at full length; the arms were nearly so, and reposed on the bed at a moderate distance from the loins. The head was very slightly elevated.

When I had accomplished this, it was fully midnight, and I requested the gentlemen present to examine M. Valdemar's condition. After a few experiments, they admitted him to be in an unusually perfect state of mesmeric trance. The curiosity of both the physicians was greatly excited. Dr. D— resolved at once to remain with the patient all night, while Dr. F— took leave with a promise to return at daybreak. Mr. L—l and the nurses remained.

We left M. Valdemar entirely undisturbed until about three o'clock in the morning, when I approached him and found him in precisely the same condition as when Dr. F— went away—that is to say, he lay in the same position; the pulse was imperceptible; the breathing was gentle (scarcely noticeable, unless through the application of a mirror to the lips); the eyes were closed naturally; and the limbs were as rigid and as cold as marble. Still, the general appearance was certainly not that of death.

As I approached M. Valdemar I made a kind of half effort to influence his right arm into pursuit of my own, as I passed the latter gently to and fro above his person. In such experiments with this patient I had never perfectly succeeded before, and assuredly I had little thought of succeeding now; but to my astonishment, his arm very readily, although feebly, followed every direction I assigned it with mine. I determined to hazard a few words of conversation.

"M. Valdemar," I said, "are you asleep?" He made no answer, but I perceived a tremor about the lips, and was thus induced to repeat the question, again and again. At its third repetition, his whole frame was agitated by a very slight shivering; the eyelids un-closed themselves so far as to display a white line of the ball; the lips moved sluggishly, and from between them, in a barely audible whisper, issued the words:

"Yes;—asleep now. Do not wake me!—let me die so!"

I here felt the limbs and found them as rigid as ever. The right arm, as before, obeyed the direction of my hand. I questioned the sleep-waker again:

"Do you still feel pain in the breast, M. Valdemar?"

The answer now was immediate, but even less audible than be-fore:

"No pain—I am dying."

I did not think it advisable to disturb him farther just then, and nothing more was said or done until the arrival of Dr. F——, who came a little before sunrise, and expressed unbounded astonish-ment at finding the patient still alive. After feeling the pulse and applying a mirror to the lips, he requested me to speak to the sleep-waker again. I did so, saying:

"M. Valdemar, do you still sleep?"

As before, some minutes elapsed ere a reply was made; and dur-ing the interval the dying man seemed to be collecting his energies to speak. At my fourth repetition of the question, he said very faintly, almost inaudibly:

"Yes; still asleep—dying."

It was now the opinion, or rather the wish, of the physicians, that M. Valdemar should be suffered to remain undisturbed in his present apparently tranquil condition, until death should supervene—and this, it was generally agreed, must now take place within a few minutes. I concluded, however, to speak to him once more, and merely repeated my previous question.

While I spoke, there came a marked change over the counte-nance of the sleep-waker. The eyes rolled themselves slowly open, the pupils disappearing upwardly; the skin generally assumed a ca-daverous hue, resembling not so much parchment as white paper; and the circular hectic spots which, hitherto, had been strongly defined in the centre of each cheek, *went out* at once. I use this ex-pression, because the suddenness of their departure put me in mind of nothing so much as the extinguishment of a candle by a puff of the breath. The upper lip, at the same time, writhed itself away from the teeth, which it had previously covered completely; while the lower jaw fell with an audible jerk, leaving the mouth widely extended, and disclosing in full view the swollen and blackened tongue. I presume that no member of the party then present had been unaccustomed to death-bed horrors; but so hideous beyond conception was the appearance of M. Valdemar at this moment, that there was a general shrinking back from the region of the bed.

I now feel that I have reached a point of this narrative at which every reader will be startled into positive disbelief. It is my business, however, simply to proceed.

There was no longer the faintest sign of vitality in M. Valdemar; and concluding him to be dead, we were consigning him to the charge of the nurses, when a strong vibratory motion was observable in the tongue. This continued for perhaps a minute. At the expiration of this period, there issued from the distended and motionless jaws a voice—such as it would be madness in me to attempt describing. There are, indeed, two or three epithets which might be considered as applicable to it in part; I might say, for example, that the sound was harsh, and broken and hollow; but the hideous whole is indescribable, for the simple reason that no similar sounds have ever jarred upon the ear of humanity. There were two particulars, nevertheless, which I thought then, and still think, might fairly be stated as characteristic of the intonation—as well adapted to convey some idea of its unearthly peculiarity. In the first place, the voice seemed to reach our ears—at least mine—from a vast distance, or from some deep cavern within the earth. In the second place, it impressed me (I fear, indeed, that it will be impossible to make myself comprehended) as gelatinous or glutinous matters impress the sense of touch.

I have spoken both of "sound" and of "voice." I mean to say that the sound was one of distinct—of even wonderfully, thrillingly distinct—syllabification. M. Valdemar *spoke*—obviously in reply to the question I had propounded to him a few minutes before. I had asked him, it will be remembered, if he still slept. He now said:

"Yes;—no;—I *have been* sleeping—and now—now—*I am dead*."

No person present even affected to deny, or attempted to repress, the unutterable, shuddering horror which these few words, thus uttered, were so well calculated to convey. Mr. L—l (the student) swooned. The nurses immediately left the chamber, and could not be induced to return. My own impressions I would not pretend to render intelligible to the reader. For nearly an hour, we busied ourselves, silently—without the utterance of a word—in endeavors to revive Mr. L—l. When he came to himself, we addressed ourselves again to an investigation of M. Valdemar's condition.

It remained in all respects as I have last described it, with the exception that the mirror no longer afforded evidence of respiration. An attempt to draw blood from the arm failed. I should mention, too, that this limb was no farther subject to my will. I endeavored in vain to make it follow the direction of my hand. The only real indication, indeed, of the mesmeric influence, was now found in the vibratory movement of the tongue, whenever I addressed M. Valdemar a question. He seemed to be making an effort to reply, but had no longer sufficient volition. To queries put to him by any other person than myself he seemed utterly insensible—although I endeavored to place each member of the company in mesmeric *rapport* with him. I believe that I have now related all that is necessary to an understanding of the sleep-waker's state at this epoch. Other nurses were procured; and at ten o'clock I left the house in company with the two physicians and Mr. L—l.

In the afternoon we all called again to see the patient. His condition remained precisely the same. We had now some discussion as to the propriety and feasibility of awakening him; but we had little difficulty in agreeing that no good purpose would be served by so doing. It was evident that, so far, death (or what is usually termed death) had been arrested by the mesmeric process. It seemed clear to us all that to awaken M. Valdemar would be merely to insure his instant, or at least his speedy dissolution.

From this period until the close of last week—*an interval of nearly seven months*—we continued to make daily calls at M. Valdemar's house, accompanied, now and then, by medical and other friends. All this time the sleep-waker remained *exactly* as I have last described him. The nurses' attentions were continual.

It was on Friday last that we finally resolved to make the experiment of awakening, or attempting to awaken him; and it is the (perhaps) unfortunate result of this latter experiment which has given rise to so much discussion in private circles—to so much of what I cannot help thinking unwarranted popular feeling.

For the purpose of relieving M. Valdemar from the mesmeric trance, I made use of the customary passes. These, for a time, were unsuccessful. The first indication of revival was afforded by a partial descent of the iris. It was observed, as especially remarkable, that this lowering of the pupil was accompanied by the profuse out-flowing of a yellowish ichor (from beneath the lids) of a pungent and highly offensive odor.

It was now suggested that I should attempt to influence the patient's arm, as heretofore. I made the attempt and failed. Dr. F— then intimated a desire to have me put a question. I did so, as follows:

"M. Valdemar, can you explain to us what are your feelings or wishes now?"

There was an instant return of the hectic circles on the cheeks; the tongue quivered, or rather rolled violently in the mouth (although the jaws and lips remained rigid as before;) and at length the same hideous voice which I have already described, broke forth:

"For God's sake!—quick!—quick!—put me to sleep—or, quick!—waken me!—quick!—*I say to you that I am dead!*"

I was thoroughly unnerved, and for an instant remained undecided what to do. At first I made an endeavor to re-compose the patient; but, failing in this through total abeyance of the will, I retraced my steps and as earnestly struggled to awaken him. In this attempt I soon saw that I should be successful—or at least I soon fancied that my success would be complete—and I am sure that all in the room were prepared to see the patient awaken.

For what really occurred, however, it is quite impossible that any human being could have been prepared.

As I rapidly made the mesmeric passes, amid ejaculations of "dead! dead!" absolutely *bursting* from the tongue and not from the lips of the sufferer, his whole frame at once—within the space of a single minute, or even less, shrunk—crumbled—absolutely *rotted* away beneath my hands. Upon the bed, before that whole company, there lay a nearly liquid mass of loathsome—of detestable putridity.

Bereavements

Although Poe found poetic inspiration in a beautiful woman's death, he tended in fiction to portray her passing as an unromantic agony. Indeed, the fiction tends to emphasize the recoil of a male narrator from a dying woman whose return from the grave sometimes savors of revenge. The tales of loss surely owe something to Poe's own recurrent bereavements—the deaths of his mother, of the beloved Mrs. Stanard, and of Frances Allan—and weirdly anticipate the early demise of his wife. But unlike the poems, which underscore grief and longing, the tales typically reflect a complicated loathing of mortality itself.

The early tale "The Assignation" introduces a succession of fated young women in Poe's fiction and unfolds from the viewpoint of an interested spectator. When the Marchesa Aphrodite dejectedly casts her baby into a Venetian canal, her paramour, a Byronic visionary, foils the infanticide and so wins a mysterious wager. Unable to escape her marriage to the cruel Mentoni, the woman honors her vow to the visionary in a manner that the narrator comprehends too late.

More provocatively Poe narrates "Berenice" from the twisted perspective of Egaeus, who traces the decline of his cousin by dwelling on revolting changes in her appearance and "personal identity." Berenice figures mostly as a cadaverous abstraction, yet her dazzling teeth become, in the narrator's alienated mind, obsessive emblems of her individuality. Reacting to her reported demise, Egaeus betrays his madness by performing a bizarre, unconscious outrage.

Identity figures again in "Morella," where the unloving narrator marries his "friend" and joins her in metaphysical studies on the fate of "personal identity." Her wasting illness so intensifies his antipathy toward her that she makes a dying vow: she will compel him to "adore" in death the one whom he abhorred in life. The daughter whom Morella delivers on her deathbed incarnates her appearance and identity so exactly that the horrifying outcome of the girl's belated christening fulfills the curse and dooms her adoring father to endless melancholy.

"Ligeia" marks Poe's most intriguing variation, however, on the bereavement plot. When Ligeia grows ill, her narrator-husband agonizes at her "pitiable" decline and marvels at her determination to resist death by force of will. In the "mental alienation" provoked by her loss, he marries blonde Rowena Trevanion but cannot hide his loathing for her *or* his longing for Ligeia's return. In the ambiguous final scene, he witnesses the possible reincarnation of raven-haired Ligeia, yet the reviving woman shuns him, forever shrouding in ambiguity her actual identity.

Poe employs a spectatorial narrator to study the strange bond between brother and sister in "The Fall of the House of Usher." Attempting to help his childhood friend, the narrator rationalizes the terrors inspired in Roderick by the illness of Madeline. Fearing that her apparent death may be a trance, Roderick buries her beneath the house, but he perversely screws down the coffin lid. Whether by natural or supernatural means, Madeline returns from the tomb, falling upon her brother and frightening him to death as their ancestral home collapses upon itself.

The only bereavement tale with a happy ending, "Eleonora" evokes the bliss of the narrator and his cousin-wife prior to her fatal illness. Despite his vow that he will never remarry, the narrator later weds the "ethereal" Ermengarde and in a mystical moment receives absolution from the spirit of Eleonora. Conversely, in "The Oval Portrait" a traveler at an Italian chateau finds in a bedside book the story of a portrait on the wall before him. Married to a "maiden of rarest beauty," an artist-husband has subjected the woman to endless sittings and so fails to notice her decline, achieving the effect of "Life itself" in his painting at an unimaginable cost.

THE ASSIGNATION

Stay for me there! I will not fail.
To meet thee in that hollow vale.
[*Exequy on the death of his wife, by Henry King, Bishop of Chichester*.]

Ill-fated and mysterious man!—bewildered in the brilliancy of thine own imagination, and fallen in the flames of thine own youth! Again in fancy I behold thee! Once more thy form hath risen before me!—not—oh not as thou art—in the cold valley and shadow—but as thou *shouldst be*—squandering away a life of magnificent meditation in that city of dim visions, thine own Venice—which is a star-beloved Elysium of the sea, and the wide windows of whose Palladian palaces look down with a deep and bitter meaning upon the secrets of her silent waters. Yes! I repeat it—as thou *shouldst be*. There are surely other worlds than this—other thoughts than the thoughts of the multitude—other speculations than the speculations of the sophist. Who then shall call thy conduct into question? who blame thee for thy visionary hours, or denounce those occupations as a wasting away of life, which were but the overflowings of thine everlasting energies?

It was at Venice, beneath the covered archway there called the *Ponte di Sospiri*, that I met for the third or fourth time the person of whom I speak. It is with a confused recollection that I bring to mind the circumstances of that meeting. Yet I remember—ah! how should I forget?—the deep midnight, the Bridge of Sighs, the beauty of woman, and the Genius of Romance that stalked up and down the narrow canal.

It was a night of unusual gloom. The great clock of the Piazza had sounded the fifth hour of the Italian evening. The square of the Campanile lay silent and deserted, and the lights in the old Ducal Palace were dying fast away. I was returning home from the Piazetta, by way of the Grand Canal. But as my gondola arrived opposite the mouth of the canal San Marco, a female voice from its recesses broke suddenly upon the night, in one wild, hysterical, and long continued shriek. Startled at the sound, I sprang upon my feet: while the gondolier, letting slip his single oar, lost it in the pitchy darkness beyond a chance of recovery, and we were consequently left to the guidance of the current which here sets from the greater into the smaller channel. Like some huge and sable-feathered condor, we were slowly drifting down towards the Bridge of Sighs, when a thousand flambeaux flashing from the windows, and down the staircases of the Ducal Palace, turned all at once that deep gloom into a livid and preternatural day.

A child, slipping from the arms of its own mother, had fallen from an upper window of the lofty structure into the deep and dim canal. The quiet waters had closed placidly over their victim; and, although my own gondola was the only one in sight, many a stout swimmer, already in the stream, was seeking in vain upon the surface, the treasure which was to be found, alas! only within the abyss. Upon the broad black marble flagstones at the entrance of the palace, and a few steps above the water, stood a figure which none who then saw can have ever since forgotten. It was the Marchesa Aphrodite—the adoration of all Venice—the gayest of the gay—the most lovely where all were beautiful—but still the young wife of the old and intriguing Mentoni, and the mother of that fair child, her first and only one, who now, deep beneath the murky water, was thinking in bitterness of heart upon her sweet caresses, and exhausting its little life in struggles to call upon her name.

She stood alone. Her small, bare and silvery feet gleamed in the black mirror of marble beneath her. Her hair, not as yet more than half loosened for the night from its ballroom array, clustered, amid a shower of diamonds, round and round her classical head, in curls like those of the young hyacinth. A snowy-white and gauze-like drapery seemed to be nearly the sole covering to her delicate form; but the mid-summer and midnight air was hot, sullen, and still, and no motion in the statue-like form itself, stirred even the folds of that raiment of very vapor which hung around it as the heavy marble hangs around the Niobe. Yet— strange to say!—her large lustrous eyes were not turned downwards upon that grave wherein her brightest hope lay buried—but riveted in a widely different direction! The prison of the Old Re-public is, I think, the stateliest building in all Venice—but how could that lady gaze so fixedly upon it, when beneath her lay sti-fling her own child? Yon dark, gloomy niche, too, yawns right op-posite her chamber window—what, then, *could* there be in its shadows—in its architecture—in its ivy-wreathed and solemn cornices—that the Marchesa di Mentoni had not wondered at a thousand times before? Nonsense!—Who does not remember that, at such a time as this, the eye, like a shattered mirror, multiplies the images of its sorrow, and sees in innumerable far off places, the woe which is close at hand?

Many steps above the Marchesa, and within the arch of the water-gate, stood, in full dress, the Satyr-like figure of Mentoni himself. He was occasionally occupied in thrumming a guitar, and seemed *ennuyé* to the very death, as at intervals he gave directions for the recovery of his child. Stupified and aghast, I had myself no power to move from the upright position I had assumed upon first hearing the shriek, and must have presented to the eyes of the agi-tated group a spectral and ominous appearance, as with pale coun-tenance and rigid limbs, I floated down among them in that funereal gondola.

All efforts proved in vain. Many of the most energetic in the search were relaxing their exertions, and yielding to a gloomy sor-row. There seemed but little hope for the child; (how much less than for the mother!) but now, from the interior of that dark niche which has been already mentioned as forming a part of the Old Republican prison, and as fronting the lattice of the Marchesa, a figure muffled in a cloak, stepped out within reach of the light, and, pausing a moment upon the verge of the giddy descent, plunged head-long into the canal. As, in an instant afterwards, he stood with the still living and breathing child within his grasp, upon the marble flagstones by the side of the Marchesa, his cloak, heavy with the drenching water, became unfastened, and, falling in folds about his feet, discovered to the wonder-stricken specta-tors the graceful person of a very young man, with the sound of whose name the greater part of Europe was then ringing.

No word spoke the deliverer. But the Marchesa! She will now receive her child—she will press it to her heart—she will cling to its little form, and smother it with her caresses. Alas! *another's* arms have taken it from the stranger—*another's* arms have taken it away, and borne it afar off, unnoticed, into the palace! And the Marchesa! Her lip—her beautiful lip trembles: tears are gathering in her eyes—those eyes which, like Pliny's acanthus, are "soft and almost liquid." Yes! tears are gathering in those eyes—and see! the entire woman thrills throughout the soul, and the statue has started into life! The pallor of the marble countenance, the swelling of the marble bosom, the very purity of the marble feet, we behold suddenly flushed over with a tide of ungovernable crimson; and a slight shudder quivers about her delicate frame, as a gentle air at Napoli about the rich silver lilies in the grass.

Why *should* that lady blush! To this demand there is no answer—except that, having left, in the eager haste and terror of a mother's heart, the privacy of her own *boudoir,* she has neglected to enthral her tiny feet in their slippers, and utterly forgotten to throw over her Venetian shoulders that drapery which is their due. What other possible reason could there have been for her so blushing?—for the glance of those wild appealing eyes? for the unusual tumult of that throbbing bosom?—for the convulsive pressure of that trembling hand?—that hand which fell, as Mentoni turned into the palace, accidentally, upon the hand of the stranger. What reason could there have been for the low—the singularly low tone of those unmeaning words which the lady uttered hurriedly in bidding him adieu? "Thou hast conquered," she said, or the murmurs of the water deceived me; "thou hast conquered—one hour after sunrise—we shall meet—so let it be!"

The tumult had subsided, the lights had died away within the palace, and the stranger, whom I now recognized, stood alone upon the flags. He shook with inconceivable agitation, and his eye glanced around in search of a gondola. I could not do less than offer him the service of my own; and he accepted the civility. Having obtained an oar at the water-gate, we proceeded together to his residence, while he rapidly recovered his self-possession, and spoke of our former slight acquaintance in terms of great apparent cordiality.

There are some subjects upon which I take pleasure in being minute. The person of the stranger—let me call him by this title, who to all the world was still a stranger—the person of the

stranger is one of these subjects. In height he might have been be-
low rather than above the medium size: although there were mo-
ments of intense passion when his frame actually *expanded* and
belied the assertion. The light, almost slender symmetry of his fig-
ure, promised more of that ready activity which he evinced at the
Bridge of Sighs, than of that Herculean strength which he has
been known to wield without an effort, upon occasions of more
dangerous emergency. With the mouth and chin of a deity—
singular, wild, full, liquid eyes, whose shadows varied from pure
hazel to intense and brilliant jet—and a profusion of curling,
black hair, from which a forehead of unusual breadth gleamed
forth at intervals all light and ivory—his were features than which
I have seen none more classically regular, except, perhaps, the
marble ones of the Emperor Commodus. Yet his countenance was,
nevertheless, one of those which all men have seen at some period
of their lives, and have never afterwards seen again. It had no
peculiar—it had no settled predominant expression to be fastened
upon the memory; a countenance seen and instantly forgotten—
but forgotten with a vague and never-ceasing desire of recalling it
to mind. Not that the spirit of each rapid passion failed, at any
time, to throw its own distinct image upon the mirror of that
face—but that the mirror, mirror-like, retained no vestige of the
passion, when the passion had departed.

Upon leaving him on the night of our adventure, he solicited
me, in what I thought an urgent manner, to call upon him *very*
early the next morning. Shortly after sunrise, I found myself ac-
cordingly at his Palazzo, one of those huge structures of gloomy,
yet fantastic pomp, which tower above the waters of the Grand
Canal in the vicinity of the Rialto. I was shown up a broad wind-
ing staircase of mosaics, into an apartment whose unparalleled
splendor burst through the opening door with an actual glare,
making me blind and dizzy with luxuriousness.

I knew my acquaintance to be wealthy. Report had spoken of
his possessions in terms which I had even ventured to call terms of
ridiculous exaggeration. But as I gazed about me, I could not bring
myself to believe that the wealth of any subject in Europe could
have supplied the princely magnificence which burned and blazed
around.

Although, as I say, the sun had arisen, yet the room was still brilliantly lighted up. I judge from this circumstance, as well as from an air of exhaustion in the countenance of my friend, that he had not retired to bed during the whole of the preceding night. In the architecture and embellishments of the chamber, the evident design had been to dazzle and astound. Little attention had been paid to the *decora* of what is technically called *keeping*, or to the proprieties of nationality. The eye wandered from object to object, and rested upon none—neither the *grotesques* of the Greek painters, nor the sculptures of the best Italian days, nor the huge carvings of untutored Egypt. Rich draperies in every part of the room trembled to the vibration of low, melancholy music, whose origin was not to be discovered. The senses were oppressed by mingled and conflicting perfumes, reeking up from strange convolute censers, together with multitudinous flaring and flickering tongues of emerald and violet fire. The rays of the newly risen sun poured in upon the whole, through windows, formed each of a single pane of crimson-tinted glass. Glancing to and fro, in a thousand reflections, from curtains which rolled from their cornices like cataracts of molten silver, the beams of natural glory mingled at length fitfully with the artificial light, and lay weltering in subdued masses upon a carpet of rich, liquid-looking cloth of Chili gold.

"Ha! ha! ha!—ha! ha! ha!"—laughed the proprietor, motioning me to a seat as I entered the room, and throwing himself back at full-length upon an ottoman. "I see," said he, perceiving that I could not immediately reconcile myself to the *bienséance*[1] of so singular a welcome—"I see you are astonished at my apartment—at my statues—my pictures—my originality of conception in architecture and upholstery! absolutely drunk, eh, with my magnificence? But pardon me, my dear sir, (here his tone of voice dropped to the very spirit of cordiality,) pardon me for my uncharitable laughter. You appeared so *utterly* astonished. Besides, some things are so completely ludicrous, that a man *must* laugh, or die. To die laughing, must be the most glorious of all glorious deaths! Sir Thomas More—a very fine man was Sir Thomas More—Sir Thomas More died laughing, you remember. Also in the *Absurdities* of Ravisius Textor, there is a long list of characters who came to the same magnificent end.[2] Do you know, however," continued he, musingly, "that at Sparta (which is now Palæaochori,) at Sparta, I say, to the west of the citadel, among a chaos of scarcely visible ruins, is a kind of *socle*, upon which are still legible the letters ΛΑΣΜ. They are undoubtedly part of ΓΕΛΑΣΜΑ. Now, at Sparta were a thousand temples and shrines to a thousand different divinities. How exceedingly strange that the altar of Laughter should have survived all the others! But in the present instance," he resumed, with a singular alteration of voice and manner, "I have no right to be merry at your expense. You might well have been amazed. Europe cannot produce anything so fine as this, my little regal cabinet. My other apartments are by no means of the same order—mere *ultras* of fashionable insipidity. This is better than fashion—is it not? Yet this has but to be seen to become the rage—that is, with those who could afford it at the cost of their entire patrimony. I have guarded, however, against any such profanation. With one exception, you are the only human being besides myself and my *valet*, who has been admitted within the mysteries of these imperial precincts, since they have been bedizzened as you see!"

I bowed in acknowledgment—for the overpowering sense of splendor and perfume, and music, together with the unexpected eccentricity of his address and manner, prevented me from expressing, in words, my appreciation of what I might have construed into a compliment.

"Here," he resumed, arising and leaning on my arm as he sauntered around the apartment, "here are paintings from the Greeks to Cimabue, and from Cimabue to the present hour. Many are chosen, as you see, with little deference to the opinions of Virtu. They are all, however, fitting tapestry for a chamber such as this. Here, too, are some *chefs d'œuvre* of the unknown great; and here, unfinished designs by men, celebrated in their day, whose very names the perspicacity of the academies has left to silence and to me. What think you," said he, turning abruptly as he spoke— "what think you of this Madonna della Pietà?"

"It is Guido's own!" I said, with all the enthusiasm of my nature, for I had been poring intently over its surpassing loveliness. "It is Guido's own!—how *could* you have obtained it? she is undoubtedly in painting what the Venus is in sculpture."

"Ha!" said he, thoughtfully, "the Venus—the beautiful Venus?— the Venus of the Medici?—she of the diminutive head and the gilded hair? Part of the left arm (here his voice dropped so as to be heard with difficulty,) and all the right, are restorations; and in the co-quetry of that right arm lies, I think, the quintessence of all affecta-tion. Give *me* the Canova! The Apollo, too, is a copy—there can be no doubt of it—blind fool that I am, who cannot behold the boasted inspiration of the Apollo! I cannot help—pity me!—I cannot help preferring the Antinous. Was it not Socrates who said that the statu-ary found his statue in the block of marble? Then Michael Angelo was by no means original in his couplet—

> *Non ha l'ottimo artista alcun concetto*
> *Ch'un marmo solo in sé non circonscriva.*"[3]

It has been, or should be remarked, that, in the manner of the true gentleman, we are always aware of a difference from the bearing of the vulgar, without being at once precisely able to de-termine in what such difference consists. Allowing the remark to have applied in its full force to the outward demeanor of my ac-quaintance, I felt it, on that eventful morning, still more fully ap-plicable to his moral temperament and character. Nor can I better define that peculiarity of spirit which seemed to place him so es-sentially apart from all other human beings, than by calling it a *habit* of intense and continual thought, pervading even his most trivial actions—intruding upon his moments of dalliance—and in-terweaving itself with his very flashes of merriment—like adders which writhe from out the eyes of the grinning masks in the cor-nices around the temples of Persepolis.

I could not help, however, repeatedly observing, through the min-gled tone of levity and solemnity with which he rapidly descanted upon matters of little importance, a certain air of trepidation—a degree of nervous *unction* in action and in speech—an unquiet excitability of manner which appeared to me at all times unac-countable, and upon some occasions even filled me with alarm. Frequently, too, pausing in the middle of a sentence whose com-mencement he had apparently forgotten, he seemed to be listening in the deepest attention, as if either in momentary expectation of a visiter, or to sounds which must have had existence in his imagina-tion alone.

It was during one of these reveries or pauses of apparent

abstraction, that, in turning over a page of the poet and scholar Politian's beautiful tragedy "The Orfeo," (the first native Italian tragedy,) which lay near me upon an ottoman, I discovered a passage underlined in pencil. It was a passage towards the end of the third act—a passage of the most heart-stirring excitement—a passage which, although tainted with impurity, no man shall read without a thrill of novel emotion—no woman without a sigh. The whole page was blotted with fresh tears; and, upon the opposite interleaf, were the following English lines, written in a hand so very different from the peculiar characters of my acquaintance, that I had some difficulty in recognising it as his own:—

> Thou wast that all to me, love,
>   For which my soul did pine—
> A green isle in the sea, love,
>   A fountain and a shrine,
> All wreathed with fairy fruits and flowers;
>   And all the flowers were mine.
>
> Ah, dream too bright to last!
>   Ah, starry Hope, that didst arise
> But to be overcast!
>   A voice from out the Future cries,
> "Onward!"—but o'er the Past
>   (Dim gulf!) my spirit hovering lies,
> Mute—motionless—aghast!
>
> For alas! alas! with me
>   The light of life is o'er.
> "No more—no more—no more,"
> (Such language holds the solemn sea
>   To the sands upon the shore,)
> Shall bloom the thunder-blasted tree,
>   Or the stricken eagle soar!
>
> Now all my hours are trances;
>   And all my nightly dreams
> Are where the dark eye glances,

> And where thy footstep gleams,
> In what ethereal dances,
> By what Italian streams.
>
> Alas! for that accursed time
> They bore thee o'er the billow,
> From Love to titled age and crime,
> And an unholy pillow!—
> From me, and from our misty clime,
> Where weeps the silver willow!

That these lines were written in English—a language with which I had not believed their author acquainted—afforded me little matter for surprise. I was too well aware of the extent of his acquirements, and of the singular pleasure he took in concealing them from observation, to be astonished at any similar discovery; but the place of date, I must confess, occasioned me no little amazement. It had been originally written *London*, and afterwards carefully overscored—not, however, so effectually as to conceal the word from a scrutinizing eye. I say, this occasioned me no little amazement; for I well remember that, in a former conversation with my friend, I particularly inquired if he had at any time met in London the Marchesa di Mentoni, (who for some years previous to her marriage had resided in that city,) when his answer, if I mistake not, gave me to understand that he had never visited the metropolis of Great Britain. I might as well here mention, that I have more than once heard, (without, of course, giving credit to a report involving so many improbabilities,) that the person of whom I speak was not only by birth, but in education, an *Englishman*.

"There is one painting," said he, without being aware of my notice of the tragedy—"there is still one painting which you have not seen." And throwing aside a drapery, he discovered a full-length portrait of the Marchesa Aphrodite.

Human art could have done no more in the delineation of her superhuman beauty. The same ethereal figure which stood before me the preceding night upon the steps of the Ducal Palace, stood before me once again. But in the expression of the countenance, which was beaming all over with smiles, there still lurked (incomprehensible anomaly!) that fitful stain of melancholy which will ever be found inseparable from the perfection of the beautiful. Her right arm lay folded over her bosom. With her left she pointed downward to a curiously fashioned vase. One small, fairy foot, alone visible, barely touched the earth; and, scarcely discernible in the brilliant atmosphere which seemed to encircle and enshrine her loveliness, floated a pair of the most delicately imagined wings. My glance fell from the painting to the figure of my friend, and the vigorous words of Chapman's *Bussy D'Ambois*, quivered instinctively upon my lips:

> "He is up
> There like a Roman statue! He will stand
> 'Till Death hath made him marble!"

"Come," he said at length, turning towards a table of richly enamelled and massive silver, upon which were a few goblets fantastically stained, together with two large Etruscan vases, fashioned in the same extraordinary model as that in the foreground of the portrait, and filled with what I supposed to be Johannisberger. "Come," he said, abruptly, "let us drink! It is early—but let us drink. It is *indeed* early," he continued, musingly, as a cherub with a heavy golden hammer made the apartment ring with the first hour after sunrise: "It is *indeed* early—but what matters it? let us drink! Let us pour out an offering to yon solemn sun which the gaudy lamps and censers are so eager to subdue!" And, having made me pledge him in a bumper, he swallowed in rapid succession several goblets of the wine.

"To dream," he continued, resuming the tone of his desultory conversation, as he held up to the rich light of a censer one of the magnificent vases—"to dream has been the business of my life. I have therefore framed for myself, as you see, a bower of dreams. In the heart of Venice could I have erected a better? You behold around you, it is true, a medley of architectural embellishments. The chastity of Ionia is offended by antediluvian devices, and the sphynxes of Egypt are outstretched upon carpets of gold. Yet the effect is incongruous to the timid alone. Proprieties of place, and especially of time, are the bugbears which terrify mankind from the contemplation of the magnificent. Once I was myself a decorist; but that sublimation of folly has palled upon my soul. All this is now the fitter for my purpose. Like these arabesque censers, my spirit is writhing in fire, and the delirium of this scene is fashioning me for the wilder visions of that land of real dreams whither I am now rapidly departing." He here paused abruptly, bent his head to his bosom, and seemed to listen to a sound which I could not hear. At length, erecting his frame, he looked upwards, and ejaculated the lines of the Bishop of Chichester:

> "Stay for me there! I will not fail
> To meet thee in that hollow vale."

In the next instant, confessing the power of the wine, he threw himself at full-length upon an ottoman.

A quick step was now heard upon the staircase, and a loud knock at the door rapidly succeeded. I was hastening to anticipate a second disturbance, when a page of Mentoni's household burst into the room, and faltered out, in a voice choking with emotion the incoherent words, "My mistress!—my mistress!—Poisoned!—poisoned! Oh, beautiful—oh, beautiful Aphrodite!"

Bewildered, I flew to the ottoman, and endeavored to arouse the sleeper to a sense of the startling intelligence. But his limbs were rigid—his lips were livid—his lately beaming eyes were riveted in *death*. I staggered back towards the table—my hand fell upon a cracked and blackened goblet—and a consciousness of the entire and terrible truth flashed suddenly over my soul.

BERENICE

*Dicebant mihi sodales, si sepulchrum amicae visitarem, curas meas
aliquantulum fore levatas.*
—EBN ZAIAT[1]

Misery is manifold. The wretchedness of earth is multiform. Over-
reaching the wide horizon as the rainbow, its hues are as various
as the hues of that arch—as distinct too, yet as intimately blended.
Overreaching the wide horizon as the rainbow! How is it that
from beauty I have derived a type of unloveliness?—from the
covenant of peace, a simile of sorrow? But as, in ethics, evil is a
consequence of good, so, in fact, out of joy is sorrow born. Either
the memory of past bliss is the anguish of to-day, or the agonies
which *are*, have their origin in the ecstasies which *might have
been*.

My baptismal name is Egaeus; that of my family I will not men-
tion. Yet there are no towers in the land more time-honored than
my gloomy, gray, hereditary halls. Our line has been called a race of
visionaries; and in many striking particulars—in the character of
the family mansion—in the frescos of the chief saloon—in the tap-
estries of the dormitories—in the chiselling of some buttresses in the
armory—but more especially in the gallery of antique paintings—in
the fashion of the library chamber—and, lastly, in the very peculiar
nature of the library's contents—there is more than sufficient evi-
dence to warrant the belief.

The recollections of my earliest years are connected with that
chamber, and with its volumes—of which latter I will say no
more. Here died my mother. Herein was I born. But it is mere
idleness to say that I had not lived before—that the soul has no
previous existence. You deny it?—let us not argue the matter. Con-
vinced myself, I seek not to convince. There is, however, a remem-
brance of aerial forms—of spiritual and meaning eyes—of sounds,
musical yet sad; a remembrance which will not be excluded; a
memory like a shadow—vague, variable, indefinite, unsteady; and

like a shadow, too, in the impossibility of my getting rid of it while the sunlight of my reason shall exist.

In that chamber was I born. Thus awaking from the long night of what seemed, but was not, nonentity, at once into the very regions of fairy land—into a palace of imagination—into the wild dominions of monastic thought and erudition—it is not singular that I gazed around me with a startled and ardent eye—that I loitered away my boyhood in books, and dissipated my youth in reverie; but it *is* singular that as years rolled away, and the noon of manhood found me still in the mansion of my fathers—it *is* wonderful what stagnation there fell upon the springs of my life—wonderful how total an inversion took place in the character of my commonest thought. The realities of the world affected me as visions, and as visions only, while the wild ideas of the land of dreams became, in turn, not the material of my every-day existence, but in very deed that existence utterly and solely in itself.

Berenice and I were cousins, and we grew up together in my paternal halls. Yet differently we grew—I, ill of health, and buried in gloom—she, agile, graceful, and overflowing with energy; hers, the ramble on the hill-side—mine the studies of the cloister; I, living within my own heart, and addicted, body and soul, to the most intense and painful meditation—she, roaming carelessly through life, with no thought of the shadows in her path, or the silent flight of the raven-winged hours. Berenice!—I call upon her name—Berenice!—and from the gray ruins of memory a thousand tumultuous recollections are startled at the sound! Ah, vividly is her image before me now, as in the early days of her light-heartedness and joy! Oh, gorgeous yet fantastic beauty! Oh, sylph amid the shrubberies of Arnheim! Oh, Naiad among its fountains! And then—then all is mystery and terror, and a tale which should not be told. Disease—a fatal disease, fell like the simoon upon her frame; and, even while I gazed upon her, the spirit of change swept over her, pervading her mind, her habits, and her character, and, in a manner the most subtle and terrible, disturbing even the identity of her person! Alas! the destroyer came and went!—and the victim—where is she? I knew her not—or knew her no longer as Berenice!

Among the numerous train of maladies superinduced by that

fatal and primary one which effected a revolution of so horrible a kind in the moral and physical being of my cousin, may be mentioned as the most distressing and obstinate in its nature, a species of epilepsy not unfrequently terminating in *trance* itself—trance very nearly resembling positive dissolution, and from which her manner of recovery was, in most instances, startlingly abrupt. In the mean time my own disease—for I have been told that I should call it by no other appelation—my own disease, then, grew rapidly upon me, and assumed finally a monomaniac character of a novel and extraordinary form—hourly and momently gaining vigor—and at length obtaining over me the most incomprehensible ascendancy. This monomania, if I must so term it, consisted in a morbid irritability of those properties of the mind in metaphysical science termed the *attentive*. It is more than probable that I am not understood; but I fear, indeed, that it is in no manner possible to convey to the mind of the merely general reader, an adequate idea of that nervous *intensity of interest* with which, in my case, the powers of meditation (not to speak technically) busied and buried themselves, in the contemplation of even the most ordinary objects of the universe.

To muse for long unwearied hours, with my attention riveted to some frivolous device on the margin or in the typography of a book; to become absorbed, for the better part of a summer's day, in a quaint shadow falling aslant upon the tapestry or upon the floor; to lose myself, for an entire night, in watching the steady flame of a lamp, or the embers of a fire; to dream away whole days over the perfume of a flower; to repeat, monotonously, some common word, until the sound, by dint of frequent repetition, ceased to convey any idea whatever to the mind; to lose all sense of motion or physical existence, by means of absolute bodily quiescence long and obstinately persevered in: such were a few of the most common and least pernicious vagaries induced by a condition of the mental faculties, not, indeed, altogether unparalleled, but certainly bidding defiance to anything like analysis or explanation.

Yet let me not be misapprehended. The undue, earnest, and morbid attention thus excited by objects in their own nature frivolous, must not be confounded in character with that ruminating propensity common to all mankind, and more especially indulged in by persons of ardent imagination. It was not even, as might be at first supposed, an extreme condition, or exaggeration of such propensity, but primarily and essentially distinct and different. In the one instance, the dreamer, or enthusiast, being interested by an object usually *not* frivolous, imperceptibly loses sight of this object in a wilderness of deductions and suggestions issuing therefrom, until, at the conclusion of a day-dream *often replete with luxury*, he finds the *incitamentum*, or first cause of his musings, entirely vanished and forgotten. In my case, the primary object was *invariably frivolous*, although assuming, through the medium of my distempered vision, a refracted and unreal importance. Few deductions, if any, were made; and those few pertinaciously returning in upon the original object as a centre. The meditations were *never* pleasurable; and, at the termination of the reverie, the first cause, so far from being out of sight, had attained that supernaturally exaggerated interest which was the prevailing feature of the disease. In a word, the powers of mind more particularly exercised were, with me, as I have said before, the *attentive*, and are, with the day-dreamer, the *speculative*.

My books, at this epoch, if they did not actually serve to irritate the disorder, partook, it will be perceived, largely, in their imaginative and inconsequential nature, of the characteristic qualities of the disorder itself. I well remember, among others, the treatise of the noble Italian, Caelius Secundus Curio, "*de Amplitudine Beati Regni Dei;*" St. Augustin's great work, the "City of God;" and Tertullian's "*de Carne Christi,*" in which the paradoxical sentence "*Mortuus est Dei filius; credible est quia ineptum est; et sepultus resurrexit; certum est quia impossibile est,*"[2] occupied my undivided time, for many weeks of laborious and fruitless investigation.

Thus it will appear that, shaken from its balance only by trivial things, my reason bore resemblance to that ocean-crag spoken of by Ptolemy Hephestion, which, steadily resisting the attacks of human violence, and the fiercer fury of the waters and the winds, trembled only to the touch of the flower called Asphodel. And although, to a careless thinker, it might appear a matter beyond doubt, that the alteration produced by her unhappy malady, in the *moral* condition of Berenice, would afford me many objects for the exercise of that intense and abnormal meditation whose nature I have been at some trouble in explaining, yet such was not in any degree the case. In the lucid intervals of my infirmity, her calamity, indeed, gave me pain, and, taking deeply to heart that total wreck of her fair and gentle life, I did not fail to ponder, frequently and bitterly, upon the wonder-working means by which so strange a revolution had been so suddenly brought to pass. But these reflections partook not of the idiosyncrasy of my disease, and were such as would have occurred, under similar circumstances, to the ordinary mass of mankind. True to its own character, my disorder revelled in the less important but more startling changes wrought in the *physical* frame of Berenice—in the singular and most appalling distortion of her personal identity.

During the brightest days of her unparalleled beauty, most surely I had never loved her. In the strange anomaly of my existence, feelings, with me, *had never been* of the heart, and my passions *always were* of the mind. Through the gray of the early morning—among the trellised shadows of the forest at noonday—and in the silence of my library at night—she had flitted by my eyes, and I had seen her—not as the living and breathing Berenice, but as the Berenice of a dream; not as a being of the earth, earthy, but as the abstraction of such a being; not as a thing to admire, but to analyze; not as an object of love, but as the theme of the most abstruse although desultory speculation. And *now*—now I shuddered in her presence, and grew pale at her approach; yet, bitterly lamenting her fallen and desolate condition, I called to mind that she had loved me long, and, in an evil moment, I spoke to her of marriage.

And at length the period of our nuptials was approaching, when, upon an afternoon in the winter of the year—one of those unseasonably warm, calm, and misty days which are the nurse of the beautiful Halcyon,*—I sat, (and sat, as I thought, alone,) in the inner apartment of the library. But, uplifting my eyes, I saw that Berenice stood before me.

Was it my own excited imagination—or the misty influence of the atmosphere—or the uncertain twilight of the chamber—or the gray draperies which fell around her figure—that caused in it so

*For as Jove, during the winter season, gives twice seven days of warmth, men have called this clement and temperate time the nurse of the beautiful Halcyon— *Simonides.* [Poe's note]

vacillating and indistinct an outline? I could not tell. She spoke no word; and I—not for worlds could I have uttered a syllable. An icy chill ran through my frame; a sense of insufferable anxiety oppressed me; a consuming curiosity pervaded my soul; and sinking back upon the chair, I remained for some time breathless and motionless, with my eyes riveted upon her person. Alas! its emaciation was excessive, and not one vestige of the former being lurked in any single line of the contour. My burning glances at length fell upon the face.

The forehead was high, and very pale, and singularly placid; and the once jetty hair fell partially over it, and overshadowed the hollow temples with innumerable ringlets, now of a vivid yellow, and jarring discordantly, in their fantastic character, with the reigning melancholy of the countenance. The eyes were lifeless, and lustreless, and seemingly pupilless, and I shrank involuntarily from their glassy stare to the contemplation of the thin and shrunken lips. They parted; and in a smile of peculiar meaning, *the teeth* of the changed Berenice disclosed themselves slowly to my view. Would to God that I had never beheld them, or that, having done so, I had died!

The shutting of a door disturbed me, and, looking up, I found that my cousin had departed from the chamber. But from the disordered chamber of my brain, had not, alas! departed, and would not be driven away, the white and ghastly *spectrum* of the teeth. Not a speck on their surface—not a shade on their enamel—not an indenture in their edges—but what that period of her smile had sufficed to brand in upon my memory. I saw them *now* even more unequivocally than I beheld them *then*. The teeth!—the teeth!—they were here, and there, and everywhere, and visibly and palpably before me; long, narrow, and excessively white, with the pale lips writhing about them, as in the very moment of their first terrible development. Then came the full fury of my *monomania*, and I struggled in vain against its strange and irresistible influence. In the multiplied objects of the external world I had no thoughts but for the teeth. For these I longed with a frenzied desire. All other matters and all different interests became absorbed in their single contemplation. They—they alone were present to the mental eye, and they, in their sole individuality, became the essence of my mental life. I held them in every light. I turned them in every attitude.

I surveyed their characteristics. I dwelt upon their peculiarities. I pondered upon their conformation. I mused upon the alteration in their nature. I shuddered as I assigned to them in imagination a sensitive and sentient power, and, even when unassisted by the lips, a capability of moral expression. Of Mademoiselle Sallé it has been well said, "*Que tous ses pas étaient des sentiments,*" and of Berenice I more seriously believed *que toutes ses dents étaient des idées.*[3] *Des idées!*—ah, here was the idiotic thought that destroyed me! *Des idées!*—ah *therefore* it was that I coveted them so madly! I felt that their possession could alone ever restore me to peace, in giving me back to reason.

And the evening closed in upon me thus—and then the darkness came, and tarried, and went—and the day again dawned—and the mists of a second night were now gathering around—and still I sat motionless in that solitary room—and still I sat buried in meditation—and still the *phantasma* of the teeth maintained its terrible ascendancy, as, with the most vivid and hideous distinctness, it floated about amid the changing lights and shadows of the chamber. At length there broke in upon my dreams a cry as of horror and dismay; and thereunto, after a pause, succeeded the sound of troubled voices, intermingled with many low moanings of sorrow or of pain. I arose from my seat, and, throwing open one of the doors of the library, saw standing out in the antechamber a servant maiden, all in tears, who told me that Berenice was—no more! She had been seized with epilepsy in the early morning, and now, at the closing in of the night, the grave was ready for its tenant, and all the preparations for the burial were completed.

I found myself sitting in the library, and again sitting there alone. It seemed that I had newly awakened from a confused and exciting dream. I knew that it was now midnight, and I was well aware, that since the setting of the sun, Berenice had been interred. But of that dreary period which intervened I had no positive, at least no definite comprehension. Yet its memory was replete with horror—horror more horrible from being vague, and terror more terrible from ambiguity. It was a fearful page in the record my existence, written all over with dim, and hideous, and unintelligible recollections. I strived to decypher them, but in vain; while ever and anon,

like the spirit of a departed sound, the shrill and piercing shriek of
a female voice seemed to be ringing in my ears. I had done a
deed—what was it? I asked myself the question aloud, and the
whispering echoes of the chamber answered me,—"*What was it?*"

On the table beside me burned a lamp, and near it lay a little box.
It was of no remarkable character, and I had seen it frequently be-
fore, for it was the property of the family physician; but how came
it *there*, upon my table, and why did I shudder in regarding it?
These things were in no manner to be accounted for, and my eyes at
length dropped to the open pages of a book, and to a sentence un-
derscored therein. The words were the singular but simple ones of
the poet Ebn Zaiat:—"*Dicebant mihi sodales si sepulchrum amicae
visitarem, curas meas aliquantulum fore levatas.*" Why, then, as I
perused them, did the hairs of my head erect themselves on end, and
the blood of my body become congealed within my veins?

There came a light tap at the library door—and, pale as the ten-
ant of a tomb, a menial entered upon tiptoe. His looks were wild
with terror, and he spoke to me in a voice tremulous, husky, and
very low. What said he?—some broken sentences I heard. He told
of a wild cry disturbing the silence of the night—of the gathering
together of the household—of a search in the direction of the
sound; and then his tones grew thrillingly distinct as he whispered
me of a violated grave—of a disfigured body enshrouded, yet still
breathing—still palpitating—*still alive!*

He pointed to garments; they were muddy and clotted with
gore. I spoke not, and he took me gently by the hand: it was in-
dented with the impress of human nails. He directed my attention
to some object against the wall. I looked at it for some minutes: it
was a spade. With a shriek I bounded to the table, and grasped the
box that lay upon it. But I could not force it open; and, in my
tremor, it slipped from my hands, and fell heavily, and burst into
pieces; and from it, with a rattling sound, there rolled out some in-
struments of dental surgery, intermingled with thirty-two small,
white, and ivory-looking substances that were scattered to and fro
about the floor.

MORELLA

With a feeling of deep yet most singular affection I regarded my friend Morella. Thrown by accident into her society many years ago, my soul from our first meeting, burned with fires it had never before known; but the fires were not of Eros, and bitter and tormenting to my spirit was the gradual conviction that I could in no manner define their unusual meaning, or regulate their vague intensity. Yet we met; and fate bound us together at the altar; and I never spoke of passion, nor thought of love. She, however, shunned society, and, attaching herself to me alone, rendered me happy. It is a happiness to wonder;—it is a happiness to dream.

Morella's erudition was profound. As I hope to live, her talents were of no common order—her powers of mind were gigantic. I felt this, and, in many matters, became her pupil. I soon, however, found that, perhaps on account of her Presburg education, she placed before me a number of those mystical writings which are usually considered the mere dross of the early German literature. These, for what reason I could not imagine, were her favourite and constant study—and that, in process of time they became my own, should be attributed to the simple but effectual influence of habit and example.

In all this, if I err not, my reason had little to do. My convictions, or I forget myself, were in no manner acted upon by the ideal, nor was any tincture of the mysticism which I read, to be discovered, unless I am greatly mistaken, either in my deeds or in my thoughts. Persuaded of this, I abandoned myself implicitly to the guidance of my wife, and entered with an unflinching heart into the intricacies of her studies. And then—then, when, poring over forbidden pages, I felt a forbidden spirit enkindling within

me—would Morella place her cold hand upon my own, and rake
up from the ashes of a dead philosophy some low, singular words,
whose strange meaning burned themselves in upon my memory.
And then, hour after hour, would I linger by her side, and dwell
upon the music of her voice—until, at length, its melody was
tainted with terror,—and there fell a shadow upon my soul—and I
grew pale, and shuddered inwardly at those too unearthly tones.
And thus, joy suddenly faded into horror, and the most beautiful
became the most hideous, as Hinnom became Ge-Henna.[1]

It is unnecessary to state the exact character of those dis-
quisitions which, growing out of the volumes I have mentioned,
formed, for so long a time, almost the sole conversation of Morella
and myself. By the learned in what might be termed theological
morality they will be readily conceived, and by the unlearned they
would, at all events, be little understood. The wild Pantheism of
Fichte; the modified $\Pi\alpha\lambda\iota\gamma\gamma\epsilon\nu\epsilon\sigma\iota\alpha$[2] of the Pythagoreans; and,
above all, the doctrines of *Identity* as urged by Schelling, were
generally the points of discussion presenting the most of beauty to
the imaginative Morella. That identity which is termed personal,
Mr. Locke, I think, truly defines to consist in the sameness of a ra-
tional being. And since by person we understand an intelligent
essence having reason, and since there is a consciousness which al-
ways accompanies thinking, it is this which makes us all to be that
which we call *ourselves*, thereby distinguishing us from other be-
ings that think, and giving us our personal identity. But the *prin-
cipium individuationis*, the notion of that identity *which at death
is or is not lost for ever*, was to me, at all times, a consideration of
intense interest; not more from the perplexing and exciting nature
of its consequences, than from the marked and agitated manner in
which Morella mentioned them.

But, indeed, the time had now arrived when the mystery of my
wife's manner oppressed me as a spell. I could no longer bear the
touch of her wan fingers, nor the low tone of her musical lan-
guage, nor the lustre of her melancholy eyes. And she knew all
this, but did not upbraid; she seemed conscious of my weakness or
my folly, and, smiling, called it Fate. She seemed, also, conscious
of a cause, to me unknown, for the gradual alienation of my re-
gard; but she gave me no hint or token of its nature. Yet was she
woman, and pined away daily. In time, the crimson spot settled

steadily upon the cheek, and the blue veins upon the pale forehead became prominent; and, one instant my nature melted into pity, but, in the next I met the glance of her meaning eyes, and then my soul sickened and became giddy with the giddiness of one who gazes downward into some dreary and unfathomable abyss.

Shall I then say that I longed with an earnest and consuming desire for the moment of Morella's decease? I did; but the fragile spirit clung to its tenement of clay for many days—for many weeks and irksome months—until my tortured nerves obtained the mastery over my mind, and I grew furious through delay, and, with the heart of a fiend, cursed the days, and the hours, and the bitter moments, which seemed to lengthen and lengthen as her gentle life declined—like shadows in the dying of the day.

But one autumnal evening, when the winds lay still in heaven, Morella called me to her bed-side. There was a dim mist over all the earth, and a warm glow upon the waters, and, amid the rich October leaves of the forest, a rainbow from the firmament had surely fallen.

"It is a day of days," she said, as I approached; "a day of all days either to live or die. It is a fair day for the sons of earth and life—ah, more fair for the daughters of heaven and death!"

I kissed her forehead, and she continued:

"I am dying, yet shall I live."

"Morella!"

"The days have never been when thou couldst love me—but her whom in life thou didst abhor, in death thou shalt adore."

"Morella!"

"I repeat that I am dying. But within me is a pledge of that affection—ah, how little!—which thou didst feel for me, Morella. And when my spirit departs shall the child live—thy child and mine, Morella's. But thy days shall be days of sorrow—that sorrow which is the most lasting of impressions, as the cypress is the most enduring of trees. For the hours of thy happiness are over and joy is not gathered twice in a life, as the roses of Pæstum twice in a year. Thou shalt no longer, then, play the Teian with time, but, being ignorant of the myrtle and the vine, thou shalt bear about with thee thy shroud on earth, as do the Moslemin at Mecca."

"Morella!" I cried, "Morella! how knowest thou this?"—but

she turned away her face upon the pillow, and, a slight tremor coming over her limbs, she thus died, and I heard her voice no more.

Yet, as she had foretold, her child—to which in dying she had given birth, and which breathed not until the mother breathed no more—her child, a daughter, lived. And she grew strangely in stature and intellect, and was the perfect resemblance of her who had departed, and I loved her with a love more fervent than I had believed it possible to feel for any denizen of earth.

But, ere long, the heaven of this pure affection became darkened, and gloom, and horror, and grief, swept over it in clouds. I said the child grew strangely in stature and intelligence. Strange indeed was her rapid increase in bodily size—but terrible, oh! terrible were the tumultuous thoughts which crowded upon me while watching the development of her mental being. Could it be otherwise, when I daily discovered in the conceptions of the child the adult powers and faculties of the woman?—when the lessons of experience fell from the lips of infancy? and when the wisdom or the passions of maturity I found hourly gleaming from its full and speculative eye? When, I say, all this became evident to my appalled senses—when I could no longer hide it from my soul, nor throw it off from those perceptions which trembled to receive it—is it to be wondered at that suspicions, of a nature fearful and exciting, crept in upon my spirit, or that my thoughts fell back aghast upon the wild tales and thrilling theories of the entombed Morella? I snatched from the scrutiny of the world a being whom destiny compelled me to adore, and in the rigorous seclusion of my home, watched with an agonizing anxiety over all which concerned the beloved.

And, as years rolled away, and I gazed, day after day, upon her holy, and mild, and eloquent face, and poured over her maturing form, day after day did I discover new points of resemblance in the child to her mother, the melancholy and the dead. And, hourly, grew darker these shadows of similitude, and more full, and more definite, and more perplexing, and more hideously terrible in their aspect. For that her smile was like her mother's I could bear; but then I shuddered at its too perfect *identity*—that her eyes were like Morella's I could endure; but then they too often looked down into the depths of my soul with Morella's own intense and bewildering meaning. And in the contour of the high forehead, and in the ringlets of the silken hair, and in the wan fingers which buried themselves therein, and in the sad musical tones of her speech, and above all—oh, above all—in the phrases and expressions of the dead on the lips of the loved and the living, I found food for consuming thought and horror—for a worm that *would* not die.

Thus passed away two lustra of her life, and, as yet, my daughter remained nameless upon the earth. "My child" and "my love" were the designations usually prompted by a father's affection, and the rigid seclusion of her days precluded all other intercourse. Morella's name died with her at her death. Of the mother I had never spoken to the daughter;—it was impossible to speak. Indeed, during the brief period of her existence the latter had received no impressions from the outward world save such as might have been afforded by the narrow limits of her privacy. But at length the ceremony of baptism presented to my mind, in its unnerved and agitated condition, a present deliverance from the terrors of my destiny. And at the baptismal font I hesitated for a name. And many titles of the wise and beautiful, of old and modern times, of my own and foreign lands, came thronging to my lips, with many, many fair titles of the gentle, and the happy, and the good. What prompted me, then, to disturb the memory of the buried dead? What demon urged me to breathe that sound, which, in its very recollection was wont to make ebb the purple blood in torrents from the temples to the heart? What fiend spoke from the recesses of my soul, when, amid those dim aisles, and in the silence of the night, I whispered within the ears of the holy man the syllables—Morella? What more than fiend convulsed the features of my child, and overspread them with hues of death, as, starting at that scarcely audible sound, she turned her glassy eyes from the earth to heaven, and falling prostrate on the black slabs of our ancestral vault, responded—"I am here!"

Distinct, coldly, calmly distinct, fell those few simple sounds within my ear, and thence, like molten lead, rolled hissingly into my brain. Years—years may pass away, but the memory of that epoch—never! Nor was I indeed ignorant of the flowers and the vine—but the hemlock and the cypress overshadowed me night and day. And I kept no reckoning of time or place, and the stars of my fate faded from heaven, and therefore the earth grew dark, and its figures passed by me, like flitting shadows, and among them all I beheld only—Morella. The winds of the firmament breathed but one sound within my ears, and the ripples upon the sea murmured evermore—Morella. But she died; and with my own hands I bore her to the tomb; and I laughed with a long and bitter laugh as I found no traces of the first, in the charnel where I laid the second—Morella.

LIGEIA

And the will therein lieth, which dieth not. Who knoweth the mysteries of the will, with its vigor? For God is but a great will pervading all things by nature of its intentness. Man doth not yield himself to the angels, nor unto death utterly, save only through the weakness of his feeble will.

JOSEPH GLANVILL[1]

I cannot, for my soul, remember how, when, or even precisely where, I first became acquainted with the lady Ligeia. Long years have since elapsed, and my memory is feeble through much suffering. Or, perhaps, I cannot *now* bring these points to mind, because, in truth, the character of my beloved, her rare learning, her singular yet placid cast of beauty, and the thrilling and enthralling eloquence of her low musical language, made their way into my heart by paces so steadily and stealthily progressive that they have been unnoticed and unknown. Yet I believe that I met her first and most frequently in some large, old, decaying city near the Rhine. Of her family—I have surely heard her speak. That it is of a remotely ancient date cannot be doubted. Ligeia! Ligeia! Buried in studies of a nature more than all else adapted to deaden impressions of the outward world, it is by that sweet word alone—by Ligeia—that I bring before mine eyes in fancy the image of her who is no more. And now, while I write, a recollection flashes upon me that I have *never known* the paternal name of her who was my friend and my betrothed, and who became the partner of my studies, and finally the wife of my bosom. Was it a playful charge on the part of my Ligeia? or was it a test of my strength of affection, that I should institute no inquiries upon this point? or was it rather a caprice of my own—a wildly romantic offering on the shrine of the most passionate devotion? I but indistinctly recall the fact itself—what wonder that I have utterly forgotten the circumstances which originated or attended it? And, indeed, if ever that spirit which is entitled *Romance*—if ever she, the wan and the misty-winged *Ashtophet* of idolatrous Egypt, presided, as they tell, over marriages ill-omened, then most surely she presided over mine.

There is one dear topic, however, on which my memory fails me not. It is the *person* of Ligeia. In stature she was tall, somewhat slender, and, in her latter days, even emaciated. I would in vain attempt to portray the majesty, the quiet ease, of her demeanor, or the incomprehensible lightness and elasticity of her footfall. She came and departed as a shadow. I was never made aware of her entrance into my closed study save by the dear music of her low sweet voice, as she placed her marble hand upon my shoulder. In beauty of face no maiden ever equalled her. It was the radiance of an opium dream—an airy and spirit-lifting vision more wildly divine than the phantasies which hovered about the slumbering souls of the daughters of Delos. Yet her features were not of that regular mould which we have been falsely taught to worship in the classical labors of the heathen. "There is no exquisite beauty," says Bacon, Lord Verulam, speaking truly of all the forms and *genera* of beauty, "without some *strangeness* in the proportion." Yet, although I saw that the features of Ligeia were not of a classic regularity—although I perceived that her loveliness was indeed "exquisite," and felt that there was much of "strangeness" pervading it, yet I have tried in vain to detect the irregularity and to trace home my own perception of "the strange." I examined the contour of the lofty and pale forehead—it was faultless—how cold indeed that word when applied to a majesty so divine!—the skin rivalling the purest ivory, the commanding extent and repose, the gentle prominence of the regions above the temples; and then the raven-black, the glossy, the luxuriant and naturally-curling tresses, setting forth the full force of the Homeric epithet, "hyacinthine!" I looked at the delicate outlines of the nose—and nowhere but in the graceful medallions of the Hebrews had I beheld a similar perfection. There were the same luxurious smoothness of surface, the same scarcely perceptible tendency to the aquiline, the same harmoniously curved nostrils speaking the free spirit. I regarded the sweet mouth. Here was indeed the triumph of all things heavenly—the magnificent turn of the short upper lip—the soft, voluptuous slumber of the under—the dimples which sported, and the color which spoke—the teeth glancing back, with a brilliancy almost startling, every ray of the holy light which fell upon them in her serene and placid, yet most exultingly radiant of all smiles. I scrutinized the formation of the chin—and here, too, I found the gentleness of breadth, the softness and the majesty, the fullness and the spirituality, of the Greek—the contour which the god Apollo revealed but in a dream, to Cleomenes, the son of the Athenian. And then I peered into the large eyes of Ligeia.

For eyes we have no models in the remotely antique. It might have been, too, that in these eyes of my beloved lay the secret to which Lord Verulam alludes. They were, I must believe, far larger than the ordinary eyes of our own race. They were even fuller than the fullest of the gazelle eyes of the tribe of the valley of Nourjahad. Yet it was only at intervals—in moments of intense excitement—that this peculiarity became more than slightly noticeable in Ligeia. And at such moments was her beauty—in my heated fancy thus it appeared perhaps—the beauty of beings either above or apart from the earth— the beauty of the fabulous Houri of the Turk. The hue of the orbs was the most brilliant of black, and, far over them, hung jetty lashes of great length. The brows, slightly irregular in outline, had the same tint. The "strangeness," however, which I found in the eyes, was of a nature distinct from the formation, or the color, or the brilliancy of the features, and must, after all, be referred to the *expression*. Ah, word of no meaning! behind whose vast latitude of mere sound we intrench our ignorance of so much of the spiritual. The expression of the eyes of Ligeia! How for long hours have I pondered upon it! How have I, through the whole of a midsummer night, struggled to fathom it! What was it—that something more profound than the well of Democritus—which lay far within the pupils of my beloved? What *was* it? I was possessed with a passion to discover. Those eyes! those large, those shining, those divine orbs! they became to me twin stars of Leda, and I to them devoutest of astrologers.

There is no point, among the many incomprehensible anomalies of the science of mind, more thrillingly exciting than the fact— never, I believe, noticed in the schools—that, in our endeavors to recall to memory something long forgotten, we often find ourselves *upon the very verge* of remembrance, without being able, in the end, to remember. And thus how frequently, in my intense scrutiny of Ligeia's eyes, have I felt approaching the full knowledge of their expression—felt it approaching—yet not quite be mine—and so at length entirely depart! And (strange, oh strangest mystery of all!) I found, in the commonest objects of the universe, a circle of analogies to that expression. I mean to say that, subsequently to the period when Ligeia's beauty passed into my spirit, there dwelling as in a shrine, I derived, from many existences in the material world, a sentiment such as I felt always aroused within me by her large and luminous orbs. Yet not the more could I define that sentiment, or analyze, or even steadily view it. I recognized it, let me repeat, sometimes in the survey of a rapidly-growing vine—in the contemplation of a moth, a butterfly, a chrysalis, a stream of running water. I have felt it in the ocean; in the falling of a meteor. I have felt it in the glances of unusually aged people. And there are one or two stars in heaven—(one especially, a star of the sixth magnitude, double and changeable, to be found near the large star in Lyra) in a telescopic scrutiny of which I have been made aware of the feeling. I have been filled with it by certain sounds from stringed instruments, and not unfrequently by passages from books. Among innumerable other instances, I well remember something in a volume of Joseph Glanvill, which (perhaps merely from its quaintness—who shall say?) never failed to inspire me with the sentiment;—"And the will therein lieth, which dieth not. Who knoweth the mysteries of the will, with its vigor? For God is but a great will pervading all things by nature of its intentness. Man doth not yield him to the angels, nor unto death utterly, save only through the weakness of his feeble will."

Length of years, and subsequent reflection, have enabled me to trace, indeed, some remote connection between this passage in the English moralist and a portion of the character of Ligeia. An *intensity* in thought, action, or speech, was possibly, in her, a result, or at least an index, of that gigantic volition which, during our long intercourse, failed to give other and more immediate evidence of its existence. Of all the women whom I have ever known, she, the outwardly calm, the ever-placid Ligeia, was the most violently a prey to the tumultuous vultures of stern passion. And of such passion I could form no estimate, save by the miraculous expansion of those eyes which at once so delighted and appalled me—by the almost magical melody, modulation, distinctness and placidity of her very low voice—and by the fierce energy (rendered doubly effective by contrast with her manner of utterance) of the wild words which she habitually uttered.

I have spoken of the learning of Ligeia: it was immense—such as I have never known in woman. In the classical tongues was she deeply proficient, and as far as my own acquaintance extended in regard to the modern dialects of Europe, I have never known her at fault. Indeed upon any theme of the most admired, because simply the most abstruse of the boasted erudition of the academy, have I *ever* found Ligeia at fault? How singularly—how thrillingly, this one point in the nature of my wife has forced itself, at this late period only, upon my attention! I said her knowledge was such as I have never known in woman—but where breathes the man who has traversed, and successfully, *all* the wide areas of moral, physical, and mathematical science? I saw not then what I now clearly perceive, that the acquisitions of Ligeia were gigantic, were astounding; yet I was sufficiently aware of her infinite supremacy to resign myself, with a child-like confidence, to her guidance through the chaotic world of metaphysical investigation at which I was most busily occupied during the earlier years of our marriage. With how vast a triumph—with how vivid a delight—with how much of all that is ethereal in hope—did I *feel*, as she bent over me in studies but little sought—but less known—that delicious vista by slow degrees expanding before me, down whose long, gorgeous, and all untrodden path, I might at length pass onward to the goal of a wisdom too divinely precious not to be forbidden!

How poignant, then, must have been the grief with which, after some years, I beheld my well-grounded expectations take wings to themselves and fly away! Without Ligeia I was but as a child groping benighted. Her presence, her readings alone, rendered vividly luminous the many mysteries of the transcendentalism in which we were immersed. Wanting the radiant lustre of her eyes, letters, lambent and golden, grew duller than Saturnian lead. And now those eyes shone less and less frequently upon the pages over which I pored. Ligeia grew ill. The wild eyes blazed with a too—too glorious effulgence; the pale fingers became of the transparent waxen hue of the grave, and the blue veins upon the lofty forehead swelled and sank impetuously with the tides of the most gentle emotion. I saw that she must die—and I struggled desperately in spirit with the grim Azrael. And the struggles of the passionate wife were, to my astonishment, even more energetic than my own. There had been much in her stern nature to impress me with the belief that, to her, death would have come without its terrors;—but not so. Words are impotent to convey any just idea of the fierceness of resistance with which she wrestled with the Shadow. I groaned in anguish at the pitiable spectacle. I would have soothed—I would have reasoned; but, in the intensity of her wild desire for life,—for life—*but* for life—solace and reason were the uttermost of folly. Yet not until the last instance, amid the most convulsive writhings of her fierce spirit, was shaken the external placidity of her demeanor. Her voice grew more gentle—grew more low—yet I would not wish to dwell upon the wild meaning of the quietly uttered words. My brain reeled as I hearkened, entranced, to a melody more than mortal—to assumptions and aspirations which mortality had never before known.

That she loved me I should not have doubted; and I might have been easily aware that, in a bosom such as hers, love would have reigned no ordinary passion. But in death only, was I fully impressed with the strength of her affection. For long hours, detaining my hand, would she pour out before me the overflowing of a heart whose more than passionate devotion amounted to idolatry. How had I deserved to be so blessed by such confessions?—how had I deserved to be so cursed with the removal of my beloved in the hour of her making them? But upon this subject I cannot bear to dilate. Let me say only, that in Ligeia's more than womanly abandonment to a love, alas! all unmerited, all unworthily bestowed, I at length recognized the principle of her longing with so wildly earnest a desire for the life which was now fleeing so rapidly away. It is this wild longing—it is this eager vehemence of desire for life—*but* for life—that I have no power to portray—no utterance capable of expressing.

At high noon of the night in which she departed, beckoning me, peremptorily, to her side, she bade me repeat certain verses composed by herself not many days before. I obeyed her.—They were these:

> Lo! 'tis a gala night
>   Within the lonesome latter years!
> An angel throng, bewinged, bedight
>   In veils, and drowned in tears,
>   Sit in a theatre, to see

A play of hopes and fears,
While the orchestra breathes fitfully
        The music of the spheres.

Mimes, in the form of God on high,
        Mutter and mumble low,
And hither and thither fly—
        Mere puppets they, who come and go
At bidding of vast formless things
        That shift the scenery to and fro,
Flapping from out their
        Condor wings Invisible Wo!

That motley drama!—oh, be sure
        It shall not be forgot!
With its Phantom chased forevermore,
        By a crowd that seize it not,
Through a circle that ever returneth in
        To the self-same spot,
And much of Madness and more of Sin
        And Horror the soul of the plot.

But see, amid the mimic rout,
        A crawling shape intrude!
A blood-red thing that writhes from out
        The scenic solitude!
It writhes!—it writhes!—with mortal pangs
        The mimes become its food,
And the seraphs sob at vermin fangs
        In human gore imbued.

Out—out are the lights—out all!
        And over each quivering form,
The curtain, a funeral pall,
        Comes down with the rush of a storm,
And the angels, all pallid and wan,
        Uprising, unveiling, affirm
That the play is the tragedy, "Man,"
        And its hero the Conqueror Worm.

"O God!" half shrieked Ligeia, leaping to her feet and extending her arms aloft with a spasmodic movement, as I made an end of these lines—"O God! O Divine Father!—shall these things be undeviatingly so?—shall this Conqueror be not once conquered? Are we not part and parcel in Thee? Who—who knoweth the mysteries of the will with its vigor? Man doth not yield him to the angels, *nor unto death utterly*, save only through the weakness of his feeble will."

And now, as if exhausted with emotion, she suffered her white arms to fall, and returned solemnly to her bed of Death. And as she breathed her last sighs, there came mingled with them a low murmur from her lips. I bent to them my ear and distinguished, again, the concluding words of the passage in Glanvill—*"Man doth not yield him to the angels, nor unto death utterly, save only through the weakness of his feeble will."*

She died;—and I, crushed into the very dust with sorrow, could no longer endure the lonely desolation of my dwelling in the dim and decaying city by the Rhine. I had no lack of what the world calls wealth. Ligeia had brought me far more, very far more than ordinarily falls to the lot of mortals. After a few months, therefore, of weary and aimless wandering, I purchased, and put in some repair, an abbey, which I shall not name, in one of the wildest and least frequented portions of fair England. The gloomy and dreary grandeur of the building, the almost savage aspect of the domain, the many melancholy and time-honored memories connected with both, had much in unison with the feelings of utter abandonment which had driven me into that remote and unsocial region of the country. Yet although the external abbey, with its verdant decay hanging about it, suffered but little alteration, I gave way, with a child-like perversity, and perchance with a faint hope of alleviating my sorrows, to a display of more than regal magnificence within. For such follies, even in childhood, I had imbibed a taste, and now they came back to me as if in the dotage of grief. Alas, I feel how much even of incipient madness might have been discovered in the gorgeous and fantastic draperies, in the solemn carvings of Egypt, in the wild cornices and furniture, in the Bedlam patterns of the carpets of tufted gold! I had become a bounden slave in the trammels of opium, and my labors and my orders had taken a coloring from my dreams. But these absurdities

I must not pause to detail. Let me speak only of that one chamber, ever accursed, whither in a moment of mental alienation, I led from the altar as my bride—as the successor of the unforgotten Ligeia—the fair-haired and blue-eyed Lady Rowena Trevanion, of Tremaine.

There is no individual portion of the architecture and decoration of that bridal chamber which is not now visibly before me. Where were the souls of the haughty family of the bride, when, through thirst of gold, they permitted to pass the threshold of an apartment *so* bedecked, a maiden and a daughter so beloved? I have said that I minutely remember the details of the chamber—yet I am sadly forgetful on topics of deep moment—and here there was no system, no keeping, in the fantastic display, to take hold upon the memory. The room lay in a high turret of the castellated abbey, was pentagonal in shape, and of capacious size. Occupying the whole southern face of the pentagon was the sole window—an immense sheet of unbroken glass from Venice—a single pane, and tinted of a leaden hue, so that the rays of either the sun or moon, passing through it, fell with a ghastly lustre on the objects within. Over the upper portion of this huge window, extended the trellice-work of an aged vine, which clambered up the massy walls of the turret. The ceiling, of gloomy-looking oak, was excessively lofty, vaulted, and elaborately fretted with the wildest and most grotesque specimens of a semi-Gothic, semi-Druidical device. From out the most central recess of this melancholy vaulting, depended, by a single chain of gold with long links, a huge censer of the same metal, Saracenic in pattern, and with many perforations so contrived that there writhed in and out of them, as if endued with a serpent vitality, a continual succession of parti-colored fires.

Some few ottomans and golden candelabra, of Eastern figure, were in various stations about—and there was the couch, too—the bridal couch—of an Indian model, and low, and sculptured of solid ebony, with a pall-like canopy above. In each of the angles of the chamber stood on end a gigantic sarcophagus of black granite, from the tombs of the kings over against Luxor, with their aged lids full of immemorial sculpture. But in the draping of the apartment lay, alas! the chief phantasy of all. The lofty walls, gigantic in height—even unproportionably so—were hung from summit to

foot, in vast folds, with a heavy and massive-looking tapestry—
tapestry of a material which was found alike as a carpet on the
floor, as a covering for the ottomans and the ebony bed, as a
canopy for the bed, and as the gorgeous volutes of the curtains
which partially shaded the window. The material was the richest
cloth of gold. It was spotted all over, at irregular intervals, with
arabesque figures, about a foot in diameter, and wrought upon the
cloth in patterns of the most jetty black. But these figures partook
of the true character of the arabesque only when regarded from a
single point of view. By a contrivance now common, and indeed
traceable to a very remote period of antiquity, they were made
changeable in aspect. To one entering the room, they bore the ap-
pearance of simple monstrosities; but upon a farther advance, this
appearance gradually departed; and step by step, as the visiter
moved his station in the chamber, he saw himself surrounded by an
endless succession of the ghastly forms which belong to the super-
stition of the Norman, or arise in the guilty slumbers of the monk.
The phantasmagoric effect was vastly heightened by the artificial
introduction of a strong continual current of wind behind the
draperies—giving a hideous and uneasy animation to the whole.

In halls such as these—in a bridal chamber such as this—I
passed, with the Lady of Tremaine, the unhallowed hours of the
first month of our marriage—passed them with but little disqui-
etude. That my wife dreaded the fierce moodiness of my temper—
that she shunned me and loved me but little—I could not help
perceiving; but it gave me rather pleasure than otherwise. I loathed
her with a hatred belonging more to demon than to man. My
memory flew back, (oh, with what intensity of regret!) to Ligeia,
the beloved, the august, the beautiful, the entombed. I revelled in
recollections of her purity, of her wisdom, of her lofty, her ethereal
nature, of her passionate, her idolatrous love. Now, then, did my
spirit fully and freely burn with more than all the fires of her own.
In the excitement of my opium dreams (for I was habitually fet-
tered in the shackles of the drug) I would call aloud upon her
name, during the silence of the night, or among the sheltered re-
cesses of the glens by day, as if, through the wild eagerness, the
solemn passion, the consuming ardor of my longing for the de-
parted, I could restore her to the pathway she had abandoned—ah,
could it be forever?—upon the earth.

About the commencement of the second month of the mar-
riage, the Lady Rowena was attacked with sudden illness, from
which her recovery was slow. The fever which consumed her ren-
dered her nights uneasy; and in her perturbed state of half-
slumber, she spoke of sounds, and of motions, in and about the
chamber of the turret, which I concluded had no origin save in
the distemper of her fancy, or perhaps in the phantasmagoric in-
fluences of the chamber itself. She became at length convalescent—
finally well. Yet but a brief period elapsed, ere a second more
violent disorder again threw her upon a bed of suffering; and
from this attack her frame, at all times feeble, never altogether
recovered. Her illnesses were, after this epoch, of alarming char-
acter, and of more alarming recurrence, defying alike the knowl-
edge and the great exertions of her physicians. With the increase
of the chronic disease which had thus, apparently, taken too
sure hold upon her constitution to be eradicated by human
means, I could not fail to observe a similar increase in the nervous
irritation of her temperament, and in her excitability by trivial
causes of fear. She spoke again, and now more frequently and
pertinaciously, of the sounds—of the slight sounds—and of the
unusual motions among the tapestries, to which she had formerly
alluded.

One night, near the closing in of September, she pressed this dis-
tressing subject with more than usual emphasis upon my attention.
She had just awakened from an unquiet slumber, and I had been
watching, with feelings half of anxiety, half of a vague terror, the
workings of her emaciated countenance. I sat by the side of her
ebony bed, upon one of the ottomans of India. She partly arose,
and spoke, in an earnest low whisper, of sounds which she *then*
heard, but which I could not hear—of motions which she *then* saw,
but which I could not perceive. The wind was rushing hurriedly be-
hind the tapestries, and I wished to show her (what, let me confess
it, I could not *all* believe) that those almost inarticulate breathings,
and those very gentle variations of the figures upon the wall, were
but the natural effects of that customary rushing of the wind. But a
deadly pallor, overspreading her face, had proved to me that my ex-
ertions to reassure her would be fruitless. She appeared to be faint-
ing, and no attendants were within call. I remembered where was
deposited a decanter of light wine which had been ordered by her

physicians, and hastened across the chamber to procure it. But, as I stepped beneath the light of the censer, two circumstances of a startling nature attracted my attention. I had felt that some palpable although invisible object had passed lightly by my person; and I saw that there lay upon the golden carpet, in the very middle of the rich lustre thrown from the censer, a shadow—a faint, indefinite shadow of angelic aspect—such as might be fancied for the shadow of a shade. But I was wild with the excitement of an immoderate dose of opium, and heeded these things but little, nor spoke of them to Rowena. Having found the wine, I recrossed the chamber, and poured out a goblet-ful, which I held to the lips of the fainting lady. She had now partially recovered, however, and took the vessel herself, while I sank upon an ottoman near me, with my eyes fastened upon her person. It was then that I became distinctly aware of a gentle foot-fall upon the carpet, and near the couch; and in a second thereafter, as Rowena was in the act of raising the wine to her lips, I saw, or may have dreamed that I saw, fall within the goblet, as if from some invisible spring in the atmosphere of the room, three or four large drops of a brilliant and ruby colored fluid. If this I saw—not so Rowena. She swallowed the wine unhesitatingly, and I forbore to speak to her of a circumstance which must, after all, I considered, have been but the suggestion of a vivid imagination, rendered morbidly active by the terror of the lady, by the opium, and by the hour.

Yet I cannot conceal it from my own perception that, immediately subsequent to the fall of the ruby-drops, a rapid change for the worse took place in the disorder of my wife; so that, on the third subsequent night, the hands of her menials prepared her for the tomb, and on the fourth, I sat alone, with her shrouded body, in that fantastic chamber which had received her as my bride. Wild visions, opium-engendered, flitted, shadow-like, before me. I gazed with unquiet eye upon the sarcophagi in the angles of the room, upon the varying figures of the drapery, and upon the writhing of the parti-colored fires in the censer overhead. My eyes then fell, as I called to mind the circumstances of a former night, to the spot beneath the glare of the censer where I had seen the faint traces of the shadow. It was there, however, no longer; and breathing with greater freedom, I turned my glances to the pallid and rigid figure upon the bed. Then rushed upon me a thousand memories of Ligeia—and then came back upon my heart, with the turbulent violence of a flood, the whole of that unutterable wo with which I had regarded *her* thus enshrouded. The night waned; and still, with a bosom full of bitter thoughts of the one only and supremely beloved, I remained gazing upon the body of Rowena.

It might have been midnight, or perhaps earlier, or later, for I had taken no note of time, when a sob, low, gentle, but very distinct, startled me from my revery. I *felt* that it came from the bed of ebony—the bed of death. I listened in an agony of superstitious terror—but there was no repetition of the sound. I strained my vision to detect any motion in the corpse—but there was not the slightest perceptible. Yet I could not have been deceived. I *had* heard the noise, however faint, and my soul was awakened within me. I resolutely and perseveringly kept my attention riveted upon the body. Many minutes elapsed before any circumstance occurred tending to throw light upon the mystery. At length it became evident that a slight, a very feeble, and barely noticeable tinge of color had flushed up within the cheeks, and along the sunken small veins of the eyelids. Through a species of unutterable horror and awe, for which the language of mortality has no sufficiently energetic expression, I felt my heart cease to beat, my limbs grow rigid where I sat. Yet a sense of duty finally operated to restore my self-possession. I could no longer doubt that we had been precipitate in our preparations—that Rowena still lived. It was necessary that some immediate exertion be made; yet the turret was altogether apart from the portion of the abbey tenanted by the servants—there were none within call—I had no means of summoning them to my aid without leaving the room for many minutes—and this I could not venture to do. I therefore struggled alone in my endeavors to call back the spirit still hovering. In a short period it was certain, however, that a relapse had taken place; the color disappeared from both eyelid and cheek, leaving a wanness even more than that of marble; the lips became doubly shrivelled and pinched up in the ghastly expression of death; a repulsive clamminess and coldness overspread rapidly the surface of the body; and all the usual rigorous stiffness immediately supervened. I fell back with a shudder upon the couch from which I had been so startlingly aroused, and again gave myself up to passionate waking visions of Ligeia.

An hour thus elapsed when (could it be possible?) I was a second time aware of some vague sound issuing from the region of the bed. I listened—in extremity of horror. The sound came again—it was a sigh. Rushing to the corpse, I saw—distinctly saw—a tremor upon the lips. In a minute afterward they relaxed, disclosing a bright line of the pearly teeth. Amazement now struggled in my bosom with the profound awe which had hitherto reigned there alone. I felt that my vision grew dim, that my reason wandered; and it was only by a violent effort that I at length succeeded in nerving myself to the task which duty thus once more had pointed out. There was now a partial glow upon the forehead and upon the cheek and throat; a perceptible warmth pervaded the whole frame; there was even a slight pulsation at the heart. The lady *lived*; and with redoubled ardor I betook myself to the task of restoration. I chafed and bathed the temples and the hands, and used every exertion which experience, and no little medical reading, could suggest. But in vain. Suddenly, the color fled, the pulsation ceased, the lips resumed the expression of the dead, and, in an instant afterward, the whole body took upon itself the icy chilliness, the livid hue, the intense rigidity, the sunken outline, and all the loathsome peculiarities of that which has been, for many days, a tenant of the tomb.

And again I sunk into visions of Ligeia—and again, (what marvel that I shudder while I write,) *again* there reached my ears a low sob from the region of the ebony bed. But why shall I minutely detail the unspeakable horrors of that night? Why shall I pause to relate how, time after time, until near the period of the gray dawn, this hideous drama of revivification was repeated; how each terrific relapse was only into a sterner and apparently more irredeemable death; how each agony wore the aspect of a struggle with some invisible foe; and how each struggle was succeeded by I know not what of wild change in the personal appearance of the corpse? Let me hurry to a conclusion.

The greater part of the fearful night had worn away, and she who had been dead, once again stirred—and now more vigorously than hitherto, although arousing from a dissolution more appalling in its utter hopelessness than any. I had long ceased to struggle or to move, and remained sitting rigidly upon the ottoman, a helpless prey to a whirl of violent emotions, of which extreme awe was perhaps the least terrible, the least consuming. The corpse, I repeat, stirred, and now more vigorously than before. The hues of life flushed up with unwonted energy into the countenance—the limbs relaxed—and, save that the eyelids were yet pressed heavily together, and that the bandages and draperies of the grave still imparted their charnel character to the figure, I might have dreamed that Rowena had indeed shaken off, utterly, the fetters of Death. But if this idea was not, even then, altogether adopted, I could at least doubt no longer, when, arising from the bed, tottering, with feeble steps, with closed eyes, and with the manner of one bewildered in a dream, the thing that was enshrouded advanced bodily and palpably into the middle of the apartment.

I trembled not—I stirred not—for a crowd of unutterable fancies connected with the air, the stature, the demeanor of the figure, rushing hurriedly through my brain, had paralyzed—had chilled me into stone. I stirred not—but gazed upon the apparition. There was a mad disorder in my thoughts—a tumult unappeasable. Could it, indeed, be the *living* Rowena who confronted me? Could it indeed be Rowena *at all*—the fair-haired, the blue-eyed Lady Rowena Trevanion of Tremaine? Why, *why* should I doubt it? The bandage lay heavily about the mouth—but then might it not be the mouth of the breathing Lady of Tremaine? And the cheeks—there were the roses as in her noon of life—yes, these might indeed be the fair cheeks of the living Lady of Tremaine. And the chin, with its dimples, as in health, might it not be hers?—but *had she then grown taller since her malady?* What inexpressible madness seized me with that thought? One bound, and I had reached her feet! Shrinking from my touch, she let fall from her head the ghastly cerements which had confined it, and there streamed forth, into the rushing atmosphere of the chamber, huge masses of long and dishevelled hair; *it was blacker than the wings of the midnight!* And now slowly opened *the eyes* of the figure which stood before me. "Here then, at least," I shrieked aloud, "can I never—can I never be mistaken—these are the full, and the black, and the wild eyes—of my lost love—of the lady—of the LADY LIGEIA."

THE FALL OF THE HOUSE
OF USHER

Son cœur est un luth suspendu;
Sitôt qu'on le touche il résonne.
DE BÉRANGER.[1]

During the whole of a dull, dark, and soundless day in the autumn
of the year, when the clouds hung oppressively low in the heavens,
I had been passing alone, on horseback, through a singularly
dreary tract of country; and at length found myself, as the shades
of the evening drew on, within view of the melancholy House of
Usher. I know not how it was—but, with the first glimpse of the
building, a sense of insufferable gloom pervaded my spirit. I say
insufferable; for the feeling was unrelieved by any of that half-
pleasurable, because poetic, sentiment, with which the mind usu-
ally receives even the sternest natural images of the desolate or
terrible. I looked upon the scene before me—upon the mere house,
and the simple landscape features of the domain—upon the bleak
walls—upon the vacant eye-like windows—upon a few rank
sedges—and upon a few white trunks of decayed trees—with an
utter depression of soul which I can compare to no earthly sensa-
tion more properly than to the after-dream of the reveller upon
opium—the bitter lapse into everyday life—the hideous dropping
off of the veil. There was an iciness, a sinking, a sickening of the
heart—an unredeemed dreariness of thought which no goading of
the imagination could torture into aught of the sublime. What was
it—I paused to think—what was it that so unnerved me in the con-
templation of the House of Usher? It was a mystery all insoluble;
nor could I grapple with the shadowy fancies that crowded upon
me as I pondered. I was forced to fall back upon the unsatisfactory
conclusion, that while, beyond doubt, there *are* combinations of
very simple natural objects which have the power of thus affecting

us, still the analysis of this power lies among considerations beyond our depth. It was possible, I reflected, that a mere different arrangement of the particulars of the scene, of the details of the picture, would be sufficient to modify, or perhaps to annihilate its capacity for sorrowful impression; and, acting upon this idea, I reined my horse to the precipitous brink of a black and lurid tarn that lay in unruffled lustre by the dwelling, and gazed down—but with a shudder even more thrilling than before—upon the remodelled and inverted images of the gray sedge, and the ghastly tree-stems, and the vacant and eye-like windows.

Nevertheless, in this mansion of gloom I now proposed to myself a sojourn of some weeks. Its proprietor, Roderick Usher, had been one of my boon companions in boyhood; but many years had elapsed since our last meeting. A letter, however, had lately reached me in a distant part of the country—a letter from him—which, in its wildly importunate nature, had admitted of no other than a personal reply. The MS. gave evidence of nervous agitation. The writer spoke of acute bodily illness—of a mental disorder which oppressed him—and of an earnest desire to see me, as his best, and indeed his only personal friend, with a view of attempting, by the cheerfulness of my society, some alleviation of his malady. It was the manner in which all this, and much more, was said—it was the apparent *heart* that went with his request—which allowed me no room for hesitation; and I accordingly obeyed forthwith what I still considered a very singular summons.

Although, as boys, we had been even intimate associates, yet I really knew little of my friend. His reserve had been always excessive and habitual. I was aware, however, that his very ancient family had been noted, time out of mind, for a peculiar sensibility of temperament, displaying itself, through long ages, in many works of exalted art, and manifested, of late, in repeated deeds of munificent yet unobtrusive charity, as well as in a passionate devotion to the intricacies, perhaps even more than to the orthodox and easily recognisable beauties, of musical science. I had learned, too, the very remarkable fact, that the stem of the Usher race, all time-honored as it was, had put forth, at no period, any enduring branch; in other words, that the entire family lay in the direct line of descent, and had always, with very trifling and very temporary variation, so lain. It was this deficiency, I considered, while running over in thought the perfect keeping of the character of the premises with the accredited character of the people, and while speculating upon the possible influence which the one, in the long lapse of centuries, might have exercised upon the other—it was this deficiency, perhaps, of collateral issue, and the consequent undeviating transmission, from sire to son, of the patrimony with the name, which had, at length, so identified the two as to merge the original title of the estate in the quaint and equivocal appellation of the "House of Usher"—an appellation which seemed to include, in the minds of the peasantry who used it, both the family and the family mansion.

I have said that the sole effect of my somewhat childish experiment—that of looking down within the tarn—had been to deepen the first singular impression. There can be no doubt that the consciousness of the rapid increase of my superstition—for why should I not so term it?—served mainly to accelerate the increase itself. Such, I have long known, is the paradoxical law of all sentiments having terror as a basis. And it might have been for this reason only, that, when I again uplifted my eyes to the house itself, from its image in the pool, there grew in my mind a strange fancy—a fancy so ridiculous, indeed, that I but mention it to show the vivid force of the sensations which oppressed me. I had so worked upon my imagination as really to believe that about the whole mansion and domain there hung an atmosphere peculiar to themselves and their immediate vicinity—an atmosphere which had no affinity with the air of heaven, but which had reeked up from the decayed trees, and the gray wall, and the silent tarn—a pestilent and mystic vapor, dull, sluggish, faintly discernible, and leaden-hued.

Shaking off from my spirit what *must* have been a dream, I scanned more narrowly the real aspect of the building. Its principal feature seemed to be that of an excessive antiquity. The discoloration of ages had been great. Minute fungi overspread the whole exterior, hanging in a fine tangled web-work from the eaves. Yet all this was apart from any extraordinary dilapidation. No portion of the masonry had fallen; and there appeared to be a wild inconsistency between its still perfect adaptation of parts, and the crumbling condition of the individual stones. In this there was much that reminded me of the specious totality of old wood-work which has rotted for long years in some neglected vault, with no disturbance from the breath of the external air. Beyond this indication of extensive decay, however, the fabric gave little token of instability. Perhaps the eye of a scrutinizing observer might have discovered a barely perceptible fissure, which, extending from the roof of the building in front, made its way down the wall in a zigzag direction, until it became lost in the sullen waters of the tarn.

Noticing these things, I rode over a short causeway to the house. A servant in waiting took my horse, and I entered the Gothic archway of the hall. A valet, of stealthy step, thence conducted me, in silence, through many dark and intricate passages in my progress to the *studio* of his master. Much that I encountered on the way contributed, I know not how, to heighten the vague sentiments of which I have already spoken. While the objects around me—while the carvings of the ceilings, the sombre tapestries of the walls, the ebon blackness of the floors, and the phantasmagoric armorial trophies which rattled as I strode, were but matters to which, or to such as which, I had been accustomed from my infancy—while I hesitated not to acknowledge how familiar was all this—I still wondered to find how unfamiliar were the fancies which ordinary images were stirring up. On one of the staircases, I met the physician of the family. His countenance, I thought, wore a mingled expression of low cunning and perplexity. He accosted me with trepidation and passed on. The valet now threw open a door and ushered me into the presence of his master.

The room in which I found myself was very large and lofty. The windows were long, narrow, and pointed, and at so vast a distance from the black oaken floor as to be altogether inaccessible from within. Feeble gleams of encrimsoned light made their way through the trellissed panes, and served to render sufficiently distinct the more prominent objects around; the eye, however, struggled in vain to reach the remoter angles of the chamber, or the recesses of the vaulted and fretted ceiling. Dark draperies hung upon the walls. The general furniture was profuse, comfortless, antique, and tattered. Many books and musical instruments lay scattered about, but failed to give any vitality to the scene. I felt that I breathed an atmosphere of sorrow. An air of stern, deep, and irredeemable gloom hung over and pervaded all.

Upon my entrance, Usher arose from a sofa on which he had been lying at full length, and greeted me with a vivacious warmth which had much in it, I at first thought, of an overdone cordiality—of the constrained effort of the *ennuyé* man of the world. A glance, however, at his countenance, convinced me of his perfect sincerity. We sat down; and for some moments, while he spoke not, I gazed upon him with a feeling half of pity, half of awe. Surely, man had never before so terribly altered, in so brief a period, as had Roderick Usher! It was with difficulty that I could bring myself to admit the identity of the wan being before me with the companion of my early boyhood. Yet the character of his face had been at all times remarkable. A cadaverousness of complexion; an eye large, liquid, and luminous beyond comparison; lips somewhat thin and very pallid, but of a surpassingly beautiful curve; a nose of a delicate Hebrew model, but with a breadth of nostril unusual in similar formations; a finely moulded chin, speaking, in its want of prominence, of a want of moral energy; hair of a more than web-like softness and tenuity; these features, with an inordinate expansion above the regions of the temple, made up altogether a countenance not easily to be forgotten. And now in the mere exaggeration of the prevailing character of these features, and of the expression they were wont to convey, lay so much of change that I doubted to whom I spoke. The now ghastly pallor of the skin, and the now miraculous lustre of the eye, above all things startled and even awed me. The silken hair, too, had been suffered to grow all unheeded, and as, in its wild gossamer texture, it floated rather than fell about the face, I could not, even with effort, connect its Arabesque expression with any idea of simple humanity.

In the manner of my friend I was at once struck with an incoherence—an inconsistency; and I soon found this to arise from a series of feeble and futile struggles to overcome an habitual trepidancy—an excessive nervous agitation. For something of this nature I had indeed been prepared, no less by his letter, than by reminiscences of certain boyish traits, and by conclusions deduced from his peculiar physical conformation and temperament. His action was alternately vivacious and sullen. His voice varied rapidly from a tremulous indecision (when the animal spirits seemed utterly in abeyance) to that species of energetic concision—that abrupt, weighty, unhurried, and hollow-sounding enunciation—that leaden, self-balanced and perfectly modulated guttural utterance, which may be observed in the lost drunkard, or the irreclaimable eater of opium, during the periods of his most intense excitement.

It was thus that he spoke of the object of my visit, of his earnest desire to see me, and of the solace he expected me to afford him. He entered, at some length, into what he conceived to be the nature of his malady. It was, he said, a constitutional and a family evil, and one for which he despaired to find a remedy—a mere nervous affection, he immediately added, which would undoubtedly soon pass off. It displayed itself in a host of unnatural sensations. Some of these, as he detailed them, interested and bewildered me; although, perhaps, the terms, and the general manner of the narration had their weight. He suffered much from a morbid acuteness of the senses; the most insipid food was alone endurable; he could wear only garments of certain texture; the odors of all flowers were oppressive; his eyes were tortured by even a faint light; and there were but peculiar sounds, and these from stringed instruments, which did not inspire him with horror.

To an anomalous species of terror I found him a bounden slave. "I shall perish," said he, "I *must* perish in this deplorable folly. Thus, thus, and not otherwise, shall I be lost. I dread the events of the future, not in themselves, but in their results. I shudder at the thought of any, even the most trivial, incident, which may operate upon this intolerable agitation of soul. I have, indeed, no abhorrence of danger, except in its absolute effect—in terror. In this unnerved—in this pitiable condition—I feel that the period will sooner or later arrive when I must abandon life and reason together, in some struggle with the grim phantasm, FEAR."

I learned, moreover, at intervals, and through broken and equivocal hints, another singular feature of his mental condition. He was enchained by certain superstitious impressions in regard to the dwelling which he tenanted, and whence, for many years, he had never ventured forth—in regard to an influence whose supposititious force was conveyed in terms too shadowy here to be re-stated—an influence which some peculiarities in the mere form and substance of his family mansion, had, by dint of long sufferance, he said, obtained over his spirit—an effect which the *physique* of the gray walls and turrets, and of the dim tarn into which they all looked down, had, at length, brought about upon the *morale* of his existence.

He admitted, however, although with hesitation, that much of the peculiar gloom which thus afflicted him could be traced to a more natural and far more palpable origin—to the severe and long-continued illness—indeed to the evidently approaching dissolution—of a tenderly beloved sister—his sole companion for long years—his last and only relative on earth. "Her decease," he said, with a bitterness which I can never forget, "would leave him (him the hopeless and the frail) the last of the ancient race of the Ushers." While he spoke, the lady Madeline (for so was she called) passed slowly through a remote portion of the apartment, and, without having noticed my presence, disappeared. I regarded her with an utter astonishment not unmingled with dread—and yet I found it impossible to account for such feelings. A sensation of stupor oppressed me, as my eyes followed her retreating steps. When a door, at length, closed upon her, my glance sought instinctively and eagerly the countenance of the brother—but he had buried his face in his hands, and I could only perceive that a far more than ordinary wanness had overspread the emaciated fingers through which trickled many passionate tears.

The disease of the lady Madeline had long baffled the skill of her physicians. A settled apathy, a gradual wasting away of the person, and frequent although transient affections of a partially cataleptical character, were the unusual diagnosis. Hitherto she had steadily borne up against the pressure of her malady, and had not betaken herself finally to bed; but, on the closing in of the evening of my arrival at the house, she succumbed (as her brother told me at night with inexpressible agitation) to the prostrating power of the destroyer; and I learned that the glimpse I had obtained of her person would thus probably be the last I should obtain—that the lady, at least while living, would be seen by me no more.

For several days ensuing, her name was unmentioned by either Usher or myself: and during this period I was busied in earnest endeavors to alleviate the melancholy of my friend. We painted and read together; or I listened, as if in a dream, to the wild improvisations of his speaking guitar. And thus, as a closer and still closer intimacy admitted me more unreservedly into the recesses of his spirit, the more bitterly did I perceive the futility of all attempt at cheering a mind from which darkness, as if an inherent positive quality, poured forth upon all objects of the moral and physical universe, in one unceasing radiation of gloom.

I shall ever bear about me a memory of the many solemn hours I thus spent alone with the master of the House of Usher. Yet I should fail in any attempt to convey an idea of the exact character of the studies, or of the occupations, in which he involved me, or led me the way. An excited and highly distempered ideality threw a sulphureous lustre over all. His long improvised dirges will ring forever in my ears. Among other things, I hold painfully in mind a certain singular perversion and amplification of the wild air of the last waltz of Von Weber. From the paintings over which his elaborate fancy brooded, and which grew, touch by touch, into vaguenesses at which I shuddered the more thrillingly, because I shuddered knowing not why;—from these paintings (vivid as their images now are before me) I would in vain endeavor to educe more than a small portion which should lie within the compass of merely written words. By the utter simplicity, by the nakedness of his designs, he arrested and overawed attention. If ever mortal painted an idea, that mortal was Roderick Usher. For me at least—in the circumstances then surrounding me—there arose out of the pure abstractions which the hypochondriac contrived to throw upon his canvass, an intensity of intolerable awe, no shadow of which felt I ever yet in the contemplation of the certainly glowing yet too concrete reveries of Fuseli.

One of the phantasmagoric conceptions of my friend, partaking not so rigidly of the spirit of abstraction, may be shadowed forth, although feebly, in words. A small picture presented the interior of an immensely long and rectangular vault or tunnel, with low walls, smooth, white, and without interruption or device. Certain accessory points of the design served well to convey the idea that this excavation lay at an exceeding depth below the surface of the earth. No outlet was observed in any portion of its vast extent, and no torch, or other artificial source of light was discernible; yet a flood of intense rays rolled throughout, and bathed the whole in a ghastly and inappropriate splendor.

I have just spoken of that morbid condition of the auditory nerve which rendered all music intolerable to the sufferer, with the exception of certain effects of stringed instruments. It was, perhaps, the narrow limits to which he thus confined himself upon the guitar, which gave birth, in great measure, to the fantastic character of his performances. But the fervid *facility* of his *impromptus* could not be so accounted for. They must have been, and were, in the notes, as well as in the words of his wild fantasias (for he not unfrequently accompanied himself with rhymed verbal improvisations), the result of that intense mental collectedness and concentration to which I have previously alluded as observable only in particular moments of the highest artificial excitement. The words of one of these rhapsodies I have easily remembered. I was, perhaps, the more forcibly impressed with it, as he gave it, because, in the under or mystic current of its meaning, I fancied that I perceived, and for the first time, a full consciousness on the part of Usher, of the tottering of his lofty reason upon her throne. The verses, which were entitled "The Haunted Palace," ran very nearly, if not accurately, thus:

I.

In the greenest of our valleys,
    By good angels tenanted,
Once a fair and stately palace—
    Radiant palace—reared its head.
In the monarch Thought's dominion—
    It stood there!
Never seraph spread a pinion
    Over fabric half so fair.

II.

Banners yellow, glorious, golden,
    On its roof did float and flow;
(This—all this—was in the olden
    Time long ago)
And every gentle air that dallied,
    In that sweet day,
Along the ramparts plumed and pallid,
    A winged odor went away.

III.

Wanderers in that happy valley
    Through two luminous windows saw
Spirits moving musically

> To a lute's well-tunéd law,
> Round about a throne, where sitting
>   (Porphyrogene!)
> In state his glory well befitting,
>   The ruler of the realm was seen.
>
> ### IV.
>
> And all with pearl and ruby glowing
>   Was the fair palace door,
> Through which came flowing, flowing, flowing,
>   And sparkling evermore,
> A troop of Echoes whose sweet duty
>   Was but to sing,
> In voices of surpassing beauty,
>   The wit and wisdom of their king.
>
> ### V.
>
> But evil things, in robes of sorrow,
>   Assailed the monarch's high estate;
> (Ah, let us mourn, for never morrow
>   Shall dawn upon him, desolate!)
> And, round about his home, the glory
>   That blushed and bloomed
> Is but a dim-remembered story
>   Of the old time entombed.
>
> ### VI.
>
> And travellers now within that valley,
>   Through the red-litten windows, see
> Vast forms that move fantastically
>   To a discordant melody;
> While, like a rapid ghastly river,
>   Through the pale door,
> A hideous throng rush out forever,
>   And laugh—but smile no more.

I well remember that suggestions arising from this ballad led us into a train of thought wherein there became manifest an opinion of Usher's which I mention not so much on account of its novelty, (for other men* have thought thus,) as on account of the pertinacity with which he maintained it. This opinion, in its general form, was that of the sentience of all vegetable things. But, in his disordered fancy, the idea had assumed a more daring character, and trespassed, under certain conditions, upon the kingdom of inorganization. I lack words to express the full extent, or the earnest *abandon* of his persuasion. The belief, however, was connected (as I have previously hinted) with the gray stones of the home of his forefathers. The conditions of the sentience had been here, he imagined, fulfilled in the method of collocation of these stones—in the order of their arrangement, as well as in that of the many *fungi* which overspread them, and of the decayed trees which stood around—above all, in the long undisturbed endurance of this arrangement, and in its reduplication in the still waters of the tarn. Its evidence—the evidence of the sentience—was to be seen, he said, (and I here started as he spoke,) in the gradual yet certain condensation of an atmosphere of their own about the waters and the walls. The result was discoverable, he added, in that silent, yet importunate and terrible influence which for centuries had moulded the destinies of his family, and which made *him* what I now saw him—what he was. Such opinions need no comment, and I will make none.

Our books—the books which, for years, had formed no small portion of the mental existence of the invalid—were, as might be supposed, in strict keeping with this character of phantasm. We pored together over such works as the Ververt et Chartreuse of Gresset; the Belphegor of Machiavelli; the Heaven and Hell of Swedenborg; the Subterranean Voyage of Nicholas Klimm by Holberg; the Chiromancy of Robert Flud, of Jean D'Indaginé, and of De la Chambre; the Journey into the Blue Distance of Tieck; and the City of the Sun of Campanella. One favorite volume was a small octavo edition of the *Directorium Inquisitorium*, by the Dominican Eymeric de Gironne; and there were passages in Pomponius Mela, about the old African Satyrs and Œgipans, over which Usher would sit dreaming for hours. His chief delight, however, was found in the perusal of an exceedingly rare and curious book

*Watson, Dr. Percival, Spallanzani, and especially the Bishop of Landaff.—See "Chemical Essays," vol v. [Poe's note]

in quarto Gothic—the manual of a forgotten church—the *Vigiliae Mortuorum secundum Chorum Ecclesiae Maguntinae.*[2]

I could not help thinking of the wild ritual of this work, and of its probable influence upon the hypochondriac, when, one evening, having informed me abruptly that the lady Madeline was no more, he stated his intention of preserving her corpse for a fortnight, (previously to its final interment,) in one of the numerous vaults within the main walls of the building. The worldly reason, however, assigned for this singular proceeding, was one which I did not feel at liberty to dispute. The brother had been led to his resolution (so he told me) by consideration of the unusual character of the malady of the deceased, of certain obtrusive and eager inquiries on the part of her medical men, and of the remote and exposed situation of the burial-ground of the family. I will not deny that when I called to mind the sinister countenance of the person whom I met upon the staircase, on the day of my arrival at the house, I had no desire to oppose what I regarded as at best but a harmless, and by no means an unnatural, precaution.

At the request of Usher, I personally aided him in the arrangements for the temporary entombment. The body having been encoffined, we two alone bore it to its rest. The vault in which we placed it (and which had been so long unopened that our torches, half smothered in its oppressive atmosphere, gave us little opportunity for investigation) was small, damp, and entirely without means of admission for light; lying, at great depth, immediately beneath that portion of the building in which was my own sleeping apartment. It had been used, apparently, in remote feudal times, for the worst purposes of a donjon-keep, and, in later days, as a place of deposit for powder, or some other highly combustible substance, as a portion of its floor, and the whole interior of a long archway through which we reached it, were carefully sheathed with copper. The door, of massive iron, had been, also, similarly protected. Its immense weight caused an unusually sharp grating sound, as it moved upon its hinges.

Having deposited our mournful burden upon tressels within this region of horror, we partially turned aside the yet unscrewed lid of the coffin, and looked upon the face of the tenant. A striking similitude between the brother and sister now first arrested my attention; and Usher, divining, perhaps, my thoughts, murmured out some few words from which I learned that the deceased and himself had been twins, and that sympathies of a scarcely intelligible nature had always existed between them. Our glances, however, rested not long upon the dead—for we could not regard her unawed. The disease which had thus entombed the lady in the maturity of youth, had left, as usual in all maladies of a strictly cataleptical character, the mockery of a faint blush upon the bosom and the face, and that suspiciously lingering smile upon the lip which is so terrible in death. We replaced and screwed down the lid, and, having secured the door of iron, made our way, with toil, into the scarcely less gloomy apartments of the upper portion of the house.

And now, some days of bitter grief having elapsed, an observable change came over the features of the mental disorder of my friend. His ordinary manner had vanished. His ordinary occupations were neglected or forgotten. He roamed from chamber to chamber with hurried, unequal, and objectless step. The pallor of his countenance had assumed, if possible, a more ghastly hue—but the luminousness of his eye had utterly gone out. The once occasional huskiness of his tone was heard no more; and a tremulous quaver, as if of extreme terror, habitually characterized his utterance. There were times, indeed, when I thought his unceasingly agitated mind was laboring with some oppressive secret, to divulge which he struggled for the necessary courage. At times, again, I was obliged to resolve all into the mere inexplicable vagaries of madness, for I beheld him gazing upon vacancy for long hours, in an attitude of the profoundest attention, as if listening to some imaginary sound. It was no wonder that his condition terrified—that it infected me. I felt creeping upon me, by slow yet certain degrees, the wild influences of his own fantastic yet impressive superstitions.

It was, especially, upon retiring to bed late in the night of the seventh or eighth day after the placing of the lady Madeline within the donjon, that I experienced the full power of such feelings. Sleep came not near my couch—while the hours waned and waned away. I struggled to reason off the nervousness which had dominion over me. I endeavored to believe that much, if not all of what I felt, was due to the bewildering influence of the gloomy furniture of the room—of the dark and tattered draperies, which, tortured into motion by the breath of a rising tempest, swayed fitfully to and fro upon the walls, and rustled uneasily about the decorations of the bed. But my efforts were fruitless. An irrepressible tremor gradually pervaded my frame; and, at length, there sat upon my very heart an incubus of utterly causeless alarm. Shaking this off with a gasp and a struggle, I uplifted myself upon the pillows, and, peering earnestly within the intense darkness of the chamber, harkened—I know not why, except that an instinctive spirit prompted me—to certain low and indefinite sounds which came, through the pauses of the storm, at long intervals, I knew not whence. Overpowered by an intense sentiment of horror, unaccountable yet unendurable, I threw on my clothes with haste (for I felt that I should sleep no more during the night), and endeavored to arouse myself from the pitiable condition into which I had fallen, by pacing rapidly to and fro through the apartment.

I had taken but few turns in this manner, when a light step on an adjoining staircase arrested my attention. I presently recognised it as that of Usher. In an instant afterward he rapped, with a gentle touch, at my door, and entered, bearing a lamp. His countenance was, as usual, cadaverously wan—but, moreover, there was a species of mad hilarity in his eyes—an evidently restrained *hysteria* in his whole demeanor. His air appalled me—but anything was preferable to the solitude which I had so long endured, and I even welcomed his presence as a relief.

"And you have not seen it?" he said abruptly, after having stared about him for some moments in silence—"you have not then seen it?—but, stay! you shall." Thus speaking, and having carefully shaded his lamp, he hurried to one of the casements, and threw it freely open to the storm.

The impetuous fury of the entering gust nearly lifted us from our feet. It was, indeed, a tempestuous yet sternly beautiful night, and one wildly singular in its terror and its beauty. A whirlwind had apparently collected its force in our vicinity; for there were frequent and violent alterations in the direction of the wind; and the exceeding density of the clouds (which hung so low as to press upon the turrets of the house) did not prevent our perceiving the life-like velocity with which they flew careering from all points against each other, without passing away into the distance. I say that even their exceeding density did not prevent our perceiving this—yet we had no glimpse of the moon or stars—nor was there any flashing forth of the lightning. But the under surfaces of the huge masses of agitated vapor, as well as all terrestrial objects immediately around us, were glowing in the unnatural light of a faintly luminous and distinctly visible gaseous exhalation which hung about and enshrouded the mansion.

"You must not—you shall not behold this!" said I, shudderingly, to Usher, as I led him, with a gentle violence, from the window to a seat. "These appearances, which bewilder you, are merely electrical phenomena not uncommon—or it may be that they have their ghastly origin in the rank miasma of the tarn. Let us close this casement;—the air is chilling and dangerous to your frame. Here is one of your favorite romances. I will read, and you shall listen;—and so we will pass away this terrible night together."

The antique volume which I had taken up was the "Mad Trist" of Sir Launcelot Canning;[3] but I had called it a favorite of Usher's more in sad jest than in earnest; for, in truth, there is little in its uncouth and unimaginative prolixity which could have had interest for the lofty and spiritual ideality of my friend. It was, however, the only book immediately at hand; and I indulged a vague hope that the excitement which now agitated the hypochondriac, might find relief (for the history of mental disorder is full of similar anomalies) even in the extremeness of the folly which I should read. Could I have judged, indeed, by the wild overstrained air of vivacity with which he harkened, or apparently harkened, to the words of the tale, I might well have congratulated myself upon the success of my design.

I had arrived at that well-known portion of the story where Ethelred, the hero of the Trist, having sought in vain for peaceable admission into the dwelling of the hermit, proceeds to make good an entrance by force. Here, it will be remembered, the words of the narrative run thus:

"And Ethelred, who was by nature of a doughty heart, and who was now mighty withal, on account of the powerfulness of the wine which he had drunken, waited no longer to hold parley with the hermit, who, in sooth, was of an obstinate and maliceful turn, but, feeling the rain upon his shoulders, and fearing the rising of the tempest, uplifted his mace outright, and, with blows, made quickly room in the plankings of the door for his gauntleted hand; and now pulling therewith sturdily, he so cracked, and ripped, and tore all asunder, that the noise of the dry and hollow-sounding wood alarummed and reverberated throughout the forest."

At the termination of this sentence I started, and for a moment, paused; for it appeared to me (although I at once concluded that my excited fancy had deceived me)—it appeared to me that, from some very remote portion of the mansion, there came, indistinctly, to my ears, what might have been, in its exact similarity of character, the echo (but a stifled and dull one certainly) of the very cracking and ripping sound which Sir Launcelot had so particularly described. It was, beyond doubt, the coincidence alone which had arrested my attention; for, amid the rattling of the sashes of the casements, and the ordinary commingled noises of the still increasing storm, the sound, in itself, had nothing, surely, which should have interested or disturbed me. I continued the story:

"But the good champion Ethelred, now entering within the door, was sore enraged and amazed to perceive no signal of the maliceful hermit; but, in the stead thereof, a dragon of a scaly and prodigious demeanor, and of a fiery tongue, which sate in guard before a palace of gold, with a floor of silver; and upon the wall there hung a shield of shining brass with this legend enwritten—

"Who entereth herein, a conqueror hath bin;
Who slayeth the dragon, the shield he shall win;

"And Ethelred uplifted his mace, and struck upon the head of the dragon, which fell before him, and gave up his pesty breath, with a shriek so horrid and harsh, and withal so piercing, that Ethelred had fain to close his ears with his hands against the dreadful noise of it, the like whereof was never before heard."

Here again I paused abruptly, and now with a feeling of wild amazement—for there could be no doubt whatever that, in this instance, I did actually hear (although from what direction it proceeded I found it impossible to say) a low and apparently distant, but harsh, protracted, and most unusual screaming or grating sound—the exact counterpart of what my fancy had already conjured up for the dragon's unnatural shriek as described by the romancer.

Oppressed, as I certainly was, upon the occurrence of this second and most extraordinary coincidence, by a thousand conflicting sensations, in which wonder and extreme terror were predominant, I still retained sufficient presence of mind to avoid exciting, by any observation, the sensitive nervousness of my companion. I was by no means certain that he had noticed the sounds in question; although, assuredly, a strange alteration had, during the last few minutes, taken place in his demeanor. From a position fronting my own, he had gradually brought round his chair, so as to sit with his face to the door of the chamber; and thus I could but partially perceive his features, although I saw that his lips trembled as if he were murmuring inaudibly. His head had dropped upon his breast—yet I knew that he was not asleep, from the wide and rigid opening of the eye as I caught a glance of it in profile. The motion of his body, too, was at variance with this idea—for he rocked from side to side with a gentle yet constant and uniform sway. Having rapidly taken notice of all this, I resumed the narrative of Sir Launcelot, which thus proceeded:

"And now, the champion, having escaped from the terrible fury of the dragon, bethinking himself of the brazen shield, and of the breaking up of the enchantment which was upon it, removed the carcass from out of the way before him, and approached valorously over the silver pavement of the castle to where the shield was upon the wall; which in sooth tarried not for his full coming, but fell down at his feet upon the silver floor, with a mighty great and terrible ringing sound."

No sooner had these syllables passed my lips, than—as if a shield of brass had indeed, at the moment, fallen heavily upon a floor of silver—I became aware of a distinct, hollow, metallic, and clangorous, yet apparently muffled reverberation. Completely unnerved, I leaped to my feet; but the measured rocking movement of Usher was undisturbed. I rushed to the chair in which he sat. His eyes were bent fixedly before him, and throughout his whole countenance there reigned a stony rigidity. But, as I placed my hand upon his shoulder, there came a strong shudder over his whole person; a sickly smile quivered about his lips; and I saw that he spoke in a low, hurried, and gibbering murmur, as if unconscious of my presence. Bending closely over him, I at length drank in the hideous import of his words.

"Not hear it?—yes, I hear it, and *have* heard it. Long—long—long—many minutes, many hours, many days, have I heard it—yet I dared not—oh, pity me, miserable wretch that I am!—I dared not—I *dared* not speak! *We have put her living in the tomb!* Said I not that my senses were acute? I *now* tell you that I heard her first feeble movements in the hollow coffin. I heard them—many, many days ago—yet I dared not—*I dared not speak!* And now—to-night—Ethelred—ha! ha!—the breaking of the hermit's door, and the death-cry of the dragon, and the clangor of the shield!—say, rather, the rending of her coffin, and the grating of the iron hinges of her prison, and her struggles within the coppered arch-way of the vault! Oh whither shall I fly? Will she not be here anon? Is she not hurrying to upbraid me for my haste? Have I not heard her footstep on the stair? Do I not distinguish that heavy and horrible beating of her heart? Madman!"—here he sprang furiously to his feet, and shrieked out his syllables, as if in the effort he were giving up his soul—*"Madman! I tell you that she now stands without the door!"*

As if in the superhuman energy of his utterance there had been found the potency of a spell—the huge antique pannels to which the speaker pointed, threw slowly back, upon the instant, their ponderous and ebony jaws. It was the work of the rushing gust—but then without those doors there *did* stand the lofty and en-shrouded figure of the lady Madeline of Usher. There was blood upon her white robes, and the evidence of some bitter struggle upon every portion of her emaciated frame. For a moment she re-mained trembling and reeling to and fro upon the threshold—then, with a low moaning cry, fell heavily inward upon the person of her brother, and in her violent and now final death-agonies, bore him to the floor a corpse, and a victim to the terrors he had anticipated.

From that chamber, and from that mansion, I fled aghast. The storm was still abroad in all its wrath as I found myself crossing the old causeway. Suddenly there shot along the path a wild light, and I turned to see whence a gleam so unusual could have issued; for the vast house and its shadows were alone behind me. The ra-diance was that of the full, setting, and blood-red moon, which now shone vividly through that once barely-discernible fissure, of which I have before spoken as extending from the roof of the building, in a zigzag direction, to the base. While I gazed, this fissure rapidly widened—there came a fierce breath of the whirlwind—the entire orb of the satellite burst at once upon my sight—my brain reeled as I saw the mighty walls rushing asunder—there was a long tumultuous shouting sound like the voice of a thousand waters—and the deep and dank tarn at my feet closed sullenly and silently over the fragments of the *"House of Usher."*

ELEONORA

Sub conservatione formae specificae salva anima.

RAYMOND LULLY[1]

I am come of a race noted for vigor of fancy and ardor of passion. Men have called me mad; but the question is not yet settled, whether madness is or is not the loftiest intelligence—whether much that is glorious—whether all that is profound—does not spring from disease of thought—from *moods* of mind exalted at the expense of the general intellect. They who dream by day are cognizant of many things which escape those who dream only by night. In their gray visions they obtain glimpses of eternity, and thrill, in waking, to find that they have been upon the verge of the great secret. In snatches, they learn something of the wisdom which is of good, and more of the mere knowledge which is of evil. They penetrate, however, rudderless or compassless, into the vast ocean of the "light ineffable," and again, like the adventurers of the Nubian geographer, *"agressi sunt mare tenebrarum, quid in eo esset exploraturi."*[2]

We will say, then, that I am mad. I grant, at least, that there are two distinct conditions of my mental existence—the condition of a lucid reason, not to be disputed, and belonging to the memory of events forming the first epoch of my life—and a condition of shadow and doubt, appertaining to the present, and to the recollection of what constitutes the second great era of my being. Therefore, what I shall tell of the earlier period, believe; and to what I may relate of the later time, give only such credit as may seem due; or doubt it altogether; or, if doubt it ye cannot, then play unto its riddle the Oedipus.

She whom I loved in youth, and of whom I now pen calmly and distinctly these remembrances, was the sole daughter of the only sister of my mother long departed. Eleonora was the name of my cousin. We had always dwelled together, beneath a tropical sun, in the Valley of the Many-Colored Grass. No unguided footstep ever came upon that vale; for it lay far away up among a range of giant hills that hung beetling around about it, shutting out the sunlight from its sweetest recesses. No path was trodden in its vicinity; and, to reach our happy home, there was need of putting back, with force, the foliage of many thousands of forest trees, and of crushing to death the glories of many millions of fragrant flowers. Thus it was that we lived all alone, knowing nothing of the world without the valley—I, and my cousin, and her mother.

From the dim regions beyond the mountains at the upper end of our encircled domain, there crept out a narrow and deep river, brighter than all save the eyes of Eleonora; and, winding stealthily about in mazy courses, it passed away, at length, through a shadowy gorge, among hills still dimmer than those whence it had issued. We called it the "River of Silence:" for there seemed to be a hushing influence in its flow. No murmur arose from its bed, and so gently it wandered along, that the pearly pebbles upon which we loved to gaze, far down within its bosom, stirred not at all, but lay in a motionless content, each in its own old station, shining on gloriously forever.

The margin of the river, and of the many dazzling rivulets that glided through devious ways into its channel, as well as the spaces that extended from the margins away down into the depths of the streams until they reached the bed of pebbles at the bottom,— these spots, not less than the whole surface of the valley, from the river to the mountains that girdled it in, were carpeted all by a soft green grass, thick, short, perfectly even, and vanilla-perfumed, but so besprinkled throughout with the yellow buttercup, the white daisy, the purple violet, and the ruby-red asphodel, that its exceeding beauty spoke to our hearts in loud tones, of the love and of the glory of God.

And, here and there, in groves about this grass, like wildernesses of dreams, sprang up fantastic trees, whose tall slender stems stood not upright, but slanted gracefully towards the light that peered at noon-day into the centre of the valley. Their bark was speckled with the vivid alternate splendor of ebony and silver, and was smoother than all save the cheeks of Eleonora; so that but for the brilliant green of the huge leaves that spread from their summits in long, tremulous lines, dallying with the Zephyrs, one might have fancied them giant serpents of Syria doing homage to their Sovereign the Sun.

Hand in hand about this valley, for fifteen years, roamed I with Eleonora before Love entered within our hearts. It was one evening at the close of the third lustrum of her life, and of the fourth of my own, that we sat, locked in each other's embrace, beneath the serpent-like trees, and looked down within the waters of the River of Silence at our images therein. We spoke no words during the rest of that sweet day; and our words even upon the morrow were tremulous and few. We had drawn the God Eros from that wave, and now we felt that he had enkindled within us the fiery souls of our forefathers. The passions which had for centuries distinguished our race, came thronging with the fancies for which they had been equally noted, and together breathed a delirious bliss over the Valley of the Many-Colored Grass. A change fell upon all things. Strange, brilliant flowers, star-shaped, burst out upon the trees where no flowers had been known before. The tints of the green carpet deepened; and when, one by one, the white daisies shrank away, there sprang up, in place of them, ten by ten of the ruby-red asphodel. And life arose in our paths; for the tall flamingo, hitherto unseen, with all gay glowing birds, flaunted his scarlet plumage before us. The golden and silver fish haunted the river, out of the bosom of which issued, little by little, a murmur that swelled, at length, into a lulling melody more divine than that of the harp of Aeolus—sweeter than all save the voice of Eleonora. And now, too, a voluminous cloud, which we had long watched in the regions of Hesper, floated out thence, all gorgeous in crimson and gold, and settling in peace above us, sank, day by day, lower and lower, until its edges rested upon the tops of the mountains, turning all their dimness into magnificence, and shutting us up, as if forever, within a magic prison-house of grandeur and of glory.

The loveliness of Eleonora was that of the Seraphim; but she was a maiden artless and innocent as the brief life she had led among the flowers. No guile disguised the fervor of love which animated her heart, and she examined with me its inmost recesses as we walked together in the Valley of the Many-Colored Grass, and discoursed of the mighty changes which had lately taken place therein.

At length, having spoken one day, in tears, of the last sad change which must befall Humanity, she thenceforward dwelt only upon this one sorrowful theme, interweaving it into all our converse, as, in the songs of the bard of Schiraz, the same images are found occurring, again and again, in every impressive variation of phrase.

She had seen that the finger of Death was upon her bosom—that, like the ephemeron, she had been made perfect in loveliness only to die; but the terrors of the grave, to her, lay solely in a consideration which she revealed to me, one evening at twilight, by the banks of the River of Silence. She grieved to think that, having entombed her in the Valley of the Many-Colored Grass, I would quit forever its happy recesses, transferring the love which now was so passionately her own to some maiden of the outer and everyday world. And, then and there, I threw myself hurriedly at the feet of Eleonora, and offered up a vow, to herself and to Heaven, that I would never bind myself in marriage to any daughter of Earth— that I would in no manner prove recreant to her dear memory, or to the memory of the devout affection with which she had blessed me. And I called the Mighty Ruler of the Universe to witness the pious solemnity of my vow. And the curse which I invoked of *Him* and of her, a saint in Helusion, should I prove traitorous to that promise, involved a penalty the exceeding great horror of which will not permit me to make record of it here. And the bright eyes of Eleonora grew brighter at my words; and she sighed as if a deadly burthen had been taken from her breast; and she trembled and very bitterly wept; but she made acceptance of the vow, (for what was she but a child?) and it made easy to her the bed of her death. And she said to me, not many days afterward, tranquilly dying, that, because of what I had done for the comfort of her spirit, she would watch over me in that spirit when departed, and, if so it were permitted her return to me visibly in the watches of the night; but, if this thing were, indeed, beyond the power of the souls in Paradise, that she would, at least, give me frequent indications of her presence; sighing upon me in the evening winds, or filling the air which I breathed with perfume from the censers of the angels. And, with these words upon her lips, she yielded up her innocent life, putting an end to the first epoch of my own.

Thus far I have faithfully said. But as I pass the barrier in Time's path, formed by the death of my beloved, and proceed with the second era of my existence, I feel that a shadow gathers over my brain, and I mistrust the perfect sanity of the record. But let me on.—Years dragged themselves along heavily, and still I dwelled within the Valley of the Many-Colored Grass; but a second change had come upon all things. The star-shaped flowers shrank into the stems of the trees, and appeared no more. The tints of the green carpet faded; and, one by one, the ruby-red asphodels withered away; and there sprang up, in place of them, ten by ten, dark, eye-like violets that writhed uneasily and were ever encumbered with dew. And Life departed from our paths; for the tall flamingo flaunted no longer his scarlet plumage before us, but flew sadly from the vale into the hills, with all the gay glowing birds that had arrived in his company. And the golden and silver fish swam down through the gorge at the lower end of our domain and bedecked the sweet river never again. And the lulling melody that had been softer than the wind-harp of Aeolus, and more divine than all save the voice of Eleonora, it died little by little away, in murmurs growing lower and lower, until the stream returned, at length, utterly, into the solemnity of its original silence. And then, lastly, the voluminous cloud uprose, and, abandoning the tops of the mountains to the dimness of old, fell back into the regions of Hesper, and took away all its manifold golden and gorgeous glories from the Valley of the Many-Colored Grass.

Yet the promises of Eleonora were not forgotten; for I heard the sounds of the swinging of the censers of the angels; and streams of a holy perfume floated ever and ever about the valley; and at lone hours, when my heart beat heavily, the winds that bathed my brow came unto me laden with soft sighs; and indistinct murmurs filled often the night air; and once—oh, but once only! I was awakened from a slumber, like the slumber of death, by the pressing of spiritual lips upon my own.

But the void within my heart refused, even thus, to be filled. I longed for the love which had before filled it to overflowing. At length the valley *pained* me through its memories of Eleonora, and I left it forever for the vanities and the turbulent triumphs of the world.

I found myself within a strange city, where all things might have served to blot from recollection the sweet dreams I had dreamed so long in the Valley of the Many-Colored Grass. The pomps and pageantries of a stately court, and the mad clangor of arms, and the radiant loveliness of women, bewildered and intoxicated my brain. But as yet my soul had proved true to its vows, and the indications of the presence of Eleonora were still given me in the silent hours of the night. Suddenly, these manifestations they ceased; and the world grew dark before mine eyes; and I stood aghast at the burning thoughts which possessed—at the terrible temptations which beset me; for there came from some far, far distant and unknown land, into the gay court of the king I served, a maiden to whose beauty my whole recreant heart yielded at once—at whose footstool I bowed down without a struggle, in the most ardent, in the most abject worship of love. What indeed was my passion for the young girl of the valley in comparison with the fervor, and the delirium, and the spirit-lifting ecstasy of adoration with which I poured out my whole soul in tears at the feet of the ethereal Ermengarde?—Oh, bright was the seraph Ermengarde! and in that knowledge I had room for none other.—Oh, divine was the angel Ermengarde! and as I looked down into the depths of her memorial eyes, I thought only of them—and *of her*.

I wedded;—nor dreaded the curse I had invoked; and its bitterness was not visited upon me. And once—but once again in the silence of the night; there came through my lattice the soft sighs which had forsaken me; and they modelled themselves into familiar and sweet voice, saying:

"Sleep in peace!—for the Spirit of Love reigneth and ruleth, and, in taking to thy passionate heart her who is Ermengarde, thou art absolved, for reasons which shall be made known to thee in Heaven, of thy vows unto Eleonora."

THE OVAL PORTRAIT

The chateau into which my valet had ventured to make forcible entrance, rather than permit me, in my desperately wounded condition, to pass a night in the open air, was one of those piles of commingled gloom and grandeur which have so long frowned among the Appennines, not less in fact than in the fancy of Mrs. Radcliffe. To all appearance it had been temporarily and very lately abandoned. We established ourselves in one of the smallest and least sumptuously furnished apartments. It lay in a remote turret of the building. Its decorations were rich, yet tattered and antique. Its walls were hung with tapestry and bedecked with manifold and multiform armorial trophies, together with an unusually great number of very spirited modern paintings in frames of rich golden arabesque. In these paintings, which depended from the walls not only in their main surfaces, but in very many nooks which the bizarre architecture of the chateau rendered necessary—in these paintings my incipient delirium, perhaps, had caused me to take deep interest; so that I bade Pedro to close the heavy shutters of the room—since it was already night—to light the tongues of a tall candelabrum which stood by the head of my bed—and to throw open far and wide the fringed curtains of black velvet which enveloped the bed itself. I wished all this done that I might resign myself, if not to sleep, at least alternately to the contemplation of these pictures, and the perusal of a small volume which had been found upon the pillow, and which purported to criticise and describe them.

Long—long I read—and devoutly, devotedly I gazed. Rapidly and gloriously the hours flew by, and the deep midnight came. The position of the candelabrum displeased me, and outreaching my hand with difficulty, rather than disturb my slumbering valet, I placed it so as to throw its rays more fully upon the book.

But the action produced an effect altogether unanticipated. The rays of the numerous candles (for there were many) now fell within a niche of the room which had hitherto been thrown into deep shade by one of the bed-posts. I thus saw in vivid light a picture all unnoticed before. It was the portrait of a young girl just ripening into womanhood. I glanced at the painting hurriedly, and then closed my eyes. Why I did this was not at first apparent even to my own perception. But while my lids remained thus shut, I ran over in my mind my reason for so shutting them. It was an impulsive movement to gain time for thought—to make sure that my vision had not deceived me—to calm and subdue my fancy for a more sober and more certain gaze. In a very few moments I again looked fixedly at the painting.

That I now saw aright I could not and would not doubt; for the first flashing of the candles upon that canvas had seemed to dissipate the dreamy stupor which was stealing over my senses, and to startle me at once into waking life.

The portrait, I have already said, was that of a young girl. It was a mere head and shoulders, done in what is technically termed a *vignette* manner; much in the style of the favorite heads of Sully. The arms, the bosom and even the ends of the radiant hair, melted imperceptibly into the vague yet deep shadow which formed the back-ground of the whole. The frame was oval, richly gilded and filigreed in *Moresque*. As a thing of art nothing could be more admirable than the painting itself. But it could have been neither the execution of the work, nor the immortal beauty of the countenance, which had so suddenly and so vehemently moved me. Least of all, could it have been that my fancy, shaken from its half slumber, had mistaken the head for that of a living person. I saw at once that the peculiarities of the design, of the *vignetting*, and of the frame, must have instantly dispelled such idea—must have prevented even its momentary entertainment. Thinking earnestly upon these points, I remained, for an hour perhaps, half sitting, half reclining, with my vision riveted upon the portrait. At length, satisfied with the true secret of its effect, I fell back within the bed. I had found the spell of the picture in an absolute *life-likeliness* of expression, which, at first startling, finally confounded, subdued and appalled me. With deep and reverent awe I replaced the candelabrum in its former position. The cause of my deep agitation being thus shut from view, I sought eagerly the volume which discussed the paintings and their histories. Turning to the number which designated the oval portrait, I there read the vague and quaint words which follow:

"She was a maiden of rarest beauty, and not more lovely than full of glee. And evil was the hour when she saw, and loved, and wedded the painter. He, passionate, studious, austere, and having already a bride in his Art; she a maiden of rarest beauty, and not more lovely than full of glee: all light and smiles, and frolicsome as the young fawn: loving and cherishing all things: hating only the Art which was her rival: dreading only the pallet and brushes and other untoward instruments which deprived her of the countenance of her lover. It was thus a terrible thing for this lady to hear the painter speak of his desire to portray even his young bride. But she was humble and obedient, and sat meekly for many weeks in the dark high turret-chamber where the light dripped upon the pale canvas only from overhead. But he, the painter, took glory in his work, which went on from hour to hour, and from day to day. And he was a passionate, and wild, and moody man, who became lost in reveries; so that he *would* not see that the light which fell so ghastly in that lone turret withered the health and the spirits of his bride, who pined visibly to all but him. Yet she smiled on and still on, uncomplainingly, because she saw that the painter, (who had high renown,) took a fervid and burning pleasure in his task, and wrought day and night to depict her who so loved him, yet who grew daily more dispirited and weak. And in sooth some who beheld the portrait spoke of its resemblance in low words, as of a mighty marvel, and a proof not less of the power of the painter than of his deep love for her whom he depicted so surpassingly well. But at length, as the labor drew nearer to its conclusion, there were admitted none into the turret; for the painter had grown wild with the ardor of his work, and turned his eyes from the canvas rarely, even to regard the countenance of his wife. And he *would* not see that the tints which he spread upon the canvas were drawn from the cheeks of her who sat beside him. And when many weeks had passed, and but little remained to do, save one brush upon the mouth and one tint upon the eye, the spirit of the lady again flickered up as the flame within the socket of the lamp. And then the brush was given, and then the tint was placed; and, for one moment, the painter stood entranced before the work which he had wrought; but in the next, while he yet gazed, he grew tremulous and very pallid, and aghast, and crying with a loud voice, 'This is indeed *Life* itself!' turned suddenly to regard his beloved:—*She was dead!*"

Antagonisms

Antagonisms

During his turbulent professional career, Poe counted among his enemies shameless editors, exploitative publishers, hostile reviewers, hated coteries, and acquaintances who had (in his view) insulted or betrayed him in private life. His indignation at perceived injustices sprang in part from clashes with his foster father that culminated in Poe's abandonment and disinheritance.

Adopting the motto of John Allan's native Scotland, *"Nemo me impune lacessit"* (no one wounds me with impunity), Poe turned instinctively as a writer to themes of hostility, rivalry, and revenge. His first published story, "Metzengerstein," savors of German romanticism in evoking "metempsychosis"—the soul's transmigration at death to a human or animal form. An "ancient prophecy" portends the outcome of a feud between warring families, and Poe hints that after Count Berlifitzing dies in a fire, trying to rescue his prized horses, he avenges himself against Baron Metzengerstein (the presumed arsonist) by taking the form of a gigantic "fiery-colored horse."

A more intimate struggle informs "William Wilson," a tale based in part on Poe's memories of an English boarding school. The narrator's antipathy for his nemesis, a youth whose name is identical to his own, ends in pathological derangement as Poe finally puts in question the existence of the hated rival. Doubling abounds in Poe, but here the doppelgänger motif elaborates the conflict of a self torn between impulsive depravity and ineluctable conscience.

The intensity of "The Tell-Tale Heart" develops as much from the narrator's mad need to contradict an assumed imputation of madness as from his account of murdering and dismembering an old man. When he succumbs, under police questioning, to the delusion that he hears the dead man's beating heart, his confession discloses more derangement than remorse. His admitted need to rid himself of the old man's "vulture eye" hints that he shares his victim's dread of death.

In "The Black Cat," Poe calls the irrational urge to commit gratuitous atrocities "the spirit of PERVERSENESS." The debauched narrator's temperance tale recounts the "household events" that lead him to hang a pet cat and then to kill his wife for thwarting his assault on a second feline. By walling up the still-living creature with his wife's corpse, the murderer dooms the obscure object of his antagonism: himself. Curiously, Poe composed this domestic tale soon after the bloody onset of his wife's tuberculosis.

Poe philosophizes further on compulsive self-destruction in "The Imp of the Perverse," which begins as an essay on the impulse to defy reason and morality. This reflection leads to a brief narrative, which (as in "The Black Cat") proves to be the confession of a condemned criminal. Having committed an undetectable crime, murdering a man to inherit his estate, the narrator becomes consumed by an irrational, irrepressible need to confess his homicidal ingenuity.

Another story of doubling, "The Cask of Amontillado," presents a more intricate "perfect crime," Montresor's entrapment and living entombment of Fortunato. Spurred by his rival's insults, the narrator vows to punish with impunity and walls up his enemy among the bones of the Montresors, signaling an odd bond underlying their rivalry and thus explaining his obstinate need to confess. Poe wrote this tale in the midst of a raging feud with writer-editor Thomas Dunn English.

In Poe's last tale of antagonism, "Hop-Frog," a spectator recounts the jester Hop-Frog's revenge against the cruel king for humiliating Trippetta, another dwarf "forcibly carried off" from her home. Composed for a Boston antislavery newspaper, the tale alludes crudely to the threat of slave revolt in Hop-Frog's ploy of dressing the king and ministers as "ourang-outangs" before putting them to the torch. The story unfolds, however, from a perspective sympathetic to the jester, who exposes the true character of his longtime oppressors by carrying out his deadly masquerade.

METZENGERSTEIN

Pestis eram vivus—moriens tua mors ero.

MARTIN LUTHER[1]

Horror and fatality have been stalking abroad in all ages. Why then give a date to this story I have to tell? Let it suffice to say, that at the period of which I speak, there existed, in the interior of Hungary, a settled although hidden belief in the doctrines of the Metempsychosis. Of the doctrines themselves—that is, of their falsity, or of their probability—I say nothing. I assert, however, that much of our incredulity (as La Bruyère says of all our unhappiness) *"vient de ne pouvoir être seuls."* *[2]

But there are some points in the Hungarian superstition which were fast verging to absurdity. They—the Hungarians—differed very essentially from their Eastern authorities. For example, *"The soul,"* said the former—I give the words of an acute and intelligent Parisian—*"ne demeure qu'une seule fois dans un corps sensible: au reste—un cheval, un chien, un homme même, n'est que la ressemblance peu tangible de ces animaux."*[3]

The families of Berlifitzing and Metzengerstein had been at variance for centuries. Never before were two houses so illustrious, mutually embittered by hostility so deadly. The origin of this enmity seems to be found in the words of an ancient prophecy—"A lofty name shall have a fearful fall when, as the rider over his horse, the mortality of Metzengerstein shall triumph over the immortality of Berlifitzing."

To be sure the words themselves had little or no meaning. But more trivial causes have given rise—and that no long while ago—to

*Mercier, in *"L'an deux mille quarte cents quarante,"* seriously maintains the doctrines of Metempsychosis, and I. D'Israeli says that "no system is so simple and so little repugnant to the understanding." Colonel Ethan Allen, the "Green Mountain Boy," is also said to have been a serious metempsychosist. [Poe's note]

consequences equally eventful. Besides, the estates, which were contiguous, had long exercised a rival influence in the affairs of a busy government. Moreover, near neighbors are seldom friends; and the inhabitants of the Castle Berlifitzing might look, from their lofty buttresses, into the very windows of the Palace Metzengerstein. Least of all had the more than feudal magnificence, thus discovered, a tendency to allay the irritable feelings of the less ancient and less wealthy Berlifitzings. What wonder, then, that the words, however silly, of that prediction, should have succeeded in setting and keeping at variance two families already predisposed to quarrel by every instigation of hereditary jealousy? The prophecy seemed to imply—if it implied anything—a final triumph on the part of the already more powerful house; and was of course remembered with the more bitter animosity by the weaker and less influential.

Wilhelm, Count Berlifitzing, although loftily descended, was, at the epoch of this narrative, an infirm and doting old man, remarkable for nothing but an inordinate and inveterate personal antipathy to the family of his rival, and so passionate a love of horses, and of hunting, that neither bodily infirmity, great age, nor mental incapacity, prevented his daily participation in the dangers of the chase.

Frederick, Baron Metzengerstein, was, on the other hand, not yet of age. His father, the Minister G———, died young. His mother, the Lady Mary, followed him quickly. Frederick was, at that time, in his eighteenth year. In a city, eighteen years are no long period: but in a wilderness—in so magnificent a wilderness as that old principality, the pendulum vibrates with a deeper meaning.

From some peculiar circumstances attending the administration of his father, the young Baron, at the decease of the former, entered immediately upon his vast possessions. Such estates were seldom held before by a nobleman of Hungary. His castles were without number. The chief in point of splendor and extent was the "Palace Metzengerstein." The boundary line of his dominions was never clearly defined; but his principal park embraced a circuit of fifty miles.

Upon the succession of a proprietor so young, with a character so well known, to a fortune so unparalleled, little speculation was afloat in regard to his probable course of conduct. And, indeed, for the space of three days, the behavior of the heir out-heroded

Herod, and fairly surpassed the expectations of his most enthusiastic admirers. Shameful debaucheries—flagrant treacheries—unheard-of atrocities—gave his trembling vassals quickly to understand that no servile submission on their part—no punctilios of conscience on his own—were thenceforward to prove any security against the remorseless fangs of a petty Caligula. On the night of the fourth day, the stables of the Castle Berlifitzing were discovered to be on fire; and the unanimous opinion of the neighborhood added the crime of the incendiary to the already hideous list of the Baron's misdemeanors and enormities.

But during the tumult occasioned by this occurrence, the young nobleman himself sat apparently buried in meditation, in a vast and desolate upper apartment of the family palace of Metzengerstein. The rich although faded tapestry hangings which swung gloomily upon the walls, represented the shadowy and majestic forms of a thousand illustrious ancestors. *Here*, rich-ermined priests, and pontifical dignitaries, familiarly seated with the autocrat and the sovereign, put a veto on the wishes of a temporal king, or restrained with the fiat of papal supremacy the rebellious sceptre of the Arch-enemy. *There*, the dark, tall statures of the Princes Metzengerstein—their muscular war-coursers plunging over the carcasses of fallen foes—startled the steadiest nerves with their vigorous expression; and *here*, again, the voluptuous and swan-like figures of the dames of days gone by, floated away in the mazes of an unreal dance to the strains of imaginary melody.

But as the Baron listened, or affected to listen, to the gradually increasing uproar in the stables of Berlifitzing—or perhaps pondered upon some more novel, some more decided act of audacity—his eyes were turned unwittingly to the figure of an enormous, and unnaturally colored horse, represented in the tapestry as belonging to a Saracen ancestor of the family of his rival. The horse itself, in the fore-ground of the design, stood motionless and statue-like—while, farther back, its discomfited rider perished by the dagger of a Metzengerstein.

On Frederick's lip arose a fiendish expression, as he became aware of the direction which his glance had, without his consciousness, assumed. Yet he did not remove it. On the contrary, he could by no means account for the overwhelming anxiety which appeared falling like a pall upon his senses. It was with difficulty that he reconciled his dreamy and incoherent feelings with the certainty of being awake. The longer he gazed, the more absorbing became the spell—the more impossible did it appear that he could ever withdraw his glance from the fascination of that tapestry. But the tumult without becoming suddenly more violent, with a compulsory exertion he diverted his attention to the glare of ruddy light thrown full by the flaming stables upon the windows of the apartment.

The action, however, was but momentary; his gaze returned mechanically to the wall. To his extreme horror and astonishment, the head of the gigantic steed had, in the meantime, altered its position. The neck of the animal, before arched, as if in compassion, over the prostrate body of its lord, was now extended, at full length, in the direction of the Baron. The eyes, before invisible, now wore an energetic and human expression, while they gleamed with a fiery and unusual red; and the distended lips of the apparently enraged horse left in full view his sepulchral and disgusting teeth.

Stupified with terror, the young nobleman tottered to the door. As he threw it open, a flash of red light, streaming far into the chamber, flung his shadow with a clear outline against the quivering tapestry; and he shuddered to perceive that shadow—as he staggered awhile upon the threshold—assuming the exact position, and precisely filling up the contour, of the relentless and triumphant murderer of the Saracen Berlifitzing.

To lighten the depression of his spirits, the Baron hurried into the open air. At the principal gate of the palace he encountered three equerries. With much difficulty, and at the imminent peril of their lives, they were restraining the convulsive plunges of a gigantic and fiery-colored horse.

"Whose horse? Where did you get him?" demanded the youth, in a querulous and husky tone, as he became instantly aware that the mysterious steed in the tapestried chamber was the very counterpart of the furious animal before his eyes.

"He is your own property, sire," replied one of the equerries, "at least he is claimed by no other owner. We caught him flying, all smoking and foaming with rage, from the burning stables of the Castle Berlifitzing. Supposing him to have belonged to the old Count's stud of foreign horses, we led him back as an estray. But the grooms there disclaim any title to the creature; which is

strange, since he bears evident marks of having made a narrow es-
cape from the flames.

"The letters W. V. B. are also branded very distinctly on his
forehead," interrupted a second equerry, "I supposed them, of
course, to be the initials of Wilhelm Von Berlifitzing—but all at
the castle are positive in denying any knowledge of the horse."

"Extremely singular!" said the young Baron, with a musing air,
and apparently unconscious of the meaning of his words. "He is,
as you say, a remarkable horse—a prodigious horse! although, as
you very justly observe, of a suspicious and untractable character;
let him be mine, however," he added, after a pause, "perhaps a
rider like Frederick of Metzengerstein, may tame even the devil
from the stables of Berlifitzing."

"You are mistaken, my lord; the horse, as I think we mentioned,
is *not* from the stables of the Count. If such had been the case, we
know our duty better than to bring him into the presence of a no-
ble of your family."

"True!" observed the Baron, dryly; and at that instant a page of
the bed-chamber came from the palace with a heightened color, and
a precipitate step. He whispered into his master's ear an account of
the sudden disappearance of a small portion of the tapestry, in an
apartment which he designated; entering, at the same time, into par-
ticulars of a minute and circumstantial character; but from the low
tone of voice in which these latter were communicated, nothing es-
caped to gratify the excited curiosity of the equerries.

The young Frederick, during the conference, seemed agitated by
a variety of emotions. He soon, however, recovered his compo-
sure, and an expression of determined malignancy settled upon his
countenance, as he gave peremptory orders that the apartment in
question should be immediately locked up, and the key placed in
his own possession.

"Have you heard of the unhappy death of the old hunter Berli-
fitzing?" said one of his vassals to the Baron, as, after the depar-
ture of the page, the huge steed which that nobleman had adopted
as his own, plunged and curveted, with redoubled fury, down the
long avenue which extended from the palace to the stables of Met-
zengerstein.

"No!" said the Baron, turning abruptly toward the speaker,
"dead! say you?"

"It is indeed true, my lord; and, to the noble of your name, will be, I imagine, no unwelcome intelligence."

A rapid smile shot over the countenance of the listener. "How died he?"

"In his rash exertions to rescue a favorite portion of his hunting stud, he has himself perished miserably in the flames."

"I-n-d-e-e-d-!" ejaculated the Baron, as if slowly and deliberately impressed with the truth of some exciting idea.

"Indeed;" repeated the vassal.

"Shocking!" said the youth, calmly, and turned quietly into the palace.

From this date a marked alteration took place in the outward demeanor of the dissolute young Baron Frederick Von Metzengerstein. Indeed, his behaviour disappointed every expectation, and proved little in accordance with the views of many a manœuvering mamma; while his habits and manner, still less than formerly, offered anything congenial with those of the neighboring aristocracy. He was never to be seen beyond the limits of his own domain, and, in this wide and social world, was utterly companionless—unless, indeed, that unnatural, impetuous, and fiery-colored horse, which he henceforward continually bestrode, had any mysterious right to the title of his friend.

Numerous invitations on the part of the neighborhood for a long time, however, periodically came in. "Will the Baron honor our festivals with his presence?" "Will the Baron join us in a hunting of the boar?"—"Metzengerstein does not hunt;" "Metzengerstein will not attend," were the haughty and laconic answers.

These repeated insults were not to be endured by an imperious nobility. Such invitations became less cordial—less frequent—in time they ceased altogether. The widow of the unfortunate Count Berlifitzing was even heard to express a hope "that the Baron might be at home when he did not wish to be at home, since he disdained the company of his equals; and ride when he did not wish to ride, since he preferred the society of a horse." This to be sure was a very silly explosion of hereditary pique; and merely proved how singularly unmeaning our sayings are apt to become, when we desire to be unusually energetic.

The charitable, nevertheless, attributed the alteration in the conduct of the young nobleman to the natural sorrow of a son for the untimely loss of his parents;—forgetting, however, his atrocious and reckless behavior during the short period immediately succeeding that bereavement. Some there were, indeed, who suggested a too haughty idea of self-consequence and dignity. Others again (among them may be mentioned the family physician) did not hesitate in speaking of morbid melancholy, and hereditary ill-health; while dark hints, of a more equivocal nature, were current among the multitude.

Indeed, the Baron's perverse attachment to his lately-acquired charger—an attachment which seemed to attain new strength from every fresh example of the animal's ferocious and demon-like propensities—at length became, in the eyes of all reasonable men, a hideous and unnatural fervor. In the glare of noon—at the dead hour of night—in sickness or in health—in calm or in tempest—the young Metzengerstein seemed riveted to the saddle of that colossal horse, whose intractable audacities so well accorded with his own spirit.

There were circumstances, moreover, which coupled with late events, gave an unearthly and portentous character to the mania of the rider, and to the capabilities of the steed. The space passed over in a single leap had been accurately measured, and was found to exceed by an astounding difference, the wildest expectations of the most imaginative. The Baron, besides, had no particular *name* for the animal, although all the rest in his collection were distinguished by characteristic appellations. His stable, too, was appointed at a distance from the rest; and with regard to grooming and other necessary offices, none but the owner in person had ventured to officiate, or even to enter the enclosure of that particular stall. It was also to be observed, that although the three grooms, who had caught the steed as he fled from the conflagration at Berlifitzing, had succeeded in arresting his course, by means of a chain-bridle and noose—yet no one of the three could with any certainty affirm that he had, during that dangerous struggle, or at any period thereafter, actually placed his hand upon the body of the beast. Instances of peculiar intelligence in the demeanor of a noble and high-spirited horse are not to be supposed capable of exciting unreasonable attention, but there were certain circumstances which intruded themselves per force upon the most skeptical and phlegmatic; and it is said there were times when the animal caused the gaping crowd who stood around to recoil in horror from the deep and impressive meaning of his terrible stamp—times when the young Metzengerstein turned pale and shrunk away from the rapid and searching expression of his earnest and human-looking eye.

Among all the retinue of the Baron, however, none were found to doubt the ardor of that extraordinary affection which existed on the part of the young nobleman for the fiery qualities of his horse; at least, none but an insignificant and misshapen little page, whose deformities were in every body's way, and whose opinions were of the least possible importance. He (if his ideas are worth mentioning at all,) had the effrontery to assert that his master never vaulted into the saddle without an unaccountable and almost imperceptible shudder; and that, upon his return from every long-continued and habitual ride, an expression of triumphant malignity distorted every muscle in his countenance.

One tempestuous night, Metzengerstein, awaking from a heavy slumber, descended like a maniac from his chamber, and, mounting in hot haste, bounded away into the mazes of the forest. An occurrence so common attracted no particular attention, but his return was looked for with intense anxiety on the part of his domestics, when, after some hours' absence, the stupendous and magnificent battlements of the Palace Metzengerstein, were discovered crackling and rocking to their very foundation, under the influence of a dense and livid mass of ungovernable fire.

As the flames, when first seen, had already made so terrible a progress that all efforts to save any portion of the building were evidently futile, the astonished neighborhood stood idly around in silent, if not apathetic wonder. But a new and fearful object soon riveted the attention of the multitude, and proved how much more intense is the excitement wrought in the feelings of a crowd by the contemplation of human agony, than that brought about by the most appalling spectacles of inanimate matter.

Up the long avenue of aged oaks which led from the forest to the main entrance of the Palace Metzengerstein, a steed, bearing an unbonneted and disordered rider, was seen leaping with an impetuosity which outstripped the very Demon of the Tempest.

The career of the horseman was indisputably, on his own part, uncontrollable. The agony of his countenance, the convulsive struggle of his frame, gave evidence of superhuman exertion: but no sound, save a solitary shriek, escaped from his lacerated lips, which were bitten through and through in the intensity of terror. One instant, and the clattering of hoofs resounded sharply and shrilly above the roaring of the flames and the shrieking of the winds—another, and, clearing at a single plunge the gate-way and the moat, the steed bounded far up the tottering staircases of the palace, and, with its rider, disappeared amid the whirlwind of chaotic fire.

The fury of the tempest immediately died away, and a dead calm sullenly succeeded. A white flame still enveloped the building like a shroud, and, streaming far away into the quiet atmosphere, shot forth a glare of preternatural light; while a cloud of smoke settled heavily over the battlements in the distinct colossal figure of—*a horse.*

WILLIAM WILSON

What say of it? what say of CONSCIENCE grim,
That spectre in my path?

Chamberlayne's PHARRONIDA[1]

Let me call myself, for the present, William Wilson. The fair page now lying before me need not be sullied with my real appellation. This has been already too much an object for the scorn—for the horror—for the detestation of my race. To the uttermost regions of the globe have not the indignant winds bruited its unparalleled infamy? Oh, outcast of all outcasts most abandoned!—to the earth art thou not forever dead? to its honors, to its flowers, to its golden aspirations?—and a cloud, dense, dismal, and limitless, does it not hang eternally between thy hopes and heaven?

I would not, if I could, here or to-day, embody a record of my later years of unspeakable misery, and unpardonable crime. This epoch—these later years—took unto themselves a sudden elevation in turpitude, whose origin alone it is my present purpose to assign. Men usually grow base by degrees. From me, in an instant, all virtue dropped bodily as a mantle. From comparatively trivial wickedness I passed, with the stride of a giant, into more than the enormities of an Elah-Gabalus. What chance—what one event brought this evil thing to pass, bear with me while I relate. Death approaches; and the shadow which foreruns him has thrown a softening influence over my spirit. I long, in passing through the dim valley, for the sympathy—I had nearly said for the pity—of my fellow men. I would fain have them believe that I have been, in some measure, the slave of circumstances beyond human control. I would wish them to seek out for me, in the details I am about to give, some little oasis of *fatality* amid a wilderness of error. I would have them allow—what they cannot refrain from allowing—that, although temptation may have ere-while existed as great, man was never *thus*, at least, tempted before—certainly, never *thus* fell. And is it therefore that he has never thus suffered? Have I not indeed been living in a dream? And am I not now dying a victim to the horror and the mystery of the wildest of all sublunary visions?

I am the descendant of a race whose imaginative and easily excitable temperament has at all times rendered them remarkable; and, in my earliest infancy, I gave evidence of having fully inherited the family character. As I advanced in years it was more strongly developed; becoming, for many reasons, a cause of serious disquietude to my friends, and of positive injury to myself. I grew self-willed, addicted to the wildest caprices, and a prey to the most ungovernable passions. Weak-minded, and beset with constitutional infirmities akin to my own, my parents could do but little to check the evil propensities which distinguished me. Some feeble and ill-directed efforts resulted in complete failure on their part, and, of course, in total triumph on mine. Thenceforward my voice was a household law; and at an age when few children have abandoned their leading-strings, I was left to the guidance of my own will, and became, in all but name, the master of my own actions.

My earliest recollections of a school-life are connected with a large, rambling, Elizabethan house, in a misty-looking village of England, where were a vast number of gigantic and gnarled trees, and where all the houses were excessively ancient. In truth, it was a dream-like and spirit-soothing place, that venerable old town. At this moment, in fancy, I feel the refreshing chilliness of its deeply-shadowed avenues, inhale the fragrance of its thousand shrubberies, and thrill anew with undefinable delight, at the deep hollow note of the church-bell, breaking, each hour, with sullen and sudden roar, upon the stillness of the dusky atmosphere in which the fretted Gothic steeple lay imbedded and asleep.

It gives me, perhaps, as much of pleasure as I can now in any manner experience, to dwell upon minute recollections of the school and its concerns. Steeped in misery as I am—misery, alas! only too real—I shall be pardoned for seeking relief, however slight and temporary, in the weakness of a few rambling details. These, moreover, utterly trivial, and even ridiculous in themselves, assume, to my fancy, adventitious importance, as connected with a period and a locality when and where I recognise the first ambiguous monitions of the destiny which afterwards so fully overshadowed me. Let me then remember.

The house, I have said, was old and irregular. The grounds were extensive, and a high and solid brick wall, topped with a bed of mortar and broken glass, encompassed the whole. This prison-like rampart formed the limit of our domain; beyond it we saw but thrice a week—once every Saturday afternoon, when, attended by two ushers, we were permitted to take brief walks in a body through some of the neighboring fields—and twice during Sunday, when we were paraded in the same formal manner to the morning and evening service in the one church of the village. Of this church the principal of our school was pastor. With how deep a spirit of wonder and perplexity was I wont to regard him from our remote pew in the gallery, as, with step solemn and slow, he ascended the pulpit! This reverend man, with countenance so demurely benign, with robes so glossy and so clerically flowing, with wig so minutely powdered, so rigid and so vast,—could this be he who, of late, with sour visage, and in snuffy habiliments, administered, ferule in hand, the Draconian Laws of the academy? Oh, gigantic paradox, too utterly monstrous for solution!

At an angle of the ponderous wall frowned a more ponderous gate. It was riveted and studded with iron bolts, and surmounted with jagged iron spikes. What impressions of deep awe did it inspire! It was never opened save for the three periodical egressions and ingressions already mentioned; then, in every creak of its mighty hinges, we found a plenitude of mystery—a world of matter for solemn remark, or for more solemn meditation.

The extensive enclosure was irregular in form, having many capacious recesses. Of these, three or four of the largest constituted the play-ground. It was level, and covered with fine hard gravel. I well remember it had no trees, nor benches, nor anything similar within it. Of course it was in the rear of the house. In front lay a small parterre, planted with box and other shrubs; but through this sacred division we passed only upon rare occasions indeed—such as a first advent to school or final departure thence, or perhaps, when a parent or friend having called for us, we joyfully took our way home for the Christmas or Midsummer holy-days.

But the house!—how quaint an old building was this!—to me how veritably a palace of enchantment! There was really no end to its windings—to its incomprehensible subdivisions. It was difficult, at any given time, to say with certainty upon which of its two stories one happened to be. From each room to every other there were sure to be found three or four steps either in ascent or descent. Then the lateral branches were innumerable—inconceivable—and so returning in upon themselves, that our most exact ideas in regard to the whole mansion were not very far different from those with which we pondered upon infinity. During the five years of my residence here, I was never able to ascertain with precision, in what remote locality lay the little sleeping apartment assigned to myself and some eighteen or twenty other scholars.

The school-room was the largest in the house—I could not help thinking, in the world. It was very long, narrow, and dismally low, with pointed Gothic windows and a ceiling of oak. In a remote and terror-inspiring angle was a square enclosure of eight or ten feet, comprising the *sanctum*, "during hours," of our principal, the Reverend Dr. Bransby. It was a solid structure, with massy door, sooner than open which in the absence of the "Dominie," we would all have willingly perished by the *peine forte et dure*.[2] In other angles were two other similar boxes, far less reverenced, indeed, but still greatly matters of awe. One of these was the pulpit of the "classical" usher, one of the "English and mathematical." Interspersed about the room, crossing and recrossing in endless irregularity, were innumerable benches and desks, black, ancient, and time-worn, piled desperately with much-bethumbed books, and so beseamed with initial letters, names at full length, grotesque figures, and other multiplied efforts of the knife, as to have entirely lost what little of original form might have been their portion in days long departed. A huge bucket with water stood at one extremity of the room, and a clock of stupendous dimensions at the other.

Encompassed by the massy walls of this venerable academy, I passed, yet not in tedium or disgust, the years of the third lustrum of my life. The teeming brain of childhood requires no external world of incident to occupy or amuse it; and the apparently dismal monotony of a school was replete with more intense excitement than my riper youth has derived from luxury, or my full manhood from crime. Yet I must believe that my first mental development had in it much of the uncommon—even much of the *outré*. Upon mankind at large the events of very early existence rarely leave in mature age any definite impression. All is gray shadow—a weak and irregular remembrance—an indistinct regathering of feeble pleasures and phantasmagoric pains. With me this is not so. In childhood I must have felt with the energy of a man what I now find stamped upon memory in lines as vivid, as deep, and as durable as the *exergues* of the Carthaginian medals.

Yet in fact—in the fact of the world's view—how little was there to remember! The morning's awakening, the nightly summons to bed; the connings, the recitations; the periodical half-holidays, and perambulations; the play-ground, with its broils, its pastimes, its intrigues;—these, by a mental sorcery long forgotten, were made to involve a wilderness of sensation, a world of rich incident, an universe of varied emotion, of excitement the most passionate and spirit-stirring. *"Oh, le bon temps, que ce siècle de fer!"*[3]

In truth, the ardor, the enthusiasm, and the imperiousness of my disposition, soon rendered me a marked character among my schoolmates, and by slow, but natural gradations, gave me an ascendancy over all not greatly older than myself;—over all with a single exception. This exception was found in the person of a scholar, who, although no relation, bore the same Christian and surname as myself;—a circumstance, in fact, little remarkable; for, notwithstanding a noble descent, mine was one of those everyday appellations which seem, by prescriptive right, to have been, time out of mind, the common property of the mob. In this narrative I have therefore designated myself as William Wilson,—a fictitious title not very dissimilar to the real. My namesake alone, of those who in school-phraseology constituted "our set," presumed to compete with me in the studies of the class—in the sports and broils of the play-ground—to refuse implicit belief in my assertions, and submission to my will—indeed, to interfere with my arbitrary dictation in any respect whatsoever. If there is on earth a supreme and unqualified despotism, it is the despotism of a master-mind in boyhood over the less energetic spirits of its companions.

Wilson's rebellion was to me a source of the greatest embarrassment; the more so as, in spite of the bravado with which in public I made a point of treating him and his pretensions, I secretly felt that I feared him, and could not help thinking the equality which he maintained so easily with myself, a proof of his true superiority; since not to be overcome cost me a perpetual struggle. Yet this superiority—even this equality—was in truth acknowledged by no one but myself; our associates, by some unaccountable blindness, seemed not even to suspect it. Indeed, his competition, his resistance, and especially his impertinent and dogged interference with my purposes, were not more pointed than private. He appeared to be destitute alike of the ambition which urged, and of the passionate energy of mind which enabled me to excel. In his rivalry he might have been supposed actuated solely by a whimsical desire to thwart, astonish, or mortify myself; although there were times when I could not help observing, with a feeling made up of wonder, abasement, and pique, that he mingled with his injuries, his insults, or his contradictions, a certain most inappropriate, and assuredly most unwelcome *affectionateness* of manner. I could only conceive this singular behavior to arise from a consummate self-conceit assuming the vulgar airs of patronage and protection.

Perhaps it was this latter trait in Wilson's conduct, conjoined with our identity of name, and the mere accident of our having entered the school upon the same day, which set afloat the notion that we were brothers, among the senior classes in the academy. These do not usually inquire with much strictness into the affairs of their juniors. I have before said, or should have said, that Wilson was not, in the most remote degree, connected with my family. But assuredly if we *had* been brothers we must have been twins; for, after leaving Dr. Bransby's, I casually learned that my namesake was born on the nineteenth of January, 1813—and this is a somewhat remarkable coincidence; for the day is precisely that of my own nativity.

It may seem strange that in spite of the continual anxiety occasioned me by the rivalry of Wilson, and his intolerable spirit of contradiction, I could not bring myself to hate him altogether. We had, to be sure, nearly every day a quarrel in which, yielding me publicly the palm of victory, he, in some manner, contrived to make me feel that it was he who had deserved it; yet a sense of pride on my part, and a veritable dignity on his own, kept us always upon what are called "speaking terms," while there were many points of strong congeniality in our tempers, operating to awake in me a sentiment which our position alone, perhaps, prevented from ripening into friendship. It is difficult, indeed, to define, or even to describe, my real feelings towards him. They formed a motley and heterogeneous admixture;—some petulant animosity, which was not yet hatred, some esteem, more respect, much fear, with a world of uneasy curiosity. To the moralist it will be unnecessary to say, in addition, that Wilson and myself were the most inseparable of companions.

It was no doubt the anomalous state of affairs existing between us, which turned all my attacks upon him, (and they were many, either open or covert) into the channel of banter or practical joke (giving pain while assuming the aspect of mere fun) rather than into a more serious and determined hostility. But my endeavours on this head were by no means uniformly successful, even when my plans were the most wittily concocted; for my namesake had much about him, in character, of that unassuming and quiet austerity which, while enjoying the poignancy of its own jokes, has no heel of Achilles in itself, and absolutely refuses to be laughed at. I could find, indeed, but one vulnerable point, and that, lying in a personal peculiarity, arising, perhaps, from constitutional disease, would have been spared by any antagonist less at his wit's end than myself;—my rival had a weakness in the faucial or guttural organs, which precluded him from raising his voice at any time *above a very low whisper*. Of this defect I did not fail to take what poor advantage lay in my power.

Wilson's retaliations in kind were many; and there was one form of his practical wit that disturbed me beyond measure. How his sagacity first discovered at all that so petty a thing would vex me, is a question I never could solve; but, having discovered, he habitually practised the annoyance. I had always felt aversion to my uncourtly patronymic, and its very common, if not plebeian prænomen. The words were venom in my ears; and when, upon the day of my arrival, a second William Wilson came also to the academy, I felt angry with him for bearing the name, and doubly disgusted with the name because a stranger bore it, who would be the cause of its twofold repetition, who would be constantly in my presence, and whose concerns, in the ordinary routine of the school business, must inevitably, on account of the detestable coincidence, be often confounded with my own.

The feeling of vexation thus engendered grew stronger with every circumstance tending to show resemblance, moral or physical, between my rival and myself. I had not then discovered the remarkable fact that we were of the same age; but I saw that we were of the same height, and I perceived that we were even singularly alike in general contour of person and outline of feature. I was galled, too, by the rumor touching a relationship, which had grown current in the upper forms. In a word, nothing could more seriously disturb me, (although I scrupulously concealed such disturbance,) than any allusion to a similarity of mind, person, or condition existing between us. But, in truth, I had no reason to believe that (with the exception of the matter of relationship, and in the case of Wilson himself,) this similarity had ever been made a subject of comment, or even observed at all by our schoolfellows. That *he* observed it in all its bearings, and as fixedly as I, was apparent; but that he could discover in such circumstances so fruitful a field of annoyance, can only be attributed, as I said before, to his more than ordinary penetration.

His cue, which was to perfect an imitation of myself, lay both in words and in actions; and most admirably did he play his part. My dress it was an easy matter to copy; my gait and general manner were, without difficulty, appropriated; in spite of his constitutional defect, even my voice did not escape him. My louder tones were, of course, unattempted, but then the key, it was identical; *and his singular whisper, it grew the very echo of my own.*

How greatly this most exquisite portraiture harassed me, (for it could not justly be termed a caricature,) I will not now venture to describe. I had but one consolation—in the fact that the imitation, apparently, was noticed by myself alone, and that I had to endure only the knowing and strangely sarcastic smiles of my namesake himself. Satisfied with having produced in my bosom the intended effect, he seemed to chuckle in secret over the sting he had inflicted, and was characteristically disregardful of the public applause which the success of his witty endeavours might have so easily elicited. That the school, indeed, did not feel his design, perceive its accomplishment, and participate in his sneer, was, for many anxious months, a riddle I could not resolve. Perhaps the *gradation* of his copy rendered it not so readily perceptible; or, more possibly, I owed my security to the masterly air of the copyist, who, disdaining the letter, (which in a painting is all the obtuse can see,) gave but the full spirit of his original for my individual contemplation and chagrin.

I have already more than once spoken of the disgusting air of patronage which he assumed toward me, and of his frequent officious interference with my will. This interference often took the ungracious character of advice; advice not openly given, but hinted or insinuated. I received it with a repugnance which gained strength as I grew in years. Yet, at this distant day, let me do him the simple justice to acknowledge that I can recall no occasion when the suggestions of my rival were on the side of those errors or follies so usual to his immature age and seeming inexperience; that his moral sense, at least, if not his general talents and worldly wisdom, was far keener than my own; and that I might, to-day, have been a better, and thus a happier man, had I less frequently rejected the counsels embodied in those meaning whispers which I then but too cordially hated and too bitterly despised.

As it was, I at length grew restive in the extreme under his distasteful supervision, and daily resented more and more openly what I considered his intolerable arrogance. I have said that, in the first years of our connexion as schoolmates, my feelings in regard to him might have been easily ripened into friendship: but, in the latter months of my residence at the academy, although the intrusion of his ordinary manner had, beyond doubt, in some measure, abated, my sentiments, in nearly similar proportion, partook very much of positive hatred. Upon one occasion he saw this, I think, and afterwards avoided, or made a show of avoiding me.

It was about the same period, if I remember aright, that, in an altercation of violence with him, in which he was more than usually thrown off his guard, and spoke and acted with an openness of demeanor rather foreign to his nature, I discovered, or fancied I discovered, in his accent, his air, and general appearance, a something which first startled, and then deeply interested me, by bringing to mind dim visions of my earliest infancy—wild, confused and thronging memories of a time when memory herself was yet unborn. I cannot better describe the sensation which oppressed me than by saying that I could with difficulty shake off the belief of my having been acquainted with the being who stood before me, at some epoch very long ago—some point of the past even infinitely remote. The delusion, however, faded rapidly as it came; and I mention it at all but to define the day of the last conversation I there held with my singular namesake.

The huge old house, with its countless subdivisions, had several large chambers communicating with each other, where slept the greater number of the students. There were, however, (as must necessarily happen in a building so awkwardly planned,) many little nooks or recesses, the odds and ends of the structure; and these the economic ingenuity of Dr. Bransby had also fitted up as dormitories; although, being the merest closets, they were capable of accommodating but a single individual. One of these small apartments was occupied by Wilson.

One night, about the close of my fifth year at the school, and immediately after the altercation just mentioned, finding every one wrapped in sleep, I arose from bed, and, lamp in hand, stole through a wilderness of narrow passages from my own bedroom to that of my rival. I had long been plotting one of those ill-natured pieces of practical wit at his expense in which I had hitherto been so uniformly unsuccessful. It was my intention, now, to put my scheme in operation, and I resolved to make him feel the whole extent of the malice with which I was imbued. Having reached his closet, I noiselessly entered, leaving the lamp, with a shade over it, on the outside. I advanced a step, and listened to the sound of his tranquil breathing. Assured of his being asleep, I returned, took the light, and with it again approached the bed. Close curtains were around it, which, in the prosecution of my plan, I slowly and quietly withdrew, when the bright rays fell vividly upon the sleeper, and my eyes, at the same moment, upon his countenance. I looked;—and a numbness, an iciness of feeling instantly pervaded my frame. My breast heaved, my knees tottered, my whole spirit became possessed with an objectless yet intolerable horror. Gasping for breath, I lowered the lamp in still nearer proximity to the face. Were these,—*these* the lineaments of William Wilson? I saw, indeed, that they were his, but I shook as if with a fit of the ague, in fancying they were not. What *was* there about them to confound me in this manner? I gazed;—while my brain reeled with a multitude of incoherent thoughts. Not thus he appeared—assuredly not *thus*—in the vivacity of his waking hours. The same name! the same contour of person! the same day of arrival at the academy! And then his dogged and meaningless imitation of my gait, my voice, my habits, and my manner! Was it, in truth, within the bounds of human possibility, that what I now saw was the result, merely, of the habitual practice of this sarcastic imitation? Awe-stricken, and with a creeping shudder, I extinguished the lamp, passed silently from the chamber, and left, at once, the halls of that old academy, never to enter them again.

After a lapse of some months, spent at home in mere idleness, I found myself a student at Eton. The brief interval had been sufficient to enfeeble my remembrance of the events at Dr. Bransby's, or at least to effect a material change in the nature of the feelings with which I remembered them. The truth—the tragedy—of the drama was no more. I could now find room to doubt the evidence of my senses; and seldom called up the subject at all but with wonder at the extent of human credulity, and a smile at the vivid force of the imagination which I hereditarily possessed. Neither was this species of scepticism likely to be diminished by the character of the life I led at Eton. The vortex of thoughtless folly into which I there so immediately and so recklessly plunged, washed away all but the froth of my past hours, ingulfed at once every solid or serious impression, and left to memory only the veriest levities of a former existence.

I do not wish, however, to trace the course of my miserable profligacy here—a profligacy which set at defiance the laws, while it eluded the vigilance of the institution. Three years of folly, passed without profit, had but given me rooted habits of vice, and added, in a somewhat unusual degree, to my bodily stature, when, after a week of soulless dissipation, I invited a small party of the most dissolute students to a secret carousal in my chambers. We met at a late hour of the night; for our debaucheries were to be faithfully protracted until morning. The wine flowed freely, and there were not wanting other and perhaps more dangerous seductions; so that the gray dawn had already faintly appeared in the east, while our delirious extravagance was at its height. Madly flushed with cards and intoxication, I was in the act of insisting upon a toast of more than wonted profanity, when my attention was suddenly diverted by the violent, although partial unclosing of the door of the apartment, and by the eager voice of a servant from without. He said that some person, apparently in great haste, demanded to speak with me in the hall.

Wildly excited with wine, the unexpected interruption rather delighted than surprised me. I staggered forward at once, and a few steps brought me to the vestibule of the building. In this low and small room there hung no lamp; and now no light at all was admitted, save that of the exceedingly feeble dawn which made its way through the semi-circular window. As I put my foot over the threshold, I became aware of the figure of a youth about my own height, and habited in a white kerseymere morning frock, cut in the novel fashion of the one I myself wore at the moment. This the faint light enabled me to perceive; but the features of his face I could not distinguish. Upon my entering, he strode hurriedly up to me, and, seizing me by the arm with a gesture of petulant impatience, whispered the words "William Wilson!" in my ear.

I grew perfectly sober in an instant.

There was that in the manner of the stranger, and in the tremulous shake of his uplifted finger, as he held it between my eyes and the light, which filled me with unqualified amazement; but it was not this which had so violently moved me. It was the pregnancy of solemn admonition in the singular, low, hissing utterance; and, above all, it was the character, the tone, *the key*, of those few, simple, and familiar, yet *whispered* syllables, which came with a thousand thronging memories of bygone days, and struck upon my soul with the shock of a galvanic battery. Ere I could recover the use of my senses he was gone.

Although this event failed not of a vivid effect upon my disordered imagination, yet was it evanescent as vivid. For some weeks, indeed, I busied myself in earnest inquiry, or was wrapped in a cloud of morbid speculation. I did not pretend to disguise from my perception the identity of the singular individual who thus perseveringly interfered with my affairs, and harassed me with his insinuated counsel. But who and what was this Wilson?—and whence came he?—and what were his purposes? Upon neither of these points could I be satisfied—merely ascertaining, in regard to him, that a sudden accident in his family had caused his removal from Dr. Bransby's academy on the afternoon of the day in which I myself had eloped. But in a brief period I ceased to think upon the subject, my attention being all absorbed in a contemplated departure for Oxford. Thither I soon went; the uncalculating vanity of my parents furnishing me with an outfit and annual establishment, which would enable me to indulge at will in the luxury already so dear to my heart—to vie in profuseness of expenditure with the haughtiest heirs of the wealthiest earldoms in Great Britain.

Excited by such appliances to vice, my constitutional temperament broke forth with redoubled ardor, and I spurned even the common restraints of decency in the mad infatuation of my revels. But it were absurd to pause in the detail of my extravagance. Let it suffice, that among spendthrifts I out-Heroded Herod, and that, giving name to a multitude of novel follies, I added no brief appendix to the long catalogue of vices then usual in the most dissolute university of Europe.

It could hardly be credited, however, that I had, even here, so utterly fallen from the gentlemanly estate, as to seek acquaintance with the vilest arts of the gambler by profession, and, having become an adept in his despicable science, to practise it habitually as a means of increasing my already enormous income at the expense of the weak-minded among my fellow-collegians. Such, nevertheless, was the fact. And the very enormity of this offence against all manly and honorable sentiment proved, beyond doubt, the main if not the sole reason of the impunity with which it was committed. Who, indeed, among my most abandoned associates, would not rather have disputed the clearest evidence of his senses, than have suspected of such courses, the gay, the frank, the generous William Wilson—the noblest and most liberal commoner at Oxford—him whose follies (said his parasites) were but the follies of youth and unbridled fancy—whose errors but inimitable whim—whose darkest vice but a careless and dashing extravagance?

I had been now two years successfully busied in this way, when there came to the university a young *parvenu* nobleman, Glendinning—rich, said report, as Herodes Atticus—his riches, too, as easily acquired. I soon found him of weak intellect, and, of course, marked him as a fitting subject for my skill. I frequently engaged him in play, and contrived, with the gambler's usual art, to let him win considerable sums, the more effectually to entangle him in my snares. At length, my schemes being ripe, I met him (with the full intention that this meeting should be final and decisive) at the chambers of a fellow-commoner, (Mr. Preston,) equally intimate with both, but who, to do him justice, entertained not even a remote suspicion of my design. To give to this a better coloring, I had contrived to have assembled a party of some eight or ten, and was solicitously careful that the introduction of cards should appear accidental, and originate in the proposal of my contemplated dupe himself. To be brief upon a vile topic, none of the low finesse was omitted, so customary upon similar occasions that it is a just matter for wonder how any are still found so besotted as to fall its victim.

We had protracted our sitting far into the night, and I had at length effected the manœuvre of getting Glendinning as my sole antagonist. The game, too, was my favorite *écarté*. The rest of the company, interested in the extent of our play, had abandoned their own cards, and were standing around us as spectators. The *parvenu*, who had been induced by my artifices in the early part of the evening, to drink deeply, now shuffled, dealt, or played, with a wild nervousness of manner for which his intoxication, I thought, might partially, but could not altogether account. In a very short period he had become my debtor to a large amount, when, having taken a long draught of port, he did precisely what I had been coolly anticipating—he proposed to double our already extravagant stakes. With a well-feigned show of reluctance, and not until after my repeated refusal had seduced him into some angry words which gave a color of *pique* to my compliance, did I finally comply. The result, of course, did but prove how entirely the prey was in my toils; in less than an hour he had quadrupled his debt. For some time his countenance had been losing the florid tinge lent it by the wine; but now, to my astonishment, I perceived that it had grown to a pallor truly fearful. I say, to my astonishment. Glendinning had been represented to my eager inquiries as immeasurably wealthy; and the sums which he had as yet lost, although in themselves vast, could not, I supposed, very seriously annoy, much less so violently affect him. That he was overcome by the wine just swallowed, was the idea which most readily presented itself; and, rather with a view to the preservation of my own character in the eyes of my associates, than from any less interested motive, I was about to insist, peremptorily, upon a discontinuance of the play, when some expressions at my elbow from among the company, and an ejaculation evincing utter despair on the part of Glendinning, gave me to understand that I had effected his total ruin under circumstances which, rendering him an object for the pity of all, should have protected him from the ill offices even of a fiend.

What now might have been my conduct it is difficult to say. The pitiable condition of my dupe had thrown an air of embarrassed gloom over all; and, for some moments, a profound silence was maintained, during which I could not help feeling my cheeks tingle with the many burning glances of scorn or reproach cast upon me by the less abandoned of the party. I will even own that an intolerable weight of anxiety was for a brief instant lifted from my bosom by the sudden and extraordinary interruption which ensued. The wide, heavy folding doors of the apartment were all at once thrown open, to their full extent, with a vigorous and rushing impetuosity that extinguished, as if by magic, every candle in the room. Their light, in dying, enabled us just to perceive that a stranger had entered, about my own height, and closely muffled in a cloak. The darkness, however, was now total; and we could only *feel* that he was standing in our midst. Before any one of us could recover from the extreme astonishment into which this rudeness had thrown all, we heard the voice of the intruder.

"Gentlemen," he said, in a low, distinct, and never-to-be-forgotten *whisper* which thrilled to the very marrow of my bones, "Gentlemen, I make no apology for this behaviour, because in thus behaving, I am but fulfilling a duty. You are, beyond doubt, uninformed of the true character of the person who has to-night won at *écarté* a large sum of money from Lord Glendinning. I will therefore put you upon an expeditious and decisive plan of obtaining this very necessary information. Please to examine, at your leisure, the inner linings of the cuff of his left sleeve, and the several little packages which may be found in the somewhat capacious pockets of his embroidered morning wrapper."

While he spoke, so profound was the stillness that one might have heard a pin drop upon the floor. In ceasing, he departed at once, and as abruptly as he had entered. Can I—shall I describe my sensations? Must I say that I felt all the horrors of the damned? Most assuredly I had little time given for reflection. Many hands roughly seized me upon the spot, and lights were immediately reprocured. A search ensued. In the lining of my sleeve were found all the court cards essential in *écarté*, and, in the pockets of my wrapper, a number of packs, fac-similes of those used at our sittings, with the single exception that mine were of the species called, technically, *arrondées*; the honors being slightly convex at the ends, the lower cards slightly convex at the sides. In this dispo-sition, the dupe who cuts, as customary, at the length of the pack, will invariably find that he cuts his antagonist an honor; while the gambler, cutting at the breadth, will, as certainly, cut nothing for his victim which may count in the records of the game.

Any burst of indignation upon this discovery would have af-fected me less than the silent contempt, or the sarcastic compo-sure, with which it was received.

"Mr. Wilson," said our host, stooping to remove from beneath his feet an exceedingly luxurious cloak of rare furs, "Mr. Wilson, this is your property." (The weather was cold; and, upon quitting my own room, I had thrown a cloak over my dressing wrapper, putting it off upon reaching the scene of play.) "I presume it is supererogatory to seek here (eyeing the folds of the garment with a bitter smile) for any farther evidence of your skill. Indeed, we have had enough. You will see the necessity, I hope, of quitting Oxford—at all events, of quitting instantly my chambers."

Abased, humbled to the dust as I then was, it is probable that I should have resented this galling language by immediate personal violence, had not my whole attention been at the moment arrested by a fact of the most startling character. The cloak which I had worn was of a rare description of fur; how rare, how extrava-gantly costly, I shall not venture to say. Its fashion, too, was of my own fantastic invention; for I was fastidious to an absurd degree of coxcombry, in matters of this frivolous nature. When, there-fore, Mr. Preston reached me that which he had picked up upon the floor, and near the folding-doors of the apartment, it was with an astonishment nearly bordering upon terror, that I perceived my own already hanging on my arm, (where I had no doubt unwit-tingly placed it,) and that the one presented me was but its exact counterpart in every, in even the minutest possible particular. The singular being who had so disastrously exposed me, had been muffled, I remembered, in a cloak; and none had been worn at all by any of the members of our party with the exception of myself. Retaining some presence of mind, I took the one offered me by Preston; placed it, unnoticed, over my own; left the apartment with a resolute scowl of defiance; and, next morning ere dawn of day, commenced a hurried journey from Oxford to the continent, in a perfect agony of horror and of shame.

I fled in vain. My evil destiny pursued me as if in exultation, and proved, indeed, that the exercise of its mysterious dominion had as yet only begun. Scarcely had I set foot in Paris ere I had fresh evidence of the detestable interest taken by this Wilson in my concerns. Years flew, while I experienced no relief. Villain!—at Rome, with how untimely, yet with how spectral an officiousness, stepped he in between me and my ambition! At Vienna, too—at Berlin—and at Moscow! Where, in truth, had I *not* bitter cause to curse him within my heart? From his inscrutable tyranny did I at length flee, panic-stricken, as from a pestilence; and to the very ends of the earth *I fled in vain.*

And again, and again, in secret communion with my own spirit, would I demand the questions "Who is he?—whence came he?—and what are his objects?" But no answer was there found. And now I scrutinized, with a minute scrutiny, the forms, and the methods, and the leading traits of his impertinent supervision. But even here there was very little upon which to base a conjecture. It was noticeable, indeed, that, in no one of the multiplied instances in which he had of late crossed my path, had he so crossed it except to frustrate those schemes, or to disturb those actions, which, if fully carried out, might have resulted in bitter mischief. Poor justification this, in truth, for an authority so imperiously assumed! Poor indemnity for natural rights of self-agency so pertinaciously, so insultingly denied!

I had also been forced to notice that my tormentor, for a very long period of time, (while scrupulously and with miraculous dexterity maintaining his whim of an identity of apparel with myself,) had so contrived it, in the execution of his varied interference with my will, that I saw not, at any moment, the features of his face. Be Wilson what he might, *this*, at least, was but the veriest of affectation, or of folly. Could he, for an instant, have supposed that, in my admonisher at Eton—in the destroyer of my honor at Oxford,—in him who thwarted my ambition at Rome, my revenge at Paris, my passionate love at Naples, or what he falsely termed my avarice in Egypt,—that in this, my arch-enemy and evil genius, could fail to recognise the William Wilson of my school-boy days,—the namesake, the companion, the rival,—the hated and dreaded rival at Dr. Bransby's? Impossible!—But let me hasten to the last eventful scene of the drama.

Thus far I had succumbed supinely to this imperious domination. The sentiment of deep awe with which I habitually regarded the elevated character, the majestic wisdom, the apparent omnipresence and omnipotence of Wilson, added to a feeling of even terror, with which certain other traits in his nature and assumptions inspired me, had operated, hitherto, to impress me with an idea of my own utter weakness and helplessness, and to suggest an implicit, although bitterly reluctant submission to his arbitrary will. But, of late days, I had given myself up entirely to wine; and its maddening influence upon my hereditary temper rendered me more and more impatient of control. I began to murmur,—to hesitate,—to resist. And was it only fancy which induced me to believe that, with the increase of my own firmness, that of my tormentor underwent a proportional diminution? Be this as it may, I now began to feel the inspiration of a burning hope, and at length nurtured in my secret thoughts a stern and desperate resolution that I would submit no longer to be enslaved.

It was at Rome, during the Carnival of 18—, that I attended a masquerade in the palazzo of the Neapolitan Duke Di Broglio. I had indulged more freely than usual in the excesses of the wine-table; and now the suffocating atmosphere of the crowded rooms irritated me beyond endurance. The difficulty, too, of forcing my way through the mazes of the company contributed not a little to the ruffling of my temper; for I was anxiously seeking, (let me not say with what unworthy motive) the young, the gay, the beautiful wife of the aged and doting Di Broglio. With a too unscrupulous confidence she had previously communicated to me the secret of the costume in which she would be habited, and now, having caught a glimpse of her person, I was hurrying to make my way into her presence. At this moment I felt a light hand placed upon my shoulder, and that ever-remembered, low, damnable *whisper* within my ear.

In an absolute frenzy of wrath, I turned at once upon him who had thus interrupted me, and seized him violently by the collar. He was attired, as I had expected, in a costume altogether similar to my own; wearing a Spanish cloak of blue velvet, begirt about the waist with a crimson belt sustaining a rapier. A mask of black silk entirely covered his face.

"Scoundrel!" I said, in a voice husky with rage, while every syllable I uttered seemed as new fuel to my fury; "scoundrel! impostor! accursed villain! you shall not—you *shall not* dog me unto death! Follow me, or I stab you where you stand!"—and I broke my way from the ball-room into a small ante-chamber adjoining—dragging him unresistingly with me as I went.

Upon entering, I thrust him furiously from me. He staggered against the wall, while I closed the door with an oath, and commanded him to draw. He hesitated but for an instant; then, with a slight sigh, drew in silence, and put himself upon his defence.

The contest was brief indeed. I was frantic with every species of wild excitement, and felt within my single arm the energy and power of a multitude. In a few seconds I forced him by sheer strength against the wainscoting, and thus, getting him at mercy, plunged my sword, with brute ferocity, repeatedly through and through his bosom.

At that instant some person tried the latch of the door. I hastened to prevent an intrusion, and then immediately returned to my dying antagonist. But what human language can adequately portray *that* astonishment, *that* horror which possessed me at the spectacle then presented to view? The brief moment in which I averted my eyes had been sufficient to produce, apparently, a material change in the arrangements at the upper or farther end of the room. A large mirror,—so at first it seemed to me in my confusion—now stood where none had been perceptible before; and, as I stepped up to it in extremity of terror, mine own image, but with features all pale and dabbled in blood, advanced to meet me with a feeble and tottering gait.

Thus it appeared, I say, but was not. It was my antagonist—it was Wilson, who then stood before me in the agonies of his dissolution. His mask and cloak lay, where he had thrown them, upon the floor. Not a thread in all his raiment—not a line in all the marked and singular lineaments of his face which was not, even in the most absolute identity, *mine own!*

It was Wilson; but he spoke no longer in a whisper, and I could have fancied that I myself was speaking while he said:

"*You have conquered, and I yield. Yet, henceforward art thou also dead—dead to the World, to Heaven and to Hope! In me didst thou exist—and, in my death, see by this image, which is thine own, how utterly thou hast murdered thyself.*"

THE TELL-TALE HEART

True!—nervous—very, very dreadfully nervous I had been and am; but why *will* you say that I am mad? The disease had sharpened my senses—not destroyed—not dulled them. Above all was the sense of hearing acute. I heard all things in the heaven and in the earth. I heard many things in hell. How, then, am I mad? Hearken! and observe how healthily—how calmly I can tell you the whole story.

It is impossible to say how first the idea entered my brain; but once conceived, it haunted me day and night. Object there was none. Passion there was none. I loved the old man. He had never wronged me. He had never given me insult. For his gold I had no desire. I think it was his eye! yes, it was this! One of his eyes resembled that of a vulture—a pale blue eye, with a film over it. Whenever it fell upon me, my blood ran cold; and so by degrees—very gradually—I made up my mind to take the life of the old man, and thus rid myself of the eye forever.

Now this is the point. You fancy me mad. Madmen know nothing. But you should have seen *me*. You should have seen how wisely I proceeded—with what caution—with what foresight—with what dissimulation I went to work! I was never kinder to the old man than during the whole week before I killed him. And every night, about midnight, I turned the latch of his door and opened it—oh, so gently! And then, when I had made an opening sufficient for my head, I put in a dark lantern, all closed, closed, so that no light shone out, and then I thrust in my head. Oh, you would have laughed to see how cunningly I thrust it in! I moved it slowly—very, very slowly, so that I might not disturb the old man's sleep. It took me an hour to place my whole head within the opening so far that I could see him as he lay upon his bed. Ha!—

would a madman have been so wise as this? And then, when my head was well in the room, I undid the lantern cautiously—oh, so cautiously—cautiously (for the hinges creaked)—I undid it just so much that a single thin ray fell upon the vulture eye. And this I did for seven long nights—every night just at midnight—but I found the eye always closed; and so it was impossible to do the work; for it was not the old man who vexed me, but his Evil Eye. And every morning, when the day broke, I went boldly into the chamber, and spoke courageously to him, calling him by name in a hearty tone, and inquiring how he had passed the night. So you see he would have been a very profound old man, indeed, to suspect that every night, just at twelve, I looked in upon him while he slept.

Upon the eighth night I was more than usually cautious in opening the door. A watch's minute hand moves more quickly than did mine. Never before that night had I *felt* the extent of my own powers—of my sagacity. I could scarcely contain my feelings of triumph. To think that there I was, opening the door, little by little, and he not even to dream of my secret deeds or thoughts. I fairly chuckled at the idea; and perhaps he heard me; for he moved on the bed suddenly, as if startled. Now you may think that I drew back—but no. His room was as black as pitch with the thick darkness, (for the shutters were close fastened, through fear of robbers,) and so I knew that he could not see the opening of the door, and I kept pushing it on steadily, steadily.

I had my head in, and was about to open the lantern, when my thumb slipped upon the tin fastening, and the old man sprang up in the bed, crying out—"Who's there?"

I kept quite still and said nothing. For a whole hour I did not move a muscle, and in the meantime I did not hear him lie down. He was still sitting up in the bed listening;—just as I have done, night after night, hearkening to the death watches in the wall.[1]

Presently I heard a slight groan, and I knew it was the groan of mortal terror. It was not a groan of pain or of grief—oh, no!—it was the low stifled sound that arises from the bottom of the soul when overcharged with awe. I knew the sound well. Many a night, just at midnight, when all the world slept, it has welled up from my own bosom, deepening, with its dreadful echo, the terrors that distracted me. I say I knew it well. I knew what the old man felt, and pitied him, although I chuckled at heart. I knew that he had been lying awake ever since the first slight noise, when he had turned in the bed. His fears had been ever since growing upon him. He had been trying to fancy them causeless, but could not. He had been saying to himself—"It is nothing but the wind in the chimney—it is only a mouse crossing the floor," or "it is merely a cricket which has made a single chirp." Yes, he has been trying to comfort himself with these suppositions: but he had found all in vain. *All in vain*; because Death, in approaching him, had stalked with his black shadow before him, and enveloped the victim. And it was the mournful influence of the unperceived shadow that caused him to feel—although he neither saw nor heard—to *feel* the presence of my head within the room.

When I had waited a long time, very patiently, without hearing him lie down, I resolved to open a little—a very, very little crevice in the lantern. So I opened it—you cannot imagine how stealthily, stealthily—until, at length a single dim ray, like the thread of the spider, shot from out the crevice and fell upon the vulture eye.

It was open—wide, wide open—and I grew furious as I gazed upon it. I saw it with perfect distinctness—all a dull blue, with a hideous veil over it that chilled the very marrow in my bones; but I could see nothing else of the old man's face or person: for I had directed the ray as if by instinct, precisely upon the damned spot.

And now have I not told you that what you mistake for madness is but over acuteness of the senses?—now, I say, there came to my ears a low, dull, quick sound, such as a watch makes when enveloped in cotton. I knew *that* sound well, too. It was the beating of the old man's heart. It increased my fury, as the beating of a drum stimulates the soldier into courage.

But even yet I refrained and kept still. I scarcely breathed. I held the lantern motionless. I tried how steadily I could maintain the ray upon the eye. Meantime the hellish tattoo of the heart increased. It grew quicker and quicker, and louder and louder every instant. The old man's terror *must* have been extreme! It grew louder, I say, louder every moment!—do you mark me well? I have told you that I am nervous: so I am. And now at the dead hour of the night, amid the dreadful silence of that old house, so strange a noise as this excited me to uncontrollable terror. Yet, for some minutes longer I refrained and stood still. But the beating grew louder, louder! I thought the heart must burst. And now a new anxiety seized me—the sound would be heard by a neighbor! The old man's hour had come! With a loud yell, I threw open the lantern and leaped into the room. He shrieked once—once only. In an instant I dragged him to the floor, and pulled the heavy bed over him. I then smiled gaily, to find the deed so far done. But, for many minutes, the heart beat on with a muffled sound. This, however, did not vex me; it would not be heard through the wall. At length it ceased. The old man was dead. I removed the bed and examined the corpse. Yes, he was stone, stone dead. I placed my hand upon the heart and held it there many minutes. There was no pulsation. He was stone dead. His eye would trouble me no more.

If still you think me mad, you will think so no longer when I describe the wise precautions I took for the concealment of the body. The night waned, and I worked hastily, but in silence. First of all I dismembered the corpse. I cut off the head and the arms and the legs.

I then took up three planks from the flooring of the chamber, and deposited all between the scantlings. I then replaced the boards so cleverly, so cunningly, that no human eye—not even *his*—could have detected any thing wrong. There was nothing to wash out—no stain of any kind—no blood-spot whatever. I had been too wary for that. A tub had caught all—ha! ha!

When I had made an end of these labors, it was four o'clock—still dark as midnight. As the bell sounded the hour, there came a knocking at the street door. I went down to open it with a light heart,—for what had I *now* to fear? There entered three men, who introduced themselves, with perfect suavity, as officers of the police. A shriek had been heard by a neighbor during the night; suspicion of foul play had been aroused; information had been lodged at the police office, and they (the officers) had been deputed to search the premises.

I smiled,—for *what* had I to fear? I bade the gentlemen welcome. The shriek, I said, was my own in a dream. The old man, I mentioned, was absent in the country. I took my visitors all over the house. I bade them search—search *well*. I led them, at length, to *his* chamber. I showed them his treasures, secure, undisturbed. In the enthusiasm of my confidence, I brought chairs into the room, and desired them *here* to rest from their fatigues, while

I myself, in the wild audacity of my perfect triumph, placed my own seat upon the very spot beneath which reposed the corpse of the victim.

The officers were satisfied. My *manner* had convinced them. I was singularly at ease. They sat, and while I answered cheerily, they chatted of familiar things. But, ere long, I felt myself getting pale and wished them gone. My head ached, and I fancied a ringing in my ears: but still they sat and still chatted. The ringing became more distinct:—it continued and became more distinct: I talked more freely to get rid of the feeling: but it continued and gained definitiveness—until, at length, I found that the noise was *not* within my ears.

No doubt I now grew *very* pale;—but I talked more fluently, and with a heightened voice. Yet the sound increased—and what could I do? It was *a low, dull, quick sound—much such a sound as a watch makes when enveloped in cotton.* I gasped for breath—and yet the officers heard it not. I talked more quickly—more vehemently; but the noise steadily increased. I arose and argued about trifles, in a high key and with violent gesticulations; but the noise steadily increased. Why *would* they not be gone? I paced the floor to and fro with heavy strides, as if excited to fury by the observations of the men—but the noise steadily increased. Oh God! what *could* I do? I foamed—I raved—I swore! I swung the chair upon which I had been sitting, and grated it upon the boards, but the noise arose over all and continually increased. It grew louder—louder—*louder!* And still the men chatted pleasantly, and smiled. Was it possible they heard not? Almighty God!—no, no! They heard!—they suspected!—they *knew!*—they were making a mockery of my horror!—this I thought, and this I think. But anything was better than this agony! Anything was more tolerable than this derision! I could bear those hypocritical smiles no longer! I felt that I must scream or die!—and now—again!—hark! louder! louder! louder! *louder!*—

"Villains!" I shrieked, "dissemble no more! I admit the deed!—tear up the planks!—here, here!—it is the beating of his hideous heart!"

THE BLACK CAT

For the most wild, yet most homely narrative which I am about to pen, I neither expect nor solicit belief. Mad indeed would I be to expect it, in a case where my very senses reject their own evidence. Yet, mad am I not—and very surely do I not dream. But to-morrow I die, and to-day I would unburthen my soul. My immediate purpose is to place before the world, plainly, succinctly, and without comment, a series of mere household events. In their consequences, these events have terrified—have tortured—have destroyed me. Yet I will not attempt to expound them. To me, they have presented little but Horror—to many they will seem less terrible than *baroques*. Hereafter, perhaps, some intellect may be found which will reduce my phantasm to the common-place—some intellect more calm, more logical, and far less excitable than my own, which will perceive, in the circumstances I detail with awe, nothing more than an ordinary succession of very natural causes and effects.

From my infancy I was noted for the docility and humanity of my disposition. My tenderness of heart was even so conspicuous as to make me the jest of my companions. I was especially fond of animals, and was indulged by my parents with a great variety of pets. With these I spent most of my time, and never was so happy as when feeding and caressing them. This peculiarity of character grew with my growth, and, in my manhood, I derived from it one of my principal sources of pleasure. To those who have cherished an affection for a faithful and sagacious dog, I need hardly be at the trouble of explaining the nature or the intensity of the gratification thus derivable. There is something in the unselfish and self-sacrificing love of a brute, which goes directly to the heart of him who has had frequent occasion to test the paltry friendship and gossamer fidelity of mere *Man*.

I married early, and was happy to find in my wife a disposition not uncongenial with my own. Observing my partiality for domestic pets, she lost no opportunity of procuring those of the most agreeable kind. We had birds, gold-fish, a fine dog, rabbits, a small monkey, and *a cat*.

This latter was a remarkably large and beautiful animal, entirely black, and sagacious to an astonishing degree. In speaking of his intelligence, my wife, who at heart was not a little tinctured with superstition, made frequent allusion to the ancient popular notion, which regarded all black cats as witches in disguise. Not that she was ever *serious* upon this point—and I mention the matter at all for no better reason than that it happens, just now, to be remembered.

Pluto—this was the cat's name—was my favorite pet and playmate. I alone fed him, and he attended me wherever I went about the house. It was even with difficulty that I could prevent him from following me through the streets.

Our friendship lasted, in this manner, for several years, during which my general temperament and character—through the instrumentality of the Fiend Intemperance—had (I blush to confess it) experienced a radical alteration for the worse. I grew, day by day, more moody, more irritable, more regardless of the feelings of others. I suffered myself to use intemperate language to my wife. At length, I even offered her personal violence. My pets, of course, were made to feel the change in my disposition. I not only neglected, but ill-used them. For Pluto, however, I still retained sufficient regard to restrain me from maltreating him, as I made no scruple of maltreating the rabbits, the monkey, or even the dog, when by accident, or through affection, they came in my way. But my disease grew upon me—for what disease is like Alcohol!—and at length even Pluto, who was now becoming old, and consequently somewhat peevish—even Pluto began to experience the effects of my ill temper.

One night, returning home, much intoxicated, from one of my haunts about town, I fancied that the cat avoided my presence. I seized him; when, in his fright at my violence, he inflicted a slight wound upon my hand with his teeth. The fury of a demon instantly possessed me. I knew myself no longer. My original soul seemed, at once, to take its flight from my body; and a more than fiendish malevolence, gin-nurtured, thrilled every fibre of my frame. I took from my waistcoat-pocket a pen-knife, opened it, grasped the poor beast by the throat, and deliberately cut one of its eyes from the socket! I blush, I burn, I shudder, while I pen the damnable atrocity.

When reason returned with the morning—when I had slept off the fumes of the night's debauch—I experienced a sentiment half of horror, half of remorse, for the crime of which I had been guilty; but it was, at best, a feeble and equivocal feeling, and the soul remained untouched. I again plunged into excess, and soon drowned in wine all memory of the deed.

In the meantime the cat slowly recovered. The socket of the lost eye presented, it is true, a frightful appearance, but he no longer appeared to suffer any pain. He went about the house as usual, but, as might be expected, fled in extreme terror at my approach. I had so much of my old heart left, as to be at first grieved by this evident dislike on the part of a creature which had once so loved me. But this feeling soon gave place to irritation. And then came, as if to my final and irrevocable overthrow, the spirit of PERVERSE-NESS. Of this spirit philosophy takes no account. Yet I am not more sure that my soul lives, than I am that perverseness is one of the primitive impulses of the human heart—one of the indivisible primary faculties, or sentiments, which give direction to the character of Man. Who has not, a hundred times, found himself committing a vile or a silly action, for no other reason than because he knows he should *not*? Have we not a perpetual inclination, in the teeth of our best judgment, to violate that which is *Law*, merely because we understand it to be such? This spirit of perverseness, I say, came to my final overthrow. It was this unfathomable longing of the soul *to vex itself*—to offer violence to its own nature—to do wrong for the wrong's sake only—that urged me to continue and finally to consummate the injury I had inflicted upon the unoffending brute. One morning, in cool blood, I slipped a noose about its neck and hung it to the limb of a tree;—hung it with the tears streaming from my eyes, and with the bitterest remorse at my heart;—hung it *because* I knew that it had loved me, and *because* I felt it had given me no reason of offence;—hung it *because* I knew that in so doing I was committing a sin—a deadly sin that would so jeopardize my immortal soul as to place it—if such a thing were possible—even beyond the reach of the infinite mercy of the Most Merciful and Most Terrible God.

On the night of the day on which this cruel deed was done, I was aroused from sleep by the cry of fire. The curtains of my bed were in flames. The whole house was blazing. It was with great difficulty that my wife, a servant, and myself, made our escape from the conflagration. The destruction was complete. My entire worldly wealth was swallowed up, and I resigned myself thenceforward to despair.

I am above the weakness of seeking to establish a sequence of cause and effect, between the disaster and the atrocity. But I am detailing a chain of facts—and wish not to leave even a possible link imperfect. On the day succeeding the fire, I visited the ruins. The walls, with one exception, had fallen in. This exception was found in a compartment wall, not very thick, which stood about the middle of the house, and against which had rested the head of my bed. The plastering had here, in great measure, resisted the action of the fire—a fact which I attributed to its having been recently spread. About this wall a dense crowd were collected, and many persons seemed to be examining a particular portion of it with very minute and eager attention. The words "strange!" "singular!" and other similar expressions, excited my curiosity. I approached and saw, as if graven in *bas relief* upon the white surface, the figure of a gigantic *cat*. The impression was given with an accuracy truly marvellous. There was a rope about the animal's neck.

When I first beheld this apparition—for I could scarcely regard it as less—my wonder and my terror were extreme. But at length reflection came to my aid. The cat, I remembered, had been hung in a garden adjacent to the house. Upon the alarm of fire, this garden had been immediately filled by the crowd—by some one of whom the animal must have been cut from the tree and thrown, through an open window, into my chamber. This had probably been done with the view of arousing me from sleep. The falling of other walls had compressed the victim of my cruelty into the substance of the freshly-spread plaster; the lime of which, with the flames, and the *ammonia* from the carcass, had then accomplished the portraiture as I saw it.

Although I thus readily accounted to my reason, if not altogether to my conscience, for the startling fact just detailed, it did not the less fail to make a deep impression upon my fancy. For months I could not rid myself of the phantasm of the cat; and, during this period, there came back into my spirit a half-sentiment that seemed, but was not, remorse. I went so far as to regret the loss of the animal, and to look about me, among the vile haunts which I now habitually frequented, for another pet of the same species, and of somewhat similar appearance, with which to supply its place.

One night as I sat, half stupified, in a den of more than infamy, my attention was suddenly drawn to some black object, reposing upon the head of one of the immense hogsheads of Gin, or of Rum, which constituted the chief furniture of the apartment. I had been looking steadily at the top of this hogshead for some minutes, and what now caused me surprise was the fact that I had not sooner perceived the object thereupon. I approached it, and touched it with my hand. It was a black cat—a very large one—fully as large as Pluto, and closely resembling him in every respect but one. Pluto had not a white hair upon any portion of his body; but this cat had a large, although indefinite splotch of white, covering nearly the whole region of the breast.

Upon my touching him, he immediately arose, purred loudly, rubbed against my hand, and appeared delighted with my notice. This, then, was the very creature of which I was in search. I at once offered to purchase it off the landlord; but this person made no claim to it—knew nothing of it—had never seen it before.

I continued my caresses, and, when I prepared to go home, the animal evinced a disposition to accompany me. I permitted it to do so; occasionally stooping and patting it as I proceeded. When it reached the house it domesticated itself at once, and became immediately a great favorite with my wife.

For my own part, I soon found a dislike to it arising within me. This was just the reverse of what I had anticipated; but—I know not how or why it was—its evident fondness for myself rather disgusted and annoyed. By slow degrees, these feelings of disgust and annoyance rose into the bitterness of hatred. I avoided the creature; a certain sense of shame, and the remembrance of my former deed of cruelty, preventing me from physically abusing it. I did not, for some weeks, strike, or otherwise violently ill use it; but gradually—very gradually—I came to look upon it with unutterable loathing, and to flee silently from its odious presence, as from the breath of a pestilence.

What added, no doubt, to my hatred of the beast, was the discovery, on the morning after I brought it home, that, like Pluto, it also had been deprived of one of its eyes. This circumstance, however, only endeared it to my wife, who, as I have already said, possessed, in a high degree, that humanity of feeling which had once been my distinguishing trait, and the source of many of my simplest and purest pleasures.

With my aversion to this cat, however, its partiality for myself seemed to increase. It followed my footsteps with a pertinacity which it would be difficult to make the reader comprehend. Whenever I sat, it would crouch beneath my chair, or spring upon my knees, covering me with its loathsome caresses. If I arose to walk it would get between my feet and thus nearly throw me down, or, fastening its long and sharp claws in my dress, clamber, in this manner, to my breast. At such times, although I longed to destroy it with a blow, I was yet withheld from so doing, partly by a memory of my former crime, but chiefly—let me confess it at once—by absolute *dread* of the beast.

This dread was not exactly a dread of physical evil—and yet I should be at a loss how otherwise to define it. I am almost ashamed to own—yes, even in this felon's cell, I am almost ashamed to own—that the terror and horror with which the animal inspired me, had been heightened by one of the merest chimæras it would be possible to conceive. My wife had called my attention, more than once, to the character of the mark of white hair, of which I have spoken, and which constituted the sole visible difference between the strange beast and the one I had destroyed. The reader will remember that this mark, although large, had been originally very indefinite; but, by slow degrees—degrees nearly imperceptible, and which for a long time my Reason struggled to reject as fanciful—it had, at length, assumed a rigorous distinctness of outline. It was now the representation of an object that I shudder to name—and for this, above all, I loathed, and dreaded, and would have rid myself of the monster *had I dared*—it was now, I say, the image of a hideous—of a ghastly thing—of the GALLOWS!—oh, mournful and terrible engine of Horror and of Crime—of Agony and of Death !

And now was I indeed wretched beyond the wretchedness of mere Humanity. And *a brute beast*—whose fellow I had contemptuously destroyed—*a brute beast* to work out for *me*—for me a man, fashioned in the image of the High God—so much of insufferable wo! Alas! neither by day nor by night knew I the blessing of Rest any more! During the former the creature left me no moment alone; and, in the latter, I started, hourly, from dreams of unutterable fear, to find the hot breath of *the thing* upon my face, and its vast weight—an incarnate Night-Mare that I had no power to shake off—incumbent eternally upon my *heart*!

Beneath the pressure of torments such as these, the feeble remnant of the good within me succumbed. Evil thoughts became my sole intimates—the darkest and most evil of thoughts. The moodiness of my usual temper increased to hatred of all things and of all mankind; while, from the sudden, frequent, and ungovernable outbursts of a fury to which I now blindly abandoned myself, my uncomplaining wife, alas! was the most usual and the most patient of sufferers.

One day she accompanied me, upon some household errand, into the cellar of the old building which our poverty compelled us to inhabit. The cat followed me down the steep stairs, and, nearly throwing me headlong, exasperated me to madness. Uplifting an axe, and forgetting, in my wrath, the childish dread which had hitherto stayed my hand, I aimed a blow at the animal which, of course, would have proved instantly fatal had it descended as I wished. But this blow was arrested by the hand of my wife. Goaded, by the interference, into a rage more than demoniacal, I withdrew my arm from her grasp and buried the axe in her brain. She fell dead upon the spot, without a groan.

This hideous murder accomplished, I set myself forthwith, and with entire deliberation, to the task of concealing the body. I knew that I could not remove it from the house, either by day or by night, without the risk of being observed by the neighbors. Many projects entered my mind. At one period I thought of cutting the corpse into minute fragments, and destroying them by fire. At another, I resolved to dig a grave for it in the floor of the cellar. Again, I deliberated about casting it in the well in the yard—about packing it in a box, as if merchandize, with the usual arrangements, and so getting a porter to take it from the house. Finally

I hit upon what I considered a far better expedient than either of these. I determined to wall it up in the cellar—as the monks of the middle ages are recorded to have walled up their victims.

For a purpose such as this the cellar was well adapted. Its walls were loosely constructed, and had lately been plastered throughout with a rough plaster, which the dampness of the atmosphere had prevented from hardening. Moreover, in one of the walls was a projection, caused by a false chimney, or fireplace, that had been filled up, and made to resemble the rest of the cellar. I made no doubt that I could readily displace the bricks at this point, insert the corpse, and wall the whole up as before, so that no eye could detect any thing suspicious.

And in this calculation I was not deceived. By means of a crowbar I easily dislodged the bricks, and, having carefully deposited the body against the inner wall, I propped it in that position, while, with little trouble, I re-laid the whole structure as it originally stood. Having procured mortar, sand, and hair, with every possible precaution, I prepared a plaster which could not be distinguished from the old, and with this I very carefully went over the new brick-work. When I had finished, I felt satisfied that all was right. The wall did not present the slightest appearance of having been disturbed. The rubbish on the floor was picked up with the minutest care. I looked around triumphantly, and said to myself—"Here at least, then, my labor has not been in vain."

My next step was to look for the beast which had been the cause of so much wretchedness; for I had, at length, firmly resolved to put it to death. Had I been able to meet with it, at the moment, there could have been no doubt of its fate; but it appeared that the crafty animal had been alarmed at the violence of my previous anger, and forebore to present itself in my present mood. It is impossible to describe, or to imagine, the deep, the blissful sense of relief which the absence of the detested creature occasioned in my bosom. It did not make its appearance during the night—and thus for one night at least, since its introduction into the house, I soundly and tranquilly slept; aye, *slept* even with the burden of murder upon my soul!

The second and the third day passed, and still my tormentor came not. Once again I breathed as a freeman. The monster, in terror, had fled the premises forever! I should behold it no more!

My happiness was supreme! The guilt of my dark deed disturbed me but little. Some few inquiries had been made, but these had been readily answered. Even a search had been instituted—but of course nothing was to be discovered. I looked upon my future felicity as secured.

Upon the fourth day of the assassination, a party of the police came, very unexpectedly, into the house, and proceeded again to make rigorous investigation of the premises. Secure, however, in the inscrutability of my place of concealment, I felt no embarrassment whatever. The officers bade me accompany them in their search. They left no nook or corner unexplored. At length, for the third or fourth time, they descended into the cellar. I quivered not in a muscle. My heart beat calmly as that of one who slumbers in innocence. I walked the cellar from end to end. I folded my arms upon my bosom, and roamed easily to and fro. The police were thoroughly satisfied and prepared to depart. The glee at my heart was too strong to be restrained. I burned to say if but one word, by way of triumph, and to render doubly sure their assurance of my guiltlessness.

"Gentlemen," I said at last, as the party ascended the steps, "I delight to have allayed your suspicions. I wish you all health, and a little more courtesy. By the bye, gentlemen, this—this is a very well constructed house." [In the rabid desire to say something easily, I scarcely knew what I uttered at all.]—"I may say an *excellently* well constructed house. These walls—are you going, gentlemen?—these walls are solidly put together;" and here, through the mere phrenzy of bravado, I rapped heavily, with a cane which I held in my hand, upon that very portion of the brick-work behind which stood the corpse of the wife of my bosom.

But may God shield and deliver me from the fangs of the Arch-Fiend! No sooner had the reverberation of my blows sunk into silence, than I was answered by a voice from within the tomb!—by a cry, at first muffled and broken, like the sobbing of a child, and then quickly swelling into one long, loud, and continuous scream, utterly anomalous and inhuman—a howl—a wailing shriek, half of horror and half of triumph, such as might have arisen only out of hell, conjointly from the throats of the damned in their agony and of the demons that exult in the damnation.

Of my own thoughts it is folly to speak. Swooning, I staggered to the opposite wall. For one instant the party upon the stairs remained motionless, through extremity of terror and of awe. In the next, a dozen stout arms were toiling at the wall. It fell bodily. The corpse, already greatly decayed and clotted with gore, stood erect before the eyes of the spectators. Upon its head, with red extended mouth and solitary eye of fire, sat the hideous beast whose craft had seduced me into murder, and whose informing voice had consigned me to the hangman. I had walled the monster up within the tomb!

THE IMP OF THE PERVERSE

In the consideration of the faculties and impulses—of the *prima mobilia* of the human soul, the phrenologists have failed to make room for a propensity which, although obviously existing as a radical, primitive, irreducible sentiment, has been equally overlooked by all the moralists who have preceded them. In the pure arrogance of the reason, we have all overlooked it. We have suffered its existence to escape our senses, solely through want of belief—of faith;—whether it be faith in Revelation, or faith in the Kabbala. The idea of it has never occurred to us, simply because of its supererogation. We saw no *need* of the impulse—for the propensity. We could not perceive its necessity. We could not understand, that is to say, we could not have understood, had the notion of this *primum mobile* ever obtruded itself;—we could not have understood in what manner it might be made to further the objects of humanity, either temporal or eternal. It cannot be denied that phrenology and, in great measure, all metaphysicianism have been concocted *à priori*. The intellectual or logical man, rather than the understanding or observant man, set himself to imagine designs—to dictate purposes to God. Having thus fathomed, to his satisfaction, the intentions of Jehovah, out of these intentions he built his innumerable systems of mind. In the matter of phrenology, for example, we first determined, naturally enough, that it was the design of the Deity that man should eat. We then assigned to man an organ of alimentiveness, and this organ is the scourge with which the Deity compels man, will-I nill-I, into eating. Secondly, having settled it to be God's will that man should continue his species, we discovered an organ of amativeness, forthwith. And so with combativeness, with ideality, with causality, with constructiveness,—so, in short, with every organ, whether representing a propensity, a moral sentiment, or a faculty of the pure intellect. And in these arrangements of the *principia* of human action, the Spurzheimites, whether right or wrong, in part, or upon the whole, have but followed, in principle, the footsteps of their predecessors; deducing and establishing everything from the preconceived destiny of man, and upon the ground of the objects of his Creator.[1]

It would have been wiser, it would have been safer to classify (if classify we must,) upon the basis of what man usually or occasionally did, and was always occasionally doing, rather than upon the basis of what we took it for granted the Deity intended him to do. If we cannot comprehend God in his visible works, how then in his inconceivable thoughts, that call the works into being? If we cannot understand him in his objective creatures, how then in his substantive moods and phases of creation?

Induction, *à posteriori,* would have brought phrenology to admit, as an innate and primitive principle of human action, a paradoxical something, which we may call *perverseness,* for want of a more characteristic term. In the sense I intend, it is, in fact, a *mobile* without motive, a motive not *motivirt.* Through its promptings we act without comprehensible object; or, if this shall be understood as a contradiction in terms, we may so far modify the proposition as to say, that through its promptings we act, for the reason that we should not. In theory, no reason can be more unreasonable, but, in fact, there is none more strong. With certain minds, under certain conditions, it becomes absolutely irresistible. I am not more certain that I breathe, than that the assurance of the wrong or error of any action is often the one unconquerable *force* which impels us, and alone impels us to its prosecution. Nor will this overwhelming tendency to do wrong for the wrong's sake, admit of analysis, or resolution into ulterior elements. It is a radical, a primitive impulse—elementary. It will be said, I am aware, that when we persist in acts because we feel we should *not* persist in them, our conduct is but a modification of that which ordinarily springs from the *combativeness* of phrenology. But a glance will show the fallacy of this idea. The phrenological combativeness has for its essence, the necessity of self-defence. It is our safeguard against injury. Its principle regards our well-being; and thus the desire to be well is excited simultaneously with its development. It follows, that the desire to be well must be excited simultaneously with any principle which shall be merely a modification of combativeness, but in the case of that something which I term *perverseness,* the desire to be well is not only not aroused, but a strongly antagonistical sentiment exists.

An appeal to one's own heart is, after all, the best reply to the sophistry just noticed. No one who trustingly consults and thoroughly questions his own soul, will be disposed to deny the entire radicalness of the propensity in question. It is not more incomprehensible than distinctive. There lives no man who at some period has not been tormented, for example, by an earnest desire to tantalize a listener by circumlocution. The speaker is aware that he displeases; he has every intention to please, he is usually curt, precise, and clear; the most laconic and luminous language is struggling for utterance upon his tongue, it is only with difficulty that he restrains himself from giving it flow; he dreads and deprecates the anger of him whom he addresses; yet, the thought strikes him, that by certain involutions and parentheses this anger may be engendered. That single thought is enough. The impulse increases to a wish, the wish to a desire, the desire to an uncontrollable longing, and the longing, (to the deep regret and mortification of the speaker, and in defiance of all consequences,) is indulged.

We have a task before us which must be speedily performed. We know that it will be ruinous to make delay. The most important crisis of our life calls, trumpet-tongued, for immediate energy and action. We glow, we are consumed with eagerness to commence the work, with the anticipation of whose glorious result our whole souls are on fire. It must, it shall be undertaken to-day, and yet we put it off until to-morrow; and why? There is no answer, except that we feel *perverse,* using the word with no comprehension of the principle. To-morrow arrives, and with it a more impatient anxiety to do our duty, but with this very increase of anxiety arrives, also, a nameless, a positively fearful, because unfathomable, craving for delay. This craving gathers strength as the moments fly. The last hour for action is at hand. We tremble with the violence of the conflict within us,—of the definite with the indefinite—of the substance with the shadow. But, if the contest have proceeded thus far, it is the shadow which prevails,—we struggle in vain. The clock strikes, and is the knell of our welfare. At the same time, it is the chanticleer-note to the ghost that has so long overawed us. It flies—it disappears—we are free. The old energy returns. We will labor now. Alas, it is *too late*!

We stand upon the brink of a precipice. We peer into the abyss—we grow sick and dizzy. Our first impulse is to shrink from the danger. Unaccountably we remain. By slow degrees our sickness, and dizziness, and horror, become merged in a cloud of unnameable feeling. By gradations, still more imperceptible, this cloud assumes shape, as did the vapor from the bottle out of which arose the genius in the Arabian Nights. But out of this *our* cloud upon the precipice's edge, there grows into palpability, a shape, far more terrible than any genius, or any demon of a tale, and yet it is but a thought, although a fearful one, and one which chills the very marrow of our bones with the fierceness of the delight of its horror. It is merely the idea of what would be our sensations during the sweeping precipitancy of a fall from such a height. And this fall—this rushing annihilation—for the very reason that it involves that one most ghastly and loathsome of all the most ghastly and loathsome images of death and suffering which have ever presented themselves to our imagination—for this very cause do we now the most vividly desire it. And because our reason violently deters us from the brink, *therefore*, do we the more impetuously approach it. There is no passion in nature so demoniacally impatient, as that of him who, shuddering upon the edge of a precipice, thus meditates a plunge. To indulge for a moment, in any attempt *at thought*, is to be inevitably lost; for reflection but urges us to forbear, and *therefore* it is, I say, that we *cannot*. If there be no friendly arm to check us, or if we fail in a sudden effort to prostrate ourselves backward from the abyss, we plunge, and are destroyed.

Examine these similar actions as we will, we shall find them resulting solely from the spirit of the *Perverse*. We perpetrate them merely because we feel that we should not. Beyond or behind this, there is no intelligible principle: and we might, indeed, deem this perverseness a direct instigation of the arch-fiend, were it not occasionally known to operate in furtherance of good.

I have said thus much, that in some measure I may answer your question—that I may explain to you why I am here—that I may assign to you something that shall have at least the faint aspect of a cause for my wearing these fetters, and for my tenanting this cell of the condemned. Had I not been thus prolix, you might either have misunderstood me altogether, or, with the rabble, have fancied me mad. As it is, you will easily perceive that I am one of the many uncounted victims of the Imp of the Perverse.

It is impossible that any deed could have been wrought with a more thorough deliberation. For weeks, for months, I pondered upon the means of the murder. I rejected a thousand schemes, because their accomplishment involved a *chance* of detection. At length, in reading some French memoirs, I found an account of a nearly fatal illness that occurred to Madame Pilau, through the agency of a candle accidentally poisoned. The idea struck my fancy at once. I knew my victim's habit of reading in bed. I knew, too, that his apartment was narrow and ill-ventilated. But I need not vex you with impertinent details. I need not describe the easy artifices by which I substituted, in his bed-room candlestand, a wax-light of my own making, for the one which I there found. The next morning he was discovered dead in his bed, and the coroner's verdict was,—"Death by the visitation of God."

Having inherited his estate, all went well with me for years. The idea of detection never once entered my brain. Of the remains of the fatal taper I had myself carefully disposed. I had left no shadow of a clue by which it would be possible to convict, or even to suspect me of the crime. It is inconceivable how rich a sentiment of satisfaction arose in my bosom as I reflected upon my absolute security. For a very long period of time, I was accustomed to revel in this sentiment. It afforded me more real delight than all the mere worldly advantages accruing from my sin. But there arrived at length an epoch, from which the pleasurable feeling grew, by scarcely perceptible gradations, into a haunting and harassing thought. It harassed because it haunted. I could scarcely get rid of it for an instant. It is quite a common thing to be thus annoyed with the ringing in our ears, or rather in our memories, of the burthen of some ordinary song, or some unimpressive snatches from an opera. Nor will we be the less tormented if the song in itself be good, or the opera air meritorious. In this manner, at last, I would perpetually catch myself pondering upon my security, and repeating, in a low under-tone, the phrase, "I am safe."

One day, whilst sauntering along the streets, I arrested myself in the act of murmuring, half aloud, these customary syllables. In a fit of petulance, I remodelled them thus:—"I am safe—I am safe—yes—if I be not fool enough to make open confession!"

No sooner had I spoken these words, than I felt an icy chill creep to my heart. I had had some experience in these fits of perversity, (whose nature I have been at some trouble to explain,) and I remembered well, that in no instance, I had successfully resisted their attacks. And now my own casual self-suggestion, that I might possibly be fool enough to confess the murder of which I had been guilty, confronted me, as if the very ghost of him whom I had murdered—and beckoned me on to death.

At first, I made an effort to shake off this nightmare of the soul. I walked vigorously—faster—still faster—at length I ran. I felt a maddening desire to shriek aloud. Every succeeding wave of thought overwhelmed me with new terror, for, alas! I well, too well understood that, *to think*, in my situation, was to be lost. I still quickened my pace. I bounded like a madman through the crowded thoroughfares. At length, the populace took the alarm, and pursued me. I felt *then* the consummation of my fate. Could I have torn out my tongue, I would have done it—but a rough voice resounded in my ears—a rougher grasp seized me by the shoulder. I turned—I gasped for breath. For a moment, I experienced all the pangs of suffocation; I became blind, and deaf, and giddy; and then, some invisible fiend, I thought, struck me with his broad palm upon the back. The long-imprisoned secret burst forth from my soul.

They say that I spoke with a distinct enunciation, but with marked emphasis and passionate hurry, as if in dread of interruption before concluding the brief but pregnant sentences that consigned me to the hangman and to hell.

Having related all that was necessary for the fullest judicial conviction, I fell prostrate in a swoon.

But why shall I say more? To-day I wear these chains, and am *here!* To-morrow I shall be fetterless!—*but where?*

THE CASK OF
AMONTILLADO

The thousand injuries of Fortunato I had borne as I best could; but when he ventured upon insult, I vowed revenge. You, who so well know the nature of my soul, will not suppose, however, that I gave utterance to a threat. *At length* I would be avenged; this was a point definitively settled—but the very definitiveness with which it was resolved, precluded the idea of risk. I must not only punish, but punish with impunity. A wrong is unredressed when retribution overtakes its redresser. It is equally unredressed when the avenger fails to make himself felt as such to him who has done the wrong.

It must be understood that neither by word nor deed had I given Fortunato cause to doubt my good will. I continued, as was my wont, to smile in his face, and he did not perceive that my smile *now* was at the thought of his immolation.

He had a weak point—this Fortunato—although in other regards he was a man to be respected and even feared. He prided himself on his connoisseurship in wine. Few Italians have the true virtuoso spirit. For the most part their enthusiasm is adopted to suit the time and opportunity—to practise imposture upon the British and Austrian *millionaires*. In painting and gemmary, Fortunato, like his countrymen, was a quack—but in the matter of old wines he was sincere. In this respect I did not differ from him materially: I was skilful in the Italian vintages myself, and bought largely whenever I could.

It was about dusk, one evening during the supreme madness of the carnival season, that I encountered my friend. He accosted me with excessive warmth, for he had been drinking much. The man wore motley. He had on a tight-fitting parti-striped dress, and his head was surmounted by the conical cap and bells. I was so

pleased to see him, that I thought I should never have done wring-
ing his hand.

I said to him—"My dear Fortunato, you are luckily met. How
remarkably well you are looking to-day! But I have received a pipe
of what passes for Amontillado, and I have my doubts."

"How?" said he. "Amontillado? A pipe? Impossible! And in the
middle of the carnival!"

"I have my doubts," I replied; "and I was silly enough to pay the
full Amontillado price without consulting you in the matter. You
were not to be found, and I was fearful of losing a bargain."

"Amontillado!"

"I have my doubts."

"Amontillado!"

"And I must satisfy them."

"Amontillado!"

"As you are engaged, I am on my way to Luchesi. If any one has
a critical turn, it is he. He will tell me—"

"Luchesi cannot tell Amontillado from Sherry."

"And yet some fools will have it that his taste is a match for
your own."

"Come, let us go."

"Whither?"

"To your vaults."

"My friend, no; I will not impose upon your good nature. I per-
ceive you have an engagement. Luchesi—"

"I have no engagement;—come."

"My friend, no. It is not the engagement, but the severe cold
with which I perceive you are afflicted. The vaults are insufferably
damp. They are encrusted with nitre."

"Let us go, nevertheless. The cold is merely nothing. Amontil-
lado! You have been imposed upon. And as for Luchesi, he cannot
distinguish Sherry from Amontillado."

Thus speaking, Fortunato possessed himself of my arm. Putting
on a mask of black silk, and drawing a *roquelaire* closely about
my person, I suffered him to hurry me to my palazzo.

There were no attendants at home; they had absconded to make
merry in honor of the time. I had told them that I should not re-
turn until the morning, and had given them explicit orders not to
stir from the house. These orders were sufficient, I well knew, to

insure their immediate disappearance, one and all, as soon as my back was turned.

I took from their sconces two flambeaux, and giving one to Fortunato, bowed him through several suites of rooms to the archway that led into the vaults. I passed down a long and winding staircase, requesting him to be cautious as he followed. We came at length to the foot of the descent, and stood together on the damp ground of the catacombs of the Montresors.

The gait of my friend was unsteady, and the bells upon his cap jingled as he strode.

"The pipe," said he.

"It is farther on," said I; "but observe the white web-work which gleams from these cavern walls."

He turned towards me, and looked into my eyes with two filmy orbs that distilled the rheum of intoxication.

"Nitre?" he asked, at length.

"Nitre," I replied. "How long have you had that cough?"

"Ugh! ugh! ugh!—ugh! ugh! ugh!—ugh! ugh! ugh!—ugh! ugh! ugh!—ugh! ugh! ugh!"

My poor friend found it impossible to reply for many minutes.

"It is nothing," he said, at last.

"Come," I said, with decision, "we will go back; your health is precious. You are rich, respected, admired, beloved; you are happy, as once I was. You are a man to be missed. For me it is no matter. We will go back; you will be ill, and I cannot be responsible. Besides, there is Luchesi—"

"Enough," he said; "the cough is a mere nothing; it will not kill me. I shall not die of a cough."

"True—true," I replied; "and, indeed, I had no intention of alarming you unnecessarily—but you should use all proper caution. A draught of this Medoc will defend us from the damps."

Here I knocked off the neck of a bottle which I drew from a long row of its fellows that lay upon the mould.

"Drink," I said, presenting him the wine.

He raised it to his lips with a leer. He paused and nodded to me familiarly, while his bells jingled.

"I drink," he said, "to the buried that repose around us."

"And I to your long life."

He again took my arm, and we proceeded.

"These vaults," he said, "are extensive."

"The Montresors," I replied, "were a great and numerous family."

"I forget your arms."

"A huge human foot d'or, in a field azure; the foot crushes a serpent rampant whose fangs are imbedded in the heel."

"And the motto?"

"*Nemo me impune lacessit.*"[1]

"Good!" he said.

The wine sparkled in his eyes and the bells jingled. My own fancy grew warm with the Medoc. We had passed through walls of piled bones, with casks and puncheons intermingling, into the inmost recesses of the catacombs. I paused again, and this time I made bold to seize Fortunato by an arm above the elbow.

"The nitre!" I said; "see, it increases. It hangs like moss upon the vaults. We are below the river's bed. The drops of moisture trickle among the bones. Come, we will go back ere it is too late. Your cough—"

"It is nothing," he said; "let us go on. But first, another draught of the Medoc."

I broke and reached him a flaçon of De Grâve. He emptied it at a breath. His eyes flashed with a fierce light. He laughed and threw the bottle upwards with a gesticulation I did not understand.

I looked at him in surprise. He repeated the movement—a grotesque one.

"You do not comprehend?" he said.

"Not I," I replied.

"Then you are not of the brotherhood."

"How?"

"You are not of the masons."

"Yes, yes," I said, "yes, yes."

"You? Impossible! A mason?"

"A mason," I replied.

"A sign," he said.

"It is this," I answered, producing a trowel from beneath the folds of my *roquelaire*.

"You jest," he exclaimed, recoiling a few paces. "But let us proceed to the Amontillado."

"Be it so," I said, replacing the tool beneath the cloak, and again offering him my arm. He leaned upon it heavily. We continued our route in search of the Amontillado. We passed through a range of low arches, descended, passed on, and descending again, arrived at a deep crypt, in which the foulness of the air caused our flambeaux rather to glow than flame.

At the most remote end of the crypt there appeared another less spacious. Its walls had been lined with human remains, piled to the vault overhead, in the fashion of the great catacombs of Paris. Three sides of this interior crypt were still ornamented in this manner. From the fourth the bones had been thrown down, and lay promiscuously upon the earth, forming at one point a mound of some size. Within the wall thus exposed by the displacing of the bones, we perceived a still interior recess, in depth about four feet, in width three, in height six or seven. It seemed to have been constructed for no especial use within itself, but formed merely the interval between two of the colossal supports of the roof of the catacombs, and was backed by one of their circumscribing walls of solid granite.

It was in vain that Fortunato, uplifting his dull torch, endeavored to pry into the depth of the recess. Its termination the feeble light did not enable us to see.

"Proceed," I said; "herein is the Amontillado. As for Luchesi—"

"He is an ignoramus," interrupted my friend, as he stepped unsteadily forward, while I followed immediately at his heels. In an instant he had reached the extremity of the niche, and finding his progress arrested by the rock, stood stupidly bewildered. A moment more and I had fettered him to the granite. In its surface were two iron staples, distant from each other about two feet, horizontally. From one of these depended a short chain, from the other a padlock. Throwing the links about his waist, it was but the work of a few seconds to secure it. He was too much astounded to resist. Withdrawing the key I stepped back from the recess.

"Pass your hand," I said, "over the wall; you cannot help feeling the nitre. Indeed it is *very* damp. Once more let me *implore* you to return. No? Then I must positively leave you. But I must first render you all the little attentions in my power."

"The Amontillado!" ejaculated my friend, not yet recovered from his astonishment.

"True," I replied; "the Amontillado."

As I said these words I busied myself among the pile of bones of which I have before spoken. Throwing them aside, I soon uncovered a quantity of building stone and mortar. With these materials and with the aid of my trowel, I began vigorously to wall up the entrance of the niche.

I had scarcely laid the first tier of the masonry when I discovered that the intoxication of Fortunato had in a great measure worn off. The earliest indication I had of this was a low moaning cry from the depth of the recess. It was *not* the cry of a drunken man. There was then a long and obstinate silence. I laid the second tier, and the third, and the fourth; and then I heard the furious vibrations of the chain. The noise lasted for several minutes, during which, that I might hearken to it with the more satisfaction, I ceased my labors and sat down upon the bones. When at last the clanking subsided, I resumed the trowel, and finished without interruption the fifth, the sixth, and the seventh tier. The wall was now nearly upon a level with my breast. I again paused, and holding the flambeaux over the mason-work, threw a few feeble rays upon the figure within.

A succession of loud and shrill screams, bursting suddenly from the throat of the chained form, seemed to thrust me violently back. For a brief moment I hesitated—I trembled. Unsheathing my rapier, I began to grope with it about the recess: but the thought of an instant reassured me. I placed my hand upon the solid fabric of the catacombs, and felt satisfied. I reapproached the wall. I replied to the yells of him who clamored. I re-echoed—I aided—I surpassed them in volume and in strength. I did this, and the clamorer grew still.

It was now midnight, and my task was drawing to a close. I had completed the eighth, the ninth, and the tenth tier. I had finished a portion of the last and the eleventh; there remained but a single stone to be fitted and plastered in. I struggled with its weight; I placed it partially in its destined position. But now there came from out the niche a low laugh that erected the hairs upon my head. It was succeeded by a sad voice, which I had difficulty in recognising as that of the noble Fortunato. The voice said—

"Ha! ha! ha!—he! he!—a very good joke indeed—an excellent jest. We will have many a rich laugh about it at the palazzo—he! he! he!—over our wine—he! he! he!"

"The Amontillado!" I said.

"He! he! he!—he! he! he!—yes, the Amontillado. But is it not getting late? Will not they be awaiting us at the palazzo, the Lady Fortunato and the rest? Let us be gone."

"Yes," I said, "let us be gone."

"For the love of God, Montressor!"

"Yes," I said, "for the love of God!"

But to these words I hearkened in vain for a reply. I grew impatient. I called aloud—

"Fortunato!"

No answer. I called again—

"Fortunato!"

No answer still. I thrust a torch through the remaining aperture and let it fall within. There came forth in return only a jingling of the bells. My heart grew sick—on account of the dampness of the catacombs. I hastened to make an end of my labor. I forced the last stone into its position; I plastered it up. Against the new masonry I re-erected the old rampart of bones. For the half of a century no mortal has disturbed them. *In pace requiescat!*[2]

HOP-FROG

I never knew anyone so keenly alive to a joke as the king was. He seemed to live only for joking. To tell a good story of the joke kind, and to tell it well, was the surest road to his favor. Thus it happened that his seven ministers were all noted for their accomplishments as jokers. They all took after the king, too, in being large, corpulent, oily men, as well as inimitable jokers. Whether people grow fat by joking, or whether there is something in fat itself which predisposes to a joke, I have never been quite able to determine; but certain it is that a lean joker is a *rara avis in terris.*[1]

About the refinements, or, as he called them, the "ghosts" of wit, the king troubled himself very little. He had an especial admiration for *breadth* in a jest, and would often put up with *length*, for the sake of it. Over-niceties wearied him. He would have preferred Rabelais's "Gargantua" to the "Zadig" of Voltaire: and, upon the whole, practical jokes suited his taste far better than verbal ones.

At the date of my narrative, professing jesters had not altogether gone out of fashion at court. Several of the great continental "powers" still retained their "fools," who wore motley, with caps and bells, and who were expected to be always ready with sharp witticisms, at a moment's notice, in consideration of the crumbs that fell from the royal table.

Our king, as a matter of course, retained his "fool." The fact is, he *required* something in the way of folly—if only to counterbalance the heavy wisdom of the seven wise men who were his ministers—not to mention himself.

His fool, or professional jester, was not *only* a fool, however. His value was trebled in the eyes of the king, by the fact of his being also a dwarf and a cripple. Dwarfs were as common at court, in those days, as fools; and many monarchs would have found it difficult to get through their days (days are rather longer at court than elsewhere) without both a jester to laugh *with*, and a dwarf to laugh *at*. But, as I have already observed, your jesters, in ninety-nine cases out of a hundred, are fat, round, and unwieldy—so that it was no small source of self-gratulation with our king that, in Hop-Frog (this was the fool's name,) he possessed a triplicate treasure in one person.

I believe the name "Hop-Frog" was *not* that given to the dwarf by his sponsors at baptism, but it was conferred upon him, by general consent of the seven ministers, on account of his inability to walk as other men do. In fact, Hop-Frog could only get along by a sort of interjectional gait—something between a leap and a wriggle—a movement that afforded illimitable amusement, and of course consolation, to the king, for (notwithstanding the protuberance of his stomach and a constitutional swelling of the head) the king, by his whole court, was accounted a capital figure.

But although Hop-Frog, through the distortion of his legs, could move only with great pain and difficulty along a road or floor, the prodigious muscular power which nature seemed to have bestowed upon his arms, by way of compensation for deficiency in the lower limbs, enabled him to perform many feats of wonderful dexterity, where trees or ropes were in question, or anything else to climb. At such exercises he certainly much more resembled a squirrel, or a small monkey, than a frog.

I am not able to say, with precision, from what country Hop-Frog originally came. It was from some barbarous region, however, that no person ever heard of—a vast distance from the court of our king. Hop-Frog, and a young girl very little less dwarfish than himself (although of exquisite proportions, and a marvellous dancer,) had been forcibly carried off from their respective homes in adjoining provinces, and sent as presents to the king, by one of his ever-victorious generals.

Under these circumstances, it is not to be wondered at that a close intimacy arose between the two little captives. Indeed, they soon became sworn friends. Hop-Frog, who, although he made a great deal of sport, was by no means popular, had it not in his power to render Trippetta many services; but *she*, on account of her grace and exquisite beauty (although a dwarf,) was universally admired and petted: so she possessed much influence; and never failed to use it, whenever she could, for the benefit of Hop-Frog.

On some grand state occasion—I forget what—the king determined to have a masquerade, and whenever a masquerade or any thing of that kind, occurred at our court, then the talents, both of Hop-Frog and Trippetta were sure to be called into play. Hop-Frog, in especial, was so inventive in the way of getting up pageants, suggesting novel characters, and arranging costume, for masked balls, that nothing could be done, it seems, without his assistance.

The night appointed for the *fête* had arrived. A gorgeous hall had been fitted up, under Trippetta's eye, with every kind of device which could possibly give *éclat* to a masquerade. The whole court was in a fever of expectation. As for costumes and characters, it might well be supposed that everybody had come to a decision on such points. Many had made up their minds (as to what *rôles* they should assume) a week, or even a month, in advance; and, in fact, there was not a particle of indecision anywhere—except in the case of the king and his seven minsters. Why *they* hesitated I never could tell, unless they did it by way of a joke. More probably, they found it difficult, on account of being so fat, to make up their minds. At all events, time flew; and, as a last resource they sent for Trippetta and Hop-Frog.

When the two little friends obeyed the summons of the king, they found him sitting at his wine with the seven members of his cabinet council; but the monarch appeared to be in a very ill humor. He knew that Hop-Frog was not fond of wine; for it excited the poor cripple almost to madness; and madness is no comfortable feeling. But the king loved his practical jokes, and took pleasure in forcing Hop-Frog to drink and (as the king called it) "to be merry."

"Come here, Hop-Frog," said he, as the jester and his friend entered the room: "swallow this bumper to the health of your absent friends, [here Hop-Frog sighed,] and then let us have the benefit of your invention. We want characters—*characters*, man—something novel—out of the way. We are wearied with this everlasting sameness. Come, drink! the wine will brighten your wits."

Hop-Frog endeavored, as usual, to get up a jest in reply to these advances from the king; but the effort was too much. It happened to be the poor dwarf's birthday, and the command to drink to his "absent friends" forced the tears to his eyes. Many large, bitter drops fell into the goblet as he took it, humbly, from the hand of the tyrant.

"Ah! ha! ha! ha!" roared the latter, as the dwarf reluctantly drained the beaker. "See what a glass of good wine can do! Why, your eyes are shining already!"

Poor fellow! his large eyes *gleamed*, rather than shone; for the effect of wine on his excitable brain was not more powerful than instantaneous. He placed the goblet nervously on the table, and looked round upon the company with a half-insane stare. They all seemed highly amused at the success of the king's "*joke*."

"And now to business," said the prime minister, a *very* fat man.

"Yes," said the king; "come, Hop-Frog, lend us your assistance. Characters, my fine fellow; we stand in need of characters—all of us—ha! ha! ha!" and as this was seriously meant for a joke, his laugh was chorused by the seven.

Hop-Frog also laughed although feebly and somewhat vacantly.

"Come, come," said the king, impatiently, "have you nothing to suggest?"

"I am endeavoring to think of something *novel*," replied the dwarf, abstractedly, for he was quite bewildered by the wine.

"Endeavoring!" cried the tyrant, fiercely; "what do you mean by *that*? Ah, I perceive. You are sulky, and want more wine. Here, drink this!" and he poured out another goblet full and offered it to the cripple, who merely gazed at it, gasping for breath.

"Drink, I say!" shouted the monster, "or by the fiends—"

The dwarf hesitated. The king grew purple with rage. The courtiers smirked. Trippetta, pale as a corpse, advanced to the monarch's seat, and, falling on her knees before him, implored him to spare her friend.

The tyrant regarded her, for some moments, in evident wonder at her audacity. He seemed quite at a loss what to do or say—how most becomingly to express his indignation. At last, without uttering a syllable, he pushed her violently from him, and threw the contents of the brimming goblet in her face.

The poor girl got up the best she could, and, not daring even to sigh, resumed her position at the foot of the table.

There was a dead silence for about a half a minute, during which the falling of a leaf, or of a feather, might have been heard. It was interrupted by a low, but harsh and protracted *grating* sound which seemed to come at once from every corner of the room.

"What—what—*what* are you making that noise for?" demanded the king, turning furiously to the dwarf.

The latter seemed to have recovered, in great measure, from his intoxication, and looking fixedly but quietly into the tyrant's face, merely ejaculated:

"I—I? How could it have been me?"

"The sound appeared to come from without," observed one of the courtiers. "I fancy it was the parrot at the window, whetting his bill upon his cage-wires."

"True," replied the monarch, as if much relieved by the suggestion; "but, on the honor of a knight, I could have sworn that it was the gritting of this vagabond's teeth."

Hereupon the dwarf laughed (the king was too confirmed a joker to object to any one's laughing), and displayed a set of large, powerful, and very repulsive teeth. Moreover, he avowed his perfect willingness to swallow as much wine as desired. The monarch was pacified; and having drained another bumper with no very perceptible ill effect, Hop-Frog entered at once, and with spirit, into the plans for the masquerade.

"I cannot tell what was the association of idea," observed he, very tranquilly, and as if he had never tasted wine in his life, "but *just after* your majesty had struck the girl and thrown the wine in her face—*just after* your majesty had done this, and while the parrot was making that odd noise outside the window, there came into my mind a capital diversion—one of my own country frolics—often enacted among us, at our masquerades: but here it will be new altogether. Unfortunately, however, it requires a company of eight persons, and—"

"Here we *are*!" cried the king, laughing at his acute discovery of the coincidence; "eight to a fraction—I and my seven ministers. Come! what is the diversion?"

"We call it," replied the cripple, "the Eight Chained Ourang-Outangs, and it really is excellent sport if well enacted."

"*We* will enact it," remarked the king, drawing himself up, and lowering his eyelids.

"The beauty of the game," continued Hop-Frog, "lies in the fright it occasions among the women."

"Capital!" roared in chorus the monarch and his ministry.

"*I* will equip you as ourang-outangs," proceeded the dwarf; "leave all that to me. The resemblance shall be so striking, that the company of masqueraders will take you for real beasts—and of course, they will be as much terrified as astonished."

"O, this is exquisite!" exclaimed the king. "Hop-Frog! I will make a man of you."

"The chains are for the purpose of increasing the confusion by their jangling. You are supposed to have escaped, *en masse*, from your keepers. Your majesty cannot conceive the *effect* produced, at a masquerade, by eight chained ourang-outangs, imagined to be real ones by most of the company; and rushing in with savage cries, among the crowd of delicately and gorgeously habited men and women. The *contrast* is inimitable!"

"It *must* be," said the king: and the council arose hurriedly (as it was growing late), to put in execution the scheme of Hop-Frog.

His mode of equipping the party as ourang-outangs was very simple, but effective enough for his purposes. The animals in question had, at the epoch of my story, very rarely been seen in any part of the civilized world; and as the imitations made by the dwarf were sufficiently beast-like and more than sufficiently hideous, their truthfulness to nature was thus thought to be secured.

The king and his ministers were first encased in tight-fitting stockinet shirts and drawers. They were then saturated with tar. At this stage of the process, some one of the party suggested feathers; but the suggestion was at once overruled by the dwarf, who soon convinced the eight, by ocular demonstration, that the hair of such a brute as the ourang-outang was much more efficiently represented by *flax*. A thick coating of the latter was accordingly plastered upon the coating of tar. A long chain was now procured. First, it was passed about the waist of the king, *and tied*; then about another of the party, and also tied; then about all successively, in the same manner. When this chaining arrangement was complete, and the party stood as far apart from each other as possible, they formed a circle; and to make all things appear natural, Hop-Frog passed the residue of the chain in two diameters, at right angles, across the circle, after the fashion adopted, at the present day, by those who capture Chimpanzees, or other large apes, in Borneo.

The grand saloon in which the masquerade was to take place, was a circular room, very lofty, and receiving the light of the sun only through a single window at top. At night (the season for which the apartment was especially designed,) it was illuminated principally by a large chandelier, depending by a chain from the centre of the sky-light, and lowered, or elevated, by means of a counter-balance as usual; but (in order not to look unsightly) this latter passed outside the cupola and over the roof.

The arrangements of the room had been left to Trippetta's super-intendence; but, in some particulars, it seems, she had been guided by the calmer judgment of her friend the dwarf. At his suggestion it was that, on this occasion, the chandelier was removed. Its waxen drippings (which, in weather so warm, it was quite impossible to prevent) would have been seriously detrimental to the rich dresses of the guests, who, on account of the crowded state of the saloon, could not *all* be expected to keep from out its centre—that is to say, from under the chandelier. Additional sconces were set in various parts of the hall, out of the way; and a flambeau, emitting sweet odor, was placed in the right hand of each of the Caryatides that stood against the wall—some fifty or sixty altogether.

The eight ourang-outangs, taking Hop-Frog's advice, waited pa-tiently until midnight (when the room was thoroughly filled with masqueraders) before making their appearance. No sooner had the clock ceased striking, however, than they rushed, or rather rolled in, all together—for the impediments of their chains caused most of the party to fall, and all to stumble as they entered.

The excitement among the masqueraders was prodigious, and filled the heart of the king with glee. As had been anticipated, there were not a few of the guests who supposed the ferocious-looking creatures to be beasts of *some* kind in reality, if not precisely ourang-outangs. Many of the women swooned with affright; and had not the king taken the precaution to exclude all weapons from the saloon, his party might soon have expiated their frolic in their blood. As it was, a general rush was made for the doors; but the king had ordered them to be locked immediately upon his entrance; and, at the dwarf's suggestion, the keys had been deposited with *him*.

While the tumult was at its height, and each masquerader atten-
tive only to his own safety—(for, in fact, there was much *real* danger
from the pressure of the excited crowd,)—the chain by which the
chandelier ordinarily hung, and which had been drawn up on its re-
moval, might have been seen very gradually to descend, until its
hooked extremity came within three feet of the floor.

Soon after this, the king and his seven friends having reeled
about the hall in all directions, found themselves, at length, in its
centre, and, of course, in immediate contact with the chain.
While they were thus situated, the dwarf, who had followed
closely at their heels, inciting them to keep up the commotion,
took hold of their own chain at the intersection of the two por-
tions which crossed the circle diametrically and at right angles.
Here, with the rapidity of thought, he inserted the hook from
which the chandelier had been wont to depend; and, in an in-
stant, by some unseen agency, the chandelier-chain was drawn so
far upward as to take the hook out of reach, and, as an inevitable
consequence, to drag the ourang-outangs together in close con-
nection, and face to face.

The masqueraders, by this time, had recovered, in some mea-
sure, from their alarm; and, beginning to regard the whole matter
as a well-contrived pleasantry, set up a loud shout of laughter at
the predicament of the apes.

"Leave them to *me*!" now screamed Hop-Frog, his shrill voice
making itself easily heard through all the din. "Leave them to *me*.
I fancy *I* know them. If I can only get a good look at them, *I* can
soon tell who they are."

Here, scrambling over the heads of the crowd, he managed to
get to the wall; when, seizing a flambeau from one of the Cary-
atides, he returned, as he went, to the centre of the room—leaped,
with the agility of a monkey, upon the king's head—and thence
clambered a few feet up the chain—holding down the torch to ex-
amine the group of ourang-outangs, and still screaming: "*I* shall
soon find out who they are!"

And now, while the whole assembly (the apes included) were
convulsed with laughter, the jester suddenly uttered a shrill whis-
tle; when the chain flew violently up for about thirty feet—
dragging with it the dismayed and struggling ourang-outangs,

and leaving them suspended in mid-air between the sky-light and the floor. Hop-Frog, clinging to the chain as it rose, still maintained his relative position in respect to the eight maskers, and still (as if nothing were the matter) continued to thrust his torch down toward them, as though endeavoring to discover who they were.

So thoroughly astonished was the whole company at this ascent, that a dead silence, of about a minute's duration, ensued. It was broken by just such a low, harsh, *grating* sound, as had before attracted the attention of the king and his councillors when the former threw the wine in the face of Trippetta. But, on the present occasion, there could be no question as to *whence* the sound issued. It came from the fang-like teeth of the dwarf, who ground them and gnashed them as he foamed at the mouth, and glared, with an expression of maniacal rage, into the upturned countenances of the king and his seven companions.

"Ah, ha!" said at length the infuriated jester. "Ah, ha! I begin to see who these people *are* now!" Here, pretending to scrutinize the king more closely, he held the flambeau to the flaxen coat which enveloped him, and which instantly burst into a sheet of vivid flame. In less than half a minute the whole eight ourang-outangs were blazing fiercely, amid the shrieks of the multitude who gazed at them from below, horror-stricken, and without the power to render them the slightest assistance.

At length the flames, suddenly increasing in virulence, forced the jester to climb higher up the chain, to be out of their reach; and, as he made this movement, the crowd again sank, for a brief instant, into silence. The dwarf seized his opportunity, and once more spoke:

"I now see *distinctly*," he said, "what manner of people these maskers are. They are a great king and his seven privy-councillors— a king who does not scruple to strike a defenceless girl, and his seven councillors who abet him in the outrage. As for myself, I am simply Hop-Frog, the jester—and *this is my last jest*."

Owing to the high combustibility of both the flax and the tar to which it adhered, the dwarf had scarcely made an end of his brief speech before the work of vengeance was complete. The eight corpses swung in their chains, a fetid, blackened, hideous, and indistinguishable mass. The cripple hurled his torch at them, clambered leisurely to the ceiling, and disappeared through the sky-light.

It is supposed that Trippetta, stationed on the roof of the saloon, had been the accomplice of her friend in his fiery revenge, and that, together, they effected their escape to their own country; for neither was seen again.

Mysteries

Poe revealed his passion for solving puzzles in an early essay by deducing the human intelligence operating a chess-playing automaton. His exercises in "autography" identified crucial personality traits revealed by handwritten signatures, and he flaunted his virtuosity as a cryptographer by promising to solve any simple-substitution cryptogram devised by readers. About the same time he also encountered in translation the serialized memoirs of Vidocq, a French criminal-turned-detective, whose exploits aroused his interest in criminal investigation.

After probing the alienated consciousness of a fiend pursued by his double in "William Wilson," Poe developed in "The Man of the Crowd" a parallel narrative in which an analytical narrator stalks a stranger said to be "the type and the genius of deep crime." In the streets of nocturnal London, the would-be detective and his counterpart both lay claim to the title "the man of the crowd" as they reveal a shared compulsion: neither city-dweller can abide human solitude.

Borrowing from Vidocq to create an imaginary Paris, Poe established in "The Murders in the Rue Morgue" the basic conventions of the detective story: an eccentric sleuth, an admiring but less perceptive companion, an inept police chief, and a seemingly insoluble crime—here the murder of two women inside a locked room. C. Auguste Dupin cracks the case (which savors of antebellum racial fears) and then ensnares the sailor, who reveals the awful truth.

Poe turned from murder to buried treasure in "The Gold-Bug" and in an American tale portrayed the South Carolina island where he served in the U.S. Army. The eccentric protagonist, William Legrand, solves a cryptogram inscribed on parchment in invisible ink, and with the help of Jupiter, a manumitted slave, performs a bizarre, Gothic ritual that enables him to locate the dazzling contents of a buried chest.

In a similarly playful vein, Poe conceived "The Oblong Box," a tale of grief, shipwreck, and death narrated by an aspiring sleuth who misconstrues every bit of evidence connected with Cornelius Wyatt and the box he brings aboard a ship bound from Charleston to New York. The unexpected sinking of the *Independence* (near the site of the first English settlement in America) injects a subtle hint of national allegory as it exposes Wyatt's elaborate charade.

An esoteric mystery surrounds the death of Augustus Bedloe, who in "A Tale of the Ragged Mountains" travels through time and space to relive an insurrection in India nearly fifty years earlier. Poe invokes reincarnation when Dr. Templeton (who witnessed the revolt against British imperialism) explains Bedloe's odd resemblance to a friend killed in India. Allusions to "Indian summer" and the "fierce races" native to Virginia may imply an analogy to U.S. Indian removal.

After the inconclusive "Mystery of Marie Rogêt," Poe crafted his most brilliant detective story in "The Purloined Letter." Here, the theft of an incriminating love letter from the queen's boudoir by the Minister D— triggers first the methodical search by the Prefect of Police and then Dupin's ingenious recovery of the letter. He deduces the principle of concealment by identifying with the thief, against whom he seeks private revenge.

Poe ascribed the popularity of his ratiocinative tales partly to novelty: "I do not mean to say that they are not ingenious—but people think them more ingenious than they are—on account of their method and *air* of method." After "The Purloined Letter" he wrote only one more crime story, a modest backwoods satire called "Thou Art the Man." But by virtue of the Dupin stories alone, Poe's name has remained forever associated with tales of mystery and detection.

THE MAN OF THE CROWD

Ce grand malheur, de ne pouvoir être seul.

LA BRUYÈRE[1]

It was well said of a certain German book that *"es lässt sich nicht lesen"*[2]—it does not permit itself to be read. There are some secrets which do not permit themselves to be told. Men die nightly in their beds, wringing the hands of ghostly confessors, and looking them piteously in the eyes—die with despair of heart and convulsion of throat, on account of the hideousness of mysteries which will not *suffer themselves* to be revealed. Now and then, alas, the conscience of man takes up a burthen so heavy in horror that it can be thrown down only into the grave. And thus the essence of all crime is undivulged.

Not long ago, about the closing in of an evening in autumn, I sat at the large bow window of the D—— Coffee-House in London. For some months I had been ill in health, but was now convalescent, and, with returning strength, found myself in one of those happy moods which are so precisely the converse of *ennui*—moods of the keenest appetency, when the film from the mental vision departs—the αχλυς ος πριν επμεν[3]—and the intellect, electrified, surpasses as greatly its every-day condition, as does the vivid yet candid reason of Leibnitz, the mad and flimsy rhetoric of Gorgias. Merely to breathe was enjoyment; and I derived positive pleasure even from many of the legitimate sources of pain. I felt a calm but inquisitive interest in every thing. With a cigar in my mouth and a newspaper in my lap, I had been amusing myself for the greater part of the afternoon, now in poring over advertisements, now in observing the promiscuous company in the room, and now in peering through the smoky panes into the street.

This latter is one of the principal thoroughfares of the city, and had been very much crowded during the whole day. But, as the darkness came on, the throng momently increased; and, by the time the lamps were well lighted, two dense and continuous tides of population were rushing past the door. At this particular period of the evening I had never before been in a similar situation, and the tumultuous sea of human heads filled me, therefore, with a delicious novelty of emotion. I gave up, at length, all care of things within the hotel, and became absorbed in contemplation of the scene without.

At first my observations took an abstract and generalizing turn. I looked at the passengers in masses, and thought of them in their aggregate relations. Soon, however, I descended to details, and regarded with minute interest the innumerable varieties of figure, dress, air, gait, visage, and expression of countenance.

By far the greater number of those who went by had a satisfied business-like demeanor, and seemed to be thinking only of making their way through the press. Their brows were knit, and their eyes rolled quickly; when pushed against by fellow-wayfarers they evinced no symptom of impatience, but adjusted their clothes and hurried on. Others, still a numerous class, were restless in their movements, had flushed faces, and talked and gesticulated to themselves, as if feeling in solitude on account of the very denseness of the company around. When impeded in their progress, these people suddenly ceased muttering, but redoubled their gesticulations, and awaited, with an absent and overdone smile upon the lips, the course of the persons impeding them. If jostled, they bowed profusely to the jostlers, and appeared overwhelmed with confusion.— There was nothing very distinctive about these two large classes beyond what I have noted. Their habiliments belonged to that order which is pointedly termed the decent. They were undoubtedly noblemen, merchants, attorneys, tradesmen, stock-jobbers—the Eupatrids and the common-places of society—men of leisure and men actively engaged in affairs of their own—conducting business upon their own responsibility. They did not greatly excite my attention.

The tribe of clerks was an obvious one and here I discerned two remarkable divisions. There were the junior clerks of flash houses—young gentlemen with tight coats, bright boots, well-oiled hair, and supercilious lips. Setting aside a certain dapperness of carriage, which may be termed *deskism* for want of a better word, the manner of these persons seemed to me an exact fac-simile of what had been the perfection of *bon ton* about twelve or eighteen months before. They wore the cast-off graces of the gentry;—and this, I believe, involves the best definition of the class.

The division of the upper clerks of staunch firms, or of the "steady old fellows," it was not possible to mistake. These were known by their coats and pantaloons of black or brown, made to sit comfortably, with white cravats and waistcoats, broad solid-looking shoes, and thick hose or gaiters.—They had all slightly bald heads, from which the right ears, long used to pen-holding, had an odd habit of standing off on end. I observed that they always removed or settled their hats with both hands, and wore watches, with short gold chains of a substantial and ancient pattern. Theirs was the affectation of respectability;—if indeed there be an affectation so honorable.

There were many individuals of dashing appearance, whom I easily understood as belonging to the race of swell pick-pockets, with which all great cities are infested. I watched these gentry with much inquisitiveness, and found it difficult to imagine how they should ever be mistaken for gentlemen by gentlemen themselves. Their voluminousness of wristband, with an air of excessive frankness, should betray them at once.

The gamblers, of whom I descried not a few, were still more easily recognisable. They wore every variety of dress, from that of the desperate thimble-rig bully, with velvet waistcoat, fancy neckerchief, gilt chains, and filagreed buttons, to that of the scrupulously inornate clergyman, than which nothing could be less liable to suspicion. Still all were distinguished by a certain sodden swarthiness of complexion, a filmy dimness of eye, and pallor and compression of lip. There were two other traits, moreover, by which I could always detect them;—a guarded lowness of tone in conversation, and a more than ordinary extension of the thumb in a direction at right angles with the fingers.—Very often, in company with these sharpers, I observed an order of men somewhat different in habits, but still birds of a kindred feather. They may be defined as the gentlemen who live by their wits. They seem to prey upon the public in two battalions—that of the dandies and that of the military men. Of the first grade the leading features are long locks and smiles; of the second frogged coats and frowns.

Descending in the scale of what is termed gentility, I found darker and deeper themes for speculation. I saw Jew pedlars, with hawk eyes flashing from countenances whose every other feature wore only an expression of abject humility; sturdy professional street beggars scowling upon mendicants of a better stamp, whom despair alone had driven forth into the night for charity; feeble and ghastly invalids, upon whom death had placed a sure hand, and who sidled and tottered through the mob, looking every one beseechingly in the face, as if in search of some chance consolation, some lost hope; modest young girls returning from long and late labor to a cheerless home, and shrinking more tearfully than indignantly from the glances of ruffians, whose direct contact, even, could not be avoided; women of the town of all kinds and of all ages—the unequivocal beauty in the prime of her womanhood, putting one in mind of the statue in Lucian, with the surface of Parian marble, and the interior filled with filth—the loathsome and utterly lost leper in rags—the wrinkled, bejewelled and paint-begrimed beldame, making a last effort at youth—the mere child of immature form, yet, from long association, an adept in the dreadful coquetries of her trade, and burning with a rabid ambition to be ranked the equal of her elders in vice; drunkards innumerable and indescribable—some in shreds and patches, reeling, inarticulate, with bruised visage and lack-lustre eyes—some in whole although filthy garments, with a slightly unsteady swagger, thick sensual lips, and hearty-looking rubicund faces—others clothed in materials which had once been good, and which even now were scrupulously well brushed—men who walked with a more than naturally firm and springy step, but whose countenances were fearfully pale, whose eyes hideously wild and red, and who clutched with quivering fingers, as they strode through the crowd, at every object which came within their reach; beside these, pie-men, porters, coal-heavers, sweeps; organ-grinders, monkey-exhibiters and ballad mongers, those who vended with those who sang; ragged artizans and exhausted laborers of every description, and all full of a noisy and inordinate vivacity which jarred discordantly upon the ear, and gave an aching sensation to the eye.

As the night deepened, so deepened to me the interest of the scene; for not only did the general character of the crowd materially alter (its gentler features retiring in the gradual withdrawal of the more orderly portion of the people, and its harsher ones coming out into bolder relief, as the late hour brought forth every species of infamy from its den,) but the rays of the gas-lamps, feeble at first in their struggle with the dying day, had now at length gained ascendancy, and threw over every thing a fitful and garish lustre. All was dark yet splendid—as that ebony to which has been likened the style of Tertullian.

The wild effects of the light enchained me to an examination of individual faces; and although the rapidity with which the world of light flitted before the window, prevented me from casting more than a glance upon each visage, still it seemed that, in my then peculiar mental state, I could frequently read, even in that brief interval of a glance, the history of long years.

With my brow to the glass, I was thus occupied in scrutinizing the mob, when suddenly there came into view a countenance (that of a decrepid old man, some sixty-five or seventy years of age,)—a countenance which at once arrested and absorbed my whole attention, on account of the absolute idiosyncrasy of its expression. Any thing even remotely resembling that expression I had never seen before. I well remember that my first thought, upon beholding it, was that Retzch, had he viewed it, would have greatly preferred it to his own pictural incarnations of the fiend. As I endeavored, during the brief minute of my original survey, to form some analysis of the meaning conveyed, there arose confusedly and paradoxically within my mind, the ideas of vast mental power, of caution, of penuriousness, of avarice, of coolness, of malice, of blood-thirstiness, of triumph, of merriment, of excessive terror, of intense—of supreme despair. I felt singularly aroused, startled, fascinated. "How wild a history," I said to myself, "is written within that bosom!" Then came a craving desire to keep the man in view—to know more of him. Hurriedly putting on an overcoat, and seizing my hat and cane, I made my way into the street, and pushed through the crowd in the direction which I had seen him take; for he had already disappeared. With some little difficulty I at length came within sight of him, approached, and followed him closely, yet cautiously, so as not to attract his attention.

I had now a good opportunity of examining his person. He was short in stature, very thin, and apparently very feeble. His clothes, generally, were filthy and ragged; but as he came, now and then, within the strong glare of a lamp, I perceived that his linen, although dirty, was of beautiful texture; and my vision deceived me, or, through a rent in a closely-buttoned and evidently second-handed *roquelaire* which enveloped him, I caught a glimpse both of a diamond and of a dagger. These observations heightened my curiosity, and I resolved to follow the stranger whithersoever he should go.

It was now fully night-fall, and a thick humid fog hung over the city, soon ending in a settled and heavy rain. This change of weather had an odd effect upon the crowd, the whole of which was at once put into new commotion, and overshadowed by a world of umbrellas. The waver, the jostle, and the hum increased in a tenfold degree. For my own part I did not much regard the rain—the lurking of an old fever in my system rendering the moisture somewhat too dangerously pleasant. Tying a handkerchief about my mouth, I kept on. For half an hour the old man held his way with difficulty along the great thoroughfare; and I here walked close at his elbow through fear of losing sight of him. Never once turning his head to look back, he did not observe me. By and bye he passed into a cross street, which, although densely filled with people, was not quite so much thronged as the main one he had quitted. Here a change in his demeanor became evident. He walked more slowly and with less object than before—more hesitatingly. He crossed and re-crossed the way repeatedly without apparent aim; and the press was still so thick that, at every such movement, I was obliged to follow him closely. The street was a narrow and long one, and his course lay within it for nearly an hour, during which the passengers had gradually diminished to about that number which is ordinarily seen at noon in Broadway near the Park—so vast a difference is there between a London populace and that of the most frequented American city. A second turn brought us into a square, brilliantly lighted, and overflowing with life. The old manner of the stranger re-appeared. His chin fell upon his breast, while his eyes rolled wildly from under his knit brows, in every direction, upon those who hemmed him in. He urged his way steadily and perseveringly. I was surprised, however, to find, upon his having made the circuit of the square, that he turned and retraced his steps. Still more was I astonished to see him repeat the same walk several times—once nearly detecting me as he came round with a sudden movement.

In this exercise he spent another hour, at the end of which we met with far less interruption from passengers than at first. The rain fell fast; the air grew cool; and the people were retiring to their homes. With a gesture of impatience, the wanderer passed into a bye-street comparatively deserted. Down this, some quarter of a mile long, he rushed with an activity I could not have dreamed of seeing in one so aged, and which put me to much trouble in pursuit. A few minutes brought us to a large and busy bazaar, with the localities of which the stranger appeared well acquainted, and where his original demeanor again became apparent, as he forced his way to and fro, without aim, among the host of buyers and sellers.

During the hour and a half, or thereabouts, which we passed in this place, it required much caution on my part to keep him within reach without attracting his observation. Luckily I wore a pair of caoutchouc over-shoes, and could move about in perfect silence. At no moment did he see that I watched him. He entered shop after shop, priced nothing, spoke no word, and looked at all objects with a wild and vacant stare. I was now utterly amazed at his behaviour, and firmly resolved that we should not part until I had satisfied myself in some measure respecting him.

A loud-toned clock struck eleven, and the company were fast deserting the bazaar. A shop-keeper, in putting up a shutter, jostled the old man, and at the instant I saw a strong shudder come over his frame. He hurried into the street, looked anxiously around him for an instant, and then ran with incredible swiftness through many crooked and people-less lanes, until we emerged once more upon the great thoroughfare whence we had started— the street of the D——— Hotel. It no longer wore, however, the same aspect. It was still brilliant with gas; but the rain fell fiercely, and there were few persons to be seen. The stranger grew pale. He walked moodily some paces up the once populous avenue, then, with a heavy sigh, turned in the direction of the river, and, plunging through a great variety of devious ways, came out, at length, in view of one of the principal theatres. It was about being closed, and the audience were thronging from the doors. I saw the old man gasp as if for breath while he threw himself amid the crowd;

but I thought that the intense agony of his countenance had, in some measure, abated. His head again fell upon his breast; he appeared as I had seen him at first. I observed that he now took the course in which had gone the greater number of the audience—but, upon the whole, I was at a loss to comprehend the waywardness of his actions.

As he proceeded, the company grew more scattered, and his old uneasiness and vacillation were resumed. For some time he followed closely a party of some ten or twelve roisterers; but from this number one by one dropped off, until three only remained together, in a narrow and gloomy lane little frequented. The stranger paused, and, for a moment, seemed lost in thought; then, with every mark of agitation, pursued rapidly a route which brought us to the verge of the city, amid regions very different from those we had hitherto traversed. It was the most noisome quarter of London, where every thing wore the worst impress of the most deplorable poverty, and of the most desperate crime. By the dim light of an accidental lamp, tall, antique, worm-eaten, wooden tenements were seen tottering to their fall, in directions so many and capricious that scarce the semblance of a passage was discernible between them. The paving-stones lay at random, displaced from their beds by the rankly-growing grass. Horrible filth festered in the dammed-up gutters. The whole atmosphere teemed with desolation. Yet, as we proceeded, the sounds of human life revived by sure degrees, and at length large bands of the most abandoned of a London populace were seen reeling to and fro. The spirits of the old man again flickered up, as a lamp which is near its death-hour. Once more he strode onward with elastic tread. Suddenly a corner was turned, a blaze of light burst upon our sight, and we stood before one of the huge suburban temples of Intemperance—one of the palaces of the fiend, Gin.

It was now nearly day-break; but a number of wretched inebriates still pressed in and out of the flaunting entrance. With a half shriek of joy the old man forced a passage within, resumed at once his original bearing, and stalked backward and forward, without apparent object, among the throng. He had not been thus long occupied, however, before a rush to the doors gave token that the host was closing them for the night. It was something even more intense than despair that I then observed upon the countenance of the singular being whom I had watched so pertinaciously. Yet he did not hesitate in his career, but, with a mad energy, retraced his steps at once, to the heart of the mighty London. Long and swiftly he fled, while I followed him in the wildest amazement, resolute not to abandon a scrutiny in which I now felt an interest all-absorbing. The sun arose while we proceeded, and, when we had once again reached that most thronged mart of the populous town, the street of the D——— Hotel, it presented an appearance of human bustle and activity scarcely inferior to what I had seen on the evening before. And here, long, amid the momently increasing confusion, did I persist in my pursuit of the stranger. But, as usual, he walked to and fro, and during the day did not pass from out the turmoil of that street. And, as the shades of the second evening came on, I grew wearied unto death, and, stopping fully in front of the wanderer, gazed at him steadfastly in the face. He noticed me not, but resumed his solemn walk, while I, ceasing to follow, remained absorbed in contemplation. "This old man," I said at length, "is the type and the genius of deep crime. He refuses to be alone. *He is the man of the crowd.* It will be in vain to follow; for I shall learn no more of him, nor of his deeds. The worst heart of the world is a grosser book than the 'Hortulus Animæ,'* and perhaps it is but one of the great mercies of God that '*es lässt sich nicht lesen.*'"

---

*The "*Hortulus Animæ cum Oratiunculis Aliquibus Superadditis*" of Grün-ninger.[4] [Poe's note]

THE MURDERS IN THE RUE MORGUE

What song the Syrens sang, or what name Achilles assumed when he hid himself among women, although puzzling questions, are not beyond *all* conjecture.

SIR THOMAS BROWNE

The mental features discoursed of as the analytical are, in themselves, but little susceptible of analysis. We appreciate them only in their effects. We know of them, among other things, that they are always to their possessor, when inordinately possessed, a source of the liveliest enjoyment. As the strong man exults in his physical ability, delighting in such exercises as call his muscles into action, so glories the analyst in that moral activity which *disentangles*. He derives pleasure from even the most trivial occupations bringing his talent into play. He is fond of enigmas, of conundrums, of hieroglyphics; exhibiting in his solutions of each a degree of *acumen* which appears to the ordinary apprehension præternatural. His results, brought about by the very soul and essence of method, have, in truth, the whole air of intuition.

The faculty of re-solution is possibly much invigorated by mathematical study, and especially by that highest branch of it which, unjustly, and merely on account of its retrograde operations, has been called, as if *par excellence*, analysis. Yet to calculate is not in itself to analyse. A chess-player, for example, does the one without effort at the other. It follows that the game of chess, in its effects upon mental character, is greatly misunderstood. I am not now writing a treatise, but simply prefacing a somewhat peculiar narrative by observations very much at random; I will, therefore, take occasion to assert that the higher powers of the reflective intellect are more decidedly and more usefully tasked by the unostentatious game of draughts than by all the elaborate frivolity of chess.

In this latter, where the pieces have different and *bizarre* motions, with various and variable values, what is only complex is mistaken (a not unusual error) for what is profound. The *attention* is here called powerfully into play. If it flag for an instant, an oversight is committed, resulting in injury or defeat. The possible moves being not only manifold but involute, the chances of such oversights are multiplied; and in nine cases out of ten it is the more concentrative rather than the more acute player who conquers. In draughts, on the contrary, where the moves are *unique* and have but little variation, the probabilities of inadvertence are diminished, and the mere attention being left comparatively unemployed, what advantages are obtained by either party are obtained by superior *acumen*. To be less abstract—Let us suppose a game of draughts where the pieces are reduced to four kings, and where, of course, no oversight is to be expected. It is obvious that here the victory can be decided (the players being at all equal) only by some *recherché* movement, the result of some strong exertion of the intellect. Deprived of ordinary resources, the analyst throws himself into the spirit of his opponent, identifies himself therewith, and not unfrequently sees thus, at a glance, the sole methods (sometimes indeed absurdly simple ones) by which he may seduce into error or hurry into miscalculation.

Whist has long been noted for its influence upon what is termed the calculating power; and men of the highest order of intellect have been known to take an apparently unaccountable delight in it, while eschewing chess as frivolous. Beyond doubt there is nothing of a similar nature so greatly tasking the faculty of analysis. The best chess-player in Christendom *may* be little more than the best player of chess; but proficiency in whist implies capacity for success in all those more important undertakings where mind struggles with mind. When I say proficiency, I mean that perfection in the game which includes a comprehension of *all* the sources whence legitimate advantage may be derived. These are not only manifold but multiform, and lie frequently among recesses of thought altogether inaccessible to the ordinary understanding. To observe attentively is to remember distinctly; and, so far, the concentrative chess-player will do very well at whist; while the rules of Hoyle (themselves based upon the mere mechanism of the game) are sufficiently and generally comprehensible. Thus to have a retentive memory, and to proceed by "the book," are points commonly regarded as the sum total of good playing. But it is in matters beyond the limits of mere rule that the skill of the analyst is evinced. He makes, in silence, a host of observations and inferences. So, perhaps, do his companions; and the difference in the extent of the information obtained, lies not so much in the validity of the inference as in the quality of the observation. The necessary knowledge is that of *what* to observe. Our player confines himself not at all; nor, because the game is the object, does he reject deductions from things external to the game. He examines the countenance of his partner, comparing it carefully with that of each of his opponents. He considers the mode of assorting the cards in each hand; often counting trump by trump, and honor by honor, through the glances bestowed by their holders upon each. He notes every variation of face as the play progresses, gathering a fund of thought from the differences in the expression of certainty, of surprise, of triumph, or of chagrin. From the manner of gathering up a trick he judges whether the person taking it can make another in the suit. He recognises what is played through feint, by the air with which it is thrown upon the table. A casual or inadvertent word; the accidental dropping or turning of a card, with the accompanying anxiety or carelessness in regard to its concealment; the counting of the tricks, with the order of their arrangement; embarrassment, hesitation, eagerness or trepidation— all afford, to his apparently intuitive perception, indications of the true state of affairs. The first two or three rounds having been played, he is in full possession of the contents of each hand, and thenceforward puts down his cards with as absolute a precision of purpose as if the rest of the party had turned outward the faces of their own.

The analytical power should not be confounded with simple ingenuity; for while the analyst is necessarily ingenious, the ingenious man is often remarkably incapable of analysis. The constructive or combining power, by which ingenuity is usually manifested, and to which the phrenologists (I believe erroneously) have assigned a separate organ, supposing it a primitive faculty, has been so frequently seen in those whose intellect bordered otherwise upon idiocy, as to have attracted general observation among writers on morals. Between ingenuity and the analytic ability there exists a difference far greater, indeed, than that be-tween the fancy and the imagination, but of a character very strictly analogous. It will be found, in fact, that the ingenious are always fanciful, and the *truly* imaginative never otherwise than analytic.

The narrative which follows will appear to the reader somewhat in the light of a commentary upon the propositions just advanced.

Residing in Paris during the spring and part of the summer of 18—, I there became acquainted with a Monsieur C. Auguste Dupin. This young gentleman was of an excellent—indeed of an illustrious family, but, by a variety of untoward events, had been reduced to such poverty that the energy of his character suc-cumbed beneath it, and he ceased to bestir himself in the world, or to care for the retrieval of his fortunes. By courtesy of his credi-tors, there still remained in his possession a small remnant of his patrimony; and, upon the income arising from this, he managed, by means of a rigorous economy, to procure the necessaries of life, without troubling himself about its superfluities. Books, indeed, were his sole luxuries, and in Paris these are easily obtained.

Our first meeting was at an obscure library in the Rue Mont-martre, where the accident of our both being in search of the same very rare and very remarkable volume, brought us into closer com-munion. We saw each other again and again. I was deeply inter-ested in the little family history which he detailed to me with all that candor which a Frenchman indulges whenever mere self is his theme. I was astonished, too, at the vast extent of his reading; and, above all, I felt my soul enkindled within me by the wild fervor, and the vivid freshness of his imagination. Seeking in Paris the ob-jects I then sought, I felt that the society of such a man would be to me a treasure beyond price; and this feeling I frankly confided to him. It was at length arranged that we should live together dur-ing my stay in the city; and as my worldly circumstances were somewhat less embarrassed than his own, I was permitted to be at the expense of renting, and furnishing in a style which suited the rather fantastic gloom of our common temper, a time-eaten and grotesque mansion, long deserted through superstitions into which we did not inquire, and tottering to its fall in a retired and desolate portion of the Faubourg St. Germain.

Had the routine of our life at this place been known to the world, we should have been regarded as madmen—although, perhaps, as madmen of a harmless nature. Our seclusion was perfect. We admitted no visitors. Indeed the locality of our retirement had been carefully kept a secret from my own former associates; and it had been many years since Dupin had ceased to know or be known in Paris. We existed within ourselves alone.

It was a freak of fancy in my friend (for what else shall I call it?) to be enamored of the Night for her own sake; and into this *bizarrerie*, as into all his others, I quietly fell; giving myself up to his wild whims with a perfect *abandon*. The sable divinity would not herself dwell with us always; but we could counterfeit her presence. At the first dawn of the morning we closed all the massy shutters of our old building; lighting a couple of tapers which, strongly perfumed, threw out only the ghastliest and feeblest of rays. By the aid of these we then busied our souls in dreams—reading, writing, or conversing, until warned by the clock of the advent of the true Darkness. Then we sallied forth into the streets, arm in arm, continuing the topics of the day, or roaming far and wide until a late hour, seeking, amid the wild lights and shadows of the populous city, that infinity of mental excitement which quiet observation can afford.

At such times I could not help remarking and admiring (although from his rich ideality I had been prepared to expect it) a peculiar analytic ability in Dupin. He seemed, too, to take an eager delight in its exercise—if not exactly in its display—and did not hesitate to confess the pleasure thus derived. He boasted to me, with a low chuckling laugh, that most men, in respect to himself, wore windows in their bosoms, and was wont to follow up such assertions by direct and very startling proofs of his intimate knowledge of my own. His manner at these moments was frigid and abstract; his eyes were vacant in expression; while his voice, usually a rich tenor, rose into a treble which would have sounded petulantly but for the deliberateness and entire distinctness of the enunciation. Observing him in these moods, I often dwelt meditatively upon the old philosophy of the Bi-Part Soul, and amused myself with the fancy of a double Dupin—the creative and the re-solvent.

Let it not be supposed, from what I have just said, that I am detailing any mystery, or penning any romance. What I have described in the Frenchman, was merely the result of an excited, or perhaps of a diseased intelligence. But of the character of his remarks at the periods in question an example will best convey the idea.

We were strolling one night down a long dirty street, in the vicinity of the Palais Royal. Being both, apparently, occupied with thought, neither of us had spoken a syllable for fifteen minutes at least. All at once Dupin broke forth with these words:

"He is a very little fellow, that's true, and would do better for the *Théâtre des Variétés.*"

"There can be no doubt of that," I replied unwittingly, and not at first observing (so much had I been absorbed in reflection) the extraordinary manner in which the speaker had chimed in with my meditations. In an instant afterward I recollected myself, and my astonishment was profound.

"Dupin," said I, gravely, "this is beyond my comprehension. I do not hesitate to say that I am amazed, and can scarcely credit my senses. How was it possible you should know I was thinking of ———?" Here I paused, to ascertain beyond a doubt whether he really knew of whom I thought.

——— "of Chantilly," said he, "why do you pause? You were remarking to yourself that his diminutive figure unfitted him for tragedy."

This was precisely what had formed the subject of my reflections. Chantilly was a *quondam* cobbler of the Rue St. Denis, who, becoming stage-mad, had attempted the *rôle* of Xerxes, in Crébillon's tragedy so called, and been notoriously Pasquinaded for his pains.

"Tell me, for Heaven's sake," I exclaimed, "the method—if method there is—by which you have been enabled to fathom my soul in this matter." In fact I was even more startled than I would have been willing to express.

"It was the fruiterer," replied my friend, "who brought you to the conclusion that the mender of soles was not of sufficient height for Xerxes *et id genus omne.*"[1]

"The fruiterer!—you astonish me—I know no fruiterer whomsoever."

"The man who ran up against you as we entered the street—it may have been fifteen minutes ago."

I now remembered that, in fact, a fruiterer, carrying upon his head a large basket of apples, had nearly thrown me down, by accident, as we passed from the Rue C—— into the thoroughfare where we stood; but what this had to do with Chantilly I could not possibly understand.

There was not a particle of *charlatanerie* about Dupin. "I will explain," he said, "and that you may comprehend all clearly, we will first retrace the course of your meditations, from the moment in which I spoke to you until that of the *rencontre* with the fruiterer in question. The larger links of the chain run thus— Chantilly, Orion, Dr. Nichols, Epicurus, Stereotomy, the street stones, the fruiterer."

There are few persons who have not, at some period of their lives, amused themselves in retracing the steps by which particular conclusions of their own minds have been attained. The occupation is often full of interest; and he who attempts it for the first time is astonished by the apparently illimitable distance and incoherence between the starting-point and the goal. What, then, must have been my amazement when I heard the Frenchman speak what he had just spoken, and when I could not help acknowledging that he had spoken the truth. He continued:

"We had been talking of horses, if I remember aright, just before leaving the Rue C——. This was the last subject we discussed. As we crossed into this street, a fruiterer, with a large basket upon his head, brushing quickly past us, thrust you upon a pile of paving-stones collected at a spot where the causeway is undergoing repair. You stepped upon one of the loose fragments, slipped, slightly strained your ankle, appeared vexed or sulky, muttered a few words, turned to look at the pile, and then proceeded in silence. I was not particularly attentive to what you did; but observation has become with me, of late, a species of necessity.

"You kept your eyes upon the ground—glancing, with a petulant expression, at the holes and ruts in the pavement, (so that I saw you were still thinking of the stones,) until we reached the little alley called Lamartine, which has been paved, by way of experiment, with the overlapping and riveted blocks. Here your countenance brightened up, and, perceiving your lips move, I could not doubt that you murmured the word 'stereotomy,' a term very affectedly applied to this species of pavement. I knew that you could not say to yourself 'stereotomy' without being brought to think of atomies, and thus of the theories of Epicurus; and since, when we discussed this subject not very long ago, I mentioned to you how singularly, yet with how little notice, the vague guesses of that noble Greek had met with confirmation in the late nebular cosmogony, I felt that you could not avoid casting your eyes upward to the great *nebula* in Orion, and I certainly expected that you would do so. You did look up; and I was now assured that I had correctly followed your steps. But in that bitter *tirade* upon Chantilly, which appeared in yesterday's '*Musée*,' the satirist, making some disgraceful allusions to the cobbler's change of name upon assuming the buskin, quoted a Latin line about which we have often conversed. I mean the line

Perdidit antiquum litera prima sonum[2]

I had told you that this was in reference to Orion, formerly written Urion; and, from certain pungencies connected with this explanation, I was aware that you could not have forgotten it. It was clear, therefore, that you would not fail to combine the two ideas of Orion and Chantilly. That you did combine them I saw by the character of the smile which passed over your lips. You thought of the poor cobbler's immolation. So far, you had been stooping in your gait; but now I saw you draw yourself up to your full height. I was then sure that you reflected upon the diminutive figure of Chantilly. At this point I interrupted your meditations to remark that as, in fact, he *was* a very little fellow—that Chantilly—he would do better at the *Théâtre des Variétés*."

Not long after this, we were looking over an evening edition of the "Gazette des Tribunaux," when the following paragraphs arrested our attention.

"EXTRAORDINARY MURDERS.—This morning, about three o'clock, the inhabitants of the Quartier St. Roch were aroused from sleep by a succession of terrific shrieks, issuing, apparently, from the fourth story of a house in the Rue Morgue, known to be in the sole occupancy of one Madame L'Espanaye, and her daughter, Mademoiselle Camille L'Espanaye. After some delay, occasioned by a fruitless attempt to procure admission in the usual manner, the gateway was broken in with a crowbar, and eight or ten of the neighbors entered, accompanied by two *gendarmes*. By this time the cries had ceased; but, as the party rushed up the first flight of stairs, two or more rough voices, in angry contention, were distinguished, and seemed to proceed from the upper part of the house. As the second landing was reached, these sounds, also, had ceased, and everything remained perfectly quiet. The party spread themselves, and hurried from room to room. Upon arriving at a large back chamber in the fourth story, (the door of which, being found locked, with the key inside, was forced open,) a spectacle presented itself which struck every one present not less with horror than with astonishment.

"The apartment was in the wildest disorder—the furniture broken and thrown about in all directions. There was only one bedstead; and from this the bed had been removed, and thrown into the middle of the floor. On a chair lay a razor, besmeared with blood. On the hearth were two or three long and thick tresses of grey human hair, also dabbled in blood, and seeming to have been pulled out by the roots. Upon the floor were found four Napoleons, an ear-ring of topaz, three large silver spoons, three smaller of *métal d'Alger,* and two bags, containing nearly four thousand francs in gold. The drawers of a *bureau,* which stood in one corner, were open, and had been, apparently, rifled, although many articles still remained in them. A small iron safe was discovered under the *bed* (not under the bedstead). It was open, with the key still in the door. It had no contents beyond a few old letters, and other papers of little consequence.

"Of Madame L'Espanaye no traces were here seen; but an unusual quantity of soot being observed in the fire-place, a search was made in the chimney, and (horrible to relate!) the corpse of the daughter, head downward, was dragged therefrom; it having been thus forced up the narrow aperture for a considerable distance. The body was quite warm. Upon examining it, many excoriations were perceived, no doubt occasioned by the violence with which it had been thrust up and disengaged. Upon the face were many severe scratches, and, upon the throat, dark bruises, and deep indentations of finger nails, as if the deceased had been throttled to death.

"After a thorough investigation of every portion of the house, without farther discovery, the party made its way into a small paved yard in the rear of the building, where lay the corpse of the old lady, with her throat so entirely cut that, upon an attempt to raise her, the head fell off. The body, as well as the head, was fearfully mutilated—the former so much so as scarcely to retain any semblance of humanity.

"To this horrible mystery there is not as yet, we believe, the slightest clew."

The next day's paper had these additional particulars.

"*The Tragedy in the Rue Morgue.* Many individuals have been examined in relation to this most extraordinary and frightful affair." [The word '*affaire*' has not yet, in France, that levity of import which it conveys with us,] "but nothing whatever has transpired to throw light upon it. We give below all the material testimony elicited.

"*Pauline Dubourg*, laundress, deposes that she has known both the deceased for three years, having washed for them during that period. The old lady and her daughter seemed on good terms—very affectionate towards each other. They were excellent pay. Could not speak in regard to their mode or means of living. Believed that Madame L. told fortunes for a living. Was reputed to have money put by. Never met any persons in the house when she called for the clothes or took them home. Was sure that they had no servant in employ. There appeared to be no furniture in any part of the building except in the fourth story.

"*Pierre Moreau*, tobacconist, deposes that he has been in the habit of selling small quantities of tobacco and snuff to Madame L'Espanaye for nearly four years. Was born in the neighborhood, and has always resided there. The deceased and her daughter had occupied the house in which the corpses were found, for more than six years. It was formerly occupied by a jeweller, who underlet the upper rooms to various persons. The house was the property of Madame L. She became dissatisfied with the abuse of the premises by her tenant, and moved into them herself, refusing to let any portion. The old lady was childish. Witness had seen the daughter some five or six times during the six years. The two lived an exceedingly retired life—were reputed to have money. Had heard it said among the neighbors that Madame L. told fortunes—did not believe it. Had never seen any person enter the door except the old lady and her daughter, a porter once or twice, and a physician some eight or ten times.

"Many other persons, neighbors, gave evidence to the same effect. No one was spoken of as frequenting the house. It was not known whether there were any living connexions of Madame L. and her daughter. The shutters of the front windows were seldom opened. Those in the rear were always closed, with the exception of the large back room, fourth story. The house was a good house—not very old.

"*Isidore Musèt, gendarme*, deposes that he was called to the house about three o'clock in the morning, and found some twenty or thirty persons at the gateway, endeavoring to gain admittance. Forced it open, at length, with a bayonet—not with a crowbar. Had but little difficulty in getting it open, on account of its being a double or folding gate, and bolted neither at bottom nor top. The shrieks were continued until the gate was forced—and then suddenly ceased. They seemed to be screams of some person (or persons) in great agony—were loud and drawn out, not short and quick. Witness led the way up stairs. Upon reaching the first landing, heard two voices in loud and angry contention—the one a gruff voice, the other much shriller—a very strange voice. Could distinguish some words of the former, which was that of a Frenchman. Was positive that it was not a woman's voice. Could distinguish the words '*sacré*' and '*diable*.' The shrill voice was that of a foreigner. Could not be sure whether it was the voice of a man or of a woman. Could not make out what was said, but believed the language to be Spanish. The state of the room and of the bodies was described by this witness as we described them yesterday.

"*Henri Duval*, a neighbor, and by trade a silver-smith, deposes that he was one of the party who first entered the house. Corroborates the testimony of Musèt in general. As soon as they forced an entrance, they reclosed the door, to keep out the crowd, which collected very fast, notwithstanding the lateness of the hour. The shrill voice, this witness thinks, was that of an Italian. Was certain it was not French. Could not be sure that it was a man's voice. It might have been a woman's. Was not acquainted with the Italian language. Could not distinguish the words, but was convinced by the intonation that the speaker was an Italian. Knew Madame L. and her daughter. Had conversed with both frequently. Was sure that the shrill voice was not that of either of the deceased.

"—— *Odenheimer, restaurateur*. This witness volunteered his testimony. Not speaking French, was examined through an interpreter. Is a native of Amsterdam. Was passing the house at the time of the shrieks. They lasted for several minutes—probably ten. They were long and loud—very awful and distressing. Was one of those who entered the building. Corroborated the previous evidence in every respect but one. Was sure that the shrill voice was that of a man—of a Frenchman. Could not distinguish the words uttered. They were loud and quick—unequal—spoken apparently in fear as well as in anger. The voice was harsh—not so much shrill as harsh. Could not call it a shrill voice. The gruff voice said repeatedly 'sacré,' 'diable,' and once 'mon Dieu.'

"*Jules Mignaud*, banker, of the firm of Mignaud et Fils, Rue Deloraine. Is the elder Mignaud. Madame L'Espanaye had some property. Had opened an account with his banking house in the spring of the year — (eight years previously). Made frequent deposits in small sums. Had checked for nothing until the third day before her death, when she took out in person the sum of 4000 francs. This sum was paid in gold, and a clerk went home with the money.

"*Adolphe Le Bon*, clerk to Mignaud et Fils, deposes that on the day in question, about noon, he accompanied Madame L'Espanaye to her residence with the 4000 francs, put up in two bags. Upon the door being opened, Mademoiselle L. appeared and took from his hands one of the bags, while the old lady relieved him of the other. He then bowed and departed. Did not see any person in the street at the time. It is a bye-street—very lonely.

"*William Bird*, tailor, deposes that he was one of the party who entered the house. Is an Englishman. Has lived in Paris two years. Was one of the first to ascend the stairs. Heard the voices in contention. The gruff voice was that of a Frenchman. Could make out several words, but cannot now remember all. Heard distinctly 'sacré' and 'mon Dieu.' There was a sound at the moment as if of several persons struggling—a scraping and scuffling sound. The shrill voice was very loud—louder than the gruff one. Is sure that it was not the voice of an Englishman. Appeared to be that of a German. Might have been a woman's voice. Does not understand German.

"Four of the above-named witnesses, being recalled, deposed that the door of the chamber in which was found the body of Mademoiselle L. was locked on the inside when the party reached it. Every thing was perfectly silent—no groans or noises of any kind. Upon forcing the door no person was seen. The windows, both of the back and front room, were down and firmly fastened from within. A door between the two rooms was closed, but not locked. The door leading from the front room into the passage was locked, with the key on the inside. A small room in the front of the house, on the fourth story, at the head of the passage, was open, the door being ajar. This room was crowded with old beds, boxes, and so forth. These were carefully removed and searched. There was not an inch of any portion of the house which was not carefully searched. Sweeps were sent up and down the chimneys. The house was a four story one, with garrets (*mansardes*.) A trap-door on the roof was nailed down very securely—did not appear to have been opened for years. The time elapsing between the hearing of the voices in contention and the breaking open of the room door, was variously stated by the witnesses. Some made it as short as three minutes—some as long as five. The door was opened with difficulty.

"*Alfonzo Garcio*, undertaker, deposes that he resides in the Rue Morgue. Is a native of Spain. Was one of the party who entered the house. Did not proceed up stairs. Is nervous, and was apprehensive of the consequences of agitation. Heard the voices in contention. The gruff voice was that of a Frenchman. Could not distinguish what was said. The shrill voice was that of an Englishman—is sure of this. Does not understand the English language, but judges by the intonation.

"*Alberto Montani*, confectioner, deposes that he was among the first to ascend the stairs. Heard the voices in question. The gruff voice was that of a Frenchman. Distinguished several words. The speaker appeared to be expostulating. Could not make out the words of the shrill voice. Spoke quick and unevenly. Thinks it the voice of a Russian. Corroborates the general testimony. Is an Italian. Never conversed with a native of Russia.

"Several witnesses, recalled, here testified that the chimneys of all the rooms on the fourth story were too narrow to admit the passage of a human being. By 'sweeps' were meant cylindrical sweeping-brushes, such as are employed by those who clean chimneys. These brushes were passed up and down every flue in the house. There is no back passage by which any one could have descended while the party proceeded up stairs. The body of Mademoiselle L'Espanaye was so firmly wedged in the chimney that it could not be got down until four or five of the party united their strength.

"*Paul Dumas*, physician, deposes that he was called to view the bodies about day-break. They were both then lying on the sacking of the bedstead in the chamber where Mademoiselle L. was found. The corpse of the young lady was much bruised and excoriated. The fact that it had been thrust up the chimney would sufficiently account for these appearances. The throat was greatly chafed. There were several deep scratches just below the chin, together with a series of livid spots which were evidently the impression of fingers. The face was fearfully discolored, and the eye-balls protruded. The tongue had been partially bitten through. A large bruise was discovered upon the pit of the stomach, produced, apparently, by the pressure of a knee. In the opinion of M. Dumas, Mademoiselle L'Espanaye had been throttled to death by some person or persons unknown. The corpse of the mother was horribly mutilated. All the bones of the right leg and arm were more or less shattered. The left *tibia* much splintered, as well as all the ribs of the left side. Whole body dreadfully bruised and discolored. It was not possible to say how the injuries had been inflicted. A heavy club of wood, or a broad bar of iron—a chair—any large, heavy, and obtuse weapon would have produced such results, if wielded by the hands of a very powerful man. No woman could have inflicted the blows with any weapon. The head of the deceased, when seen by witness, was entirely separated from the body, and was also greatly shattered. The throat had evidently been cut with some very sharp instrument—probably with a razor.

"*Alexandre Etienne*, surgeon, was called with M. Dumas to view the bodies. Corroborated the testimony, and the opinions of M. Dumas.

"Nothing farther of importance was elicited, although several other persons were examined. A murder so mysterious, and so perplexing in all its particulars, was never before committed in Paris—if indeed a murder has been committed at all. The police are entirely at fault—an unusual occurrence in affairs of this nature. There is not, however, the shadow of a clew apparent."

The evening edition of the paper stated that the greatest excitement still continued in the Quartier St. Roch—that the premises in question had been carefully re-searched, and fresh examinations

of witnesses instituted, but all to no purpose. A postscript, how-
ever, mentioned that Adolphe Le Bon had been arrested and
imprisoned—although nothing appeared to criminate him, be-
yond the facts already detailed.

Dupin seemed singularly interested in the progress of this
affair—at least so I judged from his manner, for he made no com-
ments. It was only after the announcement that Le Bon had been
imprisoned, that he asked me my opinion respecting the murders.

I could merely agree with all Paris in considering them an insol-
uble mystery. I saw no means by which it would be possible to
trace the murderer.

"We must not judge of the means," said Dupin, "by this shell of
an examination. The Parisian police, so much extolled for *acu-
men*, are cunning, but no more. There is no method in their pro-
ceedings, beyond the method of the moment. They make a vast
parade of measures; but, not unfrequently, these are so ill adapted
to the objects proposed, as to put us in mind of Monsieur Jour-
dain's calling for his *robe-de-chambre—pour mieux entendre la
musique.*[3] The results attained by them are not unfrequently sur-
prising, but, for the most part, are brought about by simple dili-
gence and activity. When these qualities are unavailing, their
schemes fail. Vidocq, for example, was a good guesser, and a per-
severing man. But, without educated thought, he erred continually
by the very intensity of his investigations.[4] He impaired his vision
by holding the object too close. He might see, perhaps, one or two
points with unusual clearness, but in so doing he, necessarily, lost
sight of the matter as a whole. Thus there is such a thing as being
too profound. Truth is not always in a well. In fact, as regards the
more important knowledge, I do believe that she is invariably su-
perficial. The depth lies in the valleys where we seek her, and not
upon the mountain-tops where she is found. The modes and
sources of this kind of error are well typified in the contemplation
of the heavenly bodies. To look at a star by glances—to view it in
a side-long way, by turning toward it the exterior portions of the
retina (more susceptible of feeble impressions of light than the in-
terior), is to behold the star distinctly—is to have the best appreci-
ation of its lustre—a lustre which grows dim just in proportion as
we turn our vision *fully* upon it. A greater number of rays actually
fall upon the eye in the latter case, but, in the former, there is the

more refined capacity for comprehension. By undue profundity we perplex and enfeeble thought; and it is possible to make even Venus herself vanish from the firmanent by a scrutiny too sustained, too concentrated, or too direct.

"As for these murders, let us enter into some examinations for ourselves, before we make up an opinion respecting them. An inquiry will afford us amusement," [I thought this an odd term, so applied, but said nothing] "and, besides, Le Bon once rendered me a service for which I am not ungrateful. We will go and see the premises with our own eyes. I know G——, the Prefect of Police, and shall have no difficulty in obtaining the necessary permission."

The permission was obtained, and we proceeded at once to the Rue Morgue. This is one of those miserable thoroughfares which intervene between the Rue Richelieu and the Rue St. Roch. It was late in the afternoon when we reached it; as this quarter is at a great distance from that in which we resided. The house was readily found; for there were still many persons gazing up at the closed shutters, with an objectless curiosity, from the opposite side of the way. It was an ordinary Parisian house, with a gateway, on one side of which was a glazed watch-box, with a sliding panel in the window, indicating a *loge de concierge*. Before going in we walked up the street, turned down an alley, and then, again turning, passed in the rear of the building—Dupin, meanwhile, examining the whole neighborhood, as well as the house, with a minuteness of attention for which I could see no possible object.

Retracing our steps, we came again to the front of the dwelling, rang, and, having shown our credentials, were admitted by the agents in charge. We went up stairs—into the chamber where the body of Mademoiselle L'Espanaye had been found, and where both the deceased still lay. The disorders of the room had, as usual, been suffered to exist. I saw nothing beyond what had been stated in the "Gazette des Tribunaux." Dupin scrutinized every thing—not excepting the bodies of the victims. We then went into the other rooms, and into the yard; a *gendarme* accompanying us throughout. The examination occupied us until dark, when we took our departure. On our way home my companion stepped in for a moment at the office of one of the daily papers.

I have said that the whims of my friend were manifold, and that

Je les ménagais:—for this phrase there is no English equivalent.[5] It was his humor, now, to decline all conversation on the subject of the murder, until about noon the next day. He then asked me, suddenly, if I had observed any thing *peculiar* at the scene of the atrocity.

There was something in his manner of emphasizing the word "peculiar," which caused me to shudder, without knowing why.

"No, nothing *peculiar*," I said; "nothing more, at least, than we both saw stated in the paper."

"The 'Gazette,' " he replied, "has not entered, I fear, into the unusual horror of the thing. But dismiss the idle opinions of this print. It appears to me that this mystery is considered insoluble, for the very reason which should cause it to be regarded as easy of solution—I mean for the *outré* character of its features. The police are confounded by the seeming absence of motive—not for the murder itself—but for the atrocity of the murder. They are puzzled, too, by the seeming impossibility of reconciling the voices heard in contention, with the facts that no one was discovered up stairs but the assassinated Mademoiselle L'Espanaye, and that there were no means of egress without the notice of the party ascending. The wild disorder of the room; the corpse thrust, with the head downward, up the chimney; the frightful mutilation of the body of the old lady; these considerations, with those just mentioned, and others which I need not mention, have sufficed to paralyze the powers, by putting completely at fault the boasted *acumen*, of the government agents. They have fallen into the gross but common error of confounding the unusual with the abstruse. But it is by these deviations from the plane of the ordinary, that reason feels its way, if at all, in its search for the true. In investigations such as we are now pursuing, it should not be so much asked 'what has occurred,' as 'what has occurred that has never occurred before.' In fact, the facility with which I shall arrive, or have arrived, at the solution of this mystery, is in the direct ratio of its apparent insolubility in the eyes of the police."

I stared at the speaker in mute astonishment.

"I am now awaiting," continued he, looking toward the door of our apartment—"I am now awaiting a person who, although perhaps not the perpetrator of these butcheries, must have been in some measure implicated in their perpetration. Of the worst portion of the crimes committed, it is probable that he is innocent. I hope that I am right in this supposition; for upon it I build my expectation of reading the entire riddle. I look for the man here— in this room—every moment. It is true that he may not arrive; but the probability is that he will. Should he come, it will be necessary to detain him. Here are pistols; and we both know how to use them when occasion demands their use."

I took the pistols, scarcely knowing what I did, or believing what I heard, while Dupin went on, very much as if in a soliloquy. I have already spoken of his abstract manner at such times. His discourse was addressed to myself; but his voice, although by no means loud, had that intonation which is commonly employed in speaking to some one at a great distance. His eyes, vacant in expression, regarded only the wall.

"That the voices heard in contention," he said, "by the party upon the stairs, were not the voices of the women themselves, was fully proved by the evidence. This relieves us of all doubt upon the question whether the old lady could have first destroyed the daughter, and afterward have committed suicide. I speak of this point chiefly for the sake of method; for the strength of Madame L'Espanaye would have been utterly unequal to the task of thrusting her daughter's corpse up the chimney as it was found; and the nature of the wounds upon her own person entirely preclude the idea of self-destruction. Murder, then, has been committed by some third party; and the voices of this third party were those heard in contention. Let me now advert—not to the whole testimony respecting these voices—but to what was *peculiar* in that testimony. Did you observe any thing peculiar about it?"

I remarked that, while all the witnesses agreed in supposing the gruff voice to be that of a Frenchman, there was much disagreement in regard to the shrill, or, as one individual termed it, the harsh voice.

"That was the evidence itself," said Dupin, "but it was not the peculiarity of the evidence. You have observed nothing distinctive. Yet there *was* something to be observed. The witnesses, as you remark, agreed about the gruff voice; they were here unanimous. But in regard to the shrill voice, the peculiarity is—not that they disagreed—but that, while an Italian, an Englishman, a Spaniard, a Hollander, and a Frenchman attempted to describe it, each one spoke of it as that *of a foreigner*. Each is sure that it was not the voice of one of his own countrymen. Each likens it—not to the voice of an individual of any nation with whose language he is conversant—but the converse. The Frenchman supposes it the voice of a Spaniard, and 'might have distinguished some words *had he been acquainted with the Spanish*.' The Dutchman maintains it to have been that of a Frenchman; but we find it stated that '*not understanding French this witness was examined through an interpreter*.' The Englishman thinks it the voice of a German, and '*does not understand German*.' The Spaniard 'is sure' that it was that of an Englishman, but 'judges by the intonation' altogether, '*as he has no knowledge of the English*.' The Italian believes it the voice of a Russian, but '*has never conversed with a native of Russia*.' A second Frenchman differs, moreover, with the first, and is positive that the voice was that of an Italian; but, *not being cognizant of that tongue*, is, like the Spaniard, 'convinced by the intonation.' Now, how strangely unusual must that voice have really been, about which such testimony as this *could* have been elicited!—in whose *tones*, even, denizens of the five great divisions of Europe could recognise nothing familiar! You will say that it might have been the voice of an Asiatic—of an African. Neither Asiatics nor Africans abound in Paris; but, without denying the inference, I will now merely call your attention to three points. The voice is termed by one witness 'harsh rather than shrill.' It is represented by two others to have been 'quick and *unequal*.' No words—no sounds resembling words—were by any witness mentioned as distinguishable.

"I know not," continued Dupin, "what impression I may have made, so far, upon your own understanding; but I do not hesitate to say that legitimate deductions even from this portion of the testimony—the portion respecting the gruff and shrill voices—are in themselves sufficient to engender a suspicion which should give direction to all farther progress in the investigation of the mystery. I said 'legitimate deductions;' but my meaning is not thus fully expressed. I designed to imply that the deductions are the *sole* proper ones, and that the suspicion arises *inevitably* from them as the single result. What the suspicion is, however, I will not say just yet. I merely wish you to bear in mind that, with myself, it was sufficiently forcible to give a definite form—a certain tendency—to my inquiries in the chamber.

"Let us now transport ourselves, in fancy, to this chamber. What shall we first seek here? The means of egress employed by the murderers. It is not too much to say that neither of us believe in præternatural events. Madame and Mademoiselle L'Espanaye were not destroyed by spirits. The doers of the deed were material, and escaped materially. Then how? Fortunately, there is but one mode of reasoning upon the point, and that mode *must* lead us to a definite decision.—Let us examine, each by each, the possible means of egress. It is clear that the assassins were in the room where Mademoiselle L'Espanaye was found, or at least in the room adjoining, when the party ascended the stairs. It is then only from these two apartments that we have to seek issues. The police have laid bare the floors, the ceilings, and the masonry of the walls, in every direction. No *secret* issues could have escaped their vigilance. But, not trusting to *their* eyes, I examined with my own. There were, then, *no* secret issues. Both doors leading from the rooms into the passage were securely locked, with the keys inside. Let us turn to the chimneys. These, although of ordinary width for some eight or ten feet above the hearths, will not admit, throughout their extent, the body of a large cat. The impossibility of egress, by means already stated, being thus absolute, we are reduced to the windows. Through those of the front room no one could have escaped without notice from the crowd in the street. The murderers *must* have passed, then, through those of the back room. Now, brought to this conclusion in so unequivocal a manner as we are, it is not our part, as reasoners, to reject it on account of apparent impossibilities. It is only left for us to prove that these apparent 'impossibilities' are, in reality, not such.

"There are two windows in the chamber. One of them is unobstructed by furniture, and is wholly visible. The lower portion of the other is hidden from view by the head of the unwieldy bedstead which is thrust close up against it. The former was found securely fastened from within. It resisted the utmost force of those who endeavored to raise it. A large gimlet-hole had been pierced in its frame to the left, and a very stout nail was found fitted therein, nearly to the head. Upon examining the other window, a similar nail was seen similarly fitted in it; and a vigorous attempt to raise this sash, failed also. The police were now entirely satisfied that egress had not been in these directions. And, *therefore*, it was thought a matter of supererogation to withdraw the nails and open the windows.

"My own examination was somewhat more particular, and was so for the reason I have just given—because here it was, I knew, that all apparent impossibilities *must* be proved to be not such in reality.

"I proceeded to think thus—*à posteriori.*[6] The murderers *did* escape from one of these windows. This being so, they could not have re-fastened the sashes from the inside, as they were found fastened;—the consideration which put a stop, through its obviousness, to the scrutiny of the police in this quarter. Yet the sashes *were* fastened. They *must*, then, have the power of fastening themselves. There was no escape from this conclusion. I stepped to the unobstructed casement, withdrew the nail with some difficulty, and attempted to raise the sash. It resisted all my efforts, as I had anticipated. A concealed spring must, I now knew, exist; and this corroboration of my idea convinced me that my premises, at least, were correct, however mysterious still appeared the circumstances attending the nails. A careful search soon brought to light the hidden spring. I pressed it, and, satisfied with the discovery, forbore to upraise the sash.

"I now replaced the nail and regarded it attentively. A person passing out through this window might have reclosed it, and the spring would have caught—but the nail could not have been replaced. The conclusion was plain, and again narrowed in the field of my investigations. The assassins *must* have escaped through the other window. Supposing, then, the springs upon each sash to be the same, as was probable, there *must* be found a difference between the nails, or at least between the modes of their fixture. Getting upon the sacking of the bedstead, I looked over the headboard minutely at the second casement. Passing my hand down behind the board, I readily discovered and pressed the spring, which was, as I had supposed, identical in character with its neighbor. I now looked at the nail. It was as stout as the other, and apparently fitted in the same manner—driven in nearly up to the head.

"You will say that I was puzzled; but, if you think so, you must have misunderstood the nature of the inductions. To use a sporting phrase, I had not been once 'at fault.' The scent had never for an instant been lost. There was no flaw in any link of the chain. I had traced the secret to its ultimate result,—and that result was *the nail*. It had, I say, in every respect, the appearance of its fellow in the other window; but this fact was an absolute nullity (conclusive as it might seem to be) when compared with the consideration that here, at this point, terminated the clew. 'There *must* be something wrong,' I said, 'about the nail.' I touched it; and the head, with about a quarter of an inch of the shank, came off in my fingers. The rest of the shank was in the gimlet-hole, where it had been broken off. The fracture was an old one (for its edges were incrusted with rust), and had apparently been accomplished by the blow of a hammer, which had partially imbedded, in the top of the bottom sash, the head portion of the nail. I now carefully replaced this head portion in the indentation whence I had taken it, and the resemblance to a perfect nail was complete—the fissure was invisible. Pressing the spring, I gently raised the sash for a few inches; the head went up with it, remaining firm in its bed. I closed the window, and the semblance of the whole nail was again perfect.

"The riddle, so far, was now unriddled. The assassin had escaped through the window which looked upon the bed. Dropping of its own accord upon his exit (or perhaps purposely closed), it had become fastened by the spring; and it was the retention of this spring which had been mistaken by the police for that of the nail,—farther inquiry being thus considered unnecessary.

"The next question is that of the mode of descent. Upon this point I had been satisfied in my walk with you around the building. About five feet and a half from the casement in question there runs a lightning-rod. From this rod it would have been impossible for any one to reach the window itself, to say nothing of entering it. I observed, however, that the shutters of the fourth story were of the peculiar kind called by Parisian carpenters *ferrades*—a kind rarely employed at the present day, but frequently seen upon very old mansions at Lyons and Bordeaux. They are in the form of an ordinary door, (a single, not a folding door) except that the lower half is latticed or worked in open trellis—thus affording an excellent hold for the hands. In the present instance these shutters are fully three feet and a half broad. When we saw them from the rear of the house, they were both about half open—that is to say, they stood off at right angles from the wall. It is probable that the police, as well as myself, examined the back of the tenement; but, if so, in looking at these *ferrades* in the line of their breadth (as they must have done), they did not perceive this great breadth itself, or, at all events, failed to take it into due consideration. In fact, having once satisfied themselves that no egress could have been made in this quarter, they would naturally bestow here a very cursory examination. It was clear to me, however, that the shutter belonging to the window at the head of the bed, would, if swung fully back to the wall, reach to within two feet of the lightning-rod. It was also evident that, by exertion of a very unusual degree of activity and courage, an entrance into the window, from the rod, might have been thus effected.—By reaching to the distance of two feet and a half (we now suppose the shutter open to its whole extent) a robber might have taken a firm grasp upon the trellis-work. Letting go, then, his hold upon the rod, placing his feet securely against the wall, and springing boldly from it, he might have swung the shutter so as to close it, and, if we imagine the window open at the time, might even have swung himself into the room.

"I wish you to bear especially in mind that I have spoken of a *very* unusual degree of activity as requisite to success in so hazardous and so difficult a feat. It is my design to show you, first, that the thing might possibly have been accomplished:—but, secondly and *chiefly*, I wish to impress upon your understanding the *very extraordinary*—the almost præternatural character of that agility which could have accomplished it.

"You will say, no doubt, using the language of the law, that 'to make out my case,' I should rather undervalue, than insist upon a full estimation of the activity required in this matter. This may be the practice in law, but it is not the usage of reason. My ultimate object is only the truth. My immediate purpose is to lead you to place in juxta-position, that *very unusual* activity of which I have just spoken, with that *very peculiar* shrill (or harsh) and *unequal* voice, about whose nationality no two persons could be found to agree, and in whose utterance no syllabification could be detected."

At these words a vague and half-formed conception of the meaning of Dupin flitted over my mind. I seemed to be upon the verge of comprehension, without power to comprehend—as men, at times, find themselves upon the brink of remembrance, without being able, in the end, to remember. My friend went on with his discourse.

"You will see," he said, "that I have shifted the question from the mode of egress to that of ingress. It was my design to convey the idea that both were effected in the same manner, at the same point. Let us now revert to the interior of the room. Let us survey the appearances here. The drawers of the bureau, it is said, had been rifled, although many articles of apparel still remained within them. The conclusion here is absurd. It is a mere guess—a very silly one—and no more. How are we to know that the articles found in the drawers were not all these drawers had originally contained? Madame L'Espanaye and her daughter lived an exceedingly retired life—saw no company—seldom went out—had little use for numerous changes of habiliment. Those found were at least of as good quality as any likely to be possessed by these ladies. If a thief had taken any, why did he not take the best—why did he not take all? In a word, why did he abandon four thousand francs in gold to encumber himself with a bundle of linen? The gold *was* abandoned. Nearly the whole sum mentioned by Monsieur Mignaud, the banker, was discovered, in bags, upon the floor. I wish you, therefore, to discard from your thoughts the blundering idea of *motive*, engendered in the brains of the police by that portion of the evidence which speaks of money delivered at the door of the house. Coincidences ten times as remarkable as this (the delivery of the money, and murder committed within three days upon the party receiving it), happen to all of us every hour of our lives, without attracting even momentary notice. Coincidences, in general, are great stumbling-blocks in the way of that class of thinkers who have been educated to know nothing of the theory of probabilities—that theory to which the most glorious objects of human research are indebted for the most glorious of illustration. In the present instance, had the gold been gone, the fact of its delivery three days before would have formed something more than a coincidence. It would have been corroborative of this idea of motive. But, under the real circumstances of the case, if we are to suppose gold the motive of this outrage, we must also imagine the perpetrator so vacillating an idiot as to have abandoned his gold and his motive together.

"Keeping now steadily in mind the points to which I have drawn your attention—that peculiar voice, that unusual agility, and that startling absence of motive in a murder so singularly atrocious as this—let us glance at the butchery itself. Here is a woman strangled to death by manual strength, and thrust up a chimney, head downward. Ordinary assassins employ no such modes of murder as this. Least of all, do they thus dispose of the murdered. In the manner of thrusting the corpse up the chimney, you will admit that there was something *excessively outré*—something altogether irreconcilable with our common notions of human action, even when we suppose the actors the most depraved of men. Think, too, how great must have been that strength which could have thrust the body *up* such an aperture so forcibly that the united vigor of several persons was found barely sufficient to drag it *down*!

"Turn, now, to other indications of the employment of a vigor most marvellous. On the hearth were thick tresses—very thick tresses—of grey human hair. These had been torn out by the roots. You are aware of the great force necessary in tearing thus from the head even twenty or thirty hairs together. You saw the locks in question as well as myself. Their roots (a hideous sight!) were clotted with fragments of the flesh of the scalp—sure token of the prodigious power which had been exerted in uprooting perhaps half a million of hairs at a time. The throat of the old lady was not merely cut, but the head absolutely severed from the body: the instrument was a mere razor. I wish you also to look at the *brutal* ferocity of these deeds. Of the bruises upon the body of Madame L'Espanaye I do not speak. Monsieur Dumas, and his worthy coadjutor Monsieur Etienne, have pronounced that they were inflicted by some obtuse instrument; and so far these gentlemen are very correct. The obtuse instrument was clearly the stone pavement in the yard, upon which the victim had fallen from the window which looked in upon the bed. This idea, however simple it may now seem, escaped the police for the same reason that the breadth of the shutters escaped them—because, by the affair of the nails, their perceptions had been hermetically sealed against the possibility of the windows having ever been opened at all.

"If now, in addition to all these things, you have properly reflected upon the odd disorder of the chamber, we have gone so far as to combine the ideas of an agility astounding, a strength superhuman, a ferocity brutal, a butchery without motive, a *grotesquerie* in horror absolutely alien from humanity, and a voice foreign in tone to the ears of men of many nations, and devoid of all distinct or intelligible syllabification. What result, then, has ensued? What impression have I made upon your fancy?"

I felt a creeping of the flesh as Dupin asked me the question. "A madman," I said, "has done this deed—some raving maniac, escaped from a neighboring *Maison de Santé.*"

"In some respects," he replied, "your idea is not irrelevant. But the voices of madmen, even in their wildest paroxysms, are never found to tally with that peculiar voice heard upon the stairs. Madmen are of some nation, and their language, however incoherent in its words, has always the coherence of syllabification. Besides, the hair of a madman is not such as I now hold in my hand. I disentangled this little tuft from the rigidly clutched fingers of Madame L'Espanaye. Tell me what you can make of it."

"Dupin!" I said, completely unnerved; "this hair is most unusual—this is no *human* hair."

"I have not asserted that it is," said he; "but, before we decide this point, I wish you to glance at the little sketch I have here traced upon this paper. It is a *fac-simile* drawing of what has been described in one portion of the testimony as 'dark bruises, and deep indentations of finger nails,' upon the throat of Mademoiselle L'Espanaye, and in another, (by Messrs. Dumas and Etienne,) as a 'series of livid spots, evidently the impression of fingers.'

"You will perceive," continued my friend, spreading out the paper upon the table before us, "that this drawing gives the idea of a firm and fixed hold. There is no *slipping* apparent. Each finger has retained—possibly until the death of the victim—the fearful grasp by which it originally imbedded itself. Attempt, now, to place all your fingers, at the same time, in the respective impressions as you see them."

I made the attempt in vain.

"We are possibly not giving this matter a fair trial," he said. "The paper is spread out upon a plane surface; but the human throat is cylindrical. Here is a billet of wood, the circumference of which is about that of the throat. Wrap the drawing around it, and try the experiment again."

I did so; but the difficulty was even more obvious than before. "This," I said, "is the mark of no human hand."

"Read now," replied Dupin, "this passage from Cuvier."

It was a minute anatomical and generally descriptive account of the large fulvous Ourang-Outang of the East Indian Islands. The gigantic stature, the prodigious strength and activity, the wild ferocity, and the imitative propensities of these mammalia are sufficiently well known to all. I understood the full horrors of the murder at once.

"The description of the digits," said I, as I made an end of reading, "is in exact accordance with this drawing. I see that no animal but an Ourang-Outang, of the species here mentioned, could have impressed the indentations as you have traced them. This tuft of tawny hair, too, is identical in character with that of the beast of Cuvier. But I cannot possibly comprehend the particulars of this frightful mystery. Besides, there were *two* voices heard in contention, and one of them was unquestionably the voice of a Frenchman."

"True; and you will remember an expression attributed almost unanimously, by the evidence, to this voice,—the expression, *'mon Dieu!'* This, under the circumstances, has been justly characterized by one of the witnesses (Montani, the confectioner,) as an expression of remonstrance or expostulation. Upon these two words, therefore, I have mainly built my hopes of a full solution of the riddle. A Frenchman was cognizant of the murder. It is possible—indeed it is far more than probable—that he was innocent of all participation in the bloody transactions which took place. The Ourang-Outang may have escaped from him. He may have traced it to the chamber; but, under the agitating circumstances which ensued, he could never have re-captured it. It is still at large. I will not pursue these guesses—for I have no right to call them more—since the shades of reflection upon which they are based are scarcely of sufficient depth to be appreciable by my own intellect, and since I could not pretend to make them intelligible to the understanding of another. We will call them guesses then, and speak of them as such. If the Frenchman in question is indeed, as I suppose, innocent of this atrocity, this advertisement, which I left last night, upon our return home, at the office of 'Le Monde,' (a paper devoted to the shipping interest, and much sought by sailors,) will bring him to our residence."

He handed me a paper, and I read thus:

CAUGHT—*In the Bois de Boulogne, early in the morning of the —— inst.,* (the morning of the murder,) *a very large, tawny Ourang-Outang of the Bornese species. The owner, (who is ascertained to be a sailor, belonging to a Maltese vessel,) may have the animal again, upon identifying it satisfactorily, and paying a few charges arising from its capture and keeping. Call at No. ——, Rue ——, Faubourg St. Germain—au troisième.*

"How was it possible," I asked, "that you should know the man to be a sailor, and belonging to a Maltese vessel?"

"I do *not* know it," said Dupin. "I am not *sure* of it. Here, however, is a small piece of ribbon, which from its form, and from its greasy appearance, has evidently been used in tying the hair in one of those long *queues* of which sailors are so fond. Moreover, this knot is one which few besides sailors can tie, and is peculiar to the Maltese. I picked the ribbon up at the foot of the lightning-rod. It could not have belonged to either of the deceased. Now if, after all, I am wrong in my induction from this ribbon, that the Frenchman was a sailor belonging to a Maltese vessel, still I can have done no harm in saying what I did in the advertisement. If I am in error, he will merely suppose that I have been misled by some circumstance into which he will not take the trouble to inquire. But if I am right, a great point is gained. Cognizant although innocent of the murder, the Frenchman will naturally hesitate about replying to the advertisement—about demanding the Ourang-Outang. He will reason thus:—'I am innocent; I am poor; my Ourang-Outang is of great value—to one in my circumstances a fortune of itself—why should I lose it through idle apprehensions of danger? Here it is, within my grasp. It was found in the Bois de Boulogne—at a vast distance from the scene of that butchery. How can it ever be suspected that a brute beast should have done the deed? The police are at fault—they have failed to procure the slightest clew. Should they even trace the animal, it would be impossible to prove me cognizant of the murder, or to implicate me in guilt on account of that cognizance. Above all, *I am known*. The advertiser designates me as the possessor of the beast. I am not sure to what limit his knowledge may extend. Should I avoid claiming a property of so great value, which it is known that I possess, I will render the animal at least, liable to suspicion. It is not my policy to attract attention either to myself or to the beast. I will answer the advertisement, get the Ourang-Outang, and keep it close until this matter has blown over.'"

At this moment we heard a step upon the stairs.

"Be ready," said Dupin, "with your pistols, but neither use them nor show them until at a signal from myself."

The front door of the house had been left open, and the visiter had entered, without ringing, and advanced several steps upon the staircase. Now, however, he seemed to hesitate. Presently we heard him descending. Dupin was moving quickly to the door, when we again heard him coming up. He did not turn back a second time, but stepped up with decision, and rapped at the door of our chamber.

"Come in," said Dupin, in a cheerful and hearty tone.

A man entered. He was a sailor, evidently,—a tall, stout, and muscular-looking person, with a certain dare-devil expression of countenance, not altogether unprepossessing. His face, greatly sunburnt, was more than half hidden by whisker and *mustachio*. He had with him a huge oaken cudgel, but appeared to be otherwise unarmed. He bowed awkwardly, and bade us "good evening," in French accents, which, although somewhat Neufchatel-ish, were still sufficiently indicative of a Parisian origin.

"Sit down, my friend," said Dupin. "I suppose you have called about the Ourang-Outang. Upon my word, I almost envy you the possession of him; a remarkably fine, and no doubt a very valuable animal. How old do you suppose him to be?"

The sailor drew a long breath, with the air of a man relieved of some intolerable burden, and then replied, in an assured tone:

"I have no way of telling—but he can't be more than four or five years old. Have you got him here?"

"Oh no; we had no conveniences for keeping him here. He is at a livery stable in the Rue Dubourg, just by. You can get him in the morning. Of course you are prepared to identify the property?"

"To be sure I am, sir."

"I shall be sorry to part with him," said Dupin.

"I don't mean that you should be at all this trouble for nothing, sir," said the man. "Couldn't expect it. Am very willing to pay a reward for the finding of the animal—that is to say, any thing in reason."

"Well," replied my friend, "that is all very fair, to be sure. Let me think!—what should I have? Oh! I will tell you. My reward shall be this. You shall give me all the information in your power about these murders in the Rue Morgue."

Dupin said the last words in a very low tone, and very quietly. Just as quietly, too, he walked toward the door, locked it, and put the key in his pocket. He then drew a pistol from his bosom and placed it, without the least flurry, upon the table.

The sailor's face flushed up as if he were struggling with suffocation. He started to his feet and grasped his cudgel; but the next moment he fell back into his seat, trembling violently, and with the countenance of death itself. He spoke not a word. I pitied him from the bottom of my heart.

"My friend," said Dupin, in a kind tone, "you are alarming yourself unnecessarily—you are indeed. We mean you no harm whatever. I pledge you the honor of a gentleman, and of a Frenchman, that we intend you no injury. I perfectly well know that you are innocent of the atrocities in the Rue Morgue. It will not do, however, to deny that you are in some measure implicated in them. From what I have already said, you must know that I have had means of information about this matter—means of which you could never have dreamed. Now the thing stands thus. You have done nothing which you could have avoided—nothing, certainly, which renders you culpable. You were not even guilty of robbery, when you might have robbed with impunity. You have nothing to conceal. You have no reason for concealment. On the other hand, you are bound by every principle of honor to confess all you know. An innocent man is now imprisoned, charged with that crime of which you can point out the perpetrator."

The sailor had recovered his presence of mind, in a great measure, while Dupin uttered these words; but his original boldness of bearing was all gone.

"So help me God," said he, after a brief pause, "I *will* tell you all I know about this affair;—but I do not expect you to believe one half I say—I would be a fool indeed if I did. Still, I *am* innocent, and I will make a clean breast if I die for it."

What he stated was, in substance, this. He had lately made a voyage to the Indian Archipelago. A party, of which he formed one, landed at Borneo, and passed into the interior on an excursion of pleasure. Himself and a companion had captured the

Ourang-Outang. This companion dying, the animal fell into his own exclusive possession. After great trouble, occasioned by the intractable ferocity of his captive during the home voyage, he at length succeeded in lodging it safely at his own residence in Paris, where, not to attract toward himself the unpleasant curiosity of his neighbors, he kept it carefully secluded, until such time as it should recover from a wound in the foot, received from a splinter on board ship. His ultimate design was to sell it.

Returning home from some sailors' frolic the night, or rather in the morning of the murder, he found the beast occupying his own bed-room, into which it had broken from a closet adjoining, where it had been, as was thought, securely confined. Razor in hand, and fully lathered, it was sitting before a looking-glass, attempting the operation of shaving, in which it had no doubt previously watched its master through the key-hole of the closet. Terrified at the sight of so dangerous a weapon in the possession of an animal so ferocious, and so well able to use it, the man, for some moments, was at a loss what to do. He had been accustomed, however, to quiet the creature, even in its fiercest moods, by the use of a whip, and to this he now resorted. Upon sight of it, the Ourang-Outang sprang at once through the door of the chamber, down the stairs, and thence, through a window, unfortunately open, into the street.

The Frenchman followed in despair; the ape, razor still in hand, occasionally stopping to look back and gesticulate at its pursuer, until the latter had nearly come up with it. It then again made off. In this manner the chase continued for a long time. The streets were profoundly quiet, as it was nearly three o'clock in the morning. In passing down an alley in the rear of the Rue Morgue, the fugitive's attention was arrested by a light gleaming from the open window of Madame L'Espanaye's chamber, in the fourth story of her house. Rushing to the building, it perceived the lightning-rod, clambered up with inconceivable agility, grasped the shutter, which was thrown fully back against the wall, and, by its means, swung itself directly upon the headboard of the bed. The whole feat did not occupy a minute. The shutter was kicked open again by the Ourang-Outang as it entered the room.

The sailor, in the meantime, was both rejoiced and perplexed. He had strong hopes of now recapturing the brute, as it could scarcely escape from the trap into which it had ventured, except by the rod, where it might be intercepted as it came down. On the other hand, there was much cause for anxiety as to what it might do in the house. This latter reflection urged the man still to follow the fugitive. A lightning-rod is ascended without difficulty, especially by a sailor; but, when he had arrived as high as the window, which lay far to his left, his career was stopped; the most that he could accomplish was to reach over so as to obtain a glimpse of the interior of the room. At this glimpse he nearly fell from his hold through excess of horror. Now it was that those hideous shrieks arose upon the night, which had startled from slumber the inmates of the Rue Morgue. Madame L'Espanaye and her daughter, habited in their night clothes, had apparently been occupied in arranging some papers in the iron chest already mentioned, which had been wheeled into the middle of the room. It was open, and its contents lay beside it on the floor. The victims must have been sitting with their backs toward the window; and, from the time elapsing between the ingress of the beast and the screams, it seems probable that it was not immediately perceived. The flapping-to of the shutter would naturally have been attributed to the wind.

As the sailor looked in, the gigantic animal had seized Madame L'Espanaye by the hair, (which was loose, as she had been combing it,) and was flourishing the razor about her face, in imitation of the motions of a barber. The daughter lay prostrate and motionless; she had swooned. The screams and struggles of the old lady (during which the hair was torn from her head) had the effect of changing the probably pacific purposes of the Ourang-Outang into those of wrath. With one determined sweep of its muscular arm it nearly severed her head from her body. The sight of blood inflamed its anger into phrenzy. Gnashing its teeth, and flashing fire from its eyes, it flew upon the body of the girl, and imbedded its fearful talons in her throat, retaining its grasp until she expired. Its wandering and wild glances fell at this moment upon the head of the bed, over which the face of its master, rigid with horror, was just discernible. The fury of the beast, who no doubt bore still in mind the dreaded whip, was instantly converted into fear. Conscious of having deserved punishment, it seemed desirous of concealing its bloody deeds, and skipped about the chamber in an agony of nervous agitation; throwing down and breaking the furniture as it moved, and dragging the bed from the bedstead. In conclusion, it seized first the corpse of the daughter, and thrust it up the chimney, as it was found; then that of the old lady, which it immediately hurled through the window headlong.

As the ape approached the casement with its mutilated burden, the sailor shrank aghast to the rod, and, rather gliding than clambering down it, hurried at once home—dreading the consequences of the butchery, and gladly abandoning, in his terror, all solicitude about the fate of the Ourang-Outang. The words heard by the party upon the staircase were the Frenchman's exclamations of horror and affright, commingled with the fiendish jabberings of the brute.

I have scarcely anything to add. The Ourang-Outang must have escaped from the chamber, by the rod, just before the breaking of the door. It must have closed the window as it passed through it. It was subsequently caught by the owner himself, who obtained for it a very large sum at the *Jardin des Plantes*. Le Bon was instantly released, upon our narration of the circumstances (with some comments from Dupin) at the *bureau* of the Prefect of Police. This functionary, however well disposed to my friend, could not altogether conceal his chagrin at the turn which affairs had taken, and was fain to indulge in a sarcasm or two, about the propriety of every person minding his own business.

"Let him talk," said Dupin, who had not thought it necessary to reply. "Let him discourse; it will ease his conscience. I am satisfied with having defeated him in his own castle. Nevertheless, that he failed in the solution of this mystery, is by no means that matter for wonder which he supposes it; for, in truth, our friend the Prefect is somewhat too cunning to be profound. In his wisdom is no *stamen*. It is all head and no body, like the pictures of the Goddess Laverna,—or, at best, all head and shoulders, like a codfish. But he is a good creature after all. I like him especially for one master stroke of cant, by which he has attained his reputation for ingenuity. I mean the way he has '*de nier ce qui est, et d'expliquer ce qui n'est pas.*' "*[7]

*Rousseau—Nouvelle Heloise. [Poe's note]

THE GOLD-BUG

What ho! what ho! this fellow is dancing mad!
He hath been bitten by the Tarantula.
                                                    All in the Wrong

Many years ago, I contracted an intimacy with a Mr. William Legrand. He was of an ancient Huguenot family, and had once been wealthy; but a series of misfortunes had reduced him to want. To avoid the mortification consequent upon his disasters, he left New Orleans, the city of his forefathers, and took up his residence at Sullivan's Island, near Charleston, South Carolina.

This Island is a very singular one. It consists of little else than the sea sand, and is about three miles long. Its breadth at no point exceeds a quarter of a mile. It is separated from the main land by a scarcely perceptible creek, oozing its way through a wilderness of reeds and slime, a favorite resort of the marsh-hen. The vegetation, as might be supposed, is scant, or at least dwarfish. No trees of any magnitude are to be seen. Near the western extremity, where Fort Moultrie stands, and where are some miserable frame buildings, tenanted, during summer, by the fugitives from Charleston dust and fever, may be found, indeed, the bristly palmetto; but the whole island, with the exception of this western point, and a line of hard, white beach on the seacoast, is covered with a dense undergrowth of the sweet myrtle, so much prized by the horticulturists of England. The shrub here often attains the height of fifteen or twenty feet, and forms an almost impenetrable coppice, burthening the air with its fragrance.

In the inmost recesses of this coppice, not far from the eastern or more remote end of the island, Legrand had built himself a small hut, which he occupied when I first, by mere accident, made his acquaintance. This soon ripened into friendship—for there was much in the recluse to excite interest and esteem. I found him well educated, with unusual powers of mind, but infected with

misanthropy, and subject to perverse moods of alternate enthusi-
asm and melancholy. He had with him many books, but rarely
employed them. His chief amusements were gunning and fishing,
or sauntering along the beach and through the myrtles, in quest of
shells or entomological specimens;—his collection of the latter
might have been envied by a Swammerdamm.[1] In these excursions
he was usually accompanied by an old negro, called Jupiter, who
had been manumitted before the reverses of the family, but who
could be induced, neither by threats nor by promises, to abandon
what he considered his right of attendance upon the footsteps of
his young "Massa Will."[2] It is not improbable that the relatives of
Legrand, conceiving him to be somewhat unsettled in intellect,
had contrived to instil this obstinacy into Jupiter, with a view to
the supervision and guardianship of the wanderer.

The winters in the latitude of Sullivan's Island are seldom very
severe, and in the fall of the year it is a rare event indeed when a
fire is considered necessary. About the middle of October, 18—,
there occurred, however, a day of remarkable chilliness. Just be-
fore sunset I scrambled my way through the evergreens to the hut
of my friend, whom I had not visited for several weeks—my resi-
dence being, at that time, in Charleston, a distance of nine miles
from the Island, while the facilities of passage and re-passage were
very far behind those of the present day. Upon reaching the hut I
rapped, as was my custom, and getting no reply, sought for the
key where I knew it was secreted, unlocked the door and went in.
A fine fire was blazing upon the hearth. It was a novelty, and by no
means an ungrateful one. I threw off an overcoat, took an arm-
chair by the crackling logs, and awaited patiently the arrival of my
hosts.

Soon after dark they arrived, and gave me a most cordial wel-
come. Jupiter, grinning from ear to ear, bustled about to prepare
some marsh-hens for supper. Legrand was in one of his fits—how
else shall I term them?—of enthusiasm. He had found an un-
known bivalve, forming a new genus, and, more than this, he had
hunted down and secured, with Jupiter's assistance, a *scarabæus*
which he believed to be totally new, but in respect to which he
wished to have my opinion on the morrow.

"And why not to-night?" I asked, rubbing my hands over the
blaze, and wishing the whole tribe of *scarabæi* at the devil.

"Ah, if I had only known you were here!" said Legrand, "but it's so long since I saw you; and how could I foresee that you would pay me a visit this very night of all others? As I was coming home I met Lieutenant G—, from the fort, and, very foolishly, I lent him the bug; so it will be impossible for you to see it until the morning. Stay here to-night, and I will send Jup down for it at sunrise. It is the loveliest thing in creation!"

"What?—sunrise?"

"Nonsense! no!—the bug. It is of a brilliant gold color—about the size of a large hickory-nut—with two jet black spots near one extremity of the back, and another, somewhat longer, at the other. The *antennæ* are—"

"Dey aint *no* tin in him, Massa Will, I keep a tellin on you," here interrupted Jupiter; "de bug is a goole bug, solid, ebery bit of him, inside and all, sep him wing—neber feel half so hebby a bug in my life."

"Well, suppose it is, Jup," replied Legrand, somewhat more earnestly, it seemed to me, than the case demanded, "is that any reason for your letting the birds burn? The color"—here he turned to me—"is really almost enough to warrant Jupiter's idea. You never saw a more brilliant metallic lustre than the scales emit—but of this you cannot judge till to-morrow. In the mean time I can give you some idea of the shape." Saying this, he seated himself at a small table, on which were a pen and ink, but no paper. He looked for some in a drawer, but found none.

"Never mind," said he at length, "this will answer;" and he drew from his waistcoat pocket a scrap of what I took to be very dirty foolscap, and made upon it a rough drawing with the pen. While he did this, I retained my seat by the fire, for I was still chilly. When the design was complete, he handed it to me without rising. As I received it, a loud growl was heard, succeeded by a scratching at the door. Jupiter opened it, and a large Newfoundland, belonging to Legrand, rushed in, leaped upon my shoulders, and loaded me with caresses; for I had shown him much attention during previous visits. When his gambols were over, I looked at the paper, and, to speak the truth, found myself not a little puzzled at what my friend had depicted.

"Well!" I said, after contemplating it for some minutes, "this *is* a strange *scarabæus*, I must confess: new to me: never saw anything

like it before—unless it was a skull, or a death's-head—which it
more nearly resembles than anything else that has come under *my*
observation."

"A death's-head!" echoed Legrand—"Oh—yes—well, it has
something of that appearance upon paper, no doubt. The two up-
per black spots look like eyes, eh? and the longer one at the bot-
tom like a mouth—and then the shape of the whole is oval."

"Perhaps so," said I; "but, Legrand, I fear you are no artist. I
must wait until I see the beetle itself, if I am to form any idea of its
personal appearance."

"Well, I don't know," said he, a little nettled, "I draw
tolerably—*should* do it at least—have had good masters, and flat-
ter myself that I am not quite a blockhead."

"But, my dear fellow, you are joking then," said I, "this is a very
passable *skull*—indeed, I may say that it is a very *excellent* skull, ac-
cording to the vulgar notions about such specimens of physiology—
and your *scarabæus* must be the queerest *scarabæus* in the world if
it resembles it. Why, we may get up a very thrilling bit of supersti-
tion upon this hint. I presume you will call the bug *scarabæus ca-
put hominis*,³ or something of that kind—there are many similar
titles in the Natural Histories. But where are the *antennæ* you
spoke of?"

"The *antennæ*!" said Legrand, who seemed to be getting unac-
countably warm upon the subject; "I am sure you must see the *an-
tennæ*. I made them as distinct as they are in the original insect,
and I presume that is sufficient."

"Well, well," I said, "perhaps you have—still I don't see them;"
and I handed him the paper without additional remark, not wishing
to ruffle his temper; but I was much surprised at the turn affairs had
taken; his ill humor puzzled me—and, as for the drawing of the bee-
tle, there were positively *no antennæ* visible, and the whole *did* bear
a very close resemblance to the ordinary cuts of a death's-head.

He received the paper very peevishly, and was about to crumple
it, apparently to throw it in the fire, when a casual glance at the de-
sign seemed suddenly to rivet his attention. In an instant his face
grew violently red—in another as excessively pale. For some min-
utes he continued to scrutinize the drawing minutely where he sat.
At length he arose, took a candle from the table, and proceeded to
seat himself upon a sea-chest in the farthest corner of the room.

Here again he made an anxious examination of the paper; turning it in all directions. He said nothing, however, and his conduct greatly astonished me; yet I thought it prudent not to exacerbate the growing moodiness of his temper by any comment. Presently he took from his coat pocket a wallet, placed the paper carefully in it, and deposited both in a writing-desk, which he locked. He now grew more composed in his demeanor; but his original air of enthusiasm had quite disappeared. Yet he seemed not so much sulky as abstracted. As the evening wore away he became more and more absorbed in reverie, from which no sallies of mine could arouse him. It had been my intention to pass the night at the hut, as I had frequently done before, but, seeing my host in this mood, I deemed it proper to take leave. He did not press me to remain, but, as I departed, he shook my hand with even more than his usual cordiality.

It was about a month after this (and during the interval I had seen nothing of Legrand) when I received a visit, at Charleston, from his man, Jupiter. I had never seen the good old negro look so dispirited, and I feared that some serious disaster had befallen my friend.

"Well, Jup," said I, "what is the matter now?—how is your master?"

"Why, to speak de troof, massa, him not so berry well as mought be."

"Not well! I am truly sorry to hear it. What does he complain of?"

"Dar! dat's it!—him neber plain of notin—but him berry sick for all dat."

"*Very* sick, Jupiter!—why didn't you say so at once? Is he confined to bed?"

"No, dat he aint!—he aint find nowhar—dat's just whar de shoe pinch—my mind is got to be berry hebby bout poor Massa Will."

"Jupiter, I should like to understand what it is you are talking about. You say your master is sick. Hasn't he told you what ails him?"

"Why, massa, taint worf while for to git mad bout de matter—Massa Will say noffin at all aint de matter wid him—but den what make him go about looking dis here way, wid he head down and he soldiers up, and as white as a gose? And den he keep a syphon all de time—"

"Keeps a what, Jupiter?"

"Keeps a syphon wid de figgurs on de slate—de queerest figgurs I ebber did see. Ise gittin to be skeered, I tell you. Hab for to keep mighty tight eye pon him noovers. Todder day he gib me slip fore de sun up and was gone de whole ob de blessed day. I had a big stick ready cut for to gib him d—d good beating when he did come—but Ise sich a fool dat I hadn't de heart arter all—he look so berry poorly."

"Eh?—what?—ah yes!—upon the whole I think you had better not be too severe with the poor fellow—don't flog him, Jupiter—he can't very well stand it—but can you form no idea of what has occasioned this illness, or rather this change of conduct? Has anything unpleasant happened since I saw you?"

"No, massa, dey aint bin noffin onpleasant *since* den—'twas *fore* den I'm feared—'twas *fore* den I'm feared—'twas de berry day you was dare."

"How? what do you mean?"

"Why, massa, I mean de bug—dare now."

"The what?"

"De bug,—I'm berry sartain dat Massa Will bin bit somewhere bout de head by dat goole-bug."

"And what cause have you, Jupiter, for such a supposition?"

"Claws enuff, massa, and mouff too. I nebber did see sich a d—d bug—he kick and he bite ebery ting what cum near him. Massa Will cotch him fuss, but had for to let him go gin mighty quick, I tell you—den was de time he must ha got de bite. I didn't like de look ob de bug mouff, myself, no how, so I wouldn't take hold ob him wid my finger, but I cotch him wid a piece ob paper dat I found. I rap him up in de paper and stuff piece ob it in he mouff—dat was de way."

"And you think, then, that your master was really bitten by the beetle, and that the bite made him sick?"

"I don't tink noffin about it—I nose it. What make him dream bout de goole so much, if taint cause he bit by de goole-bug? Ise heerd bout dem goole-bugs fore dis."

"But how do you know he dreams about gold?"

"How I know? why cause he talk about it in he sleep—dat's how I nose."

"Well, Jup, perhaps you are right; but to what fortunate

circumstance am I to attribute the honor of a visit from you to-day?"

"What de matter, massa?"

"Did you bring any message from Mr. Legrand?"

"No, massa, I bring dis here pissel;" and here Jupiter handed me a note which ran thus:

MY DEAR—

Why have I not seen you for so long a time? I hope you have not been so foolish as to take offence at any little *brusquerie* of mine; but no, that is improbable.

Since I saw you I have had great cause for anxiety. I have something to tell you, yet scarcely know how to tell it, or whether I should tell it at all.

I have not been quite well for some days past, and poor old Jup annoys me, almost beyond endurance, by his well-meant attentions. Would you believe it?—he had prepared a huge stick, the other day, with which to chastise me for giving him the slip, and spending the day, *solus*, among the hills on the main land. I verily believe that my ill looks alone saved me a flogging.

I have made no addition to my cabinet since we met.

If you can, in any way, make it convenient, come over with Jupiter. *Do* come. I wish to see you *to-night*, upon business of importance. I assure you that it is of the *highest* importance.

EVER YOURS,
WILLIAM LEGRAND

There was something in the tone of this note which gave me great uneasiness. Its whole style differed materially from that of Legrand. What could he be dreaming of? What new crotchet possessed his excitable brain? What "business of the highest importance" could *he* possibly have to transact? Jupiter's account of him boded no good. I dreaded lest the continued pressure of misfortune had, at length, fairly unsettled the reason of my friend. Without a moment's hesitation, therefore, I prepared to accompany the negro.

Upon reaching the wharf, I noticed a scythe and three spades, all apparently new, lying in the bottom of the boat in which we were to embark.

"What is the meaning of all this, Jup?" I inquired.

"Him syfe, massa, and spade."

"Very true; but what are they doing here?"

"Him de syfe and de spade what Massa Will sis pon my buying for him in de town, and de debbil's own lot of money I had to gib for em."

"But what, in the name of all that is mysterious, is your 'Massa Will' going to do with scythes and spades?"

"Dat's more dan I know, and debbil take me if I don't blieve 'tis more dan he know, too. But it's all cum ob de bug."

Finding that no satisfaction was to be obtained of Jupiter, whose whole intellect seemed to be absorbed by "de bug," I now stepped into the boat and made sail. With a fair and strong breeze we soon ran into the little cove to the northward of Fort Moultrie, and a walk of some two miles brought us to the hut. It was about three in the afternoon when we arrived. Legrand had been awaiting us in eager expectation. He grasped my hand with a nervous *empressement*[4] which alarmed me and strengthened the suspicions already entertained. His countenance was pale even to ghastliness, and his deep-set eyes glared with unnatural lustre. After some inquiries respecting his health, I asked him, not knowing what better to say, if he had yet obtained the *scarabæus* from Lieutenant G——.

"Oh, yes," he replied, coloring violently, "I got it from him the next morning. Nothing should tempt me to part with that *scarabæus*. Do you know that Jupiter is quite right about it?"

"In what way?" I asked, with a sad foreboding at heart.

"In supposing it to be a bug of *real gold*." He said this with an air of profound seriousness, and I felt inexpressibly shocked.

"This bug is to make my fortune," he continued, with a triumphant smile, "to reinstate me in my family possessions. Is it any wonder, then, that I prize it? Since Fortune has thought fit to bestow it upon me, I have only to use it properly and I shall arrive at the gold of which it is the index. Jupiter; bring me that *scarabæus*!"

"What! de bug, massa? I'd rudder not go fer trubble dat bug—you mus git him for your own self." Here upon Legrand arose, with a grave and stately air, and brought me the beetle from a glass case in which it was enclosed. It was a beautiful *scarabæus*, and, at that time, unknown to naturalists—of course a great prize in a scientific point of view. There were two round, black spots near one extremity of the back, and a long one near the other. The scales were exceedingly hard and glossy, with all the appearance of burnished gold. The weight of the insect was very remarkable, and, taking all things into consideration, I could hardly blame Jupiter for his opinion respecting it; but what to make of Legrand's agreement with that opinion, I could not, for the life of me, tell.

"I sent for you," said he, in a grandiloquent tone, when I had completed my examination of the beetle, "I sent for you, that I might have your counsel and assistance in furthering the views of Fate and of the bug"—

"My dear Legrand," I cried, interrupting him, "you are certainly unwell, and had better use some little precautions. You shall go to bed, and I will remain with you a few days, until you get over this. You are feverish and"—

"Feel my pulse," said he.

I felt it, and, to say the truth, found not the slightest indication of fever.

"But you may be ill and yet have no fever. Allow me this once to prescribe for you. In the first place, go to bed. In the next"—

"You are mistaken," he interposed, "I am as well as I can expect to be under the excitement which I suffer. If you really wish me well, you will relieve this excitement."

"And how is this to be done?"

"Very easily. Jupiter and myself are going upon an expedition into the hills, upon the main land, and, in this expedition, we shall need the aid of some person in whom we can confide. You are the only one we can trust. Whether we succeed or fail, the excitement which you now perceive in me will be equally allayed."

"I am anxious to oblige you in any way," I replied; "but do you mean to say that this infernal beetle has any connection with your expedition into the hills?"

"It has."

"Then, Legrand, I can become a party to no such absurd proceeding."

"I am sorry—very sorry—for we shall have to try it by ourselves."

"Try it by yourselves! The man is surely mad!—but stay!—how long do you propose to be absent?"

"Probably all night. We shall start immediately, and be back, at all events, by sunrise."

"And will you promise me, upon your honor, that when this freak of yours is over, and the bug business (good God!) settled to your satisfaction, you will then return home and follow my advice implicitly, as that of your physician?"

"Yes; I promise; and now let us be off, for we have no time to lose."

With a heavy heart I accompanied my friend. We started about four o'clock—Legrand, Jupiter, the dog, and myself. Jupiter had with him the scythe and spades—the whole of which he insisted upon carrying—more through fear, it seemed to me, of trusting either of the implements within reach of his master, than from any excess of industry or complaisance. His demeanor was dogged in the extreme, and "dat d—d bug" were the sole words which escaped his lips during the journey. For my own part, I had charge of a couple of dark lanterns, while Legrand contented himself with the *scarabæus*, which he carried attached to the end of a bit of whip-cord; twirling it to and fro, with the air of a conjuror, as he went. When I observed this last, plain evidence of my friend's aberration of mind, I could scarcely refrain from tears. I thought it best, however, to humor his fancy, at least for the present, or until I could adopt some more energetic measures with a chance of success. In the mean time I endeavored, but all in vain, to sound him in regard to the object of the expedition. Having succeeded in inducing me to accompany him, he seemed unwilling to hold conversation upon any topic of minor importance, and to all my questions vouchsafed no other reply than "we shall see!"

We crossed the creek at the head of the island by means of a skiff, and, ascending the high grounds on the shore of the main land, proceeded in a northwesterly direction, through a tract of country excessively wild and desolate, where no trace of a human footstep was to be seen. Legrand led the way with decision; pausing only for an instant, here and there, to consult what appeared to be certain landmarks of his own contrivance upon a former occasion.

In this manner we journeyed for about two hours, and the sun was just setting when we entered a region infinitely more dreary than any yet seen. It was a species of table land, near the summit of an almost inaccessible hill, densely wooded from base to pinnacle, and interspersed with huge crags that appeared to lie loosely upon the soil, and in many cases were prevented from precipitating themselves into the valleys below, merely by the support of the trees against which they reclined. Deep ravines, in various directions, gave an air of still sterner solemnity to the scene.

The natural platform to which we had clambered was thickly overgrown with brambles, through which we soon discovered that it would have been impossible to force our way but for the scythe; and Jupiter, by direction of his master, proceeded to clear for us a path to the foot of an enormously tall tulip-tree, which stood, with some eight or ten oaks, upon the level, and far surpassed them all, and all other trees which I had then ever seen, in the beauty of its foliage and form, in the wide spread of its branches, and in the general majesty of its appearance. When we reached this tree, Legrand turned to Jupiter, and asked him if he thought he could climb it. The old man seemed a little staggered by the question, and for some moments made no reply. At length he approached the huge trunk, walked slowly around it, and examined it with minute attention. When he had completed his scrutiny, he merely said,

"Yes, massa, Jup climb any tree he ebber see in he life."

"Then up with you as soon as possible, for it will soon be too dark to see what we are about."

"How far mus go up, massa?" inquired Jupiter.

"Get up the main trunk first, and then I will tell you which way to go—and here—stop! take this beetle with you."

"De bug, Massa Will!—de goole bug!" cried the negro, drawing back in dismay—"what for mus tote de bug way up de tree?—d—n if I do!"

"If you are afraid, Jup, a great big negro like you, to take hold of a harmless little dead beetle, why you can carry it up by this string—but, if you do not take it up with you in some way, I shall be under the necessity of breaking your head with this shovel."

"What de matter now, massa?" said Jup, evidently shamed into compliance; "always want for to raise fuss wid old nigger. Was only funnin any how. Me feered de bug! what I keer for de bug?" Here he took cautiously hold of the extreme end of the string, and, maintaining the insect as far from his person as circumstances would permit, prepared to ascend the tree.

In youth, the tulip-tree, or *Liriodendron Tulipiferum*, the most magnificent of American foresters, has a trunk peculiarly smooth, and often rises to a great height without lateral branches; but, in its riper age, the bark becomes gnarled and uneven, while many short limbs make their appearance on the stem. Thus the difficulty of ascension, in the present case, lay more in semblance than in reality. Embracing the huge cylinder, as closely as possible, with his arms and knees, seizing with his hands some projections, and resting his naked toes upon others, Jupiter, after one or two narrow escapes from falling, at length wriggled himself into the first great fork, and seemed to consider the whole business as virtually accomplished. The *risk* of the achievement was, in fact, now over, although the climber was some sixty or seventy feet from the ground.

"Which way mus go now, Massa Will?" he asked.

"Keep up the largest branch—the one on this side," said Legrand. The negro obeyed him promptly, and apparently with but little trouble; ascending higher and higher, until no glimpse of his squat figure could be obtained through the dense foliage which enveloped it. Presently his voice was heard in a sort of halloo.

"How much fudder is got for go?"

"How high up are you?" asked Legrand.

"Ebber so fur," replied the negro; "can see de sky fru de top ob de tree."

"Never mind the sky, but attend to what I say. Look down the trunk and count the limbs below you on this side. How many limbs have you passed?"

"One, two, tree, four, fibe—I done pass fibe big limb, massa, pon dis side."

"Then go one limb higher."

In a few minutes the voice was heard again, announcing that the seventh limb was attained.

"Now, Jup," cried Legrand, evidently much excited, "I want you to work your way out upon that limb as far as you can. If you see anything strange, let me know."

By this time what little doubt I might have entertained of my poor friend's insanity, was put finally at rest. I had no alternative but to conclude him stricken with lunacy, and I became seriously anxious about getting him home. While I was pondering upon what was best to be done, Jupiter's voice was again heard.

"Mos feerd for to ventur pon dis limb berry far—tis dead limb putty much all de way."

"Did you say it was a *dead* limb, Jupiter?" cried Legrand in a quavering voice.

"Yes, massa, him dead as de door-nail—done up for sartain—done departed dis here life."

"What in the name of heaven shall I do?" asked Legrand, seemingly in the greatest distress.

"Do!" said I, glad of an opportunity to interpose a word, "why come home and go to bed. Come now!—that's a fine fellow. It's getting late, and, besides, you remember your promise."

"Jupiter," cried he, without heeding me in the least, "do you hear me?"

"Yes, Massa Will, hear you ebber so plain."

"Try the wood well, then, with your knife, and see if you think it *very* rotten."

"Him rotten, massa, sure nuff," replied the negro in a few moments, "but not so berry rotten as mought be. Mought ventur out leetle way pon de limb by myself, dat's true."

"By yourself!—what do you mean?"

"Why I mean de bug. 'Tis *berry* hebby bug. Spose I drop him down fuss, and den de limb won't break wid just de weight ob one nigger."

"You infernal scoundrel!" cried Legrand, apparently much relieved, "what do you mean by telling me such nonsense as that? As sure as you let that beetle fall I'll break your neck. Look here, Jupiter!—do you hear me?"

"Yes, massa, needn't hollo at poor nigger dat style."

"Well! now listen!—if you will venture out on the limb as far as you think safe, and not let go the beetle, I'll make you a present of a silver dollar as soon as you get down."

"I'm gwine, Massa Will—deed I is," replied the negro very promptly—"mos out to the eend now."

"*Out to the end!*" here fairly screamed Legrand, "do you say you are out to the end of that limb?"

"Soon be to de eend, massa,—o-o-o-o-oh! Lor-gol-a-marcy! what *is* dis here pon de tree?"

"Well!" cried Legrand, highly delighted, "what is it?"

"Why taint noffin but a skull—somebody bin lef him head up de tree, and de crows done gobble ebery bit ob de meat off."

"A skull, you say!—very well!—how is it fastened to the limb?—what holds it on?"

"Sure nuff, massa; mus look. Why dis berry curous sarcumstance, pon my word—dare's a great big nail in de skull, what fastens ob it on to de tree."

"Well now, Jupiter, do exactly as I tell you—do you hear?"

"Yes, massa."

"Pay attention, then!—find the left eye of the skull."

"Hum! hoo! dat's good! why dar aint no eye lef at all."

"Curse your stupidity! do you know your right hand from your left?"

"Yes, I nose dat—nose all bout dat—tis my lef hand what I chops de wood wid."

"To be sure! you are left-handed; and your left eye is on the same side as your left hand. Now, I suppose, you can find the left eye of the skull, or the place where the left eye has been. Have you found it?"

Here was a long pause. At length the negro asked,

"Is de lef eye of de skull pon de same side as de lef hand of de skull, too?—cause de skull aint got not a bit ob a hand at all—nebber mind! I got de lef eye now—here de lef eye! what mus do wid it?"

"Let the beetle drop through it, as far as the string will reach—but be careful and not let go your hold of the string."

"All dat done, Massa Will; mighty easy ting for to put de bug fru de hole—look out for him dar below!"

During this colloquy no portion of Jupiter's person could be seen; but the beetle, which he had suffered to descend, was now visible at the end of the string, and glistened, like a globe of burnished gold, in the last rays of the setting sun, some of which still faintly illumined the eminence upon which we stood. The *scarabæus* hung quite clear of any branches, and, if allowed to fall, would have fallen at our feet. Legrand immediately took the scythe, and cleared with it a circular space, three or four yards in diameter, just beneath the insect, and, having accomplished this, ordered Jupiter to let go the string and come down from the tree.

Driving a peg, with great nicety, into the ground, at the precise spot where the beetle fell, my friend now produced from his pocket a tape-measure. Fastening one end of this at that point of the trunk of the tree which was nearest the peg, he unrolled it till it reached the peg, and thence farther unrolled it, in the direction already established by the two points of the tree and the peg, for the distance of fifty feet—Jupiter clearing away the brambles with the scythe. At the spot thus attained a second peg was driven, and about this, as a centre, a rude circle, about four feet in diameter, described. Taking now a spade himself, and giving one to Jupiter and one to me, Legrand begged us to set about digging as quickly as possible.

To speak the truth, I had no especial relish for such amusement at any time, and, at that particular moment, would most willingly have declined it; for the night was coming on, and I felt much fatigued with the exercise already taken; but I saw no mode of escape, and was fearful of disturbing my poor friend's equanimity by a refusal. Could I have depended, indeed, upon Jupiter's aid, I would have had no hesitation in attempting to get the lunatic home by force; but I was too well assured of the old negro's disposition, to hope that he would assist me, under any circumstances, in a personal contest with his master. I made no doubt that the latter had been infected with some of the innumerable Southern superstitions about money buried, and that his phantasy had received confirmation by the finding of the *scarabæus*, or, perhaps, by Jupiter's obstinacy in maintaining it to be "a bug of real gold." A mind disposed to lunacy would readily be led away by such suggestions—especially if chiming in with favorite preconceived ideas—and then I called to mind the poor fellow's speech about the beetle's being "the index of his fortune." Upon the whole, I was sadly vexed and puzzled, but, at length, I concluded to make a virtue of necessity—to dig with a good will, and thus the sooner to convince the visionary, by ocular demonstration, of the fallacy of the opinions he entertained.

The lanterns having been lit, we all fell to work with a zeal worthy a more rational cause; and, as the glare fell upon our persons and implements, I could not help thinking how picturesque a group we composed, and how strange and suspicious our labors must have appeared to any interloper who, by chance, might have stumbled upon our whereabouts.

We dug very steadily for two hours. Little was said; and our chief embarrassment lay in the yelpings of the dog, who took exceeding interest in our proceedings. He, at length, became so obstreperous that we grew fearful of his giving the alarm to some stragglers in the vicinity;—or, rather, this was the apprehension of Legrand;—for myself, I should have rejoiced at any interruption which might have enabled me to get the wanderer home. The noise was, at length, very effectually silenced by Jupiter, who, getting out of the hole with a dogged air of deliberation, tied the brute's mouth up with one of his suspenders, and then returned, with a grave chuckle, to his task.

When the time mentioned had expired, we had reached a depth of five feet, and yet no signs of any treasure became manifest. A general pause ensued, and I began to hope that the farce was at an end. Legrand, however, although evidently much disconcerted, wiped his brow thoughtfully and recommenced. We had excavated the entire circle of four feet diameter, and now we slightly enlarged the limit, and went to the farther depth of two feet. Still nothing appeared. The gold-seeker, whom I sincerely pitied, at length clambered from the pit, with the bitterest disappointment imprinted upon every feature, and proceeded, slowly and reluctantly, to put on his coat, which he had thrown off at the beginning of his labor. In the mean time I made no remark. Jupiter, at a signal from his master, began to gather up his tools. This done, and the dog having been unmuzzled, we turned in profound silence towards home.

We had taken, perhaps, a dozen steps in this direction, when, with a loud oath, Legrand strode up to Jupiter, and seized him by the collar. The astonished negro opened his eyes and mouth to the fullest extent, let fall the spades, and fell upon his knees.

"You scoundrel," said Legrand, hissing out the syllables from between his clenched teeth—"you infernal black villain!—speak, I tell you!—answer me this instant, without prevarication!—which—which is your left eye?"

"Oh, my golly, Massa Will! aint dis here my lef eye for sartain?" roared the terrified Jupiter, placing his hand upon his *right* organ of vision, and holding it there with a desperate pertinacity, as if in immediate dread of his master's attempt at a gouge.

"I thought so!—I knew it!—hurrah!" vociferated Legrand, letting the negro go, and executing a series of curvets and caracols, much to the astonishment of his valet, who, arising from his knees, looked, mutely, from his master to myself, and then from myself to his master.

"Come! we must go back," said the latter, "the game's not up yet;" and he again led the way to the tulip-tree.

"Jupiter," said he, when we reached its foot, "come here! was the skull nailed to the limb with the face outward, or with the face to the limb?"

"De face was out, massa, so dat de crows could get at de eyes good, widout any trouble."

"Well, then, was it this eye or that through which you let fall the beetle?"—here Legrand touched each of Jupiter's eyes.

"'Twas dis eye, massa—de lef eye—jis as you tell me," and here it was his right eye that the negro indicated.

"That will do—we must try it again."

Here my friend, about whose madness I now saw, or fancied that I saw, certain indications of method, removed the peg which marked the spot where the beetle fell, to a spot about three inches to the westward of its former position. Taking, now, the tape-measure from the nearest point of the trunk to the peg, as before, and continuing the extension in a straight line to the distance of fifty feet, a spot was indicated, removed, by several yards, from the point at which we had been digging.

Around the new position a circle, somewhat larger than in the former instance, was now described, and we again set to work with the spades. I was dreadfully weary, but, scarcely understanding what had occasioned the change in my thoughts, I felt no longer any great aversion from the labor imposed. I had become most unaccountably interested—nay, even excited. Perhaps there was something, amid all the extravagant demeanor of Legrand— some air of forethought, or of deliberation, which impressed me. I dug eagerly, and now and then caught myself actually looking, with something that very much resembled expectation, for the fan-cied treasure, the vision of which had demented my unfortunate companion. At a period when such vagaries of thought most fully possessed me, and when we had been at work perhaps an hour and a half, we were again interrupted by the violent howlings of the dog. His uneasiness, in the first instance, had been, evidently, but the result of playfulness or caprice, but he now assumed a bitter and serious tone. Upon Jupiter's again attempting to muzzle him, he made furious resistance, and, leaping into the hole, tore up the mould frantically with his claws. In a few seconds he had uncovered a mass of human bones, forming two complete skeletons, intermingled with several buttons of metal, and what appeared to be the dust of decayed woollen. One or two strokes of a spade upturned the blade of a large Spanish knife, and, as we dug farther, three or four loose pieces of gold and silver coin came to light.

At sight of these the joy of Jupiter could scarcely be restrained, but the countenance of his master wore an air of extreme disappointment. He urged us, however, to continue our exertions, and the words were hardly uttered when I stumbled and fell forward, having caught the toe of my boot in a large ring of iron that lay half buried in the loose earth.

We now worked in earnest, and never did I pass ten minutes of more intense excitement. During this interval we had fairly unearthed an oblong chest of wood, which, from its perfect preservation and wonderful hardness, had plainly been subjected to some mineralizing process—perhaps that of the Bi-chloride of Mercury. This box was three feet and a half long, three feet broad, and two and a half feet deep. It was firmly secured by bands of wrought iron, riveted, and forming a kind of trellis-work over the whole. On each side of the chest, near the top, were three rings of iron—six in all—by means of which a firm hold could be obtained by six persons. Our utmost united endeavors served only to disturb the coffer very slightly in its bed. We at once saw the impossibility of removing so great a weight. Luckily, the sole fastenings of the lid consisted of two sliding bolts. These we drew back—trembling and panting with anxiety. In an instant, a treasure of incalculable value lay gleaming before us. As the rays of the lanterns fell within the pit, there flashed upwards from a confused heap of gold and of jewels, a glow and a glare that absolutely dazzled our eyes.

I shall not pretend to describe the feelings with which I gazed. Amazement was, of course, predominant. Legrand appeared exhausted with excitement, and spoke very few words. Jupiter's countenance wore, for some minutes, as deadly a pallor as it is possible, in the nature of things, for any negro's visage to assume.

He seemed stupified—thunderstricken. Presently he fell upon his knees in the pit, and, burying his naked arms up to the elbows in gold, let them there remain, as if enjoying the luxury of a bath. At length, with a deep sigh, he exclaimed, as if in a soliloquy,

"And dis all cum ob de goole-bug! de putty goole bug! de poor little goole-bug, what I boosed in dat sabage kind ob style! Aint you shamed ob yourself, nigger?—answer me dat!"

It became necessary, at last, that I should arouse both master and valet to the expediency of removing the treasure. It was growing late, and it behooved us to make exertion, that we might get every thing housed before daylight. It was difficult to say what should be done; and much time was spent in deliberation—so confused were the ideas of all. We, finally, lightened the box by removing two thirds of its contents, when we were enabled, with some trouble, to raise it from the hole. The articles taken out were deposited among the brambles, and the dog left to guard them, with strict orders from Jupiter neither, upon any pretence, to stir from the spot, nor to open his mouth until our return. We then hurriedly made for home with the chest; reaching the hut in safety, but after excessive toil, at one o'clock in the morning. Worn out as we were, it was not in human nature to do more just then. We rested until two, and had supper; starting for the hills immediately afterwards, armed with three stout sacks, which, by good luck, were upon the premises. A little before four we arrived at the pit, divided the remainder of the booty, as equally as might be, among us, and, leaving the holes unfilled, again set out for the hut, at which, for the second time, we deposited our golden burthens, just as the first streaks of the dawn gleamed from over the tree-tops in the East.

We were now thoroughly broken down; but the intense excitement of the time denied us repose. After an unquiet slumber of some three or four hours' duration, we arose, as if by preconcert, to make examination of our treasure.

The chest had been full to the brim, and we spent the whole day, and the greater part of the next night, in a scrutiny of its contents. There had been nothing like order or arrangement. Every thing had been heaped in promiscuously. Having assorted all with care, we found ourselves possessed of even vaster wealth than we had at first supposed. In coin there was rather more than four hundred and fifty thousand dollars—estimating the value of the pieces, as accurately as we could, by the tables of the period. There was not a particle of silver. All was gold of antique date and of great variety—French, Spanish, and German money, with a few English guineas, and some counters, of which we had never seen specimens before. There were several very large and heavy coins, so worn that we could make nothing of their inscriptions. There was no American money. The value of the jewels we found more difficulty in estimating. There were diamonds—some of them exceedingly large and fine—a hundred and ten in all, and not one of them small; eighteen rubies of remarkable brilliancy;—three hundred and ten emeralds, all very beautiful; and twenty-one sapphires, with an opal. These stones had all been broken from their settings and thrown loose in the chest. The settings themselves, which we picked out from among the other gold, appeared to have been beaten up with hammers, as if to prevent identification. Besides all this, there was a vast quantity of solid gold ornaments;— nearly two hundred massive finger and earrings;—rich chains— thirty of these, if I remember;—eighty-three very large and heavy crucifixes;—five gold censers of great value;—a prodigious golden punch-bowl, ornamented with richly chased vine-leaves and Bacchanalian figures; with two sword-handles exquisitely embossed, and many other smaller articles which I cannot recollect. The weight of these valuables exceeded three hundred and fifty pounds avoirdupois; and in this estimate I have not included one hundred and ninety-seven superb gold watches; three of the number being worth each five hundred dollars, if one. Many of them were very old, and as time keepers valueless; the works having suffered, more or less, from corrosion—but all were richly jewelled and in cases of great worth. We estimated the entire contents of the chest, that night, at a million and a half of dollars; and, upon the subsequent disposal of the trinkets and jewels (a few being retained for our own use), it was found that we had greatly undervalued the treasure.

When, at length, we had concluded our examination, and the intense excitement of the time had, in some measure, subsided, Legrand, who saw that I was dying with impatience for a solution of this most extraordinary riddle, entered into a full detail of all the circumstances connected with it.

"You remember;" said he, "the night when I handed you the rough sketch I had made of the *scarabæus*. You recollect also, that I became quite vexed at you for insisting that my drawing resembled a death's-head. When you first made this assertion I thought you were jesting; but afterwards I called to mind the peculiar spots on the back of the insect, and admitted to myself that your remark had some little foundation in fact. Still, the sneer at my graphic powers irritated me—for I am considered a good artist—and, therefore, when you handed me the scrap of parchment, I was about to crumple it up and throw it angrily into the fire."

"The scrap of paper, you mean," said I.

"No; it had much of the appearance of paper, and at first I supposed it to be such, but when I came to draw upon it, I discovered it, at once, to be a piece of very thin parchment. It was quite dirty, you remember. Well, as I was in the very act of crumpling it up, my glance fell upon the sketch at which you had been looking, and you may imagine my astonishment when I perceived, in fact, the figure of a death's-head just where, it seemed to me, I had made the drawing of the beetle. For a moment I was too much amazed to think with accuracy. I knew that my design was very different in detail from this—although there was a certain similarity in general outline. Presently I took a candle, and seating myself at the other end of the room, proceeded to scrutinize the parchment more closely. Upon turning it over, I saw my own sketch upon the reverse, just as I had made it. My first idea, now, was mere surprise at the really remarkable similarity of outline—at the singular coincidence involved in the fact, that unknown to me, there should have been a skull upon the other side of the parchment, immediately beneath my figure of the *scarabæus*, and that this skull, not only in outline, but in size, should so closely resemble my drawing. I say the singularity of this coincidence absolutely stupified me for a time. This is the usual effect of such coincidences. The mind struggles to establish a connexion—a sequence of cause and effect—and, being unable to do so, suffers a species of temporary paralysis. But, when I recovered from this stupor, there dawned upon me gradually a conviction which startled me even far more than the coincidence. I began distinctly, positively, to remember that there had been *no* drawing on the parchment when I made my sketch of the *scarabæus*. I became perfectly certain of this; for

I recollected turning up first one side and then the other, in search of the cleanest spot. Had the skull been then there, of course I could not have failed to notice it. Here was indeed a mystery which I felt it impossible to explain; but, even at that early moment, there seemed to glimmer, faintly, within the most remote and secret chambers of my intellect, a glow-worm-like conception of that truth which last night's adventure brought to so magnificent a demonstration. I arose at once, and putting the parchment securely away, dismissed all farther reflection until I should be alone.

"When you had gone, and when Jupiter was fast asleep, I betook myself to a more methodical investigation of the affair. In the first place I considered the manner in which the parchment had come into my possession. The spot where we discovered the *scarabæus* was on the coast of the main land, about a mile eastward of the island, and but a short distance above high water mark. Upon my taking hold of it, it gave me a sharp bite, which caused me to let it drop. Jupiter, with his accustomed caution, before seizing the insect, which had flown towards him, looked about him for a leaf, or something of that nature, by which to take hold of it. It was at this moment that his eyes, and mine also, fell upon the scrap of parchment, which I then supposed to be paper. It was lying half buried in the sand, a corner sticking up. Near the spot where we found it, I observed the remnants of the hull of what appeared to have been a ship's long boat. The wreck seemed to have been there for a very great while; for the resemblance to boat timbers could scarcely be traced.

"Well, Jupiter picked up the parchment, wrapped the beetle in it, and gave it to me. Soon afterwards we turned to go home, and on the way met Lieutenant G——. I showed him the insect, and he begged me to let him take it to the fort. On my consenting, he thrust it forthwith into his waistcoat pocket, without the parchment in which it had been wrapped, and which I had continued to hold in my hand during his inspection. Perhaps he dreaded my changing my mind, and thought it best to make sure of the prize at once—you know how enthusiastic he is on all subjects connected with Natural History. At the same time, without being conscious of it, I must have deposited the parchment in my own pocket.

"You remember that when I went to the table, for the purpose of making a sketch of the beetle, I found no paper where it was usually kept. I looked in the drawer, and found none there. I searched my pockets, hoping to find an old letter—and then my hand fell upon the parchment. I thus detail the precise mode in which it came into my possession; for the circumstances impressed me with peculiar force.

"No doubt you will think me fanciful—but I had already established a kind of *connexion*. I had put together two links of a great chain. There was a boat lying on a sea-coast, and not far from the boat was a parchment—*not a paper*—with a skull depicted on it. You will, of course, ask 'where is the connexion?' I reply that the skull, or death's-head, is the well-known emblem of the pirate. The flag of the death's-head is hoisted in all engagements.

"I have said that the scrap was parchment, and not paper. Parchment is durable—almost imperishable. Matters of little moment are rarely consigned to parchment; since, for the mere ordinary purposes of drawing or writing, it is not nearly so well adapted as paper. This reflection suggested some meaning—some relevancy—in the death's-head. I did not fail to observe, also, the *form* of the parchment. Although one of its corners had been, by some accident, destroyed, it could be seen that the original form was oblong. It was just such a slip, indeed, as might have been chosen for a memorandum—for a record of something to be long remembered and carefully preserved."

"But," I interposed, "you say that the skull was *not* upon the parchment when you made the drawing of the beetle. How then do you trace any connexion between the boat and the skull—since this latter, according to your own admission, must have been designed (God only knows how or by whom) at some period subsequent to your sketching the *scarabæus*?"

"Ah, hereupon turns the whole mystery; although the secret, at this point, I had comparatively little difficulty in solving. My steps were sure, and could afford but a single result. I reasoned, for example, thus: When I drew the *scarabæus*, there was no skull apparent on the parchment. When I had completed the drawing, I gave it to you, and observed you narrowly until you returned it. *You*, therefore, did not design the skull, and no one else was present to do it. Then it was not done by human agency. And nevertheless it was done.

"At this stage of my reflections I endeavored to remember, and *did* remember, with entire distinctness, every incident which occurred about the period in question. The weather was chilly (oh rare and happy accident!), and a fire was blazing on the hearth. I was heated with exercise and sat near the table. You, however, had drawn a chair close to the chimney. Just as I placed the parchment in your hand, and as you were in the act of inspecting it, Wolf, the Newfoundland, entered, and leaped upon your shoulders. With your left hand you caressed him and kept him off, while your right, holding the parchment, was permitted to fall listlessly between your knees, and in close proximity to the fire. At one moment I thought the blaze had caught it, and was about to caution you, but, before I could speak, you had withdrawn it, and were engaged in its examination. When I considered all these particulars, I doubted not for a moment that *heat* had been the agent in bringing to light, on the parchment, the skull which I saw designed on it. You are well aware that chemical preparations exist, and have existed time out of mind, by means of which it is possible to write on either paper or vellum, so that the characters shall become visible only when subjected to the action of fire. Zaffre, digested in *aqua regia*, and diluted with four times its weight of water, is sometimes employed; a green tint results. The regulus of cobalt, dissolved in spirit of nitre, gives a red. These colors disappear at longer or shorter intervals after the material written on cools, but again become apparent upon the reapplication of heat.

"I now scrutinized the death's-head with care. Its outer edges—the edges of the drawing nearest the edge of the vellum—were far more *distinct* than the others. It was clear that the action of the caloric had been imperfect or unequal. I immediately kindled a fire, and subjected every portion of the parchment to a glowing heat. At first, the only effect was the strengthening of the faint lines in the skull; but, on persevering in the experiment, there became visible, at the corner of the slip, diagonally opposite to the spot in which the death's-head was delineated, the figure of what I at first supposed to be a goat. A closer scrutiny, however, satisfied me that it was intended for a kid."

"Ha! ha!" said I, "to be sure I have no right to laugh at you—a million and a half of money is too serious a matter for mirth—but you are not about to establish a third link in your chain—you will

not find any especial connexion between your pirates and a goat—
pirates, you know, have nothing to do with goats; they appertain
to the farming interest."

"But I have just said that the figure was *not* that of a goat."

"Well, a kid then—pretty much the same thing."

"Pretty much, but not altogether," said Legrand. "You may
have heard of one *Captain* Kidd. I at once looked on the figure of
the animal as a kind of punning or hieroglyphical signature. I say
signature; because its position on the vellum suggested this idea.
The death's-head at the corner diagonally opposite, had, in the
same manner, the air of a stamp, or seal. But I was sorely put out by
the absence of all else—of the body to my imagined instrument—of
the text for my context."

"I presume you expected to find a letter between the stamp and
the signature."

"Something of that kind. The fact is, I felt irresistibly impressed
with a presentiment of some vast good fortune impending. I can
scarcely say why. Perhaps, after all, it was rather a desire than an
actual belief;—but do you know that Jupiter's silly words, about
the bug being of solid gold, had a remarkable effect on my fancy?
And then the series of accidents and coincidences—these were so
very extraordinary. Do you observe how mere an accident it was
that these events should have occurred on the *sole* day of all the
year in which it has been, or may be, sufficiently cool for fire, and
that without the fire, or without the intervention of the dog at the
precise moment in which he appeared, I should never have become
aware of the death's-head, and so never the possessor of the trea-
sure?"

"But proceed—I am all impatience."

"Well; you have heard, of course, the many stories current—the
thousand vague rumors afloat about money buried, somewhere on
the Atlantic coast, by Kidd and his associates. These rumors must
have had some foundation in fact. And that the rumors have ex-
isted so long and so continuously, could have resulted, it appeared
to me, only from the circumstance of the buried treasure still *re-
maining* entombed. Had Kidd concealed his plunder for a time,
and afterwards reclaimed it, the rumors would scarcely have
reached us in their present unvarying form. You will observe that
the stories told are all about money-seekers, not about money-finders.

Had the pirate recovered his money, there the affair would have dropped. It seemed to me that some accident—say the loss of a memorandum indicating its locality—had deprived him of the means of recovering it, and that this accident had become known to his followers, who otherwise might never have heard that treasure had been concealed at all, and who, busying themselves in vain, because unguided attempts, to regain it, had given first birth, and then universal currency, to the reports which are now so common. Have you ever heard of any important treasure being unearthed along the coast?"

"Never."

"But that Kidd's accumulations were immense, is well known. I took it for granted, therefore, that the earth still held them; and you will scarcely be surprised when I tell you that I felt a hope, nearly amounting to certainty, that the parchment so strangely found, involved a lost record of the place of deposit."

"But how did you proceed?"

"I held the vellum again to the fire, after increasing the heat; but nothing appeared. I now thought it possible that the coating of dirt might have something to do with the failure; so I carefully rinsed the parchment by pouring warm water over it, and, having done this, I placed it in a tin pan, with the skull downwards, and put the pan upon a furnace of lighted charcoal. In a few minutes, the pan having become thoroughly heated, I removed the slip, and, to my inexpressible joy, found it spotted, in several places, with what appeared to be figures arranged in lines. Again I placed it in the pan, and suffered it to remain another minute. On taking it off, the whole was just as you see it now."

Here Legrand, having re-heated the parchment, submitted it to my inspection. The following characters were rudely traced, in a red tint, between the death's-head and the goat:

53‡‡†305))6*;4826)4‡.)4‡);806*;48†8¶60))85;;]8*;:‡*8†83(88)
5*†;46(;88*96*?;8)*‡(;485);5*†2:*‡(;4956*2(5*—4)8¶8*;40692
85);)6†8)4‡‡;1(‡9;48081;8:8‡1;48†85;4)485†528806*81(‡9;48;
(88;4(‡?34;48)4‡;161;:188;‡?;5

"But," said I, returning him the slip, "I am as much in the dark as ever. Were all the jewels of Golconda awaiting me on my solution of this enigma, I am quite sure that I should be unable to earn them."

"And yet," said Legrand, "the solution is by no means so difficult as you might be led to imagine from the first hasty inspection of the characters. These characters, as any one might readily guess, form a cipher—that is to say, they convey a meaning; but then, from what is known of Kidd, I could not suppose him capable of constructing any of the more abstruse cryptographs. I made up my mind, at once, that this was of a simple species—such, however, as would appear, to the crude intellect of the sailor, absolutely insoluble without the key."

"And you really solved it?"

"Readily; I have solved others of an abstruseness ten thousand times greater. Circumstances, and a certain bias of mind, have led me to take interest in such riddles, and it may well be doubted whether human ingenuity can construct an enigma of the kind which human ingenuity may not, by proper application, resolve. In fact, having once established connected and legible characters, I scarcely gave a thought to the mere difficulty of developing their import.

"In the present case—indeed in all cases of secret writing—the first question regards the *language* of the cipher; for the principles of solution, so far, especially, as the more simple ciphers are concerned, depend upon, and are varied by, the genius of the particular idiom. In general, there is no alternative but experiment (directed by probabilities) of every tongue known to him who attempts the solution, until the true one be attained. But, with the cipher now before us, all difficulty is removed by the signature. The pun on the word 'Kidd' is appreciable in no other language than the English. But for this consideration I should have begun my attempts with the Spanish and French, as the tongues in which a secret of this kind would most naturally have been written by a pirate of the Spanish main. As it was, I assumed the cryptograph to be English.

"You observe there are no divisions between the words. Had there been divisions, the task would have been comparatively easy. In such case I should have commenced with a collation and analysis of the shorter words, and, had a word of a single letter occurred, as is most likely, (*a* or *I*, for example,) I should have considered the solution as assured. But, there being no division, my first step was to ascertain the predominant letters, as well as the least frequent. Counting all, I constructed a table, thus:

Of the character 8 there are 33.

;	"	26.
4	"	19.
‡)	"	16.
*	"	13.
5	"	12.
6	"	11.
†1	"	8.
0	"	6.
9 2	"	5.
: 3	"	4.
?	"	3.
¶	"	2.
] —.	"	1.

"Now, in English, the letter which most frequently occurs is *e*. Afterwards, the succession runs thus: *a o i d h n r s t u y c f g l m w b k p q x z. E*, however, predominates so remarkably that an individual sentence of any length is rarely seen, in which it is not the prevailing character.

"Here, then, we have, in the very beginning, the groundwork for something more than a mere guess. The general use which may be made of the table is obvious—but, in this particular cipher, we shall only very partially require its aid. As our predominant character is 8, we will commence by assuming it as the *e* of the natural alphabet. To verify the supposition, let us observe if the 8 be seen often in couples—for *e* is doubled with great frequency in English—in such words, for example, as 'meet,' 'fleet,' 'speed,' 'seen,' 'been,' 'agree,' &c. In the present instance we see it doubled no less than five times, although the cryptograph is brief.

"Let us assume 8, then, as *e*. Now, of all *words* in the language, 'the' is most usual; let us see, therefore, whether there are not repetitions of any three characters, in the same order of collocation, the last of them being 8. If we discover repetitions of such letters, so arranged, they will most probably represent the word 'the.' On inspection, we find no less than seven such arrangements, the characters being ;48. We may, therefore, assume that the semi-colon represents *t*, that 4 represents *h*, and that 8 represents *e*—the last being now well confirmed. Thus a great step has been taken.

"But, having established a single word, we are enabled to estab-lish a vastly important point; that is to say, several commence-ments and terminations of other words. Let us refer, for example, to the last instance but one, in which the combination ;48 occurs—not far from the end of the cipher. We know that the semicolon immediately ensuing is the commencement of a word, and, of the six characters succeeding this 'the,' we are cognizant of no less than five. Let us set these characters down, thus, by the let-ters we know them to represent, leaving a space for the un-known—

t eeth.

"Here we are enabled, at once, to discard the '*th*,' as forming no portion of the word commencing with the first *t*; since, by experi-ment of the entire alphabet for a letter adapted to the vacancy, we perceive that no word can be formed of which this *th* can be a part. We are thus narrowed into

t ee,

and, going through the alphabet, if necessary, as before, we arrive at the word 'tree,' as the sole possible reading. We thus gain an-other letter, *r*, represented by (, with the words 'the tree' in juxta-position.

"Looking beyond these words, for a short distance, we again see the combination ;48, and employ it by way of *termination* to what immediately precedes. We have thus this arrangement:

the tree ;4(‡?34 the,

or, substituting the natural letters, where known, it reads thus:

the tree thr‡?3h the.

"Now, if, in place of the unknown characters, we leave blank spaces, or substitute dots, we read thus:

the tree thr . . . h the,

when the word '*through*' makes itself evident at once. But this discovery gives us three new letters, *o, u* and *g*, represented by ‡ ? and 3.

"Looking now, narrowly, through the cipher for combinations of known characters, we find, not very far from the beginning, this arrangement,

83(88, or egree,

which, plainly, is the conclusion of the word 'degree,' and gives us another letter, *d*, represented by †.

"Four letters beyond the word 'degree,' we perceive the combination

;4 >>8<< <6> (;88.

"Translating the known characters, and representing the unknown by dots, as before, we read thus:

th . rtee.

an arrangement immediately suggestive of the word 'thirteen,' and again furnishing us with two new characters, *i* and *n*, represented by 6 and *.

"Referring, now, to the beginning of the cryptograph, we find the combination,

53‡‡†.

"Translating, as before, we obtain

. good,

which assures us that the first letter is *A*, and that the first two
words are 'A good.'

"To avoid confusion, it is now time that we arrange our key, as
far as discovered, in a tabular form. It will stand thus:

5	represents	a
†	"	d
8	"	e
3	"	g
4	"	h
6	"	i
*	"	n
‡	"	o
(	"	r
;	"	t

"We have, therefore, no less than ten of the most important
letters represented, and it will be unnecessary to proceed with
the details of the solution. I have said enough to convince you
that ciphers of this nature are readily soluble, and to give you
some insight into the *rationale* of their development. But be as-
sured that the specimen before us appertains to the very simplest
species of cryptograph. It now only remains to give you the full
translation of the characters upon the parchment, as unriddled.
Here it is:

*'A good glass in the bishop's hostel in the devil's seat twenty-one
degrees and thirteen minutes northeast and by north main branch
seventh limb east side shoot from the left eye of the death's-head a
bee line from the tree through the shot fifty feet out.'*"

"But," said I, "the enigma seems still in as bad a condition as
ever. How is it possible to extort a meaning from all this jargon
about 'devil's seats,' 'death's heads,' and 'bishop's hotels?'"

"I confess," replied Legrand, "that the matter still wears a seri-
ous aspect, when regarded with a casual glance. My first endeavor
was to divide the sentence into the natural division intended by the
cryptographist."

"You mean, to punctuate it?"

"Something of that kind."

"But how was it possible to effect this?"

"I reflected that it had been a *point* with the writer to run his words together without division, so as to increase the difficulty of solution. Now, a not over-acute man, in pursuing such an object, would be nearly certain to overdo the matter. When, in the course of his composition, he arrived at a break in his subject which would naturally require a pause, or a point, he would be exceedingly apt to run his characters, at this place, more than usually close together. If you will observe the MS., in the present instance, you will easily detect five such cases of unusual crowding. Acting on this hint, I made the division thus:

'*A good glass in the Bishop's hostel in the Devil's seat—twenty-one degrees and thirteen minutes—northeast and by north—main branch seventh limb east side—shoot from the left eye of the death's-head—a bee-line from the tree through the shot fifty feet out.*'"

"Even this division," said I, "leaves me still in the dark."

"It left me also in the dark," replied Legrand, "for a few days; during which I made diligent inquiry, in the neighborhood of Sullivan's Island, for any building which went by the name of the 'Bishop's Hotel;' for, of course, I dropped the obsolete word 'hostel.' Gaining no information on the subject, I was on the point of extending my sphere of search, and proceeding in a more systematic manner, when, one morning, it entered into my head, quite suddenly, that this 'Bishop's Hostel' might have some reference to an old family, of the name of Bessop, which, time out of mind, had held possession of an ancient manor-house, about four miles to the northward of the Island. I accordingly went over to the plantation, and re-instituted my inquiries among the older negroes of the place. At length one of the most aged of the women said that she had heard of such a place as *Bessop's Castle*, and thought that she could guide me to it, but that it was not a castle, nor a tavern, but a high rock.

"I offered to pay her well for her trouble, and, after some demur, she consented to accompany me to the spot. We found it without much difficulty, when, dismissing her, I proceeded to examine the place. The 'castle' consisted of an irregular assemblage of cliffs and rocks—one of the latter being quite remarkable for its height as well as for its insulated and artificial appearance. I clambered to its apex, and then felt much at a loss as to what should be next done.

"While I was busied in reflection, my eyes fell upon a narrow ledge in the eastern face of the rock, perhaps a yard below the summit on which I stood. This ledge projected about eighteen inches, and was not more than a foot wide, while a niche in the cliff just above it, gave it a rude resemblance to one of the hollow-backed chairs used by our ancestors. I made no doubt that here was the 'devil's seat' alluded to in the MS., and now I seemed to grasp the full secret of the riddle.

"The 'good glass,' I knew, could have reference to nothing but a telescope; for the word 'glass' is rarely employed in any other sense by seamen. Now here, I at once saw, was a telescope to be used, and a definite point of view, *admitting no variation*, from which to use it. Nor did I hesitate to believe that the phrases, 'twenty-one degrees and thirteen minutes,' and 'northeast and by north,' were intended as directions for the levelling of the glass. Greatly excited by these discoveries, I hurried home, procured a telescope, and returned to the rock.

"I let myself down to the ledge, and found that it was impossible to retain a seat on it unless in one particular position. This fact confirmed my preconceived idea. I proceeded to use the glass. Of course, the 'twenty-one degrees and thirteen minutes' could allude to nothing but elevation above the visible horizon, since the horizontal direction was clearly indicated by the words, 'northeast and by north.' This latter direction I at once established by means of a pocket-compass; then, pointing the glass as nearly at an angle of twenty-one degrees of elevation as I could do it by guess, I moved it cautiously up or down, until my attention was arrested by a circular rift or opening in the foliage of a large tree that overtopped its fellows in the distance. In the centre of this rift I perceived a white spot, but could not, at first, distinguish what it was. Adjusting the focus of the telescope, I again looked, and now made it out to be a human skull.

"On this discovery I was so sanguine as to consider the enigma solved; for the phrase 'main branch, seventh limb, east side,' could refer only to the position of the skull on the tree, while 'shoot from the left eye of the death's head' admitted, also, of but one interpretation, in regard to a search for buried treasure. I perceived that the design was to drop a bullet from the left eye of the skull, and that a bee-line, or, in other words, a straight line, drawn from the nearest point of the trunk through 'the shot,' (or the spot where the bullet fell,) and thence extended to a distance of fifty feet, would indicate a definite point—and beneath this point I thought it at least *possible* that a deposit of value lay concealed."

"All this," I said, "is exceedingly clear, and, although ingenious, still simple and explicit. When you left the Bishop's Hotel, what then?"

"Why, having carefully taken the bearings of the tree, I turned homewards. The instant that I left 'the devil's seat,' however, the circular rift vanished; nor could I get a glimpse of it afterwards, turn as I would. What seems to me the chief ingenuity in this whole business, is the fact (for repeated experiment has convinced me it *is* a fact) that the circular opening in question is visible from no other attainable point of view than that afforded by the narrow ledge on the face of the rock.

"In this expedition to the 'Bishop's Hotel' I had been attended by Jupiter, who had, no doubt, observed, for some weeks past, the abstraction of my demeanor, and took especial care not to leave me alone. But, on the next day, getting up very early, I contrived to give him the slip, and went into the hills in search of the tree. After much toil I found it. When I came home at night my valet proposed to give me a flogging. With the rest of the adventure I believe you are as well acquainted as myself."

"I suppose," said I, "you missed the spot, in the first attempt at digging, through Jupiter's stupidity in letting the bug fall through the right instead of through the left eye of the skull."

"Precisely. This mistake made a difference of about two inches and a half in the 'shot'—that is to say, in the position of the peg nearest the tree; and had the treasure been *beneath* the 'shot,' the error would have been of little moment; but 'the shot,' together with the nearest point of the tree, were merely two points for the establishment of a line of direction; of course the error, however trivial in the beginning, increased as we proceeded with the line, and by the time we had gone fifty feet, threw us quite off the scent. But for my deep-seated conviction that treasure was here somewhere actually buried, we might have had all our labor in vain."

"I presume the fancy of *the skull*—of letting fall a bullet through the skull's-eye—was suggested to Kidd by the piratical flag. No doubt he felt a kind of poetical consistency in recovering his money through this ominous insignium."

"Perhaps so; still I cannot help thinking that common-sense had quite as much to do with the matter as poetical consistency. To be visible from the Devil's seat, it was necessary that the object, if small, should be *white*; and there is nothing like your human skull for retaining and even increasing its whiteness under exposure to all vicissitudes of weather."

"But your grandiloquence, and your conduct in swinging the beetle—how excessively odd! I was sure you were mad. And why did you insist on letting fall the bug, instead of a bullet, from the skull?"

"Why, to be frank, I felt somewhat annoyed by your evident suspicions touching my sanity, and so resolved to punish you quietly, in my own way, by a little bit of sober mystification. For this reason I swung the beetle, and for this reason I let it fall from the tree. An observation of yours about its great weight suggested the latter idea."

"Yes, I perceive; and now there is only one point which puzzles me. What are we to make of the skeletons found in the hole?"

"That is a question I am no more able to answer than yourself. There seems, however, only one plausible way of accounting for them—and yet it is dreadful to believe in such atrocity as my suggestion would imply. It is clear that Kidd—if Kidd indeed secreted this treasure, which I doubt not—it is clear that he must have had assistance in the labor. But, the worst of this labor concluded, he may have thought it expedient to remove all participants in his secret. Perhaps a couple of blows with a mattock were sufficient, while his coadjutors were busy in the pit; perhaps it required a dozen—who shall tell?"

THE OBLONG BOX

Some years ago, I engaged passage from Charleston, S. C., to the city of New York, in the fine packet-ship "Independence," Captain Hardy. We were to sail on the fifteenth of the month (June), weather permitting; and, on the fourteenth, I went on board to arrange some matters in my state-room.

I found that we were to have a great many passengers, including a more than usual number of ladies. On the list were several of my acquaintances; and among other names, I was rejoiced to see that of Mr. Cornelius Wyatt, a young artist, for whom I entertained feelings of warm friendship. He had been with me a fellow student at C—— University, where we were very much together. He had the ordinary temperament of genius, and was a compound of misanthropy, sensibility, and enthusiasm. To these qualities he united the warmest and truest heart which ever beat in a human bosom.

I observed that his name was carded upon *three* state-rooms; and, upon again referring to the list of passengers, I found that he had engaged passage for himself, wife, and two sisters—his own. The state-rooms were sufficiently roomy, and each had two berths, one above the other. These berths, to be sure, were so exceedingly narrow as to be insufficient for more than one person; still, I could not comprehend why there were *three* state-rooms for these four persons. I was, just at that epoch, in one of those moody frames of mind which make a man abnormally inquisitive about trifles: and I confess, with shame, that I busied myself in a variety of ill-bred and preposterous conjectures about this matter of the supernumerary state-room. It was no business of mine, to be sure; but with none the less pertinacity did I occupy myself in attempts to resolve the enigma. At last I reached a conclusion which wrought in me great wonder why I had not arrived at it before. "It is a servant, of course," I said; "what a fool I am, not sooner to have thought of so obvious a solution!" And then I again repaired to the list—but here I saw distinctly that *no* servant was to come with the party; although, in fact, it had been the original design to bring one—for the words "and servant" had been first written and then overscored. "Oh, extra baggage, to be sure," I now said to myself—"something he wishes not to be put in the hold—something to be kept under his own eye—ah, I have it—a painting or so—and this is what he has been bargaining about with Nicolino, the Italian Jew." This idea satisfied me, and I dismissed my curiosity for the nonce.

Wyatt's two sisters I knew very well, and most amiable and clever girls they were. His wife he had newly married, and I had never yet seen her. He had often talked about her in my presence, however, and in his usual style of enthusiasm. He described her as of surpassing beauty, wit, and accomplishment. I was, therefore, quite anxious to make her acquaintance.

On the day in which I visited the ship, (the fourteenth,) Wyatt and party were also to visit it—so the captain informed me—and I waited on board an hour longer than I had designed, in hope of being presented to the bride, but then an apology came. "Mrs. W. was a little indisposed, and would decline coming on board until to-morrow, at the hour of sailing."

The morrow having arrived, I was going from my hotel to the wharf, when Captain Hardy met me and said that, "owing to circumstances," (a stupid but convenient phrase,) "he rather thought the 'Independence' would not sail for a day or two, and that when all was ready, he would send up and let me know." This I thought strange, for there was a stiff southerly breeze; but as "the circumstances" were not forthcoming, although I pumped for them with much perseverance, I had nothing to do but to return home and digest my impatience at leisure.

I did not receive the expected message from the captain for nearly a week. It came at length, however, and I immediately went on board. The ship was crowded with passengers, and every thing was in the bustle attendant upon making sail. Wyatt's party arrived in about ten minutes after myself. There were the two sisters, the bride, and the artist—the latter in one of his customary fits of moody misanthropy. I was too well used to these, however, to pay them any special attention. He did not even introduce me to his wife;—this courtesy devolving, per force, upon his sister Marian— a very sweet and intelligent girl, who, in a few hurried words, made us acquainted.

Mrs. Wyatt had been closely veiled; and when she raised her veil, in acknowledging my bow, I confess that I was very profoundly astonished. I should have been much more so, however, had not long experience advised me not to trust, with too implicit a reliance, the enthusiastic descriptions of my friend, the artist, when indulging in comments upon the loveliness of woman. When beauty was the theme, I well knew with what facility he soared into the regions of the purely ideal.

The truth is, I could not help regarding Mrs. Wyatt as a decidedly plain-looking woman. If not positively ugly, she was not, I think, very far from it. She was dressed, however, in exquisite taste—and then I had no doubt that she had captivated my friend's heart by the more enduring graces of the intellect and soul. She said very few words, and passed at once into her state-room with Mr. W.

My old inquisitiveness now returned. There was *no* servant— *that* was a settled point. I looked, therefore, for the extra baggage. After some delay, a cart arrived at the wharf, with an oblong pine box, which was everything that seemed to be expected. Immediately upon its arrival we made sail, and in a short time were safely over the bar and standing out to sea.

The box in question was, as I say, oblong. It was about six feet in length by two and a half in breadth;—I observed it attentively, and like to be precise. Now this shape was *peculiar*; and no sooner had I seen it, than I took credit to myself for the accuracy of my guessing. I had reached the conclusion, it will be remembered, that the extra baggage of my friend, the artist, would prove to be pictures, or at least a picture; for I knew he had been for several weeks in conference with Nicolino:—and now here was a box which, from its shape, *could* possibly contain nothing in the world but a copy of Leonardo's "Last Supper;" and a copy of this very "Last Supper," done by Rubini the younger, at Florence, I had known, for some time, to be in the possession of Nicolino. This point, therefore, I considered as sufficiently settled. I chuckled excessively when I thought of my acumen. It was the first time I had ever known Wyatt to keep from me any of his artistical secrets; but here he evidently intended to steal a march upon me, and smuggle a fine picture to New York, under my very nose; expecting me to know nothing of the matter. I resolved to quiz him *well*, now and hereafter.

One thing, however, annoyed me not a little. The box did *not* go into the extra state-room. It was deposited in Wyatt's own; and there, too, it remained, occupying very nearly the whole of the floor—no doubt to the exceeding discomfort of the artist and his wife;—this the more especially as the tar or paint with which it was lettered in sprawling capitals, emitted a strong, disagreeable, and, to *my* fancy, a peculiarly disgusting odor. On the lid were painted the words—*"Mrs. Adelaide Curtis, Albany, New York. Charge of Cornelius Wyatt, Esq. This side up. To be handled with care."*

Now, I was aware that Mrs. Adelaide Curtis, of Albany, was the artist's wife's mother;—but then I looked upon the whole address as a mystification, intended especially for myself. I made up my mind, of course, that the box and contents would never get farther north than the studio of my misanthropic friend, in Chambers Street, New York.

For the first three or four days we had fine weather, although the wind was dead ahead; having chopped round to the northward, immediately upon our losing sight of the coast. The passengers were, consequently, in high spirits and disposed to be social. I *must* except, however, Wyatt and his sisters, who behaved stiffly, and, I could not help thinking, uncourteously to the rest of the party. *Wyatt's* conduct I did not so much regard. He was gloomy, even beyond his usual habit—in fact he was *morose*—but in him I was prepared for eccentricity. For the sisters, however, I could make no excuse. They secluded themselves in their staterooms during the greater part of the passage, and absolutely refused, although I repeatedly urged them, to hold communication with any person on board.

Mrs. Wyatt herself was far more agreeable. That is to say, she was *chatty*; and to be chatty is no slight recommendation at sea. She became *excessively* intimate with most of the ladies; and, to my profound astonishment, evinced no equivocal disposition to coquet with the men. She amused us all very much. I say *"amused"*—and scarcely know how to explain myself. The truth is, I soon found that Mrs. W. was far oftener laughed *at* than *with*. The gentlemen said little about her; but the ladies, in a little while, pronounced her "a good-hearted thing, rather indifferent looking, totally uneducated, and decidedly vulgar." The great wonder was, how Wyatt had been entrapped into such a match. Wealth was the general solution—but this I knew to be no solution at all; for Wyatt had told me that she neither brought him a dollar nor had any expectations from any source whatever. "He had married," he said, "for love, and for love only; and his bride was far more than worthy of his love." When I thought of these expressions, on the part of my friend, I confess that I felt indescribably puzzled. Could it be possible that he was taking leave of his senses? What else could I think? *He*, so refined, so intellectual, so fastidious, with so exquisite a perception of the faulty, and so keen an appreciation of the beautiful! To be sure, the lady seemed especially fond of *him*—particularly so in his absence—when she made herself ridiculous by frequent quotations of what had been said by her "beloved husband, Mr. Wyatt." The word "husband" seemed forever—to use one of her own delicate expressions—forever "on the tip of her tongue." In the meantime, it was observed by all on board, that he avoided *her* in the most pointed manner, and, for the most part, shut himself up alone in his stateroom, where, in fact, he might have been said to live altogether, leaving his wife at full liberty to amuse herself as she thought best, in the public society of the main cabin.

My conclusion, from what I saw and heard, was, that, the artist, by some unaccountable freak of fate, or perhaps in some fit of enthusiastic and fanciful passion, had been induced to unite himself with a person altogether beneath him, and that the natural result, entire and speedy disgust, had ensued. I pitied him from the bottom of my heart—but could not, for that reason, quite forgive his incommunicativeness in the matter of the "Last Supper." For this I resolved to have my revenge.

One day he came upon deck, and, taking his arm as had been my wont, I sauntered with him backwards and forwards. His gloom, however, (which I considered quite natural under the circumstances,) seemed entirely unabated. He said little, and that moodily, and with evident effort. I ventured a jest or two, and he made a sickening attempt at a smile. Poor fellow!—as I thought of *his wife*,

I wondered that he could have heart to put on even the semblance of mirth. I determined to commence a series of covert insinuations, or innuendoes, about the oblong box—just to let him perceive, gradually, that I was *not* altogether the butt, or victim, of his little bit of pleasant mystification. My first observation was by way of opening a masked battery. I said something about the "peculiar shape of *that* box;" and, as I spoke the words, I smiled knowingly, winked, and touched him gently with my fore-finger in the ribs.

The manner in which Wyatt received this harmless pleasantry, convinced me, at once, that he was mad. At first he stared at me as if he found it impossible to comprehend the witticism of my remark; but as its point seemed slowly to make its way into his brain, his eyes, in the same proportion, seemed protruding from their sockets. Then he grew very red—then hideously pale—then, as if highly amused with what I had insinuated, he began a loud and boisterous laugh, which, to my astonishment, he kept up, with gradually increasing vigor, for ten minutes or more. In conclusion, he fell flat and heavily upon the deck. When I ran to uplift him, to all appearance he was *dead*.

I called assistance, and, with much difficulty, we brought him to himself. Upon reviving he spoke incoherently for some time. At length we bled him and put him to bed. The next morning he was quite recovered, so far as regarded his mere bodily health. Of his mind I say nothing, of course. I avoided him during the rest of the passage, by advice of the captain, who seemed to coincide with me altogether in my views of his insanity, but cautioned me to say nothing on this head to any person on board.

Several circumstances occurred immediately after this fit of Wyatt's, which contributed to heighten the curiosity with which I was already possessed. Among other things, this: I had been nervous—drank too much strong green tea, and slept ill at night—in fact, for two nights I could not be properly said to sleep at all. Now, my state-room opened into the main cabin, or dining-room, as did those of all the single men on board. Wyatt's three rooms were in the after-cabin, which was separated from the main one by a slight sliding door, never locked even at night. As we were almost constantly on a wind, and the breeze was not a little stiff, the ship heeled to leeward very considerably; and whenever her starboard side was to leeward, the sliding door between the cabins slid open, and so remained, nobody taking the trouble to get up and shut it. But my berth was in such a position, that when my own stateroom door was open, as well as the sliding door in question, (and my own door was *always* open on account of the heat,) I could see into the after-cabin quite distinctly, and just at that portion of it, too, where were situated the state-rooms of Mr. Wyatt. Well, during two nights (*not* consecutive) while I lay awake, I clearly saw Mrs. W., about eleven o'clock upon each night, steal cautiously from the state-room of Mr. W., and enter the extra room, where she remained until day break, when she was called by her husband and went back. That they were virtually separated was clear. They had separate apartments—no doubt in contemplation of a more permanent divorce; and here, after all, I thought, was the mystery of the extra state-room.

There was another circumstance, too, which interested me much. During the two wakeful nights in question, and immediately after the disappearance of Mrs. Wyatt into the extra stateroom, I was attracted by certain singular cautious, subdued noises in that of her husband. After listening to them for some time, with thoughtful attention, I at length succeeded perfectly in translating their import. They were sounds occasioned by the artist in prying open the oblong box, by means of a chisel and mallet—the latter being apparently muffled, or deadened, by some soft woollen or cotton substance in which its head was enveloped.

In this manner I fancied I could distinguish the precise moment when he fairly disengaged the lid—also, that I could determine when he removed it altogether, and when he deposited it upon the lower berth in his room; this latter point I knew, for example, by certain slight taps which the lid made in striking against the wooden edges of the berth, as he endeavored to lay it down *very* gently—there being no room for it on the floor. After this there was a dead stillness, and I heard nothing more, upon either occasion, until nearly daybreak; unless, perhaps, I may mention a low sobbing, or murmuring sound, so very much suppressed as to be nearly inaudible—if, indeed, the whole of this latter noise were not rather produced by my own imagination. I say it seemed to *resemble* sobbing or sighing—but, of course, it could not have been either. I rather think it was a ringing in my own ears. Mr. Wyatt, no doubt, according to custom, was merely giving the rein to one of his hobbies—indulging in one of his fits of artistic enthusiasm. He had opened his oblong box, in order to feast his eyes on the pictorial treasure within. There was nothing in this, however, to make him *sob*. I repeat therefore, that it must have been simply a freak of my own fancy, distempered by good Captain Hardy's green tea. Just before dawn, on each of the two nights of which I speak, I distinctly heard Mr. Wyatt replace the lid upon the oblong box, and force the nails into their old places, by means of the muffled mallet. Having done this, he issued from his state-room, fully dressed, and proceeded to call Mrs. W. from hers.

We had been at sea seven days, and were now off Cape Hatteras, when there came a tremendously heavy blow from the southwest. We were, in a measure, prepared for it, however, as the weather had been holding out threats for some time. Every thing was made snug, alow and aloft; and as the wind steadily freshened, we lay to, at length, under spanker and foretopsail, both double-reefed.

In this trim, we rode safely enough for forty-eight hours—the ship proving herself an excellent sea-boat, in many respects, and shipping no water of any consequence. At the end of this period, however, the gale had freshened into a hurricane, and our after-sail split into ribbons, bringing us so much in the trough of the water that we shipped several prodigious seas, one immediately after the other. By this accident we lost three men overboard, with the caboose, and nearly the whole of the larboard bulwarks. Scarcely had we recovered our senses, before the foretopsail went into shreds, when we got up a storm stay-sail and with this did pretty well for some hours, the ship heading the sea much more steadily than before.

The gale still held on, however, and we saw no signs of its abating. The rigging was found to be ill-fitted, and greatly strained; and on the third day of the blow, about five in the afternoon, our mizzen-mast, in a heavy lurch to windward, went by the board. For an hour or more, we tried in vain to get rid of it, on account of the prodigious rolling of the ship; and, before we had succeeded, the carpenter came aft and announced four feet of water in the hold. To add to our dilemma, we found the pumps choked and nearly useless.

All was now confusion and despair—but an effort was made to lighten the ship by throwing overboard as much of her cargo as could be reached, and by cutting away the two masts that remained.

This we at last accomplished—but we were still unable to do any thing at the pumps; and, in the meantime, the leak gained on us very fast.

At sundown, the gale had sensibly diminished in violence, and, as the sea went down with it, we still entertained faint hopes of saving ourselves in the boats. At eight P.M., the clouds broke away to windward, and we had the advantage of a full moon—a piece of good fortune which served wonderfully to cheer our drooping spirits.

After incredible labor we succeeded, at length, in getting the longboat over the side without material accident, and into this we crowded the whole of the crew and most of the passengers. This party made off immediately, and, after undergoing much suffering, finally arrived, in safety, at Ocracoke Inlet, on the third day after the wreck.[1]

Fourteen passengers, with the Captain, remained on board, resolving to trust their fortunes to the jolly-boat at the stern. We lowered it without difficulty, although it was only by a miracle that we prevented it from swamping as it touched the water. It contained, when afloat, the captain and his wife, Mr. Wyatt and party, a Mexican officer, wife, four children, and myself, with a negro valet.

We had no room, of course, for any thing except a few positively necessary instruments, some provisions, and the clothes upon our backs. No one had thought of even attempting to save any thing more. What must have been the astonishment of all, then, when having proceeded a few fathoms from the ship, Mr. Wyatt stood up in the stern-sheets, and coolly demanded of Captain Hardy that the boat should be put back for the purpose of taking in his oblong box!

"Sit down, Mr. Wyatt," replied the Captain, somewhat sternly; "you will capsize us if you do not sit quite still. Our gunwhale is almost in the water now."

"The box!" vociferated Mr. Wyatt, still standing—"the box, I say! Captain Hardy, you cannot, you *will* not refuse me. Its weight will be but a trifle—it is nothing—mere nothing. By the mother who bore you—for the love of Heaven—by your hope of salvation, I *implore* you to put back for the box!"

The Captain, for a moment, seemed touched by the earnest appeal of the artist, but he regained his stern composure, and merely said—

"Mr. Wyatt, you are *mad*. I cannot listen to you. Sit down, I say, or you will swamp the boat. Stay—hold him—seize him!—he is about to spring overboard! There—I knew it—he is over!"

As the Captain said this, Mr. Wyatt, in fact, sprang from the boat, and, as we were yet in the lee of the wreck, succeeded, by almost superhuman exertion, in getting hold of a rope which hung from the fore-chains. In another moment he was on board, and rushing frantically down into the cabin.

In the meantime, we had been swept astern of the ship, and being quite out of her lee, were at the mercy of the tremendous sea which was still running. We made a determined effort to put back, but our little boat was like a feather in the breath of the tempest. We saw at a glance that the doom of the unfortunate artist was sealed.

As our distance from the wreck rapidly increased, the madman (for as such only could we regard him) was seen to emerge from the companion-way, up which, by dint of strength that appeared gigantic, he dragged, bodily, the oblong box. While we gazed in the extremity of astonishment, he passed, rapidly, several turns of a three-inch rope, first around the box and then around his body. In another instant both body and box were in the sea—disappearing suddenly, at once and forever.

We lingered awhile sadly upon our oars, with our eyes riveted upon the spot. At length we pulled away. The silence remained unbroken for an hour. Finally, I hazarded a remark.

"Did you observe, Captain, how suddenly they sank? Was not that an exceedingly singular thing? I confess that I entertained some feeble hope of his final deliverance, when I saw him lash himself to the box, and commit himself to the sea."

"They sank as a matter of course," replied the Captain, "and that like a shot. They will soon rise again, however—*but not till the salt melts*."

"The salt!" I ejaculated.

"Hush!" said the Captain, pointing to the wife and sisters of the deceased. "We must talk of these things at some more appropriate time."

We suffered much, and made a narrow escape; but fortune befriended *us*, as well as our mates in the long-boat. We landed, in fine, more dead than alive, after four days of intense distress, upon the beach opposite Roanoke Island. We remained here a week, were not ill-treated by the wreckers, and at length obtained a passage to New York.

About a month after the loss of the "Independence," I happened to meet Captain Hardy in Broadway. Our conversation turned, naturally, upon the disaster, and especially upon the sad fate of poor Wyatt. I thus learned the following particulars.

The artist had engaged passage for himself, wife, two sisters and a servant. His wife was, indeed, as she had been represented, a most lovely, and most accomplished woman. On the morning of the fourteenth of June (the day in which I first visited the ship,) the lady suddenly sickened and died. The young husband was frantic with grief—but circumstances imperatively forbade the deferring his voyage to New York. It was necessary to take to her mother the corpse of his adored wife, and, on the other hand, the universal prejudice which would prevent his doing so openly was well known. Nine-tenths of the passengers would have abandoned the ship rather than take passage with a dead body.

In this dilemma, Captain Hardy arranged that the corpse, being first partially embalmed, and packed, with a large quantity of salt, in a box of suitable dimensions, should be conveyed on board as merchandise. Nothing was to be said of the lady's decease; and, as it was well understood that Mr. Wyatt had engaged passage for his wife, it became necessary that some person should personate her during the voyage. This the deceased's lady's-maid was easily prevailed on to do. The extra state-room, originally engaged for this girl, during her mistress' life, was now merely retained. In this state-room the pseudo wife slept, of course, every night. In the day-time she performed, to the best of her ability, the part of her mistress—whose person, it had been carefully ascertained, was unknown to any of the passengers on board.

My own mistake arose, naturally enough, through too careless, too inquisitive, and too impulsive a temperament. But of late, it is a rare thing that I sleep soundly at night. There is a countenance which haunts me, turn as I will. There is an hysterical laugh which will forever ring within my ears.

A TALE OF THE RAGGED MOUNTAINS

During the fall of the year 1827, while residing near Charlottesville, Virginia, I casually made the acquaintance of Mr. Augustus Bedloe. This young gentleman was remarkable in every respect, and excited in me a profound interest and curiosity. I found it impossible to comprehend him either in his moral or his physical relations. Of his family I could obtain no satisfactory account. Whence he came, I never ascertained. Even about his age—although I call him a young gentleman—there was something which perplexed me in no little degree. He certainly *seemed* young—and he made a point of speaking about his youth—yet there were moments when I should have had little trouble in imagining him a hundred years of age. But in no regard was he more peculiar than in his personal appearance. He was singularly tall and thin. He stooped much. His limbs were exceedingly long and emaciated. His forehead was broad and low. His complexion was absolutely bloodless. His mouth was large and flexible, and his teeth were more wildly uneven, although sound, than I had ever before seen teeth in a human head. The expression of his smile, however, was by no means unpleasing, as might be supposed; but it had no variation whatever. It was one of profound melancholy—of a phaseless and unceasing gloom. His eyes were abnormally large, and round like those of a cat. The pupils, too, upon any accession or diminution of light, underwent contraction or dilation, just such as is observed in the feline tribe. In moments of excitement the orbs grew bright to a degree almost inconceivable; seeming to emit luminous rays, not of a reflected but of an intrinsic lustre, as does a candle or the sun; yet their ordinary condition was so totally vapid, filmy, and dull, as to convey the idea of the eyes of a long-interred corpse.

These peculiarities of person appeared to cause him much annoyance, and he was continually alluding to them in a sort of half explanatory, half apologetic strain, which, when I first heard it, impressed me very painfully. I soon, however, grew accustomed to it, and my uneasiness wore off. It seemed to be his design rather to insinuate than directly to assert that, physically, he had not always been what he was—that a long series of neuralgic attacks had reduced him from a condition of more than usual personal beauty, to that which I saw. For many years past he had been attended by a physician, named Templeton—an old gentleman, perhaps seventy years of age—whom he had first encountered at Saratoga, and from whose attention, while there, he either received, or fancied that he received, great benefit. The result was that Bedloe, who was wealthy, had made an arrangement with Dr. Templeton, by which the latter, in consideration of a liberal annual allowance, had consented to devote his time and medical experience exclusively to the care of the invalid.

Doctor Templeton had been a traveller in his younger days, and, at Paris had become a convert, in great measure, to the doctrines of Mesmer.[1] It was altogether by means of magnetic remedies that he had succeeded in alleviating the acute pains of his patient; and this success had very naturally inspired the latter with a certain degree of confidence in the opinions from which the remedies had been educed. The Doctor, however, like all enthusiasts, had struggled hard to make a thorough convert of his pupil, and finally so far gained his point as to induce the sufferer to submit to numerous experiments. By a frequent repetition of these, a result had arisen, which of late days has become so common as to attract little or no attention, but which, at the period of which I write, had very rarely been known in America. I mean to say, that between Doctor Templeton and Bedloe there had grown up, little by little, a very distinct and strongly marked *rapport*, or magnetic relation. I am not prepared to assert, however, that this *rapport* extended beyond the limits of the simple sleep-producing power; but this power itself had attained great intensity. At the first attempt to induce the magnetic somnolency, the mesmerist entirely failed. In the fifth or sixth he succeeded very partially, and after long continued effort. Only at the twelfth was the triumph complete. After this the will of the patient succumbed rapidly to that of the physician, so that, when I first became acquainted with the two, sleep was brought about almost instantaneously, by the mere voli-tion of the operator, even when the invalid was unaware of his presence. It is only now, in the year 1845, when similar miracles are witnessed daily by thousands, that I dare venture to record this apparent impossibility as a matter of serious fact.

The temperament of Bedloe was, in the highest degree, sensitive, excitable, enthusiastic. His imagination was singularly vigorous and creative; and no doubt it derived additional force from the ha-bitual use of morphine, which he swallowed in great quantity, and without which he would have found it impossible to exist. It was his practice to take a very large dose of it immediately after break-fast, each morning—or rather immediately after a cup of strong coffee, for he ate nothing in the forenoon—and then set forth alone, or attended only by a dog, upon a long ramble among the chain of wild and dreary hills that lie westward and southward of Charlottesville, and are there dignified by the title of the Ragged Mountains.

Upon a dim, warm, misty day, toward the close of November, and during the strange *interregnum* of the seasons which in Amer-ica is termed the Indian Summer, Mr. Bedloe departed, as usual, for the hills. The day passed, and still he did not return.

About eight o'clock at night, having become seriously alarmed at his protracted absence, we were about setting out in search of him, when he unexpectedly made his appearance, in health no worse than usual, and in rather more than ordinary spirits. The account which he gave of his expedition, and of the events which had detained him, was a singular one indeed.

"You will remember," said he, "that it was about nine in the morning when I left Charlottesville. I bent my steps immediately to the mountains, and, about ten, entered a gorge which was en-tirely new to me. I followed the windings of this pass with much interest. The scenery which presented itself on all sides, although scarcely entitled to be called grand, had about it an indescribable and to me, a delicious aspect of dreary desolation. The solitude seemed absolutely virgin. I could not help believing that the green sods and the gray rocks upon which I trod, had been trodden never before by the foot of a human being. So entirely secluded, and in fact inaccessible, except through a series of accidents, is the entrance of the ravine, that it is by no means impossible that I was indeed the first adventurer—the very first and sole adventurer who had ever penetrated its recesses.

"The thick and peculiar mist, or smoke, which distinguishes the Indian Summer, and which now hung heavily over all objects, served, no doubt, to deepen the vague impressions which these objects created. So dense was this pleasant fog that I could at no time see more than a dozen yards of the path before me. This path was excessively sinuous, and as the sun could not be seen, I soon lost all idea of the direction in which I journeyed. In the meantime the morphine had its customary effect—that of enduing all the external world with an intensity of interest. In the quivering of a leaf—in the hue of a blade of grass—in the shape of a trefoil—in the humming of a bee—in the gleaming of a dew-drop—in the breathing of the wind—in the faint odors that came from the forest—there came a whole universe of suggestion—a gay and motley train of rhapsodical and immethodical thought.

"Busied in this, I walked on for several hours, during which the mist deepened around me to so great an extent, that at length I was reduced to an absolute groping of the way. And now an indescribable uneasiness possessed me—a species of nervous hesitation and tremor. I feared to tread, lest I should be precipitated into some abyss. I remembered, too, strange stories told about these Ragged Hills, and of the uncouth and fierce races of men who tenanted their groves and caverns.[2] A thousand vague fancies oppressed and disconcerted me—fancies the more distressing because vague. Very suddenly my attention was arrested by the loud beating of a drum.

"My amazement was, of course, extreme. A drum in these hills was a thing unknown. I could not have been more surprised at the sound of the trump of the Archangel. But a new and still more astounding source of interest and perplexity arose. There came a wild rattling or jingling sound, as if of a bunch of large keys—and upon the instant a dusky-visaged and half-naked man rushed past me with a shriek. He came so close to my person that I felt his hot breath upon my face. He bore in one hand an instrument composed of an assemblage of steel rings, and shook them vigorously as he ran. Scarcely had he disappeared in the mist, before, panting after him, with open mouth and glaring eyes, there darted a huge beast. I could not be mistaken in its character. It was a hyena.

"The sight of this monster rather relieved than heightened my terrors—for I now made sure that I dreamed, and endeavored to arouse myself to waking consciousness. I stepped boldly and briskly forward. I rubbed my eyes. I called aloud. I pinched my limbs. A small spring of water presented itself to my view, and here, stooping, I bathed my hands and my head and neck. This seemed to dissipate the equivocal sensations which had hitherto annoyed me. I arose, as I thought, a new man, and proceeded steadily and complacently on my unknown way.

"At length, quite overcome by exertion, and by a certain oppressive closeness of the atmosphere, I seated myself beneath a tree. Presently there came a feeble gleam of sunshine, and the shadow of the leaves of the tree fell faintly but definitely upon the grass. At this shadow I gazed wonderingly for many minutes. Its character stupefied me with astonishment. I looked upward. The tree was a palm.

"I now arose hurriedly, and in a state of fearful agitation—for the fancy that I dreamed would serve me no longer. I saw—I felt that I had perfect command of my senses—and these senses now brought to my soul a world of novel and singular sensation. The heat became all at once intolerable. A strange odor loaded the breeze. A low, continuous murmur, like that arising from a full, but gently-flowing river, came to my ears, intermingled with the peculiar hum of multitudinous human voices.

"While I listened in an extremity of astonishment which I need not attempt to describe, a strong and brief gust of wind bore off the incumbent fog as if by the wand of an enchanter.

"I found myself at the foot of a high mountain, and looking down into a vast plain, through which wound a majestic river. On the margin of this river stood an Eastern-looking city, such as we read of in the Arabian Tales, but of a character even more singular than any there described. From my position, which was far above the level of the town, I could perceive its every nook and corner, as if delineated on a map. The streets seemed innumerable, and crossed each other irregularly in all directions, but were rather long winding alleys than streets, and absolutely swarmed with inhabitants. The houses were wildly picturesque. On every hand was a wilderness of balconies, of verandahs, of minarets, of shrines, and fantastically carved oriels. Bazaars abounded; and in these were displayed rich wares in infinite variety and profusion—silks, muslins, the most dazzling cutlery, the most magnificent jewels and gems. Besides these things, were seen, on all sides, banners and palanquins, litters with stately dames close veiled, elephants gorgeously caparisoned, idols grotesquely hewn, drums, banners, and gongs, spears, silver and gilded maces. And amid the crowd, and the clamor, and the general intricacy and confusion—amid the million of black and yellow men, turbaned and robed, and of flowing beard, there roamed a countless multitude of holy filleted bulls, while vast legions of the filthy but sacred ape clambered, chattering and shrieking, about the cornices of the mosques, or clung to the minarets and oriels. From the swarming streets to the banks of the river, there descended innumerable flights of steps leading to bathing places, while the river itself seemed to force a passage with difficulty through the vast fleets of deeply-burthened ships that far and wide encountered its surface. Beyond the limits of the city arose, in frequent majestic groups, the palm and the co-coa, with other gigantic and weird trees of vast age; and here and there might be seen a field of rice, the thatched hut of a peasant, a tank, a stray temple, a gypsy camp, or a solitary graceful maiden taking her way, with a pitcher upon her head, to the banks of the magnificent river.

"You will say now, of course, that I dreamed; but not so. What I saw—what I heard—what I felt—what I thought—had about it nothing of the unmistakable idiosyncrasy of the dream. All was rigorously self-consistent. At first, doubting that I was really awake, I entered into a series of tests, which soon convinced me that I really was. Now, when one dreams, and, in the dream, suspects that he dreams, the suspicion *never fails to confirm itself*, and the sleeper is almost immediately aroused. Thus Novalis errs not in saying that 'we are near waking when we dream that we dream.' Had the vision occurred to me as I describe it, without my suspecting it as a dream, then a dream it might absolutely have been, but, occurring as it did, and suspected and tested as it was, I am forced to class it among other phenomena."

"In this I am not sure that you are wrong," observed Dr. Tem-pleton, "but proceed. You arose and descended into the city."

"I arose," continued Bedloe, regarding the Doctor with an air of profound astonishment "I arose, as you say, and descended into the city. On my way I fell in with an immense populace, crowding through every avenue, all in the same direction, and exhibiting in every action the wildest excitement. Very suddenly, and by some inconceivable impulse, I became intensely imbued with personal interest in what was going on. I seemed to feel that I had an important part to play, without exactly understanding what it was. Against the crowd which environed me, however, I experienced a deep sentiment of animosity. I shrank from amid them, and, swiftly, by a circuitous path, reached and entered the city. Here all was the wildest tumult and contention. A small party of men, clad in garments half Indian, half European, and officered by gentlemen in a uniform partly British, were engaged, at great odds, with the swarming rabble of the alleys. I joined the weaker party, arming myself with the weapons of a fallen officer, and fighting I knew not whom with the nervous ferocity of despair. We were soon overpowered by numbers, and driven to seek refuge in a species of kiosk. Here we barricaded ourselves, and, for the present were secure. From a loop-hole near the summit of the kiosk, I perceived a vast crowd, in furious agitation, surrounding and assaulting a gay palace that overhung the river. Presently, from an upper window of this place, there descended an effeminate-looking person, by means of a string made of the turbans of his attendants. A boat was at hand, in which he escaped to the opposite bank of the river.

"And now a new object took possession of my soul. I spoke a few hurried but energetic words to my companions, and, having succeeded in gaining over a few of them to my purpose made a frantic sally from the kiosk. We rushed amid the crowd that surrounded it. They retreated, at first, before us. They rallied, fought madly, and retreated again. In the mean time we were borne far from the kiosk, and became bewildered and entangled among the narrow streets of tall, overhanging houses, into the recesses of which the sun had never been able to shine. The rabble pressed impetuously upon us, harrassing us with their spears, and overwhelming us with flights of arrows. These latter were very remarkable, and resembled in some respects the writhing creese of the Malay. They were made to imitate the body of a creeping serpent, and were long and black, with a poisoned barb. One of them struck me upon the right temple. I reeled and fell. An instantaneous and deadly sickness seized me. I struggled—I gasped—I died."

"You will hardly persist *now*," said I, smiling, "that the whole of your adventure was not a dream. You are not prepared to maintain that you are dead?"

When I said these words, I of course expected some lively sally from Bedloe in reply; but, to my astonishment, he hesitated, trembled, became fearfully pallid, and remained silent. I looked toward Templeton. He sat erect and rigid in his chair—his teeth chattered, and his eyes were starting from their sockets. "Proceed!" he at length said hoarsely to Bedloe.

"For many minutes," continued the latter, "my sole sentiment—my sole feeling—was that of darkness and nonentity, with the consciousness of death. At length there seemed to pass a violent and sudden shock through my soul, as if of electricity. With it came the sense of elasticity and of light. This latter I felt—not saw. In an instant I seemed to rise from the ground. But I had no bodily, no visible, audible, or palpable presence. The crowd had departed. The tumult had ceased. The city was in comparative repose. Beneath me lay my corpse, with the arrow in my temple, the whole head greatly swollen and disfigured. But all these things I felt—not saw. I took interest in nothing. Even the corpse seemed a matter in which I had no concern. Volition I had none, but appeared to be impelled into motion, and flitted buoyantly out of the city, retracing the circuitous path by which I had entered it. When I had attained that point of the ravine in the mountains at which I had encountered the hyena, I again experienced a shock as of a galvanic battery; the sense of weight, of volition, of substance, returned. I became my original self, and bent my steps eagerly homeward—but the past had not lost the vividness of the real—and not now, even for an instant, can I compel my understanding to regard it as a dream."

"Nor was it," said Templeton, with an air of deep solemnity, "yet it would be difficult to say how otherwise it should be termed. Let us suppose only, that the soul of the man of to-day is upon the verge of some stupendous psychal discoveries. Let us content ourselves with this supposition. For the rest I have some explanation to make. Here is a water-colour drawing, which I should have shown you before, but which an unaccountable sentiment of horror has hitherto prevented me from showing."

We looked at the picture which he presented. I saw nothing in it of an extraordinary character; but its effect upon Bedloe was prodigious. He nearly fainted as he gazed. And yet it was but a miniature portrait—a miraculously accurate one, to be sure—of his own very remarkable features. At least this was my thought as I regarded it.

"You will perceive," said Templeton, "the date of this picture— it is here, scarcely visible, in this corner—1780. In this year was the portrait taken. It is the likeness of a dead friend—a Mr. Oldeb—to whom I became much attached at Calcutta, during the administration of Warren Hastings. I was then only twenty years old. When I first saw you, Mr. Bedloe, at Saratoga, it was the miraculous similarity which existed between yourself and the painting which induced me to accost you, to seek your friendship, and to bring about those arrangements which resulted in my becoming your constant companion. In accomplishing this point, I was urged partly, and perhaps principally, by a regretful memory of the deceased, but also, in part, by an uneasy, and not altogether horrorless curiosity respecting yourself.

"In your detail of the vision which presented itself to you amid the hills, you have described, with the minutest accuracy, the Indian city of Benares, upon the Holy River. The riots, the combats, the massacre, were the actual events of the insurrection of Cheyte Sing, which took place in 1780, when Hastings was put in imminent peril of his life. The man escaping by the string of turbans, was Cheyte Sing himself. The party in the kiosk were sepoys and British officers, headed by Hastings. Of this party I was one, and did all I could to prevent the rash and fatal sally of the officer who fell, in the crowded alleys, by the poisoned arrow of a Bengalee. That officer was my dearest friend. It was Oldeb. You will perceive by these manuscripts," (here the speaker produced a note-book in which several pages appeared to have been freshly written,) "that at the very period in which you fancied these things amid the hills, I was engaged in detailing them upon paper here at home."

In about a week after this conversation, the following paragraphs appeared in a Charlottesville paper:

"We have the painful duty of announcing the death of Mr. AUGUSTUS BEDLO, a gentleman whose amiable manners and many virtues have long endeared him to the citizens of Charlottesville.

"Mr. B., for some years past, has been subject to neuralgia, which has often threatened to terminate fatally; but this can be regarded only as the mediate cause of his decease. The proximate cause was one of especial singularity. In an excursion to the Ragged Mountains, a few days since, a slight cold and fever were contracted, attended with great determination of blood to the head. To relieve this, Dr. Templeton resorted to topical bleeding. Leeches were applied to the temples. In a fearfully brief period the patient died, when it appeared that, in the jar containing the leeches, had been introduced, by accident, one of the venomous vermicular sangsues which are now and then found in the neighboring ponds. This creature fastened itself upon a small artery in the right temple. Its close resemblance to the medicinal leech caused the mistake to be overlooked until too late.

"N. B. The poisonous sangsue of Charlottesville may always be distinguished from the medicinal leech by its blackness, and especially by its writhing or vermicular motions, which very nearly resemble those of a snake."[3]

I was speaking with the editor of the paper in question, upon the topic of this remarkable accident, when it occurred to me to ask how it happened that the name of the deceased had been given as Bedlo.

"I presume," I said, "you have authority for this spelling, but I have always supposed the name to be written with an e at the end."

"Authority?—no," he replied. "It is a mere typographical error. The name is Bedlo with an e, all the world over, and I never knew it to be spelt otherwise in my life."

"Then," said I mutteringly, as I turned upon my heel, "then indeed has it come to pass that one truth is stranger than any fiction—for Bedlo, without the e, what is it but Oldeb conversed? And this man tells me it is a typographical error."

THE PURLOINED LETTER

Nil sapientiae odiosius acumine nimio.

SENECA[1]

At Paris, just after dark one gusty evening in the autumn of 18——, I was enjoying the twofold luxury of meditation and a meer-schaum, in company with my friend C. Auguste Dupin, in his lit-tle back library, or book-closet, *au troisième, No. 33, Rue Dunôt, Faubourg St. Germain*. For one hour at least we had maintained a profound silence; while each, to any casual observer, might have seemed intently and exclusively occupied with the curling eddies of smoke that oppressed the atmosphere of the chamber. For my-self, however, I was mentally discussing certain topics which had formed matter for conversation between us at an earlier period of the evening; I mean the affair of the Rue Morgue, and the mystery attending the murder of Marie Rogêt. I looked upon it, therefore, as something of a coincidence, when the door of our apartment was thrown open and admitted our old acquaintance, Monsieur G——, the Prefect of the Parisian police.

We gave him a hearty welcome; for there was nearly half as much of the entertaining as of the contemptible about the man, and we had not seen him for several years. We had been sitting in the dark, and Dupin now arose for the purpose of lighting a lamp, but sat down again, without doing so, upon G.'s saying that he had called to consult us, or rather to ask the opinion of my friend, about some official business which had occasioned a great deal of trouble.

"If it is any point requiring reflection," observed Dupin, as he forebore to enkindle the wick, "we shall examine it to better pur-pose in the dark."

"That is another of your odd notions," said the Prefect, who had a fashion of calling every thing "odd" that was beyond his compre-hension, and thus lived amid an absolute legion of "oddities."

"Very true," said Dupin, as he supplied his visiter with a pipe, and rolled towards him a comfortable chair.

"And what is the difficulty now?" I asked. "Nothing more in the assassination way, I hope?"

"Oh no; nothing of that nature. The fact is, the business is *very* simple indeed, and I make no doubt that we can manage it sufficiently well ourselves; but then I thought Dupin would like to hear the details of it, because it is so excessively *odd*."

"Simple and odd," said Dupin.

"Why, yes; and not exactly that, either. The fact is, we have all been a good deal puzzled because the affair *is* so simple, and yet baffles us altogether."

"Perhaps it is the very simplicity of the thing which puts you at fault," said my friend.

"What nonsense you *do* talk!" replied the Prefect, laughing heartily.

"Perhaps the mystery is a little *too* plain," said Dupin.

"Oh, good heavens! who ever heard of such an idea?"

"A little *too* self-evident."

"Ha! ha! ha!—ha! ha! ha!—ho! ho! ho!" roared our visiter, profoundly amused, "oh, Dupin, you will be the death of me yet!"

"And what, after all, *is* the matter on hand?" I asked.

"Why, I will tell you," replied the Prefect, as he gave a long, steady, and contemplative puff, and settled himself in his chair. "I will tell you in a few words; but, before I begin, let me caution you that this is an affair demanding the greatest secrecy, and that I should most probably lose the position I now hold, were it known that I confided it to any one."

"Proceed," said I.

"Or not," said Dupin.

"Well, then; I have received personal information, from a very high quarter, that a certain document of the last importance, has been purloined from the royal apartments. The individual who purloined it is known; this beyond a doubt; he was seen to take it. It is known, also, that it still remains in his possession."

"How is this known?" asked Dupin.

"It is clearly inferred," replied the Prefect, "from the nature of the document, and from the non-appearance of certain results which would at once arise from its passing *out* of the robber's possession;—that is to say, from his employing it as he must design in the end to employ it."

"Be a little more explicit," I said.

"Well, I may venture so far as to say that the paper gives its holder a certain power in a certain quarter where such power is immensely valuable." The Prefect was fond of the cant of diplomacy.

"Still I do not quite understand," said Dupin.

"No? Well; the disclosure of the document to a third person, who shall be nameless, would bring in question the honor of a personage of most exalted station; and this fact gives the holder of the document an ascendancy over the illustrious personage whose honor and peace are so jeopardized."

"But this ascendancy," I interposed, "would depend upon the robber's knowledge of the loser's knowledge of the robber. Who would dare—"

"The thief," said G——, "is the Minister D——, who dares all things, those unbecoming as well as those becoming a man. The method of the theft was not less ingenious than bold. The document in question—a letter, to be frank—had been received by the personage robbed while alone in the royal *boudoir*. During its perusal she was suddenly interrupted by the entrance of the other exalted personage from whom especially it was her wish to conceal it. After a hurried and vain endeavor to thrust it in a drawer, she was forced to place it, open as it was, upon a table. The address, however, was uppermost, and, the contents thus unexposed, the letter escaped notice. At this juncture enters the Minister D——. His lynx eye immediately perceives the paper, recognises the handwriting of the address, observes the confusion of the personage addressed, and fathoms her secret. After some business transactions, hurried through in his ordinary manner, he produces a letter somewhat similar to the one in question, opens it, pretends to read it, and then places it in close juxtaposition to the other. Again he converses, for some fifteen minutes, upon the public affairs. At length, in taking leave, he takes also from the table the letter to which he had no claim. Its rightful owner saw, but, of course, dared not call attention to the act, in the presence of the third personage who stood at her elbow. The minister decamped; leaving his own letter—one of no importance—upon the table."

"Here, then," said Dupin to me, "you have precisely what you demand to make the ascendancy complete—the robber's knowledge of the loser's knowledge of the robber."

"Yes," replied the Prefect; "and the power thus attained has, for some months past, been wielded, for political purposes, to a very dangerous extent. The personage robbed is more thoroughly convinced, every day, of the necessity of reclaiming her letter. But this, of course, cannot be done openly. In fine, driven to despair, she has committed the matter to me."

"Than whom," said Dupin, amid a perfect whirlwind of smoke, "no more sagacious agent could, I suppose, be desired, or even imagined."

"You flatter me," replied the Prefect; "but it is possible that some such opinion may have been entertained."

"It is clear," said I, "as you observe, that the letter is still in possession of the minister; since it is this possession, and not any employment of the letter, which bestows the power. With the employment the power departs."

"True," said G.; "and upon this conviction I proceeded. My first care was to make thorough search of the minister's hotel; and here my chief embarrassment lay in the necessity of searching without his knowledge. Beyond all things, I have been warned of the danger which would result from giving him reason to suspect our design."

"But," said I, "you are quite *au fait* in these investigations. The Parisian police have done this thing often before."

"O yes; and for this reason I did not despair. The habits of the minister gave me, too, a great advantage. He is frequently absent from home all night. His servants are by no means numerous. They sleep at a distance from their master's apartment, and, being chiefly Neapolitans, are readily made drunk. I have keys, as you know, with which I can open any chamber or cabinet in Paris. For three months a night has not passed, during the greater part of which I have not been engaged, personally, in ransacking the D—— Hotel. My honor is interested, and, to mention a great secret, the reward is enormous. So I did not abandon the search until I had become fully satisfied that the thief is a more astute man than myself. I fancy that I have investigated every nook and corner of the premises in which it is possible that the paper can be concealed."

"But is it not possible," I suggested, "that although the letter may be in possession of the minister, as it unquestionably is, he may have concealed it elsewhere than upon his own premises?"

"This is barely possible," said Dupin. "The present peculiar condition of affairs at court, and especially of those intrigues in which D—— is known to be involved, would render the instant availability of the document—its susceptibility of being produced at a moment's notice—a point of nearly equal importance with its possession."

"Its susceptibility of being produced?" said I.

"That is to say, of being *destroyed*," said Dupin.

"True," I observed; "the paper is clearly then upon the premises. As for its being upon the person of the minister, we may consider that as out of the question."

"Entirely," said the Prefect. "He has been twice waylaid, as if by footpads, and his person rigorously searched under my own inspection."

"You might have spared yourself this trouble," said Dupin. "D——, I presume, is not altogether a fool, and, if not, must have anticipated these waylayings, as a matter of course."

"Not *altogether* a fool," said G., "but then he's a poet, which I take to be only one remove from a fool."

"True," said Dupin, after a long and thoughtful whiff from his meerschaum, "although I have been guilty of certain doggrel myself."

"Suppose you detail," said I, "the particulars of your search."

"Why the fact is, we took our time, and we searched *every where*. I have had long experience in these affairs. I took the entire building, room by room; devoting the nights of a whole week to each. We examined, first, the furniture of each apartment. We opened every possible drawer; and I presume you know that, to a properly trained police agent, such a thing as a *secret* drawer is impossible. Any man is a dolt who permits a 'secret' drawer to escape him in a search of this kind. The thing is *so* plain. There is a certain amount of bulk—of space—to be accounted for in every cabinet. Then we have accurate rules. The fiftieth part of a line could not escape us. After the cabinets we took the chairs. The cushions we probed with the fine long needles you have seen me employ. From the tables we removed the tops."

"Why so?"

"Sometimes the top of a table, or other similarly arranged piece of furniture, is removed by the person wishing to conceal an article; then the leg is excavated, the article deposited within the cavity, and the top replaced. The bottoms and tops of bedposts are employed in the same way."

"But could not the cavity be detected by sounding?" I asked.

"By no means, if, when the article is deposited, a sufficient wadding of cotton be placed around it. Besides, in our case, we were obliged to proceed without noise."

"But you could not have removed—you could not have taken to pieces *all* articles of furniture in which it would have been possible to make a deposit in the manner you mention. A letter may be compressed into a thin spiral roll, not differing much in shape or bulk from a large knitting-needle, and in this form it might be inserted into the rung of a chair, for example. You did not take to pieces all the chairs?"

"Certainly not; but we did better—we examined the rungs of every chair in the hotel, and, indeed the jointings of every description of furniture, by the aid of a most powerful microscope. Had there been any traces of recent disturbance we should not have failed to detect it instantly. A single grain of gimlet-dust, for example, would have been as obvious as an apple. Any disorder in the glueing—any unusual gaping in the joints—would have sufficed to insure detection."

"I presume you looked to the mirrors, between the boards and the plates, and you probed the beds and the bed-clothes, as well as the curtains and carpets."

"That of course; and when we had absolutely completed every particle of the furniture in this way, then we examined the house itself. We divided its entire surface into compartments, which we numbered, so that none might be missed; then we scrutinized each individual square inch throughout the premises, including the two houses immediately adjoining, with the microscope, as before."

"The two houses adjoining!" I exclaimed; "you must have had a great deal of trouble."

"We had; but the reward offered is prodigious."

"You include the *grounds* about the houses?"

"All the grounds are paved with brick. They gave us comparatively little trouble. We examined the moss between the bricks, and found it undisturbed."

"You looked among D——'s papers, of course, and into the books of the library?"

"Certainly; we opened every package and parcel; we not only opened every book, but we turned over every leaf in each volume, not contenting ourselves with a mere shake, according to the fashion of some of our police officers. We also measured the thickness of every book-*cover*, with the most accurate admeasurement, and applied to each the most jealous scrutiny of the microscope. Had any of the bindings been recently meddled with, it would have been utterly impossible that the fact should have escaped observation. Some five or six volumes, just from the hands of the binder, we carefully probed, longitudinally, with the needles."

"You explored the floors beneath the carpets?"

"Beyond doubt. We removed every carpet, and examined the boards with the microscope."

"And the paper on the walls?"

"Yes."

"You looked into the cellars?"

"We did."

"Then," I said, "you have been making a miscalculation, and the letter is *not* upon the premises, as you suppose."

"I fear you are right there," said the Prefect. "And now, Dupin, what would you advise me to do?"

"To make a thorough re-search of the premises."

"That is absolutely needless," replied G——. "I am not more sure that I breathe than I am that the letter is not at the Hotel."

"I have no better advice to give you," said Dupin. "You have, of course, an accurate description of the letter?"

"Oh yes!"—And here the Prefect, producing a memorandum-book proceeded to read aloud a minute account of the internal, and especially of the external appearance of the missing document. Soon after finishing the perusal of this description, he took his departure, more entirely depressed in spirits than I had ever known the good gentleman before.

In about a month afterwards he paid us another visit, and found us occupied very nearly as before. He took a pipe and a chair and entered into some ordinary conversation. At length I said,—

"Well, but G——, what of the purloined letter? I presume you have at last made up your mind that there is no such thing as over-reaching the Minister?"

"Confound him, say I—yes; I made the re-examination, how-ever, as Dupin suggested—but it was all labor lost, as I knew it would be."

"How much was the reward offered, did you say?" asked Dupin.

"Why, a very great deal—a *very* liberal reward—I don't like to say how much, precisely; but one thing I *will* say, that I wouldn't mind giving my individual check for fifty thousand francs to any one who could obtain me that letter. The fact is, it is becoming of more and more importance every day; and the reward has been lately doubled. If it were trebled, however, I could do no more than I have done."

"Why, yes," said Dupin, drawlingly, between the whiffs of his meerschaum, "I really—think, G——, you have not exerted yourself—to the utmost in this matter. You might—do a little more, I think, eh?"

"How?—in what way?"

"Why—puff, puff—you might—puff, puff—employ counsel in the matter, eh?—puff, puff, puff. Do you remember the story they tell of Abernethy?"

"No; hang Abernethy!"

"To be sure! hang him and welcome. But, once upon a time, a certain rich miser conceived the design of spunging upon this Abernethy for a medical opinion. Getting up, for this purpose, an ordinary conversation in a private company, he insinuated his case to the physician, as that of an imaginary individual.

" 'We will suppose,' said the miser, 'that his symptoms are such and such; now, doctor, what would *you* have directed him to take?'

" 'Take!' said Abernethy, 'why, take *advice*, to be sure.' "

"But," said the Prefect, a little discomposed, "I am *perfectly* willing to take advice, and to pay for it. I would *really* give fifty thousand francs to any one who would aid me in the matter."

"In that case," replied Dupin, opening a drawer, and producing a check-book, "you may as well fill me up a check for the amount mentioned. When you have signed it, I will hand you the letter."

I was astounded. The Prefect appeared absolutely thunder-stricken. For some minutes he remained speechless and motion-less, looking incredulously at my friend with open mouth, and eyes that seemed starting from their sockets; then, apparently recover-ing himself in some measure, he seized a pen, and after several pauses and vacant stares, finally filled up and signed a check for fifty thousand francs, and handed it across the table to Dupin. The latter examined it carefully and deposited it in his pocket-book; then, unlocking an *escritoire*, took thence a letter and gave it to the Prefect. This functionary grasped it in a perfect agony of joy, opened it with a trembling hand, cast a rapid glance at its con-tents, and then, scrambling and struggling to the door, rushed at length unceremoniously from the room and from the house, with-out having uttered a syllable since Dupin had requested him to fill up the check.

When he had gone, my friend entered into some explanations.

"The Parisian police," he said, "are exceedingly able in their way. They are persevering, ingenious, cunning, and thoroughly versed in the knowledge which their duties seem chiefly to de-mand. Thus, when G—— detailed to us his mode of searching the premises at the Hotel D——, I felt entire confidence in his having made a satisfactory investigation—so far as his labors extended."

"So far as his labors extended?" said I.

"Yes," said Dupin. "The measures adopted were not only the best of their kind, but carried out to absolute perfection. Had the letter been deposited within the range of their search, these fellows would, beyond a question, have found it."

I merely laughed—but he seemed quite serious in all that he said.

"The measures, then," he continued, "were good in their kind, and well executed; their defect lay in their being inapplicable to the case, and to the man. A certain set of highly ingenious re-sources are, with the Prefect, a sort of Procrustean bed, to which he forcibly adapts his designs. But he perpetually errs by being too deep or too shallow, for the matter in hand; and many a schoolboy is a better reasoner than he. I knew one about eight years of age, whose success at guessing in the game of 'even and odd' attracted universal admiration. This game is simple, and is played with marbles. One player holds in his hand a number of these toys, and demands of another whether that number is even or odd. If the guess is right, the guesser wins one; if wrong, he loses one. The boy to whom I allude won all the marbles of the school. Of course he had some principle of guessing; and this lay in mere observation and admeasurement of the astuteness of his opponents. For example, an arrant simpleton is his opponent, and, holding up his closed hand, asks, 'are they even or odd?' Our schoolboy replies, 'odd,' and loses; but upon the second trial he wins, for he then says to himself, 'the simpleton had them even upon the first trial, and his amount of cunning is just sufficient to make him have them odd upon the second; I will therefore guess odd;' —he guesses odd, and wins. Now, with a simpleton a degree above the first, he would have reasoned thus: 'This fellow finds that in the first instance I guessed odd, and, in the second, he will propose to himself, upon the first impulse, a simple variation from even to odd, as did the first simpleton; but then a second thought will suggest that this is too simple a variation, and finally he will decide upon putting it even as before. I will therefore guess even;' —he guesses even, and wins. Now this mode of reasoning in the schoolboy, whom his fellows termed 'lucky,' —what, in its last analysis, is it?"

"It is merely," I said, "an identification of the reasoner's intellect with that of his opponent."

"It is," said Dupin; "and, upon inquiring of the boy by what means he effected the *thorough* identification in which his success consisted, I received answer as follows: 'When I wish to find out how wise, or how stupid, or how good, or how wicked is any one, or what are his thoughts at the moment, I fashion the expression of my face, as accurately as possible, in accordance with the expression of his, and then wait to see what thoughts or sentiments arise in my mind or heart, as if to match or correspond with the expression.' This response of the schoolboy lies at the bottom of all the spurious profundity which has been attributed to Rochefoucault, to La Bruyère, to Machiavelli, and to Campanella."

"And the identification," I said, "of the reasoner's intellect with that of his opponent, depends, if I understand you aright, upon the accuracy with which the opponent's intellect is admeasured."

"For its practical value it depends upon this," replied Dupin; "and the Prefect and his cohort fail so frequently, first, by default of this identification, and, secondly, by ill-admeasurement, or rather through non-admeasurement, of the intellect with which they are engaged. They consider only their *own* ideas of ingenuity; and, in searching for anything hidden, advert only to the modes in which *they* would have hidden it. They are right in this much—that their own ingenuity is a faithful representative of that of *the mass*; but when the cunning of the individual felon is diverse in character from their own, the felon foils them, of course. This always happens when it is above their own, and very usually when it is below. They have no variation of principle in their investigations; at best, when urged by some unusual emergency—by some extraordinary reward—they extend or exaggerate their old modes of *practice*, without touching their principles. What, for example, in this case of D——, has been done to vary the principle of action? What is all this boring, and probing, and sounding, and scrutinizing with the microscope, and dividing the surface of the building into registered square inches— what is it all but an exaggeration *of the application* of the one principle or set of principles of search, which are based upon the one set of notions regarding human ingenuity, to which the Prefect, in the long routine of his duty, has been accustomed? Do you not see he has taken it for granted that *all* men proceed to conceal a letter,— not exactly in a gimlet-hole bored in a chair-leg—but, at least, in *some* out-of-the-way hole or corner suggested by the same tenor of thought which would urge a man to secrete a letter in a gimlet-hole bored in a chair-leg? And do you not see also, that such *recherchés* nooks for concealment are adapted only for ordinary occasions, and would be adopted only by ordinary intellects; for, in all cases of concealment, a disposal of the article concealed—a disposal of it in this *recherché* manner,—is, in the very first instance, presumable and presumed; and thus its discovery depends, not at all upon the acumen, but altogether upon the mere care, patience, and determination of the seekers; and where the case is of importance—or, what amounts to the same thing in the policial eyes, when the reward is of magnitude,—the qualities in question have *never* been known to fail. You will now understand what I meant in suggesting that, had the purloined letter been hidden any where within the limits of the Prefect's examination—in other words, had the principle of its concealment been comprehended within the principles of the Prefect— its discovery would have been a matter altogether beyond question. This functionary, however, has been thoroughly mystified; and the remote source of his defeat lies in the supposition that the Minister is a fool, because he has acquired renown as a poet. All fools are poets; this the Prefect *feels*; and he is merely guilty of a *non distributio medii*[2] in thence inferring that all poets are fools."

"But is this really the poet?" I asked. "There are two brothers, I know; and both have attained reputation in letters. The Minister I believe has written learnedly on the Differential Calculus. He is a mathematician, and no poet."

"You are mistaken; I know him well; he is both. As poet *and* mathematician, he would reason well; as mere mathematician, he could not have reasoned at all, and thus would have been at the mercy of the Prefect."

"You surprise me," I said, "by these opinions, which have been contradicted by the voice of the world. You do not mean to set at naught the well-digested idea of centuries. The mathematical reason has long been regarded as *the* reason *par excellence*."

" '*Il y a à parier*,' " replied Dupin, quoting from Chamfort, "'*que toute idée publique, toute convention reçue, est une sottise, car elle a convenu au plus grand nombre.*'[3] The mathematicians, I grant you, have done their best to promulgate the popular error to which you allude, and which is none the less an error for its promulgation as truth. With an art worthy a better cause, for example, they have insinuated the term 'analysis' into application to algebra. The French are the originators of this particular deception; but if a term is of any importance—if words derive any value from applicability—then 'analysis' conveys 'algebra' about as much as, in Latin, '*ambitus*' implies 'ambition,' '*religio*' 'religion,' or '*homines honesti*,' a set of *honorable* men."[4]

"You have a quarrel on hand, I see," said I, "with some of the algebraists of Paris; but proceed."

"I dispute the availability, and thus the value, of that reason which is cultivated in any especial form other than the abstractly logical. I dispute, in particular, the reason educed by mathematical study. The mathematics are the science of form and quantity; mathematical reasoning is merely logic applied to observation upon form and quantity. The great error lies in supposing that even the truths of what is called *pure* algebra, are abstract or general truths. And this error is so egregious that I am confounded at the universality with which it has been received. Mathematical axioms are *not* axioms of general truth. What is true of *relation*—of form and quantity—is often grossly false in regard to morals, for example. In this latter science it is very usually *un*true that the aggregated parts are equal to the whole. In chemistry also the axiom fails. In the consideration of motive it fails; for two motives, each of a given value, have not, necessarily, a value when united, equal to the sum of their values apart. There are numerous other mathematical truths which are only truths within the limits of *relation*. But the mathematician argues, from his *finite truths*, through habit, as if they were of an absolutely general applicability—as the world indeed imagines them to be. Bryant, in his very learned 'Mythology,' mentions an analogous source of error, when he says that 'although the Pagan fables are not believed, yet we forget ourselves continually, and make inferences from them as existing realities.' With the algebraists, however, who are Pagans themselves, the 'Pagan fables' *are* believed, and the inferences are made, not so much through lapse of memory, as through an unaccountable addling of the brains. In short, I never yet encountered the mere mathematician who could be trusted out of equal roots, or one who did not clandestinely hold it as a point of his faith that x^2+px was absolutely and unconditionally equal to q. Say to one of these gentlemen, by way of experiment, if you please, that you believe occasions may occur where x^2+px is *not* altogether equal to q, and, having made him understand what you mean, get out of his reach as speedily as convenient, for, beyond doubt, he will endeavor to knock you down.

"I mean to say," continued Dupin, while I merely laughed at his last observations, "that if the Minister had been no more than a mathematician, the Prefect would have been under no necessity of giving me this check. I knew him, however, as both mathematician and poet, and my measures were adapted to his capacity, with reference to the circumstances by which he was surrounded. I knew him as a courtier, too, and as a bold *intriguant*. Such a man, I considered, could not fail to be aware of the ordinary policial modes of action. He could not have failed to anticipate—and events have proved that he did not fail to anticipate—the waylayings to which he was subjected. He must have foreseen, I reflected, the secret investigations of his premises. His frequent absences from home at night, which were hailed by the Prefect as certain aids to his success, I regarded only as *ruses*, to afford opportunity for thorough search to the police, and thus the sooner to impress them with the conviction to which G——, in fact, did finally arrive—the conviction that the letter was not upon the premises. I felt, also, that the whole train of thought, which I was at some pains in detailing to you just now, concerning the invariable principle of policial action in searches for articles concealed—I felt that this whole train of thought would necessarily pass through the mind of the Minister. It would imperatively lead him to despise all the ordinary *nooks* of concealment. *He* could not, I reflected, be so weak as not to see that the most intricate and remote recess of his hotel would be as open as his commonest closets to the eyes, to the probes, to the gimlets, and to the microscopes of the Prefect. I saw, in fine, that he would be driven, as a matter of course, to *simplicity*, if not deliberately induced to it as a matter of choice. You will remember, perhaps, how desperately the Prefect laughed when I suggested, upon our first interview, that it was just possible this mystery troubled him so much on account of its being so *very* self-evident."

"Yes," said I, "I remember his merriment well. I really thought he would have fallen into convulsions."

"The material world," continued Dupin, "abounds with very strict analogies to the immaterial; and thus some color of truth has been given to the rhetorical dogma, that metaphor, or simile, may be made to strengthen an argument, as well as to embellish a description. The principle of the *vis inertiæ*,⁵ for example, seems to be identical in physics and metaphysics. It is not more true in the former, that a large body is with more difficulty set in motion than a smaller one, and that its subsequent *momentum* is commensurate with this difficulty, than it is, in the latter, that intellects of the vaster capacity, while more forcible, more constant, and more eventful in their movements than those of inferior grade, are yet the less readily moved, and more embarrassed and full of hesitation in the first few steps of their progress. Again: have you ever noticed which of the street signs, over the shop-doors, are the most attractive of attention?"

"I have never given the matter a thought," I said.

"There is a game of puzzles," he resumed, "which is played upon a map. One party playing requires another to find a given word—the name of town, river, state or empire—any word, in short, upon the motley and perplexed surface of the chart. A novice in the game generally seeks to embarrass his opponents by giving them the most minutely lettered names; but the adept selects such words as stretch, in large characters, from one end of the chart to the other. These, like the over-largely lettered signs and placards of the street, escape observation by dint of being excessively obvious; and here the physical oversight is precisely analogous with the moral inapprehension by which the intellect suffers to pass unnoticed those considerations which are too obtrusively and too palpably self-evident. But this is a point, it appears, somewhat above or beneath the understanding of the Prefect. He never once thought it probable, or possible, that the Minister had deposited the letter immediately beneath the nose of the whole world, by way of best preventing any portion of that world from perceiving it.

"But the more I reflected upon the daring, dashing, and discriminating ingenuity of D——; upon the fact that the document must always have been *at hand*, if he intended to use it to good purpose; and upon the decisive evidence, obtained by the Prefect, that it was not hidden within the limits of that dignitary's ordinary search—the more satisfied I became that, to conceal this letter, the Minister had resorted to the comprehensive and sagacious expedient of not attempting to conceal it at all.

"Full of these ideas, I prepared myself with a pair of green spectacles, and called one fine morning, quite by accident, at the Ministerial hotel. I found D—— at home, yawning, lounging, and dawdling, as usual, and pretending to be in the last extremity of *ennui*. He is, perhaps, the most really energetic human being now alive—but that is only when nobody sees him.

"To be even with him, I complained of my weak eyes, and lamented the necessity of the spectacles, under cover of which I cautiously and thoroughly surveyed the apartment, while seemingly intent only upon the conversation of my host.

"I paid especial attention to a large writing-table near which he sat, and upon which lay confusedly, some miscellaneous letters and other papers, with one or two musical instruments and a few books. Here, however, after a long and very deliberate scrutiny, I saw nothing to excite particular suspicion.

"At length my eyes, in going the circuit of the room, fell upon a trumpery fillagree card-rack of pasteboard, that hung dangling by a dirty blue ribbon, from a little brass knob just beneath the middle of the mantel-piece. In this rack, which had three or four compartments, were five or six visiting cards and a solitary letter. This last was much soiled and crumpled. It was torn nearly in two, across the middle—as if a design, in the first instance, to tear it entirely up as worthless, had been altered, or stayed, in the second. It had a large black seal, bearing the D—— cipher *very* conspicuously, and was addressed, in a diminutive female hand, to D——, the minister, himself. It was thrust carelessly, and even, as it seemed, contemptuously, into one of the upper divisions of the rack.

"No sooner had I glanced at this letter, than I concluded it to be that of which I was in search. To be sure, it was, to all appearance, radically different from the one of which the Prefect had read us so minute a description. Here the seal was large and black, with the D—— cipher; there it was small and red, with the ducal arms of the S—— family. Here, the address, to the Minister, was diminutive and feminine; there the superscription, to a certain royal personage, was markedly bold and decided; the size alone formed a point of correspondence. But, then, the *radicalness* of these differences, which was excessive; the dirt; the soiled and torn condition of the paper, so inconsistent with the *true* methodical habits of D——, and so suggestive of a design to delude the beholder into an idea of the worthlessness of the document; these things, together with the hyper-obtrusive situation of this document, full in the view of every visiter, and thus exactly in accordance with the conclusions to which I had previously arrived; these things, I say, were strongly corroborative of suspicion, in one who came with the intention to suspect.

"I protracted my visit as long as possible, and, while I maintained a most animated discussion with the Minister, on a topic which I knew well had never failed to interest and excite him, I kept my attention really riveted upon the letter. In this examination, I committed to memory its external appearance and arrangement in the rack; and also fell, at length, upon a discovery which set at rest whatever trivial doubt I might have entertained. In scrutinizing the edges of the paper, I observed them to be more *chafed* than seemed necessary. They presented the *broken* appearance which is manifested when a stiff paper, having been once folded and pressed with a folder, is refolded in a reversed direction, in the same creases or edges which had formed the original fold. This discovery was sufficient. It was clear to me that the letter had been turned, as a glove, inside out, re-directed, and re-sealed. I bade the Minister good morning, and took my departure at once, leaving a gold snuff-box upon the table.

"The next morning I called for the snuff-box, when we resumed, quite eagerly, the conversation of the preceding day. While thus engaged, however, a loud report, as if of a pistol, was heard immediately beneath the windows of the hotel, and was succeeded by a series of fearful screams, and the shoutings of a mob. D——rushed to a casement, threw it open, and looked out. In the meantime, I stepped to the card-rack, took the letter, put it in my pocket, and replaced it by a *fac-simile*, (so far as regards externals,) which I had carefully prepared at my lodgings; imitating the D—— cipher, very readily, by means of a seal formed of bread.

"The disturbance in the street had been occasioned by the frantic behavior of a man with a musket. He had fired it among a crowd of women and children. It proved, however, to have been without ball, and the fellow was suffered to go his way as a lunatic or a drunkard. When he had gone, D—— came from the window, whither I had followed him immediately upon securing the object in view. Soon afterwards I bade him farewell. The pretended lunatic was a man in my own pay."

"But what purpose had you," I asked, "in replacing the letter by a *fac-simile*? Would it not have been better, at the first visit, to have seized it openly, and departed?"

"D——," replied Dupin, "is a desperate man, and a man of nerve. His hotel, too, is not without attendants devoted to his interests. Had I made the wild attempt you suggest, I might never have left the Ministerial presence alive. The good people of Paris might have heard of me no more. But I had an object apart from these considerations. You know my political prepossessions. In this matter, I act as a partisan of the lady concerned. For eighteen months the Minister has had her in his power. She has now him in hers; since, being unaware that the letter is not in his possession, he will proceed with his exactions as if it was. Thus will he inevitably commit himself, at once, to his political destruction. His downfall, too, will not be more precipitate than awkward. It is all very well to talk about the *facilis descensus Averni*;[6] but in all kinds of climbing, as Catalani said of singing, it is far more easy to get up than to come down. In the present instance I have no sympathy—at least no pity—for him who descends. He is that *monstrum horrendum*,[7] an unprincipled man of genius. I confess, however, that I should like very well to know the precise character of his thoughts, when, being defied by her whom the Prefect terms 'a certain personage,' he is reduced to opening the letter which I left for him in the card-rack."

"How? did you put any thing particular in it?"

"Why—it did not seem altogether right to leave the interior blank—that would have been insulting. D——, at Vienna once, did me an evil turn, which I told him, quite good-humoredly, that I should remember. So, as I knew he would feel some curiosity in regard to the identity of the person who had outwitted him, I thought it a pity not to give him a clue. He is well acquainted with my MS., and I just copied into the middle of the blank sheet the words—

—Un dessein si funeste,
S'il n'est digne d'Atrée, est digne de Thyeste.[8]

They are to be found in Crébillon's 'Atrée.'"

Grotesqueries

Poe considered the "grotesque" a less serious mode in which disfiguration or repulsiveness usually signals satirical purpose. Of course he sometimes used deformity to make a character seem dangerous ("Hop-Frog") or horrifying ("The Facts in the Case of M. Valdemar"). But as if mocking his own anxieties about death, decay, living entombment, mutilation, or dismemberment, Poe created a number of farces in which grotesque transformations become laughably outrageous. In an early satire—not included here—a protagonist's "loss of breath" causes him to be thrown from a coach (fracturing his arms and skull), jolted by an electrical charge, hung as a robber, and buried alive. In another tale, a hapless fellow loses his head—literally—in a wager with the devil. Poe's comic imagining of unthinkable atrocities perhaps sustained an illusion of authorial control over human frailty. Yet his grotesque tales sometimes point to deformities in the nation itself.

Poe's first truly "American" tale, "The Man That Was Used Up," subtitled "A Tale of the Late Bugaboo and Kickapoo Campaign," evokes the controversy of Indian removal as it alludes to the mysterious condition of General John A. B. C. Smith. In quest of the legendary Indian fighter, the narrator receives tantalizing hints about the indefinable oddity of Smith's appearance. The general's friends invariably blame his condition on those "terrible wretches," the Indians, yet by conflating the Kickapoos (a real tribe) with bugaboos (groundless fears) Poe hints that Smith has been victimized by his own genocidal hatred of Native Americans. Ironically, a black servant assembles the prosthetic devices that now constitute the artificial American hero.

Caught between regional loyalties and national ambitions, Poe was more equivocal on the subject of slavery and sometimes (as in

"The Gold-Bug") caricatured African Americans. But in "The System of Doctor Tarr and Professor Fether," which depicts a mental asylum in the south of France, he also created a farcical version of the Southern plantation as reformed by abolitionism. Here the satire cuts two ways, for although the "soothing system" of M. Maillard frees the inmates and encourages unbridled lunacy, their incarcerated attendants—tarred, feathered, and resembling "big black baboons"—break free and attack the lunatics, confirming the inevitability of insurrection under slavery.

Poe composed "Some Words with a Mummy" during the presidential election of 1844 when the annexation of Texas (and impending war with Mexico) stirred national fantasies of imperial destiny. The debate between a resuscitated Egyptian mummy and a group of Anglo-American savants actually turns on questions of cultural and racial superiority—issues at the forefront of U.S. expansionist arguments. When the mummy recalls the failed experiment of thirteen Egyptian provinces trying to set "a magnificent example" for "the rest of mankind," he delivers a critique of Jacksonian democracy as mob rule. The narrator finally decides to get himself embalmed like the mummy to escape from a time and place where everything seems to be "going wrong."

THE MAN THAT
WAS USED UP[1]

A Tale of the Late Bugaboo and Kickapoo Campaign[2]

Pleurez, pleurez, mes yeux, et fondez-vous en eau!
La moitié de ma vie a mis l'autre au tombeau.

CORNEILLE[3]

I cannot just now remember when or where I first made the acquaintance of that truly fine-looking fellow, Brevet Brigadier General John A. B. C. Smith. Some one *did* introduce me to the gentleman, I am sure—at some public meeting, I know very well—held about something of great importance, no doubt—at some place or other, I feel convinced,—whose name I have unaccountably forgotten. The truth is—that the introduction was attended, upon my part, with a degree of anxious embarrassment which operated to prevent any definite impressions of either time or place. I am constitutionally nervous—this, with me, is a family failing, and I can't help it. In especial, the slightest appearance of mystery—of any point I cannot exactly comprehend—puts me at once into a pitiable state of agitation.

There was something, as it were, remarkable—yes, *remarkable*, although this is but a feeble term to express my full meaning—about the entire individuality of the personage in question. He was, perhaps, six feet in height, and of a presence singularly commanding. There was an *air distingué* pervading the whole man, which spoke of high breeding, and hinted at high birth. Upon this topic—the topic of Smith's personal appearance—I have a kind of melancholy satisfaction in being minute. His head of hair would have done honor to a Brutus;—nothing could be more richly flowing, or possess a brighter gloss. It was of a jetty black;—which was also the color, or more properly the no color of his unimaginable whiskers.

You perceive I cannot speak of these latter without enthusiasm; it is not too much to say that they were the handsomest pair of whiskers under the sun. At all events, they encircled, and at times partially overshadowed, a mouth utterly unequalled. Here were the most entirely even, and the most brilliantly white of all conceivable teeth. From between them, upon every proper occasion, issued a voice of surpassing clearness, melody, and strength. In the matter of eyes, also, my acquaintance was pre-eminently endowed. Either one of such a pair was worth a couple of the ordinary ocular organs. They were of a deep hazel, exceedingly large and lustrous; and there was perceptible about them, ever and anon, just that amount of interesting obliquity which gives pregnancy to expression.

The bust of the General was unquestionably the finest bust I ever saw. For your life you could not have found a fault with its wonderful proportion. This rare peculiarity set off to great advantage a pair of shoulders which would have called up a blush of conscious inferiority into the countenance of the marble Apollo. I have a passion for fine shoulders, and may say that I never beheld them in perfection before. The arms altogether were admirably modelled. Nor were the lower limbs less superb. These were, indeed, the *ne plus ultra* of good legs. Every connoisseur in such matters admitted the legs to be good. There was neither too much flesh, nor too little,— neither rudeness nor fragility. I could not imagine a more graceful curve than that of the *os femoris*, and there was just that due gentle prominence in the rear of the *fibula* which goes to the conformation of a properly proportioned calf. I wish to God my young and talented friend Chiponchipino, the sculptor, had but seen the legs of Brevet Brigadier General John A. B. C. Smith.

But although men so absolutely fine-looking are neither as plenty as reasons or blackberries, still I could not bring myself to believe that *the remarkable* something to which I alluded just now,—that the odd air of *je ne sais quoi* which hung about my new acquaintance,—lay altogether, or indeed at all, in the supreme excellence of his bodily endowments. Perhaps it might be traced to the *manner*;—yet here again I could not pretend to be positive. There *was* a primness, not to say stiffness, in his carriage—a degree of measured, and, if I may so express it, of rectangular precision, attending his every movement, which, observed in a more diminutive figure, would have had the least little savor in the world, of affectation, pomposity or constraint, but which noticed in a gentleman of his undoubted dimensions, was readily placed to the account of reserve, *hauteur*—of a commendable sense, in short, of what is due to the dignity of colossal proportion.

The kind friend who presented me to General Smith whispered in my ear some few words of comment upon the man. He was a *remarkable* man—a *very* remarkable man—indeed one of the *most* remarkable men of the age. He was an especial favorite, too, with the ladies—chiefly on account of his high reputation for courage.

"In *that* point he is unrivalled—indeed he is a perfect desperado—a downright fire-eater, and no mistake," said my friend, here dropping his voice excessively low, and thrilling me with the mystery of his tone.

"A downright fire-eater, and *no* mistake. Showed *that*, I should say, to some purpose, in the late tremendous swamp-fight away down South, with the Bugaboo and Kickapoo Indians." [Here my friend opened his eyes to some extent.] "Bless my soul!—blood and thunder, and all that!—*prodigies* of valor!—heard of him of course?—you know he's the man"—

"Man alive, how *do* you do? why how *are* ye? *very* glad to see ye, indeed!" here interrupted the General himself, seizing my companion by the hand as he drew near, and bowing stiffly but profoundly, as I was presented. I then thought, (and I think so still,) that I never heard a clearer nor a stronger voice nor beheld a finer set of teeth: but I *must* say that I was sorry for the interruption just at that moment, as, owing to the whispers and insinuations aforesaid, my interest had been greatly excited in the hero of the Bugaboo and Kickapoo campaign.

However, the delightfully luminous conversation of Brevet Brigadier General John A. B. C. Smith soon completely dissipated this chagrin. My friend leaving us immediately, we had quite a long *tête-à-tête*, and I was not only pleased but *really*—instructed. I never heard a more fluent talker, or a man of greater general information. With becoming modesty, he forebore, nevertheless, to touch upon the theme I had just then most at heart—I mean the mysterious circumstances attending the Bugaboo war—and, on my own part, what I conceive to be a proper sense of delicacy forbade me to broach the subject; although, in truth, I was exceedingly tempted to do so. I perceived, too, that the gallant soldier preferred topics of philosophical interest, and that he delighted, especially, in commenting upon the rapid march of mechanical invention. Indeed, lead him where I would, this was a point to which he invariably came back.

"There is nothing at all like it," he would say; "we are a wonderful people, and live in a wonderful age.[4] Parachutes and railroads—man-traps and spring-guns! Our steam-boats are upon every sea, and the Nassau balloon packet is about to run regular trips (fare either way only twenty pounds sterling) between London and Timbuctoo. And who shall calculate the immense influence upon social life—upon arts—upon commerce—upon literature—which will be the immediate result of the great principles of electro magnetics! Nor, is this all, let me assure you! There is really no end to the march of invention. The most wonderful—the most ingenious—and let me add, Mr.—Mr.—Thompson, I believe, is your name—let me add, I say, the most *useful*—the most truly *useful* mechanical contrivances, are daily springing up like mushrooms, if I may so express myself, or, more figuratively, like—ah—grasshoppers—like grasshoppers, Mr. Thompson—about us and ah—ah—ah—around us!"

Thompson, to be sure, is not my name; but it is needless to say that I left General Smith with a heightened interest in the man, with an exalted opinion of his conversational powers, and a deep sense of the valuable privileges we enjoy in living in this age of mechanical invention. My curiosity, however, had not been altogether satisfied, and I resolved to prosecute immediate inquiry among my acquaintances touching the Brevet Brigadier General himself, and particularly respecting the tremendous events *quorum pars magna fuit*,[5] during the Bugaboo and Kickapoo campaign.

The first opportunity which presented itself, and which (*horresco referens*) I did not in the least scruple to seize, occurred at the Church of the Reverend Doctor Drummummupp, where I found myself established, one Sunday, just at sermon time, not only in the pew, but by the side, of that worthy and communicative little friend of mine, Miss Tabitha T. Thus seated, I congratulated myself, and with much reason, upon the very flattering state of affairs. If any person knew anything about Brevet Brigadier General John A. B. C. Smith, that person, it was clear to me, was Miss Tabitha T. We telegraphed a few signals, and then commenced, *sotto voce*, a brisk *tête-à-tête*.

"Smith!" said she, in reply to my very earnest inquiry; "Smith!—why, not General John A. B. C.? Bless me, I thought you *knew* all about *him*! This is a wonderfully inventive age! Horrid affair that!—a bloody set of wretches, those Kickapoos!—fought like a hero—prodigies of valor—immortal renown. Smith!— Brevet Brigadier General John A. B. C.! why, you know he's the man"—

"Man," here broke in Doctor Drummummupp, at the top of his voice, and with a thump that came near knocking the pulpit about our ears; "man that is born of a woman hath but a short time to live; he cometh up and is cut down like a flower!" I started to the extremity of the pew, and perceived by the animated looks of the divine, that the wrath which had nearly proved fatal to the pulpit had been excited by the whispers of the lady and myself. There was no help for it; so I submitted with a good grace, and listened, in all the martyrdom of dignified silence, to the balance of that very capital discourse.

Next evening found me a somewhat late visitor at the Rantipole theatre, where I felt sure of satisfying my curiosity at once, by merely stepping into the box of those exquisite specimens of affability and omniscience, the Misses Arabella and Miranda Cognoscenti. That fine tragedian, Climax, was doing Iago to a very crowded house, and I experienced some little difficulty in making my wishes understood; especially, as our box was next the slips, and completely overlooked the stage.

"Smith?" said Miss Arabella, as she at length comprehended the purport of my query; "Smith?—why, not General John A. B. C.?"

"Smith?" inquired Miranda, musingly. "God bless me, did you ever behold a finer figure?"

"Never, madam, but *do* tell me"—

"Or so inimitable grace?"

"Never, upon my word!—but pray inform me"—

"Or so just an appreciation of stage effect?"

"Madam!"

"Or a more delicate sense of the true beauties of Shakespeare? Be so good as to look at that leg!"

"The devil!" and I turned again to her sister.

"Smith?" said she, "why, not General John A. B. C.? Horrid affair that, wasn't it?—great wretches, those Bugaboos—savage and so on—but we live in a wonderfully inventive age!—Smith!—O yes! great man!—perfect desperado—immortal renown—prodigies of valor! *Never heard!*" [This was given in a scream.] "Bless my soul! why, he's the man"—

> "—mandragora
> Nor all the drowsy syrups of the world
> Shall ever medicine thee to that sweet sleep
> Which thou owd'st yesterday!"[6]

here roared out Climax just in my ear, and shaking his fist in my face all the time, in a way that I *couldn't* stand, and I *wouldn't*. I left the Misses Cognoscenti immediately, went behind the scenes forthwith, and gave the beggarly scoundrel such a thrashing as I trust he will remember to the day of his death.

At the *soirée* of the lovely widow, Mrs. Kathleen O'Trump, I was confident that I should meet with no similar disappointment. Accordingly, I was no sooner seated at the card-table, with my pretty hostess for a *vis-à-vis*, than I propounded those questions the solution of which had become a matter so essential to my peace.

"Smith?" said my partner, "why, not General John A. B. C.? Horrid affair that, wasn't it?—diamonds, did you say?—terrible wretches those Kickapoos!—we are playing *whist*, if you please, Mr. Tattle—however, this is the age of invention, most certainly *the* age, one may say—*the* age *par excellence*—speak French?—oh, quite a hero—perfect desperado!—*no hearts*, Mr. Tattle? I don't believe it!—immortal renown and all that!—prodigies of valor! *Never heard!!*—why, bless me, he's the man"—

"Mann?—*Captain* Mann?" here screamed some little feminine interloper from the farthest corner of the room. "Are you talking about Captain Mann and the duel?—oh, I *must* hear—do tell—go on, Mrs. O'Trump!—do now go on!" And go on Mrs. O'Trump did—all about a certain Captain Mann, who was either shot or hung, or should have been both shot and hung. Yes! Mrs. O'Trump, she went on, and I—I went off. There was no chance of hearing anything farther that evening in regard to Brevet Brigadier General John A. B. C. Smith.

Still I consoled myself with the reflection that the tide of ill luck would not run against me forever, and so determined to make a bold push for information at the rout of that bewitching little angel, the graceful Mrs. Pirouette.

"Smith?" said Mrs. P., as we twirled about together in a *pas de zephyr*, "Smith?—why, not General John A. B. C.? Dreadful business that of the Bugaboos, wasn't it?—dreadful creatures, those Indians!—*do* turn out your toes! I really am ashamed of you—man of great courage, poor fellow!—but this is a wonderful age for invention—O dear me, I'm out of breath—quite a desperado—prodigies of valor—*never heard!!*—can't believe it—I shall have to sit down and enlighten you—Smith! why, he's the man"—

"Man-*Fred*, I tell you!" here bawled out Miss Bas-Bleu, as I led Mrs. Pirouette to a seat. "Did ever anybody hear the like? It's Man-*Fred*, I say, and not at all by any means Man-*Friday*." Here Miss Bas-Bleu beckoned to me in a very peremptory manner; and I was obliged, will I nill I, to leave Mrs. P. for the purpose of deciding a dispute touching the title of a certain poetical drama of Lord Byron's. Although I pronounced, with great promptness, that the true title was Man-*Friday*, and not by any means Man-*Fred*, yet when I returned to seek Mrs. Pirouette she was not to be discovered, and I made my retreat from the house in a very bitter spirit of animosity against the whole race of the Bas-Bleus.

Matters had now assumed a really serious aspect, and I resolved to call at once upon my particular friend, Mr. Theodore Sinivate; for I knew that here at least I should get something like definite information.

"Smith?" said he, in his well-known peculiar way of drawling out his syllables; "Smith?—why, not General John A. B. C.? Savage affair that with the Kickapo-o-o-os, wasn't it? Say! don't you think so?—perfect despera-a-ado—great pity, 'pon my honor!—wonderfully inventive age!—pro-o-odigies of valor! By the by, did you ever hear about Captain Ma-a-a-a-n?"

"Captain Mann be d—d!" said I; "please to go on with your story."

"Hem!—oh well!—quite *la même cho-o-ose*, as we say in France. Smith, eh? Brigadier-General John A. B. C.? I say"—[here Mr. S. thought proper to put his finger to the side of his nose]—"I say, you don't mean to insinuate now, really and truly, and conscientiously, that you don't know all about that affair of Smith's, as well as I do, eh? Smith? John A—B—C.? Why, bless me, he's the ma-a-an"—

"*Mr*. Sinivate," said I, imploringly, "*is* he the man in the mask?"

"No-o-o!" said he, looking wise, "nor the man in the mo-o-on."

This reply I considered a pointed and positive insult, and so left the house at once in high dudgeon, with a firm resolve to call my friend, Mr. Sinivate, to a speedy account for his ungentlemanly conduct and ill-breeding.

In the meantime, however, I had no notion of being thwarted touching the information I desired. There was one resource left me yet. I would go to the fountain-head. I would call forthwith upon the General himself, and demand, in explicit terms, a solution of this abominable piece of mystery. Here, at least, there should be no chance for equivocation. I would be plain, positive, peremptory— as short as pie-crust—as concise as Tacitus or Montesquieu.

It was early when I called, and the General was dressing; but I pleaded urgent business, and was shown at once into his bed-room by an old negro valet, who remained in attendance during my visit. As I entered the chamber, I looked about, of course, for the occupant, but did not immediately perceive him. There was a large and exceedingly odd-looking bundle of something which lay close by my feet on the floor, and, as I was not in the best humor in the world, I gave it a kick out of the way.

"Hem! ahem! rather civil that, I should say!" said the bundle, in one of the smallest, and altogether the funniest little voices, between a squeak and a whistle, that I ever heard in all the days of my existence.

"Ahem! rather civil that, I should observe."

I fairly shouted with terror, and made off, at a tangent, into the farthest extremity of the room.

"God bless me! my dear fellow," here again whistled the bundle, "what—what—what—why, what *is* the matter? I really believe you don't know me at all."

What *could* I say to all this—what *could* I? I staggered into an arm-chair, and, with staring eyes and open mouth, awaited the solution of the wonder.

"Strange you shouldn't know me though, isn't it?" presently re-squeaked the nondescript, which I now perceived was performing, upon the floor, some inexplicable evolution, very analogous to the drawing on of a stocking. There was only a single leg, however, apparent.

"Strange you shouldn't know me, though, isn't it? Pompey, bring me that leg!" Here Pompey handed the bundle, a very capital cork leg, already dressed, which it screwed on in a trice; and then it stood up before my eyes.

"And a bloody action it *was*," continued the thing, as if in a soliloquy; "but then one mustn't fight with the Bugaboos and Kickapoos, and think of coming off with a mere scratch. Pompey, I'll thank you now for that arm. Thomas" [turning to me] "is decidedly the best hand at a cork leg; but if you should ever want an arm, my dear fellow, you must really let me recommend you to Bishop." Here Pompey screwed on an arm.

"We had rather hot work of it, that you may say. Now, you dog, slip on my shoulders and bosom! Pettitt makes the best shoulders, but for a bosom you will have to go to Ducrow."

"Bosom!" said I.

"Pompey, will you *never* be ready with that wig? Scalping is a rough process after all; but then you can procure such a capital scratch at De L'Orme's."

"Scratch!"

"Now, you nigger, my teeth! For a *good* set of these you had better go to Parmly's at once; high prices, but excellent work. I swallowed some very capital articles, though, when the big Bugaboo rammed me down with the butt end of his rifle."

"Butt end! ram down!! my eye!!"

"O yes, by-the-by, my eye—here, Pompey, you scamp, screw it in! Those Kickapoos are not so very slow at a gouge; but he's a belied man, that Dr. Williams, after all; you can't imagine how well I see with the eyes of his make."

I now began very clearly to perceive that the object before me was nothing more nor less than my new acquaintance, Brevet Brigadier General John A. B. C. Smith. The manipulations of Pompey had made, I must confess, a very striking difference in the appearance of the personal man. The voice, however, still puzzled me no little; but even this apparent mystery was speedily cleared up.

"Pompey, you black rascal," squeaked the General, "I really do believe you would let me go out without my palate."

Hereupon the negro, grumbling out an apology, went up to his master, opened his mouth with the knowing air of a horse-jockey, and adjusted therein a somewhat singular-looking machine, in a very dexterous manner, that I could not altogether comprehend. The alteration, however, in the entire expression of the General's countenance was instantaneous and surprising. When he again spoke, his voice had resumed all that rich melody and strength which I had noticed upon our original introduction.

"D—n the vagabonds!" said he, in so clear a tone that I positively started at the change, "D—n the vagabonds! they not only knocked in the roof of my mouth, but took the trouble to cut off at least seven-eighths of my tongue. There isn't Bonfanti's equal, however, in America, for really good articles of this description. I can recommend you to him with confidence, [here the General bowed,] and assure you that I have the greatest pleasure in so doing."

I acknowledged his kindness in my best manner, and took leave of him at once, with a perfect understanding of the true state of affairs—with a full comprehension of the mystery which had troubled me so long. It was evident. It was a clear case. Brevet Brigadier General John A. B. C. Smith was the man—was *the man that was used up*.

THE SYSTEM OF
DOCTOR TARR AND
PROFESSOR FETHER

During the autumn of 18—, while on a tour through the extreme Southern provinces of France, my route led me within a few miles of a certain *Maison de Santé*, or private Mad House, about which I had heard much, in Paris from my medical friends. As I had never visited a place of the kind, I thought the opportunity too good to be lost; and so proposed to my travelling companion (a gentleman with whom I had made casual acquaintance a few days before,) that we should turn aside, for an hour or so, and look through the establishment. To this he objected—pleading haste, in the first place, and, in the second, a very usual horror at the sight of a lunatic. He begged me, however, not to let any mere courtesy towards himself interfere with the gratification of my curiosity, and said that he would ride on leisurely, so that I might overtake him during the day, or, at all events, during the next. As he bade me good-bye, I bethought me that there might be some difficulty in obtaining access to the premises, and mentioned my fears on this point. He replied that, in fact, unless I had personal knowledge of the superintendent, Monsieur Maillard, or some credential in the way of a letter, a difficulty might be found to exist, as the regulations of these private mad-houses were more rigid than the public hospital laws. For himself, he added, he had, some years since, made the acquaintance of Maillard, and would so far assist me as to ride up to the door and introduce me; although his feelings on the subject of lunacy would not permit of his entering the house.

I thanked him, and, turning from the main-road, we entered a grass-grown by-path, which, in half an hour, nearly lost itself in a dense forest, clothing the base of a mountain. Through this dank and gloomy wood we rode some two miles, when the *Maison de Santé* came in view. It was a fantastic *château*, much dilapidated, and indeed scarcely tenantable through age and neglect. Its aspect inspired me with absolute dread, and, checking my horse, I half resolved to turn back. I soon, however, grew ashamed of my weakness, and proceeded.

As we rode up to the gate-way, I perceived it slightly open, and the visage of a man peering through. In an instant afterward, this man came forth, accosted my companion by name, shook him cordially by the hand, and begged him to alight. It was Monsieur Maillard himself. He was a portly, fine-looking gentleman of the old school, with a polished manner, and a certain air of gravity, dignity, and authority which was very impressive.

My friend, having presented me, mentioned my desire to inspect the establishment, and received Monsieur Maillard's assurance that he would show me all attention, now took leave, and I saw him no more.

When he had gone, the superintendent ushered me into a small and exceedingly neat parlor, containing, among other indications of refined taste, many books, drawings, pots of flowers, and musical instruments. A cheerful fire blazed upon the hearth. At a piano, singing an aria from Bellini, sat a young and very beautiful woman, who, at my entrance, paused in her song, and received me with graceful courtesy. Her voice was low, and her whole manner subdued. I thought, too, that I perceived the traces of sorrow in her countenance, which was excessively, although to my taste, not unpleasingly, pale. She was attired in deep mourning, and excited in my bosom a feeling of mingled respect, interest, and admiration.

I had heard, at Paris, that the institution of Monsieur Maillard was managed upon what is vulgarly termed the "system of soothing"—that all punishments were avoided—that even confinement was seldom resorted to—that the patients, while secretly watched, were left much apparent liberty, and that most of them were permitted to roam about the house and grounds in the ordinary apparel of persons in right mind.

Keeping these impressions in view, I was cautious in what I said before the young lady; for I could not be sure that she was sane; and, in fact, there was a certain restless brilliancy about her eyes which half led me to imagine she was not. I confined my remarks, therefore, to general topics, and to such as I thought would not be displeasing or exciting even to a lunatic. She replied in a perfectly rational manner to all that I said; and even her original observations were marked with the soundest good sense; but a long acquaintance with the metaphysics of *mania*, had taught me to put no faith in such evidence of sanity, and I continued to practise, throughout the interview, the caution with which I commenced it.

Presently a smart footman in livery brought in a tray with fruit, wine, and other refreshments, of which I partook, the lady soon afterwards leaving the room. As she departed I turned my eyes in an inquiring manner towards my host.

"No," he said, "oh, no—a member of my family—my niece, and a most accomplished woman."

"I beg a thousand pardons for the suspicion," I replied, "but of course you will know how to excuse me. The excellent administration of your affairs here is well understood in Paris, and I thought it just possible, you know—"

"Yes, yes—say no more—or rather it is myself who should thank you for the commendable prudence you have displayed. We seldom find so much of forethought in young men; and, more than once, some unhappy *contre-temps* has occurred in consequence of thoughtlessness on the part of our visitors. While my former system was in operation, and my patients were permitted the privilege of roaming to and fro at will, they were often aroused to a dangerous frenzy by injudicious persons who called to inspect the house. Hence I was obliged to enforce a rigid system of exclusion; and none obtained access to the premises upon whose discretion I could not rely."

"While your *former* system was in operation!" I said, repeating his words—"do I understand you, then, to say that the 'soothing system' of which I have heard so much, is no longer in force?"

"It is now," he replied, "several weeks since we have concluded to renounce it forever."

"Indeed! you astonish me!"

"We found it, sir," he said, with a sigh, "absolutely necessary to return to the old usages. The *danger* of the soothing system was, at all times, appalling; and its advantages have been much over-rated. I believe, sir, that in this house it has been given a fair trial, if ever in any. We did every thing that rational humanity could suggest. I am sorry that you could not have paid us a visit at an earlier period, that you might have judged for yourself. But

I presume you are conversant with the soothing practice—with its details."

"Not altogether. What I have heard has been at third or fourth hand."

"I may state the system then, in general terms, as one in which the patients were *ménagés*, humored. We contradicted *no* fancies which entered the brains of the mad. On the contrary, we not only indulged but encouraged them; and many of our most permanent cures have been thus effected. There is no argument which so touches the feeble reason of the madman as the *reductio ad absurdum*. We have had men, for example, who fancied themselves chickens. The cure was, to insist upon the thing as a fact—to accuse the patient of stupidity in not sufficiently perceiving it to be a fact—and thus to refuse him any other diet for a week than that which properly appertains to a chicken. In this manner a little corn and gravel were made to perform wonders."

"But was this species of acquiescence all?"

"By no means. We put much faith in amusements of a simple kind, such as music, dancing, gymnastic exercises generally, cards, certain classes of books, and so forth. We affected to treat each individual as if for some ordinary physical disorder; and the word 'lunacy' was never employed. A great point was to set each lunatic to guard the actions of all the others. To repose confidence in the understanding or discretion of a madman, is to gain him body and soul. In this way we were enabled to dispense with an expensive body of keepers."

"And you had no punishments of any kind?"

"None."

"And you never confined your patients?"

"Very rarely. Now and then, the malady of some individual growing to a crisis, or taking a sudden turn of fury, we conveyed him to a secret cell, lest his disorder should infect the rest, and there kept him until we could dismiss him to his friends—for with the raging maniac we have nothing to do. He is usually removed to the public hospitals."

"And you have now changed all this—and you think for the better?"

"Decidedly. The system had its disadvantages, and even its dangers. It is now, happily, exploded throughout all the *Maisons de Santé* of France."

"I am very much surprised," I said, "at what you tell me; for I made sure that, at this moment, no other method of treatment for mania existed in any portion of the country."

"You are young yet, my friend," replied my host, "but the time will arrive when you will learn to judge for yourself of what is going on in the world, without trusting to the gossip of others. Believe nothing you hear, and only one half that you see. Now about our *Maisons de Santé*, it is clear that some ignoramus has misled you. After dinner, however, when you have sufficiently recovered from the fatigue of your ride, I will be happy to take you over the house, and introduce to you a system which, in my opinion, and in that of every one who has witnessed its operation, is incomparably the most effectual as yet devised."

"Your own?" I inquired—"one of your own invention?"

"I am proud," he replied, "to acknowledge that it is—at least in some measure."

In this manner I conversed with Monsieur Maillard for an hour or two, during which he showed me the gardens and conservatories of the place.

"I cannot let you see my patients," he said, "just at present. To a sensitive mind there is always more or less of the shocking in such exhibitions; and I do not wish to spoil your appetite for dinner. We will dine. I can give you some veal *à la St. Menehoult,* with cauliflowers in *velouté* sauce—after that a glass of *Clos de Vougeôt*—then your nerves will be sufficiently steadied."

At six, dinner was announced; and my host conducted me into a large *salle à manger,* where a very numerous company were assembled—twenty-five or thirty in all. They were, apparently, people of rank—certainly of high breeding—although their habiliments, I thought, were extravagantly rich, partaking somewhat too much of the ostentatious finery of the *vieille cour.* I noticed that at least two-thirds of these guests were ladies; and some of the latter were by no means accoutred in what a Parisian would consider good taste at the present day. Many females, for example, whose age could not have been less than seventy, were bedecked with a profusion of jewelry, such as rings, bracelets, and ear-rings, and wore their bosoms and arms shamefully bare. I observed, too, that very few of the dresses were well made—or, at least, that very few of them fitted the wearers. In looking about, I discovered the interesting girl to whom Monsieur Maillard had presented me in the little parlor; but my surprise was great to see her wearing a hoop and farthingale, with high-heeled shoes, and a dirty cap of Brussels lace, so much too large for her that it gave her face a ridiculously diminutive expression. When I had first seen her, she was attired, most becomingly, in deep mourning. There was an air of oddity, in short, about the dress of the whole party, which, at first, caused me to recur to my original idea of the "soothing system," and to fancy that Monsieur Maillard had been willing to deceive me until after dinner, that I might experience no uncomfortable feelings during the repast, at finding myself dining with lunatics; but I remembered having been informed, in Paris, that the southern provincialists were a peculiarly eccentric people, with a vast number of antiquated notions;[1] and then, too, upon conversing with several members of the company, my apprehensions were immediately and fully dispelled.

The dining-room, itself, although perhaps sufficiently comfortable, and of good dimensions, had nothing too much of elegance about it. For example, the floor was uncarpeted; in France, however, a carpet is frequently dispensed with. The windows, too, were without curtains; the shutters, being shut, were securely fastened with iron bars, applied diagonally, after the fashion of our ordinary shop-shutters. The apartment, I observed, formed, in itself, a wing of the *château*, and thus the windows were on three sides of the parallelogram; the door being at the other. There were no less than ten windows in all.

The table was superbly set out. It was loaded with plate, and more than loaded with delicacies. The profusion was absolutely barbaric. There were meats enough to have feasted the Anakim.[2] Never, in all my life, had I witnessed so lavish, so wasteful an expenditure of the good things of life. There seemed very little taste, however, in the arrangements; and my eyes, accustomed to quiet lights, were sadly offended by the prodigious glare of a multitude of wax candles, which, in silver *candelabra*, were deposited upon the table, and all about the room, wherever it was possible to find a place. There were several active servants in attendance; and, upon a large table, at the farther end of the apartment, were seated seven or eight people with fiddles, fifes, trombones, and a drum. These fellows annoyed me very much, at intervals, during the repast, by an infinite variety of noises, which were intended for music, and which appeared to afford much entertainment to all present, with the exception of myself.

Upon the whole, I could not help thinking that there was much of the *bizarre* about every thing I saw—but then the world is made up of all kinds of persons, with all modes of thought, and all sorts of conventional customs. I had travelled, too, so much as to be quite an adept at the *nil admirari*; so I took my seat very coolly at the right hand of my host, and, having an excellent appetite, did justice to the good cheer set before me.

The conversation, in the meantime, was spirited and general. The ladies, as usual, talked a great deal. I soon found that nearly all the company were well educated; and my host was a world of good-humored anecdote in himself. He seemed quite willing to speak of his position as superintendent of a *Maison de Santé*; and, indeed, the topic of lunacy was, much to my surprise, a favorite one with all present. A great many amusing stories were told, having reference to the *whims* of the patients.

"We had a fellow here once," said a fat little gentleman, who sat at my right—"a fellow that fancied himself a tea-pot; and by the way, is it not especially singular how often this particular crotchet has entered the brain of the lunatic? There is scarcely an insane asylum in France which cannot supply a human tea-pot. *Our* gentleman was a Britannia-ware tea-pot, and was careful to polish himself every morning with buckskin and whiting."

"And then," said a tall man, just opposite, "we had here, not long ago, a person who had taken it into his head that he was a donkey—which, allegorically speaking, you will say, was quite true. He was a troublesome patient; and we had much ado to keep him within bounds. For a long time he would eat nothing but thistles; but of this idea we soon cured him by insisting upon his eating nothing else. Then he was perpetually kicking out his heels—so—so—"

"Mr. De Kock! I will thank you to behave yourself!" here interrupted an old lady, who sat next to the speaker. "Please keep your feet to yourself! You have spoiled my brocade! Is it necessary, pray, to illustrate a remark in so practical a style? Our friend, here, can surely comprehend you without all this. Upon my word, you are nearly as great a donkey as the poor unfortunate imagined himself. Your acting is very natural, as I live."

"*Mille pardons! Ma'm'selle!*" replied Monsieur De Kock, thus addressed—"a thousand pardons! I had no intention of offending. Ma'm'selle Laplace—Monsieur De Kock will do himself the honor of taking wine with you."

Here Monsieur De Kock bowed low, kissed his hand with much ceremony, and took wine with Ma'm'selle Laplace.

"Allow me, *mon ami*," now said Monsieur Maillard, addressing myself, "allow me to send you a morsel of this veal *à la St. Menehoult*—you will find it particularly fine."

At this instant three sturdy waiters had just succeeded in depositing safely upon the table an enormous dish, or trencher, containing what I supposed to be the *"monstrum, horrendum, informe, ingens, cui lumen ademptum."*[3] A closer scrutiny assured me, however, that it was only a small calf roasted whole, and set upon its knees, with an apple in its mouth, as is the English fashion of dressing a hare.

"Thank you, no," I replied; "to say the truth, I am not particularly partial to veal *à la St.*—what is it?—for I do not find that it altogether agrees with me. I will change my plate, however, and try some of the rabbit."

There were several side-dishes on the table, containing what appeared to be the ordinary French rabbit—a very delicious *morceau*, which I can recommend.

"Pierre," cried the host, "change this gentleman's plate, and give him a side-piece of this rabbit *au-chat.*"

"This what?" said I.

"This rabbit *au-chat.*"

"Why, thank you—upon second thoughts, no. I will just help myself to some of the ham."

There is no knowing what one eats, thought I to myself, at the tables of these people of the province. I will have none of their rabbit *au-chat*—and, for the matter of that, none of their *cat-au-rabbit* either.

"And then," said a cadaverous-looking personage, near the foot of the table, taking up the thread of the conversation where it had

been broken off—"and then, among other oddities, we had a pa-
tient, once upon a time, who very pertinaciously maintained him-
self to be a Cordova cheese, and went about, with a knife in his
hand, soliciting his friends to try a small slice from the middle of
his leg."

"He was a great fool, beyond doubt," interposed some one,
"but not to be compared with a certain individual whom we all
know, with the exception of this strange gentleman. I mean the
man who took himself for a bottle of champagne, and always
went off with a pop and a fizz, in this fashion."

Here the speaker, very rudely, as I thought, put his right thumb
in his left cheek, withdrew it with a sound resembling the popping
of a cork, and then, by a dexterous movement of the tongue upon
the teeth, created a sharp hissing and fizzing, which lasted for sev-
eral minutes, in imitation of the frothing of champagne. This be-
havior, I saw plainly, was not very pleasing to Monsieur Maillard;
but that gentleman said nothing, and the conversation was re-
sumed by a very lean little man in a big wig.

"And then there was an ignoramus," said he, "who mistook
himself for a frog; which, by the way, he resembled in no little de-
gree. I wish you could have seen him, sir,"—here the speaker ad-
dressed myself—"it would have done your heart good to see the
natural airs that he put on. Sir, if that man was *not* a frog, I can only
observe that it is a pity he was not. His croak thus—o-o-o-o-gh—
o-o-o-o-gh! was the finest note in the world—B flat; and when he
put his elbows upon the table thus—after taking a glass or two of
wine—and distended his mouth, thus, and rolled up his eyes, thus,
and winked them with excessive rapidity, thus, why then, sir, I
take it upon myself to say, positively, that you would have been
lost in admiration of the genius of the man."

"I have no doubt of it," I said.

"And then," said somebody else, "then there was Petit Gaillard,
who thought himself a pinch of snuff, and was truly distressed be-
cause he could not take himself between his own finger and
thumb."

"And then there was Jules Desoulières, who was a very singular
genius, indeed, and went mad with the idea that he was a pump-
kin. He persecuted the cook to make him up into pies—a thing
which the cook indignantly refused to do. For my part, I am by no

means sure that a pumpkin pie *à la Desoulières* would not have been very capital eating, indeed!"

"You astonish me!" said I; and I looked inquisitively at Monsieur Maillard.

"Ha! ha! ha!" said that gentleman—"he! he! he!—hi! hi! hi!—ho! ho! ho!—hu! hu! hu! hu!—very good indeed! You must not be astonished, *mon ami*; our friend here is a wit—a *drôle*—you must not understand him to the letter."

"And then," said some other one of the party,—"then there was Bouffon Le Grand—another extraordinary personage in his way. He grew deranged through love, and fancied himself possessed of two heads. One of these he maintained to be the head of Cicero; the other he imagined a composite one, being Demosthenes' from the top of the forehead to the mouth, and Lord Brougham from the mouth to the chin. It is not impossible that he was wrong; but he would have convinced you of his being in the right; for he was a man of great eloquence. He had an absolute passion for oratory, and could not refrain from display. For example, he used to leap upon the dinner-table thus, and—and—"

Here a friend, at the side of the speaker, put a hand upon his shoulder, and whispered a few words in his ear; upon which he ceased talking with great suddenness, and sank back within his chair.

"And then," said the friend, who had whispered, "there was Boullard, the tee-totum. I call him the tee-totum, because, in fact, he was seized with the droll but not altogether irrational crotchet, that he had been converted into a tee-totum. You would have roared with laughter to see him spin. He would turn round upon one heel by the hour, in this manner—so—"

Here the friend whom he had just interrupted by a whisper, performed an exactly similar office for himself.

"But then," cried the old lady, at the top of her voice, "your Monsieur Boullard was a madman, and a very silly madman at best; for who, allow me to ask you, ever heard of a human tee-totum? The thing is absurd. Madame Joyeuse was a more sensible person, as you know. She had a crotchet, but it was instinct with common sense, and gave pleasure to all who had the honor of her acquaintance. She found, upon mature deliberation, that, by some accident, she had been turned into a chicken-cock; but, as such, she behaved with propriety. She flapped her wings with prodigious effect—so—so—so—and, as for her crow, it was delicious! Cock-a-doodle-doo!—cock-a-doodle-doo!—cock-a-doodle-de-doo-doo-dooo-do-o-o-o-o-o-o-!"

"Madame Joyeuse, I will thank you to behave yourself!" here interrupted our host, very angrily. "You can either conduct yourself as a lady should do, or you can quit the table forthwith—take your choice."

The lady, (whom I was much astonished to hear addressed as Madame Joyeuse, after the description of Madame Joyeuse she had just given) blushed up to the eyebrows, and seemed exceedingly abashed at the reproof. She hung down her head, and said not a syllable in reply. But another and younger lady resumed the theme. It was my beautiful girl of the little parlor.

"Oh, Madame Joyeuse *was* a fool!" she exclaimed, "but there was really much sound sense, after all, in the opinion of Eugénie Salsafette. She was a very beautiful and painfully modest young lady, who thought the ordinary mode of habiliment indecent, and wished to dress herself, always, by getting outside instead of inside of her clothes. It is a thing very easily done, after all. You have only to do so—and then so—so—so—and then so—so—so—and then so—so—and then—"

"Mon dieu! Ma'm'selle Salsafette!" here cried a dozen voices at once. "What *are* you about?—forbear!—that is sufficient!—we see, very plainly, how it is done!—hold! hold!" and several persons were already leaping from their seats to withhold Ma'm'selle Salsafette from putting herself upon a par with the Medicean Venus, when the point was very effectually and suddenly accomplished by a series of loud screams, or yells, from some portion of the main body of the *château*.

My nerves were very much affected, indeed, by these yells; but the rest of the company I really pitied. I never saw any set of reasonable people so thoroughly frightened in my life. They all grew as pale as so many corpses, and, shrinking within their seats, sat quivering and gibbering with terror, and listening for a repetition of the sound. It came again—louder and seemingly nearer—and then a third time *very* loud, and then a fourth time with a vigor evidently diminished. At this apparent dying away of the noise, the spirits of the company were immediately regained, and all was life and anecdote as before. I now ventured to inquire the cause of the disturbance.

"A mere *bagatelle*," said Monsieur Maillard. "We are used to these things, and care really very little about them. The lunatics, every now and then, get up a howl in concert; one starting another, as is sometimes the case with a bevy of dogs at night. It occasionally happens, however, that the *concerto* yells are succeeded by a simultaneous effort at breaking loose; when, of course, some little danger is to be apprehended."

"And how many have you in charge?"

"At present we have not more than ten, altogether."

"Principally females, I presume?"

"Oh, no—every one of them men, and stout fellows, too, I can tell you."

"Indeed! I have always understood that the majority of lunatics were of the gentler sex."

"It is generally so, but not always. Some time ago, there were about twenty-seven patients here; and, of that number, no less than eighteen were women; but, lately, matters have changed very much, as you see."

"Yes—have changed very much, as you see," here interrupted the gentleman who had broken the shins of Ma'm'selle Laplace.

"Yes—have changed very much, as you see!" chimed in the whole company at once.

"Hold your tongues, every one of you!" said my host, in a great rage. Whereupon the whole company maintained a dead silence for nearly a minute. As for one lady, she obeyed Monsieur Maillard to the letter, and thrusting out her tongue, which was an excessively long one, held it very resignedly, with both hands, until the end of the entertainment.

"And this gentlewoman," said I, to Monsieur Maillard, bending over and addressing him in a whisper—"this good lady who has just spoken, and who gives us the cock-a-doodle-de-doo—she, I presume, is harmless—quite harmless, eh?"

"Harmless!" ejaculated he, in unfeigned surprise, "why—why, what *can* you mean?"

"Only slightly touched?" said I, touching my head. "I take it for granted that she is not particularly—not dangerously affected, eh?"

"*Mon dieu!* what *is* it you imagine? This lady, my particular old friend Madame Joyeuse, is as absolutely sane as myself. She has her little eccentricities, to be sure—but then, you know, all old women—all *very* old women are more or less eccentric!"

"To be sure," said I,—"to be sure—and then the rest of these ladies and gentlemen—"

"Are my friends and keepers," interrupted Monsieur Maillard, drawing himself up with *hauteur*,—"my very good friends and assistants."

"What! all of them?" I asked,—"the women and all?"

"Assuredly," he said,—"we could not do at all without the women; they are the best lunatic nurses in the world; they have a way of their own, you know; their bright eyes have a marvellous effect;—something like the fascination of the snake, you know."

"To be sure," said I,—"to be sure! They behave a little odd, eh?—they are a little *queer*, eh?—don't you think so?"

"Odd!—queer!—why, do you *really* think so? We are not very prudish, to be sure, here in the South—do pretty much as we please—enjoy life, and all that sort of thing, you know—"

"To be sure," said I,—"to be sure."

"And then, perhaps, this *Clos de Vougeôt* is a little heady, you know—a little strong—you understand, eh?"

"To be sure," said I,—"to be sure. By-the-bye, Monsieur, did I understand you to say that the system you have adopted, in place of the celebrated soothing system, was one of very rigorous severity?"

"By no means. Our confinement is necessarily close; but the treatment—the medical treatment, I mean—is rather agreeable to the patients than otherwise."

"And the new system is one of your own invention?"

"Not altogether. Some portions of it are referable to Professor Tarr, of whom you have, necessarily, heard; and, again, there are modifications in my plan which I am happy to acknowledge as belonging of right to the celebrated Fether, with whom, if I mistake not, you have the honor of an intimate acquaintance."

"I am quite ashamed to confess," I replied, "that I have never even heard the names of either gentleman before."

"Good heavens!" ejaculated my host, drawing back his chair abruptly, and uplifting his hands. "I surely do not hear you aright! You did not intend to say, eh? that you had never *heard* either of the learned Doctor Tarr, or of the celebrated Professor Fether?"

"I am forced to acknowledge my ignorance," I replied; "but the truth should be held inviolate above all things. Nevertheless, I feel humbled to the dust, not to be acquainted with the works of these, no doubt, extraordinary men. I will seek out their writings forthwith, and peruse them with deliberate care. Monsieur Maillard, you have really—I must confess it—you have *really*—made me ashamed of myself!"

And this was the fact.

"Say no more, my good young friend," he said kindly, pressing my hand—"join me now in a glass of Sauterne."

We drank. The company followed our example, without stint. They chatted—they jested—they laughed—they perpetrated a thousand absurdities—the fiddles shrieked—the drum row-de-dowed—the trombones bellowed like so many brazen bulls of Phalaris[4]—and the whole scene, growing gradually worse and worse, as the wines gained the ascendancy, became at length a sort of Pandemonium *in petto*. In the meantime, Monsieur Maillard and myself, with some bottles of Sauterne and Vougeôt between us, continued our conversation at the top of the voice. A word spoken in an ordinary key stood no more chance of being heard than the voice of a fish from the bottom of Niagara Falls.

"And, sir," said I, screaming in his ear, "you mentioned something before dinner about the danger incurred in the old system of soothing. How is that?"

"Yes," he replied, "there was, occasionally, very great danger indeed. There is no accounting for the caprices of madmen; and, in my opinion as well as in that of Doctor Tarr and Professor Fether, it is *never* safe to permit them to run at large unattended. A lunatic may be 'soothed,' as it is called, for a time, but, in the end, he is very apt to become obstreperous. His cunning, too, is proverbial, and great. If he has a project in view, he conceals his design with a marvellous wisdom; and the dexterity with which he counterfeits sanity, presents, to the metaphysician, one of the most singular problems in the study of mind. When a madman appears *thoroughly* sane, indeed, it is high time to put him in a straitjacket."

"But the *danger*, my dear sir, of which you were speaking—in your own experience—during your control of this house—have you had practical reason to think liberty hazardous, in the case of a lunatic?"

"Here?—in my own experience?—why, I may say, yes. For example:—no *very* long while ago, a singular circumstance occurred in this very house. The 'soothing system,' you know, was then in operation, and the patients were at large. They behaved remarkably well—especially so—any one of sense might have known that some devilish scheme was brewing from that particular fact, that the fellows behaved so *remarkably* well. And, sure enough, one fine morning the keepers found themselves pinioned hand and foot, and thrown into the cells, where they were attended, as if *they* were the lunatics, by the lunatics themselves, who had usurped the offices of the keepers."

"You don't tell me so! I never heard of any thing so absurd in my life!"

"Fact—it all came to pass by means of a stupid fellow—a lunatic—who, by some means, had taken it into his head that he had invented a better system of government than any ever heard of before—of lunatic government, I mean. He wished to give his invention a trial, I suppose—and so he persuaded the rest of the patients to join him in a conspiracy for the overthrow of the reigning powers."

"And he really succeeded?"

"No doubt of it. The keepers and kept were soon made to exchange places. Not that exactly either—for the madmen had been free, but the keepers were shut up in cells forthwith, and treated, I am sorry to say, in a very cavalier manner."

"But I presume a counter revolution was soon effected. This condition of things could not have long existed. The country people in the neighborhood—visitors coming to see the establishment—would have given the alarm."

"There you are out. The head rebel was too cunning for that. He admitted no visitors at all—with the exception, one day, of a very stupid-looking young gentleman of whom he had no reason to be afraid. He let him in to see the place—just by way of variety—to have a little fun with him. As soon as he had gammoned him sufficiently, he let him out, and sent him about his business."

"And *how* long, then, did the madmen reign?"

"Oh, a very long time, indeed—a month certainly—how much

longer I can't precisely say. In the meantime, the lunatics had a jolly season of it—that you may swear. They doffed their own shabby clothes, and made free with the family wardrobe and jewels. The cellars of the *château* were well stocked with wine; and these madmen are just the devils that know how to drink it. They lived well, I can tell you."

"And the treatment—what was the particular species of treatment which the leader of the rebels put into operation?"

"Why, as for that, a madman is not necessarily a fool, as I have already observed; and it is my honest opinion that his treatment was a much better treatment than that which it superseded. It was a very capital system indeed—simple—neat—no trouble at all—in fact it was delicious—it was—"

Here my host's observations were cut short by another series of yells, of the same character as those which had previously disconcerted us. This time, however, they seemed to proceed from persons rapidly approaching.

"Gracious Heavens!" I ejaculated—"the lunatics have most undoubtedly broken loose."

"I very much fear it is so," replied Monsieur Maillard, now becoming excessively pale. He had scarcely finished the sentence, before loud shouts and imprecations were heard beneath the windows; and, immediately afterward, it became evident that some persons outside were endeavoring to gain entrance into the room. The door was beaten with what appeared to be a sledge-hammer, and the shutters were wrenched and shaken with prodigious violence.

A scene of the most terrible confusion ensued. Monsieur Maillard, to my excessive astonishment, threw himself under the sideboard. I had expected more resolution at his hands. The members of the orchestra, who, for the last fifteen minutes, had been seemingly too much intoxicated to do duty, now sprang all at once to their feet and to their instruments, and, scrambling upon their table, broke out, with one accord, into "Yankee Doodle,"[5] which they performed, if not exactly in tune, at least with an energy superhuman, during the whole of the uproar.

Meantime, upon the main dining-table, among the bottles and glasses, leaped the gentleman, who, with such difficulty, had been restrained from leaping there before. As soon as he fairly settled himself, he commenced an oration, which, no doubt, was a very capital one, if it could only have been heard. At the same moment, the man with the tee-totum predilections, set himself to spinning around the apartment, with immense energy, and with arms out-stretched at right angles with his body; so that he had all the air of a tee-totum in fact, and knocked every body down that happened to get in his way. And now, too, hearing an incredible popping and fizzing of champagne, I discovered at length, that it proceeded from the person who performed the bottle of that delicate drink during dinner. And then, again, the frog-man croaked away as if the salvation of his soul depended upon every note that he uttered. And, in the midst of all this, the continuous braying of a donkey arose over all. As for my old friend, Madame Joyeuse, I really could have wept for the poor lady, she appeared so terribly per-plexed. All she did, however, was to stand up in a corner, by the fire-place, and sing out incessantly at the top of her voice, "Cock-a-doodle-de-dooooooh!"

And now came the climax—the catastrophe of the drama. As no resistance, beyond whooping and yelling and cock-a-doodleing, was offered to the encroachments of the party without, the ten windows were very speedily, and almost simultaneously, broken in. But I shall never forget the emotions of wonder and horror with which I gazed, when, leaping through these windows, and down among us *pêle-mêle*, fighting, stamping, scratching, and howling, there rushed a perfect army of what I took to be Chim-panzees, Ourang-Outangs, or big black baboons of the Cape of Good Hope.

I received a terrible beating—after which I rolled under a sofa and lay still. After lying there some fifteen minutes, however, dur-ing which time I listened with all my ears to what was going on in the room, I came to some satisfactory *dénouement* of this tragedy. Monsieur Maillard, it appeared, in giving me the account of the lunatic who had excited his fellows to rebellion, had been merely relating his own exploits. This gentleman had, indeed, some two or three years before, been the superintendent of the establish-ment; but grew crazy himself, and so became a patient. This fact was unknown to the travelling companion who introduced me. The keepers, ten in number, having been suddenly overpowered, were first well tarred, then carefully feathered, and then shut up in underground cells. They had been so imprisoned for more than a month, during which period Monsieur Maillard had generously allowed them not only the tar and feathers (which constituted his "system"), but some bread and abundance of water. The latter was pumped on them daily. At length, one escaping through a sewer, gave freedom to all the rest.

The "soothing system," with important modifications, has been resumed at the *château*; yet I cannot help agreeing with Monsieur Maillard, that his own "treatment" was a very capital one of its kind. As he justly observed, it was "simple—neat—and gave no trouble at all—not the least."

I have only to add that, although I have searched every library in Europe for the works of Doctor *Tarr* and Professor *Fether*, I have, up to the present day, utterly failed in my endeavors at procuring an edition.

SOME WORDS
WITH A MUMMY [1]

The symposium of the preceding evening had been a little too much for my nerves. I had a wretched headache, and was desperately drowsy. Instead of going out, therefore, to spend the evening as I had proposed, it occurred to me that I could not do a wiser thing than just eat a mouthful of supper and go immediately to bed.

A *light* supper of course. I am exceedingly fond of Welsh rabbit. More than a pound at once, however, may not at all times be advisable. Still, there can be no material objection to two. And really between two and three, there is merely a single unit of difference. I ventured, perhaps, upon four. My wife will have it five;—but, clearly, she has confounded two very distinct affairs. The abstract number, five, I am willing to admit; but, concretely, it has reference to bottles of Brown Stout, without which, in the way of condiment, Welsh rabbit is to be eschewed.

Having thus concluded a frugal meal, and donned my nightcap, with the serene hope of enjoying it till noon the next day, I placed my head upon the pillow, and through the aid of a capital conscience, fell into a profound slumber forthwith.

But when were the hopes of humanity fulfilled? I could not have completed my third snore when there came a furious ringing at the street-door bell, and then an impatient thumping at the knocker, which awakened me at once. In a minute afterward, and while I was still rubbing my eyes, my wife thrust in my face a note from my old friend, Doctor Ponnonner. It ran thus:

Come to me by all means, my dear good friend, as soon as you receive this. Come and help us to rejoice. At last, by long persevering diplomacy, I have gained the assent of the Directors of the City

Museum, to my examination of the Mummy—you know the one I mean. I have permission to unswathe it and open it, if desirable. A few friends only will be present—you, of course. The Mummy is now at my house, and we shall begin to unroll it at eleven to-night.

Yours ever,
PONNONNER.

By the time I had reached the "Ponnonner," it struck me that I was as wide awake as a man need be. I leaped out of bed in an ecstasy, overthrowing all in my way; dressed myself with a rapidity truly marvellous; and set off, at the top of my speed, for the Doctor's.

There I found a very eager company assembled. They had been awaiting me with much impatience; the Mummy was extended upon the dining table; and the moment I entered, its examination was commenced.

It was one of a pair brought, several years previously, by Captain Arthur Sabretash, a cousin of Ponnonner's from a tomb near Eleithias, in the Lybian mountains, a considerable distance above Thebes on the Nile. The grottoes at this point, although less magnificent than the Theban sepulchres, are of higher interest, on account of affording more numerous illustrations of the private life of the Egyptians. The chamber from which our specimen was taken, was said to be very rich in such illustrations; the walls being completely covered with fresco paintings and bas-reliefs, while statues, vases, and Mosaic work of rich patterns, indicated the vast wealth of the deceased.

The treasure had been deposited in the Museum precisely in the same condition in which Captain Sabretash had found it;—that is to say, the coffin had not been disturbed. For eight years it had thus stood, subject only externally to public inspection. We had now, therefore, the complete Mummy at our disposal; and to those who are aware how very rarely the unransacked antique reaches our shores, it will be evident, at once that we had great reason to congratulate ourselves upon our good fortune.

Approaching the table, I saw on it a large box, or case, nearly seven feet long, and perhaps three feet wide, by two feet and a half deep. It was oblong—not coffin-shaped. The material was at first supposed to be the wood of the sycamore (platanus), but, upon cutting into it, we found it to be pasteboard, or more properly, *papier maché*, composed of papyrus. It was thickly ornamented with paintings, representing funeral scenes, and other mournful subjects, interspersed among which, in every variety of position, were certain series of hieroglyphical characters intended, no doubt, for the name of the departed. By good luck, Mr. Gliddon formed one of our party;[2] and he had no difficulty in translating the letters, which were simply phonetic, and represented the word *Allamistakeo*.

We had some difficulty in getting this case open without injury; but, having at length accomplished the task, we came to a second, coffin-shaped, and very considerably less in size than the exterior one, but resembling it precisely in every other respect. The interval between the two was filled with resin, which had, in some degree, defaced the colors of the interior box.

Upon opening this latter (which we did quite easily,) we arrived at a third case, also coffin-shaped, and varying from the second one in no particular, except in that of its material, which was cedar, and still emitted the peculiar and highly aromatic odor of that wood. Between the second and the third case there was no interval; the one fitting accurately within the other.

Removing the third case, we discovered and took out the body itself. We had expected to find it, as usual, enveloped in frequent rolls, or bandages, of linen, but, in place of these, we found a sort of sheath, made of papyrus, and coated with a layer of plaster, thickly gilt and painted. The paintings represented subjects connected with the various supposed duties of the soul, and its presentation to different divinities, with numerous identical human figures, intended, very probably, as portraits of the persons embalmed. Extending from head to foot was a columnar, or perpendicular, inscription, in phonetic hieroglyphics, giving again his name and titles, and the names and titles of his relations.

Around the neck thus ensheathed, was a collar of cylindrical glass beads, diverse in color, and so arranged as to form images of deities, of the scarabæus, etc, with the winged globe. Around the small of the waist was a similar collar, or belt.

Stripping off the papyrus, we found the flesh in excellent preservation, with no perceptible odor. The color was reddish. The skin was hard, smooth, and glossy. The teeth and hair were in good condition. The eyes (it seemed) had been removed, and glass ones substituted, which were very beautiful and wonderfully life-like, with the exception of somewhat too determined a stare. The fingers and the nails were brilliantly gilded.

Mr. Gliddon was of opinion, from the redness of the epidermis, that the embalmment had been effected altogether by asphaltum; but, on scraping the surface with a steel instrument, and throwing into the fire some of the powder thus obtained, the flavor of camphor and other sweet-scented gums became apparent.

We searched the corpse very carefully for the usual openings through which the entrails are extracted, but, to our surprise, we could discover none. No member of the party was at that period aware that entire or unopened mummies are not infrequently met. The brain it was customary to withdraw through the nose; the intestines through an incision in the side; the body was then shaved, washed, and salted; then laid aside for several weeks, when the operation of embalming, properly so called, began.

As no trace of an opening could be found, Doctor Ponnonner was preparing his instruments for dissection, when I observed that it was then past two o'clock. Hereupon it was agreed to postpone the internal examination until the next evening; and we were about to separate for the present, when some one suggested an experiment or two with the Voltaic pile.

The application of electricity to a Mummy three or four thousand years old at the least, was an idea, if not very sage, still sufficiently original, and we all caught at it at once. About one-tenth in earnest and nine-tenths in jest, we arranged a battery in the Doctor's study, and conveyed thither the Egyptian.

It was only after much trouble that we succeeded in laying bare some portions of the temporal muscle which appeared of less stony rigidity than other parts of the frame, but which, as we had anticipated, of course, gave no indication of galvanic susceptibility when brought in contact with the wire. This the first trial, indeed, seemed decisive, and, with a hearty laugh at our own absurdity, we were bidding each other good night, when my eyes, happening to fall upon those of the Mummy, were there immediately riveted in amazement. My brief glance, in fact, had sufficed to assure me that the orbs which we had all supposed to be glass, and which were originally noticeable for a certain wild stare, were now so far covered by the lids, that only a small portion of the *tunica albuginea* remained visible.

With a shout I called attention to the fact, and it became immediately obvious to all.

I cannot say that I was *alarmed* at the phenomenon, because "alarmed" is, in my case, not exactly the word. It is possible, however, that, but for the Brown Stout, I might have been a little nervous. As for the rest of the company, they really made no attempt at concealing the downright fright which possessed them. Doctor Ponnonner was a man to be pitied. Mr. Gliddon, by some peculiar process, rendered himself invisible. Mr. Silk Buckingham,[3] I fancy, will scarcely be so bold as to deny that he made his way, upon all fours, under the table.

After the first shock of astonishment, however, we resolved, as a matter of course, upon further experiment forthwith. Our operations were now directed against the great toe of the right foot. We made an incision over the outside of the exterior *os sesamoideum pollicis pedis*, and thus got at the root of the *abductor* muscle. Readjusting the battery, we now applied the fluid to the bisected nerves—when, with a movement of exceeding life-likeness, the Mummy first drew up its right knee so as to bring it nearly in contact with the abdomen, and then, straightening the limb with inconceivable force, bestowed a kick upon Doctor Ponnonner, which had the effect of discharging that gentleman, like an arrow from a catapult, through a window into the street below.

We rushed out *en masse* to bring in the mangled remains of the victim, but had the happiness to meet him upon the staircase, coming up in an unaccountable hurry, brimful of the most ardent philosophy, and more than ever impressed with the necessity of prosecuting our experiment with vigor and with zeal.

It was by his advice, accordingly, that we made, upon the spot, a profound incision into the tip of the subject's nose, while the Doctor himself, laying violent hands upon it, pulled it into vehement contact with the wire.

Morally and physically—figuratively and literally—was the effect electric. In the first place, the corpse opened its eyes and winked very rapidly for several minutes, as does Mr. Barnes in the pantomime; in the second place, it sneezed; in the third, it sat upon end; in the fourth, it shook its fist in Doctor Ponnonner's face; in the fifth, turning to Messieurs Gliddon and Buckingham, it addressed them, in very capital Egyptian, thus:

"I must say, gentlemen, that I am as much surprised as I am mortified at your behaviour. Of Doctor Ponnonner nothing better was to be expected. He is a poor little fat fool who *knows* no better. I pity and forgive him. But you, Mr. Gliddon—and you, Silk—who have travelled and resided in Egypt until one might imagine you to the manor born—you, I say, who have been so much among us that you speak Egyptian fully as well, I think, as you write your mother tongue—you, whom I have always been led to regard as the firm friend of the mummies—I really did anticipate more gentlemanly conduct from you. What am I to think of your standing quietly by and seeing me thus unhandsomely used? What am I to suppose by your permitting Tom, Dick, and Harry to strip me of my coffins, and my clothes, in this wretchedly cold climate? In what light (to come to the point) am I to regard your aiding and abetting that miserable little villain, Doctor Ponnonner, in pulling me by the nose?"

It will be taken for granted, no doubt, that upon hearing this speech under the circumstances, we all either made for the door, or fell into violent hysterics, or went off in a general swoon. One of these three things was, I say, to be expected. Indeed each and all of these lines of conduct might have been very plausibly pursued. And, upon my word, I am at a loss to know how or why it was that we pursued neither the one or the other. But, perhaps, the true reason is to be sought in the spirit of the age, which proceeds by the rule of contraries altogether, and is now usually admitted as the solution of everything in the way of paradox and impossibility. Or, perhaps, after all, it was only the Mummy's exceedingly natural and matter-of-course air that divested his words of the terrible. However this may be, the facts are clear, and no member of our party betrayed any very particular trepidation, or seemed to consider that any thing had gone very especially wrong.

For my part I was convinced it was all right, and merely stepped aside, out of the range of the Egyptian's fist. Doctor Ponnonner thrust his hands into his breeches' pockets, looked hard at the Mummy, and grew excessively red in the face. Mr. Gliddon stroked his whiskers and drew up the collar of his shirt. Mr. Buckingham hung down his head, and put his right thumb into the left corner of his mouth.

The Egyptian regarded him with a severe countenance for some minutes, and at length, with a sneer, said:

"Why don't you speak, Mr. Buckingham? Did you hear what I asked you, or not? *Do* take your thumb out of your mouth!"

Mr. Buckingham, hereupon, gave a slight start, took his right thumb out of the left corner of his mouth, and, by way of indemnification inserted his left thumb in the right corner of the aperture above-mentioned.

Not being able to get an answer from Mr. B., the figure turned peevishly to Mr. Gliddon, and, in a peremptory tone, demanded in general terms what we all meant.

Mr. Gliddon replied at great length, in phonetics; and but for the deficiency of American printing-offices in hieroglyphical type, it would afford me much pleasure to record here, in the original, the whole of his very excellent speech.

I may as well take this occasion to remark, that all the subsequent conversation in which the Mummy took a part, was carried on in primitive Egyptian, through the medium (so far as concerned myself and other untravelled members of the company)—through the medium, I say, of Messieurs Gliddon and Buckingham, as interpreters. These gentlemen spoke the mother-tongue of the Mummy with inimitable fluency and grace; but I could not help observing that (owing, no doubt, to the introduction of images entirely modern, and, of course, entirely novel to the stranger,) the two travellers were reduced, occasionally, to the employment of sensible forms for the purpose of conveying a particular meaning. Mr. Gliddon, at one period, for example, could not make the Egyptian comprehend the term "politics," until he sketched upon the wall, with a bit of charcoal, a little carbuncle-nosed gentleman, out at elbows, standing upon a stump, with his left leg drawn back, right arm thrown forward, with his fist shut, the eyes rolled up toward Heaven, and the mouth open at an angle of ninety degrees. Just in the same way Mr. Buckingham failed to convey the absolutely modern idea, "wig," until, (at Doctor Ponnonner's suggestion,) he grew very pale in the face, and consented to take off his own.

It will be readily understood that Mr. Gliddon's discourse turned chiefly upon the vast benefits accruing to science from the unrolling and disembowelling of mummies; apologizing, upon this score, for any disturbance that might have been occasioned *him*, in particular, the individual Mummy called Allamistakeo; and concluding with a mere hint (for it could scarcely be considered more,) that, as these little matters were now explained, it might be as well to proceed with the investigation intended. Here Doctor Ponnonner made ready his instruments.

In regard to the latter suggestions of the orator, it appears that Allamistakeo had certain scruples of conscience, the nature of which I did not distinctly learn; but he expressed himself satisfied with the apologies tendered, and, getting down from the table, shook hands with the company all round.

When this ceremony was at an end, we immediately busied ourselves in repairing the damages which our subject had sustained from the scalpel. We sewed up the wound in his temple, bandaged his foot, and applied a square inch of black plaster to the tip of his nose.

It was now observed that the Count, (this was the title, it seems, of Allamistakeo,) had a slight fit of shivering—no doubt from the cold. The Doctor immediately repaired to his wardrobe, and soon returned with a black dress coat, made in Jennings' best manner, a pair of sky-blue plaid pantaloons with straps, a pink gingham *chemise*, a flapped vest of brocade, a white sack overcoat, a walking cane with a hook, a hat with no brim, patent-leather boots, straw-colored kid gloves, an eye-glass, a pair of whiskers, and a waterfall cravat. Owing to the disparity of size between the Count and the doctor, (the proportion being as two to one,) there was some little difficulty in adjusting these habiliments upon the person of the Egyptian; but when all was arranged, he might have been said to be dressed. Mr. Gliddon, therefore, gave him his arm, and led him to a comfortable chair by the fire, while the Doctor rang the bell upon the spot and ordered a supply of cigars and wine.

The conversation soon grew animated. Much curiosity was, of course, expressed in regard to the somewhat remarkable fact of Allamistakeo's still remaining alive.

"I should have thought," observed Mr. Buckingham, "that it is high time you were dead."

"Why," replied the Count, very much astonished, "I am little more than seven hundred years old! My father lived a thousand, and was by no means in his dotage when he died."

Here ensued a brisk series of questions and computations, by means of which it became evident that the antiquity of the Mummy had been grossly misjudged. It had been five thousand and fifty years and some months since he had been consigned to the catacombs at Eleithias.

"But my remark," resumed Mr. Buckingham, "had no reference to your age at the period of interment (I am willing to grant, in fact, that you are still a young man,) and my allusion was to the immensity of time during which, by your own showing, you must have been done up in asphaltum."

"In what?" said the Count.

"In asphaltum," persisted Mr. B.

"Ah, yes; I have some faint notion of what you mean; it might be made to answer, no doubt,—but in my time we employed scarcely anything else than the Bichloride of Mercury."

"But what we are especially at a loss to understand," said Doctor Ponnonner, "is how it happens that, having been dead and buried in Egypt five thousand years ago, you are here to-day all alive and looking so delightfully well."

"Had I been, as you say, *dead*," replied the Count, "it is more than probable that dead I should still be; for I perceive you are yet in the infancy of Galvanism, and cannot accomplish with it what was a common thing among us in the old days. But the fact is, I fell into catalepsy, and it was considered by my best friends that I was either dead or should be; they accordingly embalmed me at once—I presume you are aware of the chief principle of the embalming process?"

"Why not altogether."

"Ah, I perceive;—a deplorable condition of ignorance! Well, I cannot enter into details just now: but it is necessary to explain that to embalm (properly speaking,) in Egypt, was to arrest indefinitely *all* the animal functions subjected to the process. I use the word 'animal' in its widest sense, as including the physical not more than the moral and *vital* being. I repeat that the leading principle of embalmment consisted, with us, in the immediately arresting, and holding in perpetual *abeyance*, *all* the animal functions subjected to the process. To be brief, in whatever condition the individual was, at the period of embalmment, in that condition he remained. Now, as it is my good fortune to be of the blood of the Scarabæus, I was embalmed *alive*, as you see me at present."

"The blood of the Scarabæus!" exclaimed Doctor Ponnonner.

"Yes. The Scarabæus was the *insignium*, or the 'arms,' of a very distinguished and a very rare patrician family. To be 'of the blood of the Scarabæus,' is merely to be one of that family of which the Scarabæus is the *insignium*. I speak figuratively."

"But what has this to do with you being alive?"

"Why it is the general custom, in Egypt, to deprive a corpse, before embalmment, of its bowels and brains; the race of the Scarabæi alone did not coincide with the custom. Had I not been a Scarabæus, therefore, I should have been without bowels and brains; and without either it is inconvenient to live."

"I perceive that;" said Mr. Buckingham, "and I presume that all the *entire* mummies that come to hand are of the race of Scarabæi."

"Beyond doubt."

"I thought," said Mr. Gliddon, very meekly, "that the Scarabæus was one of the Egyptian gods."

"One of the Egyptian *what*?" exclaimed the Mummy, starting to its feet.

"Gods!" repeated the traveller.

"Mr. Gliddon, I really am astonished to hear you talk in this style," said the Count, resuming his chair. "No nation upon the face of the earth has ever acknowledged more than *one god*. The Scarabæus, the Ibis, etc., were with us (as similar creatures have been with others) the symbols, or *media*, through which we offered worship to a Creator too august to be more directly approached."

There was here a pause. At length the colloquy was renewed by Doctor Ponnonner.

"It is not improbable, then, from what you have explained," said he, "that among the catacombs near the Nile there may exist other mummies of the Scarabæus tribe, in a condition of vitality?"

"There can be no question of it," replied the Count; "all the Scarabæi embalmed accidentally while alive, are alive now. Even some of those *purposely* so embalmed, may have been overlooked by their executors, and still remain in the tombs."

"Will you be kind enough to explain," I said, "what you mean by 'purposely so embalmed'?"

"With great pleasure," answered the Mummy, after surveying

me leisurely through his eye-glass—for it was the first time I had ventured to address him a direct question.

"With great pleasure," he said. "The usual duration of man's life, in my time, was about eight hundred years. Few men died, unless by most extraordinary accident, before the age of six hundred; few lived longer than a decade of centuries; but eight were considered the natural term. After the discovery of the embalming principle, as I have already described it to you, it occurred to our philosophers that a laudable curiosity might be gratified, and, at the same time, the interests of science much advanced, by living this natural term in installments. In the case of history, indeed, experience demonstrated that something of this kind was indispensable. An historian, for example, having attained the age of five hundred, would write a book with great labor and then get himself carefully embalmed; leaving instructions to his executors *pro tem.*, that they should cause him to be revivified after the lapse of a certain period—say five or six hundred years. Resuming existence at the expiration of this time, he would invariably find his great work converted into a species of hap-hazard note-book—that is to say, into a kind of literary arena for the conflicting guesses, riddles, and personal squabbles of whole herds of exasperated commentators. These guesses, etc., which passed under the name of annotations or emendations, were found so completely to have enveloped, distorted, and overwhelmed the text, that the author had to go about with a lantern to discover his own book. When discovered, it was never worth the trouble of the search. After re-writing it throughout, it was regarded as the bounden duty of the historian to set himself to work, immediately, in correcting from his own private knowledge and experience, the traditions of the day concerning the epoch at which he had originally lived. Now this process of re-scription and personal rectification, pursued by various individual sages, from time to time, had the effect of preventing our history from degenerating into absolute fable."

"I beg your pardon," said Doctor Ponnonner at this point, laying his hand gently upon the arm of the Egyptian—"I beg your pardon, sir, but may I presume to interrupt you for one moment?"

"By all means, *sir*," replied the Count, drawing up.

"I merely wished to ask you a question," said the Doctor. "You mentioned the historian's personal correction of *traditions* respecting his own epoch. Pray, sir, upon an average, what proportion of these Kabbala were usually found to be right?"

"The Kabbala, as you properly term them, sir, were generally discovered to be precisely on a par with the facts recorded in the un-re-written histories themselves;—that is to say, not one individual iota of either, was ever known, under any circumstances, to be not totally and radically wrong."

"But since it is quite clear," resumed the Doctor, "that at least five thousand years have elapsed since your entombment, I take it for granted that your histories at that period, if not your traditions, were sufficiently explicit on that one topic of universal interest, the Creation, which took place, as I presume you are aware, only about ten centuries before."

"Sir!" said the Count Allamistakeo.

The Doctor repeated his remarks, but it was only after much additional explanation, that the foreigner could be made to comprehend them. The latter at length said, hesitatingly:

"The ideas you have suggested are to me, I confess, utterly novel. During my time I never knew any one to entertain so singular a fancy as that the universe (or this world if you will have it so) ever had a beginning at all. I remember, once, and once only, hearing something remotely hinted, by a man of many speculations, concerning the origin *of the human race*; and by this individual the very word *Adam*, (or Red Earth) which you make use of, was employed. He employed it, however, in a generical sense, with reference to the spontaneous germination from rank soil (just as a thousand of the lower *genera* of creatures are germinated)—the spontaneous germination, I say, of five vast hordes of men, simultaneously upspringing in five distinct and nearly equal divisions of the globe."[4]

Here, in general, the company shrugged their shoulders, and one or two of us touched our foreheads with a very significant air. Mr. Silk Buckingham, first glancing slightly at the occiput and then at the sinciput of Allamistakeo, spoke as follows:—

"The long duration of human life in your time, together with the occasional practice of passing it, as you have explained, in instalments, must have had, indeed, a strong tendency to the general development and conglomeration of knowledge. I presume, therefore, that we are to attribute the marked inferiority of the old

Egyptians in all particulars of science, when compared with the moderns, and more especially with the Yankees, altogether to the superior solidity of the Egyptian skull."[5]

"I confess again," replied the Count with much suavity, "that I am somewhat at a loss to comprehend you; pray, to what particulars of science do you allude?"

Here our whole party, joining voices, detailed, at great length, the assumptions of phrenology and the marvels of animal magnetism.

Having heard us to an end, the Count proceeded to relate a few anecdotes, which rendered it evident that prototypes of Gall and Spurzheim[6] had flourished and faded in Egypt so long ago as to have been nearly forgotten, and that the manœuvres of Mesmer were really very contemptible tricks when put in collation with the positive miracles of the Theban *savans*, who created lice and a great many other similar things.

I here asked the Count if his people were able to calculate eclipses. He smiled rather contemptuously, and said they were.

This put me a little out, but I began to make other inquiries in regard to his astronomical knowledge, when a member of the company, who had never as yet opened his mouth, whispered in my ear, that for information on this head, I had better consult Ptolemy, (whoever Ptolemy is), as well as one Plutarch *de facie lunae.*

I then questioned the Mummy about burning-glasses and lenses, and, in general, about the manufacture of glass; but I had not made an end of my queries before the silent member again touched me quietly on the elbow, and begged me for God's sake to take a peep at Diodorus Siculus. As for the Count, he merely asked me, in the way of reply, if we moderns possessed any such microscopes as would enable us to cut cameos in the style of the Egyptians. While I was thinking how I should answer this question, little Doctor Ponnonner committed himself in a very extraordinary way.

"Look at our architecture!" he exclaimed, greatly to the indignation of both the travellers, who pinched him black and blue to no purpose.

"Look," he cried with enthusiasm, "at the Bowling-Green Fountain in New York![7] or if this be too vast a contemplation, regard for a moment the Capitol at Washington, D.C.!"—and the good little medical man went on to detail very minutely, the proportions of the fabric to which he referred. He explained that the portico alone was adorned with no less than four and twenty columns, five feet in diameter, and ten feet apart.

The Count said that he regretted not being able to remember, just at that moment, the precise dimensions of any one of the principal buildings of the city of Aznac, whose foundations were laid in the night of Time, but the ruins of which were still standing, at the epoch of his entombment, in a vast plain of sand to the westward of Thebes. He recollected, however, (talking of the porticoes) that one affixed to an inferior palace in a kind of suburb called Carnac, consisted of a hundred and forty-four columns, thirty-seven feet in circumference, and twenty-five feet apart. The approach to this portico, from the Nile, was through an avenue two miles long, composed of sphynxes, statues and obelisks, twenty, sixty, and a hundred feet in height. The palace itself (as well as he could remember) was, in one direction, two miles long, and might have been altogether, about seven in circuit. Its walls were richly painted all over, within and without, with hieroglyphics. He would not pretend to *assert* that even fifty or sixty of the Doctor's Capitols might have been built within these walls, but he was by no means sure that two or three hundred of them might not have been squeezed in with some trouble. That palace at Carnac was an insignificant little building after all. He, (the Count) however, could not conscientiously refuse to admit the ingenuity, magnificence, and superiority of the Fountain at the Bowling-Green, as described by the Doctor. Nothing like it, he was forced to allow, had ever been seen in Egypt or elsewhere.

I here asked the Count what he had to say to our railroads.

"Nothing," he replied, "in particular." They were rather slight, rather ill-conceived, and clumsily put together. They could not be compared, of course, with the vast, level, direct, iron-grooved causeways, upon which the Egyptians conveyed entire temples and solid obelisks of a hundred and fifty feet in altitude.

I spoke of our gigantic mechanical forces.

He agreed that we knew something in that way, but inquired how I should have gone to work in getting up the imposts on the lintels of even the little palace at Carnac.

This question I concluded not to hear, and demanded if he had any idea of Artesian wells; but he simply raised his eye-brows; while Mr. Gliddon winked at me very hard, and said, in a low tone, that one had been recently discovered by the engineers employed to bore for water in the Great Oasis.

I then mentioned our steel; but the foreigner elevated his nose, and asked me if our steel could have executed the sharp carved work seen on the obelisks, and which was wrought altogether by edge-tools of copper.

This disconcerted us so greatly that we thought it advisable to vary the attack to Metaphysics. We sent for a copy of a book called the "Dial," and read out of it a chapter or two about something that is not very clear, but which the Bostonians call the Great Movement or Progress.[8]

The Count merely said that Great Movements were awfully common things in his day, and as for Progress, it was at one time quite a nuisance, but it never progressed.

We then spoke of the great beauty and importance of Democracy, and were at much trouble in impressing the Count with a due sense of the advantages we enjoyed in living where there was suffrage *ad libitum*, and no king.

He listened with marked interest, and in fact seemed not a little amused. When we had done, he said that, a great while ago, there had occurred something of a very similar sort. Thirteen Egyptian provinces determined all at once to be free, and so set a magnificent example to the rest of mankind.[9] They assembled their wise men, and concocted the most ingenious constitution it is possible to conceive. For a while they managed remarkably well; only their habit of bragging was prodigious. The thing ended, however, in the consolidation of the thirteen states, with some fifteen or twenty others, into the most odious and insupportable despotism that was ever heard of upon the face of the Earth.

I asked what was the name of the usurping tyrant.

As well as the Count could recollect, it was *Mob*.

Not knowing what to say to this, I raised my voice, and deplored the Egyptian ignorance of steam.

The Count looked at me with much astonishment, but made no answer. The silent gentleman, however, gave me a violent nudge in the ribs with his elbows—told me I had sufficiently exposed myself for once—and demanded if I was really such a fool as not to know that the modern steam-engine is derived from the invention of Hero, through Solomon de Caus.

We were now in imminent danger of being discomfited; but, as good luck would have it, Doctor Ponnonner, having rallied, returned to our rescue, and inquired if the people of Egypt would seriously pretend to rival the moderns in the all-important particular of dress.

The Count, at this, glanced downward to the straps of his pantaloons, and then taking hold of the end of one of his coat-tails, held it up close to his eyes for some minutes. Letting it fall, at last, his mouth extended itself very gradually from ear to ear; but I do not remember that he said any thing in the way of reply.

Hereupon we recovered our spirits, and the Doctor, approaching the Mummy with great dignity, desired it to say candidly, upon its honor as a gentleman, if the Egyptians had comprehended, at *any* period, the manufacture of either Ponnonner's lozenges, or Brandreth's pills.

We looked, with profound anxiety, for an answer;—but in vain. It was not forthcoming. The Egyptian blushed and hung down his head. Never was triumph more consummate; never was defeat borne with so ill a grace. Indeed, I could not endure the spectacle of the poor Mummy's mortification. I reached my hat, bowed to him stiffly, and took leave.

Upon getting home I found it past four o'clock, and went immediately to bed. It is now ten, A.M. I have been up since seven, penning these memoranda for the benefit of my family and of mankind. The former I shall behold no more. My wife is a shrew. The truth is, I am heartily sick of this life and of the nineteenth century in general. I am convinced that every thing is going wrong. Besides, I am anxious to know who will be President in 2045.[10] As soon, therefore, as I shave and swallow a cup of coffee, I shall just step over to Ponnonner's and get embalmed for a couple of hundred years.

POEMS

POEMS

Poe conjured strange scenes and haunting images in a dozen truly memorable poems that established his reputation in verse. Yet he achieved originality through a study of the poetic tradition; his juvenilia included imitations of the classical satirists. As a schoolboy he read Shakespeare and Milton with appreciation and studied Alexander Pope with delight. He left home at eighteen with a sheaf of verses, desperate to become a famous poet and identifying closely with the exiled Byron. In "Tamerlane," the title poem of his first volume, he envisioned a scorned Byronic hero, and in the longer "Al Aaraaf," which occasioned his second book, he emulated the orientalism of Thomas Moore's *Lalla Rookh*. His fondness for dream imagery also derived from his reading of Coleridge. Savoring of derision and self-pity, the early poems recur to themes of loneliness, rejection, and loss, and "The Lake" offers a suggestive hint of the delight in terror symptomatic of his curious fascination with death.

Although Poe published three volumes of poetry by the age of twenty-two, none met with commercial success. In his "Letter to Mr. —— ——," which introduced the *Poems* of 1831, he acknowledged "the great barrier in the path of an American writer": the popularity of established European writers, whose works sold cheaply in the absence of an international copyright law. Abandoning the idea of a career as a poet, he turned to periodical fiction and became "essentially a magazinist" but continued to write occasional poems, incorporating a few in tales such as "The Fall of the House of Usher." He returned to poetry more concertedly when "The Raven" brought literary celebrity in 1845; his last four years produced several poems that rank among his best.

Poe regarded beauty as the sole province of the poem and valued indefinite sensation. Through meter, rhyme, and sonority he created musical effects and believed the beauty of woman inspired the "elevating excitement of the soul" essential to poetry. By a logical extension, "the death of a beautiful woman" represented "the most poetical topic in the world" and many of his most memorable poems grapple with the loss of an idealized female presence. Poems about dying women abounded in the sentimental literature of the day; what sets Poe's work apart (beyond verbal brilliance) is the obsessive intensity and occult strangeness of the poet's attachment to the dead beloved.

Among the early poems included here, "Fairy-Land" epitomizes indefiniteness in its evocation of a nocturnal landscape where "huge moons wax and wane," burying the "strange woods" in "a labyrinth of light." "Alone" offers revealing self-reflection: the speaker acknowledges a strangeness or difference that from childhood has alienated him from the rest of humanity. "Introduction" extends this confessional mode, tracing the beginnings of the "dreaming-book" his poems comprise. Poe tellingly admits that he "fell in love with melancholy" and "could not love except where Death / Was mingling his with Beauty's breath"—that he felt doomed to love only dying women. A similar note of fatality informs "The Sleeper," where the poet broods on the strange "pallor" and "silentness" of his "sleeping" love. It suffuses "To Helen," where his homage to Helen of Troy privately eulogizes the late Mrs. Stanard, the nurturing, cherished confidant of Poe's early adolescence.

But two other early poems deliver notable meditations on the poetic imagination itself. "Sonnet—To Science" asks why systematic knowledge, suggestively portrayed as a "vulture," preys upon "the poet's heart," substituting "dull realities" for romantic illusions. Poe based "Israfel" on a reference in the Koran to an angel possessing "the sweetest voice of all God's creatures." Inhabiting a sphere of "perfect bliss," Israfel derives the "fire" of his "burning measures" from a lute strung by his own "heart-strings," and the poet envisions changing places with the angel so that he might sound a "bolder note" in heaven.

The 1831 *Poems* also reveal a developing fascination with unreal landscapes. "The Valley of Unrest" depicts a "silent dell" depopulated by war and changed from an idyllic place into a restless "sad valley" where trees "palpitate" supernaturally and lilies wave over "a nameless grave." "The City in the Sea" envisions a necropolis surrounded by "melancholy waters," where from a "proud tower . . . Death looks gigantically down." Perhaps alluding to an ancient natural catastrophe, the poet depicts the hellish sinking of the city beneath a reddened wave.

In several short verses composed between 1831 and 1845, Poe elaborated the notion of death as a place. The surreal terrain of an early prose-poem ("Silence—A Fable") anticipates this progression. The later "Sonnet—Silence" succinctly maps dual regions of silence—one corporeal, encountered in "lonely places / Newly with grass o'ergrown" (cemeteries) and the other situated in the "lone regions" of the soul. His poem "The Haunted Palace," ascribed in his famous tale to Roderick Usher, also evokes the symbolic topography of a "happy valley" where a "radiant" palace is irreversibly transformed by "evil things in robes of sorrow." Perhaps Poe's greatest deathscape, "Dream-Land," evokes a "wild weird clime . . . Out of SPACE—out of TIME," unmistakably identified as the realm of death when a traveler meets "shrouded forms" of long-dead friends. This "ultimate dim Thule" cannot be observed by the living or reported by the dead and must remain terra incognita.

During his last years, Poe's preoccupation with Virginia's illness and subsequent death as well as his struggle for survival gave his poems a sharper urgency. "Lenore" signals his return to the death-of-a-beautiful-woman motif and builds on an early poem ("A Paean") as Poe insinuates that the "sweet Lenore" dies unmourned by her plighted husband (Guy de Vere) and despised by his family, while an unnamed speaker "wild" with grief weeps for the "dear child" who should have been *his* bride. Both the title and long poetic lines of the 1844 version of "Lenore" anticipate the extraordinary narrative poem composed later that year, "The Raven." A sustained meditation on memory and forgetting, this much parodied verse stages a fantastic dialogue between a speaker trying to escape his grief in scholarship and a seemingly diabolical bird whose refrain of "Nevermore" leads the writer to pose insidious questions that finally betray his anxieties about a spiritual afterlife and reunion with his dead beloved. Much as the speaker wishes to "forget this lost Lenore," the bird's presence ensures his excruciating remembrance, traced in octosyllabic stanzas with relentless internal rhyming. If "The Raven" rehearses Poe's anticipated loss of

Virginia, the mystical "Ulalume," written three years later, dramatizes his experience after her demise. Using esoteric astronomical imagery, the poem stages a dialogue between the poet and his soul as it represents the speaker's unconscious, compulsive return to Ulalume's tomb on the anniversary of her death.

Something of the despair that menaced Poe can be glimpsed in the short but affecting "A Dream Within a Dream," which concludes with the question, "Is *all* that we see or seem / But a dream within an dream?" The poet's inability to save one grain of sand from time's "pitiless wave" epitomizes the futile transience of mortal life. In its final incarnation "The Bells" dates from the same period and represents a tour de force of sonority, a performance piece that evolved into a four-part poem defining a succession of bells, each representing a season of life. Alliteration, repetition, and rhyme complement the headlong metrical effect that simulates a mounting frenzy approaching derangement. By contrast, the restrained lyric "Eldorado" expresses a philosophy of defiance: The seeker of riches must "boldly ride," according to the "pilgrim shadow" who exhorts an aging, dispirited knight. In Poe's symbolic landscape, Eldorado lies not in California (the poem's implied inspiration) but "Over the Mountains / Of the Moon, / Down the Valley of the Shadow"—implicitly, beyond love and death.

Poe's last poems reflect his grasping for emotional support. "To My Mother" suggests that after his wife's death, Mrs. Clemm became his principal source of affection. Yet his insistence on his love for Virginia must also be read in the context of his feverish quest for a second wife. In addition to the unremarkable verses composed for Sarah Helen Whitman, briefly his fiancée in 1848, he wrote "For Annie" as a token of devotion to Annie Richmond, his young confidante of the same period. Apparently penned after an overdose of laudanum, the poem mirrors his emotional confusion and self-pity, contrasting the hectic "fever called 'Living' " (perhaps his multiple courtships) with the deathlike serenity he achieves in a vision of intimacy with Mrs. Richmond. The much cited "Annabel Lee" may also owe its inspiration to Annie Richmond, or to Virginia's recent death, although there is reason to suspect that Poe was recalling his childhood love, Sarah Elmira Royster Shelton, by then a widow still living in Richmond. The poet's visit there in 1848 fanned the embers of early passion; when he began courting her in 1849, he read the poem in her presence. Its poignant evocation of a fated love that outlasts death itself, compelling the speaker to "lie down" nightly beside the tomb of Annabel Lee, stands as Poe's greatest lyric poem.

THE LAKE—TO ——[1]

In spring of youth it was my lot
To haunt of the wide world a spot
The which I could not love the less—
So lovely was the loneliness
Of a wild lake, with black rock bound,
And the tall pines that towered around.

But when the Night had thrown her pall
Upon that spot, as upon all,
And the mystic wind went by
Murmuring in melody—
Then—ah then I would awake
To the terror of the lone lake.

Yet that terror was not fright,
But a tremulous delight—
A feeling not the jewelled mine
Could teach or bribe me to define—
Nor Love—although the Love were thine.

Death was in that poisonous wave,
And in its gulf a fitting grave
For him who thence could solace bring
To his lone imagining—
Whose solitary soul could make
An Eden of that dim lake.

SONNET—TO SCIENCE

Science! true daughter of Old Time thou art!
    Who alterest all things with thy peering eyes.
Why preyest thou thus upon the poet's heart,
    Vulture, whose wings are dull realities?
How should he love thee? or how deem thee wise,
    Who wouldst not leave him in his wandering
To seek for treasure in the jewelled skies,
    Albeit he soared with an undaunted wing?
Hast thou not dragged Diana[1] from her car?
    And driven the Hamadryad from the wood
To seek a shelter in some happier star?
    Hast thou not torn the Naiad from her flood,
The Elfin from the green grass, and from me
The summer dream beneath the tamarind tree?

FAIRY-LAND

Dim vales—and shadowy floods—
And cloudy-looking woods,
Whose forms we can't discover
For the tears that drip all over.
Huge moons there wax and wane—
Again—again—again—
Every moment of the night—
Forever changing places—
And they put out the star-light
With the breath from their pale faces.
About twelve by the moon-dial
One more filmy than the rest
(A kind which, upon trial,
They have found to be the best)
Comes down—still down—and down
With its centre on the crown
Of a mountain's eminence,
While its wide circumference
In easy drapery falls
Over hamlets, over halls,
Wherever they may be—
O'er the strange woods—o'er the sea—
Over spirits on the wing—
Over every drowsy thing—
And buries them up quite
In a labyrinth of light—
And then, how deep!—O, deep!
Is the passion of their sleep.
In the morning they arise,

And their moony covering
Is soaring in the skies,
With the tempests as they toss,
Like—almost any thing—
Or a yellow Albatross.
They use that moon no more
For the same end as before—
Videlicet[1] a tent—
Which I think extravagant:
Its atomies,[2] however,
Into a shower dissever,
Of which those butterflies,
Of Earth, who seek the skies,
And so come down again
(Never-contented things!)
Have brought a specimen
Upon their quivering wings.

INTRODUCTION[1]

Romance, who loves to nod and sing,
With drowsy head and folded wing,
Among the green leaves as they shake
Far down within some shadowy lake,
To me a painted paroquet
Hath been—a most familiar bird—
Taught me my alphabet to say—
To lisp my very earliest word
While in the wild-wood I did lie
A child—with a most knowing eye.

Succeeding years, too wild for song,
Then roll'd like tropic storms along,
Where, tho' the garish lights that fly
Dying along the troubled sky.
Lay bare, thro' vistas thunder-riven,
The blackness of the general Heaven,
That very blackness yet doth fling
Light on the lightning's silver wing.

For, being an idle boy lang syne,
Who read Anacreon,[2] and drank wine,
I early found Anacreon rhymes
Were almost passionate sometimes—
And by strange alchemy of brain
His pleasures always turn'd to pain—
His naivete to wild desire—
His wit to love—his wine to fire—

And so, being young and dipt in folly
I fell in love with melancholy,
And used to throw my earthly rest
And quiet all away in jest—
I could not love except where Death
Was mingling his with Beauty's breath—
Or Hymen,[3] Time, and Destiny
Were stalking between her and me.

O, then the eternal Condor years
So shook the very Heavens on high,
With tumult as they thunder'd by;
I had no time for idle cares,
Thro' gazing on the unquiet sky!
Or if an hour with calmer wing
Its down did on my spirit fling,
That little hour with lyre and rhyme
To while away—forbidden thing!
My heart half fear'd to be a crime
Unless it trembled with the string.

But *now* my soul hath too much room—
Gone are the glory and the gloom—
The black hath mellow'd into grey,
And all the fires are fading away.

My draught of passion hath been deep—
I revell'd, and I now would sleep—
And after-drunkenness of soul
Succeeds the glories of the bowl—
An idle longing night and day
To dream my very life away.

But dreams—of those who dream as I,
Aspiringly, are damned, and die:
Yet should I swear I mean alone,
By notes so very shrilly blown,
To break upon Time's monotone,

While yet my vapid joy and grief
Are tintless of the yellow leaf—
Why not an imp the greybeard hath,
Will shake his shadow in my path—
And even the greybeard will o'erlook
Connivingly my dreaming-book.

"ALONE" [1]

From childhood's hour I have not been
As others were—I have not seen
As others saw—I could not bring
My passions from a common spring—
From the same source I have not taken
My sorrow—I could not awaken
My heart to joy at the same tone—
And all I lov'd—*I* lov'd alone—
Then—in my childhood—in the dawn
Of a most stormy life—was drawn
From ev'ry depth of good and ill
The mystery which binds me still—
From the torrent, or the fountain—
From the red cliff of the mountain—
From the sun that 'round me roll'd
In its autumn tint of gold—
From the lightning in the sky
As it pass'd me flying by—
From the thunder, and the storm—
And the cloud that took the form
(When the rest of Heaven was blue)
Of a demon in my view—

TO HELEN[1]

Helen, thy beauty is to me
  Like those Nicéan barks of yore,
That gently, o'er a perfumed sea,
  The weary, way-worn wanderer bore
To his own native shore.

On desperate seas long wont to roam,
  Thy hyacinth hair, thy classic face,
Thy Naiad airs have brought me home
  To the glory that was Greece,
And the grandeur that was Rome.

Lo! in yon brilliant window-niche
  How statue-like I see thee stand,
The agate lamp within thy hand!
  Ah, Psyche, from the regions which
  Are Holy-Land!

THE SLEEPER

At midnight, in the month of June,
I stand beneath the mystic moon.
An opiate vapour, dewy, dim,
Exhales from out her golden rim,
And, softly dripping, drop by drop,
Upon the quiet mountain top,
Steals drowsily and musically
Into the universal valley.
The rosemary nods upon the grave;
The lily lolls upon the wave;
Wrapping the fog about its breast,
The ruin moulders into rest;
Looking like Lethë,[1] see! the lake
A conscious slumber seems to take,
And would not, for the world, awake.
All Beauty sleeps!—and lo! where lies
Irenë, with her Destinies!

Oh, lady bright! can it be right—
This window open to the night?
The wanton airs, from the tree-top,
Laughingly through the lattice drop—
The bodiless airs, a wizard rout,
Flit through thy chamber in and out,
And wave the curtain canopy
So fitfully—so fearfully—
Above the closed and fringéd lid
'Neath which thy slumb'ring soul lies hid,
That, o'er the floor and down the wall,

Like ghosts the shadows rise and fall!
Oh, lady dear, hast thou no fear?
Why and what art thou dreaming here?
Sure thou art come o'er far-off seas,
A wonder to these garden trees!
Strange is thy pallor! strange thy dress!
Strange, above all, thy length of tress,
And this all solemn silentness!

The lady sleeps! Oh, may her sleep,
Which is enduring, so be deep!
Heaven have her in its sacred keep!
This chamber changed for one more holy,
This bed for one more melancholy,
I pray to God that she may lie
Forever with unopened eye,
While the pale sheeted ghosts go by!

My love, she sleeps! Oh, may her sleep,
As it is lasting, so be deep!
Soft may the worms about her creep!
Far in the forest, dim and old,
For her may some tall vault unfold—
Some vault that oft hath flung its black
And wingèd pannels fluttering back,
Triumphant, o'er the crested palls,
Of her grand family funerals—
Some sepulchre, remote, alone,
Against whose portal she hath thrown,
In childhood, many an idle stone—
Some tomb from out whose sounding door
She ne'er shall force an echo more,
Thrilling to think, poor child of sin!
It was the dead who groaned within.

ISRAFEL*

In Heaven a spirit doth dwell
　"Whose heart-strings are a lute;"
None sing so wildly well
As the angel Israfel,
And the giddy stars (so legends tell)
Ceasing their hymns, attend the spell
　Of his voice, all mute.

Tottering above
　In her highest noon,
　The enamoured moon
Blushes with love,
　While, to listen, the red levin¹
　(With the rapid Pleiads, even,
　Which were seven,)
　Pauses in Heaven.

And they say (the starry choir
　And the other listening things)
That Israfeli's fire
Is owing to that lyre
　By which he sits and sings—
The trembling living wire
Of those unusual strings.

---

*And the angel Israfel, whose heart-strings are a lute, and who has the sweetest
voice of all God's creatures.—KORAN [Poe's note]

But the skies that angel trod,
  Where deep thoughts are a duty—
Where Love's a grown-up God—
  Where the Houri[2] glances are
Imbued with all the beauty
  Which we worship in a star.

Therefore, thou art not wrong,
  Israfeli, who despisest
An unimpassioned song;
To thee the laurels belong,
  Best bard, because the wisest!
Merrily live, and long!

The ecstasies above
  With thy burning measures suit—
Thy grief, thy joy, thy hate, thy love,
  With the fervour of thy lute—
  Well may the stars be mute!

Yes, Heaven is thine; but this
  Is a world of sweets and sours;
  Our flowers are merely—flowers,
And the shadow of thy perfect bliss
  Is the sunshine of ours.

If I could dwell
Where Israfel
  Hath dwelt, and he where I,
He might not sing so wildly well
  A mortal melody,
While a bolder note than this might swell
  From my lyre within the sky.

THE VALLEY OF UNREST

Once it smiled a silent dell
Where the people did not dwell;
They had gone unto the wars,
Trusting to the mild-eyed stars,
Nightly, from their azure towers,
To keep watch above the flowers,
In the midst of which all day
The red sun-light lazily lay.
Now each visiter shall confess
The sad valley's restlessness.
Nothing there is motionless.
Nothing save the airs that brood
Over the magic solitude.
Ah, by no wind are stirred those trees
That palpitate like the chill seas
Around the misty Hebrides!
Ah, by no wind those clouds are driven
That rustle through the unquiet Heaven
Uneasily, from morn till even,
Over the violets there that lie
In myriad types of the human eye—
Over the lilies there that wave
And weep above a nameless grave!
They wave:—from out their fragrant tops
Eternal dews come down in drops.
They weep:—from off their delicate stems
Perennial tears descend in gems.

THE CITY IN THE SEA [1]

Lo! Death has reared himself a throne
In a strange city lying alone
Far down within the dim West,
Where the good and the bad and the worst and the best
Have gone to their eternal rest.
There shrines and palaces and towers
(Time-eaten towers that tremble not!)
Resemble nothing that is ours.
Around, by lifting winds forgot,
Resignedly beneath the sky
The melancholy waters lie.

No rays from the holy heaven come down
On the long night-time of that town;
But light from out the lurid sea
Streams up the turrets silently—
Gleams up the pinnacles far and free—
Up domes—up spires—up kingly halls—
Up fanes—up Babylon-like walls—
Up shadowy long-forgotten bowers
Of sculptured ivy and stone flowers—
Up many and many a marvellous shrine
Whose wreathed friezes intertwine
The viol, the violet, and the vine.

Resignedly beneath the sky
The melancholy waters lie.
So blend the turrets and shadows there

That all seem pendulous in air,
While from a proud tower in the town
Death looks gigantically down.

There open fanes and gaping graves
Yawn level with the luminous waves;
But not the riches there that lie
In each idol's diamond eye—
Not the gaily-jewelled dead
Tempt the waters from their bed;
For no ripples curl, alas!
Along that wilderness of glass—
No swellings tell that winds may be
Upon some far-off happier sea—
No heavings hint that winds have been
On seas less hideously serene.

But lo, a stir is in the air!
The wave—there is a movement there!
As if the towers had thrust aside,
In slightly sinking, the dull tide—
As if their tops had feebly given
A void within the filmy Heaven.
The waves have now a redder glow—
The hours are breathing faint and low—
And when, amid no earthly moans,
Down, down that town shall settle hence,
Hell, rising from a thousand thrones,
Shall do it reverence.

LENORE

Ah, broken is the golden bowl!—the spirit flown forever!
Let the bell toll!—a saintly soul floats on the Stygian river:—
And, Guy De Vere, hast *thou* no tear?—weep now or never more!
See! on yon drear and rigid bier low lies thy love, Lenore!
Come! let the burial rite be read—the funeral song be sung!—
An anthem for the queenliest dead that ever died so young—
A dirge for her the doubly dead in that she died so young.

"Wretches! ye loved her for her wealth and ye hated her for her
    pride;
And when she fell in feeble health, ye blessed her—that she
    died:—
How *shall* the ritual then be read?—the requiem how be sung
By you—by yours, the evil eye—by yours, the slanderous tongue
That did to death the innocence that died and died so young?"

Peccavimus;[1] yet rave not thus! but let a Sabbath song
Go up to God so solemnly the dead may feel no wrong!
The sweet Lenore hath gone before, with Hope, that flew beside
Leaving thee wild for the dear child that should have been thy
    bride—
For her, the fair and debonair, that now so lowly lies,
The life upon her yellow hair, but not within her eyes—
The life still there upon her hair, the death upon her eyes.

"Avaunt!—avaunt! to friends from fiends the indignant ghost is
    riven—
From Hell unto a high estate within the utmost Heaven—

From moan and groan to a golden throne beside the King of
    Heaven:—
Let *no* bell toll, then, lest her soul, amid its hallowed mirth—
Should catch the note as it doth float up from the damnéd
    Earth!—
And I—tonight my heart is light:—no dirge will I upraise,
But waft the angel on her flight with a Pæan of old days!"

SONNET—SILENCE

There are some qualities—some incorporate things,
  That have a double life, which thus is made
A type of that twin entity which springs
  From matter and light, evinced in solid and shade.
There is a two-fold *Silence*—sea and shore—
  Body and soul. One dwells in lonely places,
  Newly with grass o'ergrown; some solemn graces,
Some human memories and tearful lore,
Render him terrorless: his name's "No More."
He is the corporate Silence: dread him not!
  No power hath he of evil in himself;
But should some urgent fate (untimely lot!)
  Bring thee to meet his shadow (nameless elf,
That haunteth the lone regions where hath trod
No foot of man,) commend thyself to God!

DREAM-LAND

By a route obscure and lonely,
Haunted by ill angels only,
Where an Eidolon,[1] named Night,
On a black throne reigns upright,
I have reached these lands but newly
From an ultimate dim Thule—
From a wild weird clime that lieth, sublime,
   Out of Space—out of Time.

Bottomless vales and boundless floods,
And chasms, and caves, and Titan woods,
With forms that no man can discover
For the dews that drip all over;
Mountains toppling evermore
Into seas without a shore;
Seas that restlessly aspire,
Surging, unto skies of fire;
Lakes that endlessly outspread
Their lone waters—lone and dead,—
Their still waters—still and chilly
With the snows of the lolling lily.

By the lakes that thus outspread
Their lone waters, lone and dead,—
Their sad waters, sad and chilly
With the snows of the lolling lily,—
By the mountains—near the river
Murmuring lowly, murmuring ever,—

By the grey woods,—by the swamp
Where the toad and the newt encamp,—
By the dismal tarns and pools
        Where dwell the Ghouls,—
By each spot the most unholy—
In each nook most melancholy,—
There the traveller meets aghast
Sheeted Memories of the Past—
Shrouded forms that start and sigh
As they pass the wanderer by—
White-robed forms of friends long given,
In agony, to the Earth—and Heaven.

For the heart whose woes are legion
'Tis a peaceful, soothing region—
For the spirit that walks in shadow
'Tis—oh 'tis an Eldorado!
But the traveller, travelling through it,
May not—dare not openly view it;
Never its mysteries are exposed
To the weak human eye unclosed;
So wills its King, who hath forbid
The uplifting of the fringed lid;
And thus the sad Soul that here passes
Beholds it but through darkened glasses.

By a route obscure and lonely,
Haunted by ill angels only,
Where an Eidolon, named NIGHT,
On a black throne reigns upright,
I have wandered home but newly
From this ultimate dim Thule.

THE RAVEN

Once upon a midnight dreary, while I pondered, weak and
   weary,
Over many a quaint and curious volume of forgotten lore—
While I nodded, nearly napping, suddenly there came a tapping,
As of some one gently rapping, rapping at my chamber door.
" 'Tis some visiter," I muttered, "tapping at my chamber door—
            Only this and nothing more."

Ah, distinctly I remember it was in the bleak December,
And each separate dying ember wrought its ghost upon the floor.
Eagerly I wished the morrow;—vainly I had sought to borrow
From my books surcease of sorrow—sorrow for the lost Lenore—
For the rare and radiant maiden whom the angels name Lenore—
            Nameless here for evermore.[1]

And the silken, sad, uncertain rustling of each purple curtain
Thrilled me—filled me with fantastic terrors never felt before;
So that now, to still the beating of my heart, I stood repeating
" 'Tis some visiter entreating entrance at my chamber door—
Some late visiter entreating entrance at my chamber door;—
            This it is and nothing more."

Presently my soul grew stronger; hesitating then no longer,
"Sir," said I, "or Madam, truly your forgiveness I implore;
But the fact is I was napping, and so gently you came rapping,
And so faintly you came tapping, tapping at my chamber door,
That I scarce was sure I heard you"—here I opened wide the
   door;—
            Darkness there and nothing more.

Deep into that darkness peering, long I stood there wondering,
  fearing,
Doubting, dreaming dreams no mortal ever dared to dream
  before;
But the silence was unbroken, and the darkness gave no token,
And the only word there spoken was the whispered word,
  "Lenore!"
This I whispered, and an echo murmured back the word,
  "Lenore!"—
                                  Merely this, and nothing more.

Back into the chamber turning, all my soul within me burning,
Soon I heard again a tapping somewhat louder than before.
"Surely," said I, "surely that is something at my window lattice;
Let me see, then, what thereat is, and this mystery explore—
Let my heart be still a moment and this mystery explore;—
                                  'Tis the wind and nothing more!"

Open here I flung the shutter, when, with many a flirt and flutter,
In there stepped a stately Raven of the saintly days of yore;
Not the least obeisance made he; not a minute stopped or stayed he;
But, with mien of lord or lady, perched above my chamber door—
Perched upon a bust of Pallas² just above my chamber door—
                                  Perched, and sat, and nothing more.

Then this ebony bird beguiling my sad fancy into smiling,
By the grave and stern decorum of the countenance it wore,
"Though thy crest be shorn and shaven, thou," I said, "art sure
  no craven,
Ghastly grim and ancient raven wandering from the Nightly shore—
Tell me what thy lordly name is on the Night's Plutonian shore!"
                                  Quoth the Raven "Nevermore."

Much I marvelled this ungainly fowl to hear discourse so plainly,
Though its answer little meaning—little relevancy bore;
For we cannot help agreeing that no living human being
Ever yet was blessed with seeing bird above his chamber door—
Bird or beast upon the sculptured bust above his chamber door,
                                  With such name as "Nevermore."

But the Raven, sitting lonely on the placid bust, spoke only
That one word, as if his soul in that one word he did outpour.
Nothing farther then he uttered—not a feather then he fluttered—
Till I scarcely more than muttered "Other friends have flown
    before—
On the morrow *he* will leave me, as my Hopes have flown before."
                     Then the bird said "Nevermore."

Startled at the stillness broken by reply so aptly spoken,
"Doubtless," said I, "what it utters is its only stock and store
Caught from some unhappy master whom unmerciful Disaster
Followed fast and followed faster till his songs one burden bore—
Till the dirges of his Hope that melancholy burden bore
                     Of 'Never—nevermore.' "

But the raven still beguiling my sad fancy into smiling,
Straight I wheeled a cushioned seat in front of bird, and bust and
    door;
Then, upon the velvet sinking, I betook myself to linking
Fancy unto fancy, thinking what this ominous bird of yore—
What this grim, ungainly, ghastly, gaunt and ominous bird of yore
                     Meant in croaking "Nevermore."

This I sat engaged in guessing, but no syllable expressing
To the fowl whose fiery eyes now burned into my bosom's core;
This and more I sat divining, with my head at ease reclining
On the cushion's velvet lining that the lamplight gloated o'er,
But whose velvet-violet lining with the lamp-light gloating o'er,
                     She shall press, ah, nevermore!

Then, methought, the air grew denser, perfumed from an unseen
    censer
Swung by seraphim whose faint foot-falls tinkled on the tufted
    floor.
"Wretch," I cried, "thy God hath lent thee—by these angels he
    hath sent thee
Respite—respite and nepenthe[3] from thy memories of Lenore;
Quaff, oh quaff this kind nepenthe and forget this lost Lenore!"
                     Quoth the Raven "Nevermore."

"Prophet!" said I, "thing of evil!—prophet still, if bird or devil!—
Whether Tempter sent, or whether tempest tossed thee here ashore,
Desolate yet all undaunted, on this desert land enchanted—
On this home by Horror haunted—tell me truly, I implore—
Is there—*is* there balm in Gilead?—tell me—tell me, I implore!"
                                        Quoth the Raven "Nevermore."

"Prophet!" said I, "thing of evil!—prophet still, if bird or devil!
By that Heaven that bends above us—by that God we both
    adore—
Tell this soul with sorrow laden if, within the distant Aidenn,[4]
It shall clasp a sainted maiden whom the angels name Lenore—
Clasp a rare and radiant maiden whom the angels name
    Lenore."
                                        Quoth the Raven "Nevermore."

"Be that word our sign of parting, bird or fiend!" I shrieked,
    upstarting—
"Get thee back into the tempest and the Night's Plutonian shore!
Leave no black plume as a token of that lie thy soul hath spoken!
Leave my loneliness unbroken!—quit the bust above my door!
Take thy beak from out my heart, and take thy form from off my
    door!"
                                        Quoth the Raven "Nevermore."

And the Raven, never flitting, still is sitting, *still* is sitting
On the pallid bust of Pallas just above my chamber door;
And his eyes have all the seeming of a demon's that is dreaming,
And the lamp-light o'er him streaming throws his shadow on the
    floor;
And my soul from out that shadow that lies floating on the floor
                                        Shall be lifted—nevermore!

ULALUME—A BALLAD[1]

The skies they were ashen and sober;
    The leaves they were crispéd and sere—
    The leaves they were withering and sere;
It was night in the lonesome October
    Of my most immemorial year:
It was hard by the dim lake of Auber,
    In the misty mid region of Weir:—
It was down by the dank tarn of Auber,
    In the ghoul-haunted woodland of Weir.

Here once, through an alley Titanic,
    Of cypress, I roamed with my Soul—
    Of cypress, with Psyche, my Soul.
There were days when my heart was volcanic
    As the scoriac rivers that roll—
    As the lavas that restlessly roll
Their sulphurous currents down Yaanek,
    In the ultimate climes of the Pole—
That groan as they roll down Mount Yaanek
    In the realms of the Boreal Pole.[2]

Our talk had been serious and sober,
    But our thoughts they were palsied and sere—
    Our memories were treacherous and sere;
For we knew not the month was October,
    And we marked not the night of the year—
    (Ah, night of all nights in the year!)[3]
We noted not the dim lake of Auber,
    (Though once we had journeyed down here)

We remembered not the dank tarn of Auber,
    Nor the ghoul-haunted woodland of Weir.

And now, as the night was senescent,
    And star-dials pointed to morn—
    As the star-dials hinted of morn—
At the end of our path a liquescent
    And nebulous lustre was born,
Out of which a miraculous crescent
    Arose with a duplicate horn—
Astarte's bediamonded crescent,
    Distinct with its duplicate horn.[4]

And I said—"She is warmer than Dian;
    She rolls through an ether of sighs—
    She revels in a region of sighs.
She has seen that the tears are not dry on
    These cheeks where the worm never dies,
And has come past the stars of the Lion,[5]
    To point us the path to the skies—
    To the Lethean peace of the skies—
Come up, in despite of the Lion,
    To shine on us with her bright eyes—
Come up, through the lair of the Lion,
    With love in her luminous eyes."

But Psyche, uplifting her finger,
    Said—"Sadly this star I mistrust—
    Her pallor I strangely mistrust—
Ah, hasten!—ah, let us not linger!
    Ah, fly!—let us fly!—for we must."
In terror she spoke; letting sink her
    Wings till they trailed in the dust—
In agony sobbed; letting sink her
    Plumes till they trailed in the dust—
    Till they sorrowfully trailed in the dust.

I replied—"This is nothing but dreaming.
    Let us on, by this tremulous light!

Let us bathe in this crystalline light!
Its Sybillic splendor is beaming
    With Hope and in Beauty to-night—
    See!—it flickers up the sky through the night!
Ah, we safely may trust to its gleaming,
    And be sure it will lead us aright—
We safely may trust to a gleaming
    That cannot but guide us aright,
    Since it flickers up to Heaven through the night."

Thus I pacified Psyche and kissed her,
    And tempted her out of her gloom—
    And conquered her scruples and gloom;
And we passed to the end of the vista—
    But were stopped by the door of a tomb—
    By the door of a legended tomb:—
And I said—"What is written, sweet sister,
    On the door of this legended tomb?"
    She replied—"Ulalume—Ulalume!—
    'T is the vault of thy lost Ulalume!"

Then my heart it grew ashen and sober
    As the leaves that were crispéd and sere—
    As the leaves that were withering and sere—
And I cried—"It was surely October
    On *this* very night of last year,
    That I journeyed—I journeyed down here!—
    That I brought a dread burden down here—
    On this night, of all nights in the year,
    Ah, what demon hath tempted me here?
Well I know, now, this dim lake of Auber—
    This misty mid region of Weir:—
Well I know, now, this dank tarn of Auber—
    This ghoul-haunted woodland of Weir."

Said we, then—the two, then—"Ah, can it
    Have been that the woodlandish ghouls—
    The pitiful, the merciful ghouls,
To bar up our way and to ban it

From the secret that lies in these wolds—
From the thing that lies hidden in these wolds—
Have drawn up the spectre of a planet
From the limbo of lunary souls—
This sinfully scintillant planet
From the Hell of planetary souls?"

THE BELLS

1.

Hear the sledges with the bells—
Silver bells!
What a world of merriment their melody foretells!
How they tinkle, tinkle, tinkle,
In the icy air of night!
While the stars that oversprinkle
All the Heavens, seem to twinkle
With a crystalline delight;
Keeping time, time, time,
In a sort of Runic rhyme,[1]
To the tintinnabulation that so musically wells
From the bells, bells, bells, bells,
Bells, bells, bells—
From the jingling and the tinkling of the bells.

2.

Hear the mellow wedding bells—
Golden bells!
What a world of happiness their harmony foretells!
Through the balmy air of night
How they ring out their delight!
From the molten-golden notes,
And all in tune,
What a liquid ditty floats
To the turtle-dove that listens, while she gloats
On the moon!
Oh, from out the sounding cells
What a gush of euphony voluminously wells!

How it swells!
How it dwells
On the Future! how it tells
Of the rapture that impels
To the swinging and the ringing
Of the bells, bells, bells,
Of the bells, bells, bells, bells,
Bells, bells, bells—
To the rhyming and the chiming of the bells!

3.

Hear the loud alarum bells—
Brazen bells!
What tale of terror, now, their turbulency tells!
In the startled ear of Night
How they scream out their affright!
Too much horrified to speak,
They can only shriek, shriek,
Out of tune,
In a clamorous appealing to the mercy of the fire—
In a mad expostulation with the deaf and frantic fire,
Leaping higher, higher, higher,
With a desperate desire,
And a resolute endeavor
Now—now to sit or never,
By the side of the pale-faced moon.
Oh, the bells, bells, bells!
What a tale their terror tells
Of despair!
How they clang and clash and roar!
What a horror they outpour
In the bosom of the palpitating air!
Yet the ear, it fully knows,
By the twanging,
And the clanging,
How the danger ebbs and flows;
Yet, the ear distinctly tells,
In the jangling,
And the wrangling,

How the danger sinks and swells,
By the sinking or the swelling in the anger of the bells—
Of the bells—
Of the bells, bells, bells, bells,
Bells, bells, bells—
In the clamor and the clangor of the bells!

4.

Hear the tolling of the bells—
Iron bells!
What a world of solemn thought their monody compels!
In the silence of the night,
How we shiver with affright
At the melancholy meaning of their tone!
For every sound that floats
From the rust within their throats
Is a groan.
And the people—ah, the people—
They that dwell up in the steeple,
All alone,
And who, tolling, tolling, tolling,
In that muffled monotone,
Feel a glory in so rolling
On the human heart a stone—
They are neither man nor woman—
They are neither brute nor human—
They are Ghouls:—
And their king it is who tolls;
And he rolls, rolls, rolls, rolls,
A Pæan from the bells!
And his merry bosom swells
With the Pæan of the bells!
And he dances, and he yells;
Keeping time, time, time,
In a sort of Runic rhyme,
To the Pæan of the bells—
Of the bells:
Keeping time, time, time,
In a sort of Runic rhyme,

To the throbbing of the bells—
Of the bells, bells, bells—
To the sobbing of the bells;
Keeping time, time, time,
As he knells, knells, knells,
In a happy Runic rhyme,
To the rolling of the bells—
Of the bells, bells, bells:—
To the tolling of the bells—
Of the bells, bells, bells, bells,
Bells, bells, bells—
To the moaning and the groaning of the bells.

A DREAM WITHIN A DREAM

Take this kiss upon the brow!
And, in parting from you now,
Thus much let me avow—
You are not wrong, who deem
That my days have been a dream;
Yet if hope has flown away
In a night, or in a day,
In a vision, or in none,
Is it therefore the less *gone*?
All that we see or seem
Is but a dream within a dream.

I stand amid the roar
Of a surf-tormented shore,
And I hold within my hand
Grains of the golden sand—
How few! yet how they creep
Through my fingers to the deep,
While I weep—while I weep!
O God! can I not grasp
Them with a tighter clasp?
O God! can I not save
One from the pitiless wave?
Is *all* that we see or seem
But a dream within a dream?

FOR ANNIE[1]

Thank Heaven! the crisis—
    The danger is past,
And the lingering illness
    Is over at last—
And the fever called "Living"
    Is conquered at last.

Sadly, I know
    I am shorn of my strength,
And no muscle I move
    As I lie at full length—
But no matter!—I feel
    I am better at length.

And I rest so composedly,
    Now, in my bed,
That any beholder
    Might fancy me dead—
Might start at beholding me,
    Thinking me dead.

The moaning and groaning,
    The sighing and sobbing,
Are quieted now,
    With that horrible throbbing
At heart:—ah, that horrible,
    Horrible throbbing!

The sickness—the nausea—
   The pitiless pain—
Have ceased, with the fever
   That maddened my brain—
With the fever called "Living"
   That burned in my brain.

And oh! of all tortures
   That torture the worst
Has abated—the terrible
   Torture of thirst
For the naphthaline river[2]
   Of Passion accurst:—
I have drank of a water
   That quenches all thirst:—

Of a water that flows,
   With a lullaby sound,
From a spring but a very few
   Feet under ground—
From a cavern not very far
   Down under ground.

And ah! let it never
   Be foolishly said
That my room it is gloomy
   And narrow my bed;
For man never slept
   In a different bed—
And, to *sleep*, you must slumber
   In just such a bed.

My tantalized spirit
   Here blandly reposes,
Forgetting, or never
   Regretting its roses—
Its old agitations
   Of myrtles and roses:

For now, while so quietly
   Lying, it fancies
A holier odor
   About it, of pansies—
A rosemary odor,
   Commingled with pansies—
With rue and the beautiful
   Puritan pansies.[3]

And so it lies happily,
   Bathing in many
A dream of the truth
   And the beauty of Annie—
Drowned in a bath
   Of the tresses of Annie.

She tenderly kissed me,
   She fondly caressed,
And then I fell gently
   To sleep on her breast—
Deeply to sleep
   From the heaven of her breast.

When the light was extinguished,
   She covered me warm,
And she prayed to the angels
   To keep me from harm—
To the queen of the angels
   To shield me from harm.

And I lie so composedly,
   Now, in my bed,
(Knowing her love)
   That you fancy me dead—
And I rest so contentedly,
   Now in my bed,
(With her love at my breast)

That you fancy me dead—
That you shudder to look at me,
　　Thinking me dead:—

But my heart it is brighter
　　Than all of the many
Stars in the sky,
　　For it sparkles with Annie—
It glows with the light
　　Of the love of my Annie—
With the thought of the light
　　Of the eyes of my Annie.

ELDORADO[1]

Gaily bedight,
A gallant knight,
In sunshine and in shadow,
Had journeyed long,
Singing a song,
In search of Eldorado.

But he grew old—
This knight so bold—
And o'er his heart a shadow
Fell, as he found
No spot of ground
That looked like Eldorado.

And, as his strength
Failed him at length,
He met a pilgrim shadow—
"Shadow," said he,
"Where can it be—
This land of Eldorado?"

"Over the Mountains
Of the Moon,
Down the Valley of the Shadow,
Ride, boldly ride,"
The shade replied,—
"If you seek for Eldorado!"

TO MY MOTHER

Because the angels in the Heavens above,
    Devoutly singing unto one another,
Can find, among their burning terms of love,
    None so devotional as that of "mother,"
Therefore by that sweet name I long have called you—
    You who are more than mother unto me,
Filling my heart of hearts, where God installed you
    In setting my Virginia's spirit free.
My mother—my own mother, who died early,
    Was but the mother of myself; but you
Are mother to the dead I loved so dearly,
    And thus more precious than the one I knew
By that infinity with which my wife
    Was dearer to my soul than its soul-life.

ANNABEL LEE

It was many and many a year ago,
    In a kingdom by the sea,
That a maiden lived whom you may know
    By the name of Annabel Lee;—
And this maiden she lived with no other thought
    Than to love and be loved by me.

She was a child and *I* was a child,
    In this kingdom by the sea,
But we loved with a love that was more than love—
    I and my Annabel Lee—
With a love that the wingéd seraphs of Heaven
    Coveted her and me.

And this was the reason that, long ago,
    In this kingdom by the sea,
A wind blew out of a cloud by night
    Chilling my Annabel Lee;
So that her high-born kinsmen came
    And bore her away from me,
To shut her up, in a sepulchre
    In this kingdom by the sea.

The angels, not half so happy in Heaven,
    Went envying her and me:—
Yes! that was the reason (as all men know,
    In this kingdom by the sea)
That the wind came out of the cloud, chilling
    And killing my Annabel Lee.

But our love it was stronger by far than the love
    Of those who were older than we—
    Of many far wiser than we—
And neither the angels in Heaven above
    Nor the demons down under the sea
Can ever dissever my soul from the soul
    Of the beautiful Annabel Lee:—

For the moon never beams without bringing me dreams
    Of the beautiful Annabel Lee;
And the stars never rise but I see the bright eyes
    Of the beautiful Annabel Lee;
And so, all the night-tide, I lie down by the side
Of my darling, my darling, my life and my bride
    In her sepulchre there by the sea—
    In her tomb by the side of the sea.

LETTERS

LETTERS

From more than eight hundred extant letters by Poe, the following selection hints at the complications of his private life and the quirks of his personality. By turns audacious and desperate, hapless and scheming, penitent and indignant, dutiful and dissolute, Poe emerges from these missives as a writer driven to dominate the "republic of letters" in America by sheer force of genius—but also as a man sporadically beset by an urge to ruin his own prospects. From his early, defiant letters to John Allan to his late communications with the women he loved, Poe reveals his impetuous need to control his own destiny—as well as his pathetic inability to do so.

I have edited the letters to produce fully readable versions of correspondence that is sometimes illegible, incomplete, or mutilated. Missing letters and words have been supplied, following the textual reconstructions of John Ward Ostrom. Some interpolated material is bracketed. I have silently corrected misspelled words that invite misreading and have allowed others to stand to reflect Poe's compositional habits. In his private letters, the author was far less concerned about punctuation, grammar, and usage than in his published writings.

EDGAR ALLAN POE TO
JOHN ALLAN

Richmond   Monday   [March 19, 1827]

Sir,

After my treatment on yesterday and what passed between us this
morning, I can hardly think you will be surprised at the contents
of this letter. My determination is at length taken—to leave your
house and indeavor to find some place in this wide world, where I
will be treated—not as you have treated me—This is not a hurried
determination, but one on which I have long considered—and
having so considered my resolution is unalterable—You may per-
haps think that I have flown off in a passion, & that I am already
wishing to return; But not so—I will give you the reasons which
have actuated me, and then judge—

Since I have been able to think on any subject, my thoughts have
aspired, and they have been taught by *you* to aspire, to eminence
in public life—this cannot be attained without a good Education,
such a one I cannot obtain at a Primary school—A collegiate Edu-
cation therefore was what I most ardently desired, and I had been
led to expect that it would at some future time be granted—but in
a moment of caprice—you have blasted my hope because forsooth
I disagreed with you in an opinion, which opinion I was forced to
express—Again, I have heard you say (when you little thought I
was listening and therefore must have said it in earnest) that you
had no affection for me—

You have moreover ordered me to quit your house, and are con-
tinually upbraiding me with eating the bread of Idleness, when
you yourself were the only person to remedy the evil by placing me
to some business—You take delight in exposing me before those
whom you think likely to advance my interest in this world—

You suffer me to be subjected to the whims & caprice, not only of
your white family, but the complete authority of the blacks—these

448 LETTERS

grievances I could not submit to; and I am gone. I request that you will send me my trunk containing my clothes & books—and if you still have the least affection for me, As the last call I shall make on your bounty, To prevent the fulfillment of the Prediction you this morning expressed, send me as much money as will defray the expences of my passage to some of the Northern cities & then support me for one month, by which time I shall be enabled to place myself in some situation where I may not only obtain a livelihood, but lay by a sum which one day or another will support me at the University—Send my trunk &c to the Court-house Tavern, send me I entreat you some money immediately—as I am in the greatest necessity—If you fail to comply with my request—I tremble for the consequence

Yours &c
EDGAR A POE

It depends upon yourself if hereafter you see or hear from me.

This letter marks Poe's break with John Allan and follows his forced withdrawal from the University of Virginia. Poe announces his decision to leave home, although the letter makes clear that he has already been evicted.

EDGAR ALLAN POE
TO JOHN ALLAN

Fortress Monroe (Va)   *December 22d 1828—*

Dear Sir;

I wrote you shortly before leaving Fort Moultrie & am much hurt
at receiving no answer. Perhaps my letter has not reached you &
under that supposition I will recapitulate its contents. It was
chiefly to sollicit your interest in freeing me from the Army of the
U.S. in which, (as Mr Lay's letter from Lieut Howard informed
you)—I am at present a soldier. I begged that you would suspend
any judgement you might be inclined to form, upon many unto-
ward circumstances, until you heard *of* me again—& begged you
to give my dearest love to Ma & solicit her not to let my wayward
disposition wear away the affection she used to have for me. I
mentioned that all that was necessary to obtain my discharge from
the army was your consent in a letter to Lieut J. Howard, who has
heard of you by report, & the high character given you by Mr
Lay; this being all that I asked at your hands, I was hurt at your
declining to answer my letter. Since arriving at Fort Moultrie Lieut
Howard has given me an introduction to Col: James House of the
1rst Arty [Artillery] to whom I was before personally known only
as a soldier of his regiment. He spoke kindly to me. told me that
he was personally acquainted with my Grandfather Genl Poe, with
yourself & family, & reassured me of my immediate discharge
upon your consent. It must have been a matter of regret to me,
that when those who were strangers took such deep interest in my
welfare, you who called me your son should refuse me even the
common civility of answering a letter. If it is your wish to forget
that I have been your son I am too proud to remind you of it
again—I only beg you to remember that you yourself cherished the
cause of my leaving your family—Ambition. If it has not taken
the channel you wished it, it is not the less certain of its object.

Richmond & the U. States were too narrow a sphere & the world shall be my theatre—

As I observed in the letter which you have not received—(you would have answered it if you had) you believe me degraded—but do not believe it—There is that within my heart which has no connection with degradation—I can walk among infection & be uncontaminated. There never was any period of my life when my bosom swelled with a deeper satisfaction, of myself & (except in the injury which I may have done to your feelings)—of my conduct—My father do not throw me aside as *degraded*. I will be an honor to your name.

Give my best love to my Ma & to all friends—

If you determine to abandon me—here take I my farewell— Neglected—I will be doubly ambitious, & the world shall hear of the son whom you have thought unworthy of your notice. But if you let the love you bear me, outweigh the offence which I have given—then write me my father, quickly. My desire is for the present to be freed from the Army—Since I have been in it my character is one that will bear scrutiny & has merited the esteem of my officers—but I have accomplished my own ends—& I wish to be gone—Write to Lieut Howard—& to Col: House, desiring my discharge—& above all to myself. Lieut Howard's direction is Lieut J. Howard, For^{ss} Monroe, Col: House's Col: Jas. House—F^{ss} Monroe—my own the same—

My dearest love to Ma & all my friends

I am Your affectionate son
EDGAR A POE

Two months before the death of his foster mother, Poe writes from Fortress Monroe to ask Allan's help in obtaining a discharge from the Army but (anticipating refusal) also announces a defiant plan to achieve global fame. Poe's ambivalent tone mirrors his conflicted feelings for Allan.

EDGAR ALLAN POE
TO JOHN ALLAN

West Point   Jany 3^d 1830. [1831]

Sir,

I suppose (altho' you desire no further communication with your-self on my part,) that your restriction does not extend to my an-swering your final letter.

Did I, when an infant, sollicit your charity and protection, or was it of your own free will, that you volunteered your services in my behalf? It is well known to respectable individuals in Balti-more, and elsewhere, that my Grandfather (my natural protector at the time you interposed) was wealthy, and that I was his fa-vorite grandchild—But the promises of adoption, and liberal edu-cation which you held forth to him in a letter which is now in possession of my family, induced him to resign all care of me into your hands. Under such circumstances, can it be said that I have no *right* to expect any thing at your hands? You may probably urge that you have given me a liberal education. I will leave the de-cision of that question to those who know how far liberal educa-tions can be obtained in 8 months at the University of Va. Here you will say that it was my own fault that I did not return—You would not let me return because bills were presented you for pay-ment which I never wished nor desired you to pay. Had you let me return, my reformation had been sure—as my conduct the last 3 months gave every reason to believe—and you would never have heard more of my extravagances. But I am not about to proclaim myself guilty of all that has been alledged against me, and which I have hitherto endured, simply because I was too proud to reply. I will boldly say that it was wholly and entirely your own mistaken parsimony that caused all the difficulties in which I was involved while at Charlottesville. The expences of the institution at the lowest estimate were $350 per annum. You sent me there with

$110. Of this $50 were to be paid immediately for board—$60 for attendance upon 2 professors—and you even then did not miss the opportunity of abusing me because I did not attend 3. Then $15 more were to be paid for room-rent—remember that all this was to be paid *in advance*, with $110.—$12 more for a bed—and $12 more for room furniture. I had, of course, the mortification of running in debt for public property—against the known rules of the institution, and was immediately regarded in the light of a beggar. You will remember that in a week after my arrival, I wrote to you for some more money, and for books—You replied in terms of the utmost abuse—if I had been the vilest wretch on earth you could not have been more abusive than you were because I could not contrive to pay $150 with $110. I had enclosed to you in my letter (according to your express commands) an account of the expences incurred amounting to $149—the balance to be paid was $39—You enclosed me $40, leaving me one dollar in pocket. In a short time afterwards I received a packet of books consisting of, Gil Blas, and the Cambridge Mathematics in 2 vols: books for which I had no earthly use since I had no means of attending the mathematical lectures. But books must be had, If I intended to remain at the institution—and they were bought accordingly *upon credit*. In this manner debts were accumulated, and money borrowed of Jews in Charlottesville at extravagant interest—for I was obliged to hire a servant, to pay for wood, for washing, and a thousand other necessaries. It was then that I became dissolute, for how could it be otherwise? I could associate with no students, except those who were in a similar situation with myself—altho' from different causes—They from drunkenness, and extravagance—I, because it was my crime to have no one on Earth who cared for me, or loved me. I call God to witness that I have never loved dissipation—Those who know me know that my pursuits and habits are very far from any thing of the kind. But I was drawn into it by my companions. Even their professions of friendship—hollow as they were—were a relief. Towards the close of the session you sent me $100—but it was too late—to be of any service in extricating me from my difficulties—I kept it for some time—thinking that if I could obtain more I could yet retrieve my character—I applied to James Galt—but he, I believe, from the best of motives refused to lend me any—I then became desperate, and gambled—until I finally involved myself irretrievably. If I have been to blame in all this—place yourself in my situation, and tell me if you would not have been equally so. But these circumstances were all unknown to my friends when I returned home—They knew that I had been extravagant—but that was all—I had no hope of returning to Charlottesville, and I waited in vain in expectation that you would, at least, obtain me some employment. I saw no prospect of this—and I could endure it no longer.—Every day threatened with a warrant &c. I left home—and after nearly 2 years conduct with which no fault could be found—in the army, as a common soldier—I *earned*, myself, by the most humiliating privations—a Cadets' warrant which you could have obtained at any time for asking. It was then that I thought I might venture to sollicit your assistance in giving me an outfit—I came home, you will remember, the night after the burial—If she had not have died while I was away there would have been nothing for me to regret—*Your* love I never valued—but she I believed loved me as her own child. You promised me to forgive all—but you soon forgot your promise. You sent me to W. Point like a beggar. The same difficulties are threatening me as before at Charlottesville—and I must resign.

As to your injunction not to trouble you with farther communication rest assured, Sir, that I will most religiously observe it. When I parted from you—at the steam-boat, I knew that I should never see you again.

As regards Sergt. Graves—I *did* write him that letter. As to the truth of its contents, I leave it to God, and your own conscience.— The time in which I wrote it was within a half hour after you had embittered every feeling of my heart against you by your abuse of my *family*, and myself, under your own roof—and at a time when you knew that my heart was almost breaking.

I have no more to say—except that my future life (which thank God will not endure long) must be passed in indigence and sickness. I have no energy left, nor health, If it was possible, to put up with the fatigues of this place, and the inconveniences which my absolute want of necessaries subject me to, and as I mentioned before it is my intention to resign. For this end it will be necessary that you (as my nominal guardian) enclose me your written permission. It will be useless to refuse me this last request—for I can leave the place without any permission—your refusal would only deprive me of the little pay which is now due as mileage.

From the time of writing this I shall neglect my studies and duties at the institution—if I do not receive your answer in 10 days— I will leave the point without—for otherwise I should subject myself to dismission.

                                                        E A POE

Hurt by Allan's failure to contact him during his recent visit to New York City (for the purpose of remarriage), Poe blames both his predicament at West Point and his debacle at the University of Virginia on Allan's parsimony while simultaneously begging permission to resign from the academy and threatening to neglect his military duties. Sgt. Graves was Poe's hired substitute in the U.S. Army; explaining the delay in paying Graves, Poe had remarked in a letter that Allan was "not very often sober."

EDGAR ALLAN POE
TO JOHN ALLAN

Baltimore   April 12ᵗʰ 1833

It has now been more than two years since you have assisted me, and more than three since you have spoken to me. I feel little hope that you will pay any regard to this letter, but still I cannot refrain from making one more attempt to interest you in my behalf. If you will only consider in what a situation I am placed you will surely pity me—without friends, without any means, consequently of obtaining employment, I am perishing—absolutely perishing for want of aid. And yet I am not idle—nor addicted to any vice—nor have I committed any offence against society which would render me deserving of so hard a fate. For God's sake pity me, and save me from destruction.

E A Poe

Two years after his court martial and discharge from West Point, now living in abject poverty and ill health with relatives in Baltimore, Poe here appeals forlornly to Allan (who would die eleven months later) for a handout.

EDGAR ALLAN POE TO THOMAS W. WHITE

[April 30, 1835]

I noticed the allusion in the Doom. The writer seems to compare my swim with that of Lord Byron, whereas there can be no comparison between them. Any swimmer "in the falls" in my days, would have swum the Hellespont, and thought nothing of the matter. I swam from Ludlam's wharf to Warwick, (six miles,) in a hot June sun, against one of the strongest tides ever known in the river. It would have been a feat comparatively easy to swim twenty miles in still water. I would not think much of attempting to swim the British Channel from Dover to Calais [. . .] to what you said concerning [MS. torn, missing text]

A word or two in relation to Berenice. Your opinion of it is very just. The subject is by far too horrible, and I confess that I hesitated in sending it you especially as a specimen of my capabilities. The Tale originated in a bet that I could produce nothing effective on a subject so singular, provided I treated it seriously. But what I wish to say relates to the character of your Magazine more than to any articles I may offer, and I beg you to believe that I have no intention of giving you *advice*, being fully confident that, upon consideration, you will agree with me. The history of all Magazines shows plainly that those which have attained celebrity were indebted for it to articles *similar in nature—to Berenice*—although, I grant you, far superior in style and execution. I say similar in *nature*. You ask me in what does this nature consist? In the ludicrous heightened into the grotesque: the fearful coloured into the horrible: the witty exaggerated into the burlesque: the singular wrought out into the strange and mystical. You may say all this is bad taste. I have my doubts about it. Nobody is more aware than I am that simplicity is the cant of the day—but take my word for it no one cares any thing about simplicity in their hearts. Believe me also, in spite of what people say to the contrary, that there is nothing easier in the world than to be extremely simple. But whether the articles of which I speak are, or are not in bad taste is little to the purpose. To be appreciated you must be *read*, and these things are invariably sought after with avidity. They are, if you will take notice, the articles which find their way into other periodicals, and into the papers, and in this manner, taking hold upon the public mind they augment the reputation of the source where they originated. Such articles are the "M.S. found in a Madhouse" and the "Monos and Daimonos" of the London New Monthly—the "Confessions of an Opium-Eater" and the "Man in the Bell" of Blackwood. The two first were written by no less a man than Bulwer—the *Confessions* [illegible] universally attributed to Coleridge—although unjustly. Thus the first men in [England] have not thought writings of this nature unworthy of their talents, and I have good reason to believe that some very high names valued themselves *principally* upon this species of literature. To be sure originality is an essential in these things—great attention must be paid to style, and much labour spent in their composition, or they will degenerate into the turgid or the absurd. If I am not mistaken you will find Mr Kennedy, whose writings you admire, and whose Swallow-Barn is unrivalled for purity of style and thought of my opinion in this matter. It is unnecessary for you to pay much attention to the many who will no doubt favour you with their critiques. In respect to Berenice individually I allow that it approaches the very verge of bad taste—but I will not sin quite so egregiously again. I propose to furnish you every month with a Tale of the nature which I have alluded to. The effect—if any—will be estimated better by the circulation of the Magazine than by any comments upon its contents. This much, however, it is necessary to premise, that no two of these Tales will have the slightest resemblance one to the other either in matter or manner—still however preserving the character which I speak of.

Mrs Butler's book will be out on the 1^rst. A life of Cicero is in press by Jno Stricker of this city—also a life of Franklin by Jared Sparks, Boston.—also Willis' Poems, and a novel by Dr Bird.

Yours sincerely
EDGAR A POE

The letter was torn, perhaps by White, who printed a portion of it (the first paragraph here—through "Calais") in the *Southern Literary Messenger*. Poe notes a recent story, not of his composition, that alludes to his famous swimming exploit. More significantly, in the unpublished body of the letter he defends his tale, "Berenice," from White's imputation of "bad taste" and articulates bold goals as a writer of magazine fiction.

EDGAR ALLAN POE TO MARIA AND VIRGINIA CLEMM

[Richmond]   Aug: 29th [1835]

My dearest Aunty,

I am blinded with tears while writing this letter—I have no wish to live another hour. Amid sorrow, and the deepest anxiety your letter reached—and you well know how little I am able to bear up under the pressure of grief. My bitterest enemy would pity me could he now read my heart. My last my last my only hold on life is cruelly torn away—I have no desire to live and *will not*. But let my duty be done. I love, *you know* I love Virginia passionately devotedly. I cannot express in words the fervent devotion I feel towards my dear little cousin—my own darling. But what can I say? Oh think for me for I am incapable of thinking. All of my thoughts are occupied with the supposition that both you & she will prefer to go with N. Poe. I do sincerely believe that your *comforts* will for the present be secured—I cannot speak as regards your peace—your happiness. You have both tender hearts—and you will always have the reflection that my agony is more than I can bear—that you have driven me to the grave—for love like mine can never be gotten over. It is useless to disguise the truth that when Virginia goes with N.P. that I shall never behold her again—that is absolutely sure. Pity me, my dear Aunty, pity me. I have no one now to fly to. I am among strangers, and my wretchedness is more than I can bear. It is useless to expect advice from me—what can I say? Can I, in honour & in truth say—Virginia! do not go!—do not go where you can be comfortable & perhaps happy—and on the other hand can I calmly resign my—life itself. If she had truly loved me would she not have rejected the offer with scorn? Oh God have mercy on me! If she goes with N.P. what are you to do, my own Aunty?

I had procured a sweet little house in a retired situation on Church Hill—newly done up and with a large garden and every convenience—at only $5 per month. I have been dreaming every day & night since of the rapture I should feel in having my only friends—all I love on Earth with me there, and the pride I would take in making you both comfortable & in calling her my wife. But the dream is over. Oh God have mercy on me. What have I *to live for*? Among strangers with *not one soul to love me*.

The situation has this morning been conferred upon another. Branch T. Saunders. but White has engaged to make my salary $60 a month, and we could live in comparative comfort & happiness—even the $4 a week I am now paying for board would support us all—but I shall have $15 a week & what need would we have of more? I had thought to send you on a little money every week until you could either hear from Hall or W^m. Poe, and then we could get a little furniture for a start for White will not be able to advance any. After that all would go well—or I would make a desperate exertion & try to borrow enough for that purpose. There is little danger of the house being taken immediately.

I would send you on $5 now—for White paid me the $8 2 days since—but you appear not to have received my last letter and I am afraid to trust it to the mail, as the letters are continually robbed. I have it *for* you & will keep it until I hear from you when I will send it & more if I get any in the meantime. I wrote you that Wm. Poe had written to me concerning you & has offered to assist you asking me questions concerning you which I answered. He will beyond doubt aid you shortly & with an effectual aid. Trust in God.

The tone of your letter wounds me to the soul—Oh Aunty, Aunty you loved me once—how can you be so cruel now? You speak of Virginia acquiring accomplishments, and entering into society— you speak in so *worldly* a tone. Are you sure she would be more happy. Do you think any one could love her more dearly than I? She will have far—very far better opportunities of entering into society here than with N.P. Every one here receives me with open arms.

Adieu my dear aunty. I *cannot advise you.* Ask Virginia. Leave it to her. Let me have, under her own hand, a letter, bidding me *good bye*—forever—and I may die—my heart will break—but I will say no more.

E A P.

Kiss her for me—a million times.

For Virginia,

My love, my own sweetest Sissy, my darling little wifey, think well before you break the heart of your cousin. Eddy.

I open this letter to enclose the 5$—I have just received another letter from you announcing the rect. of mine. My heart bleeds for you. Dearest Aunty consider my happiness while you are thinking about your own. I am saving all I can. The only money I have yet spent is 50 cts for washing—I have 2.25 left. I will shortly send you more. Write immediately. I shall be all anxiety & dread until I hear from you. Try and convince my dear Virg^a· how devotedly I love her. I wish you would get me the Republican wh: which noticed the Messenger & send it on immediately by mail. God bless & protect you both.

Poe despised his cousin Neilson Poe (then a successful newspaper publisher) and feared that if Neilson became Virginia's protector, he would thwart her marriage to Edgar. Poe notes that the teaching position he sought had been given to another man but assures Mrs. Clemm that his salary from White will support her and her daughter in Richmond.

EDGAR ALLAN POE TO PHILIP P. COOKE

Philadelphia   Sep. 21ˢᵗ· 1839.

My Dear Sir:

I recd. your letter this morning—and read it with more pleasure than I can well express. You wrong me, indeed, in supposing that I meant one word of mere flattery in what I said. I have an inveterate habit of speaking the truth—and had I not valued your opinion more highly than that of any man in America I should not have written you as I did.

I say that I read your letter with delight. In fact I am aware of no delight greater than that of feeling one's self appreciated (in such wild matters as "Ligeia") by those in whose judgment one has faith. You read my inmost spirit "like a book," and with the single exception of D'Israeli, I have had communication with no other person who does. Willis had a glimpse of it—Judge Tucker saw about one half way through—but your ideas are the very echo of my own. I am very far from meaning to flatter—I am flattered and honored. Beside me is now lying a letter from Washington Irving in which he speaks with enthusiasm of a late tale of mine, "The Fall of the House of Usher,"—and in which he promises to make his opinion public, upon the first opportunity,—but from the bottom of my heart I assure you, I regard his best word as but dust in the balance when weighed with those discriminating opinions of your own, which teach me that you feel and perceive.

Touching "Ligeia" you are right—all right—throughout. The *gradual* perception of the fact that Ligeia lives again in the person of Rowena is a far loftier and more thrilling idea than the one I have embodied. It offers in my opinion, the widest possible scope to the imagination—it might be rendered even sublime. And this idea was mine—had I never written before I should have adopted it—but then there is "Morella." Do you remember there the *gradual* conviction on the part of the parent that the spirit of the first Morella tenants the person of the second? It was necessary, since "Morella" was written, to modify "Ligeia." I was forced to be content with a sudden half-consciousness, on the part of the narrator, that Ligeia stood before him. One point I have not fully carried out—I should have intimated that the *will* did not perfect its intention—there should have been a relapse—a final one—and Ligeia (who had only succeeded in so much as to convey an idea of the truth to the narrator) should be at length entombed as Rowena—the bodily alterations having gradually faded away.

But since "Morella" is upon record I will suffer "Ligeia" to remain as it is. Your word that it is "intelligible" suffices—and your commentary sustains your word. As for the mob—let them talk on. I should be grieved if I thought they comprehended me here.

The "saith Verulam" shall be put right—your "impertinence" is quite pertinent.

I send the "Gentleman's Magazine" (July, August, September). Do not think of subscribing. The criticisms are not worth your notice. Of course I pay no attention to them—for there are two of us. It is not pleasant to be taxed with the twaddle of other people, or to let other people be taxed with ours. Therefore for the present I remain upon my oars—merely penning an occasional paragraph, without care. The critiques, such as they are, are all mine in the July number and all mine in the August and September with the exception of the three first in each—which are by Burton. As soon as Fate allows I will have a Magazine of my own—and will endeavor to kick up a dust.

Do you ever see the "Pittsburg Examiner" (a New Monthly)? I wrote a Review of "Tortesa," at some length in the July No. In the October number of the "Gentleman's Magazine" I will have "William Wilson" from "The Gift" for 1840. This Tale I think you will like—it is perhaps the best—although not the last—I have done. During the autumn I will publish all in 2 vols—and now I have done with my egoism.

It makes me laugh to hear you speaking about "romantic young persons" as of a race with whom, for the future, you have nothing to do. You need not attempt to shake off or to banter off Romance. It is an evil you will never get rid of to the end of your days. It is a part of yourself—a portion of your soul. Age will only mellow it a

little, and give it a holier tone. I will give your contributions a
hearty welcome, and the choicest position in the magazine.

Sincerely Yours

EDGAR A. POE.

This letter is notable mainly for its discussion of "Ligeia" and for
the inception of Poe's idea to found a magazine. There is no evidence
that Poe ever corresponded with the British author Benjamin D'Is-
raeli, who was (according to Lambert Wilmer) Poe's early model as
a writer.

EDGAR ALLAN POE TO
WILLIAM E. BURTON

[June 1, 1840.]

Sir:

I find myself at leisure this Monday morning, June 1, to notice
your very singular letter of Saturday. & you shall now hear what I
have to say. In the first place—your attempts to bully me excite in
my mind scarcely any other sentiment than mirth. When you ad-
dress me again preserve if you can, the dignity of a gentleman. If
by accident you have taken it into your head that I am to be in-
sulted with impunity I can only assume that you are an ass. This
one point being distinctly understood I shall feel myself more at
liberty to be explicit. As for the rest, you do me gross injustice;
and you know it. As usual you have wrought yourself into a pas-
sion with me on account of some imaginary wrong; for no real in-
jury, or attempt at injury, have you ever received at my hands. As I
live, I am utterly unable to say why you are angry, or what true
grounds of complaint you have against me. You are a man of im-
pulses; have made yourself, in consequence, some enemies; have
been in many respects ill treated by those whom you had looked
upon as friends—and these things have rendered you suspicious.
You once wrote in your magazine a sharp critique upon a book of
mine—a very silly book—Pym. Had I written a similar criticism
upon a book of yours, you feel that you would have been my en-
emy for life, and you therefore imagine in my bosom a latent hos-
tility towards yourself. This has been a mainspring in your whole
conduct towards me since our first acquaintance. It has acted to
prevent all cordiality. In a general view of human nature your idea
is just—but you will find yourself puzzled in judging me by ordi-
nary motives. Your criticism was essentially correct and therefore,
although severe, it did not occasion in me one solitary emotion ei-
ther of anger or dislike. But even while I write these words, I am

sure you will not believe them. Did I not still think you, in spite of the exceeding littleness of some of your hurried actions, a man of many honorable impulses, I should not now take the trouble to send you this letter. I cannot permit myself to suppose that you would say to me in cool blood what you said in your letter of yesterday. . . .

Upon the whole I am not willing to admit that you have greatly overpaid me. That I did not do 4 times as much as I did for the Magazine, was your own fault. At first I wrote long articles which you deemed inadmissable, & never did I suggest any to which you had not some immediate and decided objection. Of course I grew discouraged & could feel no interest in the Journal. I am at a loss to know why you call me selfish. If you mean that I borrowed money of you—you know that you offered it—and you know that I am poor. In what instance has anyone ever found me selfish? Was there selfishness in the affront I offered Benjamin (whom I respect, and who spoke well of me) because I deemed it a duty not to receive from any one commendation at your expense? I had no hesitation in making him my enemy (which he now must be) through a sense of my obligations as your coadjutor. I have said that I could not tell why you were angry. Place yourself in my situation & see whether you would not have acted as I have done. You first "enforced", as you say, a deduction of salary: giving me to understand thereby that you thought of parting company—You next spoke disrespectfully of me behind my back—this as an habitual thing—to those whom you supposed your friends, and who punctually retailed me, as a matter of course, every ill-natured word which you uttered. Lastly you advertised your magazine for sale without saying a word to me about it. I felt no anger at what you did—none in the world. Had I not firmly believed it your design to give up your Journal, with a view of attending to the Theatre, I should never have dreamed of attempting one of my own. The opportunity of doing something for myself seemed a good one—(I was about to be thrown out of business)—and I embraced it. Now I ask you as a man of honor and as a man of sense—what is there wrong in all this? What have I done at which you have any right to take offense? I can give you no definitive answer (respecting the continuation of Rodman's Journal,) until I hear from you again. The charge of 100 $ I shall not admit for an instant. If you persist

in it our intercourse is at an end, and We can each adopt our own
measures

In the meantime, I am
Y^r Obt St.
EDGAR A POE

Wm E. Burton Esqr.

Poe's angry retort to Burton, who had dismissed him, includes a
lengthy passage (deleted here) refuting Burton's accusation that Poe
owed him $100. Poe added up his monthly contributions to the
magazine and concluded that he owed only $60. Burton *had* re-
viewed *Pym* and called it "a very silly book," a criticism Poe here
seems to accept. But because Poe genuinely believed that Burton
(then building a theater) planned to sell the *Gentleman's Magazine*,
he took umbrage at the accusation of disloyalty sparked by Poe's
printing of a prospectus for *The Penn.*

EDGAR ALLAN POE TO
JOSEPH EVANS SNODGRASS

Philadelphia, April 1, 1841.

My Dear Snodgrass—

I fear you have been thinking it was not my design to answer your kind letter at all. It is now April Fool's Day, and yours is dated March 8th; but believe me, although, for good reason, I may occasionally postpone my reply to your favors, I am never in danger of forgetting them.

I am much obliged to you for permitting me to hand over your essay to Mr. Graham. It will appear in the June number. In order to understand this apparent delay, you must be informed that we go to press at a singularly early period. The *May* number is now within two days of being ready for delivery to the mails. I should be pleased to receive a brief notice of Soran's poems for the June number—if you think this will not be too late.

In regard to Burton. I feel indebted to you for the kind interest you express; but scarcely know how to reply. My situation is embarrassing. It is impossible, as you say, to notice a buffoon and a felon, as one gentleman would notice another. The law, then, is my only resource. Now, if the truth of a scandal could be admitted in justification—I mean of what the law terms a *scandal*—I would have matters all my own way. I would institute a suit, forthwith, for his personal defamation of myself. He would be unable to prove the truth of his allegations. I could prove their falsity and their malicious intent by witnesses who, seeing me at all hours of every day, would have the best right to speak—I mean Burton's own clerk, Morrell, and the compositors of the printing office. In fact, I could prove the scandal almost by acclamation. I should obtain damages. But, on the other hand, I have never been scrupulous in regard to what I have said of him. I have always told *him* to his face, and everybody else, that I looked upon him as a blackguard and a villain. This is notorious. He would meet me with a cross action. The truth of the allegation—which I could easily prove as he would find it difficult to prove the truth of his own respecting me—would not avail me. The law will not admit, as justification of my calling Billy Burton a scoundrel, that Billy Burton is really such. What then can I do? If I sue, he sues; you see how it is.

At the same time—as I may, after further reflection, be induced to sue, I would take it as an act of kindness—not to say *justice*— on your part, if you would see the gentleman of whom you spoke, and ascertain with accuracy all that may legally avail me; that is to say, what and when were the words used, and whether your friend would be willing for your sake, for my sake, and for the sake of truth, to give evidence if called upon. Will you do this for me?

So far for the matter inasmuch as it concerns Burton. I have now to thank you for your defence of myself, as stated. You are a physician, and I presume no physician can have difficulty in detecting the *drunkard* at a glance. You are, moreover, a literary man, well read in morals. You will never be brought to believe that I could write what I daily write, *as* I write it, were I as this villain would induce those who know me not, to believe. In fine, I pledge you, before God, the solemn word of a gentleman, that I am temperate even to rigor. From the hour in which I first saw this basest of calumniators to the hour in which I retired from his office in uncontrollable disgust at his chicanery, arrogance, ignorance and brutality, *nothing stronger than water ever passed my lips.*

It is, however, due to candor that I inform you upon what foundation he has erected his slanders. At no period of my life was I ever what men call intemperate. I never was in the *habit* of intoxication. I never drunk drams, &c. But, for a brief period, while I resided in Richmond, and edited the *Messenger*, I certainly did give way, at long intervals, to the temptation held out on all sides by the spirit of Southern conviviality. My sensitive temperament could not stand an excitement which was an everyday matter to my companions. In short, it sometimes happened that I was completely intoxicated. For some days after each excess I was invariably confined to bed. But it is now quite four years since I have abandoned every kind of alcoholic drink—four years, with the exception of a single deviation, which occurred shortly *after* my leaving Burton, and when I was induced to resort to the occasional use of *cider*, with the hope of relieving a nervous attack.

You will thus see, frankly stated, the whole amount of my sin. You will also see the blackness of that heart which could *revive* a slander of this nature. Neither can you fail to perceive how desperate the malignity of the slanderer must be—how resolute he must be to slander, and how slight the grounds upon which he would build up a defamation—since he can find nothing better with which to charge me than an accusation which can be disproved by each and every man with whom I am in the habit of daily intercourse.

I have now only to repeat to you, in general, my solemn assurance that my habits are as far removed from intemperance as the day from the night. My sole drink is water.

Will you do me the kindness to repeat this assurance to such of your friends as happen to speak of me in your hearing?

I feel that nothing more is requisite, and you will agree with me upon reflection.

Hoping soon to hear from you, I am,

Yours most cordially,

Dr. J. E. Snodgrass. EDGAR A. POE.

P.S.—You will receive the magazine, as a matter of course. I had supposed that you were already on our free list.

P.P.S.—The *Penn*, I hope, is only "scotched, not killed." It would have appeared under glorious auspices, and with capital at command, in March, as advertised, but for the unexpected bank suspensions. In the meantime, Mr. Graham has made me a liberal offer, which I had great pleasure in accepting. The *Penn* project will unquestionably be resumed hereafter.

> Dr. Snodgrass was a Baltimore newspaper editor who had been coeditor of the *American Museum* when Poe published "Ligeia" there in 1838. Poe summarizes his continuing feud with Burton and seeks advice about a prospective (but never pursued) defamation lawsuit; he also responds to Burton's charges of Poe's insobriety by denying recent intemperance while confessing past lapses.

EDGAR ALLAN POE TO FREDERICK W. THOMAS

[Philadelphia, June 26, 1841]

My Dear Thomas,

With this I mail you the July No: of the Mag: If you can get us a notice in the Intelligencer, as you said, I will take it as a particular favor—but if it is inconvenient, do not put yourself to any trouble about it.

I have just heard through Graham, who obtained his information from Ingraham, that you have stepped into an office at Washington—salary $1000. From the bottom of my heart I wish you joy. You can now lucubrate more at your ease & will infallibly do something worthy yourself.

For my own part, notwithstanding Graham's unceasing civility, and real kindness, I feel more & more disgusted with my situation. Would to God, I could do as you have done. Do you seriously think that an application on my part to Tyler would have a good result? My claims, to be sure, are few. I am a Virginian—at least I call myself one, for I have resided all my life, until within the last few years, in Richmond. My political principles have always been as nearly as may be, with the existing administration, and I battled with right good will for Harrison, when opportunity offered. With Mr Tyler I have some slight personal acquaintance— although this is a matter which he has possibly forgotten. For the rest, I am a literary man—and I see a disposition in government to cherish letters. Have I any chance? I would be greatly indebted to you if you reply to this as soon as you can, and tell me if it would, in your opinion, be worth my while to make an effort—and if so—put me upon the right track. This could not be better done than by detailing to me your own mode of proceeding.

It appears that Ingraham is in high dudgeon with me because I spoke ill of his "Quadroone." I am really sorry to hear it—but it

LETTERS

is a matter that cannot be helped. As a man I like him much, and wherever I could do so, without dishonor to my own sense of truth, I have praised his writings. His "South-West," for example, I lauded highly. His "Quadroone" is, in my honest opinion, trash. If I must call it a good book to preserve the friendship of Prof. Ingraham—Prof. Ingraham may go to the devil.

I am *really* serious about the office. If you can aid me in any way, I am sure you will. Remember me kindly to Dow & believe me

Yours most truly,

F. W. Thomas.   EDGAR A POE

Phil: June 26. 41

It is not impossible that you could effect my object by merely showing this letter yourself personally to the President and speaking of me as the original editor of the Messenger.

Poe met Thomas (a Whig supporter of Harrison) during the presidential campaign of 1840. The author of an 1835 novel (*Clinton Bradshaw*) reviewed unfavorably by Poe, Thomas had been a friend of Poe's brother in Baltimore and indeed received a patronage position during the presidency of Harrison's successor, John Tyler. Poe's claim to have "battled with right good will for Harrison" has never been substantiated, and his request to be identified to Tyler as the "original editor" of the *Southern Literary Messenger* is misleading at best.

EDGAR ALLAN POE TO
FREDERICK W. THOMAS

Philadelphia   Feb. 3, '42.

My dear Friend:
I am sure you will pardon me for my seeming neglect in not replying to your last when you learn what has been the cause of the delay. My dear little wife has been dangerously ill. About a fortnight since, in singing, she ruptured a blood-vessel, and it was only on yesterday that the physicians gave me any hope of her recovery. You might imagine the agony I have suffered, for you know how devotedly I love her. But to-day the prospect brightens, and I trust that this bitter cup of misery will not be my portion. I seize the first moment of hope and relief to reply to your kind words.

You ask me how I come on with Graham? Will you believe it Thomas? On the morning subsequent to the accident I called upon him, and, being entirely out of his debt, asked an advance of two months salary—when he not only flatly but discourteously refused. Now that man *knows* that I have rendered him the most important services; he cannot help knowing it, for the fact is rung in his ears by every second person who visits the office, and the comments made by the press are too obvious to be misunderstood.

The project of the new Magazine still (you may be sure) occupies my thoughts. *If I live*, I will accomplish it, and in triumph. By the way, there is one point upon which I wish to consult you. You are personally acquainted with Robert Tyler, author of "Ahasuerus." In this poem there are many evidences of power, and, what is better, of nobility of thought & feeling. In reading it, an idea struck me—"Might it not," I thought, "be possible that *he* would, or rather might be induced to feel some interest in my contemplated scheme, perhaps even to *take* an interest in something of the kind—an interest either open or secret?" The Magazine might be made to play even an important part in the politics of the day,

like Blackwood; and in this view might be worthy his considera-
tion. Could you contrive to suggest the matter to him? Provided I
am permitted a proprietary right in the journal, I shall not be very
particular about the extent of that right. If, instead of a paltry
salary, Graham had given me a tenth of his Magazine, I should feel
myself a rich man to-day. When he bought out Burton, the joint
circulation was 4,500, and we have printed of the February num-
ber last, 40,000. Godey, at the period of the junction, circulated
30,000, and, in spite of the most strenuous efforts, has not been
able to prevent his list from *falling*. *I* am sure that he does not
print more than 30,000 to-day. His absolute circulation is about
20,000. Now Godey, in this interval, has surpassed Graham in all
the *externals* of a good Magazine. His paper is better, his type far
better, and his engravings fully as good; but I fear I am getting
sadly egotistical. I would not speak so plainly to any other than
yourself. How delighted I would be to grasp you by the hand!

As regards the French—get into a French family by all means—
read much, write more, & give grammar to the dogs.

You are quizzing me about the autographs. I was afraid to say
more than one half of what I really thought of you, lest it should
be attributed to personal friendship. Those articles have had a
great run—have done wonders for the Journal—but I fear have
also done me, personally, much injury. I was weak enough to per-
mit Graham to modify my opinions (or at least their expression)
in many of the notices. In the case of Conrad, for example; he in-
sisted upon *praise* and worried me into speaking well of such nin-
nies as Holden, Peterson, Spear, &c., &c. I would not have yielded
had I thought it made much difference what one said of such pup-
pets as these, but it seems the error has been made to count against
my critical impartiality. Know better next time. Let no man accuse
me of leniency again.

I do not believe that Ingraham stole "Lafitte."

No, Benjamin does not write the political papers in the "New
World," but I cannot say who does. I cannot bring myself to like
that man, although I wished to do so, and although he made some
advances, of late, which you may have seen. He is too thorough-
souled a time-server. I would not say again what I said of him in
the "Autography."

Did you read my review of "Barnaby Rudge" in the Feb. No.?

You see that I was right throughout in my predictions about the plot. Was it not you who said you believed I would find myself mistaken?

Remember me kindly to Dow. I fear he has given me up; never writes; never sends a paper.

Will you bear in mind what I say about R. Tyler?

God bless you.
EDGAR A. POE.

F. W. Thomas

Significant for its reference to Virginia's recent pulmonary hemorrhage, this letter reveals both Poe's discontent with George Graham and his own current fantasy of establishing a quality monthly that would support—and be supported by—the Tyler administration. The president's son was an aspiring poet whose work Poe reviewed favorably in *Graham's*. In a magazine piece, Poe had correctly predicted the outcome of Dickens's serialized *Barnaby Rudge*.

EDGAR ALLAN POE TO
T. H. CHIVERS

Philadelphia   Sep. 27, 1842.

My Dear Sir,

Through some accident, I did not receive your letter of the 15th inst: until this morning, and now hasten to reply.

Allow me, in the first place, to thank you sincerely for your kindness in procuring me the subscribers to the Penn Magazine. The four names sent will aid me most materially in this early stage of the proceedings.

As yet I have taken no overt step in the measure, and have not even printed a Prospectus. As soon as I do this I will send you several. I do not wish to announce my positive resumption of the original scheme until about the middle of October. Before that period I have reason to believe that I shall have received an appointment in the Philadelphia Custom House, which will afford me a good salary and leave the greater portion of my time unemployed. With this appointment to fall back upon, as a certain resource, I shall be enabled to start the Magazine without difficulty, provided I can make an arrangement with either a practical printer possessing a small office, or some one not a printer, with about $1000 at command. (over)

It would, of course, be better for the permanent influence and success of the journal that I unite myself with a gentleman of education & similarity of thought and feeling. It was this consciousness which induced me to suggest the enterprise to yourself. I know no one with whom I would more readily enter into association than yourself.

I am not aware what are your political views. My own have reference to no one of the present parties; but it has been hinted to me that I will receive the most effectual patronage from Government, for a journal which will admit occasional papers in support of the Administration. For Mr Tyler personally, & as an honest statesman, I have the highest respect. Of the government patronage, upon the condition specified, *I am assured* and this alone will more than sustain the Magazine.

The only real difficulty lies in the beginning—in the pecuniary means for getting out the two (or three) first numbers; after this all is sure, and a great triumph may, and indeed *will* be achieved. If you can command about $1000 and say that you will join me, I will write you fully as respects the details of the plan, or we can have an immediate interview.

It would be proper to start with an edition of 1000 copies. For this number, the monthly expense, including paper (of the finest quality) composition, press-work & stitching will be about 180$. I calculate *all* expenses at about $250—which is $3000 per annum—a *very* liberal estimate. 1000 copies at $ 5 = 5000$— leaving a nett profit of 2000$, even supposing we have only 1000 subscribers. But I am sure of *beginning* with at least 500, and make no doubt of obtaining 5000 before the expiration of the 2d year. A Magazine, such as I propose, with 5000 subscribers will produce us each an income of some $10,000; and this you will acknowledge is a game worth playing. At the same time there is no earthly reason why such a Magazine may not, eventually, reach a circulation as great as that of "Graham's" at present—viz 50,000.

I repeat that it would give me the most sincere pleasure if you would make up your mind to join me. I am sure of our community of thought & feeling, and that we would accomplish *much*.

In regard to the poem on Harrison's death, I regret to say that nothing can be done with the Philadelphia publishers. The truth is that the higher order of poetry is, and always will be, in this country, unsaleable; but, even were it otherwise, the present state of the Copy-Right Laws will not warrant any publisher, in *purchasing* an American book. The only condition, I am afraid, upon which the poem can be printed, is that you print at your own expense.

I will see Griswold and endeavour to get the smaller poems from him. A precious fellow is he!

Write as soon as you receive this & believe me

Yours most truly
EDGAR A POE

A Georgia physician, poet, and plantation owner who admired Poe, Thomas Holley Chivers was a plausible prospective partner. When he penned this letter, Poe was confident that he would be receiving a government appointment. But the job failed to materialize, and Chivers declined the invitation to bankroll Poe's magazine. The passing reference to the absence of an international copyright law coincides with Poe's emerging advocacy of such protection for U.S. authors. The mention of Rufus Griswold, then working for Graham, hints at Poe's scorn for him.

EDGAR ALLAN POE TO FREDERICK W. THOMAS AND JESSE E. DOW

Philadelphia   March 16, 1843.

My Dear Thomas, & Dow

I arrived here, in perfect safety, and *sober*, about half past four last evening—nothing occurring on the road of any consequence. I shaved and breakfasted in Baltimore and lunched on the Susque-hannah, and by the time I got to Phila. felt quite decent. Mrs. Clemm was expecting me at the car-office. I went immediately home, took a warm bath & supper & then went to Clarke's. I never saw a man in my life more surprised to see another. He thought by Dow's epistle that I must not only be dead but buried & would as soon have thought of seeing his great-great-great grand-mother. He received me, therefore, very cordially & made light of the matter. I told him what had been agreed upon—that I was a lit-tle sick & that Dow, knowing I had been, in times passed, given to spreeing upon an extensive scale, had become unduly alarmed &c&c.—that when I found he had written I thought it best to come home. He said my trip had improved me & that he had never *seen me looking so well!!!*—and I don't believe I ever did.

This morning I took medicine, and, as it is a snowy day, will avail myself of the excuse to stay at home—so that by to-morrow I shall be *really* as well as ever.

Virginia's health is about the same—but her distress of mind has been even more than I had anticipated. She desires her *kindest* re-membrances to both of you—as also does Mrs. C.

Clarke, it appears, wrote to Dow, who must have received the letter this morning. Please re-inclose the letter to me, here—so that I may know how to guide myself.—and, Thomas, do write imme-diately as proposed. If *possible*, enclose a line from Rob. Tyler—

but I fear, under the circumstances, it is not so—I blame no one but myself.

The letter which I looked for & which I wished returned, is not on its way—reason, no money forthcoming—Lowell had not yet sent it—he is ill in N. York of opthalmia. Immediately upon receipt of it, or before, I will forward the money you were both so kind as to lend—which is 8 to Dow—and 3 1/2 to Thomas—What a confounded business I have got myself into, attempting to write a letter to two people at once!

However—this is for Dow. My dear fellow—Thank you a thousand times for your kindness & great forbearance, and don't say a word about the cloak turned inside out, or other peccadilloes of that nature. Also, express to your wife my deep regret for the vexation I must have occasioned her. Send me, also, if you can the letter to Blythe. Call also, at the barber's shop just above Fuller's and pay for me a levy which I believe I owe. And now God bless you—for a nobler fellow never lived.

And this is for Thomas. My dear friend. Forgive me my petulance & don't believe I think all I said. Believe me I am very grateful to you for your many attentions & forbearances and the time will never come when I shall forget either them or you. Remember me most kindly to Dr Lacey—also to the Don, whose mustachios I *do* admire after all, and who has about the finest figure I ever beheld—also to Dr Frailey. Please express my regret to Mr Fuller for making such a fool of myself in his house, and say to him (if you think it necessary) that I should not have got half so drunk on his excellent Port wine but for the rummy coffee with which I was forced to wash it down. I would be glad, too, if you would take an opportunity of saying to Mr Rob. Tyler that if he *can* look over matters & get me the Inspectorship, I will join the Washingtonians forthwith. I am as serious as a judge—& much so than many. I think it would be a feather in Mr Tyler's cap to save from the perils of mint julep—& "Port wines"—a young man of whom all the world thinks so well & who thinks so remarkably well of himself.

And now, my dear friends, good bye & believe me

Most Truly Yours.

EDGAR A. POE

Mess Dow & Thomas.

Upon getting here I found numerous letters of subscribers to my Magazine—for which no canvas has yet been made. This was un-expected & cheering. Did you say Dow that Commodore Elliot had desired me to put down his name? Is it so or did I dream it? At all events, when you see him present my respects and thanks. Thomas you will remember that Dr. Lacey wished me to put him down—but I don't know his first name—please let me have it.

This letter pertains to Poe's notorious visit to Washington in quest of a government appointment. Thomas was ill and had failed to arrange the desired interview with the president. Upon his arrival Poe began drinking heavily, and here he apologizes to two offended friends while reiterating a rationalization for Dow's letter to Thomas Clarke, who had recently agreed to publish Poe's monthly magazine. As a temperance man, Clarke would have been appalled by Poe's ac-tual escapades, which included wearing his cloak turned inside out, insulting several people (including Mr. and Mrs. Robert Tyler as well as novelist Thomas Dunn English), and walking out of a barber shop without paying.

EDGAR ALLAN POE TO
JAMES RUSSELL LOWELL

Philadelphia   *March 30, 1844.*

My Dear Friend,

Graham has been speaking to me, lately, about your Biography, and I am anxious to write it at once—always provided you have no objection. Could you forward me the materials within a day or two? I am just now quite disengaged—in fact positively idle.

I presume you have read the Memoir of Willis, in the April No: of G. It is written by a Mr Landor—but I think it full of hyperbole. Willis is *no* genius—a graceful trifler—no more. He wants force & sincerity. He is very frequently far-fetched. In me, at least, he never excites an emotion. Perhaps the best poem he has written, is a little piece called "Unseen Spirits", beginning "The Shadow lay—Along Broadway".

You inquire about my own portrait. It has been done for some time—but is better as an engraving, than as a portrait. It scarcely resembles me at all. When it will appear I cannot say. Conrad & Mrs Stephens will certainly come before me—perhaps Gen: Morris. My Life is not yet written, and I am at a sad loss for a Biographer—for Graham insists upon leaving the matter to myself.

I sincerely rejoice to hear of the success of your volume. To sell eleven hundred copies of a bound book of American poetry, is to do wonders. I hope every thing from your future endeavours. Have you read "Orion"? Have you seen the article on "American Poetry" in the "London Foreign Quarterly"? It has been denied that Dickens wrote it—but, to me, the article affords so strong internal evidence of his hand that I would as soon think of doubting my existence. He tells much truth—although he evinces much ignorance and more spleen. Among other points he accuses myself of "metrical imitation" of Tennyson, citing, by way of instance, passages from poems which were written & published by me long before

Tennyson was heard of:—but I have, at no time, made any poetical pretension. I am greatly indebted for the trouble you have taken about the Lectures, and shall be very glad to avail myself, next season, of any invitation from the "Boston Lyceum." Thank you also, for the hint about the North A. Review:—I will bear it in mind. I mail you, herewith, a "Dollar Newspaper," containing a somewhat extravagant tale of my own. I fear it will prove little to your taste.

How dreadful is the present condition of our Literature! To what are things tending? We want two things, certainly:—an International Copy-Right Law, and a well-founded Monthly Journal, of sufficient ability, circulation, and character, to control and so give tone to, our Letters. It should be, externally, a specimen of high, but not too refined Taste:—I mean, it should be boldly printed, on excellent paper, in single column, and be illustrated, not merely embellished, by spirited wood designs in the style of Grandville. Its chief aims should be Independence, Truth, Originality. It should be a journal of some 120 pp, and furnished at $5. It should have nothing to do with Agents or Agencies. Such a Magazine might be made to exercise a prodigious influence, and would be a source of vast wealth to its proprietors. There *can* be no reason why 100,000 copies might not, in one or two years, be circulated: but the means of bringing it into circulation should be radically different from those usually employed.

Such a journal might, perhaps, be set on foot by a coalition, and, thus set on foot, with proper understanding, would be irresistible. Suppose, for example, that the élite of our men of letters should combine secretly. Many of them control papers &c. Let each subscribe, say $200, for the commencement of the undertaking; furnishing other means, as required from time to time, until the work be established. The articles to be supplied by the members solely, and upon a concerted plan of action. A nominal editor to be elected from among the number. How could such a journal fail? I would like very much to hear your opinion upon this matter. Could not the "ball be set in motion"? If we do *not* defend ourselves by some such coalition, we shall be devoured, without mercy, by the Godeys, the Snowdens, et id genus omne.

Most truly your friend
EDGAR A POE

Poe refers to the biographical sketch of Lowell that he had been asked to write (but never did) and observes pointedly that he must find someone to write his own biography for *Graham's* (which Lowell eventually did). Poe signals his willingness to speak at the Boston Lyceum—where he created an uproar in 1845—and sounds out Lowell (whose *Pioneer* was short lived) on the idea of a monthly magazine published by a secret confederation of literary men.

EDGAR ALLAN POE TO MARIA CLEMM

New-York, Sunday Morning
April 7. [1844]   just after breakfast.

My dear Muddy,
We have just this minute done breakfast, and I now sit down to
write you about everything. I can't pay for the letter, because the
P.O. won't be open to-day.—In the first place, we arrived safe at
Walnut St wharf. The driver wanted to make me pay a dollar, but I
wouldn't. Then I had to pay a boy a levy to put the trunks in the
baggage car. In the meantime I took Sis in the Depot Hotel. It was
only a quarter past 6, and we had to wait till 7. We saw the Ledger
& Times—nothing in either—a few words of no account in the
Chronicle.—We started in good spirits, but did not get here until
nearly 3 o'clock. We went in the cars to Amboy about 40 miles from
N. York, and then took the steamboat the rest of the way.—Sissy
coughed none at all. When we got to the wharf it was raining hard.
I left her on board the boat, after putting the trunks in the Ladies'
Cabin, and set off to buy an umbrella and look for a boarding-
house. I met a man selling umbrellas and bought one for 62 cents.
Then I went up Greenwich St and soon found a boarding-house. It
is just before you get to Cedar St on the west side going up—the left
hand side. It has brown stone steps, with a porch with brown pil-
lars. "Morrison" is the name on the door. I made a bargain in a few
minutes and then got a hack and went for Sis. I was not gone more
than 1/2 an hour, and she was quite astonished to see me back so
soon. She didn't expect me for an hour. There were 2 other ladies
waiting on board—so she was'nt very lonely.—When we got to the
house we had to wait about 1/2 an hour before the room was ready.
The house is old & looks buggy, [missing words] The landlady is
a nice chatty old [missing words] gave us the back room on the

[missing words] night & day & attendance, for 7 $—[missing words] the cheapest board I ever knew, taking into consideration the central situation and the *living*. I wish Kate could see it—she would faint. Last night, for supper, we had the nicest tea you ever drank, strong & hot—wheat bread & rye bread—cheese—tea-cakes (elegant) a great dish (2 dishes) of elegant ham, and 2 of cold veal piled up like a mountain and large slices—3 dishes of the cakes, and every thing in the greatest profusion. No fear of starving here. The land-lady seemed as if she could'nt press us enough, and we were at home directly. Her husband is living with her—a fat good-natured old soul. There are 8 or 10 boarders—2 or 3 of them ladies—2 servants.—For breakfast we had excellent-flavored coffee, hot & strong—not very clear & no great deal of cream—veal cutlets, elegant ham & eggs & nice bread and butter. I never sat down to a more plentiful or a nicer breakfast. I wish you could have seen the eggs—and the great dishes of meat. I ate the first hearty breakfast I have eaten since I left our little home. Sis is delighted, and we are both in excellent spirits. She has coughed hardly any and had no night sweat. She is now busy mending my pants which I tore against a nail. I went out last night and bought a skein of silk, a skein of thread, & 2 buttons, a pair of slippers & a tin pan for the stove. The fire kept in all night.—We have now got 4 $ and a half left. Tomor-row I am going to try & borrow 3 $—so that I may have a fortnight to go upon. I feel in excellent spirits & have'nt drank a drop—so that I hope so on to get out of trouble. The very instant I scrape to-gether enough money I will send it on. You ca'nt imagine how much we both do miss you. Sissy had a hearty cry last night, because you and Catterina weren't here. We are resolved to get 2 rooms the first moment we can. In the meantime it is impossible we could be more comfortable or more at home than we are.—It looks as if it was go-ing to clear up now.—Be sure and go to the P.O. & have my letters forwarded. As soon as I write Lowell's article, I will send it to you, & get you to get the money from Graham. Give our best loves to Catterina.

[autograph signature clipped from letter]

Be sure & take home the Messenger, [to Henry B. Hirst]. We hope to send for you *very* soon.

After six years in Philadelphia, Poe and Virginia had gone to New York to find suitable lodging while Poe explored publishing contacts. Mrs. Clemm here receives details of a boarding house that will enable her to rejoin her daughter and son-in-law upon arrival. Poe's elaborate attention to food must be read in the context of recurrent family hardships, including hunger. Catterina is the family cat.

EDGAR ALLAN POE TO
JAMES RUSSELL LOWELL

New-York, July 2. 44.

My Dear Mr Lowell,
I can feel for the "constitutional indolence" of which you complain—for it is one of my own besetting sins. I am excessively slothful, and wonderfully industrious—by fits. There are epochs when any kind of mental exercise is torture, and when nothing yields me pleasure but solitary communion with the "mountains & the woods"—the "altars" of Byron. I have thus rambled and dreamed away whole months, and awake, at last, to a sort of mania for composition. Then I scribble all day, and read all night, so long as the disease endures. This is also the temperament of P. P. Cooke, of Va. the author of "Florence Vane", "Young Rosalie Lee", & some other sweet poems—and I should not be surprised if it were your own. Cooke writes and thinks as you—and I have been told that you resemble him personally.

I am *not* ambitious—unless negatively. I, now and then feel stirred up to excel a fool, merely because I hate to let a fool imagine that he may excel me. Beyond this I feel nothing of ambition. I really perceive that vanity about which most men merely prate—the vanity of the human or temporal life. I live continually in a reverie of the future. I have no faith in human perfectibility. I think that human exertion will have no appreciable effect upon humanity. Man is now only more active—not more happy—nor more wise, than he was 6000 years ago. The result will never vary—and to suppose that it will, is to suppose that the foregone man has lived in vain—that the foregone time is but the rudiment of the future—that the myriads who have perished have not been upon equal footing with ourselves—nor are we with our posterity. I cannot agree to lose sight of man the individual, in man the mass.—I have no belief in spirituality. I think the word a *mere* word. No one has really a conception of spirit. We cannot imagine what is not. We deceive ourselves by the idea of infinitely rarefied matter. Matter escapes the senses by degrees—a stone—a metal—a liquid—the atmosphere—a gas—the luminiferous ether. Beyond this there are other modifications more rare. But to all we attach the notion of a constitution of particles—atomic composition. For this reason only, we think spirit different; for spirit, we say is unparticled, and *therefore is* not matter. But it is clear that if we proceed sufficiently far in our ideas of rarefaction, we shall arrive at a point where the particles coalesce; for, although the particles be infinite, the infinity of littleness in the spaces between them, is an absurdity.—The unparticled matter, permeating & impelling, all things, is God. Its activity is the thought of God—which creates. Man, and other thinking beings, are individualizations of the unparticled matter. Man exists as a "person", by being clothed with matter (the particled matter) which individualizes him. Thus habited, his life is rudimental. What we call "death" is the painful metamorphosis. The stars are the habitations of rudimental beings. But for the necessity of the rudimental life, there would have been no worlds. At death, the worm is the butterfly—still material, but of a matter unrecognized by our organs—recognized, occasionally, perhaps, by the sleep-waker, directly—without organs—through the mesmeric medium. Thus a sleep-waker may see ghosts. Divested of the rudimental covering, the being inhabits *space*—what we suppose to be the immaterial universe—passing every where, and acting all things, by mere volition—cognizant of all secrets but that of the nature of God's volition—the motion, or activity, of the unparticled matter.

You speak of "an estimate of my life"—and, from what I have already said, you will see that I have none to give. I have been too deeply conscious of the mutability and evanescence of temporal things, to give any continuous effort to anything—to be consistent in anything. My life has been *whim*—impulse—passion—a longing for solitude—a scorn of all things present, in an earnest desire for the future.

I am profoundly excited by music, and by some poems—those of Tennyson especially—whom, with Keats, Shelley, Coleridge (occasionally) and a few others of like thought and expression, I regard as the *sole* poets. Music is the perfection of the soul, or idea, of Poetry. The *vagueness* of exultation aroused by a sweet air

(which should be strictly indefinite & never too strongly sugges-
tive) is precisely what we should aim at in poetry. Affectation,
within bounds, is thus no blemish.

I still adhere to Dickens as either author, or dictator, of the review.
My reasons would convince you, could I give them to you—but I
have left myself no space. I had two long interviews with Mr D.
when here. Nearly every thing in the critique, I heard from him or
suggested to him, personally. The poem of Emerson I read to him.

I have been so negligent as not to preserve copies of any of my
volumes of poems—nor was either worthy preservation. The best
passages were culled in Hirst's article. I think my best poems, "The
Sleeper", "The Conqueror Worm", "The Haunted Palace",
"Lenore", "Dreamland" & "The Coliseum"—but all have been
hurried & unconsidered. My best tales are "Ligeia"; The "Gold-
Bug"; The "Murders in the Rue Morgue", "The Fall of the House
of Usher", The "Tell-Tale Heart", The "Black Cat", "William Wil-
son", & "The Descent into the Maelström." "The Purloined Let-
ter," forthcoming in the "Gift", is, perhaps, the best of my tales of
ratiocination. I have lately written, for Godey, "The Oblong-Box",
and "Thou art the Man"—as yet unpublished. With this, I mail you
"The Gold-Bug", which is the only one of my tales I have on hand.

Graham has had, for 9 months, a review of mine on Longfel-
low's "Spanish Student", which I have "used up", and in which I
have exposed some of the grossest plagiarisms ever perpetrated. I
can't tell why he does not publish it.—I believe G. intends my Life
for the September number, which will be made up by the 10th Au-
gust. Your article shd be on hand as soon as convenient.

                                      Believe me your true friend.

                                               E A POE.

Poe's allusion to the "mania of composition" that sometimes comes
over him resonates with his manic productivity in 1844, when he
composed and published more tales than in any other year. But the
chief significance of this letter lies in Poe's articulation of his ideas
about human progress and spirituality. For Lowell, who was writing
the requested biographical essay, Poe revealed certain personal traits
and identified what he conceived to be his best writings.

EDGAR ALLAN POE TO EVERT A. DUYCKINCK

Thursday Morning—13th. [November 13, 1845.]
85 Amity St.

My Dear Mr Duyckinck,

For the first time during two months I find myself entirely myself—dreadfully sick and depressed, but still myself. I seem to have just awakened from some horrible dream, in which all was confusion, and suffering—relieved only by the constant sense of your kindness, and that of one or two other considerate friends. I really believe that I have been mad—but indeed I have had abundant reason to be so. I have made up my mind to a step which will preserve me, for the future, from at least the greater portion of the troubles which have beset me. In the meantime, I have need of the most active exertion to extricate myself from the embarrassments into which I have already fallen—and my object in writing you this note is, (once again) to beg your aid. Of course I need not say to you that my most urgent trouble is the want of ready money. I find that what I said to you about the prospects of the B. J. is strictly correct. The most trifling immediate relief would put it on an excellent footing. All that I want is time in which to look about me; and I think that it is your power to afford me this. . . .

Please send your answer to 85 Amity St. and believe me—with the most sincere friendship and ardent gratitude

Yours
EDGAR A POE.

As the *Broadway Journal* collapsed, Poe sought personal loans to meet his expenses. This letter bears witness to a period of profound exhaustion and discouragement.

EDGAR ALLAN POE TO VIRGINIA POE

June. 12th—1846   *[New York]*

My Dear Heart, My dear Virginia! our Mother will explain to you why I stay away from you this night. I trust the interview I am promised, will result in some *substantial good* for me, for your dear sake, and hers—Keep up your heart in all hopefulness, and trust yet a little longer—In my last great disappointment, I should have lost my courage *but for you*—my little darling wife you are my *greatest* and *only* stimulus now, to battle with this uncongenial, unsatisfactory and ungrateful life—I shall be with you tomorrow P.M. and be assured until I see you, I will keep in *loving remembrance* your *last words* and your fervent prayer!

Sleep well and may God grant you a peaceful summer, with your devoted

 EDGAR

The "great disappointment" Poe acknowledges is the failure of the *Broadway Journal.* No information exists about the "interview" he mentions. But as the only extant letter written solely to Virginia, it testifies to his devotion to her.

EDGAR ALLAN POE TO
PHILIP P. COOKE

New-York—August 9. 1846.

My Dear Sir,
Never think of excusing yourself (to me) for dilatoriness in answering letters—I know too well the unconquerable procrastination which besets the poet. I will place it all to the accounts of the turkeys. Were I to be seized by a rambling fit—one of my customary *passions* (nothing less) for vagabondizing through the woods for a week or a month together—I would not—in fact I *could* not be put out of my mood, were it even to answer a letter from the Grand Mogul, informing me that I had fallen heir to his possessions.

Thank you for the compliments. Were I in a serious humor just now, I would tell you, frankly, how your words of appreciation make my nerves thrill—not because you praise me (for others have praised me more lavishly) but because I feel that you comprehend and discriminate. You are right about the hair-splitting of my French friend:—that is all done for effect. These tales of ratiocination owe most of their popularity to being something in a new key. I do not mean to say that they are not ingenious—but people think them more ingenious than they are—on account of their method and *air* of method. In the "Murders in the Rue Morgue," for instance, where is the ingenuity of unravelling a web which you yourself (the author) have woven for the express purpose of unravelling? The reader is made to confound the ingenuity of the supposititious Dupin with that of the writer of the story.

Not for the world would I have had any one else to continue Lowell's Memoir until I had heard from you. I wish *you* to do it (if you will be so kind) and nobody else. By the time the book appears you will be famous, (or all my prophecy goes for nothing) and I shall have the éclat of your name to aid my sales. But, seriously, I do not think that any one so well enters into the poetical portion of my mind as yourself—and I deduce this idea from my intense appreciation of those points of your own poetry which seem lost upon others.

Should you undertake the work for me, there is one topic—there is one particular in which I have had wrong done me—and it may not be indecorous in me to call your attention to it. The last selection of my Tales was made from about 70, by Wiley & Putnam's reader, Duyckinck. He has what he thinks a taste for ratiocination, and has accordingly made up the book mostly of analytic stories. But this is not *representing* my mind in its various phases—it is not giving me fair play. In writing these Tales one by one, at long intervals, I have kept the book-unity always in mind—that is, each has been composed with reference to its effect as part of *a whole*. In this view, one of my chief aims has been the widest diversity of subject, thought, & especially *tone* & manner of handling. Were all my tales now before me in a large volume and as the composition of another—the merit which would principally arrest my attention would be the wide *diversity and* variety. You will be surprised to hear me say that (omitting one or two of my first efforts) I do not consider any one of my stories *better* than another. There is a vast variety of kinds and, in degree of value, these kinds vary—but each tale is equally good *of its kind*. The loftiest kind is that of the highest imagination—and, for this reason only, "Ligeia" may be called my *best* tale. I have much improved this last since you saw it and I mail you a copy, as well as a copy of my best specimen of analysis—"The Philosophy of Composition."

Do you ever see the British papers? Martin F. Tupper, author of "Proverbial Philosophy" has been paying me some high compliments—and indeed I have been treated more than well. There is one "British opinion", however, which I value highly— Miss Barrett's. She says:—"This vivid writing!—this power *which is felt!* The Raven has produced a sensation—'a fit horror' here in England. Some of my friends are taken by the fear of it and some by the music. I hear of persons *haunted* by the 'Nevermore', and one acquaintance of mine who has the misfortune of possessing a 'bust of Pallas' never can bear to look at it in the twilight. . . . Our great poet Mr Browning, author of Paracelsus etc is enthusiastic in his admiration of the rhythm. Then there is a tale of his which I do not find in this volume, but which is going the rounds of the news-papers, about Mesmerism [The Valdemar Case] throwing us all into most admired disorder or dreadful doubts as to whether it can be true, as the children say of ghost stories. The certain thing in the tale in question is the power of the writer & the faculty he has of making horrible improbabilities seem near and familiar." Would it be in bad taste to quote these words of Miss B. in your notice?

Forgive these egotisms (which are rendered in some measure necessary by the topic) and believe me that I will let slip *no* opportunity of reciprocating your kindness.

Griswold's new edition I have not yet seen (is it out?) but I will manage to find "Rosalie Lee". Do not forget to send me a few personal details of yourself—such as I give in "The N. Y. Literati". When your book appears I propose to review it fully in Colton's "American Review." If you ever write to him, please suggest to him that I wish to do so. I hope to get your volume before mine goes to press—so that I may speak more fully.

I will forward the papers to which I refer, *in a day or two*—not by to-day's mail.

Touching "The Stylus":—this is the one great purpose of my literary life. Undoubtedly (unless I die) I will accomplish it—but I can afford to lose nothing by precipitancy. I cannot yet say when or how I shall get to work—but when the time comes I will write to you. I wish to establish a journal in which the men of genius may fight their battles; upon some terms of equality, with those dunces the men of talent. But, apart from this, I have *magnificent* objects in view—may I but live to accomplish them!

Most cordially Your friend
EDGAR A. POE.

Famous for its demystification of the detective story Poe had created a few years earlier, this letter also reflects Poe's recruitment of Cooke as his biographer. Cooke extended James Russell Lowell's biographical sketch of Poe (published in *Graham's* in February 1845) in a piece published in the *Southern Literary Messenger* (January 1848), and he obliged Poe by inserting the flattering quote from Miss Barrett. After the *Broadway Journal* fiasco, Poe here expresses renewed determination to publish *The Stylus*.

EDGAR ALLAN POE TO
N. P. WILLIS

[December 30, 1846.]

My Dear Willis:—
The paragraph which has been put in circulation respecting my
wife's illness, my own, my poverty etc., is now lying before me; to-
gether with the beautiful lines by Mrs. Locke and those by Mrs.—,
to which the paragraph has given rise, as well as your kind and
manly comments in "The Home Journal."

The motive of the paragraph I leave to the conscience of him or
her who wrote it or suggested it. Since the thing is done, however,
and since the concerns of my family are thus pitilessly thrust be-
fore the public, I perceive no mode of escape from a public state-
ment of what is true and what erroneous in the report alluded to.

That my wife is ill, then, is true; and you may imagine with
what feeling I add that this illness, hopeless from the first, has
been heightened and precipitated by her reception, at two dif-
ferent periods, of anonymous letters—one enclosing the para-
graph now in question; the other, those published calumnies
of Messrs—, for which I yet hope to find redress in a court of
justice.

Of the facts, that I myself have been long and dangerously ill,
and that my illness has been a well understood thing among my
brethren of the press, the best evidence is afforded by the innu-
merable paragraphs of personal and literary abuse with which I
have been latterly assailed. This matter, however, will remedy it-
self. At the very first blush of my new prosperity, the gentlemen
who toadied me in the old, will recollect themselves and toady me
again. You, who know me, will comprehend that I speak of these
things only as having served, in a measure, to lighten the gloom of
unhappiness, by a gentle and not unpleasant sentiment of mingled
pity, merriment and contempt.

That, as the inevitable consequence of so long an illness, I have been in want of money, it would be folly in me to deny—but that I have ever materially suffered from privation, beyond the extent of my capacity for suffering, is not altogether true. That I am "without friends" is a gross calumny, which I am sure you never could have believed, and which a thousand noble-hearted men would have good right never to forgive me for permitting to pass unnoticed and undenied. Even in the city of New York I could have no difficulty in naming a hundred persons, to each of whom—when the hour for speaking had arrived—I could and would have applied for aid and with unbounded confidence, and with absolutely *no* sense of humiliation.

I do not think, my dear Willis, that there is any need of my saying more. I am getting better, and may add—if it be any comfort to my enemies—that I have little fear of getting worse. The truth is, I have a great deal to do; and I have made up my mind not to die till it is done.

Sincerely yours,
EDGAR A. POE.

Rumors of Poe's destitution, illness, and possible insanity swirled in the New York newspapers in late 1846. Poe here turns to his erstwhile employer to help him refute the charge that he has no friends. The paragraph in question represented Poe and his wife as "dangerously ill" and "so far reduced as to be barely able to obtain the necessaries of life." The "published calumnies" for which Poe sought (and won) legal satisfaction were promulgated by Thomas Dunn English and Hiram Fuller.

EDGAR ALLAN POE TO MARIE L. SHEW

[January 29, 1847.]

Kindest—dearest friend—

My poor Virginia still lives, although failing fast and now suffering much pain. May God grant her life until she sees you and thanks you once again! Her bosom is full to overflowing—like my own—with a boundless—inexpressible gratitude to you. Lest she may never see you more—she bids me say that she sends you her sweetest kiss of love and will die blessing you. But come—oh come to-morrow! Yes, I *will* be calm—everything you so nobly wish to see me. My mother sends you, also, her "warmest love and thanks." She begs me to ask you, if possible, to make arrangements at home so that you may stay with us tomorrow night. I enclose the order to the Postmaster.

> Heaven bless you and farewell
> EDGAR A POE.

Fordham,
Jan. 29. 47

Mrs. Shew nursed both Poe and Virginia during the worst months of their life together. This note, penned on the eve of Virginia's death, expresses the gratitude and love of both husband and wife.

EDGAR ALLAN POE TO GEORGE W. EVELETH

New-York—Jan. 4, 1848.

My Dear Sir—

Your last, dated July 26, ends with—"Write will you not"? I have been living ever since in a constant state of intention to write, and finally concluded not to write at all until I could say something definite about The Stylus and other matters. You perceive that I now send you a Prospectus—but before I speak farther on this topic, let me succinctly reply to various points in your letter. 1.—"Hawthorne" is out—how do you like it? 2—"The Rationale of Verse" was found to come down too heavily (as I forewarned you it did) upon some of poor Colton's personal friends in Frogpondium—the "pundits" you know; so I gave him "a song" for it & took it back. The song was "Ulalume a Ballad" published in the December number of the Am. Rev. I enclose it as copied by the Home Journal (Willis's paper) with the Editor's remarks—please let me know how you like "Ulalume". As for the "Rat. of Verse" I sold it to "Graham" at a round advance on Colton's price, and in Graham's hands it is still—but not to remain even there; for I mean to get it back, revise or rewrite it (since "Evangeline" has been published) and deliver it as a lecture when I go South & West on my Magazine expedition. 3—I have been "so still" on account of preparation for the magazine campaign—also have been working at my book—nevertheless I have written some trifles not yet published—some which have been. 4—My health is better—best. I have never been so well. 5—I do not well see how I could have otherwise replied to English. You must know him, (English) before you can well estimate my reply. He is so thorough a "blatherskite" that to have replied to him with *dignity* would have been the extreme of the ludicrous. The only true plan—not to have replied to him at all—was precluded on account of the nature of some of his accusations—forgery for instance. To such charges, even from the Autocrat of all the Asses—a man is *compelled* to answer. There he had me. Answer him I must. But how? Believe me there exists no such dilemma as that in which a gentleman is placed when he is forced to reply to a blackguard. If he have any genius then is the time for its display. I confess to you that I rather *like* that reply of mine in a literary sense—and so do a great many of my friends. It fully answered its purpose beyond a doubt— would to Heaven every work of art did as much! You err in supposing me to have been "peevish" when I wrote the reply:—the peevishness was all "put on" as a part of my argument—of my plan:—so was the "indignation" with which I wound up. *How* could I be either peev-ish or indignant about a matter so well adapted to further my purposes? Were I able to afford so expensive a luxury as personal and especially as *refutable* abuse, I would willingly pay any man $2000 per annum, to hammer away at me all the year round. I suppose you know that I sued the Mirror & got a verdict. English eloped. 5—The "common friend" referred to is Mrs Frances S. Osgood, the poetess.—6—I agree with you only in part as regards Miss Fuller. She has some general but no particular critical powers. She belongs to a *school* of criticism— the Gothean, esthetic, eulogistic. The creed of this school is that, in criticizing an author you must imitate him, ape him, out-Herod Herod. She is grossly dishonest. She abuses Lowell, for example, (the best of our poets, perhaps) on account of a personal quarrel with him. She has omitted all mention of me for the same reason—although, a short time before the issue of her book, she praised me highly in the Tribune. I enclose you her criticism that you may judge for yourself. She praised "Witchcraft" because Mathews (who toadies her) wrote it. In a word, she is an ill-tempered and very inconsistent old maid—avoid her. 7—Nothing was omitted in "Marie Roget" but what I omitted myself:—all *that* is mystification. The story was originally published in Snowden's "Lady's Companion". The "naval officer" who committed the murder (or rather the accidental death arising from an attempt at abortion) con*fessed* it; and the whole matter is now well understood—but, for the sake of relatives, his is a topic on which I must not speak further. 8—"The Gold Bug" was originally sent to Graham, but he not liking it, I got him to take some critical

papers instead, and sent it to The Dollar Newspaper which had of-
fered $100 for the best story. It obtained the premium and made a
great noise. 9—The "necessities" were pecuniary ones. I referred
to a sneer at my poverty on the part of the Mirror. 10—You say—
"Can you *hint* to me what was the terrible evil" which caused the
irregularities so profoundly lamented?" Yes; I can do more than
hint. This "evil" was the greatest which can befall a man. Six
years ago, a wife, whom I loved as no man ever loved before, rup-
tured a blood-vessel in singing. Her life was despaired of. I took
leave of her forever & underwent all the agonies of her death. She
recovered partially and I again hoped. At the end of a year the ves-
sel broke again—I went through precisely the same scene. Again
in about a year afterward. Then again—again—again & even once
again at varying intervals. Each time I felt all the agonies of her
death—and at each accession of the disorder I loved her more
dearly & clung to her life with more desperate pertinacity. But I
am constitutionally sensitive—nervous in a very unusual degree. I
became insane, with long intervals of horrible sanity. During these
fits of absolute unconsciousness I drank, God only knows how of-
ten or how much. As a matter of course, my enemies referred the
insanity to the drink rather than the drink to the insanity. I had in-
deed, nearly abandoned all hope of a permanent cure when I found
one in the *death* of my wife. This I can & do endure as becomes a
man—it was the horrible never-ending oscillation between hope &
despair which I could *not* longer have endured without the total
loss of reason. In the death of what was my life, then, I receive a
new but—oh God! how melancholy an existence.

And now, having replied to all your queries let me refer to The
Stylus. I am resolved to be my own publisher. To be controlled is
to be ruined. My ambition is great. If I succeed, I put myself
(within 2 years) in possession of a fortune & infinitely more. My
plan is to go through the South & West & endeavor to interest my
friends so as *to commence with a list of at least 500 subscribers.*
With this list I can take the matter into my own hands. There are
some few of my friends who have sufficient confidence in me to
advance their subscriptions—but at all events succeed I *will*. Can
you or will you help me? I have room to say no more.

Truly Yours—
E A Poe.

[Please re-enclose the printed slips when you have done with them. Have you seen the article on "The American Library" in the November No. of Blackwood, and if so, what do you think of it? E. A. Poe.]

This lengthy reply to a young admirer touches on a range of fascinating topics. Poe's enumeration of points includes two items numbered "5." Significantly he alludes to plans for *The Stylus* and to his ongoing irritation with English, "the Autocrat of the Asses," who continued to satirize Poe in the pages of a weekly newspaper called the *John-Donkey*. He also clarifies the process by which "The Gold-Bug" was withdrawn from *Graham's* for entry in the *Dollar Newspaper* contest. Most significantly, Poe explains his drinking of the mid-1840s as a reaction to Virginia's illness, here described (in terms reminiscent of "Ligeia") as a "horrible never-ending oscillation between hope & despair."

EDGAR ALLAN POE TO
GEORGE W. EVELETH

New-York—Feb. 29—48.

My Dear Sir,
I mean to start for Richmond on the 10th March. Every thing has
gone as I wished it, and my final success is certain, or I abandon all
claims to the title of Vates. The only contretemps of any moment,
lately, has been Willis's somewhat premature announcement of my
project:—but this will only force me into action a little sooner
than I had proposed. Let me now answer the points of your last
letter.

Colton acted pretty much as all mere men of the world act. I
think very little the worse of him for his endeavor to succeed with
you at my expense. I always liked him and I believe he liked me.
His intellect was o. His "I understand the matter perfectly,"
amuses me. Certainly, then, it was the only matter he *did* under-
stand. "The Rationale of Verse" will appear in "Graham" after
all:—I will stop in Phil: to see the proofs. As for Godey, he is a
good little man and means as well as he knows how. The editor of
the "Weekly Universe" speaks kindly and I find no fault with his
representing my habits as "shockingly irregular". He could not
have had the "personal acquaintance" with me of which he
writes; but has fallen into a very natural error. The fact is thus:—
My *habits* are rigorously abstemious and I omit nothing of the
natural regimen requisite for health:—i.e.—I rise early, eat moder-
ately, drink nothing but water, and take abundant and regular ex-
ercise in the open air. But this is my private life—my studious and
literary life—and of course escapes the eye of the world. The de-
sire for society comes upon me only when I have become excited
by drink. Then *only* I go—that is, at these times only *I have been*
in the practice of going among my friends: who seldom, or in fact
never, having seen me unless excited, take it for granted that I am

always so. Those who *really* know me, know better. In the mean-time I shall turn the general error to account. But enough of this: the causes which maddened me to the drinking point are no more, and I am done drinking, forever.—I do *not* know the "editors & contributors" of the "Weekly Universe" and was not aware of the existence of such a paper. Who are they? or is it a secret? The "most distinguished of American scholars" is Prof. Chas. Anthon, author of the "Classical Dictionary".

I presume you have seen some newspaper notices of my late lecture on the Universe. You could have gleaned, however, no idea of what the lecture was, from what the papers said it was. All praised it—as far as I have yet seen—and all absurdly misrepresented it. The only report of it which approaches the truth, is the one I enclose—from the "Express"—written by E. A. Hopkins—a gentleman of much scientific acquirement—son of Bishop Hopkins of Vermont—but he conveys only my general idea, and his digest is full of inaccuracies. I enclose also a slip from the "Courier & Enquirer":—*please return them.* To eke out a chance of your understanding what I really *did* say, I add a loose summary of my propositions & results:

The General Proposition is this:—Because Nothing was, *therefore* All Things are.

1—An inspection of the *universality* of Gravitation—i.e., of the fact that each particle tends, *not* to any one common point, but to *every other* particle—suggests *perfect* totality, or *absolute* unity, as the source of the phaenomenon.

2—Gravity is but the mode in which is manifested the tendency of all things to return into their original unity; is but the reaction of the first Divine Act.

3—The *law* regulating the return—i.e., the *law* of Gravitation—is but a necessary result of the necessary & sole possible mode of equable *irradiation* of matter through space:—this *equable* irradiation is necessary as a basis for the Nebular Theory of Laplace.

4—The Universe of Stars (contradistinguished from the Universe of Space) is limited.

5—Mind is cognizant of Matter *only* through its two properties, attraction and repulsion: therefore Matter *is* only attraction & repulsion: a finally consolidated globe of globes, being but *one* particle, would be without attraction, i.e., gravitation; the existence of such a globe presupposes the expulsion of the separative ether which we know to exist between the particles as at present diffused:—thus the final globe would be matter without attraction & repulsion:—but these *are* matter:—then the final globe would be matter without matter:—i.e., no matter at all:—it must disappear. Thus Unity is *Nothingness*.

6. Matter, springing from Unity, sprang from Nothingness:—i.e., was *created*.

7. All will return to Nothingness, in returning to Unity.

Read these items *after* the Report. As to the Lecture, I am very quiet about it—but, if you have ever dealt with such topics, you will recognize the novelty & *moment* of my views. What I have propounded will (in good time) revolutionize the world of Physical & Metaphysical Science. I say this calmly—but I say it.

I shall not go till I hear from you.

Truly Yours,
E A POE

By the bye, lest you infer that my views, in detail, are the same with those advanced in the *Nebular Hypothesis*, *I* venture to offer a few addenda, the substance of which was penned, though never printed, several years ago, under the head of—A Prediction. . . .

How will *that* do for a postscript?

This letter reveals Poe's utter preoccupation with the cosmological theories eventually published as *Eureka*. Poe labors to refute more accusations of insobriety but curiously refuses to disagree with the editors of the *Weekly Universe*, who have described his habits as "shockingly irregular." The lengthy post-script, condensed here, appears in Mabbott's edition of *Tales* (volume 3, pages 1320–22) as "A Prediction," and elaborates a theory of the origins of the solar system.

EDGAR ALLAN POE TO SARAH HELEN WHITMAN

[Fordham]   Sunday Night—Oct. 1—48.

I have pressed your letter again and again to my lips, sweetest Helen—bathing it in tears of joy, or of a "divine despair". But I—who so lately, in your presence, vaunted the "power of words"—of what avail are mere words to me now? *Could I* believe in the efficiency of prayers to the God of Heaven, I would indeed kneel—humbly kneel—at this the most earnest epoch of my life—kneel in entreaty for words—*but* for words that should disclose to you—that might enable me to lay bare to you my whole heart. All thoughts—all passions seem now merged in that one consuming desire—the mere wish to make you comprehend—to make you see *that* for which there is no human voice—the unutterable fervor of my love for you:—for so well do I know your poet-nature, oh Helen, Helen! that I feel sure if you could but look down *now* into the depths of my soul with your pure spiritual eyes you *could* not refuse to speak to me what, alas! you still resolutely have unspoken—you would *love* me if only for the greatness of my love. Is it not something in this cold, dreary world, *to be loved?*—Oh, if I could but burn into your spirit the deep—the *true* meaning which I attach to those three syllables underlined!—but, alas: the effort is all in vain and "I live and die unheard".

When I spoke to you of what I felt, saying that I loved now for the *first* time, I did not hope you would believe or even understand me; nor can I hope to convince you now—but if, throughout some long, dark summer night, I could but have held you close, close to my heart and whispered to you the strange secrets of its passionate history, then indeed you would have seen that I have been far from attempting to deceive you in this respect. I could have shown you that it was not and could never have been in the power of any other than yourself to move me as I am now moved—to oppress me with this ineffable emotion—to surround and bathe me in this electric light, illumining and enkindling my whole nature—filling my soul with glory, with wonder, and with awe. During our walk in the cemetery I said to you, while the bitter, bitter tears sprang into my eyes—"Helen, I love now—now—for the first and only time." I said this, I repeat, in no hope that you could believe me, but because I could not help feeling how unequal were the heart-riches we might offer each to each. . . .

And now, in the most simple words at my command, let me paint to you the impression made upon me by your personal presence.—As you entered the room, pale, timid, hesitating, and evidently oppressed at heart; as your eyes rested appealingly, for one brief moment, upon mine, I felt, for the first time in my life, and tremblingly acknowledged, the existence of spiritual influences altogether out of the reach of the reason. I saw that you were *Helen—my* Helen—the Helen of a thousand dreams—she whose visionary lips had so often lingered upon my own in the divine trance of passion—she whom the great Giver of all Good had pre-ordained to be mine—mine only—if not now, alas! then at least hereafter and *forever*, in the Heavens.—You spoke falteringly and seemed scarcely conscious of what you said. I heard no words—only the soft voice, more familiar to me than my own, and more melodious than the songs of the angels. Your hand rested within mine, and my whole soul shook with a tremulous ecstasy. And then but for very shame—but for the fear of grieving or oppress-ing you—I would have fallen at your feet in as pure—in as real a *worship* as was ever offered to Idol or to God. And when, after-wards, on those two successive evenings of all-Heavenly delight, you passed to and fro about the room—now sitting by my side, now far away, now standing with your hand resting on the back of my chair, while the praeternatural thrill of your touch vibrated even through the senseless wood into my heart—while you moved thus restlessly about the room—as if a deep Sorrow or a more pro-found Joy haunted your bosom—my brain reeled beneath the in-toxicating spell of your presence, and it was with no merely human senses that I either saw or heard you. It was my soul only that distinguished you there. I grew faint with the luxury of your voice and blind with the voluptuous lustre of your eyes.

Let me quote to you a passage from your letter:—"You will,

perhaps, attempt to convince me that my person is agreeable to you—that my countenance interests you:—but in this respect I am so variable that I should inevitably disappoint you if you hoped to find in me to-morrow the same aspect which won you to-day. And, again, although my reverence for your intellect and my admiration of your genius make me feel like a *child* in your presence, you are not, perhaps, aware that I am many years older than yourself. I *fear* you do not know it, and that if you *had* known it you would not have felt for me as you do."—To all this what shall I—what *can I* say—except that the heavenly candor with which you speak oppresses my heart with so rich a burden of love that my eyes overflow with sweet tears. You are mistaken, Helen, very far mistaken about this matter of age. I am older than you; and if illness and sorrow have made you seem older than you are—is not all this the best of reason for my loving you the more? Cannot my patient cares—my watchful, earnest attention—cannot the magic which lies in such devotion as I feel for you, win back for you much—oh, very much of the freshness of your youth? But grant that what you urge were even true. Do you not feel in your inmost heart of hearts that the "soul-love" of which the world speaks so often and so idly is, in this instance at least, but the veriest, the most absolute of realities? Do you not—I ask it of your reason, *darling*, not less than of your heart—do you not perceive that it is my diviner nature—my spiritual being—which burns and pants to commingle with your own? Has the soul *age*, Helen? Can Immortality regard Time? Can that which began *never* and shall never end, consider a few wretched years of its incarnate life? Ah, I could weep—I could *almost* be angry with you for the unwarranted wrong you offer to the purity—to the sacred reality of my affection.—And how *am* I to answer what you say of your personal appearance? Have I not *seen* you, Helen, have I not heard the more than melody of your voice? Has not my heart ceased to throb beneath the magic of your smile? Have I not held your hand in mine and looked steadily into your soul through the crystal Heaven of your eyes? Have I not done all these things?—or do I dream?—or am I mad? Were you *indeed* all that your fancy, enfeebled and perverted by illness, tempts you to suppose that you are, still, life of my life! I would but love you—but worship you the more:—it would be so glorious a happiness to be able to *prove* to you what I feel! But as it is, what can I—what *am* I to say? *Who* ever spoke of you without emotion—without praise? Who *ever* saw you and did not love?

But now a deadly terror oppresses me; for I too clearly see that these objections—so groundless—so futile when urged to one whose nature must be so well known to you as mine is—can scarcely be meant earnestly; and I tremble lest they but serve to mask others, more real, and which you hesitate—perhaps in pity—to confide to me. Alas! I too distinctly perceive, also, that in no instance you have ever permitted yourself to say that you *love me*. You are aware, sweet Helen, that on my part there are insuperable reasons forbidding me to *urge* upon you my love. Were I not poor—had not my late errors and reckless excesses justly lowered me in the esteem of the good—were I wealthy, or could I offer you worldly honors—ah then—then—how proud would I be to persevere—to sue—to plead—to kneel—to pray—to beseech you for your love—in the deepest humility—at your feet—at your feet, Helen, and with floods of passionate tears.

And now let me copy here one other passage from your letter:— "I find that I cannot now tell you all that I promised. I can only say to you that had I youth and health and beauty, I would live for you and die with you. *Now*, were I to allow myself to love you, I could only enjoy a bright, brief hour of rapture and die—perhaps [illegible]."—The last five words have been [illegible] Ah, beloved, beloved Helen the darling of my heart—my first and my real love!—may God forever shield you from the agony which these your words occasion *me*! How *selfish*—how despicably selfish seems now all—*all* that I have written! Have I not, indeed, been demanding at your hands a love which might endanger your life? You will never, *never* know—you can *never* picture to yourself the hopeless, rayless despair with which I now trace these words. Alas Helen! my soul!—what is it that I have been saying to you?—to what madness have I been urging you?—I who am *nothing* to you—*you* who have a dear mother and sister to be blessed by your life and love. But ah, darling! if I *seem* selfish, yet believe that I truly, *truly* love you, and that it is the most spiritual of love that I speak, even if I speak it from the depths of the most passionate of hearts. Think—oh, think for *me*, Helen, and for yourself! *Is there no* hope?—is there *none*? May not this terrible disease be conquered? Frequently it *has* been overcome. And more frequently are we deceived in respect to its actual existence. Long-continued nervous disorder—especially when exasperated by ether or [omitted]—will give rise to *all* the symptoms of heart-disease and so deceive the most skillful physicians—as even in my own case they were deceived. But admit that this fearful evil *has* indeed assailed you. Do you not all the more really need the devotionate care which only one who loves you as I do, could or would bestow? On my bosom could I not still the throbbings of your own? Do not mistake me, Helen! Look, with your searching—your seraphic eyes, into the soul of my soul, and see if you can discover there one taint of an ignoble nature! At your feet—if you so willed it—I would cast from me, forever, all merely human desire, and clothe myself in the glory of a pure, calm, and *unexacting* affection. I would comfort you—soothe you—tranquillize you. My love—my faith—should instil into your bosom a praeternatural calm. You would rest from care—from all worldly agitation. You would get better, and finally well. And if *not*, Helen,—if not—if you *died*— then at least would I clasp your dear hand in death, and willingly—*oh, joyfully—joyfully—joyfully*—go down *with you* into the night of the Grave.

Write soon—soon—oh, *soon!*—but not *much*. Do not weary or agitate yourself for *my* sake. Say to me those coveted words which would turn Earth into Heaven. If Hope is forbidden, I will *not* murmur if you comfort me with Love.—The papers of which you speak I will procure and forward immediately. They will cost me nothing, *dear* Helen, and I therefore re-enclose you what you so thoughtfully sent. Think that, in doing so, my lips are pressed fervently and lingeringly upon your own. And now, in closing this long, long letter, let me speak last of that which lies nearest my heart—of that precious gift which I would not exchange for the surest hope of Paradise. It seems to me too sacred that I should even whisper *to you*, the dear giver, what it is. My soul, this night, shall come to you in dreams and speak to you those fervid thanks which my pen is all powerless to utter.

EDGAR

P. S. Tuesday Morning.—I beg you to believe, dear Helen, that I replied to your letter *immediately* upon its receipt; but a most unusual storm, up to this moment, precludes all access to the City.

A lengthy section of this letter, recollecting Poe's first awareness of Mrs. Whitman and then the effect of the Valentine she sent him in 1848, has been omitted. So too is a passage in which Poe interprets as miraculously prophetic the fact that his first great poem was titled "To Helen." The author's ardent language suggests the intensity of the attraction that led him to propose marriage (in a cemetery) during his first face-to-face meeting with Mrs. Whitman, a widow six years his senior. That age difference provokes Poe's fascinating rationalization of his devotion. From the outset, Mrs. Whitman's misgivings and her mother's active mistrust of Poe doomed the courtship, in which Poe persisted through December 1848, when he received a final, definitive refusal.

EDGAR ALLAN POE TO
ANNIE L. RICHMOND

Fordham   Nov. 16th 1848—

Ah, Annie Annie! *my* Annie! what cruel thoughts about your Eddy must have been torturing your heart during the last terrible fort-night, in which you have heard *nothing* from me—not even one little word to say that I still lived & loved you. But Annie I know that you *felt* too deeply the nature of my love for you, to doubt *that,* even for one moment, & this thought has comforted me in my bitter sorrow—I could bear that you should imagine *every other evil except that one*—that my soul had been untrue to yours. Why am I not *with you* now *darling* that I might sit by your side, press your dear hand in mine, & look deep down into the clear Heaven of your eyes—so that the words which I now can only *write*, might sink into your heart, and make you comprehend what it is that I would say—And yet Annie, *all* that I wish to say—all that my soul pines to express at this instant, is included in the one word, *love*—To be with you now—so that I might whisper in your ear the divine emotions, which agitate me—I would willingly—oh *joyfully* abandon this world with all my hopes of another:—but you *believe* this, Annie—you do believe it, & will always believe it—So long as I think that you *know* I love you, as no man ever loved woman—so long as I think you comprehend in some mea-sure, the fervor with which I adore you, *so* long, no worldly trou-ble can ever render me absolutely wretched. But oh, *my darling, my* Annie, my own sweet *sister* Annie, my *pure* beautiful angel—*wife* of my soul—to be mine hereafter & *forever in the Heavens*—how shall I explain to you the *bitter, bitter* anguish which has tortured me since I left you? You saw, you *felt* the agony of grief with which I bade you farewell—You remember my expressions of gloom—of a dreadful horrible foreboding of ill—Indeed—*indeed* it seemed to me that death approached me even then, &

that I was involved in the shadow which went before him—As I clasped you to my heart, I said to myself—"it is for the last time, until we meet in Heaven"—I remember nothing distinctly, from that moment until I found myself in Providence—I went to bed & wept through a long, long, hideous night of despair—When the day broke, I arose & endeavored to quiet my mind by a rapid walk in the cold, keen air—but all *would* not do—the demon tormented me still. Finally I procured two ounces of laudanum & without returning to my Hotel, took the cars back to Boston. When I arrived, I wrote you a letter, in which I opened my whole heart to you—to *you*—my Annie, whom I so madly, so distractedly love—I told you how my struggles were more than I could bear—how my soul revolted from saying the words which were to be said—and that not even for your dear sake, could I bring myself to say them. I then reminded you of that holy promise, which was the last I exacted from you in parting—the promise that, under all circumstances, you would come to me on my bed of death—I implored you to come *then*—mentioning the place where I should be found in Boston—Having written this letter, I swallowed about half the laudanum & hurried to the Post-Office—intending not to take the rest until I saw you—for, I did not doubt for one moment, that *my own* Annie would keep her sacred promise—But I had not calculated on the strength of the laudanum, for, before I reached the Post Office my reason was entirely gone, & the letter was never put in. Let me pass over, my darling *Sister*, the awful horrors which succeeded—A friend was at hand, who aided & (if it can be called saving) saved me—but it is only within the last three days that I have been able to remember what occurred in that dreary interval—It appears that, after the laudanum was rejected from the stomach, I became calm, & to a casual observer, sane—so that I was suffered to go back to Providence—Here I saw *her, &* spoke, for *your* sake, the words which you urged me to speak— Ah Annie Annie! *my* Annie!—is your heart *so* strong?—is there *no* hope!—is there *none*?—I feel that I *must* die if I persist, & yet, how can I now retract with honor?—Ah *beloved*, think—think for *me &* for yourself—do I not *love you* Annie? do you not *love me*? Is not this *all*? Beyond this blissful thought, what other consideration *can* there be in this dreary world! It is not *much* that I ask, *sweet sister Annie*—my mother & myself would take a small

cottage at Westford—oh *so* small—so *very* humble—I should be
far away from the tumults of the world—from the ambition
which I loathe—I would labor day & night, and with industry, I
could accomplish *so* much—Annie! it would be a Paradise be-
yond my wildest hopes—I could see some of your beloved family
every day, & you often—oh VERY often—I would hear from you
continually—regularly & *our* dear mother would be with us &
love us both—ah *darling*—do not these pictures touch your in-
most heart? Think—oh *think* for me—before the words—the
vows are spoken, which put yet another terrible *bar* between us—
before the time goes by, beyond which there must be *no*
thinking—I call upon you in the name of God—in the name of
the holy love I bear you, to be *sincere* with me—*Can you, my* An-
nie, *bear* to think I am another's? *It would give me supreme—
infinite bliss* to hear you say that you could *not* bear it—I am at
home now with my dear muddie who is endeavoring to comfort
me—but the sole words which soothe me, are those in which she
speaks of *"my Annie"*—she tells me that she has written you,
begging you to come on to Fordham—ah beloved Annie, IS IT
NOT POSSIBLE? I am so *ill*—*so* terribly, hopelessly ILL in body and
mind, that I feel I CANNOT live, unless I can feel your sweet,
gentle, loving hand pressed upon my forehead—oh my *pure, vir-
tuous, generous, beautiful, beautiful sister* Annie!—is it not POS-
SIBLE for you to come—if only for one little week?—until I
subdue this fearful agitation, which if continued, will either de-
stroy my life or, drive me hopelessly mad—Farewell—here &
hereafter—

Forever your own
EDDY—

In part Poe pursued his romance with Mrs. Whitman (as this letter
makes clear) because Mrs. Nancy "Annie" Richmond, his muse and
confidante, had encouraged him to do so. Here Poe virtually begs
Annie to reverse herself and oppose the courtship; indeed, his account
of the bizarre episode in which he ingested laudanum (opium) im-
plies that he meant to create a crisis that would bring Annie to his
bedside. One cannot know whether this was a genuine suicide at-
tempt or a desperate ploy for Annie's attention, or both. Poe seems to

have no sense of impropriety in writing a love letter to Mrs. Richmond, a married woman, or of speaking of his own marriage to Mrs. Whitman as "<u>another</u> terrible *bar*" (my underscoring, Poe's italics) to a relationship with Annie. Tellingly, several romantic phrases in this letter also appear in the preceding letter to Mrs. Whitman. Understandably, Annie may have urged Poe's courtship with Mrs. Whitman to redirect his amorous attentions.

EDGAR ALLAN POE TO FREDERICK W. THOMAS

Fordham, near New-York   Feb. 14—49.

My dear friend Thomas,

Your letter, dated Nov. 27, has reached me at a little village of the Empire State, after having taken, at its leisure, a very considerable tour among the P. Offices—occasioned, I presume, by your endorsement "to forward" wherever I might be—and the fact is, where I might *not* have been, for the last three months, is the legitimate question. At all events, now that I have your well-known M.S. before me, it is most cordially welcome. Indeed, it seems an age since I heard from you and a decade of ages since I shook you by the hand—although I hear of you now and then. Right glad am I to find you once more in a true position—in the "field of Letters." Depend upon it, after all, Thomas, Literature is the most noble of professions. In fact, it is about the only one fit for a man. For my own part, there is no seducing me from the path. I shall be a *litterateur*, at least, all my life; nor would I abandon the hopes which still lead me on for all the gold in California. Talking of gold, and of the temptations at present held out to "poor-devil authors", did it ever strike you that all which is really valuable to a man of letters—to a poet in especial—is absolutely unpurchaseable? Love, fame, the dominion of intellect, the consciousness of power, the thrilling sense of beauty, the free air of Heaven, exercise of body & mind, with the physical and moral health which result—these and such as these are really all that a poet cares for:—then answer me this—*why* should he go to California? Like Brutus, "I pause for a reply"—which, like F. W. Thomas, I take it for granted you have no intention of giving me.—[I have read the Prospectus of the "Chronicle" and like it much especially the part where you talk about "letting go the finger" of that conceited body, the East—which is by no means the East out of which came the wise men mentioned in Scripture!] I wish you would come down on the Frogpondians. They are getting worse and worse, and pretend not to be aware that there *are* any literary people out of Boston. The worst and most disgusting part of the matter is, that the Bostonians are really, as a race, far inferior in point of *anything beyond mere talent*, to any other *set* upon the continent of N. A. They are decidedly the most servile imitators of the English it is possible to conceive. I always get into a passion when I think about. It would be the easiest thing in the world to use them up *en masse*. One really well-written satire would accomplish the business:—but it must not be such a dish of skimmed milk-and-water as Lowell's.

I suppose you have seen that affair—the "Fable for Critics" I mean. Miss Fuller, that detestable old maid—told him, once, that he was "so wretched a poet as to be disgusting even to his best friends". This set him off at a tangent and he has never been quite right since:—so he took to writing satire against mankind in general, with Margaret Fuller and her *protégé*, Cornelius Matthews, in particular. It is miserably weak upon the whole, but has one or two good, but by no means *original*, things—Oh, there is "*nothing* new under the sun" & Solomon is right—for once. I sent a review of the "Fable" to the "S. L. Messenger" a day or two ago, and I only hope Thompson will print it. Lowell is a ranting abolitionist and *deserves* a good using up. It is a pity that he is a poet.— I have not seen your paper yet, and hope you will mail me one—regularly if you can spare it. I will send you something whenever I get a chance.—[With your co-editor, Mr (unreadable) I am not acquainted personally but he is well known to me by reputation. Eames, I think, was talking to me about him in Washington once, and spoke very highly of him in many respects—so upon the whole you are in luck]—The rock on which most new enterprizes, in the paper way, split, is namby-pamby-ism. It never did do & never will. No yea-nay journal *ever* succeeded.—but I know there is little danger of your making the Chronicle a yea-nay one. I have been quite out of the literary world for the last three years, and have *said* little or nothing, but, like the owl, I have "taken it out in thinking". By and bye I mean to come out of the bush, and then I have *some* old scores to settle. I fancy I see some of my *friends* already stepping up to the Captain's office. The fact is,

Thomas, living buried in the country makes a man savage—
wolfish. I am just in the humor for a fight. You will be pleased to
hear that I am in better health than I ever knew myself to be—full
of energy and bent upon success. You shall hear of me again
shortly—and it is not improbable that I may soon pay you a visit
in Louisville.—If I can do anything for you in New-York, let me
know.—Mrs Clemm sends her best respects & begs to be remem-
bered to your mother's family, if they are with you.—You would
oblige me very especially if you could squeeze in what follows, ed-
itorially. The lady spoken of is a most particular friend of mine,
and deserves *all* I have said of her. I will reciprocate the favor I
ask, whenever you say the word and show me how. Address me at
N. *York City,* as usual and if you insert the following, please cut it
out & enclose it in your letter.

Truly your friend,
EDGAR A POE.

Poe here expresses his commitment to the life of writing as he re-
flects on the rush for California gold. He also urges Thomas, then a
newspaper editor in Louisville, to perform a literary service by crit-
icizing the "Frogpondians" (Bostonians) as a group; his animus to-
ward Lowell has been occasioned by Lowell's caricature of Poe in
"A Fable for Critics." Poe describes himself as "full of energy and
bent upon success" prior to a striking decline in physical and men-
tal health during the spring and summer of 1849.

EDGAR ALLAN POE TO
MARIA CLEMM

New York [Philadelphia]   July 7. [1849]

My dear, dear Mother,—
I have been *so* ill—have had the cholera, or spasms quiet as bad,
and can now hardly hold the pen. . . .
 The very instant you get this, *come* to me. The joy of seeing you
will almost compensate for our sorrows. We can but die together.
It is no use to reason with me *now*; I must die. I have no desire to
live since I have done "Eureka." I could accomplish nothing more.
For your sake it would be sweet to live, but we must die together.
You have been all in all to me, darling, ever beloved mother, and
dearest, truest friend.
 I was never *really* insane, except on occasions where my heart
was touched. . . .
 I have been taken to prison once since I came here for spreeing
drunk; but *then I* was not. It was about Virginia.

                                                        [UNSIGNED]

Poe's drinking in Philadelphia earned him a night in Moyamensing
Prison, from which he was liberated by literary friends. The illness to
which he refers may have been delirium tremens; while in prison he
reportedly had a nightmare in which Mrs. Clemm was mutilated. His
explanation of the binge drinking is poignantly succinct: "It was
about Virginia."

EDGAR ALLAN POE TO
MARIA CLEMM

Richmond Va   Tuesday—Sep 18—49.

My own darling Muddy,
On arriving here last night from Norfolk I received both your let-
ters, including Mrs Lewis's. I cannot tell you the joy they gave me—
to learn at least that you are well & hopeful. May God forever bless
you, my *dear dear* Muddy—Elmira has just got home from the
country. I spent last evening with her. I think she loves me more de-
votedly than any one I ever knew & I cannot help loving her in re-
turn. Nothing is yet definitely settled and it will not do to hurry
matters. I lectured at Norfolk on Monday & cleared enough to set-
tle my bill here at the Madison House with $2 over. I had a highly
fashionable audience, but Norfolk is a small place & there were 2
exhibitions the same night. Next Monday I lecture again here &
expect to have a large audience. On Tuesday I start for Phila to at-
tend to Mrs Loud's Poems—& *possibly* on Thursday I may start
for N. York. If I do I will go straight over to Mrs Lewis's & send for
you. It will be better for me not to go to Fordham—don't you think
so? Write immediately in reply & direct to Phila. For fear I should
not get the letter, sign no name & address it to E. S. *T. Grey Esqre.*
If possible I will get married before I start—but there is no
telling. Give my dearest love to Mrs L. My poor poor Muddy. I am
still unable to send you even one dollar—but keep up heart—I hope
that our troubles are nearly over. I saw John Beatty in Norfolk.
God bless & protect you my own darling Muddy. I showed
your letter to Elmira and she says "it is such a darling precious let-
ter that she loves you for it already"

Your own Eddy.

Don't forget to write immediately to Phila. so that your letter will
be there when I arrive.

The papers here are praising me to death—and I have been received everywhere with enthusiasm. Be sure & preserve all the printed scraps I have sent you & keep up my file of the Lit. World.

Having obtained Sarah Elmira Royster Shelton's acceptance of a marriage offer, Poe seemed in a position to launch his journal (thanks to a young Illinois publisher named Edward Patterson) and to secure domestic stability through remarriage. Poe had been lecturing successfully on American poetry in Richmond and Norfolk; and he took a pledge of temperance to convince Mrs. Shelton of his serious purpose. But his relapses into alcoholic excess were numerous that summer. He may have been planning to bring Mrs. Clemm to Virginia for the wedding, unless an earlier date could be agreed upon. His insistence that Mrs. Clemm address his mail to an alias may reflect mere prudence after his recent misadventures in Philadelphia or it may betray growing paranoia. Less than three weeks after writing this letter, he was dead.

CRITICAL PRINCIPLES

As a magazinist, Poe reviewed scores of new books and commented extensively on contemporary poetry, fiction, and nonfiction. Exacting and occasionally derisive, he became known as "the tomahawk man," stirring controversy by attacking powerful literary figures. He lampooned a novel by an editor of the *New-York Mirror* and later accused the esteemed Henry Wadsworth Longfellow of plagiarism. He deplored the shameless promotion of mediocre authors and in several fictional satires—as well as the final review in this section—indicted the practice of "puffery" then pervasive in the American publishing world. Poe believed that the literature of the United States could outgrow its provincialism only if literary critics applied rigorous standards rather than indulging in partisan favoritism. While he resented British condescension toward American writers, he himself did not hesitate to expose the "stupidity" of certain American books.

Driven by economics to write more fiction than poetry, Poe helped to shape the conventions of an emerging literary form, the short story. Yet he never used that term—which came into use only late in the nineteenth century—instead concerning himself with "the short prose tale." And although Poe grasped the peculiar demands of the form, he wrote about its generic principles only briefly in reviews of works by individual authors. His most famous statement about short fiction appears in his 1842 review of Hawthorne's *Twice-Told Tales*, where Poe devotes four extended paragraphs to a theory of the tale emphasizing "unity of effect." This "totality" reveals itself, he asserts, only in narratives that can be read at a single sitting of at most "one or two hours." Yet although this review figures as the starting point for modern short-story theory, Poe had been thinking about the importance of

unifying effect at least since 1836, when he remarked in a review
of Dickens that unity was more crucial in the "brief article" (or
short narrative) than in the novel. An 1841 review of Lytton Bul-
wer's fiction registers the same point by implication, insisting on
the impossibility of achieving "unity or totality *of effect*" in a nar-
rative as long as a novel. Here Poe suggests that plot is crucial to
unity (though curiously not "essential" to storytelling). In "A
Chapter of Suggestions" Poe returns briefly to the matter of plot
and advances a theory of narrative construction that begins with
the ending, the effect intended in the *dénouement*. In this view,
plot becomes the unifying structure from which no individual ele-
ment can be removed without destroying the totality of the tale.

Poe's critical reflections on poetry represent a more concerted
attempt to articulate basic principles. His "Letter to B—," which
introduced the 1831 volume of *Poems*, reveals much about Poe's
values as a young poet in his comparison of Wordsworth and Co-
leridge, then the giants of English poetry. Poe's disdain for
Wordsworth's philosophizing and his admiration for Coleridge's
"towering intellect" and "gigantic power" help to explain his per-
sonal definition of the poem as a work whose immediate object
is "pleasure" created by "indefinite sensations," toward which
end the "sweet sound" of music is "essential." As an editorial as-
sistant, Poe inserted passing comments on the nature of poetry in
critical notices such as the "Drake-Halleck" review of 1836, and
in 1843 he began to lecture on poetry. But not until the success of
"The Raven" did he confect a grand theory of poetry. His "Phi-
losophy of Composition" (1845) amounts to a tour de force, a
logical analysis of how he wrote his most famous poem by work-
ing backward from its intended final effect. Poe's account of the
composition process must be taken *cum grano salis* (with a grain
of salt—one of his favorite Latin expressions), but his designation
of "Beauty" as "the sole legitimate province of the poem" accords
with his own practice and helps to legitimate the subsequent (and
self-serving) claim that a beautiful woman's death constitutes "the
most poetical topic in the world." The following year he expanded
earlier notes on poetry into "The Rationale of Verse," a lengthy
and somewhat technical essay (not included here) on rhythm, rep-
etition, meter, and line length, as they affected the sound of a
poem.

Poe's late lectures included "The Poets and Poetry of America" (of which no full manuscript has been located) and "The Poetic Principle," his last and arguably most important meditation on the key elements of poetry. Here he asserts that the long poem is "a contradiction in terms" because the "elevating excitement" necessary to poetry is by nature transient. Countering the notion popular in his day that poetry must be morally instructive, Poe rails against "the heresy of the didactic" and insists again that beauty is the poem's only legitimate object. He construes poetry as the "rhythmical creation of beauty" while beauty itself is precisely the "supernal Loveliness" of "glories beyond the grave" for which the immortal soul yearns. Poe finds intimations of this heavenly beauty in many earthly images and sounds and most tellingly in the "divine majesty" of a woman's love.

If Poe's critical assumptions prevented him from fully appreciating longer forms such as novels and epic poems—to say nothing of drama, about which he occasionally wrote—they nevertheless enabled him to achieve a remarkable consonance between the literary principles that he advocated and the literature that he produced over slightly more than two decades.

ON UNITY OF EFFECT

(from a review of Watkins Tottle and Other Sketches
by Charles Dickens)

It is not every one who can put "a good thing" properly together,
although, perhaps, when thus properly put together, every tenth
person you meet with may be capable of both conceiving and ap-
preciating it. We cannot bring ourselves to believe that less actual
ability is required in the composition of a really good "brief arti-
cle," than in a fashionable novel of the usual dimensions. The
novel certainly requires what is denominated a sustained effort—
but this is a matter of mere perseverance, and has but a collateral
relation to talent. On the other hand—unity of effect, a quality
not easily appreciated or indeed comprehended by an ordinary
mind, and a *desideratum* difficult of attainment, even by those
who can conceive it—is indispensable in the "brief article," and
not so in the common novel. The latter, if admired at all, is ad-
mired for its detached passages, without reference to the work as a
whole—or without reference to any general design—which, if it
even exist in some measure, will be found to have occupied but lit-
tle of the writer's attention, and cannot, from the length of the
narrative, be taken in at one view, by the reader.

—*Southern Literary Messenger*, June 1836

ON PLOT IN NARRATIVE

(from a review of Night and Morning
by Lytton Bulwer)

The word "plot," as commonly accepted, conveys but an indefinite meaning. Most persons think of it as of simple *complexity*; and into this error even so fine a critic as Augustus William Schlegel has obviously fallen, when he confounds its idea with that of the mere *intrigue* in which the Spanish dramas of Cervantes and Calderon abound. But the greatest involution of incident will not result in plot; which, properly defined, is *that in which no part can be displaced without ruin to the whole*. It may be described as a building so dependently constructed, that to change the position of a single brick is to overthrow the entire fabric. In this definition and description, we of course refer only to that infinite perfection which the true artist bears ever in mind—that unattainable goal to which his eyes are always directed, but of the possibility of attaining which he still endeavors, if wise, to cheat himself into the belief. The reading world, however, is satisfied with a less rigid construction of the term. It is content to think that plot a good one, in which none of the *leading* incidents can be *removed* without *detriment* to the mass. Here indeed is a material difference; . . .

The interest of plot, referring, as it does, to cultivated thought in the reader, and appealing to considerations analogous with those which are the essence of sculptural taste, is by no means a popular interest; although it has the peculiarity of being appreciated in its atoms by all, while in its totality of beauty is it comprehended but by the few. The pleasure which the many derive from it is disjointed, ineffective, and evanescent; and even in the case of the critical reader it is a pleasure which may be purchased too dearly. A good tale may be written without it. Some of the finest fictions in the world have neglected it altogether. We see nothing of it in Gil Blas, in the Pilgrim's Progress, or in Robinson Crusoe. Thus it is not an essential in story-telling at all; although, well-managed, within proper limits, it is a thing to be desired. At best it is but a secondary and rigidly artistical merit, for which no merit of a higher class—no merit founded in nature—should be sacrificed. . . .

In the wire-drawn romances which have been so long fashionable, (God only knows how or why) the pleasure we derive (if any) is a composite one, and made up of the respective sums of the various pleasurable sentiments experienced in perusal. Without excessive and fatiguing exertion, inconsistent with legitimate interest, the mind cannot comprehend at one time, and in one survey, the numerous individual items which go to establish the whole. Thus the high ideal sense of the *unique* is sure to be wanting:—for, however absolute in itself be the unity of the novel, it must inevitably fail of appreciation. We speak now of that species of unity which is alone worth the attention of the critic—the unity or totality *of effect.*

—*Graham's Magazine*, April 1841

ON THE PROSE TALE

(from a review of Twice-Told Tales
by Nathaniel Hawthorne)

The tale proper, in our opinion, affords unquestionably the fairest field for the exercise of the loftiest talent, which can be afforded by the wide domains of mere prose. Were we bidden to say how the highest genius could be most advantageously employed for the best display of its own powers, we should answer, without hesitation—in the composition of a rhymed poem, not to exceed in length what might be perused in an hour. Within this limit alone can the highest order of true poetry exist. We need only here say, upon this topic, that, in almost all classes of composition, the unity of effect or impression is a point of the greatest importance. It is clear, moreover, that this unity cannot be thoroughly preserved in productions whose perusal cannot be completed at one sitting. We may continue the reading of a prose composition, from the very nature of prose itself, much longer than we can persevere, to any good purpose, in the perusal of a poem. The latter, if truly fulfilling the demands of the poetic sentiment, induces an exaltation of the soul which cannot be long sustained. All high excitements are necessarily transient. Thus a long poem is a paradox. And, without unity of impression, the deepest effects cannot be brought about. Epics were the offspring of an imperfect sense of Art, and their reign is no more. A poem *too* brief may produce a vivid, but never an intense or enduring impression. Without a certain continuity of effort—without a certain duration or repetition of purpose—the soul is never deeply moved. There must be the dropping of the water upon the rock. De Béranger has wrought brilliant things—pungent and spirit-stirring—but, like all immassive bodies, they lack *momentum*, and thus fail to satisfy the Poetic Sentiment. They sparkle and excite, but, from want of continuity, fail deeply to impress. Extreme brevity will degenerate into epigrammatism; but the sin of extreme length is even more unpardonable. *In medio tutissimus ibis.*[1]

Were we called upon however to designate that class of composition which, next to such a poem as we have suggested, should best fulfil the demands of high genius—should offer it the most advantageous field of exertion—we should unhesitatingly speak of the prose tale, as Mr. Hawthorne has here exemplified it. We allude to the short prose narrative, requiring from a half-hour to one or two hours in its perusal. The ordinary novel is objectionable, from its length, for reasons already stated in substance. As it cannot be read at one sitting, it deprives itself, of course, of the immense force derivable from *totality*. Worldly interests intervening during the pauses of perusal, modify, annul, or counteract, in a greater or less degree, the impressions of the book. But simple cessation in reading would, of itself, be sufficient to destroy the true unity. In the brief tale, however, the author is enabled to carry out the fulness of his intention, be it what it may. During the hour of perusal the soul of the reader is at the writer's control. There are no external or extrinsic influences—resulting from weariness or interruption.

A skilful literary artist has constructed a tale. If wise, he has not fashioned his thoughts to accommodate his incidents; but having conceived, with deliberate care, a certain unique or single *effect* to be wrought out, he then invents such incidents—he then combines such events as may best aid him in establishing this preconceived effect. If his very initial sentence tend not to the outbringing of this effect, then he has failed in his first step. In the whole composition there should be no word written, of which the tendency, direct or indirect, is not to the one pre-established design. And by such means, with such care and skill, a picture is at length painted which leaves in the mind of him who contemplates it with a kindred art, a sense of the fullest satisfaction. The idea of the tale has been presented unblemished, because undisturbed; and this is an end unattainable by the novel. Undue brevity is just as exceptionable here as in the poem; but undue length is yet more to be avoided.

We have said that the tale has a point of superiority even over the poem. In fact, while the *rhythm* of this latter is an essential aid in the development of the poem's highest idea—the idea of the Beautiful—the artificialities of this rhythm are an inseparable bar to the development of all points of thought or expression which have their basis in *Truth*. But Truth is often, and in very great degree, the aim of the tale. Some of the finest tales are tales of ratiocination. Thus the field of this species of composition, if not in so elevated a region on the mountain of Mind, is a table-land of far vaster extent than the domain of the mere poem. Its products are never so rich, but infinitely more numerous, and more appreciable by the mass of mankind. The writer of the prose tale, in short, may bring to his theme a vast variety of modes or inflections of thought and expression—(the ratiocinative, for example, the sarcastic or the humorous) which are not only antagonistical to the nature of the poem, but absolutely forbidden by one of its most peculiar and indispensable adjuncts; we allude of course, to rhythm. It may be added, here, *par parenthèse*, that the author who aims at the purely beautiful in a prose tale is laboring at great disadvantage. For Beauty can be better treated in the poem. Not so with terror, or passion, or horror, or a multitude of such other points. And here it will be seen how full of prejudice are the usual animadversions against those *tales of effect* many fine examples of which were found in the earlier numbers of Blackwood. The impressions produced were wrought in a legitimate sphere of action, and constituted a legitimate although sometimes an exaggerated interest. They were relished by every man of genius: although there were found many men of genius who condemned them without just ground. The true critic will but demand that the design intended be accomplished, to the fullest extent, by the means most advantageously applicable.

—*Graham's Magazine*, May 1842

ON THE DESIGN OF FICTION

(from "A Chapter of Suggestions")

An excellent Magazine paper might be written upon the subject of the progressive steps by which any great work of art—especially of literary art—attained completion. How vast a dissimilarity always exists between the germ and the fruit—between the work and its original conception! Sometimes the original conception is abandoned, or left out of sight altogether. *Most* authors sit down to write with *no* fixed design, trusting to the inspiration of the moment; it is not, therefore, to be wondered at, that *most* books are valueless. Pen should never touch paper, until at least a well-digested *general* purpose be established. In fiction, the *dénouement*—in all other composition the intended *effect*, should be definitely considered and arranged, before writing the first word; and *no* word should be then written which does not tend, or form a part of a sentence which tends, to the development of the *dénouement*, or to the strengthening of the effect. Where *plot* forms a portion of the contemplated interest, too much preconsideration cannot be had. *Plot* is very imperfectly understood, and has never been rightly defined. Many persons regard it as mere complexity of incident. In its most rigorous acceptation, it is *that from which no component atom can be removed, and in which none of the component atoms can be displaced, without ruin to the whole*; and although a sufficiently good plot may be constructed, without attention to the whole rigor of this definition, still it is the definition which the true artist should always keep in view, and always endeavor to consummate in his works. Some authors appear, however, to be totally deficient in constructiveness, and thus, even with plentiful invention, fail signally in plot. Dickens belongs to this

class. His "Barnaby Rudge" shows not the least ability to *adapt*.
Godwin and Bulwer are the best constructors of plot in English lit-
erature. The former has left a preface to his "Caleb Williams," in
which he says that the novel was *written backwards*; the author
first completing the second volume, in which the hero is involved
in a maze of difficulties, and then casting about him for suffi-
ciently probable cause of these difficulties, out of which to con-
coct volume the first. This mode cannot surely be recommended,
but evinces the idiosyncrasy of Godwin's mind. Bulwer's "Pom-
peii" is an instance of admirably managed plot. His "Night and
Morning," sacrifices to *mere* plot interests of far higher value.

—The Opal, 1845

THE OBJECT OF POETRY

(from "Letter to B———")

It has been said that a good critique on a poem may be written by one who is no poet himself. This, according to *your* idea and *mine* of poetry, I feel to be false—the less poetical the critic, the less just the critique, and the converse. On this account, and because there are but few B—'s in the world, I would be as much ashamed of the world's good opinion as proud of your own. Another than yourself might here observe, "Shakspeare is in possession of the world's good opinion, and yet Shakspeare is the greatest of poets. It appears then that the world judge correctly, why should you be ashamed of their favorable judgment?" The difficulty lies in the interpretation of the word "judgment" or "opinion." The opinion is the world's, truly, but it may be called theirs as a man would call a book his, having bought it; he did not write the book, but it is his; they did not originate the opinion, but it is theirs. A fool, for example, thinks Shakspeare a great poet—yet the fool has never read Shakspeare. But the fool's neighbor, who is a step higher on the Andes of the mind, whose head (that is to say his more exalted thought) is too far above the fool to be seen or understood, but whose feet (by which I mean his every-day actions) are sufficiently near to be discerned, and by means of which that superiority is ascertained, which *but* for them would never have been discovered—this neighbor asserts that Shakspeare is a great poet—the fool believes him, and it is henceforward his *opinion*. This neighbor's own opinion has, in like manner, been adopted from one above *him*, and so, ascendingly, to a few gifted individuals, who kneel around the summit, beholding, face to face, the master spirit who stands upon the pinnacle. * * * * * * * * * * * * *

You are aware of the great barrier in the path of an American writer. He is read, if at all, in preference to the combined and established wit of the world. I say established; for it is with literature as with law or empire—an established name is an estate in tenure, or a throne in possession. Besides, one might suppose that books, like their authors, improve by travel—their having crossed the sea is, with us, so great a distinction. Our antiquaries abandon time for distance; our very fops glance from the binding to the bottom of the title-page, where the mystic characters which spell London, Paris, or Genoa, are precisely so many letters of recommendation.

I mentioned just now a vulgar error as regards criticism. I think the notion that no poet can form a correct estimate of his own writings is another. I remarked before, that in proportion to the poetical talent, would be the justice of a critique upon poetry. Therefore, a bad poet would, I grant, make a false critique, and his self-love would infallibly bias his little judgment in his favor; but a poet, who is indeed a poet, could not, I think, fail of making a just critique. Whatever should be deducted on the score of self-love, might be replaced on account of his intimate acquaintance with the subject; in short, we have more instances of false criticism than of just, where one's own writings are the test, simply because we have more bad poets than good. There are of course many objections to what I say: Milton is a great example of the contrary; but his opinion with respect to the Paradise Regained, is by no means fairly ascertained. By what trivial circumstances men are often led to assert what they do not really believe! Perhaps an inadvertent word has descended to posterity. But, in fact, the Paradise Regained is little, if at all, inferior to the Paradise Lost, and is only supposed so to be, because men do not like epics, whatever they may say to the contrary, and reading those of Milton in their natural order, are too much wearied with the first to derive any pleasure from the second.

I dare say Milton preferred Comus to either—if so—justly.

As I am speaking of poetry, it will not be amiss to touch slightly upon the most singular heresy in its modern history—the heresy of what is called very foolishly, the Lake School. Some years ago I might have been induced, by an occasion like the present, to attempt a formal refutation of their doctrine; at present it would be a work of supererogation. The wise must bow to the wisdom of such men as Coleridge and Southey, but being wise, have laughed at poetical theories so prosaically exemplified.

Aristotle, with singular assurance, has declared poetry the most philosophical of all writing*—but it required a Wordsworth to pronounce it the most metaphysical. He seems to think that the end of poetry is, or should be, instruction—yet it is a truism that the end of our existence is happiness; if so, the end of every separate part of our existence—every thing connected with our existence should be still happiness. Therefore the end of instruction should be happiness; and happiness is another name for pleasure;—therefore the end of instruction should be pleasure: yet we see the above mentioned opinion implies precisely the reverse.

To proceed: ceteris paribus, he who pleases, is of more importance to his fellow men than he who instructs, since utility is happiness, and pleasure is the end already obtained which instruction is merely the means of obtaining.

I see no reason, then, why our metaphysical poets should plume themselves so much on the utility of their works, unless indeed they refer to instruction with eternity in view; in which case, sincere respect for their piety would not allow me to express my contempt for their judgment; contempt which it would be difficult to conceal, since their writings are professedly to be understood by the few, and it is the many who stand in need of salvation. In such case I should no doubt be tempted to think of the devil in Melmoth, who labors indefatigably through three octavo volumes, to accomplish the destruction of one or two souls, while any common devil would have demolished one or two thousand.

Against the subtleties which would make poetry a study—not a passion—it becomes the metaphysician to reason—but the poet to protest. Yet Wordsworth and Coleridge are men in years; the one imbued in contemplation from his childhood, the other a giant in intellect and learning. The diffidence, then, with which I venture to dispute their authority, would be over-whelming, did I not feel,

*Spoudiotaton kai philosophikotaton genos. [Poe's note][1]

from the bottom of my heart, that learning has little to do with the imagination—intellect with the passions—or age with poetry.   *

> "Trifles, like straws, upon the surface flow,
> He who would search for pearls must dive below,"

are lines which have done much mischief. As regards the greater truths, men oftener err by seeking them at the bottom than at the top; the depth lies in the huge abysses where wisdom is sought—not in the palpable palaces where she is found. The ancients were not always right in hiding the goddess in a well: witness the light which Bacon has thrown upon philosophy; witness the principles of our divine faith—that moral mechanism by which the simplicity of a child may overbalance the wisdom of a man.

We see an instance of Coleridge's liability to err, in his Biographia Literaria—professedly his literary life and opinions, but, in fact, a treatise *de omni scibili et quibusdam aliis*.[2] He goes wrong by reason of his very profundity, and of his error we have a natural type in the contemplation of a star. He who regards it directly and intensely sees, it is true, the star, but it is the star without a ray—while he who surveys it less inquisitively is conscious of all for which the star is useful to us below—its brilliancy and its beauty.

As to Wordsworth, I have no faith in him. That he had, in youth, the feelings of a poet I believe—for there are glimpses of extreme delicacy in his writings—(and delicacy is the poet's own kingdom—his *El Dorado*)—but they have the appearance of a better day recollected; and glimpses, at best, are little evidence of present poetic fire—we know that a few straggling flowers spring up daily in the crevices of the glacier.

He was to blame in wearing away his youth in contemplation with the end of poetizing in his manhood. With the increase of his judgment the light which should make it apparent has faded away. His judgment consequently is too correct. This may not be understood,—but the old Goths of Germany would have understood it, who used to debate matters of importance to their State twice, once when drunk, and once when sober—sober that they might not be deficient in formality—drunk lest they should be destitute of vigor.

The long wordy discussions by which he tries to reason us into admiration of his poetry, speak very little in his favor: they are full of such assertions as this—(I have opened one of his volumes at random) "Of genius the only proof is the act of doing well what is worthy to be done, and what was never done before"—indeed! then it follows that in doing what is *un*worthy to be done, or what *has* been done before, no genius can be evinced: yet the picking of pockets is an unworthy act, pockets have been picked time immemorial, and Barrington, the pick-pocket, in point of genius, would have thought hard of a comparison with William Wordsworth, the poet.

Again—in estimating the merit of certain poems, whether they be Ossian's or M'Pherson's, can surely be of little consequence, yet, in order to prove their worthlessness, Mr. W. has expended many pages in the controversy. *Tantœne animis?*[3] Can great minds descend to such absurdity? But worse still: that he may bear down every argument in favor of these poems, he triumphantly drags forward a passage, in his abomination of which he expects the reader to sympathize. It is the beginning of the epic poem *"Temora."* "The blue waves of Ullin roll in light; the green hills are covered with day; trees shake their dusky heads in the breeze." And this—this gorgeous, yet simple imagery—where all is alive and panting with immortality—this—William Wordsworth, the author of Peter Bell, has *selected* for his contempt. . . .

Of Coleridge I cannot speak but with reverence. His towering intellect! his gigantic power! He is one more evidence of the fact "que la plupart des sectes ont raison dans une bonne partie de ce qu'elles avancent, mais non pas en ce qu'elles nient."[4] He has imprisoned his own conceptions by the barrier he has erected against those of others. It is lamentable to think that such a mind should be buried in metaphysics, and, like the Nyctanthes, waste its perfume upon the night alone. In reading his poetry I tremble—like one who stands upon a volcano, conscious, from the very darkness bursting from the crater, of the fire and the light that are weltering below.

What is Poetry?—Poetry! that Proteus-like idea, with as many appellations as the nine-titled Corcyra! Give me, I demanded of a scholar some time ago, give me a definition of poetry? "Tres-volontiers,"—and he proceeded to his library, brought me a Dr.

Johnson, and overwhelmed me with a definition. Shade of the immortal Shakspeare! I imagined to myself the scowl of your spiritual eye upon the profanity of that scurrilous Ursa Major. Think of poetry, dear B—, think of poetry, and then think of—Dr. Samuel Johnson! Think of all that is airy and fairy-like, and then of all that is hideous and unwieldy; think of his huge bulk, the Elephant! and then—and then think of the Tempest—the Midsummer Night's Dream—Prospero—Oberon—and Titania!

A poem, in my opinion, is opposed to a work of science by having, for its *immediate* object, pleasure, not truth; to romance, by having for its object an *indefinite* instead of a *definite* pleasure, being a poem only so far as this object is attained; romance presenting perceptible images with definite, poetry with *in*definite sensations, to which end music is an *essential*, since the comprehension of sweet sound is our most indefinite conception. Music, when combined with a pleasurable idea, is poetry; music without the idea is simply music; the idea without the music is prose from its very definitiveness.

What was meant by the invective against him who had no music in his soul?

To sum up this long rigmarole, I have, dear B—, what you no doubt perceive, for the metaphysical poets, *as* poets, the most sovereign contempt. That they have followers proves nothing—

> No Indian prince has to his palace
> More followers than a thief to the gallows.
>   —*Southern Literary Messenger*, July 1836

"THE PHILOSOPHY OF COMPOSITION"

Charles Dickens, in a note now lying before me, alluding to an examination I once made of the mechanism of "Barnaby Rudge," says—"By the way, are you aware that Godwin wrote his 'Caleb Williams' backwards? He first involved his hero in a web of difficulties, forming the second volume, and then, for the first, cast about him for some mode of accounting for what had been done."

I cannot think this the *precise* mode of procedure on the part of Godwin—and indeed what he himself acknowledges, is not altogether in accordance with Mr. Dickens' idea—but the author of "Caleb Williams" was too good an artist not to perceive the advantage derivable from at least a somewhat similar process. Nothing is more clear than that every plot, worth the name, must be elaborated to its *dénouement* before any thing be attempted with the pen. It is only with the *dénouement* constantly in view that we can give a plot its indispensable air of consequence, or causation, by making the incidents, and especially the tone at all points, tend to the development of the intention.

There is a radical error, I think, in the usual mode of constructing a story. Either history affords a thesis—or one is suggested by an incident of the day—or, at best, the author sets himself to work in the combination of striking events to form merely the basis of his narrative—designing, generally, to fill in with description, dialogue, or autorial comment, whatever crevices of fact, or action, may, from page to page, render themselves apparent.

I prefer commencing with the consideration of an *effect*. Keeping originality *always* in view—for he is false to himself who ventures to dispense with so obvious and so easily attainable a source of interest—I say to myself, in the first place, "Of the innumerable effects, or impressions, of which the heart, the intellect, or (more generally) the soul is susceptible, what one shall I, on the present occasion, select?" Having chosen a novel, first, and secondly a vivid effect, I consider whether it can best be wrought by incident or tone—whether by ordinary incidents and peculiar tone, or the converse, or by peculiarity both of incident and tone—afterward looking about me (or rather within) for such combinations of event, or tone, as shall best aid me in the construction of the effect.

I have often thought how interesting a magazine paper might be written by any author who would—that is to say, who could—detail, step by step, the processes by which any one of his compositions attained its ultimate point of completion. Why such a paper has never been given to the world, I am much at a loss to say—but, perhaps, the autorial vanity has had more to do with the omission than any one other cause. Most writers—poets in especial—prefer having it understood that they compose by a species of fine frenzy—an ecstatic intuition—and would positively shudder at letting the public take a peep behind the scenes, at the elaborate and vacillating crudities of thought—at the true purposes seized only at the last moment—at the innumerable glimpses of idea that arrived not at the maturity of full view—at the fully matured fancies discarded in despair as unmanageable—at the cautious selections and rejections—at the painful erasures and interpolations—in a word, at the wheels and pinions—the tackle for scene-shifting—the step-ladders and demon-traps—the cock's feathers, the red paint and the black patches, which, in ninety-nine cases out of the hundred, constitute the properties of the literary *histrio*.

I am aware, on the other hand, that the case is by no means common, in which an author is at all in condition to retrace the steps by which his conclusions have been attained. In general, suggestions, having arisen pell-mell, are pursued and forgotten in a similar manner.

For my own part, I have neither sympathy with the repugnance alluded to, nor, at any time, the least difficulty in recalling to mind the progressive steps of any of my compositions; and, since the interest of an analysis, or reconstruction, such as I have considered a *desideratum*, is quite independent of any real or fancied interest in the thing analyzed, it will not be regarded as a breach of decorum on my part to show the *modus operandi* by which some one of my own works was put together. I select "The Raven," as the most generally known. It is my design to render it manifest that no one point in its composition is referrible either to accident or intuition—that the work proceeded, step by step, to its completion with the precision and rigid consequence of a mathematical problem.

Let us dismiss, as irrelevant to the poem *per se*, the circumstance—or say the necessity—which, in the first place, gave rise to the intention of composing a poem that should suit at once the popular and the critical taste.

We commence, then, with this intention.

The initial consideration was that of extent. If any literary work is too long to be read at one sitting, we must be content to dispense with the immensely important effect derivable from unity of impression—for, if two sittings be required, the affairs of the world interfere, and every thing like totality is at once destroyed. But since, *ceteris paribus*,[1] no poet can afford to dispense with *any thing* that may advance his design, it but remains to be seen whether there is, in extent, any advantage to counterbalance the loss of unity which attends it. Here I say no, at once. What we term a long poem is, in fact, merely a succession of brief ones—that is to say, of brief poetical effects. It is needless to demonstrate that a poem is such, only inasmuch as it intensely excites, by elevating, the soul; and all intense excitements are, through a psychal necessity, brief. For this reason, at least one half of the "Paradise Lost" is essentially prose—a succession of poetical excitements interspersed, *inevitably*, with corresponding depressions—the whole being deprived, through the extremeness of its length, of the vastly important artistic element, totality, or unity, of effect.

It appears evident, then, that there is a distinct limit, as regards length, to all works of literary art—the limit of a single sitting—and that, although in certain classes of prose composition, such as "Robinson Crusoe," (demanding no unity,) this limit may be advantageously overpassed, it can never properly be overpassed in a poem. Within this limit, the extent of a poem may be made to bear mathematical relation to its merit—in other words, to the excitement or elevation—again in other words, to the degree of the true poetical effect which it is capable of inducing; for it is clear that the brevity must be in direct ratio of the intensity of the intended effect:—this, with one proviso—that a certain degree of duration is absolutely requisite for the production of any effect at all.

Holding in view these considerations, as well as that degree of excitement which I deemed not above the popular, while not below the critical, taste, I reached at once what I conceived the proper *length* for my intended poem—a length of about one hundred lines. It is, in fact, a hundred and eight.

My next thought concerned the choice of an impression, or effect, to be conveyed: and here I may as well observe that, throughout the construction, I kept steadily in view the design of rendering the work *universally* appreciable. I should be carried too far out of my immediate topic were I to demonstrate a point upon which I have repeatedly insisted, and which, with the poetical, stands not in the slightest need of demonstration—the point, I mean, that Beauty is the sole legitimate province of the poem. A few words, however, in elucidation of my real meaning, which some of my friends have evinced a disposition to misrepresent. That pleasure which is at once the most intense, the most elevating, and the most pure, is, I believe, found in the contemplation of the beautiful. When, indeed, men speak of Beauty, they mean, precisely, not a quality, as is supposed, but an effect—they refer, in short, just to that intense and pure elevation of *soul*—*not* of intellect, or of heart—upon which I have commented, and which is experienced in consequence of contemplating "the beautiful." Now I designate Beauty as the province of the poem, merely because it is an obvious rule of Art that effects should be made to spring from direct causes—that objects should be attained through means best adapted for their attainment—no one as yet having been weak enough to deny that the peculiar elevation alluded to, is *most readily* attained in the poem. Now the object, Truth, or the satisfaction of the intellect, and the object Passion, or the excitement of the heart, are, although attainable, to a certain extent, in poetry, far more readily attainable in prose. Truth, in fact, demands a precision, and Passion, a *homeliness* (the truly passionate will comprehend me) which are absolutely antagonistic to that Beauty which, I maintain, is the excitement, or pleasurable elevation, of the soul. It by no means follows from any thing here said, that passion, or even truth, may not be introduced, and even profitably introduced, into a poem—for they may serve in elucidation, or aid the general effect, as do discords in music, by contrast—but the true artist will always contrive, first, to tone them into proper subservience to the predominant aim, and, secondly, to enveil them, as far as possible, in that Beauty which is the atmosphere and the essence of the poem.

Regarding, then, Beauty as my province, my next question referred to the *tone* of its highest manifestation—and all experience has shown that this tone is one of *sadness*. Beauty of whatever kind, in its supreme development, invariably excites the sensitive soul to tears. Melancholy is thus the most legitimate of all the poetical tones.

The length, the province, and the tone, being thus determined, I betook myself to ordinary induction, with the view of obtaining some artistic piquancy which might serve me as a key-note in the construction of the poem—some pivot upon which the whole structure might turn. In carefully thinking over all the usual artistic effects—or more properly *points*, in the theatrical sense—I did not fail to perceive immediately that no one had been so universally employed as that of the *refrain*. The universality of its employment sufficed to assure me of its intrinsic value, and spared me the necessity of submitting it to analysis. I considered it, however, with regard to its susceptibility of improvement, and soon saw it to be in a primitive condition. As commonly used, the *refrain*, or burden, not only is limited to lyric verse, but depends for its impression upon the force of monotone—both in sound and thought. The pleasure is deduced solely from the sense of identity—of repetition. I resolved to diversify, and so vastly heighten, the effect, by adhering, in general, to the monotone of sound, while I continually varied that of thought: that is to say, I determined to produce continuously novel effects, by the variation *of the application* of the *refrain*—the *refrain* itself remaining, for the most part, unvaried.

These points being settled, I next bethought me of the *nature* of my *refrain*. Since its application was to be repeatedly varied, it was clear that the *refrain* itself must be brief, for there would have been an insurmountable difficulty in frequent variations of application in any sentence of length. In proportion to the brevity of the sentence, would, of course, be the facility of the variation. This led me at once to a single word as the best *refrain*.

The question now arose as to the *character* of the word. Having made up my mind to a *refrain*, the division of the poem into stanzas was, of course, a corollary: the *refrain* forming the close to each stanza. That such a close, to have force, must be sonorous and susceptible of protracted emphasis, admitted no doubt: and these considerations inevitably led me to the long *o* as the most sonorous vowel, in connection with *r* as the most producible consonant.

The sound of the *refrain* being thus determined, it became necessary to select a word embodying this sound, and at the same time in the fullest possible keeping with that melancholy which I had predetermined as the tone of the poem. In such a search it would have been absolutely impossible to overlook the word "Nevermore." In fact, it was the very first which presented itself.

The next *desideratum* was a pretext for the continuous use of the one word "nevermore." In observing the difficulty which I at once found in inventing a sufficiently plausible reason for its continuous repetition, I did not fail to perceive that this difficulty arose solely from the pre-assumption that the word was to be so continuously or monotonously spoken by *a human* being—I did not fail to perceive, in short, that the difficulty lay in the reconciliation of this monotony with the exercise of reason on the part of the creature repeating the word. Here, then, immediately arose the idea of a *non*-reasoning creature capable of speech; and, very naturally, a parrot, in the first instance, suggested itself, but was superseded forthwith by a Raven, as equally capable of speech, and infinitely more in keeping with the intended *tone*.

I had now gone so far as the conception of a Raven—the bird of ill omen—monotonously repeating the one word, "Nevermore," at the conclusion of each stanza, in a poem of melancholy tone, and in length about one hundred lines. Now, never losing sight of the object *supremeness*, or perfection, at all points, I asked myself—"Of all melancholy topics, what, according to the *universal* understanding of mankind, is the *most* melancholy?" Death—was the obvious reply. "And when," I said, "is this most melancholy of topics most poetical?" From what I have already explained at some length, the answer, here also, is obvious—"When it most closely allies itself to *Beauty*: the death, then, of a beautiful woman is, unquestionably, the most poetical topic in the world—and equally is it beyond doubt that the lips best suited for such topic are those of a bereaved lover."

I had now to combine the two ideas, of a lover lamenting his deceased mistress and a Raven continuously repeating the word "Nevermore"—I had to combine these, bearing in mind my design of varying, at every turn, the *application* of the word repeated; but the only intelligible mode of such combination is that of imagining the Raven employing the word in answer to the queries of the lover. And here it was that I saw at once the opportunity afforded for the effect on which I had been depending—that is to say, the effect of the *variation of application*. I saw that I could make the first query propounded by the lover—the first query to which the Raven should reply "Nevermore"—that I could make this first query a commonplace one—the second less so—the third still less, and so on—until at length the lover, startled from his original *nonchalance* by the melancholy character of the word itself—by its frequent repetition—and by a consideration of the ominous reputation of the fowl that uttered it—is at length excited to superstition, and wildly propounds queries of a far different character—queries whose solution he has passionately at heart—propounds them half in superstition and half in that species of despair which delights in self-torture—propounds them not altogether because he believes in the prophetic or demoniac character of the bird (which, reason assures him, is merely repeating a lesson learned by rote) but because he experiences a phrenzied pleasure in so modeling his questions as to receive from the *expected* "Nevermore" the most delicious because the most intolerable of sorrow. Perceiving the opportunity thus afforded me—or, more strictly, thus forced upon me in the progress of the construction—I first established in mind the climax, or concluding query—that to which "Nevermore" should be in the last place an answer—that in reply to which this word "Nevermore" should involve the utmost conceivable amount of sorrow and despair.

Here then the poem may be said to have its beginning—at the end, where all works of art should begin—for it was here, at this point of my preconsiderations, that I first put pen to paper in the composition of the stanza:

"Prophet," said I, "thing of evil! prophet still if bird or devil!
    By that heaven that bends above us—by that God we both adore,
    Tell this soul with sorrow laden, if within the distant Aidenn,

It shall clasp a sainted maiden whom the angels name Lenore—
Clasp a rare and radiant maiden whom the angels name Lenore."
Quoth the raven "Nevermore."

I composed this stanza, at this point, first that, by establishing the climax, I might the better vary and graduate, as regards seriousness and importance, the preceding queries of the lover—and, secondly, that I might definitely settle the rhythm, the metre, and the length and general arrangement of the stanza—as well as graduate the stanzas which were to precede, so that none of them might surpass this in rhythmical effect. Had I been able, in the subsequent composition, to construct more vigorous stanzas, I should, without scruple, have purposely enfeebled them, so as not to interfere with the climacteric effect.

And here I may as well say a few words of the versification. My first object (as usual) was originality. The extent to which this has been neglected, in versification, is one of the most unaccountable things in the world. Admitting that there is little possibility of variety in mere *rhythm*, it is still clear that the possible varieties of metre and stanza are absolutely infinite—and yet, *for centuries, no man, in verse, has ever done, or ever seemed to think of doing, an original thing*. The fact is, originality (unless in minds of very unusual force) is by no means a matter, as some suppose, of impulse or intuition. In general, to be found, it must be elaborately sought, and although a positive merit of the highest class, demands in its attainment less of invention than negation.

Of course, I pretend to no originality in either the rhythm or metre of the "Raven." The former is trochaic—the latter is octameter acatalectic, alternating with heptameter catalectic repeated in the *refrain* of the fifth verse, and terminating with tetrameter catalectic. Less pedantically—the feet employed throughout (trochees) consist of a long syllable followed by a short: the first line of the stanza consists of eight of these feet—the second of seven and a half (in effect two-thirds)—the third of eight—the fourth of seven and a half—the fifth the same—the sixth three and a half. Now, each of these lines, taken individually, has been employed before, and what originality the "Raven" has, is in their *combination into stanza*; nothing even remotely approaching this combination has ever been attempted. The effect of this originality of combination is aided by other unusual, and some altogether novel effects, arising from an extension of the application of the principles of rhyme and alliteration.

The next point to be considered was the mode of bringing together the lover and the Raven—and the first branch of this consideration was the *locale*. For this the most natural suggestion might seem to be a forest, or the fields—but it has always appeared to me that a close *circumscription of space* is absolutely necessary to the effect of insulated incident:—it has the force of a frame to a picture. It has an indisputable moral power in keeping concentrated the attention, and, of course, must not be confounded with mere unity of place.

I determined, then, to place the lover in his chamber—in a chamber rendered sacred to him by memories of her who had frequented it. The room is represented as richly furnished—this in mere pursuance of the ideas I have already explained on the subject of Beauty, as the sole true poetical thesis.

The *locale* being thus determined, I had now to introduce the bird—and the thought of introducing him through the window, was inevitable. The idea of making the lover suppose, in the first instance, that the flapping of the wings of the bird against the shutter, is a "tapping" at the door, originated in a wish to increase, by prolonging, the reader's curiosity, and in a desire to admit the incidental effect arising from the lover's throwing open the door, finding all dark, and thence adopting the half-fancy that it was the spirit of his mistress that knocked.

I made the night tempestuous, first, to account for the Raven's seeking admission, and secondly, for the effect of contrast with the (physical) serenity within the chamber.

I made the bird alight on the bust of Pallas, also for the effect of contrast between the marble and the plumage—it being understood that the bust was absolutely *suggested* by the bird—the bust of *Pallas* being chosen, first, as most in keeping with the scholarship of the lover, and, secondly, for the sonorousness of the word, Pallas, itself.

About the middle of the poem, also, I have availed myself of the force of contrast, with a view of deepening the ultimate impression.

For example, an air of the fantastic—approaching as nearly to the ludicrous as was admissible—is given to the Raven's entrance. He comes in "with many a flirt and flutter."

> Not the *least obeisance made he*—not a moment stopped or
>   stayed he,
> *But with mien of lord or lady*, perched above my chamber door.

In the two stanzas which follow, the design is more obviously carried out:—

> Then this ebony bird beguiling my sad fancy into smiling
> By the *grave and stern decorum of the countenance it wore*,
> "Though thy *crest be shorn and shaven* thou," I said, "art sure
>   no craven,
> Ghastly grim and ancient Raven wandering from the nightly shore—
> Tell me what thy lordly name is on the Night's Plutonian shore!"
>   Quoth the Raven "Nevermore."

> Much I marvelled *this ungainly fowl* to hear discourse so plainly,
> Though its answer little meaning—little relevancy bore;
> For we cannot help agreeing that no living human being
> *Ever yet was blessed with seeing bird above his chamber door*—
> *Bird or beast upon the sculptured bust above his chamber door*,
>   With such name as "Nevermore."

The effect of the *dénouement* being thus provided for, I immediately drop the fantastic for a tone of the most profound seriousness:—this tone commencing in the stanza directly following the one last quoted, with the line,

> But the Raven, sitting lonely on that placid bust, spoke only, etc.

From this epoch the lover no longer jests—no longer sees any thing even of the fantastic in the Raven's demeanor. He speaks of him as a "grim, ungainly, ghastly, gaunt, and ominous bird of yore," and feels the "fiery eyes" burning into his "bosom's core." This revolution of thought, or fancy, on the lover's part, is intended to induce a similar one on the part of the reader—to bring the mind into a proper frame for the *dénouement*—which is now brought about as rapidly and as *directly* as possible.

With the *dénouement* proper—with the Raven's reply, "Nevermore," to the lover's final demand if he shall meet his mistress in another world—the poem, in its obvious phase, that of a simple narrative, may be said to have its completion. So far, every thing is within the limits of the accountable—of the real. A raven, having learned by rote the single word "Nevermore," and having escaped from the custody of its owner, is driven, at midnight, through the violence of a storm, to seek admission at a window from which a light still gleams—the chamber-window of a student, occupied half in poring over a volume, half in dreaming of a beloved mistress deceased. The casement being thrown open at the fluttering of the bird's wings, the bird itself perches on the most convenient seat out of the immediate reach of the student, who, amused by the incident and the oddity of the visiter's demeanor, demands of it, in jest and without looking for a reply, its name. The raven addressed, answers with its customary word, "Nevermore"—a word which finds immediate echo in the melancholy heart of the student, who, giving utterance aloud to certain thoughts suggested by the occasion, is again startled by the fowl's repetition of "Nevermore." The student now guesses the state of the case, but is impelled, as I have before explained, by the human thirst for self-torture, and in part by superstition, to propound such queries to the bird as will bring him, the lover, the most of the luxury of sorrow, through the anticipated answer "Nevermore." With the indulgence, to the utmost extreme, of this self-torture, the narration, in what I have termed its first or obvious phase, has a natural termination, and so far there has been no overstepping of the limits of the real.

But in subjects so handled, however skilfully, or with however vivid an array of incident, there is always a certain hardness or nakedness, which repels the artistical eye. Two things are invariably required—first, some amount of complexity, or more properly, adaptation; and, secondly, some amount of suggestiveness—some under current, however indefinite of meaning. It is this latter, in especial, which imparts to a work of art so much of that *richness* (to borrow from colloquy a forcible term) which we are too fond of confounding with *the ideal*. It is the *excess* of the suggested meaning—it is the rendering this the upper instead of the under current of the theme—which turns into prose (and that of the very flattest kind) the so called poetry of the so called transcendentalists.

Holding these opinions, I added the two concluding stanzas of the poem—their suggestiveness being thus made to pervade all the narrative which has preceded them. The under current of meaning is rendered first apparent in the lines—

"Take thy beak from out *my heart*, and take thy form from
    off my door!"
                    Quoth the Raven "Nevermore!"

It will be observed that the words, "from out my heart," involve the first metaphorical expression in the poem. They, with the answer, "Nevermore," dispose the mind to seek a moral in all that has been previously narrated. The reader begins now to regard the Raven as emblematical—but it is not until the very last line of the very last stanza, that the intention of making him emblematical of *Mournful and Never-ending Remembrance* is permitted distinctly to be seen:

And the Raven, never flitting, still is sitting, still is sitting,
On the pallid bust of Pallas just above my chamber door;
And his eyes have all the seeming of a demon's that is dreaming,
And the lamplight o'er him streaming throws his shadow on the
    floor;
And my soul *from out that shadow* that lies floating on the floor
                    Shall be lifted—nevermore.
                                    —*Graham's Magazine*, April 1846

THE EFFECT OF RHYME

(from "Marginalia")

The effect derivable from well-managed rhyme is very imperfectly understood. Conventionally "rhyme" implies merely close similarity of sound at the ends of verse, and it is really curious to observe how long mankind have been content with their limitation of the idea. What, in rhyme, first and principally pleases, may be referred to the human sense or appreciation of *equality*—the common element, as might be easily shown, of all the gratification we derive from music in its most extended sense—very especially in its modifications of metre and rhythm. We see, for example, a crystal, and are immediately interested by the equality between the sides and angles of one of its faces—but on bringing to view a second face, in all respects similar to the first, our pleasure seems to be *squared*—on bringing to view a third, it appears to be *cubed*, and so on: I have no doubt, indeed, that the delight experienced, if measurable, would be found to have exact mathematical relations, such, or nearly such, as I suggest—that is to say, as far as a certain point, beyond which there would be a decrease, in similar relations. Now here, as the ultimate result of analysis, we reach the sense of mere *equality*, or rather the human delight in this sense; and it was an instinct, rather than a clear comprehension of this delight as a principle, which, in the first instance, led the poet to attempt an increase of the effect arising from the mere similarity (that is to say equality) between two sounds—led him, I say, to attempt increasing this effect by making a secondary equalization, in placing the rhymes at equal distances—that is, at the ends of lines of equal length. In this manner, rhyme and the termination of the line grew connected in men's thoughts—grew into a conventionalism—the principle being lost sight of altogether. And it was simply because Pindaric verses had, before this epoch, existed—*i.e.* verses of unequal length—that rhymes were subsequently found at unequal distances. It was for this reason solely, I say—for none more profound—rhyme had come to be regarded as of right appertaining to the *end* of verse—and here we complain that the matter has finally rested.

But it is clear that there was much more to be considered. So far, the sense of *equality* alone, entered the effect; or, if this equality was slightly varied, it was varied only through an accident—the accident of the existence of Pindaric metres. It will be seen that the rhymes were always *anticipated*. The eye, catching the end of a verse, whether long or short, expected, for the ear, a rhyme. The great element of unexpectedness was not dreamed of—that is to say, of novelty—of originality. "But," says Lord Bacon, (how justly!) "there is no exquisite beauty without some strangeness in the proportions." Take away this element of strangeness—of unexpectedness—of novelty—of originality—call it what we will—and all that is *ethereal* in loveliness is lost at once. We lose—we miss the *unknown*—the vague—the uncomprehended, because offered before we have time to examine and comprehend. We lose, in short, all that assimilates the beauty of earth with what we dream of the beauty of Heaven.

Perfection of rhyme is attainable only in the combination of the two elements, Equality and Unexpectedness. But as evil cannot exist without good, so unexpectedness must arise from expectedness. We do not contend for mere *arbitrariness* of rhyme. In the first place, we must have equi-distant or regularly recurring rhymes, to form the basis, expectedness, out of which arises the element, unexpectedness, by the introduction of rhymes, not arbitrarily, but with an eye to the greatest amount of unexpectedness. We should not introduce them, for example, at such points that the entire line is a multiple of the syllables preceding the points. When, for instance, I write—

And the silken, sad, uncertain rustling of each purple curtain,

I produce more, to be sure, but not remarkably more than the ordinary effect of rhymes regularly recurring at the ends of lines; for the number of syllables in the whole verse is merely a multiple of the number of syllables preceding the rhyme introduced at the middle, and there is still left, therefore, a certain degree of expectedness. What there is of the element, unexpectedness, is addressed, in fact, to the eye only—for the ear divides the verse into two ordinary lines, thus:

> And the silken, sad, uncertain
> Rustling of each purple curtain.

I obtain, however, the whole effect of unexpectedness, when I write—

> *Thrilled* me, *filled* me with fantastic terrors never felt before.

N. B. It is very commonly supposed that rhyme, as it now ordinarily exists, is of modern invention—but see the "Clouds" of Aristophanes. Hebrew verse, however, did *not* include it—the terminations of the lines, where most distinct, never showing any thing of the kind.

—*Graham's Magazine*, March 1846

"THE POETIC PRINCIPLE"

(excerpts)

In speaking of the Poetic Principle, I have no design to be either thorough or profound. While discussing, very much at random, the essentiality of what we call Poetry, my principal purpose will be to cite for consideration, some few of those minor English or American poems which best suit my own taste, or which, upon my own fancy, have left the most definite impression. By "minor poems" I mean, of course, poems of little length. And here, in the beginning, permit me to say a few words in regard to a somewhat peculiar principle, which, whether rightfully or wrongfully, has always had its influence in my own critical estimate of the poem. I hold that a long poem does not exist. I maintain that the phrase, "a long poem," is simply a flat contradiction in terms.

I need scarcely observe that a poem deserves its title only inasmuch as it excites, by elevating the soul. The value of the poem is in the ratio of this elevating excitement. But all excitements are, through a psychal necessity, transient. That degree of excitement which would entitle a poem to be so called at all, cannot be sustained throughout a composition of any great length. After the lapse of half an hour, at the very utmost, it flags—fails—a revulsion ensues—and then the poem is, in effect, and in fact, no longer such.

There are, no doubt, many who have found difficulty in reconciling the critical dictum that the "Paradise Lost" is to be devoutly admired throughout, with the absolute impossibility of maintaining for it, during perusal, the amount of enthusiasm which that critical dictum would demand. This great work, in fact, is to be regarded as poetical, only when, losing sight of that vital requisite in all works of Art, Unity, we view it merely as a series of minor poems.

If, to preserve its Unity—its totality of effect or impression—we read it (as would be necessary) at a single sitting, the result is but a constant alternation of excitement and depression. After a passage of what we feel to be true poetry, there follows, inevitably, a passage of platitude which no critical pre-judgment can force us to admire; but if, upon completing the work, we read it again, omitting the first book—that is to say, commencing with the second—we shall be surprised at now finding that admirable which we before condemned—that damnable which we had previously so much admired. It follows from all this that the ultimate, aggregate, or absolute effect of even the best epic under the sun, is a nullity:—and this is precisely the fact. . . .

While the epic mania—while the idea that, to merit in poetry, prolixity is indispensable—has, for some years past, been gradually dying out of the public mind, by mere dint of its own absurdity—we find it succeeded by a heresy too palpably false to be long tolerated, but one which, in the brief period it has already endured, may be said to have accomplished more in the corruption of our Poetical Literature than all its other enemies combined. I allude to the heresy of *The Didactic*. It has been assumed, tacitly and avowedly, directly and indirectly, that the ultimate object of all Poetry is Truth. Every poem, it is said, should inculcate a moral; and by this moral is the poetical merit of the work to be adjudged. We Americans, especially, have patronised this happy idea; and we Bostonians, very especially, have developed it in full. We have taken it into our heads that to write a poem simply for the poem's sake, and to acknowledge such to have been our design, would be to confess ourselves radically wanting in the true Poetic dignity and force:—but the simple fact is, that, would we but permit ourselves to look into our own souls, we should immediately there discover that under the sun there neither exists nor *can* exist any work more thoroughly dignified—more supremely noble than this very poem—this poem *per se*—this poem which is a poem and nothing more—this poem written solely for the poem's sake.

With as deep a reverence for the True as ever inspired the bosom of man, I would, nevertheless, limit, in some measure, its modes of inculcation. I would limit to enforce them. I would not enfeeble them by dissipation. The demands of Truth are severe. She has no sympathy with the myrtles. All *that* which is so indispensable in Song, is precisely all *that* with which *she* has nothing whatever to do. It is but making her a flaunting paradox, to wreathe her in gems and flowers. In enforcing a truth, we need severity rather than efflorescence of language. We must be simple, precise, terse. We must be cool, calm, unimpassioned. In a word, we must be in that mood which, as nearly as possible, is the exact converse of the poetical. *He* must be blind, indeed, who does not perceive the radical and chasmal differences between the truthful and the poetical modes of inculcation. He must be theory-mad beyond redemption who, in spite of these differences, shall still persist in attempting to reconcile the obstinate oils and waters of Poetry and Truth.

Dividing the world of mind into its three most immediately obvious distinctions, we have the Pure Intellect, Taste, and the Moral Sense. I place Taste in the middle, because it is just this position, which, in the mind, it occupies. It holds intimate relations with either extreme; but from the Moral Sense is separated by so faint a difference that Aristotle has not hesitated to place some of its operations among the virtues themselves. Nevertheless, we find the *offices* of the trio marked with a sufficient distinction. Just as the Intellect concerns itself with Truth, so Taste informs us of the Beautiful while the Moral Sense is regardful of Duty. Of this latter, while Conscience teaches the obligation, and Reason the expediency, Taste contents herself with displaying the charms:— waging war upon Vice solely on the ground of her deformity—her disproportion—her animosity to the fitting, to the appropriate, to the harmonious—in a word, to Beauty.

An immortal instinct, deep within the spirit of man, is thus, plainly, a sense of the Beautiful. This it is which administers to his delight in the manifold forms, and sounds, and odours, and sentiments amid which he exists. And just as the lily is repeated in the lake, or the eyes of Amaryllis in the mirror, so is the mere oral or written repetition of these forms, and sounds, and colours, and odours, and sentiments, a duplicate source of delight. But this mere repetition is not poetry. He who shall simply sing, with however glowing enthusiasm, or with however vivid a truth of description, of the sights, and sounds, and odours, and colours, and sentiments, which greet *him* in common with all mankind—he, I say, has yet failed to prove his divine title. There is still a something in the distance which he has been unable to attain. We have still a thirst unquenchable, to allay which he has not shown us the crystal springs. This thirst belongs to the immortality of Man. It is at once a consequence and an indication of his perennial existence. It is the desire of the moth for the star. It is no mere appreciation of the Beauty before us—but a wild effort to reach the Beauty above. Inspired by an ecstatic prescience of the glories beyond the grave, we struggle, by multiform combinations among the things and thoughts of Time, to attain a portion of that Loveliness whose very elements, perhaps, appertain to eternity alone. And thus when by Poetry—or when by Music, the most entrancing of the Poetic moods—we find ourselves melted into tears—we weep then—not as the Abbaté Gravina supposes—through excess of pleasure, but through a certain, petulant, impatient sorrow at our inability to grasp *now*, wholly, here on earth, at once and for ever, those divine and rapturous joys, of which *through* the poem, or *through* the music, we attain to but brief and indeterminate glimpses.

The struggle to apprehend the supernal Loveliness—this struggle, on the part of souls fittingly constituted—has given to the world all *that* which it (the world) has ever been enabled at once to understand and *to feel* as poetic.

The Poetic Sentiment, of course, may develope itself in various modes—in Painting, in Sculpture, in Architecture, in the Dance—very especially in Music—and very peculiarly, and with a wide field, in the composition of the Landscape Garden. Our present theme, however, has regard only to its manifestation in words. And here let me speak briefly on the topic of rhythm. Contenting myself with the certainty that Music, in its various modes of metre, rhythm, and rhyme, is of so vast a moment in Poetry as never to be wisely rejected—is so vitally important an adjunct, that he is simply silly who declines its assistance, I will not now pause to maintain its absolute essentiality. It is in Music, perhaps, that the soul most nearly attains the great end for which, when inspired with the Poetic Sentiment, it struggles—the creation of supernal Beauty. It *may* be, indeed, that here this sublime end is, now and then, attained *in fact*. We are often made to feel, with a shivering delight, that from an earthly harp are stricken notes which *cannot* have been unfamiliar to the angels. And thus there can be little doubt that in the union of Poetry with Music in its popular sense, we shall find the widest field for the Poetic development. The old Bards and Minnesingers had advantages which we do not possess—and Thomas Moore, singing his own songs, was, in the most legitimate manner, perfecting them as poems.

To recapitulate, then:—I would define, in brief, the Poetry of words as *The Rhythmical Creation of Beauty*. Its sole arbiter is Taste. With the Intellect or with the Conscience, it has only collateral relations. Unless incidentally, it has no concern whatever either with Duty or with Truth.

A few words, however, in explanation. *That* pleasure which is at once the most pure, the most elevating, and the most intense, is derived, I maintain, from the contemplation of the Beautiful. In the contemplation of Beauty we alone find it possible to attain that pleasurable elevation, or excitement, *of the soul*, which we recognise as the Poetic Sentiment, and which is so easily distinguished from Truth, which is the satisfaction of the Reason, or from Passion, which is the excitement of the heart. I make Beauty, therefore—using the word as inclusive of the sublime—I make Beauty the province of the poem, simply because it is an obvious rule of Art that effects should be made to spring as directly as possible from their causes:—no one as yet having been weak enough to deny that the peculiar elevation in question is at least *most readily* attainable in the poem. It by no means follows, however, that the incitements of Passion, or the precepts of Duty, or even the lessons of Truth, may not be introduced into a poem, and with advantage; for they may subserve, incidentally, in various ways, the general purposes of the work:—but the true artist will always contrive to tone them down in proper subjection to that *Beauty* which is the atmosphere and the real essence of the poem. . . .

Thus, although in a very cursory and imperfect manner, I have endeavoured to convey to you my conception of the Poetic Principle. It has been my purpose to suggest that, while this Principle itself is, strictly and simply, the Human Aspiration for Supernal Beauty, the manifestation of the Principle is always found in *an elevating excitement of the Soul*—quite independent of that passion which is the intoxication of the Heart—or of that Truth which is the satisfaction of the Reason. For, in regard to Passion, alas! its tendency is to degrade, rather than to elevate the Soul. Love, on the contrary—Love—the true, the divine Eros—the Uranian, as distinguished from the Dionæan Venus—is unquestionably the purest and truest of all poetical themes. And in regard to Truth— if, to be sure, through the attainment of a truth, we are led to perceive a harmony where none was apparent before, we experience, at once, the true poetical effect—but this effect is referable to the harmony alone, and not in the least degree to the truth which merely served to render the harmony manifest.

We shall reach, however, more immediately a distinct conception of what the true Poetry is, by mere reference to a few of the simple elements which induce in the Poet himself the true poetical effect. He recognises the ambrosia which nourishes his soul, in the bright orbs that shine in Heaven—in the volutes of the flower—in the clustering of low shrubberies—in the waving of the grain-fields—in the slanting of tall, Eastern trees—in the blue distance of mountains— in the grouping of clouds—in the twinkling of half-hidden brooks—in the gleaming of silver rivers—in the repose of sequestered lakes—in the star-mirroring depths of lonely wells. He perceives it in the songs of birds—in the harp of the Æolus—in the sighing of the night-wind—in the repining voice of the forest—in the surf that complains to the shore—in the fresh breath of the woods—in the scent of the violet—in the voluptuous perfume of the hyacinth—in the suggestive odour that comes to him, at eventide, from far-distant, undiscovered islands, over dim oceans, illimitable and unexplored. He owns it in all noble thoughts—in all unworldly motives—in all holy impulses—in all chivalrous, generous, and self-sacrificing deeds. He feels it in the beauty of woman—in the grace of her step—in the lustre of her eye—in the melody of her voice—in her soft laughter—in her sigh—in the harmony of the rustling of her robes. He deeply feels it in her winning endearments—in her burning enthusiasms—in her gentle charities—in her meek and devotional endurances—but above all—ah, far above all—he kneels to it—he worships it in the faith, in the purity, in the strength, in the altogether divine majesty—of her *love*. . . . .

—*Sartain's Union Magazine*, October 1850

AMERICAN CRITICISM

(from a review of The Quacks of Helicon *by
Lambert A. Wilmer)*

The corrupt nature of our ordinary criticism has become notorious. Its powers have been prostrated by its own arm. The intercourse between critic and publisher, as it now almost universally stands, is comprised either in the paying and pocketing of black mail, as the price of a simple forbearance, or in a direct system of petty and contemptible bribery, properly so called—a system even more injurious than the former to the true interests of the public, and more degrading to the buyers and sellers of good opinion, on account of the more positive character of the service here rendered for the consideration received. We laugh at the idea of any denial of our assertions upon this topic; they are infamously true. In the charge of general corruption there are undoubtedly many noble exceptions to be made. There are, indeed, some very few editors, who, maintaining an entire independence, will receive no books from publishers at all, or who receive them with a perfect understanding, on the part the latter, that an unbiassed *critique* will be given. But these cases are insufficient to have much effect on the popular mistrust: a mistrust heightened by late exposure of the machinations of *coteries* in New York—*coteries* which, at the bidding of leading booksellers, manufacture, as required from time to time, a pseudo-public opinion by wholesale, for the benefit of any little hanger on of the party, or pettifogging protector of the firm.

We speak of these things in the bitterness of scorn. It is unnecessary to cite instances, where one is found in almost every issue of a book. It is needless to call to mind the desperate case of Fay[1]—a case where the pertinacity of the effort to gull—where the obviousness of the attempt at forestalling a judgment—where the wofully over-done be-Mirrorment of that man-of-straw, together with the pitiable platitude of his production, proved a dose somewhat too potent for even the well-prepared stomach of the mob. We say it is supererogatory to dwell upon "Norman Leslie," or other by-gone follies, when we have, before our eyes, hourly instances of the machinations in question. To so great an extent of methodical assurance has the *system* of puffery arrived, that publishers, of late, have made no scruple of keeping on hand an assortment of commendatory notices, prepared by their men of all work, and of sending these notices around to the multitudinous papers within their influence, done up within the fly-leaves of the book. The grossness of these base attempts, however, has not escaped indignant rebuke from the more honorable portion of the press; and we hail these symptoms of restiveness under the yoke of unprincipled ignorance and quackery (strong only in combination) as the harbinger of a better era for the interests of real merit, and of the national literature as a whole.

It has become, indeed the plain duty of each individual connected with our periodicals, heartily to give whatever influence he possesses, to the good cause of integrity and the truth. The results thus attainable will be found worthy his closest attention and best efforts. We shall thus frown down all conspiracies to foist inanity upon the public consideration at the obvious expense of every man of talent who is not a member of a *clique* in power. We may even arrive, in time, at that desirable point from which a distinct view of our men of letters may be obtained, and their respective pretension adjusted, by the standard of a rigorous and self-sustaining criticism alone. That their several positions are as yet properly settled; that the posts which a vast number of them now hold are maintained by any better tenure than that of the chicanery upon which we have commented, will be asserted by none but the ignorant, or the parties who have best right to feel an interest in the "good old condition of things." No two matters can be more radically different than the reputation of some of our prominent *litterateurs*, as gathered from the mouths of the people, (who glean it from the paragraphs of the papers,) and the same reputation as deduced from the private estimate of intelligent and educated men. We do not advance this fact as a new discovery. Its truth, on the contrary, is the subject, and has long been so, of every-day witticism and mirth.

Why not? Surely there can be few things more ridiculous than the general character and assumptions of the ordinary critical notices of new books! An editor, sometimes without the shadow of the commonest attainment—often without brains, always without time—does not scruple to give the world to understand that he is in the *daily* habit of critically reading and deciding upon a flood of publications one tenth of whose title-pages he may possibly have turned over, three fourths of whose contents would be Hebrew to his most desperate efforts at comprehension, and whose entire mass and amount, as might be mathematically demonstrated, would be sufficient to occupy, in the most cursory perusal, the attention of some ten or twenty readers for a month! What he wants in plausibility, however, he makes up in obsequiousness; what he lacks in time he supplies in temper. He is the most easily pleased man in the world. He admires everything, from the big Dictionary of Noah Webster to the last diamond edition of Tom Thumb. Indeed his sole difficulty is in finding tongue to express his delight. Every pamphlet is a miracle—every book in boards is an epoch in letters. His phrases, therefore, get bigger and bigger every day, and, if it were not for talking Cockney, we might call him a "regular swell."

Yet in the attempt at getting definite information in regard to any one portion of our literature, the merely general reader, or the foreigner, will turn in vain from the lighter to the heavier journals. But it is not our intention here to dwell upon the radical, antique, and systematized rigmarole of our Quarterlies. The articles here are anonymous. Who writes?—who causes to be written? Who but an ass will put faith in tirades which *may* be the result of personal hostility, or in panegyrics which nine times out of ten may be laid, directly or indirectly, to the charge of the author himself? It is in the favor of these saturnine pamphlets that they contain, now and then, a good essay *de omnibus rebus et quibusdam aliis,*[2] which may be looked into, without decided somnolent consequences, at any period not immediately subsequent to dinner. But it is useless to expect criticism from periodicals called "Reviews" from never reviewing. Besides, all men know, or should know, that these books are sadly given to verbiage. It is a part of their nature, a condition of their being, a point of their faith. A veteran reviewer loves the safety of generalities, and is therefore rarely particular. "Words, words, words" are the secret of his strength. He has one or two ideas of his own, and is both wary and fussy in giving them out. His wit lies with his truth, in a well, and there is always a world of trouble in getting it up. He is a sworn enemy to all things simple and direct. He gives no ear to the advice of the giant Moulineau—"*Belier, mon ami, commencez au commencement.*"[3] He either jumps at once into the middle of his subject, or breaks in at a back door, or sidles up to it with the gait of a crab. No other mode of approach has an air of sufficient profundity. When fairly into it, however, he becomes dazzled with the scintillations of his own wisdom, and is seldom able to see his way out. Tired of laughing at his antics, or frightened at seeing him flounder, the reader at length shuts him up, with the book. "What song the Syrens sang," says Sir Thomas Browne, "or what name Achilles assumed when he hid himself among women, though puzzling questions, are not beyond *all* conjecture"—but it would puzzle Sir Thomas, backed by Achilles and all the Syrens in Heathendom, to say, in nine cases out of ten, *what is the object* of a thorough-going Quarterly Reviewer.

Should the opinions promulgated by our press at large be taken, in their wonderful aggregate, as an evidence of what American literature absolutely is, (and it may be said that, in general, they are really so taken,) we shall find ourselves the most enviable set of people upon the face of the earth. Our fine writers are legion. Our very atmosphere is redolent of genius; and we, the nation, are a huge, well-contented chameleon, grown pursy by inhaling it. We are *teretes et rotundi*[4]—enwrapped in excellence. All our poets are Miltons, neither mute nor inglorious; all our poetesses are "American Hemanses;" nor will it do to deny that all our novelists are great Knowns or great Unknowns, and that every body who writes, in every possible and impossible department, is the admirable Crichton, or at least the admirable Crichton's ghost. We are thus in a glorious condition, and will remain so until forced to disgorge our ethereal honors. In truth, there is some danger that the jealousy of the Old World will interfere. It cannot long submit to that outrageous monopoly of "all the decency and all the talent" in which the gentlemen of the press give such undoubted assurance of our being so busily engaged.

But we feel angry with ourselves for the jesting tone of our observations upon this topic. The prevalence of the spirit of puffery is a subject far less for merriment than for disgust. Its truckling, yet dogmatical character—its bold, unsustained, yet self-sufficient and wholesale laudation—is becoming, more and more, an insult to the common sense of the community. Trivial as it essentially is, it has yet been made the instrument of the grossest abuse in the elevation of imbecility, to the manifest injury, to the utter ruin, of true merit. Is there any man of good feeling and of ordinary understanding—is there one single individual among all our readers—who does not feel a thrill of bitter indignation, apart from any sentiment of mirth, as he calls to mind instance after instance of the purest, of the most unadulterated quackery in letters, which has risen to a high post in the apparent popular estimation, and which still maintains it, by the sole means of a blustering arrogance, or of a busy wriggling conceit, or of the most barefaced plagiarism, or even through the simple immensity of its assumptions—assumptions not only unopposed by the press at large, but absolutely supported in proportion to the vociferous clamor with which they are made—in exact accordance with their utter baselessness and untenability? We should have no trouble in pointing out, today, some twenty or thirty so-called literary personages, who, if not idiots, as we half think them, or if not hardened to all sense of shame by a long course of disingenuousness, will now blush, in the perusal of these words, through consciousness of the shadowy nature of that purchased pedestal upon which they stand—will now tremble in thinking of the feebleness of the breath which will be adequate to the blowing it from beneath their feet. With the help of a hearty good will, even *we* may yet tumble them down.

So firm, through a long endurance, has been the hold taken upon the popular mind (at least so far as we may consider the popular mind reflected in ephemeral letters) by the laudatory system which we have deprecated, that what is, in its own essence, a vice, has become endowed with the appearance, and met with the reception of a virtue. Antiquity, as usual, has lent a certain degree of speciousness even to the absurd. So continuously have we puffed, that we have at length come to think puffing the duty, and plain speaking the dereliction. What we began in gross error, we persist in through habit. Having adopted, in the earlier days of our literature, the untenable idea that this literature, as a whole, could be advanced by an indiscriminate approbation bestowed on its every effort—having adopted this idea, we say, without attention to the obvious fact that praise of all was bitter although negative censure to the few alone deserving, and that the only result of the system, in the fostering way, would be the fostering of folly—we now continue our vile practices through the supineness of custom, even while, in our national self-conceit, we repudiate that necessity for patronage and protection in which originated our conduct. In a word, the press throughout the country has not been ashamed to make head against the very few bold attempts at independence which have, from time to time, been made in the face of the reigning order of things. And if, in one, or perhaps two, insulated cases, the spirit of severe truth, sustained by an unconquerable will, was not to be so put down, then, forthwith, were private chicaneries set in motion; then was had resort, on the part of those who considered themselves injured by the severity of criticism, (and who were so, if the just contempt of every ingenuous man is injury,) resort to arts of the most virulent indignity, to untraceable slanders, to ruthless assassinations in the dark. We say these things were done, while the press in general looked on, and, with a full understanding of the wrong perpetrated, spoke not against the wrong. The idea had absolutely gone abroad—had grown up little by little into toleration—that attacks however just, upon a literary reputation however obtained, however untenable, were well retaliated by the basest and most unfounded traduction of personal fame. But is this an age—is this a day—in which it can be necessary even to advert to such considerations as that the book of the author is the property of the public, and that the issue of the book is the throwing down of the gauntlet to the reviewer—to the reviewer whose duty is the plainest; the duty not even of approbation, or of censure, or of silence, at his own will, but at the sway of those sentiments and of those opinions which are derived from the author himself, through the medium of his written and published words? True criticism is the reflection of the thing criticised upon the spirit of the critic.

—*Graham's Magazine*, August 1841

OBSERVATIONS

As a magazinist Poe composed notes, squibs, short essays, and editorial comments on a wide range of topics. These pieces served several purposes, one of which (admittedly) was to fill empty column space. But these "brevities" also enabled Poe to flaunt his learning, to deliver pungent insights, to convey literary gossip, to indulge in philosophical speculation, and to play the cultural pundit. From the beginning of his tenure at the *Southern Literary Messenger*, he contributed scraps of filler, culled mainly from the classics, and in one issue supplied nine pages of scholarly tidbits that he called "Pinakidia." Poe's best known series of general observations, "Marginalia," made its 1844 debut in the *Democratic Review*, and over the next five years, installments also appeared in *Godey's*, *Graham's*, and the *Southern Literary Messenger*. As editor of the weekly *Broadway Journal* in 1845, Poe likewise composed brief miscellaneous comments, mostly concerned with contemporary literary culture.

From these stray writings, one gains both a better appreciation of Poe's intellectual range and a clearer sense of his concerns as an American man of letters. The selections included in the section cohere around several organizing ideas—art, imagination, reason, genius, insight, spiritual revelation—and reflect his preoccupations mostly during the 1840s, a period of profound uncertainty when he was increasingly drawn toward a compensatory vision of cosmic unity. Inevitably, his comments also betray the inconsistency of his thinking. Poe defines art as "the reproduction of what the senses perceive in nature through the veil of the soul," and he emphasizes the role of that "veil," which restricts conventional sight that always sees "too much" by focusing on material surfaces. Yet elsewhere he hails the "clear-sightedness" of the poet, which enables him to see injustice "where the unpoetical see no injustice whatsoever." Poe insists in these jottings that the "natural" state of humankind is not "the savage" but rather the rational; implicitly countering Rousseau, he affirms a notion of "improvement" and cultural progress that he elsewhere rejected.

Much like Emerson, Poe describes the crucial process by which the soul, in moments of heightened awareness, transcends its human particularity to apprehend its relationship to the universe. The imagination likewise offers occasional glimpses of "things supernal and eternal." The first installment of "Marginalia" includes a meditation on the "*mutuality* of adaptation" inherent in the created universe and reflective of divine perfection. In a revealing commentary from 1846 he describes his own "psychal impressions" between waking and sleep, visions of "the spirit's outer world" that he means yet to communicate with through "the power of words." Though not a fragment of "Marginalia," the last selection (from the conclusion of *Eureka*), represents the transcendental culmination of this line of speculation, the counterpart, in effect, of his dread.

The subject of genius fascinated Poe, and in one of his "Fifty Suggestions" he distinguishes between genius in the popular sense, which arises from the abnormal development of one "predominant faculty," and that highest, most irresistible form of genius, which derives from a huge intelligence whose faculties are all in "absolute proportion." In his "Marginalia" Poe argues that genius may be "far more abundant than is supposed," but most people lack the moral and analytical powers to *create* works of genius, which depend crucially upon patience, concentration, and energy. Reversing his assumption about the prevalence of genius, though, he muses elsewhere about the strange fate of an individual "accursed" with an intellect far superior to the rest of the human race, whose unconventional opinions would be taken for signs of madness. The greatest test of radical originality would be, he later conjectures, to reveal truthfully the inmost secrets of one's heart; the generality of humankind would not dare make the attempt for "the paper would shrivel and blaze at every touch of the fiery pen."

Alongside Poe's meditations on mind, soul, and imagination, his comments on the situation of the American writer and the project to create a national literature offer a revealing contrast, illuminating the obstacles to authorship and the cultural politics that circumscribed his literary career. One of his most basic convictions, expressed repeatedly in letters, informs his "Marginalia" comment on magazine literature in America: the "*rush* of the [modern] age" was creating a reading public that demanded "the curt, the condensed, the pointed, the readily diffused." Poe believed that the "whole tendency of the age is Magazine-ward" and anticipated a "geometrical" increase in the cultural importance of monthly journals. Yet in "Some Secrets of the Magazine Prison-House," one of his most trenchant critiques, Poe reveals the dark side of this publishing trend. Drawn into magazine work by the absence of an international copyright law, American writers found themselves victimized on two fronts by the pressures of literary capitalism. While book publishers spurned their work, preferring to profit from pirated works by British authors, magazine publishers likewise exploited them by delaying payment for original articles, virtually starving to death "poor devil" contributors.

Poe toiled in the magazine world at a time when, as he wrote in an 1842 "Exordium to Critical Notices," the "watchword" in American popular culture was "a national literature." The imperative to infuse literature with nationalism struck Poe as a formula for provincialism, and he mocked the tendency to praise "a stupid book" because its "stupidity" was home-grown. Again in 1845 in an editorial comment Poe questioned the value of "American themes," yet he also resented American "subserviency" to British critical opinion and closed with a ringing call for a literary "Declaration of Independence" from England, or better still, he added, a "Declaration of War." About the same time, in a "Marginalia" column for *Godey's*, he underscored his support for international copyright by pointing out the consequences of the heavy reliance on imported literature: The same system that represses the true literary genius encourages "gentlemen of elegant leisure" to produce insipid colonial imitations of British models, just as the dissemination of foreign books has promoted a "monarchical or aristocratic sentiment" ultimately "fatal to democracy."

Because Poe worried about the future of the nation and (as we see in his satires) about the fate of democracy itself, his modest proposal of 1846, inspired by Irving, to name the United States "Appalachia"—and thereby resist appropriating the general name of the Western hemisphere—shows an underappreciated aspect of his thinking about the nation. He argued that Appalachia would associate the country with its unique topography and honor those who named it—the original Native inhabitants who had been "at all points unmercifully despoiled, assassinated, and dishonored." If Poe sometimes conjured in fiction and poetry a fantastic place "out of space—out of time," he was nevertheless attuned to cultural politics and concerned that rabid nationalism was distorting American literature and criticism.

LITERARY NATIONALISM

(from "Exordium to Critical Notices")

That the public attention, in America, has, of late days, been more than usually directed to the matter of literary criticism, is plainly apparent. Our periodicals are beginning to acknowledge the importance of the science (shall we so term it?) and to disdain the flippant *opinion* which so long has been made its substitute.

Time was when we imported our critical decisions from the mother country. For many years we enacted a perfect farce of subserviency to the *dicta* of Great Britain. At last a revulsion of feeling, with self-disgust, necessarily ensued. Urged by these, we plunged into the opposite extreme. In throwing *totally* off that "authority," whose voice had so long been so sacred, we even surpassed, and by much, our original folly. But the watchword now was, "a national literature!"—as if any true literature *could be* "national"—as if the world at large were not the only proper stage for the literary *histrio*. We became, suddenly, the merest and maddest *partizans* in letters. Our papers spoke of "tariffs" and "protection." Our Magazines had habitual passages about that "truly native novelist, Mr. Cooper," or that "staunch American genius, Mr. Paulding." Unmindful of the spirit of the axioms that "a prophet has no honor in his own land" and that "a hero is never a hero to his *valet-de-chambre*"—axioms founded in reason and in truth—our reviews urged the propriety—our booksellers the necessity, of strictly "American" themes. A foreign subject, at this epoch, was a weight more than enough to drag down into the very depths of critical damnation the finest writer owning nativity in the States; while, on the reverse, we found ourselves daily in the paradoxical dilemma of liking, or pretending to like, a stupid

577

book the better because (sure enough) its stupidity was of our own growth, and discussed our own affairs.

It is, in fact, but very lately that this anomalous state of feeling has shown any signs of subsidence. Still it *is* subsiding. Our views of literature in general having expanded, we begin to demand the use—to inquire into the offices and provinces of criticism—to regard it more as an art based immoveably in nature, less as a mere system of fluctuating and conventional dogmas. And, with the prevalence of these ideas, has arrived a distaste even to the home-dictation of the bookseller-*coteries*. If our editors are not as yet *all* independent of the will of a publisher, a majority of them scruple, at least, *to confess* a subservience, and enter into no positive combinations against the minority who despise and discard it. And this is a *very* great improvement of exceedingly late date.

—*Graham's Magazine*, January 1842

"SOME SECRETS OF THE
MAGAZINE PRISON-HOUSE"

The want of an International Copy-Right Law, by rendering it
nearly impossible to obtain anything from the booksellers in the
way of remuneration for literary labor, has had the effect of forc-
ing many of our very best writers into the service of the Magazines
and Reviews, which with a pertinacity that does them credit, keep
up in a certain or uncertain degree the good old saying, that even
in the thankless field of Letters the laborer is worthy of his hire.
How—by dint of what dogged instinct of the honest and proper,
these journals have contrived to persist in their paying practices, in
the very teeth of the opposition got up by the Fosters and Leonard
Scotts, who furnish for eight dollars any four of the British peri-
odicals for a year, is a point we have had much difficulty in set-
tling to our satisfaction, and we have been forced to settle it, at
last, upon no more reasonable ground than that of a still lingering
esprit de patrie.[1] That Magazines can live, and not only live but
thrive, and not only thrive but afford to disburse money for origi-
nal contributions, are facts which can only be solved, under the
circumstances, by the really fanciful but still agreeable supposi-
tion, that there is somewhere still existing an ember not altogether
quenched among the fires of good feeling for letters and literary
men, that once animated the American bosom.

It would *not do* (perhaps this is the idea) to let our poor devil
authors absolutely starve, while we grow fat, in a literary sense, on
the good things of which we unblushingly pick the pocket of all
Europe: it would not be exactly the thing *comme il faut*, to permit
a positive atrocity of this kind: and hence we have Magazines, and
hence we have a portion of the public who subscribe to these Mag-
azines (through sheer pity), and hence we have Magazine publish-
ers (who sometimes take upon themselves the duplicate title of

"editor *and* proprietor,")—publishers, we say, who, under certain conditions of good conduct, occasional puffs, and decent subserviency at all times, make it a point of conscience to encourage the poor devil author with a dollar or two, more or less as he behaves himself properly and abstains from the indecent habit of turning up his nose.

We hope, however, that we are not so prejudiced or so vindictive as to insinuate that what certainly does look like illiberality on the part of them (the Magazine publishers) is really an illiberality chargeable to *them*. In fact, it will be seen at once, that what we have said has a tendency directly the reverse of any such accusation. These publishers pay *something*—other publishers nothing at all. Here certainly is a difference—although a mathematician might contend that the difference might be infinitesimally small. Still, these Magazine editors and proprietors *pay* (that is the word), and with your true poor-devil author the smallest favors are sure to be thankfully received. No: the illiberality lies at the door of the demagogue-ridden public, who suffer their anointed delegates (or perhaps arointed—which is it?) to insult the common sense of them (the public) by making orations in our national halls on the beauty and conveniency of robbing the Literary Europe on the highway, and on the gross absurdity in especial of admitting so unprincipled a principle, that a man has any right and title either to his own brains or the flimsy material that he chooses to spin out of them, like a confounded caterpillar as he is. If anything of this gossamer character stands in need of protection, why we have our hands full at once with the silk-worms and the *morus multicaulis*.[2]

But if we cannot, under the circumstances, complain of the absolute illiberality of the Magazine publishers (since pay they do), there is at least one particular in which we have against them good grounds of accusation. Why (since pay they must) do they not pay with a good grace, and *promptly*. Were we in an ill humor at this moment, we could a tale unfold which would erect the hair on the head of Shylock. A young author, struggling with Despair itself in the shape of a ghastly poverty, which has no alleviation—no sympathy from an everyday world, that cannot understand his necessities, and that would pretend not to understand them if it comprehended them ever so well—this young author is politely requested to compose an article, for which he will "be handsomely

paid." Enraptured, he neglects perhaps for a month the sole em-
ployment which affords him the chance of a livelihood, and hav-
ing starved through the month (he and his family) completes at
length the month of starvation and the article, and despatches the
latter (with a broad hint about the former) to the pursy "editor"
and bottle-nosed "proprietor" who has condescended to honor
him (the poor devil) with his patronage. A month (starving still),
and no reply. Another month—still none. Two months more—
still none. A second letter, modestly hinting that the article may
not have reached its destination—still no reply. At the expiration
of six additional months, personal application is made at the "ed-
itor and proprietor" 's office. Call again. The poor devil goes out,
and does not fail to call again. Still call again;—and call again is
the word for three or four months more. His patience exhausted,
the article is demanded. No—he can't have it—(the truth is, it was
too good to be given up so easily)—"it is in print," and "contri-
butions of this character are never paid for (it is a *rule* we have)
under six months after publication. Call in six months after the is-
sue of your affair, and your money is ready for you—for we are
business men, ourselves—prompt." With this the poor devil is sat-
isfied, and makes up his mind that the "editor and proprietor" is a
gentleman, and that of course he (the poor devil) will wait as re-
quested. And it is supposable that he would have waited if he
could—but Death in the meantime would not. He dies, and by the
good luck of his decease (which came by starvation) the fat "edi-
tor and proprietor" is fatter henceforward and for ever to the
amount of five and twenty dollars, very cleverly saved, to be spent
generously in canvas-backs and champagne.

There are two things which we hope the reader will not do, as
he runs over this article: first, we hope that he will not believe that
we write from any personal experience of our own, for we have
only the reports of actual sufferers to depend upon, and second,
that he will not make any personal application of our remarks to
any Magazine publisher now living, it being well known that they
are all as remarkable for their generosity and urbanity, as for their
intelligence, and appreciation of Genius.

—*Broadway Journal*, February 15, 1845

AMERICAN LITERARY INDEPENDENCE

(an editorial comment from the Broadway Journal*)*

Much has been said, of late, about the necessity of maintaining a proper *nationality* in American Letters; but what this nationality *is*, or what is to be gained by it, has never been distinctly understood. That an American should confine himself to American themes, or even prefer them, is rather a political than a literary idea—and at best is a questionable point. We would do well to bear in mind that "distance lends enchantment to the view." *Ceteris paribus*,[1] a foreign theme is, in a strictly literary sense, to be preferred. After all, the world at large is the only legitimate stage for the autorial *histrio*.

But of the need of *that* nationality which defends our own literature, sustains our own men of letters, upholds our own dignity, and depends upon our own resources, there cannot be the shadow of a doubt. Yet here is the very point at which we are most supine. We complain of our want of an International Copyright, on the ground that this want justifies our publishers in inundating us with British opinion in British books; and yet when these very publishers, at their own obvious risk, and even obvious loss, do publish an American book, we turn up our noses at it with supreme contempt (this as a general thing) until it (the American book) has been dubbed "readable" by some illiterate Cockney critic. It is too much to say that, with us, the opinion of Washington Irving—of Prescott—of Bryant—is a mere nullity in comparison with that of any anonymous sub-sub-editor of The Spectator, The Athenæum or the "London Punch"? It is *not* saying too much, to say this. It is a solemn—an absolutely awful fact. Every publisher in the country will admit it to be a fact. There is not a more disgusting spectacle under the sun than our subserviency to British criticism. It is disgusting, first, because it is truckling, servile, pusillanimous—secondly, because of its gross irrationality. We *know* the British to bear us little but ill will—we know that, in no case, do they utter unbiassed opinions of American books—we know that in the few instances in which our writers have been treated with common decency in England, these writers have either openly paid homage to English institutions, or have had lurking at bottom of their hearts a secret principle at war with Democracy:—we *know* all this, and yet, day after day, submit our necks to the degrading yoke of the crudest opinion that emanates from the fatherland. Now if we *must* have nationality let it be a nationality that will throw off this yoke.

The chief of the rhapsodists who have ridden us to death like the Old Man of the Mountain, is the ignorant and egotistical Wilson.[2] We use the term rhapsodists with perfect deliberation; for, Macaulay, and Dilke, and one or two others, excepted, there is not in Great Britain a critic who can be fairly considered worthy the name. The Germans and even the French are infinitely superior. As regards Wilson, no man ever penned worse criticism or better rhodomontade. That he is "egotistical" his works show to all men, running as they read. That he is "ignorant" let his absurd and continuous schoolboy blunders about Homer bear witness. Not long ago we ourselves pointed out a series of similar inanities in his review of Miss Barrett's poems—a series, we say, of gross blunders arising from sheer ignorance—and we defy him or any one to answer a single syllable of what we then advanced.

And yet this is the man whose simple *dictum* (to our shame be it spoken) has the power to make or to mar any American reputation! In the last number of Blackwood, he has a continuation of the dull "Specimens of the British Critics," and makes occasion wantonly to insult one of the noblest of our poets, Mr. Lowell. The point of the whole attack consists in the use of slang epithets and phrases of the most ineffably vulgar description. "Squabashes" is a pet term. "Faugh!" is another. "We are Scotsmen to *the spine*!" says Sawney—as if the thing were not more than self-evident. Mr. Lowell is called "a magpie," an "ape," a "Yankee cockney," and his name is intentionally mis-written *John* Russell Lowell. Now were these indecencies perpetrated by any American critic, that critic would be sent to Coventry by the whole press of the country, but since it is Wilson who insults, we, as in duty bound, not only submit to the insult, but echo it, as an excellent jest, throughout the length and breadth of the land. *Quamdiu Catilina?*[3] We do indeed demand the nationality of self-respect. In Letters as in Government we require a Declaration of Independence. A better thing still would be a Declaration of War—and that war should be carried forthwith "into Africa."[4]

Broadway Journal, October 4, 1845

THE SOUL AND THE SELF

(from "Chapter of Suggestions")

In the life of every man there occurs at least one epoch, when the spirit seems to abandon, for a brief period, the body, and, elevating itself above mortal affairs just so far as to get a comprehensive and *general* view, makes thus an estimate of its humanity, as accurate as is possible, under any circumstances, to that particular spirit. The soul here separates itself from its own idiosyncrasy, or individuality, and considers its own being, not as appertaining solely to itself, but as a portion of the universal Ens.[1] All the important good resolutions which we keep—all startling, marked regenerations of character—are brought about at these *crises* of life. And thus it is our intense *sense of self* which debases, and which keeps us debased.

—*The Opal*, 1845

IMAGINATION AND INSIGHT

(from "Chapter of Suggestions")

That the imagination has not been unjustly ranked as supreme among the mental faculties, appears, from the intense consciousness, on the part of the imaginative man, that the faculty in question brings his soul often to a glimpse of things supernal and eternal—to the very verge of the *great secrets*. There are moments, indeed, in which he perceives the faint perfumes, and hears the melodies of a happier world. Some of the most profound knowledge—perhaps all *very* profound knowledge—has originated from a highly stimulated imagination. Great intellects *guess* well. The laws of Kepler were, professedly, *guesses*.

—*The Opal*, 1845

POETICAL IRRITABILITY

(from "Fifty Suggestions")

That poets (using the word comprehensively, as including artists in general) are a *genus irritabile*, is well understood; but the *why*, seems not to be commonly seen. An artist *is* an artist only by dint of his exquisite sense of Beauty—a sense affording him rapturous enjoyment, but at the same time implying, or involving, an equally exquisite sense of Deformity of disproportion. Thus a wrong—an injustice—done a poet who is really a poet, excites him to a degree which, to ordinary apprehension, appears disproportionate with the wrong. Poets *see* injustice—*never* where it does not exist—but very often where the unpoetical see no injustice whatever. Thus the poetical irritability has no reference to "temper" in the vulgar sense, but merely to a more than usual clear-sightedness in respect to Wrong:—this clear-sightedness being nothing more than a corollary from the vivid perception of Right—of justice—of proportion—in a word, of το χαλον.[1] But one thing is clear—that the man who is *not* "irritable," (to the ordinary apprehension,) is *no poet.*

—*Graham's Magazine*, May 1849

GENIUS AND PROPORTIONATE INTELLECT

(from "Fifty Suggestions")

Let a man succeed ever so evidently—ever so demonstrably—in many different displays of *genius,* the envy of criticism will agree with the popular voice in denying him more than *talent* in any. Thus a poet who has achieved a great (by which I mean an effective) poem, should be cautious not to distinguish himself in any other walk of Letters. In especial—let him make no effort in Science—unless anonymously, or with the view of waiting patiently the judgment of posterity. Because universal or even versatile geniuses have rarely or never been known, *therefore,* thinks the world, none such can ever be. A "therefore" of this kind is, with the world, conclusive. But what is the *fact,* as taught us by analysis of mental power? Simply, that the *highest* genius—that the genius which all men instantaneously acknowledge as such—which acts upon individuals, as well as upon the mass, by a species of magnetism incomprehensible but irresistible and *never resisted*—that this genius which demonstrates itself in the simplest gesture—or even by the absence of all—this genius which speaks without a voice and flashes from the unopened eve—is but the result of generally large mental power existing in a state of *absolute proportion*—so that no one faculty has undue predominance. *That* factitious "genius"—that "genius" in the popular sense—which is but the manifestation of the abnormal predominance of some one faculty over all the others—and, of course, at the expense and to the detriment, of all the others—is a result of mental disease or rather, of organic malformation of mind:—it is this and nothing more. Not only will such "genius" fail, if turned aside from the path indicated by its predominant faculty; but, even when pursuing this path—when producing those works in which, certainly, it is *best* calculated to succeed—will give unmistakeable indications of *unsoundness*, in respect to general intellect. Hence, indeed, arises the just idea that

"Great wit to madness nearly is allied."

I say "just idea;" for by "great wit," in this case, the poet intends precisely the pseudo-genius to which I refer. The true genius, on the other hand, is necessarily, if not universal in its manifestations, at least capable of universality; and if, attempting all things, it succeeds in one rather better than in another, this is merely on account of a certain bias by which *Taste* leads it with more earnestness in the one direction than in the other. With equal zeal, it would succeed equally in all.

To sum up our results in respect to this very simple, but much *vexata questio:*[1]

What the world calls "genius" is the state of mental disease arising from the undue predominance of some one of the faculties. The works of such genius are never sound in themselves and, in especial, always betray the general mental insanity.

The *proportion* of the mental faculties, in a case where the general mental power is *not* inordinate, gives that result which we distinguish as *talent:*—and the talent is greater or less, first, as the general mental power is greater or less; and, secondly, as the proportion of the faculties is more or less absolute.

The proportion of the faculties, in a case where the mental power is inordinately great, gives that result which *is* the true *genius* (but which, on account of the proportion and seeming simplicity of its works, is seldom acknowledged to *be* so;) and the genius is greater or less, first, as the general mental power is more or less inordinately great; and, secondly, as the proportion of the faculties is more or less absolute.

An objection will be made:—that the greatest excess of mental power, however proportionate, does not seem to satisfy our idea of genius, unless we have, in addition, sensibility, passion, energy. The reply is, that the "absolute proportion" spoken of, when applied to inordinate mental power, gives, as a result, the appreciation of Beauty and horror of Deformity which we call sensibility, together with that intense vitality, which is implied when we speak of "Energy" or "Passion."

—*Graham's Magazine*, May 1849

REASON AND GOVERNMENT

(from "Marginalia")

The theorizers on Government, who pretend always to "begin with the beginning," commence with Man in what they call his *natural* state—the savage. What right have they to suppose this his natural state? Man's chief idiosyncrasy being reason, it follows that his savage condition—his condition of action *without* reason—is his *un*natural state. The more he reasons, the nearer he approaches the position to which this chief idiosyncrasy irresistibly impels him; and not until he attains this position with exactitude—not until his reason has exhausted itself for his improvement—not until he has stepped upon the highest pinnacle of civilisation—will his *natural* state be ultimately reached, or thoroughly determined.

—*Democratic Review*, November 1844

ADAPTATION AND THE PLOTS OF GOD

(from "Marginalia")

All the Bridgewater treatises[1] have failed in noticing *the great* idiosyncrasy in the Divine system of adaptation:—that idiosyncrasy which stamps the adaptation as Divine, in distinction from that which is the work of merely human constructiveness. I speak of the complete *mutuality* of adaptation. For example:—in human constructions, a particular cause has a particular effect—a particular purpose brings about a particular object; but we see no reciprocity. The effect does not re-act upon the cause—the object does not change relations with the purpose. In Divine constructions, the object is either object or purpose, as we choose to regard it, while the purpose is either purpose or object; so that we can never (abstractedly, without concretion—without reference to facts of the moment) decide which is which. For secondary example:—In polar climates, the human frame, to maintain its due caloric, requires, for combustion in the stomach, the most highly ammoniac food, such as train oil. Again:—In polar climates, the sole food afforded man is the oil of abundant seals and whales. Now, whether is oil at hand because imperatively demanded?—or whether is it the only thing demanded because the only thing to be obtained? It is impossible to say. There is an absolute reciprocity of adaptation, for which we seek in vain among the works of man.

The Bridgewater tractists may have avoided this point, on account of its apparent tendency to overthrow the idea of *cause* in general—consequently of a First Cause—of God. But it is more probable that they have failed to perceive what no one preceding them, has, to my knowledge, perceived.

The pleasure which we derive from any exertion of human ingenuity, is in the direct ratio of the *approach* to this species of reciprocity between cause and effect. In the construction of *plot*, for example, in fictitious literature, we should aim at so arranging the points, or incidents, that we cannot distinctly see, in respect to any one of them, whether that one depends from any one other, or upholds it. In this sense, of course, perfection of plot is unattainable *in fact*,—because Man is the constructor. The plots of God are perfect. The Universe is a Plot of God.

—*Democratic Review*, November 1844

WORKS OF GENIUS

(from "Marginal Notes")

Men of genius are far more abundant than is supposed. In fact, to appreciate thoroughly the work of what we call genius, is to possess all the genius by which the work was produced. But the person appreciating may be utterly incompetent to reproduce the work, or any thing similar, and this solely through lack of what may be termed the constructive ability—a matter quite independent of what we agree to understand in the term "genius" itself. This ability is based, to be sure, in great part, upon the faculty of analysis, enabling the artist to get full view of the machinery of his proposed effect, and thus work it and regulate it at will; but a great deal depends also upon properties strictly moral—for example, upon patience, upon concentrativeness, or the power of holding the attention steadily to the one purpose, upon self-dependence and contempt for all opinion which is opinion and no more—in especial, upon energy or industry. So vitally important is this last, that it may well be doubted if any thing to which we have been accustomed to give the title of a "work of genius" was ever accomplished without it; and it is chiefly because this quality and genius are nearly incompatible, that "works of genius" are few, while mere men of genius are, as I say, abundant. The Romans, who excelled us in acuteness of *observation*, while falling below us in induction from facts observed, seem to have been so fully aware of the inseparable connection between industry and a "work of genius," as to have adopted the error that industry, in great measure, was genius itself. The highest *compliment* is intended by a Roman, when, of an epic, or any thing similar, he says that it is written *industriâ mirabili* or *incredibili industriâ*.[1]

—*Godey's Lady's Book*, August 1845

NATIONAL LITERATURE
AND IMITATION

(from "Marginal Notes")

The question of international copyright has been overloaded with words. The right of property in a literary work is disputed merely for the sake of disputation, and no man should be at the trouble of arguing the point. Those who deny it, have made up their minds to deny every thing tending to further the law in contemplation. Nor is the question of expediency in any respect relevant. Expediency is only to be discussed where no *rights* interfere. It would no doubt be very expedient in any poor man to pick the pocket of his wealthy neighbour, (and as the poor are the majority the case is precisely parallel to the copyright case;) but what would the rich think if expediency were permitted to overrule their right?

But even the expediency is untenable, grossly so. The immediate advantage arising to the pockets of our people, in the existing condition of things, is no doubt sufficiently plain. We get more reading for less money than if the international law existed; but the remoter disadvantages are of infinitely greater weight. In brief, they are these: First, we have injury to our national literature by repressing the efforts of our men of genius; for genius, as a general rule, is poor in worldly goods and cannot write for nothing. Our genius being thus repressed, we are written *at* only by our "gentlemen of elegant leisure," and mere gentlemen of elegant leisure have been noted, time out of mind, for the insipidity of their productions. In general, too, they are obstinately conservative, and this feeling leads them into imitation of foreign, more especially of British models. This is one main source of the imitativeness with which, as a people, we have been justly charged, although the first cause is to be found in our position as a colony. Colonies have always naturally aped the mother land.

In the second place, irreparable ill is wrought by the almost exclusive dissemination among us of foreign—that is to say, of monarchical or aristocratical sentiment in foreign books; nor is this sentiment less fatal to democracy because it reaches the people themselves directly in the gilded pill of the poem or the novel.

We have next to consider the impolicy of our committing, in the national character, an open and continuous wrong on the frivolous pretext of its benefiting ourselves.

The last and by far the most important consideration of all, however, is that sense of insult and injury aroused in the whole active intellect of the world, the bitter and fatal resentment excited in the universal heart of literature—a resentment which will not and which cannot make nice distinctions between the temporary perpetrators of the wrong and that democracy in general which permits its perpetration. The autorial body is the most autocratic on the face of the earth. How, then, can those institutions even hope to be safe which systematically persist in trampling it under foot?

—*Godey's Lady's Book*, September 1845

LANGUAGE AND THOUGHT

(from "Marginalia")

Some Frenchman—possibly Montaigne—says: "People talk about thinking, but for my part I never think, except when I sit down to write." It is this never thinking, unless when we sit down to write, which is the cause of so much indifferent composition. But perhaps there is something more involved in the Frenchman's observation than meets the eye. It is certain that the mere act of inditing, tends, in a great degree, to the logicalization of thought. Whenever, on account of its vagueness, I am dissatisfied with a conception of the brain, I resort forthwith to the pen, for the purpose of obtaining, through its aid, the necessary form, consequence and precision.

How very commonly we hear it remarked, that such and such thoughts are beyond the compass of words! I do not believe that any thought, properly so called, is out of the reach of language. I fancy, rather, that where difficulty in expression is experienced, there is, in the intellect which experiences it, a want either of deliberateness or of method. For my own part, I have never had a thought which I could not set down in words, with even more distinctness than that with which I conceived it:—as I have before observed, the thought is logicalized by the effort at (written) expression.

There is, however, a class of fancies, of exquisite delicacy, which are *not* thoughts, and to which, *as yet*, I have found it absolutely impossible to adapt language. I use the word *fancies* at random, and merely because I must use *some* word; but the idea commonly attached to the term is not even remotely applicable to the shadows of shadows in question. They seem to me rather psychal than intellectual. They arise in the soul (alas, how rarely!) only at its epochs of most intense tranquillity—when the bodily and mental health are in perfection—and at those mere points of time where the confines of the waking world blend with those of the world of dreams. I am aware of these "fancies" only when I am upon the very brink of sleep, with the consciousness that I am so. I have satisfied myself that this condition exists but for an inappreciable *point* of time—yet it is crowded with these "shadows of shadows;" and for absolute *thought* there is demanded time's *endurance*.

These "fancies" have in them a pleasurable ecstasy as far beyond the most pleasurable of the world of wakefulness, or of dreams, as the Heaven of the Northman theology is beyond its Hell. I regard the visions, even as they arise, with an awe which, in some measure, moderates or tranquilizes the ecstasy—I so regard them, through a conviction (which seems a portion of the ecstasy itself) that this ecstasy, in itself, is of a character supernal to the Human Nature—is a glimpse of the spirit's outer world; and I arrive at this conclusion—if this term is at all applicable to instantaneous intuition—by a perception that the delight experienced has, as its element, but *the absoluteness of novelty*. I say the absoluteness—for in these fancies—let me now term them psychal impressions—there is really nothing even approximate in character to impressions ordinarily received. It is as if the five senses were supplanted by five myriad others alien to mortality.

Now, so entire is my faith in the *power of words*, that, at times, I have believed it possible to embody even the evanescence of fancies such as I have attempted to describe. In experiments with this end in view, I have proceeded so far as, first, to control (when the bodily and mental health are good) the existence of the condition:—that is to say, I can now (unless when ill) be sure that the condition will supervene, if I so wish it, at the point of time already described:—of its supervention, until lately, I could never be certain, even under the most favorable circumstances. I mean to say, merely, that now I can be sure, when all circumstances are favorable, of the supervention of the condition, and feel even the capacity of inducing or compelling it:—the favorable circumstances, however, are not the less rare—else had I compelled, already, the Heaven into the Earth.

I have proceeded so far, secondly, as to prevent the lapse from *the point* of which I speak—the point of blending between wakefulness and sleep—as to prevent at will, I say, the lapse from this border-ground into the dominion of sleep. Not that I can *continue* the condition—not that I can render the point more than a point—but that I can startle myself from the point into wakefulness—*and thus transfer the point itself into the realm of Memory*—convey its impressions, or more properly their recollections, to a situation where (although still for a very brief period) I can survey them with the eye of analysis.

For these reasons—that is to say, because I have been enabled to accomplish thus much—I do not altogether despair of embodying in words at least enough of the fancies in question to convey, to certain classes of intellect, a shadowy conception of their character.

In saying this I am not to be understood as supposing that the fancies, or psychal impressions, to which I allude, are confined to my individual self—are not, in a word, common to all mankind—for on this point it is quite impossible that I should form an opinion—but nothing can be more certain than that even a partial record of the impressions would startle the universal intellect of mankind, by the *supremeness of the novelty* of the material employed, and of its consequent suggestions. In a word—should I ever write a paper on this topic, the world will be compelled to acknowledge that, at last, I have done an original thing.

—*Graham's Magazine*, March 1846

MAGAZINE LITERATURE IN AMERICA

(from "Marginalia")

Whatever may be the merits or demerits, generally, of the Magazine Literature of America, there can be no question as to its extent or influence. The topic—Magazine Literature—is therefore an important one. In a few years its importance will be found to have increased in geometrical ratio. The whole tendency of the age is Magazine-ward. The Quarterly Reviews have *never* been popular. Not only are they too stilted, (by way of keeping up a due dignity,) but they make a point, with the same end in view, of discussing only topics which are *caviare* to the many, and which, for the most part, have only a conventional interest even with the few. Their issues, also, are at too long intervals; their subjects get cold before being served up. In a word, their ponderosity is quite out of keeping with the *rush* of the age. We now demand the light artillery of the intellect; we need the curt, the condensed, the pointed, the readily diffused—in place of the verbose, the detailed, the voluminous, the inaccessible. On the other hand, the lightness of the artillery should not degenerate into popgunnery—by which term we may designate the character of the greater portion of the newspaper press—their sole legitimate object being the discussion of ephemeral matters in an ephemeral manner. Whatever talent may be brought to bear upon our daily journals, (and in many cases this talent is very great,) still the imperative necessity of catching, *currente calamo*,[1] each topic as it flits before the eye of the public, must of course materially narrow the limits of their power. The bulk and the period of issue of the monthly magazines, seem to be precisely adapted, if not to all the literary wants of the day, at least to the largest and most imperative, as well as the most consequential portion of them.

—*Graham's Magazine*, December 1846

THE NAME OF THE NATION

(from "Marginalia")

It is a thousand pities that the puny witticisms of a few professional objectors should have power to prevent, even for a year, the adoption of a name for our country. At present we have, clearly, none. There should be no hesitation about "Appalachia." In the first place, it is distinctive. "America" is not, and can never be made so. We may legislate as much as we please, and assume for our country whatever name we think right—but to us it will be no name, to any purpose for which a name is needed, unless we can take it away from the regions which employ it at present. South America is "America," and will insist upon remaining so. In the second place, "Appalachia" is indigenous, springing from one of the most magnificent and distinctive features of the country itself. Thirdly, in employing this word we do honor to the Aborigines, whom, hitherto, we have at all points unmercifully despoiled, assassinated and dishonored. Fourthly, the name is the suggestion of, perhaps, the most deservedly eminent among all the pioneers of American literature. It is but just that Mr. Irving should name the land for which, in letters, he first established a name. The last, and by far the most truly important consideration of all, however, is the music of "Appalachia" itself; nothing could be more sonorous, more liquid, or of fuller volume, while its length is just sufficient for dignity. How the guttural "Alleghania" could ever have been preferred for a moment is difficult to conceive. I yet hope to find "Appalachia" assumed.

—*Graham's Magazine*, December 1846

THE UNWRITABLE BOOK

(from "Marginalia")

If any ambitious man have a fancy to revolutionize, at one effort, the universal world of human thought, human opinion, and human sentiment, the opportunity is his own—the road to immortal renown lies straight, open, and unencumbered before him. All that he has to do is to write and publish a very little book. Its title should be simple—a few plain words—"My Heart Laid Bare." But—this little book must be *true to its title*.

Now, is it not very singular that, with the rabid thirst for notoriety which distinguishes so many of mankind—so many, too, who care not a fig what is thought of them after death, there should not be found one man having sufficient hardihood to write this little book? To *write*, I say. There are ten thousand men who, if the book were once written, would laugh at the notion of being disturbed by its publication during their life, and who could not even conceive *why* they should object to its being published after their death. But to write it—*there* is the rub. No man dare write it. No man ever will dare write it. No man *could* write it, even if he dared. The paper would shrivel and blaze at every touch of the fiery pen.

—*Graham's Magazine*, January 1848

IMAGINATION

(from "Marginalia")

The *pure Imagination* chooses, from *either Beauty or Deformity*, only the most combinable things hitherto uncombined; the compound, as a general rule, partaking, in character, of beauty, or sublimity, in the ratio of the respective beauty or sublimity of the things combined—which are themselves still to be considered as atomic—that is to say, as previous combinations. But, as often analogously happens in physical chemistry, so not unfrequently does it occur in this chemistry of the intellect, that the admixture of two elements results in a something that has nothing of the qualities of one of them, or even nothing of the qualities of either. . . . Thus, the range of Imagination is unlimited. Its materials extend throughout the universe. Even out of deformities it fabricates that *Beauty* which is at once its sole object and its inevitable test. But, in general, the richness or force of the matters combined; the facility of discovering combinable novelties worth combining; and, especially the absolute "chemical combination" of the completed mass—are the particulars to be regarded in our estimate of Imagination. It is this thorough harmony of an imaginative work which so often causes it to be undervalued by the thoughtless, through the character of *obviousness* which is superinduced. We are apt to find ourselves asking *why* it is that these combinations have never been imagined before.

—*Southern Literary Messenger*, May 1849

ART AND THE SOUL

(from "Marginalia")

Were I called on to define, *very* briefly, the term "Art," I should call it "the reproduction of what the Senses perceive in Nature through the veil of the soul." The mere imitation, however accurate, of what *is* in Nature, entitles no man to the sacred name of "Artist." Denner was no artist. The grapes of Zeuxis were *in*artistic—unless in a bird's-eye view; and not even the curtain of Parrhasius could conceal his deficiency in point of genius.[1] I have mentioned "the *veil* of the soul." Something of the kind appears indispensable in Art. We can, at any time, double the true beauty of an actual landscape by half closing our eyes as we look at it. The naked Senses sometimes see too little—but then *always* they see too much.

—*Southern Literary Messenger*, June 1849

SUPERIORITY AND SUFFERING

(from "Marginalia")

I have sometimes amused myself by endeavoring to fancy what would be the fate of any individual gifted, or rather accursed, with an intellect *very* far superior to that of his race. Of course, he would be conscious of his superiority; nor could he (if otherwise constituted as man is) help manifesting his consciousness. Thus he would make himself enemies at all points. And since his opinions and speculations would widely differ from those of *all* mankind—that he would be considered a madman, is evident. How horribly painful such a condition! Hell could invent no greater torture than that of being charged with abnormal weakness on account of being abnormally strong.

In like manner, nothing can be clearer than that a *very* generous spirit—*truly* feeling what all merely profess—must inevitably find itself misconceived in every direction—its motives misinterpreted. Just as extremeness of intelligence would be thought fatuity, so excess of chivalry could not fail of being looked upon as meanness in its last degree:—and so on with other virtues. This subject is a painful one indeed. That individuals *have* so soared above the plane of their race, is scarcely to be questioned; but, in looking back through history for traces of their existence, we should pass over all biographies of "the good and the great," while we search carefully the slight records of wretches who died in prison, in Bedlam, or upon the gallows.

—*Southern Literary Messenger*, June 1849

MATTER, SPIRIT, AND DIVINE WILL

(from Eureka)

I have already alluded to that absolute *reciprocity of adaptation* which is the idiosyncrasy of the Divine Art—stamping it divine. Up to this point of our reflections, we have been regarding the electrical influence as a something by dint of whose repulsion alone Matter is enabled to exist in that state of diffusion demanded for the fulfilment of its purposes:—so far, in a word, we have been considering the influence in question as ordained for Matter's sake—to subserve the objects of matter. With a perfectly legitimate reciprocity, we are now permitted to look at Matter, as created *solely for the sake of this influence*—solely to serve the objects of this spiritual Ether. Through the aid—by the means—through the agency of Matter, and by dint of its heterogeneity—is this Ether manifested— is *Spirit individualized*. It is merely in the development of this Ether, through heterogeneity, that particular masses of Matter become animate—sensitive—and in the ratio of their heterogeneity;— some reaching a degree of sensitiveness involving what we call *Thought* and thus attaining obviously Conscious Intelligence.

In this view, we are enabled to perceive Matter as a Means—not as an End. Its purposes are thus seen to have been comprehended in its diffusion; and with the return into Unity these purposes cease. The absolutely consolidated globe of globes would be *objectless*:—therefore not for a moment could it continue to exist. Matter, created for an end, would unquestionably, on fulfilment of that end, be Matter no longer. Let us endeavor to understand that it would disappear, and that God would remain all in all.

That every work of Divine conception must cöexist and cöexpire with its particular design, seems to me especially obvious; and

I make no doubt that, on perceiving the final globe of globes to be *objectless*, the majority of my readers will be satisfied with my "*therefore* it cannot continue to exist." Nevertheless, as the startling thought of its instantaneous disappearance is one which the most powerful intellect cannot be expected readily to entertain on grounds so decidedly abstract, let us endeavor to look at the idea from some other and more ordinary point of view:—let us see how thoroughly and beautifully it is corroborated in an *à posteriori* consideration of Matter as we actually find it.

I have before said that "Attraction and Repulsion being undeniably the sole properties by which Matter is manifested to Mind, we are justified in assuming that Matter *exists* only as Attraction and Repulsion—in other words that Attraction and Repulsion *are* Matter; there being no conceivable case in which we may not employ the term 'Matter' and the terms 'Attraction' and 'Repulsion' taken together, as equivalent, and therefore convertible, expressions in Logic."

Now the very definition of Attraction implies particularity—the existence of parts, particles, or atoms; for we define it as the tendency of "each atom &c. to every other atom" &c. according to a certain law. Of course where there are *no* parts—where there is absolute Unity—where the tendency to oneness is satisfied—there can be no Attraction:—this has been fully shown, and all Philosophy admits it. When, on fulfilment of its purposes, then, Matter shall have returned into its original condition of *One*—a condition which presupposes the expulsion of the separative Ether, whose province and whose capacity are limited to keeping the atoms apart until that great day when, this Ether being no longer needed, the overwhelming pressure of the finally collective Attraction shall at length just sufficiently predominate and expel it:—when, I say, Matter, finally, expelling the Ether, shall have returned into absolute Unity,—it will then (to speak paradoxically for the moment) be Matter without Attraction and without Repulsion—in other words, Matter without Matter—in other words, again, *Matter no more*. In sinking into Unity, it will sink at once into that Nothingness which, to all finite perception, Unity must be—into that Material Nihility from which alone we can conceive it to have been evoked—to have been *created* by the Volition of God.

I repeat then—Let us endeavor to comprehend that the final

globe of globes will instantaneously disappear, and that God will remain all in all.

But are we here to pause? Not so. On the Universal agglomeration and dissolution, we can readily conceive that a new and perhaps totally different series of conditions may ensue—another creation and radiation, returning into itself—another action and reaction of the Divine Will. Guiding our imaginations by that omniprevalent law of laws, the law of periodicity, are we not, indeed, more than justified in entertaining a belief—let us say, rather, in indulging a hope—that the processes we have here ventured to contemplate will be renewed forever, and forever, and forever; a novel Universe swelling into existence, and then subsiding into nothingness, at every throb of the Heart Divine?

And now—this Heart Divine—what is it? *It is our own.*

Let not the merely seeming irreverence of this idea frighten our souls from that cool exercise of consciousness—from that deep tranquility of self-inspection—through which alone we can hope to attain the presence of this, the most sublime of truths, and look it leisurely in the face.

The *phænomena* on which our conclusions must at this point depend, are merely spiritual shadows, but not the less thoroughly substantial.

We walk about, amid the destinies of our world-existence, encompassed by dim but ever present *Memories* of a Destiny more vast—very distant in the by-gone time, and infinitely awful.

We live out a Youth peculiarly haunted by such shadows; yet never mistaking them for dreams. As Memories we *know* them. *During our Youth* the distinction is too clear to deceive us even for a moment.

So long as this Youth endures; the feeling *that we exist*, is the most natural of all feelings. We understand it *thoroughly*. That there was a period at which we did *not* exist—or, that it might so have happened that we never had existed at all—are the considerations, indeed, which *during this Youth*, we find difficulty in understanding. Why we should *not* exist, is, *up to the epoch of our Manhood*, of all queries the most unanswerable. Existence—self-existence—existence from all Time and to all Eternity—seems, up to the epoch of Manhood, a normal and unquestionable condition:—*seems, because it is.*

But now comes the period at which a conventional World-Reason awakens us from the truth of our dream. Doubt, Surprise and Incomprehensibility arrive at the same moment. They say:— "You live and the time was when you lived not. You have been created. An Intelligence exists greater than your own; and it is only through this Intelligence you live at all." These things we struggle to comprehend and cannot:—*cannot*, because these things, being untrue, are thus, of necessity, incomprehensible.

No thinking being lives who, at some luminous point of his life of thought, has not felt himself lost amid the surges of futile efforts at understanding, or believing, that anything exists *greater than his own soul*. The utter impossibility of any one's soul feeling itself inferior to another; the intense, overwhelming dissatisfaction and rebellion at the thought;—these, with the omniprevalent aspirations at perfection, are but the spiritual, coincident with the material, struggles towards the original Unity—are, to my mind at least, a species of proof far surpassing what Man terms demonstration, that no one soul *is* inferior to another—that nothing is, or can be, superior to any one soul—that each soul is, in part, its own God—its own Creator:—in a word, that God—the material *and* spiritual God—*now* exists solely in the diffused Matter and Spirit of the Universe; and that the regathering of this diffused Matter and Spirit will be but the re-constitution of the *purely Spiritual* and Individual God.

In this view, and in this view alone, we comprehend the riddles of Divine Injustice—of Inexorable Fate. In this view alone the existence of Evil becomes intelligible; but in this view it becomes more—it becomes endurable. Our souls no longer rebel at a *Sorrow* which we ourselves have imposed upon ourselves, in furtherance of our own purposes—with a view—if even with a futile view—to the extension of our own *Joy*.

I have spoken of *Memories* that haunt us during our Youth. They sometimes pursue us even into our Manhood:—assume gradually less and less indefinite shapes:—now and then speak to us with low voices, saying:

"There was an epoch in the Night of Time, when a still-existent Being existed—one of an absolutely infinite number of similar Beings that people the absolutely infinite domains of the absolutely infinite space. It was not and is not in the power of this Being—any more than it is in your own—to extend, by actual increase, the joy of his Existence; but just as it *is* in your power to expand or to concentrate your pleasures (the absolute amount of happiness remaining always the same) so did and does a similar capability appertain to this Divine Being, who thus passes his Eternity in perpetual variation of Concentrated Self and almost Infinite Self-Diffusion. What you call The Universe of Stars is but his present expansive existence. He now feels his life through an infinity of imperfect pleasures—the partial and pain-intertangled pleasures of those inconceivably numerous things which you designate as his creatures, but which are really but infinite individualizations of Himself. All these creatures—*all*—those whom you term animate, as well as those to which you deny life for no better reason than that you do not behold it in operation—*all* these creatures have, in a greater or less degree, a capacity for pleasure and for pain:—*but the general sum of their sensations is precisely that amount of Happiness which appertains by right to the Divine Being when concentrated within Himself.* These creatures are all, too, more or less, and more or less obviously, conscious Intelligences; conscious, first, of a proper identity; conscious, secondly and by faint indeterminate glimpses, of an identity with the Divine Being of whom we speak—of an identity with God. Of the two classes of consciousness, fancy that the former will grow weaker, the latter stronger, during the long succession of ages which must elapse before these myriads of individual Intelligences become blended—when the bright stars become blended—into One. Think that the sense of individual identity will be gradually merged in the general consciousness—that Man, for example, ceasing imperceptibly to feel himself Man, will at length attain that awfully triumphant epoch when he shall recognize his existence as that of Jehovah. In the meantime bear in mind that all is Life—Life—Life within Life—the less within the greater, and all within the *Spirit Divine.*"*

THE END

*Note—The pain of the consideration that we shall lose our individual identity, ceases at once when we reflect that the process, as above described, is, neither more nor less than that of the absorption, by each individual intelligence, of all other intelligences (that is, of the Universe) into its own. That God may be all in all, *each* must become God. [Poe's note]

Notes

TALES

Predicaments
MS. Found in a Bottle

1. He who has only a moment to live has nothing more to hide. Philippe Quinault wrote the lyrics for Lully's opera *Atys*.
2. Extreme skepticism.
3. Poe alludes here to the theory of Captain John Cleves Symmes (1779–1829), who believed that at the poles, gigantic vortices opened upon concentric spheres within the hollow, habitable center of the Earth.
4. This note appears for the first time in the Griswold edition of 1850; the actual publication date of Poe's story is 1833.

A Descent into the Maelström

1. Al Idrisi, in *Geographia Nubiensis* (1619), refers to the Atlantic Ocean as the *"Mare Tenebrarum,"* or sea of darkness.
2. Poe's several incorrect renderings of island names have been corrected.

The Masque of the Red Death

1. At the notorious debut of Victor Hugo's play *Hernani* in 1830, supporters of Hugo proclaimed the triumph of romanticism over classicism at the *Comédie Française* by dressing in outlandish costumes and shouting down irate traditionalists.

The Pit and the Pendulum

1. Here the furious, insatiable mob long embraced a hatred of innocent blood. Now that the nation is saved, and the fatal cave destroyed, life and health shall be where fearful death has been.

2. Literally, "act of faith." The term refers to the public condemnation and execution of those accused of heresy by the Spanish Inquisition.
3. General Colbert, Comte de Lasalle, entered Toledo in 1808, putting a temporary halt to the Inquisition that began in 1478. Trials resumed a few years later but came to a definitive end in 1834.

The Premature Burial

1. Among these famous disasters and massacres, the most recent event was Napoleon's loss in 1812 of roughly twenty-five thousand troops and at least that many civilian stragglers as his army attempted to cross makeshift bridges spanning the Beresina River in Russia.
2. William Buchan's *Domestic Medicine* (1769) went through many editions and would have encouraged the narrator's preoccupation with physical symptoms; Edward Young's *The Complaint; or Night Thoughts on Life, Death, and Immortality* (1742) was typical of the "graveyard school" of melancholy poetry.
3. Carathis explores Hell in William Beckford's *Vathek* (1786) and Afrasiab figures in Persian mythology—as does the River Oxus—but the reference is unlocated.

The Facts in the Case of M. Valdemar

1. At the point of death.

Bereavements
The Assignation

1. Propriety.
2. Poe refers, apparently, to a sixteenth-century scholar named Jean Tixtier, but no work by this title has been found.
3. The best sculptor has never had an idea that a block of marble did not contain.

Berenice

1. My companions told me that if I visited the tomb of my beloved, my grief would be in some measure relieved.
2. The "paradoxical sentence" of Tertullian may be translated: The son of God is dead; believable is that which is beyond belief; he is risen from the tomb; certain is that which is impossible.
3. Of Madame Sallé, a ballerina, it was said that every step was an emotion; the narrator says of Berenice that all of her teeth were ideas.

Morella

1. Through its association with the sacrifice of children to the god Moloch, the Valley of Hinnon near Jerusalem was renamed Gehenna (hell).
2. Reincarnation.

Ligeia

1. Poe possibly invented this quotation from Glanvill; the textual source has never been located.

The Fall of the House of Usher

1. His heart is a suspended lute; as soon as it is touched, it resonates.
2. The Latin title is *Vigils for the Dead* according to the Church at Mainz. The esoteric works cited here all allude to real books.
3. The author and volume, as well as the cited passages, were invented by Poe.

Eleonora

1. Under care of a certain sort the soul is safe.
2. Poe cites the same ancient geographer, Al Idrisi, in "A Descent into the Maelström." The quotation may be translated, They went upon the Sea of Darkness so that it might be explored.

Antagonisms
Metzengerstein

1. Living I was your plague, dying I will be your death. Luther addressed these lines to the Pope.
2. Comes from the inability to be alone.
3. The quotation, probably devised by Poe, does not make complete sense in French but suggests that although the soul inhabits a human body only once, it may, as an intangible likeness, take an animal form.

William Wilson

1. Poe apparently invented this passage, which does not appear in Chamberlayne's verse narrative, *Pharonnida* (1659).
2. Punishment strong and severe, which traditionally meant being pressed or crushed to death.
3. The quotation from Voltaire may be translated, Oh, what a good time it was, that age of iron.

The Tell-Tale Heart

1. A species of beetle that produces a clicking or ticking sound as it burrows into walls.

The Imp of the Perverse

1. In this discussion of the first causes (*prima mobile*) of human behavior, Poe includes among those explanations constructed upon theory and empirically unverifiable (hence *à priori*), the nineteenth-century "science" of phrenology, developed by Gall and Spurzheim, which analyzed human character based on the shape of the cranium.

The Cask of Amontillado

1. No one injures me with impunity.
2. Rest in peace.

Hop-Frog

1. Rare bird on earth.

Mysteries
The Man of the Crowd

1. This great misfortune, to be unable to be alone.
2. It does not permit itself to be read.
3. The darkness that was once upon them.
4. Poe alludes to an obscure devotional text from 1500 ("The Spirit of the Garden") said by Isaac D'Israeli to contain unseemly illustrations.

The Murders in the Rue Morgue

1. And all that sort of thing.
2. The first letter has lost its original sound.
3. Poe evokes a character in Molière's *Le Bourgeois Gentilhomme* who absurdly calls for his dressing gown so that he can better hear the music.
4. A former criminal who became the head of Napoleon's security forces, François Eugène Vidocq later published a memoir, which in translation was adapted and serialized in *Burton's Gentleman's Magazine*.
5. A plausible equivalent would be, I tended to them.
6. After the fact, from effect to cause.
7. Of denying that which is, and explaining that which is not.

The Gold-Bug

1. Swammerdamm was a seventeenth-century Dutch naturalist and collector of entomological specimens; the title of his major work might be translated *The Bible of Nature; or The History of Insects*.
2. Poe presumably identified Jupiter as a freed slave to avoid criticism from Northern readers that he meant to idealize slavery. Jupiter's devotion and simplicity fit a common racial stereotype; yet he later manifests his independence by threatening playfully to beat Legrand.
3. The human-head beetle.
4. Eagerness.
5. When the tale first appeared in the *Dollar Magazine*, the cipher was correctly represented; in subsequent versions (including the one followed here) Poe inadvertently introduced minor inconsistencies.

The Oblong Box

1. The ship *Independence* sinks on or about July 4 near the site of the first English settlement in the New World.

A Tale of the Ragged Mountains

1. Dr. Franz Anton Mesmer (1733–1815) developed a therapeutic treatment for nervous disorders that relied upon "animal magnetism" to place patients in a trance. The "magnetic control" of the mesmerist over the subject anticipated techniques of modern hypnosis.
2. Bedloe seems to refer here to Indian tribes that once inhabited Virginia but which had (by the 1840s) disappeared as a result of conflicts with white settlers.
3. No such venomous leech exists.

The Purloined Letter

1. There is nothing more inimical to wisdom than too much acuteness.
2. An undistributed middle term, which in formal logic produces fallacious reasoning.
3. You can bet that every public idea, every received convention, is nonsense, for it has suited the majority.
4. *Ambitus* denotes circularity; *religio* denotes superstition or (in another sense) scrupulousness; *homines honesti* was a Ciceronian epithet for partisans.
5. The force of inertia.
6. The descent into Hades is easy.
7. Horrible monster.
8. A scheme so deadly, if unworthy of Atreus, is worthy of Thyestes.

Gotesqueries
The Man That Was Used Up

1. In the magazine world of Poe's day, to "use up" someone meant to annihilate them with criticism.
2. Written during the second Seminole war, as General Zachary Taylor led the U.S. Army against combined Indian forces in Florida that included some Kickapoos, Poe injects a skeptical note by equating Bugaboo and Kickapoo: In Poe's usage, a bugaboo (or bugbear) referred to an imaginary, needless object of dread.
3. Weep, weep, my eyes, and dissolve into water! The first half of my life has put the other half in the tomb.
4. Poe here satirizes the national self-adulation that helped to justify Indian removal.
5. In which matters he figured greatly.
6. Poe cites *Othello*, III, iii, 330–33. Iago, plotting to excite in Othello doubts about Desdemona's fidelity, remarks that the hero will never again know restful sleep.

The System of Doctor Tarr and Professor Fether

1. Poe's reference to the odd eccentricities of the "southern provincialists" alludes to prejudices about the America South, inspired in part by abolitionists whose ideas of reform Poe satirizes by reversing master-slave relations.
2. Numbers 13:33 refers to a race of giants, the sons of Anak, who rule a land that devours its inhabitants.
3. A horrible monster, enormous, deformed, and sightless. In shorter form, the same phrase from Virgil also appears in "The Purloined Letter."
4. Phalaris, the tyrant who ruled Agrigentum, Sicily, in the fifth century B.C., placed prisoners in a hollow brass bull that amplified their screams.
5. The sheer incongruity of an orchestra of French lunatics playing "Yankee Doodle" in the midst of a revolt hints at American implications.

Some Words with a Mummy

1. Poe capitalized on the fascination with Egypt launched by Napoleon's plundering of the pyramids and the discovery of the Rosetta stone in 1799. Champollion's deciphering of the Rosetta stone launched the field of modern Egyptology, and by the 1830s and 1840s, museums in Europe and America were acquiring major collections of mummies and Egyptian artifacts.

2. George Robins Gliddon, a noted lecturer on Egyptology, decried the ransacking of tombs and monuments in *An Appeal to the Antiquaries of Europe* (1841).

3. James Silk Buckingham, an English traveler, had published several volumes about his excursions through the Near East.

4. Contemporary antebellum debates about the origins of the five principal races hinged on the competing theories of monogenesis (the progressive evolution of different races from a single people) and polygenesis (the simultaneous development of racially distinct peoples). Proponents of monogenesis tended to see the Anglo-Saxon race as the culmination of all evolutionary progress.

5. Emerging theories of eugenics typically focused on skull shapes.

6. See note 1 for "The Imp of the Perverse."

7. Poe ridiculed the bad taste of this monument in *Doings of Gotham*.

8. *The Dial* was the journal of the Emersonian Transcendentalists, often a target of Poe's satire.

9. Poe alludes transparently to the founding of the United States and the establishment of popular suffrage. His skepticism about Jacksonian democracy is apparent in this passage.

10. Poe wrote this tale, apparently, during the election of 1844, which hinged on territorial expansion and American destiny, issues successfully exploited by James K. Polk. The narrator's sense that "everything is going wrong" seems to allude to U.S. jingoism on the eve of the Mexican War.

POEMS

The Lake—To——

1. The place described here, Lake Drummond, is situated in the Great Dismal Swamp between Virginia and North Carolina. It was in Poe's day a site associated with mysterious disappearances by melancholy lovers—and also by fugitive slaves.

Sonnet—To Science

1. Poe identifies several mythic figures demystified by empirical science: Diana, the Roman goddess of the hunt, associated with the moon; the Hamadryad, a Greek wood nymph associated with trees; the Naiad, a Greek water nymph, associated with springs and fountains; the Elfin, elves or fairies, associated (here) with lawns and fields. The tamarind is a tropical fruit tree from India.

Fairy-Land

1. Namely.
2. Atoms.

Introduction

1. This poem incorporates lines later published as "Romance" and appeared in this form only once, as a verse introduction to *Poems* (1831).
2. Poe probably knew the Greek poet both through his early studies in the classical languages and by way of Thomas Moore's popular translations and adaptations.
3. Greek god of marriage.

Alone

1. This poem did not appear in print during Poe's lifetime. It was preserved in the album of a Baltimore woman and first published, with a title added by Eugene L. Didier, in *Scribner's Monthly* in 1875.

To Helen

1. Famously inspired by Jane Stith Stanard, the mother of a Richmond boyhood friend, the poem obviously evokes the legendary beauty of Helen of Troy. Poe's "Nicéan barks" may allude to ships either dedicated to the goddess Nike or originating from Nicea, an ancient city of Asia Minor. Psyche was the lover of the Greek god Eros and became a personification of the soul. For Naiad, see the note to "Sonnet—To Science."

The Sleeper

1. In Greek mythology, the river of forgetfulness.

Israfel

1. Lightning (archaic). The Pleiades are a cluster of seven stars, formed, according to Greek mythology, by the daughters of Atlas.
2. The Houris are the beautiful virgins said in the Koran to inhabit paradise.

The City in the Sea

1. Poe's subject was probably suggested by Sodom and Gomorrah, the biblical sunken cities of the Dead Sea. The poem complements "The Valley of Unrest."

Lenore

1. We have sinned.

Dream-Land

1. An eidolon is a phantom; Poe's subsequent allusion to "Thule" derives from Virgil's reference to an "ultima Thule," a remote island in the North Atlantic, perhaps Greenland.

The Raven

1. That is, her name must hereafter remain unspoken.
2. Pallas Athena was the Greek goddess of wisdom.
3. Legendary drug that relieved sorrow.
4. An eccentric spelling of Eden. Poe's narrator wishes to confirm the existence of a spiritual afterlife, where he may again embrace Lenore. Yet the question is perverse: He inevitably anticipates the bird's response.

Ulalume—A Ballad

1. Arguably Poe's most difficult poem, a verse narrative complicated by esoteric astrological imagery, "Ulalume" presumably fictionalizes Poe's own visits to the grave of Virginia in 1847. The name of the dead beloved here likely derives from the Latin verb *ululare*, to wail or howl.
2. Poe's Mount Yaanek may refer to an Antarctic volcano, Mt. Erebus, discovered in 1840. The "scoriac" rivers refer to lava flows.
3. Presumably Halloween. Virginia Poe died, however, in January.
4. Astarte was the Phoenician goddess of love and hence the counterpart of Venus. The moon here seems to be in a crescent phase, perhaps "bediamonded" in juxtaposition with the planet Venus.
5. The constellation Leo. The juxtaposition of Venus and Leo would have been astrologically ominous. Psyche (the soul) expresses "mistrust" about the passion of Venus.

The Bells

1. Magical verse; a rune was a letter in the archaic Anglo-Saxon alphabet.

For Annie

1. Perhaps no other poem pertains more closely to a specific event in Poe's life, here, the crisis of November 1848 in which the distraught poet swallowed laudanum hoping to bring "Annie" Richmond to his bedside.
2. Naphthaline is a clear compound derived from petroleum or tar and is used in making dyes, solvents, and explosives. Its figurative sense here seems to be that of a toxic, perhaps flammable influence.
3. Poe may be punning on the etymology of pansy, which (as he knew) derived from the French word for thought, *pensée*; the floral reference thus alludes to his thoughts of Mrs. Richmond, who lived in Massachusetts and possibly represented herself to Poe as a daughter of the Puritans.

Eldorado

1. The idea of a city of gold, a place of longed-for riches, also figures in Poe's "Dream-Land," but by 1849, "Eldorado" had become synonymous with California, and this poem hints that the quest for instant wealth may be a delusion. See Poe's letter to Frederick W. Thomas of February 14, 1849, for further reflections on the gold rush.

CRITICAL PRINCIPLES

The Prose Tale (from a review of Hawthorne's Twice-Told Tales*)*

1. The phrase may be translated, One proceeds most prudently by following a middle course.

The Object of Poetry (from "Letter to B——")

1. Poe translates Aristotle's *Poetics* somewhat inaccurately.
2. About all that can be known and certain other things.
3. Why so much anger?
4. Most sects are right in much of what they advocate but wrong in what they deny.

The Philosophy of Composition

1. All else being equal.

American Criticism

1. Theodore Fay was an editor of the *New York Mirror* and author of the novel *Norman Leslie*, which Poe savaged in 1835, as much for the extravagant "puffing" of the volume as for its flimsiness.
2. About all things and certain others.
3. Belier, my friend, begin at the beginning. Poe alludes to *Le Bélier*, an exotic tale by the Irish-French author Anthony Hamilton.
4. Smooth and round.

OBSERVATIONS

Some Secrets of the Magazine Prison-House

1. National spirit. Foster and Scott were New York publishers who reprinted cheap editions of British journals for the American literary market.
2. Mulberry tree (on which silkworms feed).

American Literary Independence

1. All else being equal.
2. Poe refers to John Wilson, editor of *Blackwood's Magazine*, who in the persona of "Christopher North" delivered dismissive opinions about American writers (such as Lowell).
3. How long, Catalina?
4. That is, to the most remote sites of competing interest.

The Soul and the Self

1. Entity or real thing.

Poetical Irritability

1. Beauty.

Genius and Proportionate Intellect

1. Vexing question.

Adaptation and the Plots of God

1. Commencing in 1833, a series of philosophical and theological monographs by different authors on the general subject of God's "power, wisdom, and goodness," especially as manifested in the natural world. The project was instituted by Reverend Francis Henry Egerton, the eighth Earl of Bridgewater.

Works of Genius

1. Wonderful diligence or incredible industry.

Magazine Literature in America

1. With a running pen.

Art and the Soul

1. Zeuxis and Parrhasius, Greek painters of the fifth century B.C., competed to produce the most realistic painting imaginable. Zeuxis painted a cluster of grapes that birds attempted to eat; Parrhasius then showed Zeuxis a veiled painting that, when Zeuxis attempted to lift the veil, proved to be part of the painting itself.

Selected Bibliography

FIRST EDITIONS OF POE'S WORKS (BOOKS)

Poe, Edgar Allan. *Tamerlane and Other Poems. By a Bostonian.* Boston: Calvin F. S. Thomas—Printer, 1827.

———. *Al Aaraaf, Tamerlane, and Minor Poems, By Edgar A. Poe.* Baltimore: Hatch & Dunning, 1829.

———. *Poems by Edgar A. Poe . . . Second Edition.* New York: Elam Bliss, 1831.

———. *The Narrative of Arthur Gordon Pym of Nantucket.* New York: Harper & Brothers, 1838.

———. *Tales of the Grotesque and Arabesque.* 2 vols. Philadelphia: Lea and Blanchard, 1840.

———. *The Prose Romances of Edgar A. Poe.* No. 1. Philadelphia: William H. Graham, 1843.

———. *Tales.* New York: Wiley and Putnam, 1845.

———. *The Raven and Other Poems.* New York: Wiley and Putnam, 1845.

———. *Eureka: A Prose Poem.* New York: Putnam, 1848.

LATER EDITIONS

Griswold, Rufus W., ed. *The Works of the Late Edgar Allan Poe.* 4 vols. New York: J. S. Redfield, 1850–56.

Harrison, James A., ed. *The Complete Works of Edgar Allan Poe.* Virginia Edition. 17 vols. New York: Thomas Y. Crowell, 1902.

Mabbott, Thomas Ollive, ed. *Collected Works of Edgar Allan Poe.* 3 vols. Cambridge: Harvard University Press, 1969, 1978.

Pollin, Burton R. *Collected Writings of Edgar Allan Poe: Imaginary Voyages.* Boston: Twayne, 1981; rpt. New York: Gordian Press, 1994.

————. *The Brevities: Pinakidia, Marginalia, and Other Works*. New York: Gordian Press, 1985.

————. *Nonfictional Writings in the Broadway Journal*. New York: Gordian Press, 1986.

————. *Broadway Journal Annotations*. New York: Gordian Press, 1986.

————. *Nonfictional Southern Literary Messenger Prose*. New York: Gordian Press, 1997.

Quinn, Patrick F., ed. *Poetry and Tales*. New York: Library of America, 1984.

Thompson, G. R., ed. *Essays and Reviews*. New York: Library of America, 1984.

LETTERS

Poe, Edgar Allan. *The Letters of Edgar Allan Poe*. Edited by John Ward Ostrom. 2 vols. 1949; rpt. New York: Gordian Press, 1966.

BIBLIOGRAPHY

Dameron, J. Lasley, and Irby B. Cauthen, Jr. *Edgar Allan Poe: A Bibliography of Criticism, 1827–1967*. Charlottesville: University Press of Virginia, 1974.

Hyneman, Esther F. *Edgar Allan Poe: An Annotated Bibliography of Books and Articles in English, 1827–1973*. Boston: G. K. Hall, 1974.

BIOGRAPHY

Bittner, William. *Poe: A Biography*. Boston: Atlantic Monthly Press, 1962.

Meyers, Jeffrey. *Edgar Allan Poe: His Life and Legacy*. New York: Charles Scribner's Sons, 1992.

Miller, John Carl. *Building Poe Biography*. Baton Rouge: Louisiana State University Press, 1977.

Quinn, Arthur Hobson. *Edgar Allan Poe: A Critical Biography*. 1941; rpt. New York: Cooper Square, 1969.

Silverman, Kenneth. *Edgar A. Poe: Mournful and Never-ending Remembrance*. New York: HarperCollins, 1991.

Thomas, Dwight, and David K. Jackson. *The Poe Log: A Documentary Life of Edgar Allan Poe 1809–1849*. Boston: G. K. Hall, 1987.

CRITICISM: BOOKS

Allen, Michael. *Poe and the British Magazine Tradition*. New York: Oxford University Press, 1969.

Auerbach, Jonathan. *The Romance of Failure: First-Person Fictions of Poe, Hawthorne, and James*. New York: Oxford University Press; 1989.

Bloom, Harold, ed. *The Tales of Poe*. New York: Chelsea House, 1987.

Bonaparte, Marie. *The Life and Works of Edgar Allan Poe: A Psychoanalytic Interpretation*. Trans. John Rodker. London: Imago Publishing Company, 1949.

Budd, Louis J., and Edwin H. Cady, eds. *On Poe*. Durham: Duke University Press, 1993.

Carlson, Eric W., ed. *Critical Essays on Edgar Allan Poe*. Boston: G. K. Hall, 1987.

———, ed. *The Recognition of Edgar Allan Poe*. Ann Arbor: University of Michigan Press, 1966.

Davidson, Edward. *Poe, a Critical Study*. Cambridge: Belknap Press of Harvard University, 1957.

Dayan, Joan. *Fables of Mind: An Inquiry into Poe's Fiction*. New York: Oxford University Press, 1987.

Fiedler, Leslie. *Love and Death in the American Novel*. New York: Dell, 1966.

Fisher IV, Benjamin Franklin, ed. *Poe and His Times*. Baltimore: Edgar Allan Poe Society, 1990.

Goddu, Teresa. *Gothic America: Narrative, History, and Nation*. New York: Columbia University Press, 1997.

Halliburton, David. *Edgar Allan Poe: A Phenomenological View*. Princeton: Princeton University Press, 1973.

Hayes, Kevin, ed. *Cambridge Companion to Edgar Allan Poe*. Cambridge: Cambridge University Press, 2002.

Hoffman, Daniel. *Poe Poe Poe Poe Poe Poe Poe*. Garden City, NY: Doubleday, 1972.

Howarth, William L., ed. *Twentieth Century Interpretations of Poe's Tales: A Collection of Critical Essays*. Englewood Cliffs, NJ: Prentice-Hall, 1971.

Irwin, John. *American Hieroglyphics: The Symbol of the Egyptian Hieroglyphics in the American Renaissance*. New Haven: Yale University Press, 1980.

————. *The Mystery to a Solution: Poe, Borges, and the Analytical Detective Story*. Baltimore: Johns Hopkins University Press, 1994.

Jacobs, Robert D. *Poe: Journalist and Critic*. Baton Rouge: Louisiana State University Press, 1969.

Kennedy, J. Gerald, ed. *A Historical Guide to Edgar Allan Poe*. New York: Oxford University Press, 2001.

————. *The Narrative of Arthur Gordon Pym and the Abyss of Interpretation*. New York: Twayne Publishers, 1995.

————. *Poe, Death, and the Life of Writing*. New Haven: Yale University Press, 1987.

Ketterer, David. *The Rationale of Deception in Poe*. Baton Rouge: Louisiana State University Press, 1979.

Kopley, Richard, ed. *Poe's Pym: Critical Explorations*. Durham: Duke University Press, 1992.

Levin, Harry. *The Power of Blackness: Hawthorne, Poe, Melville*. New York: Vintage, 1958.

Levine, Stuart. *Edgar Allan Poe: Seer and Craftsman*. Deland, FL: Everett/Edwards, 1972.

May, Charles. *Edgar Allan Poe: A Study of the Short Fiction*. Boston: Twayne, 1991.

McGill, Meredith. *American Literature and the Culture of Reprinting, 1834–1853*. Philadelphia: University of Pennsylvania Press, 2002.

Miller, Perry. *The Raven and the Whale: The War of Words and Wits in the Era of Poe and Melville*. New York: Harcourt, Brace, 1956.

Moss, Sidney. *Poe's Literary Battles*. Durham: Duke University Press, 1963.

Muller, John P., and William J. Richardson. *The Purloined Poe: Lacan, Derrida, and Psychoanalytic Reading*. Baltimore: Johns Hopkins University Press, 1988.

Nelson, Dana. *National Manhood: Capitalist Citizenship and the Imagined Fraternity of White Men*. Durham: Duke University Press, 1998.

————. *The Word in Black and White*. New York: Oxford University Press, 1992.

Peeples, Scott. *The Afterlife of Edgar Allan Poe*. Rochester: Camden House, 2004.

————. *Edgar Allan Poe Revisited*. New York: Twayne, 1998.

Person, Leland S. *Aesthetic Headaches: Women and a Masculine Poetics in Poe, Melville, and Hawthorne*. Athens: University of Georgia Press, 1988.

Pollin, Burton R. *Discoveries in Poe*. Notre Dame: University of Notre Dame Press, 1970.

Porte, Joel. *The Romance in America: Studies in Cooper, Poe, Hawthorne, Melville, and James.* Middletown, CT: Wesleyan University Press, 1969.

Quinn, Patrick F. *The French Face of Edgar Allan Poe.* Carbondale, IL: Southern Illinois University Press, 1957.

Regan, Robert, ed. *Poe: A Collection of Critical Essays.* Englewood Cliffs, NJ: Prentice-Hall, 1967.

Renza, Louis A. *Edgar Allan Poe, Wallace Stevens, and the Poetics of American Privacy.* Baton Rouge: Louisiana State University Press, 2002.

Reynolds, David. *Beneath the American Renaissance: The Subversive Imagination in the Age of Emerson and Melville.* Cambridge: Harvard University Press, 1988.

Rosenheim, Shawn. *The Cryptographic Imagination: Secret Writing from Edgar Poe to the Internet.* Baltimore: Johns Hopkins University Press, 1997.

———, and Stephen Rachman, eds. *The American Face of Edgar Allan Poe.* Baltimore: Johns Hopkins University Press, 1995.

Rowe, John Carlos. *Through the Custom-House: Nineteenth-Century American Fiction and Modern Theory.* Baltimore: Johns Hopkins University Press, 1982.

Silverman, Kenneth, ed. *New Essays on Poe's Major Tales.* New York: Cambridge University Press, 1993.

Stovall, Floyd. *Edgar Poe the Poet: Essays Old and New on the Man and his Work.* Charlottesville: University Press of Virginia, 1969.

Thompson, G. R. *Poe's Fiction: Romantic Irony in the Gothic Tales.* Madison: University of Wisconsin Press, 1973.

Vines, Lois Davis, ed. *Poe Abroad: Influence, Reputation, Affinities.* Iowa City: University of Iowa Press, 1999.

Walker, I. M. *Edgar Allan Poe: The Critical Heritage.* London: Routledge, 1986.

Whalen, Terence. *Edgar Allan Poe and the Masses: The Political Economy of Literature in Antebellum America.* Princeton: Princeton University Press, 1999.

Wilbur, Richard. *Responses. Prose Pieces: 1953–1976.* New York: Harcourt, Brace, Jovanovich, 1976.

Williams, Michael J. S. *A World of Words: Language and Displacement in the Fiction of Edgar Allan Poe.* Durham: Duke University Press, 1988.

CRITICISM: ESSAYS

Barthes, Roland. "Textual Analysis of a Tale of Poe." In *On Signs*, ed. Marshall Blonsky. Baltimore: Johns Hopkins University Press; 1985:84–97.

Dayan, Joan. "Amorous Bondage: Poe, Ladies, and Slaves." *American Literature* 66 (1994):239–73.

———. "From Romance to Modernity: Poe and the Work of Poetry." *Studies in Romanticism* 29 (1990):413–37.

Eakin, Paul John. "Poe's Sense of an Ending." *American Literature* 45 (1973):1–22.

Gargano, James. "The Question of Poe's Narrators." *College English* 25 (1963):177–81.

Hovey, Kenneth. "'These Many Pieces Are Yet One Book': The Book-Unity of Poe's Tale Collections." *Poe Studies* 31 (1998):1–16.

Jackson, Leon. "'Behold Our Literary Mohawk, Poe': Literary Nationalism and the 'Indianation' of Antebellum American Culture." *ESQ: A Journal of the American Renaissance* 48 (2002):97–133.

Jay, Gregory S. "Poe: Writing and the Unconscious." *Bucknell Review* 28 (1983):144–69.

Jordan, Cynthia S. "Poe's Re-Vision: The Recovery of the Second Story." *American Literature* 59 (1987):1–19.

Kennedy, J. Gerald. "'A Mania for Composition': Poe's *Annus Mirabilis* and the Violence of Nation Building." *American Literary History* 17 (2005):1–35.

Moldenhauer, Joseph. "Murder as a Fine Art: Basic Connections between Poe's Aesthetics, Psychology, and Moral Vision." *PMLA* 83 (1968):284–97.

Smith, Dave. "Edgar Allan Poe and the Nightmare Ode." *Southern Humanities Review* 29 (1995):1–10

Tate, Allen. "The Poetry of Edgar Allan Poe." *Sewanee Review* 76 (1968):214–25.